Author's Note

In 2001 I wrote a novel called 'The Cull'. The research took me deep into the heroin nightmare that has a grip on the town where I live; Dumfries. Things didn't stop with the book and in June 2003, my partner Carol and myself opened The First Base Agency. First Base is a small charity and we offer information and advice to the local community and support to anyone affected by drink and drugs. I know that when Dumfries people read this they will start trying to identify the characters. Forget it guys. Everyone in these pages, and I mean everyone, is completely made up. Figments of my imagination. They don't exist!

When I was younger I was lucky enough to travel all over the world. A few of the destinations turn up in the pages of this book. First Base has taught me a big lesson. Sometimes the longest journey you ever take is to places just a mile or two from where you live. We all know the places. They are the places where we don't park the car at night. And we all love to judge the people who live in these places. But when you meet many of these people, and we meet them every day, you find that they are mainly thoroughly decent human beings who have been unlucky enough to draw the short straw. This story tries to put a side of things that the Daily Mail tends to miss out. I hope so. The ball is in your court now.

I also have some people to thank. Carol, my editor-in-chief, who hopefully makes sure I keep it real. My mum and dad for proofreading. Yasmin for turning files into a book. And Detective Superintendent Bill Gillis for giving me some clues as to what the police who do if things panned out in real life as they do in the book.

A Glenmill Publication

First published in 2005

Glenmill Publishing

Dumfries

Scotland

DG2 8PX

tel: 07770 443 483

http://www.thecull.com

British Library Cataloguing in Publication Data.
A catalogue record of this book
is available from the British Library.

ISBN 0 9535944 5 9

Glenmill logo: Andrew Carroll AKA 'Gizmo'

Printed and bound in Great Britain

THE
POISONOUS
PAST

MARK FRANKLAND

Dedication

I dedicate this book to the memory of Martin Luther King

And yes, I know that sounds pretentious, but
I'm doing it anyway for two very simple reasons.

Number one. I'm white. My partner Carol
is black. Our boys are brown. Without
Dr King our family would never have happened.

Number two. He taught me that there is more to life
than chasing cash. That there is more fulfilment in
trying to expose injustice than owning a fancy car

So now I do what I do and this book is part of it. And
the car is a clapped-out Fiesta with a pancake-flat battery.

Prologue
Sunnybank Estate

The ghost of a steam train – echoes down my track
It's at the moment bound for nowhere –
Just going round and round
Playground kids and creaking swings –
Lost laughter in the breeze
I could go on for hours and I probably will –
But I'd sooner put some joy back
In this town called Malice.

The Style Council. 'A town called Malice'.

Lenny Baxter took a sip of his tea and allowed the images from the TV screen to bounce around his head. An angry crowd. A chanting crowd. Jumble-sale clothes and unshaven faces filled with a mix of rage and grief. A new pile of shattered concrete set in front of a backdrop of doleful low-rise housing. Grey skies and lingering smoke. A line of bodies roughly dumped under stained sheets looked over by a pair of washed out black American Marines with cradled guns and sunglasses.

". . . the suicide bomber struck in a busy market place. Today in Famoudi it has been twelve civilians who have become the latest victims of the upsurge in violence in this small town at the centre of the so called Sunni Triangle. Yesterday four Marines were killed when a roadside bomb . . . ."

The words from Iraq went into his head, but not to any place where they particularly registered. As ever it was the images that rang a mournful bell somewhere deep in his subconscious. Angry faces. Shouting crowds. Rage at the armed strangers in their tanks and armoured vehicles. Memories trudged around his tired brain like the inmates of a labour camp. Old memories. Poisonous memories.

"When are you off Uncle Lenny?"

He hadn't heard her come into the cold living room. He pushed the memories and images to a corner of his brain. The clock in the corner of the TV told him it was 8.21 a.m.

"About half past I suppose."

He took a look out of the window and grimaced. The wind had got up through the night and the rain had come with the dawn. Outside Sunnybank Estate looked every bit as grey as the broken concrete wasteland of Famoudi. He stood and stretched and took in the view. Sally's second floor flat enjoyed a view of playing fields with a line of three-storey pebble-dash at the far side. Out beyond the pebble-dash were the Galloway Hills. On a clear morning the view was long and fine. Not this morning. This morning the clouds from the Atlantic had swallowed the hills from sight and made the view all grey.

Grey all the way from Famoudi to Sunnybank Estate, Dumfries. A deadly grey world riddled with cancer. A world dying on its feet.

He took another sip of tea and tried to climb out of the despondency of everything. Sally joined him at the window and turned down the side of her mouth as she took in the puddles and swaying trees.

"How are you getting there?"

Lenny shrugged. "I'll walk."

"Don't be daft. Tha'll get soaked. I'll ring for a taxi. Expenses like. There'll be no problem with it. It's a justifiable cost. Volunteers can get up to £10 a day for expenses."

She made him smile. She always made him smile. Twenty years old and speaking like a walking rulebook. She was her granddad's granddaughter that way.

The thought of it made him smile. Just a small smile, but a smile all the same. Something to carry him clear of Famoudi and the puddles. His dad and his niece were a century apart but they both knew how to eat a rulebook. They were at ease with clauses and sub-sections and committees. His dad had a lifetime of it with the Haddington Branch of the Yorkshire National Union of Mineworkers. She was right there at the beginning of the road as the manager of 'The Zone', Sunnybank Estate's one and only Youth Centre. They both loved a lost cause. His dad had battled the system for fifty years without taking a backward step until a lungful of coal dust and Thatcher's heartbreak had wiped him out at fifty-two. Sally was just setting out on her own war.

The Zone Centre had three small rooms, one manager, one sixteen-hour-a-week part-timer, and a motley group of volunteers of whom he was one. It alone offered an open door to the three-and-a-half-thousand youngsters of the sprawling Sunnybank Estate. The sheer impossibility of the task would have put off just about anyone, but not Sally Baxter who had been born with an overflowing quota of

Yorkshire stubbornness. He liked to think that somewhere up in the coal grey clouds his dad could see her. He would be pleased.

"So. Am I ringing a taxi or not?"

He shook his head. "No. I'll walk. It'll do me some good. Clear the cobwebs and all that."

"Tha'll get soaked."

"Well I won't melt, will I lass."

She grinned. "Tha' don't half sound bloody old at times Uncle Lenny."

"That's because I am bloody old. Dinosaur old. Come on. Let's grab another brew and you can get me properly briefed."

He forced some enthusiasm into his legs and made his way to the small kitchen and clicked on the kettle. She followed him and threw herself down onto a chair at the table and started.

"OK. The Scottish Parliament's Anti-Social Behaviour Act is now law. OK?"

"Aye, I think I've managed that bit. No more loud music and dog dirt on the pavements right?"

She nodded and took out a packet of cigarettes. She raised an eyebrow and he nodded so she lit up two and passed him one. "That's the kind of thing. Anyway, like I told you, a big part of it is all about what they call 'Diversionary Activities'which is beaurocrat speak for giving kids something to do with themselves instead of playing their music loud and smashing school windows."

"What about the dogs?"

"How do you mean?"

"How do we divert the dogs? There has to be some way we can divert them from crapping all over the place. A spot of dog yoga, happen. Maybe canine citizen classes. Let the hounds know that their actions have an impact on the community they live in. The anti-social dogs need to be made aware of how their bodily functions interface with the recreational needs of their neighbours."

Sally gave a dismissive snort. "Hey don't go talking like that or one of those pratts will take it on."

"You reckon?"

"Oh aye. No problem. Before you can blink they'll have a steering group in place and word will get out that there are officials who are thinking all the way out of the box and driving the exciting initiative forward."

"... and then rolling it out?"

"Not half. They would roll it out all the way to Stranraer."

Lenny poured boiling water over the tea bags and took a pull on the cigarette.

"So today's a Strategy Group, right?"

"Right."

"And what exactly are you wanting me to do?"

She smiled at him. "You really don't want to go do you?"

"Well it's not that, it's just . . . I don't know . . . this is the stuff you're good at, that's all. I can't see why you want me to go."

"Because it will be good for you."

"Good for me! How the hell do you work that out?"

"How long have you been here in Dumfries, Uncle Lenny?"

He shrugged. "Don't know. Must be getting on a year now."

"Fifteen months."

"That long? So what's that got to do with the price of coal?"

She took a moment to brace herself. He did the same. The kitchen waited for one of those I'm going to say this and you are probably not going to like it moments. "You're not meeting anyone Uncle Lenny. You're either down at Zone or sitting in the flat reading. You need to meet people of your own age. Make friends. You spend all your time with kids. It's not healthy."

Bloody hell. This was a hell of a start to a grey day in May. "There's the cricket." As soon as he said it, it sounded lame. Bloody lame.

"Aye. But you never stay for a drink after the games do you?"

He shrugged. This wasn't how things were supposed to pan out. He had come up to Dumfries when his sister in law Sheila had died from cancer the year before. He had come up to help his niece Sally to arrange the funeral and everything. He had stayed on because of the words of his brother. Just a few words. Words that came to him every night when sleep wouldn't come. Words that had haunted him for twenty endless years. "You'll look after our Sheila won't you Lenny. And little 'un, when it comes . . ." Two sentences. Two decades. And he had stared all the way to the back of his brother's eyes and held his hand and nodded and promised, promised the very second that the lights had gone out.

Sheila had got by it. The baby came and it was a girl and she called it Sally. She met a Scotsman and they moved to Sunnybank Estate where he soon got to battering her every night until one night he upped and left for Falkirk. Sally grew up and Sheila died at forty-four and Lenny had come. He was here to look after his niece and keep a promise that could never be broken. Except it wasn't turning out that way. Instead it was her looking after him. For a moment he found it hard to think of much to say.

"I can't really afford a drink I suppose. Anyway what do you mean about not meeting anyone of my own age?"

Sally just smiled. The penny dropped through the slot and bounced its way to the bottom of the machine. He took a hard drag at his nicotine.

"Oh bloody hell Sally."

She grinned mock innocence. "What?"

"You bloody well know what. Tha's talking about women."

She shrugged, all innocence. "Might be."

He rolled his eyes. "This is bloody ridiculous."

"Is it?"

"Course it is. I'm your uncle for Christ's sake."

"Meaning?"

"Meaning bloody hell, that's what."

"How very articulate. I can see you're going to knock them dead today with that level of blinding repartee." She took a careful sip of tea and played her cigarette between thumb and forefinger.

Lenny sighed. "Where's all this coming from all of a sudden then?"

"I suppose it's because everyone's talking about it."

"Everyone! Who the hell is everyone?"

"All the lasses at Zone for a start."

"What bloody lasses?"

"Those that come in, those that work there."

He nearly spat out his tea. "Those that come in! They're teenagers Sally. What do you mean they're talking about it?"

She was grinning now, enjoying every last second of his growing discomfort. "They all reckon you're a proper hunk. A bit of alright. So do all my mates."

"Ah come on, this is so much crap. I'm old enough to be their dad. Their bloody granddad. This is plain stupid."

"Modern girls like an older man."

PROLOGUE

This time he actually did spit out a mouthful of tea and he covered his burning embarrassment by scrubbing at his shirt with a tea towel.

She decided to allow him off the hook. "No. Seriously Uncle Lenny. You should be meeting someone. You shouldn't be on you own like this. It's not right."

He shook his head. "And at this meeting today you reckon there'll be lots of suitable women of a proper age who will be on hand to guide me through my autumn years into retirement."

"That's better. Much more articulate. Suddenly I feel a little more hopeful of your prospects for the day." Now her smile was different. She had said it and it was said. For the umpteenth time he looked at his niece with something approaching awe. She had grown up hard. Very hard. A dad dead before she was born. A step dad packed up and away before she was in primary school in a torrent of violence and abuse. A mum dead before she turned twenty. It would have been so very easy for her to have become yet another morose and resentful Sunnybank youngster, probably already a mother herself, complaining her way through every bleak day with her pram and fortnightly benefit cheque. Instead the lass at at the table was five foot two's worth of heart. Against all the odds she had flourished at Sunnybank High School and then college. She had bulldozed her way through interviews with stale men in mediocre suits and hard faced women with their sensible shoes. By sheer dogged determination she had dragged funding from tight purses to open up The Zone and secure core funding from a resentful local Council. She was the only family he had left and she made him proud. How his brother would have loved the daughter he had never lived to hold. The Baxters had never lacked for heart and the lass carried every ounce of the family tradition. For a moment the ghosts of his past floated through the small kitchen and he felt close to tears. It was time to move away from the memories before they ran him down like a speeding truck.

Just like it had been every day for twenty endless years.

"OK. If we're done with the matchmaking, I'd best be off. Let me make sure I'm clear on my task. The Anti Social Behaviour Strategy Group is designed to write down a plan on how Dumfries and Galloway will go about how to stop its citizens being a public pain in the neck, yeah?"

Sally nodded. Lenny continued.

"The Government comes up with the cash and sends it down to the Council."

Another nod.

"And if anyone wants to apply for any of the cash it has to be written up somewhere in the strategy."

"Very, very good Uncle Lenny. I'm impressed."

"So my task of the day is get them to write down that all work involving youth work in Dumfries and Galloway can only be undertaken by projects with Z in the name."

"Spot on."

Lenny put away the last half of his tea in a gulp and shrugged himself into the anorak that was hanging on the back of the door. "Fair do's. I'll see you at Zone later."

"Enjoy yourself."

"I'm sure it'll be a gas."

As he patted down his pocket in the hallway for his keys he caught a snapshot of himself in the mirror. What was it she had said? Hunk? Another bloody Americanism. Ridiculous. The way he looked wasn't anything that he considered much. He hadn't the faintest clue what or wasn't considered a hunk by a young woman of the twenty first century. He supposed he was in reasonable sort of order for a man in his mid forties. He had passed the six foot barrier before turning sixteen and had settled out at six two. The blond hair of boyhood had never darkened and the grey hairs were still outnumbered twenty to one. He wasn't carrying any weight. He never had. He was lucky that way. Exercise had always been a blind habit. These days it was his push ups and sit ups every morning and miles of walking. His face bothered him. The only time he ever really took much of a look at it was when he shaved, and even then he tried his best to be dispassionate. He supposed that it was not a bad looking sort of a face. What bothered him was the way the lines ran. His was a face that had spent twenty years setting in all the wrong directions. Twenty years of no smiles. Twenty years of living out about fifteen tonnes of remorse. Twenty years of taking life a day at a time. He thought about the scowling faces of a variety of rap artists who stared out from the walls of the Zone and he supposed that his kind of broken down look was in some way in vogue. Bloody ridiculous.

He took the stairs two at a time and swung open the broken door.

PROLOGUE

Outside the rain hit his face like a wake up call. He was pulled up short by the sight of a used needle half hidden by the broken branches of a shrub. That was three mornings out of the last six. He was past being angry at it and stooped down to carefully pick it up. The sin bin for needle disposal had become a regular part of his morning routine.

Sunnybank was easing itself into life. The traffic was fairly light and the pedestrians were mainly kids making their way to school. He settled into his familiar brisk pace and met the youthful greetings with smiles and nods. His work at the Zone had made him a familiar face on Sunnybank and he was popular. Sally and the female volunteers handled all the agony aunt stuff. They doled out the condoms and warned of sexually transmitted diseases. Lenny focused on sports and had won his spurs when the newly founded Zone Under 14 football team had kicked their way to a local cup final only to be stopped by an over zealous referee. He had tried to generate some enthusiasm for cricket, but had failed like many an Englishman before him. The fact that he spent his summer Saturdays playing cricket was a source of endless amusement for many of his young clients.

As he turned the corner he noticed three familiar figures in a huddle in the doorway of a closed down newsagent shop. They were hooded up and their body language spoke of no good whatsoever. Their backs were half turned into the rain which meant that they didn't notice him approach.

"Morning lads."

He was met by three startled faces as bags were snapped shut.

"I'm not even going to ask."

Two of the faces were as identical as a pair of eggs. The dreaded Flint twins, Tim and Barry. Three generations of the Flint family had filled police files for as far back as anyone on Sunnybank could remember and at eleven there was little doubt that Tim and Barry were set fair to carry on the family tradition. The third face was cut from different cloth. Luke Crenshaw was different. He been one of the first kids that Lenny had spent much time with when Sally had at last persuaded him to do some work at The Zone. Luke's mum would hand deliver him through the front door and the boy would try to make himself invisible in a corner. It hadn't taken Lenny long to see the reason. Every time the staff turned their backs, something would always happen and it always involved the Flints and it always left

Luke fighting back tears. Sally told him that she kept catching them and banning them but nothing ever did much good. It took a lot for Sally to admit defeat but the Flint twins pretty well had her beat.

It turned out that football had been a turning point. It soon became apparent to Lenny that the Flint twins shared a very modest level of natural talent for the game. However they made up for this by pure unthinking aggression and a commitment borne out of blind loyalty to Sunnybank. They became his central defensive partnership and they intimidated opponents from all around the town. It hadn't taken him long to tease out the genuine talent in Luke who became the playmaker in a team made up mainly of aggression and a free and easy approach to the rules. Football soon turned the two bullies and their victim into a threesome. Lenny wondered which was the worse. Being bullied had made Luke into a miserable withdrawn child. Being a part of a three with the Flints would no doubt carry him along all the wrong tracks and lead him into bother. Somewhere there should probably have been a middle way, but Lenny hadn't found it yet.

"Alright Lenny." Was it Tim or Barry? He hadn't a clue.

"Aye. Glad to see you lot are going to school."

"It's football today."

"Ah. Not going for the Maths then."

This caused great amusement. "As if." Tim or Barry? He hadn't a clue. If it had been Tim before it was Barry now. "Where you off to then Lenny?"

"A meeting." This provoked a chorus of Ooooing

"Are you lot coming in later?"

"S'ppose so."

Lenny grinned and shook his head. "Hey don't show too much enthusiasm lads. Someone might see."

It was a pretty feeble attempt at a joke but he expected to get some kind of a reaction, derision being the most likely. Instead to his surprise he got a serious shaking of hooded heads.

"Thing is Lenny, its getting boring, ken? We saw this young people place the other night on the tele. Glasgow it was. They had pool tables and everything. Why can't we's have the likes of all that at The Zone? We're all getting fed up with just sitting and playing games and that. It's all right for they lasses, but there should be more for the lads tae do."

PROLOGUE

Lenny blew out his cheeks and then smiled. "Big speech for so early in the morning lads. Let's just say we're working on it. That's why I'm off to my meeting. Faith and patience lads. Faith and patience."

The three young faces showed little evidence of either.

"They Council bastards won't give you's any cash Lenny. They dunnae give a shite about the likes of us. All they want is the Wardens to stop us playing football and that."

Tim or Barry? He hadn't a clue. The new Community Wardens had become a burning bone of contention among the youthful clientele of the Zone. In the local media the wardens were being painted as the twenty first century knights in shining armour, protecting the old and the weak from the rampaging hordes of drug crazed teenagers. As far as the teenagers in question were concerned, the sole role of the wardens seemed to be to stop them doing anything whatsoever in any public place. No football. No sitting about in groups. No skateboarding in the Sunnybank Centre. No BMX ramps. No nothing. In the privacy of the flat, Lenny's opinion of the new wardens was pretty much in line with that of his clients. Sally had lectured him long and hard about how important it was that he kept his opinions to himself in public. If the good and the great at the Council got wind that anyone from the Zone was publicly slagging the wardens they wouldn't get funding for toilet rolls let alone a new and bigger centre. The wardens were the new jewel in the crown. Criticism would mean consequences. It was all about local politics. Lenny had suggested that some might have said similar about the Munich Council in the 1920's when their newly salaried Nazi Brownshirts went about smashing up Jewish shops. That had been local politics too. Sally had told him not to be so stupid. Once upon a time Lenny might well have argued. Once he might have fought long and hard. Not any more. Instead he had just grinned and ruffled the hair of his niece and told her he was only ragging her. Lenny Baxter had done his share of fighting the system and the system had won out. The system had taken him apart piece by piece. The system had taken twenty years.

"Faith and patience lads. Go on. You best bugger off. You'll be late for school." As if that was something that was anything of the remotest concern.

He turned and left them to it. God alone knew what they were up to. Nothing good, that was a cert. Lenny turned his face into the rain and stepped out. At times he wondered how much he actually achieved at the Zone. Sally told him that it was brilliant that the likes of Tim and Barry Flint were engaging with him., Engaging?. What the hell was that supposed to mean? Sure they talked to him and didn't mess him about. They watched their p's and q's once they were through the doors of the Zone. But what else? Was there any sign of them not following the family tradition of trouble, more trouble and prison? Not much. Not any in fact. So what exactly was he managing to achieve? He wiped the thought away. It was like most thoughts, it led nowhere worthwhile. He had come to terms many years earlier that life was all about swimming into a tide and going slowly backwards. And then you die. Thinking about it just made it worse.

The rain got a bit harder. Lenny ducked his head and walked. He turned two corners and paused. Set back a little from the road that skirted the edge of Sunnybank were the old Council Waste Collection offices. To say that they were now in a sad state of disrepair was a major understatement. Once upon a time they had been home to fifteen council employees who coordinated the collection of Dumfries' rubbish. It had been a job for three, maybe four. The fact that there had been fifteen with several offices and a large canteen was a legacy of Britain of the Sixties and Seventies when it always took a lot of people to do not a lot of Public Works. The place had been closed down when the gale force wind of Maggie Thatcher had blown through the public sector in the Eighties. It had never opened since and now it stood as a monument to the combine harvester that the infamous daughter of a Grantham grocer had driven through the public services.

Now the tired old building had become Sally's Holy Grail. She had managed to win funding from a private trust fund to hire architects to draw up plans for the full renovation of the old offices to create a new and shiny version of the Zone. The result would be along the lines of the place in Glasgow that Tim or Barry Flint had been describing. She planned a pool and table tennis room. There were quiet rooms for homework. There was a computer suite. There was a fully equipped kitchen that would be run by the kids as a cafe. There were 'one to one' talk rooms. There was even a basketball net and a half pipe for skateboarding on the car park at the back. Sally's dream was going to cost a fortune and it kept her up late most nights filling in funding applications and penning letters to politicians.

For a while there had seemed to be some hope, but then it had leaked out that the Council was on the verge of selling off the site to a development company to build ten new houses and thereby cash in on the local house price boom. The clock was ticking down and even Sally was beginning to have doubts. The economics of the situation offered little cause for optimism. Selling off the asset would throw money into the coffers. Developing it as a youth centre would cost a fortune. It wasn't hard to work out which solution would hold most attraction to the Council bean counters and the elected members who had to fight their corners at weekly surgeries when their angry constituents all had a lot to say about their rising Council Tax bills.

He cupped his hands against the damp wind and lit up his fourth cigarette of the morning. He was pretty convinced that the whole thing was just a pipe dream. The Council were just humouring Sally and ticking the boxes that proved that they had investigated and evaluated the idea. Then they would sell off the land and shrug their shoulders. He had tried to warn his niece about how much chasing rainbows could hurt. He wanted to tell her that chasing rainbows destroyed lives. His life. His dad. His brother. All those others who had once marched out to take on the system with their banners and heads held high. All those others who had in the end been broken by the police batons and the repossession orders from the HP companies. They had all chased their rainbows on beans on toast. Tea bags used three times over. Frozen fish fingers containing about as much fish as a lake by a Soviet chemical factory. And the rain had come and the rainbow had become a twenty year old memory.

His watch said 9.05. He stepped out. He didn't want to be the one who walked into the meeting late. There would be enough stares anyway. There always were. Stares and whispers. That's Lenny Baxter. Have you heard about him? His history followed his every step like a stray dog that just wouldn't give up. He tossed the smoked cigarette and walked, head down against the rain.

The three boys watched Lenny disappear around the corner before carrying on with their disturbed business at hand. Luke re-opened his bag to show off his booty, all of it lifted from his home whilst his mum was frying up the morning bacon and his dad was completing his ablutions in the bathroom. First out was a crumpled ten pack of Mayfair cigarettes which when opened revealed contents of three.

"These were in my Dad's pocket from Saturday night. He must have been well pissed because he was sick as a dog on Sunday morning. He'll not miss these."

Next came a rather dusty bottle of sherry which had been lurking at the back of one of the kitchen cupboards for as long as Luke could remember. His gran had used to enjoy a sherry at Christmas when she had come down from Motherwell to visit, but his gran had been dead for four years and the sherry had not been required since. Both of the items received approving nods from the twins. However the third item drew frowns.

"What's that all about then?" Asked Tim when Luke pulled out a can of lighter fluid.

"You spray it in your mouth. Makes you feel like you're completely pissed." Luke enjoyed the opportunity to show off his knowledge. He still couldn't quite believe that the two twins were now mates rather than tormentors.

"Says who?" Tim was a long, long way from being convinced.

"One of those leaflets from the Zone. You know. The drugs ones. It's all about sniffing glue and gas and stuff. Here. I've got it in my bag. Have a read."

Tim moved the conversation on quickly. He was barely able to read his own name, let alone a leaflet about solvent abuse, pictures or no pictures. "Bugger that. Tell you what. You can go first and we'll see what it looks like. That sounds a plan."

Luke straightened himself. He sensed a challenge and he was up for it. His whole life had changed since the Zone under 14's team and his friendship with the Flint twins. No longer was the playground a place of fear. Now he actually looked forward to break time. Being with the Flints meant respect. It meant a share in the chocolate bars and fruit shoot yoghurts they claimed as a matter of right from the boys who brought in a packed lunch. It wasn't something he was about to let go of. Not a chance.

"Nae bother boys. When do you want to have a go?"

"After school."

PROLOGUE

"We not bothering with the Zone then?"

Barry gave a dismissive shake of this head. "Na. Zone's getting shite. I'm sick of poxy games and all they stupid lasses yapping on about David Beckham. We'll go round to the old Pavilion."

"OK. Sound."

The three lads emerged from the doorway and joined the slow moving crowd of Sunnybank youth making their unenthusiastic way to another day of education.

When Zoe McGuire awoke that morning she was totally unaware of the two anniversaries that the date represented. A squinting look at the clock told her that it was barely morning at all. A few minutes before twelve. Strange. It wasn't often that she slept in. She had always been good at getting up. Her parents had never had to go through the door banging routine to prize her out of bed for school. Not Zoe. Always up and showered and bright as a button. There had always been plenty to get up for. School. Ice skating. Days out with her dad on the milk tanker. For sixteen years life had been a sunny place for Zoe McGuire. Then it had started to fall to pieces on the very day when all her dreams had seemed to come true at once.

That had been the first of the anniversaries, five months earlier, her sixteenth birthday. The day had started great. Presents. Fuss from her parents and her younger brother and all her mates at school. It had been a Friday and that evening ten of them had hit the town, dressed up to the nines in party clothes that managed to cover about fifteen percent of their fast developing bodies. They had booked a big table in a Chinese restaurant where there had been a cake and party hats and vodka passed around under the table to mix in with soft drinks. As far as her parents were concerned, they were all headed out to a friend's house whose parents lived a few miles out of the town and had converted a stable for their treasured daughter to entertain her friends. Instead, the real plan was to head into the town centre to a club where one of her mates' older brothers was on the door and had agreed to nod them all through.

Inside the place was million miles from being a theatre of dreams. It was a few years past seeing a paintbrush. The cracks were getting slightly wider. The damp spots were becoming damp patches. The owner was losing his hair and his bank manager was not the friend he

15

had once been. But the lights were low and nothing was about to interrupt the excitement of the ten lasses from Sunnybank High. This was their right of passage. They had waited a long time to make their grand entrance into the big world of adult nightlife. They had laughed and screamed and danced around their handbags as the place slowly filled up. The bar staff never asked for ID. They occasionally glanced over at the manager who responded with a small nod. He had a mortgage and jobs in the town were not that easy to come by. If the ten under-agers from Sunnybank were about to throw a couple of hundred much need quid at the till for their Alco pops, then he wasn't about to cut off his nose to spite his face.

Zoe was brimmingly the right side of ten bottles of sugary orange based Schnapps when her dream came thunderingly true. Had she glanced at the new watch her Grandpa had given her earlier in the day, she would have seen that it was more or less exactly midnight. A true fairytale and she was Cinderella for the night.

Her prince was called Kevin Peters and he had been her prince since the age of twelve when she had first made her way through the gates of Sunnybank High School. She hadn't been on her own in this. Just about every girl in her year felt the same. And the year above her. And the year above that. Kevin was two years older than her and he was everything. He was drop dead boy band gorgeous with spiked hair and a face with a permanent tough guy attitude. He was the free scoring centre forward of the all conquering school team. Of course he was the captain. His dad and big brother were both long term guests of her Majesty, one in HMP Kilmarnock, one up in Peterhead. He would have a lit fag in his mouth before he was even out of the school gates and he would walk away with lads years older than him who carried reputations.

For years, the girls of Sunnybank had watched Kevin take his pick of them as he worked the field like a combine harvester. By the time he had left school two years earlier, there were all kinds of rumours that there were already two infant Kevins being pushed around Sunnybank in prams by sour faced teenage mothers. None of them had seen much of him for a couple of years. Leaving school took him out of the immediate spotlight, but his legend lived on. He became an occasionally glimpsed figure on street corners or up the High Street on Saturday afternoons. Absence merely made all their hearts grow fonder and none of the boys in their year came close to matching him.

That was why she felt her drunken legs buckle under her when her forearm felt the electricity of his touch at 11.58 on the night of her birthday. She didn't register the looks of astonishment and seething jealousy in the eyes of her friends as he leant in close to shout in her ear.

"You the birthday girl then?"

She wanted to be cool and witty and dismissive. Instead the best she could manage was a shouted "Aye."

The next two hours were a blur. A dream. The sweat of the heaving dance floor. A table with three of his mates. The sharp burning of her first ever line of speed. More dancing. Hungry snogging and her virginity taken away in a frantic thrash in a backyard full of overflowing wheelie bins.

The next morning she had woken to a screaming hangover and a memory that was shaky at best. Her phone buzzed with eager text messages from her friends. Some were subtle. Others were frank. They all asked the same thing. Did he? Did you? How was it? She was cool and evasive and never even came close to telling the truth. It was a truth that was a million miles over frozen icecaps from the magazines of her hopeful teenage years. There had been no dazzling light of the dawn and singing of birds and heart squeezing background music. All she could remember was the bins and a thin miserable rain and a jarring pain. Later that morning she had gone into the Zone and cried as Sally gave her the morning after pill and hugged her.

But when he had asked her out again via a text two days later she had said yes. That had been five months ago and her life had slowly been coming apart at the seams ever since. After two months she had left home amidst foul mouth screaming from her dad, desperate tears from her mum, and a bemused shocked silence from her little brother. A month later she had stopped going to school. A month after that she had learned the truth about why Kevin's graceful athletic body had become a bag of bones. At first she hadn't noticed as it was hidden away under layers of baggy clothes. Only when they spent their first proper night together in the grimy sheets of his bed had she seen just how painfully skinny he was. Not that she hadn't half known already. There had been plenty of rumours. Plenty of warnings. Careful Zoe. He's a smackhead you know. A junkie. Thieving bastard. Just like his dad. Just like his brother. She had half known because one by one her mates didn't reply to her texts any more. There were several more sixteenth birthday parties, but she wasn't invited to any of them. As far as parents were concerned, she had become a no go area. Only Sally was honest with her. Only Sally sat her down and talked to her properly. She still went into the Zone even though Kevin laughed at her for it. She went when she knew it would be quiet and drank tea with Sally in the boxy little office. Sally became the go between her and her mum. Dad had laid down the law. So long as his daughter shamed the family by living with Kevin Peters she wasn't part of his family any more, and not one of them was allowed to speak with her. Her mum left messages and small packages and envelopes with £10 and £20 notes for Sally to pass on. Sally was patient. She never came right out and said it. She just hinted and made sure she left leaflets warning of the dangers of heroin where it was easy for Zoe to pick them up whilst Sally went to the kitchen to switch on the kettle.

Zoe had read the leaflets and she had been so sure that there was no way she would ever in a million years be stupid enough to use heroin. Of course she wouldn't. She had grown up amongst all the ghost figures of Sunnybank with their sunken eyes and emaciated bodies. No way. Not ever. No matter what.

But when Kevin got out foil for the first time she hadn't been able to find the words. By now she was lonely. Achingly lonely. She missed her family and her friends and the warmth of the life she had thrown up. It had only taken weeks for everything to fall apart. Kevin was all she had now. Her one possession. Her one guiding light. And so when he told her what to do in a quiet voice, she did as she was instructed and chased the dragon shaped plume of heroin smoke and took it down into her lungs.

That had been the second unseen anniversary. It had been two months earlier. The day her habit had begun. Not that she had admitted it for ages. No chance. She never injected it, did she? Never jagged. Kevin did, but she didn't. She just smoked it. It was just a couple of times a week to start with. Then three, and four until it had become every day. Kevin hadn't really had to push her too hard to get her out shoplifting. By this time she knew the ropes well enough. Shoplifting was the woman's work among her new group of acquaintances. The men tried, but they weren't any use. It was the lasses who marched out every morning to strip the dwindling number of shops on the High Street. They went in twos and threes and fours. They worked in teams. They stole to order and by eleven o clock they would return to their men who would trade in the goods for bags of smack. One night she watched a documentary from Africa about a year in the lives of a pride of Kenyan lions. Her comatose brain registered the similarities. The male lions lazed about in the sun and shook the flies from their shaggy manes whilst their women went out and brought down zebra and wildebeest. She had watched first with a small smile of recognition and then miserable tears.

Kevin hadn't come home that night. Or the next two. It had been the first time that she had known what it was to rattle. The slow blinding pain of withdrawal. The growing panic of need. Terrible need. All consuming need. She had trailed the streets looking for him only to be met with shrugged shoulders and smirks until she was told that he might be shacked up with that Sheila Benson.

She was blazing. She was going to walk out. Go home. Get her life back. Bury a kitchen knife in his scrawny stomach. But when he came back she was in such a state she would have done anything for him. Anything. She had closed her eyes in utter all consuming impossible bliss when he had pushed a needle through the wall of her vein and taken all the pain and loneliness and fear away in less than thirty seconds. No more smoking after that. He had told her they couldn't afford it. Too much waste. He wasn't wasting his time looking after her habit if she insisted on smoking. Not that she had argued any. Now she knew why almost everyone jagged it. Jagging was like nothing else. Jagging was the stairway to heaven. Jagging took everything away. All of it. The agonising guilt at what she had done to her mum and dad. The empty feeling she got when she saw her little brother heading home from school with his mates. The loneliness and loss she felt when she saw her old friends still looking smart and healthy, out shopping with their mums as she avoided their glances and waited for her chance to steal. All of it disappeared within seconds of the sharp heaven of the needle.

She pulled herself up into a sitting position and checked the time on the face of her mobile phone. Past noon. Her brain registered dull surprise. Heroin was like a drill sergeant in a training barracks. It kicked her out of her bed early and sent her out in pursuit of more.

Always more. Slowly her foggy brain started to clear and memories from the previous evening trudged in like refugees from a cold northern country. Kevin had been out most of the night. He'd got back in after midnight and cooked up straight away. Where was it that he said he'd been? That was it. He'd been to see Mog. Mog had been the talk of the High Street all day. Mog had taken a special delivery direct from Liverpool. Mog was selling the best tenner bags of smack that Dumfries had seen in two years or more. Kevin hadn't said much. He had muttered something about Mog being out most of the night.

Then what? She screwed her face up a little as she tried to remember. Nothing. A vague recollection of being in the warmest, safest place there had ever been. Then zero. Twelve whole hours of perfect oblivion. So the rumours had been right. Mog had become the man of the hour.

There was neither sight nor sound of Kevin. When had he left? No way of telling. His tolerance was way, way higher than hers. No doubt he would have been up with the larks, ready for another day or ducking and diving so that he could get back to Mog as soon as he had the cash. Something didn't make sense. Why had he let her sleep? It certainly would have nothing to do with the milk of human kindness. No way. The only reason she was still in bed was that he must have been unable to wake her up. She must have been comatose. Otherwise he would have dragged her to the High Street and her new work.

A small fission of alarm passed through her. Had she skated close to an overdose? No way of telling. It was what they all said. You never knew. The cotton wool simply wrapped you into blackness. If an ambulance got to you in time, you would awake from death to blazing lights and pain. If there was nobody there, you'd never wake up at all. Was that what had happened? No point asking Kevin. It was probably something she would never know. The thought soon floated up and away and out of sight. In its place was the memory of the perfect warmth. The nagging voice in her ear was already starting its all too familiar litany.

More.

More.

Lenny decided that it was probably best to force himself to stop looking at the clock. It was closing in on 2.30 now. The Anti Social

PROLOGUE

Behaviour Strategy Group was an all day affair. It had started with coffee and biscuits at 9.30. Three hours later they had broken for sandwiches and cakes. They were due to wrap it up at 4.30. In the front of his brain was the coffee break at 3.00 when he could escape to the porch and chew through two cigarettes, one after the other.

The day had gone downhill more or less from the very start. He was in the Prevention Group. It hadn't come as much of a surprise to find that he was the sore thumb. The odd man out. The looks had started from the minute he had walked into the room. Stolen glances. Quick, careful conversations. He's Lenny Baxter. Have you heard about him? Really? He could sense his past being the main topic of conversation. Nothing new in that. It was the way it was. He could sense it wherever he went. The group were wary of him, he in his jeans and a rather frayed check shirt, they in their non-descript suits and discount shoes. They took notes on pads held in place in folders that had been given for birthdays or Christmas. Presents for low level beaurocrats who spent their lives in meetings and focus groups. Paper for words like 'interface' and 'strategy'and 'rigorous monitoring'and 'evaluation techniques'.

It had taken him an hour to work out what was happening around him. They were defending their empires. Small, miserable little empires that encompassed two or three rooms in dreary public buildings. Empires made up of a couple of secretaries and a telephonist. Empires that meant a slathering snog at the Christmas party and a dismal affair if there was half a chance. Empires where the booty was a wage somewhere just over the National Average and a decent pension. Empires that paid for bungalows that were rising in price and mid range cars that were cleaned every weekend and holidays to places that were two steps up the ladder from Benidorm. The key to the empires was that all boxes had always to be ticked in all the right places. Never, never admit that something wasn't working. A complete washout would always be described as 'showing encouraging signs of potential'. Failure was something that could never be written down. These were people who lived their lives running from the threat of government spending cuts. If any hint of failure ever leaked out of their three room empires, then the hard faced men from Edinburgh might cut off the money. Then it could be redundancy and mid life crisis and no more holidays in places two rungs up the ladder from Benidorm.

So it was that Lenny had sat through hour after hour of fantasy. A stranger from out of town would have left with a firm impression that the youth of Dumfries must have been the most pampered young people in the western world. They listed projects that had never made it out of filing cabinets and activities that had never been more than paperwork. To admit that there was nothing for young people to do would have meant placing their empires under threat. So instead they indulged in beaurocratic Alice in Wonderland. The message they committed to paper was always going to be a very clear one. Things were good. Great. Not a penny was being wasted. Every shilling was being spent on delivering world class public services that were the envy of the world. The youngsters of Dumfries were spoiled for choice when it came to things to do. If they chose to misbehave themselves and vandalise schools and take drugs and swear at old ladies, then it was nothing to do with any lack of provision.

He silently wished that he had brought Tim and Barry with him to drive a thirty tonne truck through the tower of bullshit. Instead he kept quiet and chipped in small comments every now and then to make sure that the name of Sunnybank was written down where it needed to be. Inside he ached with shame at his politeness. Somewhere in South Yorkshire his dad must have been turning in his grave. When had a Baxter ever sat in a room full of suits and been so polite? Never. The Baxters were the scourge of suits. Always had been. The Baxters shouted in the faces of the men in suits. The Baxters stood up and told it like it was. Regardless.

Once upon a time Lenny had shouted with the best of them. He had fought until there was nothing left. Until they had dismantled him. Broken him. Destroyed him. And now here he was, sitting it out, thinking of no more than the relief of nicotine whilst out there were hundreds of Barrys and Tims and Lukes who needed him to get stuck in and fight for them. Deep down he knew that Sally was right. Kicking off would get him nowhere. If he allowed his anger and contempt to come up to the surface they would all close ranks and make sure that the Zone wouldn't get a single, lousy penny of the bounty that was to be sent down from the Government.

He pulled his wandering attention back and tried to focus on what was now being discussed. Unbelievable. They were onto the subject of bushes and shrubs. There were two schools of thought. Some said that bushes could be a good thing. They kept young people from spoiling public places with litter and mess and noise. Especially spiky bushes with big fat thorns. Others disagreed. Others felt that bushes could offer young people secluded cover to meet in secret and take their drugs and be beastly. The conclusion for the strategy was that bushes and shrubs could be a good thing and a bad thing. It all depended on individual community circumstances. There would have to be analysis and public consultation exercises. Then there would be focus groups to consider and work the issues through. Then there would be feasibility studies and risk assessment. Police and Fire would be consulted. Well of course they would. Proper linkage would have to be put in place. Partnership working would be paramount.

The image of the fast fading Hitler in his bunker in the last days of the Reich leapt into Lenny's mind. There he was with all his generals, playing make believe war with ghost armies that had been annihilated months earlier whilst the rampaging tanks of the Red Army were smashing their way though the suburbs of Berlin. The fantasy of paperwork. Write it down carefully enough and it can seem like it is really true.

They agreed that the policy on bushes and shrubs was that it was a local issue to be considered on a case by case basis. At least five empires grabbed a little piece of it. Lenny doubted whether a single bush would ever be either planted or uprooted, but there would be plenty of man hours spent on talking about it.

They moved along to the next topic and he found himself looking at the clock again. 2.45 p.m. Just a quarter of an hour to some fresh air and nicotine.

Kevin Peters was having a bad day. A lousy day. He had woken at eight and spent almost an hour trying to rouse Zoe. Stupid cow. Out for the count. In the end he had got fed up and gone up to the High Street on his own. The next few hours had been a study in failure. His face was all too familiar to the security men on the doors of the shops that had anything worth nicking. He hadn't even made it through a front door by noon. Everything was against him. All morning the grey skies had thrown down a thin drenching rain. It wasn't any kind of day for Joe Public to head for town and do a bit of shopping. The town centre was all but deserted. It seemed as if the junkies outnumbered the paying punters by at least two to one. Crowds meant a bit of cover, a chance of distraction. Today was a day for the security men who had no problem in spotting the approach of the town's more notorious faces. Most of the time he had been stopped before he had even got within five yards of the door.

The majority of the morning had been spent talking about Mog. All along the High Street small groups met and talked about the man of the hour. Had any yet have you? Too right. The business. Serious kit. Pale faces and bad skin. Baseball caps and hooded tops. Eyes gleaming with the eating desire for a wee taste of Mog's smack which was just an elusive tenner away. The Chinese could have dropped an atom bomb on San Francisco and it would not have deflected them for a second from the burning issue of the day. And the more they all talked about it, the more they all wanted it. The more they all wanted it, the more desperate they all became.

Jimmy McGuire was the first casualty. That came as no surprise to anyone. It was pretty well agreed that Jimmy McGuire was an idiot. Always had been. Jimmy always had voices in his head and by the late morning they were screaming at him. He just completely lost it and barged his way into Marks and Spencer and grabbed an armful of Tweed jackets. The security guard was a veteran of the Dumfries Rugby Club and he took Jimmy down hard whilst he was still twenty yards short of the door. It was a story that the guard would chuckle about for days. It won him four free pints in the club on the following Saturday when his back was meatily slapped in congratulation by one and all who said that was the only way to deal with the junkie bastards. The security guard weighed eighteen stones in his underpants. Jimmy McGuire couldn't tip the scales over eight stone even in the anorak his gran had given him for his fourteenth birthday. The simple physics of the fight led to Jimmy getting two cracked ribs to go with six months for shoplifting.

Kevin had known Jimmy since Primary School and he had seen all the signs. He had sensed that Jimmy was about to go down the desperado route and he had tracked him. A good move. A smart move. The commotion that followed the rugby tackle gave Kevin the chance to complete a quick hit and run. He had shovelled a handful of holiday gadgets into his pockets and ghosted out into the rain whilst Jimmy's high pitched voice cursed the world and their grandmother and the security guard in particular. The guard was so empowered by the feeling of slamming Jimmy to the floor that he at last summoned up the courage to ask out one of the assistants who was a thirty four year old divorcee who he fancied rotten. She had told him to get stuffed.

Kevin ducked into an alleyway and checked his loot. Six items, all designed for the kind of holidays taken by people looking for somewhere two steps up the ladder from Benidorm. There were two travel alarm clocks that could give the correct time in London, New York, Hong Kong and Sydney. There was an ultra light money belt. A slim-line travel torch that promised a beam of light good for a hundred yards. A compass and thermometer all in one. And a blow up neck cushion to help sleep on either bus or plane. The cheapest item was priced at £7. The dearest was the compass/thermometer which weighed in at £11. The total retail value was £56. Kevin frowned at the maths. It was going to be marginal. The going rate for stolen goods was 20% of the price ticket value. Technically that would give him about £11. The problem was that these were hardly mainstream items. They certainly weren't DVDs. On the up side he thought that the calendar was in his favour. People would be going off on their holidays soon and they might well be in the market for this kind of stuff, especially after a pint or two in the pub. These were just the kind of things that a bloke might take home with him to appease a wife when he had stayed out an hour too long and supped three pints too many. So there was a chance. A decent chance.

Half an hour later his balloon was well and truly popped. None of his contacts had been willing to buy into the holiday theory. They had just laughed at it. Two had offered him £3. One hadn't offered him a penny and told him to get lost. The last had offered £5 for old time's sake and Kevin had taken it. That left him with decisions. Two choices. He could either go back up to the High Street and try to turn £5 into £10. If not that, he could hike back to Sunnybank, score half a bag off Mog, shoot it up, go back to the flat, kick Zoe out of bed and get her out into the town in time to get some cash together for the evening. No contest. As soon as the thought of half a bag clambered into his increasingly fried brain it was never going to be much of a contest. Plan B was adopted and Kevin strode out for Sunnybank.

Mog was having a day of it. A real day of it. And it hadn't just been one day. It had almost been three weeks now. Three weeks unlike any he had ever known. All of a sudden everyone wanted to know him. He suddenly had friends and lots of them and the unbelievable, unaccustomed feeling of a bulging pocketful of cash. He was damned if he was going to take any of it for granted. Not a chance. He was going to make sure that he enjoyed every last second of it.

There hadn't been many good weeks in Mog's thirty-three years on the planet. In fact, before this three week golden era, there probably hadn't been any. His life could have been used as a template for an academic study of the most commonly trodden paths of Scottish heroin addiction. His few fleeting infant memories of his father were of towering anger and flying fists. Father had disappeared from his life before he was four. After that, there was the boyfriend. More fleeting memories, this time so blurred that they were almost nothing. Mog's brain had worked hard to do the blurring. All that was left was an image of his bedroom door opening and the silhouette of the boyfriend framed by the naked bulb on the landing. Then the door would close leaving the room lit only by the dreary orange glow of the street lamp outside. Then bad stuff. Very, very bad stuff. The worst stuff in the world.

Something had happened when he was six. He never really knew what. Suddenly his mother was gone. And the boyfriend. And he was moved to a care home for boys with problems. At that point in his life he had still been Ronald Morgan. By the time he was eight he had become Mog.

The first care home hadn't been so bad. Not when he had got used to it. It was the second one where it all started up again. The silhouette at the door. And bad stuff. Terrible stuff. Stuff that Mog's mind could never quite lose. Could never quite come to terms with. This time he wasn't alone. This time there were lots of boys going through the bad stuff. They had tried to tell people, but it had only made things worse. Who was ever about to believe them? Nobody of course. They were the bad boys. Very bad boys. And when the men and women they tried to tell left the home, the bad stuff would get worse until one day the police cars had come and it all stopped.

The bad boys had left the home together at sixteen and fallen into the hostels of Dumfries. They were still tied together by all the bad stuff they had been through and they never, ever talked about. They shared the nightmares and the sleepless nights in cold rooms in houses that would never be homes. It hadn't taken long for one of them to find the only medicine in the world that would take all the bad stuff away. Within weeks they were all using the medicine. To the outside world they were just teenage junkies. But they had found something that at last helped them to feel safe. Really, really safe. Something to take all the memories away. Something to erase the image of that silhouette framed by the naked light bulb on the landing.

And so it had all started, just a few weeks after his sixteenth birthday. The endless cycle. Mog's life had been an unbroken tale of abuse. Sixteen years of fairly unrelenting sexual abuse moved seamlessly into seventeen years of similarly unrelenting heroin abuse. The cycle. Hostel. Young Offenders Institution. Hostel. Friend's couch. Hospital. Prison. Hostel. Flat. Prison. Hostel. Prison. Rehab. Friend's couch. Prison. The cycle. Day after day of petty little crimes to come up with the next magic tenner ticket to a place of safety and no memories. The place where there was no figure on the landing.

And through all of it, all thirty three dismal years of it, he couldn't remember a single unbroken good week. Until these three. So there was no way he was about to take it for granted. He was going to milk it. Every drop. And he was going to make it last.

The tipping point had been his latest prison sentence, this time served out in Kilmarnock. He had shared a cell with a Scouser of similar age. Jerry was a junkie too. They became close in the long hours of lock up that were the main feature of the privatised prison. They chased the dragon together. They shared their nightmares with each other. Bad stuff. The same bad stuff. For Jerry it had been a home in the picture post card prettiness of the Welsh hills. Jerry was a travelling salesman. The product in his briefcase was heroin and he represented several firms from his home town.

Liverpool was the undisputed heroin capital of Britain. All the best stuff came from Liverpool. The real stuff. Purest quality. Best price. Though god help anyone who didn't pay their bill. For hundreds of years Liverpool had been the place that brought in the raw materials to make Britain tick. The cotton that had rumbled up the railways to the mills of East Lancashire. Sugar and tea and coffee and corn and spices and bananas. Liverpool had always been about bringing in commodities. Once upon a time at the very height of the British Empire all these commodities had gone through the books and the turnover had been huge. Nothing much had changed. Now the great buildings of the Albert Dock were home to yuppie flats and designer clothes shops and the cranes were just for show. No cranes required to bring in the pills and powders of the drugs industry. But the city still had the know-how. Only this time, the huge turnover was off the books.

When Mog and Jerry got out, they promised to stay in touch. And they did. Jerry fitted Mog in on his Glasgow run and got him started with a couple hundred of quid's worth. It hadn't taken long for the word to sweep the town that Mog was selling proper Scouse smack. The first batch had all gone in a single evening and Jerry had dropped off more on his way back home. Mog had been a dealer before. Lots of times. He had done three stretches as a result. But never before had he plugged into a pipeline right from the fountainhead. Never before had he had a product that knocked spots off what everybody else was peddling. Never before had he traded with a mate. A proper mate. And Jerry was one of the few proper mates he had ever known.

It had been going on for three weeks now and the delivery that Jerry had dropped off the week before had been the best yet. Mog knew it better than anyone. He had managed to keep the cash to one side to make his next payment. All the profits had gone straight into the veins of his groin. The veins of his arms had given up the ghost years before. For the very first time the figure on the landing hadn't been there for a whole week.

He had walked the High Street that afternoon and it had been like a procession. They had come to him to pay their respects. All of them with ingratiating smiles. Yellow broken teeth wrecked by years of sugary methadone. Y'aright Mog? How's it going? Still selling? Always before he had been with them. Scurrying about trying to somehow steal enough. Begging and cajoling for a bit of credit. Just to tide me over. I get my social tomorrow. Go on pal, just enough to tide me over, just enough for a wee taste. And now all of a sudden he was the man. The one they all wanted to know.

When he had been released, he had landed up at his mate Benny's flat in Sunnybank. He had been with Benny in the care home. They had been through all the bad stuff together. Benny had dived into the smack along with all the rest of them. But Benny had never really come close to dealing with things. Benny tended to get it off his chest by hitting people. And stabbing them. Umpteen anger management classes in various prisons hadn't even scratched the surface. It meant that Benny was the perfect man to stay with for Dumfries' newest entrepreneur. When you had a lot of cash floating around you needed someone like Benny about the place. The bank certainly wasn't an option.

Mog got in at three and the mobile phone never stopped. Most of his orders were delivered by a couple of youngsters who got a bag in the mornings and a bag in the afternoons and two in the evenings for their services. The mobile phone kept on ringing. And ringing. And Jerry was due back in two days time.

Kevin was one of the ones who was allowed to call round and knock the door. Mog had done time with Kevin's dad and that gave Kevin privileges. Not that many, but some. He didn't look all that good when Benny waved him inside. He had always been a handsome boy. He had certainly seemed to do well enough with the lasses. That was something that Mog had never excelled at. Even without the erosion of seventeen years of heroin addiction he would never have been a pin-up. He had always been small and skinny with a face boney in all the non-Hollywood places. Now his teeth were a line of stumps and his hair was all but gone on top. His skin was the colour of three week old mashed potato left out in the rain. His nose had never set properly after a prison beating years earlier. No. Never a pin-up. Not Mog.

It hadn't been long ago that nobody would have clocked Kevin as a junkie. He had been a tall boy of designer clothes glowing health. Not any more. The weight had all dropped off and the arrogant straight back of youth was already bent. He hadn't shaved for a day or two and his face was a field of acne. He was soaked through and his coat almost splatted when he tossed it to the floor and flopped into an armchair.

Mog shook out two fags and tossed one over to his young guest.

"Cheers Mog."

"Bit damp hey Kev."

"Aye. Shite out there."

"Grafting any good today?" Grafting was their word for the day job. The shoplifting. Seven days a week, Lots of overtime. Pay variable and no holiday entitlement.

"Nah. Terrible. All junkies and nae punters. Jimmy got lifted. M&S. That big security man flattened him. I think they had to take him to the Infirmary."

Mog chuckled. "Jimmy's always getting lifted. Jimmy's just a dickhead."

"Aye."

They smoked in silence for a moment. Benny joined them with a can of Tennants and a dangerously blank expression. Mog's was a trade where there was no need for a sales pitch. Whatever money his customer had, they would spend. That was all there was to it. He could tell by every aspect of Kevin's demeanour that here was a customer with not a lot in his pockets. He wondered if he actually had anything in his pockets. How many times had Mog been on that side of the room. The wrong side of the deal. The begging zone.

"Only got a fiver Mog."

Mog shrugged. "It's nae so bad. Half a bag of this kit's better than two of the normal shite."

"Aye s'ppose so."

Kevin stubbed his fag and fiddled with his grimy fingers. "Can I shoot it up the now Mog. That cool with you's?"

"Aye. Be my guest."

Mog pocketed the crumpled fiver and passed a half bag across. He smoked another cigarette as Kevin tried not to seem too hurried as he dug all his works out from his pockets and cooked up the brown powder on a spoon. He smiled as he watched his customer flop back in relief as the needle did its work. He left him in peace for a while. Enough to get the full bang. Enough to find the place of worship. Enough to want more of the same. Much more. As much as he could get. Enough to do just about anything to get it. Anything. Because Mog had something in mind. He decided to speak before Kevin's gouch took him off to sleep.

"Hey. Kev."

The boy's head lifted from his chest slowly, a small smile now where there had only been tight-lipped tension.

"Aye."

"Is that you out of cash then?"

"Aye. Skint. Nae a penny to my name."

Mog shook his head sadly in a manner of been there a million times before pal.

"A bastard hey. You anything coming then?"

A shake of the head. "Nah. Toss all. I'll go and get Zoe in a bit and we'll see what we can graft. Might be back later."

"Ah. Zoe. Right." There must have been something in his voice because Kevin's dull eyes suddenly sparked.

"Wha'boot Zoe?"

A careful drag. Very careful. "She's a bonnie lass, that's all."

"I suppose."

"How old is she?"

"Sixteen."

"Must be a blinder in the sack."

"She's all right."

Another careful drag. "Tell you what Kev. I'll no beat about the bush here. You bring Zoe round later. Say eight o'clock. I get to screw her and I'll give you a gramme. What do you think of that?"

Now the eyes widened. Mog looked into them carefully. Was it anger or was it greed? Benny sat up slightly. Ready. Always ready. Mog decided it was time to organise his security a wee treat.

"Two grams if Benny gets a wee turn as well." He was a big hearted employer. He felt like De Niro playing Al Capone. "So what do you reckon?"

Kevin put his head down. He hadn't expected this. He didn't care much about Zoe. Not any more. He was bored with her and she was whinging too much. But this was something else. The thought of these two jumping all over her made his skin crawl. But then again. Two grams. Two grams was twenty tenner bags. Two grams was a dream come true. He shook his head.

"She'll no do it Mog. No way."

Mog had considered this. Planned for it. He gave Kevin a slow smile. "Here." He opened his palm to show ten pills. 10 mg Valium "They're real. No that imitation junk. She'll be rattling around the flat when you get back in. Give her these to take the edge off. Give her a bag and then bring her round. We'll give her a wee drink and another hit and I don't think there will be a problem. Here. A bag on the house whilst you think about it."

As Kevin cooked up again, Mog allowed his imagination to wander onto the image of Zoe McGuire. He had watched her grow up when he had lived a few doors down a couple of years before. He had watched her coming back home in her school uniform and going out in the crop tops showing her smooth belly. He had never screwed a girl like Zoe. Sixteen and bonnie as a Hollywood starlet. The thought made him near dizzy. That was how far things had come. One month, Kilmarnock Prison. The next month, a chance of screwing Zoe McGuire. A chance of making her strip everything off. It was how things could be for the man of the hour.

Kevin slammed in the needle and left the room for a while. When his head lolled forward after a quarter of an hour he was smiling.

"Here. Give me the vallies Mog. I'll sort it out. See you later."

Kevin rose unsteadily to his feet and seemed to take an age in getting his wet coat on. Benny sat and watched without a flicker. Mog luxuriated in the sheer joy of the way his life was going and thought about Zoe McGuire.

By the time the exodus of youth piled out of the gates of Sunnybank High School at three thirty, the rain had worked up a full head of steam. Every night on the TV, the Scottish Tourist Board was sending out glossy images of the hills and lakes adorned in all the finery of sunny June. The place to take a long weekend. The place to find your soul. Come to Scotland and find yourself. It wasn't that sort of day and the vista of the unrelenting pebble-dash greyness of Sunnybank wasn't the sort of picture to inspire long weekends. It was more a come to Scotland and hang yourself afternoon.

The awfulness of the day didn't have any great effect on the spirits of Luke and the Flint twins. They were well enough used to it. They pulled up their hoods and walked fast with their heads close together. Fifteen minutes later they crossed the playing fields to the old pavilion. On a sunny day they would probably not have found the peace and quiet they needed and they would have had to hunt about for somewhere else. No such problems today. It was an afternoon for crisps in front of the TV or Playstation. They holed up at the back where the eaves of the roof covered a reasonably sheltered balcony. Each emptied their bags. Tim had risked life and limb and grabbed a handful of Club bars before leaving the house whilst his mum was telling his older sister that she looked like an under-dressed tart and that she deserved all she got. Barry had terrorised a fellow first year out of the Yorkie bar that his mum had packed in his lunch box. Luke laid out the Mayfair cigarettes, the sherry and the lighter fluid.

"What's first then lads?"

Tim assumed a careful, thoughtful kind of expression. It was a decision not worth hurrying. At last he gave his opinion in his version of a posh voice. "Well gents. Personally I think a drink and a smoke are in order. How's about you?"

His brother Barry picked up the cue. "Absolutely Bro. Quite right too. Most civilised. Don't mind if I do."

Tim took out a cigarette, lit it, and sucked in a long, appreciative lungful before attempting and failing to produce the smoke rings that the occasion merited. The whistling wind made such an enterprise all but impossible. Barry assumed the relaxed pose of a country gent at his leisure and nodded formally to his brother when he passed over the fag. "Too kind good sir. Too kind."

When his time came, Luke tried to mimic the long hard pull and exploded into a fit of coughing that all but popped his eyes out of their sockets. This sent the twins rolling around in hysterics. When Barry at last regained the power of speech the posh persona had slipped somewhat.

"Bloody hell Luke. You're such a mong."

Next came the vintage sherry. They passed it round and drank in sips. There was no hurry. They weren't about to go anywhere else. All that lay ahead was the walk home and strip tearing from their respective parents. This was their time. No teachers. No parents. No wardens. Just three lads on a dusty balcony that gave shelter from the teeming rain. Time could drift a while.

By the time Kevin walked through the door just after four, Zoe already had her coat on and was about to go out to find him. He hadn't even got the door closed before she was into him.

"You're just a complete bastard Kev. Where've you been? I'm dying here. Really dying. And you just piss off and leave me. Bet you've been with that Sheila tart haven't you. I hope you get the clap you bastard. They say that dirty bitch has just about everything, she's just a stinking . . . ."

He thumped her. Hard. Right in the face. He'd had enough. Absolutely enough. Spoilt little whining cow. It was all she ever did.

Moan. Moan. Moan. Let her go back to her poxy family. Who did they think they were anyway? All airs and graces as if they were royalty or something. And what was her bastard dad? A milk-tanker driver. That's what. A poxy milk-tanker driver and he thought he was the bees-knees just because none of his family had ever done a lump of time in the nick. And the mum. Silly cow. All done up like an overdone tart. What was she? Just because she was on the PTA she seemed to think she was some kind of local hero. Stuff that. Just another fat tart on the tills at Tesco. He bent down to the screaming figure of his soon-to-be ex and dragged her head up by the hair. He pushed his face in close. When he spoke there was no rage. No shouting. Mog's super strength smack took care of that. He was calm. He was ice. He was in complete control. He was the master of his universe. He even smiled when he spoke. He felt like a real gangster.

"Why don't you just shut up darling? I've been out sorting things out whilst you've been getting your beauty sleep. Shut up. Yeah?"

She didn't. She was in utter panic. He'd just hit her. Really hit her. With his fist. And it hurt. Christ it hurt. Nobody had ever hit her before. Never.

"Yeah?"

No.

He slapped her hard across the cheek and her eyes iced over with shock and fear.

"Yeah?"

This time she nodded and fell into trembling silence.

"Good. Sound as a pound. Now darling. Treat time. Get these down your lovely neck whilst I cook up. They'll mellow you out some. Then you can get your kit off and get into bed. We'll do the business then we'll share this bag, yeah? Now isn't that a plan my wee treasure?"

He was frightening her. Terrifying her. She only just managed not to wet herself. She took the smeared glass filled with tap water and gulped down the pills three at a time whilst he held her with an expression she had never seen on his face before.

"Good girl. Good, good girl. Come on now. Let's have your kit off now. That's it. There's a good lass."

Tears streamed down her face as she undressed. His gleaming eyes seemed to eat her. As soon as she was naked she leapt under the duvet and covered herself. Already the Valium had started its work. He decided to allow it to run its course and sat down to smoke a cigarette as he watched her eyes slowly start to glaze.

What happened next was little better than rape, but he didn't care a damn. It would be the last time. He had lost any lingering interest in Zoe the moment he'd made his mind up to sell her to Mog for two grams of Scouse smack. No way was he about to follow Mog and Benny. No way. Zoe was history. A man had his pride after all. There were plenty more fish in the sea, Sheila Benson for a start.

When he had finished, he cooked up Mog's freebie. It sent her into a bottomless gouch just like he knew it would. He wouldn't hear a peep for an hour or two, and when he woke her up she would be little better than a zombie. He smiled in contentment. What the hell.

Sally took a sip of coffee and looked out the though the open door of her boxy office. Then she glanced up at the clock on the wall. Just by six. Just by six and only three kids. It was the third time in a fortnight that they had been this quiet. She knew that she really shouldn't worry too much about it. The other two times it had been chucking it down with rain as well. The night before the place had been packed. Too full. There certainly would have been bother if anyone from the council had turned up unannounced and done a head count. It wasn't just the slow, barely perceptible drop in numbers that was bothering her. It was the moaning. When the Zone had opened two years earlier everyone had been so upbeat. The trouble was that she hadn't really been able to move the place on. There was only so much that anyone could do in the three shoe-box rooms. They only had one computer and there was always a queue. Same story with the Playstation where things nearly came to blows just about every night they were open. She had seen too many regulars drop off over the last few months.

Just like every day, her thoughts turned to the derelict old Council offices a few hundred yards away. If only. Always if only. Everything could be possible if only she could find a way to make it all happen. She would have a chance to try and do a proper job of things and actually make a real difference. The very thought of the houses they were planning on building made the anger start to burn in the pit of her stomach.

She closed her eyes for a moment and took a breath or two. She was turning into a rat-bag in her old age. Living and breathing work and flying off the handle too easily. Too much caffeine and too much work and not enough stuff turning out right. She focused her brain on being on a long white beach with palm trees and parrots. The thought brought a small smile to her face.

"Someone looks happy. That good was he?"

She hadn't heard Jane come in. Jane was her twenty-year-old assistant doing her work experience. Jane's bright orange spiked hair offering a vivid contrast to Sally's sensibly cut brown.

"Fat chance. I was merely taking my tired soul off for a few moments to a beach in Barbados."

"Oh aye. Who with?"

Sally chuckled. "For some reason my mind came up with a picture of palm trees and parrots rather than hunky beachcombers."

"Parrots? Girl, you need help."

"That's right enough. Things OK out there?"

"Fine and dandy. One doing homework and no assistance needed. One in a fully-approved chatroom and one slaughtering Nazis on the Playstation. I'm not required. Anything you need doing?"

"No. I'm fine. Here. Have a read of this."

She passed over a letter from a small Trust that had agreed to fund a day trip for six of the older girls to attend a fashion event in Glasgow. Jane nodded enthusiastically as she read. "Wow Sally, this is really cool. Who've you got in mind?"

"Dunno really."

They passed a few minutes discussing different names. Soon they had five.

"What about Zoe?"

Jane frowned and shook her head. "What, you think she'll come? She's not been around in ages, ever since she shacked up with that Kevin Peters."

"I've seen her a bit. She comes in to see me sometimes when we're closed."

"Oh I didn't realise. How is she?"

Sally shook her head. "Not good. I've got a horrible feeling that she's using."

"Oh Christ no. Not Zoe."

Sally shrugged a what the hell can you do kind of shrug.

"Maybe I'll ask her. I'll drop round tonight. He stays near me. Aye.

I'll ask her. It would do her good to get out of his clutches for a day."

"Just watch him if you call round though."

"I don't think he'd be trying anything much whilst Lenny's around. Do you?"

Jane laughed at the thought. "No. S'ppose not. He's a runty little shit when all is said and done. I wouldn't bet against you putting his lights out if you ever got the chance."

"Ooooh now there's a thought to get a girl going. How nice would it be to kick him as hard as you could, right in his balls."

The thought hit the spot. They both burst out laughing so loud that the Nazi murderer on the PS2 glanced over his shoulder to see what all the excitement was about.

Detective Sergeant Frank Dixon was feeling in unusually good spirits. He was naturally a man of good spirits. He always had been. For twenty years he had enjoyed just about every minute of being a copper. Only in the last two had things started to turn sour. When he had been transferred across to the Drugs Squad it had been a good day. A step upwards on the career ladder at long last. It was ridiculous that his career had moved at such a snail's pace. He wasn't a stupid man. He was popular. He got his fair share of results. Even the villains liked him. They always said that Frank was a proper copper. An old-fashioned copper. Hard but straight. The sort of copper where you knew where you stood.

His problem was his mouth. He had never learned the art of not speaking his mind. He was a big straightforward sort of man who played rugby in the winter and, much to his colleagues amusement, cricket in the summer. He had a nice house, a nice wife and three nice children. If he saw a problem with something, he said so. If part of that problem was the way that his superiors were handling it, then he said so. If one of the younger coppers had a problem, they would take it to Frank and he would go out to bat for them. He was no good at mincing words. He just told it as it was. And as a result he had never been promoted beyond Detective Sergeant. Not that he was overly concerned. Detective Sergeant was still one of the lads. Detective Sergeant let him spend most of his time being a hands-on copper rather than a jumped-up form-filler.

Things had changed with the drug squad. Suddenly he found

himself fighting a battle that seemed to make no sense. No matter what they did, no matter how many they caught and locked up, it just never seemed to make a difference. They only ever seemed to get the small fry, the desperate ones, often lads he had watched grow up. It was rare that they were bad lads at heart. They had taken a wrong turn and suddenly heroin had them under its control. Complete control. They did stupid things out of blind gagging desperation and Frank and his mates collared them and had them locked up for a while. They would be back out soon enough and the whole weary business would start up all over again.

They all knew exactly who the main players were. Most of the town did. The ones with the big houses and so called respectable businesses. These were the ones they never seemed to get close to. He knew that he wasn't alone in his discontent. Whenever he went away on conferences he met the same feelings at the bar. Everyone was jaded with it. The whole force. As usual Frank had opened his mouth way too much and the higher ups were a long way short of being happy with him. The drug crisis was all over the local media, just like every other small town in Scotland. The papers got the community jumping as every parent lived in a constant state of dread that the cancer would find its way into their home. That in turn got the politicians hopping as they had to be seen to be doing something to be tough on the problem or they would get voted out and have to return tail between their legs to the day job. And that in turn meant the heat was put on the police force in general and the drug squad in particular to get quick results. Visual results. Something to go in the paper and calm the community down a bit. And so everything had to be done yesterday. Policing by Press Release. It was why they spent all their time locking up the poor sods who dealt a few lousy bags a day to feed their own habits. Two years and he hadn't got close to a villain driving about in an Audi Quattro.

The reason for the higher than normal spirits was that the current operation made a bit of sense. Fair enough, at his end of things there weren't many high end cars floating about. His end was Ronald Morgan AKAMog. Normally his inner soul would have ached silently at the idea of setting up an Op to snare Mog.

Frank had been there seventeen years earlier when they had raided the care home and arrested the manager who had without doubt been the most repellent individual he had ever known. He had never forgotten the blank, sullen faces of the boys as they had watched the man who had destroyed their lives being cuffed and taken away. He could still remember Mog's face. An ugly little face, an eternity beyond emotion. He had seen most of those lads in the cells since that day. He'd watched them rattling and vomiting as they hung on through the endless hours of the night before being wheeled into court for shoplifting or credit card fraud.

It had been another reason why he had stayed a sergeant. Several times he had harangued the duty doctor to give them something. Anything. Anything to take the withdrawal pains away and make the night a little shorter. Others liked to leave them to suffer and question them in the cold hours of the dawn when they were at their weakest. Pick up a few names. Frank just couldn't do it. Always there was that image of the day at the care home. The lost faces. The empty souls.

But this time the Op wasn't just about Mog. Mog was only the sideshow. The main event was a hundred and fifty miles down the road in Liverpool. The Merseyside Police had kept a very close eye on Jerry Tanner when he came back to town after his stay in Kilmarnock. They had him pulled within three days with five grammes in his pockets and a future which read six years minimum. They knew there was no point asking him give away names in Liverpool. Jerry wasn't that daft. Doing that would have been much akin to a death sentence. Instead they offered him a different chance of redemption. The offer was that he should spend his days selling to the Jock mates he had made in the Prison. He would let the Merseyside police know where the drops were and the Scottish cops would take it from there. Once he had fed the smack into the system they would watch and note down names and contacts. When the raid eventually came it would be a good couple of days after Jerry had made his delivery. That would keep him in the clear. They had even told him he could keep his share of the cash.

Jerry had decided it was a gift horse and he hadn't looked it too closely in the mouth. No way was he ready to go back to Walton Jail on a sixer. So he had played ball. He set up supplies with Mog in Dumfries as well as two other contacts, one in Bathgate and one in Oban. One of the reasons why the Op was turning out to be so spectacularly successful was that it was almost unknown for the three small Scottish towns to receive a supply of Scouse Smack that was genuinely uncut. The quality was at least double the norm and it brought the users sprinting out of the woodwork. For three weeks the traffic to and from Mog's door in Sunnybank had been like the M25.

Frank had organised shifts in an old barn on a hillside that overlooked the estate. From the barn to Mog's door was half a mile as the crow flew, a distance that was reduced to a few feet by the high powered zoom lens they were using to take their pictures. Already they had a list that was well over a hundred. His oppo's in Bathgate and Oban reported the same story. All three towns were jumping with excitement at the sudden availability of fifty percent pure proper kit. They would run the thing for another day and then the doors would fly in. Mog would get a four minimum. Benny the same, maybe more if he resisted arrest which he probably would. Benny was a head-banger. Frank decided he wouldn't feel a twinge of remorse if Benny pulled a twenty. Benny was a public liability.

The fact that the end goal of the Op was to lock up Mog and Benny wasn't the reason for his unaccustomed motivation. The reason was what had gone down in Liverpool. Had Jerry Tanner looked his gift horse in the mouth he would have realised that there were always two sides to any story. Sure, he knew the Scottish cops were going to kick a few doors in on the back of his intelligence. That was life wasn't it? What he never did was to think the thing all the way through. If the cops knew when he was about to make a sale, then they had a pretty good idea when he was about to make a purchase. It was one of those what goes up must come down situations. The Liverpool boys had worked it all out from the very start. They knew that Jerry would be manna from heaven in the small Scottish towns. They knew there would very quickly be a massive demand for what he had to sell. They knew that as he bought more, he would start winning brownie points hand over fist with some of the big players in the Pool. That was the heartbeat of the Op. The endgame. The chance to swoop in as Jerry bought enough gear to service a run. That was where the real outcome had been. It didn't bother Frank that his end of things would just be the small fry. What counted was that the thing made sense for once. Four forces working together with some proper bad guys in their sights.

The word had come through that the Liverpool end of things had gone down without a hitch in the early hours of the morning. They had ten very serious individuals under lock and key and they had collected up a big, big quantity of Class A's. It had been a big one. Much bigger than anyone had dared to expect and Frank felt a swell of pride in the knowledge that he had played a small part in it all. Now the only thing left to do was to tie off the loose ends in Dumfries. Mog's door would fly off the hinges in the hour before dawn. It didn't really matter whether or not they found much gear in the place. They had him and Benny cold on the surveillance photos. He still felt a familiar regret that Mog would be taken down so hard. Maybe he might find some proper help in prison. It would be long enough this time. It had been many years since Frank had learnt that there would be no black and white in his work.

Inside the barn, two of the younger lads had the end of Op mood on them. They had been passed the word that their end was due to wrap up before first light the next day. After that there would hopefully be a piss up. A huge one. There had even been whispers about a mini bus and a night in a hotel in Liverpool with the lads from the other end of things. Now it was just a case of shooting off the last few photos and cleaning the place up.

Their eyes lit up when they clocked the McDonalds bag in Frank's hand and the cardboard tray with three coffees.

"Hey boss, you're the business."

"I only got them because it was buy one, get one free. Here you go."

They pulled out the Big Macs and sugared the coffees.

"Much going on this afternoon?"

"Na. Not much. Mog was out most of the time. Got back in just after four. Only Kevin Peters since then. In and out."

Frank shook his head sadly. Kevin Peters. What chance had he ever had? Frank had been there when they had pulled his dad trying to raid a petrol station with a combat knife. Eight years. Then his older brother. And now Kevin. His son had played in the same school team as Kevin for three years. Frank had watched just about every game they ever played. Kevin had stood apart. Time. Balance. Vision. Pace. Good engine. He had the lot. Maybe he could have just about made it pro. Instead he had gone down the well-trodden Sunnybank road to the smack. Now he wouldn't last ten minutes on the football pitch. What a bloody waste.

"Give it another hour and then you can put things to bed. We'll all meet up at the station at three for a briefing. We're going in at four.

I'll take a last look about this evening. You've done a good job here boys. A top job."

"Cheers boss."

As he drove back to the station he wondered if there really was a need to give the thing a last drive by later on. The geography of Sunnybank was indelibly imprinted on his brain. He had worked the mean streets and alleyways for two decades and more. He could have found his way to Benny's flat with his eyes closed. Two stairwells with broken security doors. One corridor. Middle flat of three. But he knew that he would still do it. It was his way. Always take that one last look. Never allow complacency to have its way. He decided that he would go home and have his tea then he would take a drive around. Just to be sure.

It was past six when the sherry bottle was passed round for the last time. All the three boys got was a few drips each. They were quite drunk by now. Had the bottle been full it would have been better. But it had been good anyway. The Mayfair packet was screwed up and tossed on the floor along with all the chocolate wrappers. All that was left on the menu for the evening was the lighter refill. For the last half hour it had been the centre of their attention.

Luke had been having second thoughts as the time drew nearer. The idea of it had been fine in theory. After all, it must have been something that people did or they wouldn't have had a leaflet about it in the Zone. It was just that it seemed a hell of a thing to actually stick it in his mouth and squirt.

Tim and Barry had sensed his doubt and worked it with the ease of long practice. After half an hour Luke knew he was backed up right into a corner. Suddenly everything was on the line. The friendship that had changed his life seemed to be hanging by a thread. To keep the respect of the twins he needed to take the hit. They were loving every minute of his nerves. They mocked him. Poked him. Moved him along towards the edge.

The fags were gone. The sherry was gone. The biscuits were gone. All gone. Only the lighter fluid left. No other path to walk. No middle way. Take it, or go home in shame.

No choice to be made.

One road open. And it was time.

PROLOGUE

He grabbed the can and thrust it deep into his mouth as the twins roared him on.

And he squirted.

And for a moment there was nothing really. Just a cold feeling. Like swallowing a lump of ice without chewing it. It was a cold that went down deep. Really deep. His brain started to get strange messages. It was happening. What was happening? The cold was way down now and the messages were becoming frantic. The messages were becoming klaxon calls. Warning sirens were howling through his brain.

Can't breathe.

Can't breathe.

CAN'T BREATHE!!!!!

He was writhing now. Kicking out. Eyes wide with shining terror. At first the twins cracked up. It was a hell of an act. A game. Good old Luke. Well game he was. Took the hit and playing it out. But then they started to realise that it was no game. They felt the real terror of the eyes.

And Luke started to turn blue.

"Oh Jesus Barry, what's happening."

"He can't breathe. Can't breathe . . ."

Tim jumped to his feet and looked about frantically. There had to be someone. Anyone. Had to be.

Nothing. Nobody. Just the rain splashing the puddles in muddy goal mouth of the football pitch. Just the moan of the wind in the old wooden roof of the pavilion.

Decision.

"I'll go. I'll get some help. Make him breath Barry. Just make him breathe."

"But how . . . ?"

Tim was gone. Off the verandah and running like he'd never run before. Running and screaming.

At first the screaming was just a small sound to Lenny. A normal sound. Kids playing. Nothing to warrant attention. He had taken a long route back to Sunnybank from the meeting and now he was starting to regret it. When he had set out, the fresh air had seemed like a good idea, but now the rain had worked its way all the way through his coat and he was ready for coffee and a fag and a shower.

Slowly his brain filtered the sound of the scream. Not a game. Too real. He lifted his head and scanned a hundred and eighty degrees until he spotted a small figure approaching him fast over the football pitch. Something familiar. Something bad. Something really bad.

Tim was thirty yards away when Lenny recognised him. By this time Tim had recognised him as well.

"Lenny! You've got to come. Quick. Now!"

"Whooa. Calm down for Christ's sake. Take a breath Tim. What's up?"

Tim wasn't about to take a breath. He was way beyond that. "Quick. It's Luke. I think he's dying. He can't breathe. Honest . . . ."

"Where?" Everything about the boy spoke of disaster. Not a tough kid now. Just fear. Sheer and complete. Tim gasped in breaths that were half sobs. He pointed frantically at the old pavilion and turned and ran towards it.

Lenny never hesitated. He ran after the small sprinting figure. As soon as he made it round the back he knew there was trouble. Terrible trouble. His eyes took in the elements of the scene. Barry was holding his head, tears flooding his cheeks. Luke was down. Barely moving now. Face as blue as the sea. Right by him was the can of lighter fluid. Lenny grabbed it and held it up.

"This?"

"We didn't know Lenny . . . honest . . . we never thought . . ."

Lenny wasn't listening. He grabbed his phone from his pocket and hammered in 999.

"Ambulance . . . very urgent. I'm at the old Pavilion in Sunnybank . . . just off Cairns Road . . . I have a young boy . . . he can't breathe . . . he's inhaled lighter fluid . . . Baxter. Lenny Baxter . . . be fast . . . I don't think he has long . . . ."

He dropped the phone and fell to his knees. Years earlier he had done a First Aid course and he desperately dusted off the cobwebs in his memory. He clamped his mouth over Luke's and blew as hard as he could. Then he pressed at the small chest. One. Two. Three. Blow again. One. Two. Three. And again. And again.

He tried for five minutes, every second a lifetime. He wasn't aware that he was shouting.

"Come on Luke . . . For Christ's sake Luke . . . COME . . . ON . . ."

PROLOGUE

Both twins stood and watched with all colour drained from their faces as the horror set in. At last Lenny flopped back. Luke was completely still now. Not a twitch. Somewhere about half a mile away he could hear the sound of the sirens wailing through the rain. He looked up into the terrified faces of the twins. This would finish them. They would be blamed. Never forgiven. The community would make them into lepers.

One life had already been lost. Two more hung in the balance. Lenny screwed his eyes shut. The siren was close now. He made his mind up.

"You two can't be here. Go. Now. You left Luke after school. Think about what you did. But go. You have to go."

For a moment they never moved. Shock was setting in fast. They just stood and stared into the blank eyes of their friend.

"GO!!!!!"

The ferocity of his voice broke through. They grabbed their bags and sprinted away across the wet grass and the dog dirt. The ambulance bounced its way across the field as they disappeared out of sight down an alley.

The medics worked with cold efficiency whilst Lenny stood and watched. They gave up after a few minutes. The older one gave a small shake of the head and dragged a packet of cigarettes out of his pocket. No words. He offered one to Lenny. Lenny took it. They just stared down and smoked a while.

Apolice car pulled up. The young officer's face collapsed as he took in the twelve-year-old corpse. After a while he started to do his job.

"It was you that found him sir?"

Lenny nodded. "It was. I heard him shouting. Screaming really. I found him here on the balcony. He was already bad. I rang 999 and I tried to keep him going. No good. I couldn't and . . . well . . . you know."

The constable nodded. "Was there anyone else here sir?"

"Not that I saw. Just Luke."

"You know him?"

"Aye. I do some work at the Zone. He comes in. Luke Crenshaw. Stirling Avenue I think."

"Did he say anything? I mean about what had happened?"

"No. He was past speaking. I think it was probably this." Lenny nudged the can of lighter fluid with the toe of his shoe. "I could taste it. You know. When I was doing the mouth to mouth."

There were a few more questions. Half an hour's worth, whilst the ambulance men lifted Luke onto stretcher and covered him over. Lenny gave his details and arranged to call into the station the next day to make a formal statement. The policeman offered Lenny a lift home. Lenny said it was OK. Said he would rather walk. He felt the tension in the younger man.

"Are you going round to his parents?"

A nod.

"That's hard. I'm sorry."

Another nod. The younger man made his way very slowly to his car. In the next hour he would grow up ten years. Lenny didn't notice the rain any more as he walked the last half mile. He didn't notice a thing.

Sally said her goodbyes to the Nazi-hunter and knocked off the lights and locked the door. The weather outside was dire. She hadn't walked twenty yards up the pavement before the wind had blown her umbrella inside out. She fought with it for a couple of minutes before tossing it into a bin in disgust. Another £4.99 down the drain. By the time she reached Zoe's block she was soaked through. She contemplated going home and changing and drying her hair before calling round, but decided against it. Her enthusiasm for the idea had cooled as the afternoon had worn on and she knew that if she didn't do it straight away she wouldn't do it at all.

She bashed away at the door for a couple of minutes and had pretty well made up her mind that it was a waste of time when she heard movement inside. Seconds later Kevin Peters dragged the door open, cursing as it got stuck on a pile of soggy junk mail that had clearly been there a while. He had pulled on his coat over his boxer shorts and he didn't look half way amused by the visit.

"What do you want?"

"Is Zoe in?"

"Aye. She's in."

"Can I see her?"

"No."

Zoe took a deep breath. "Any reason why?"

"She's asleep."

PROLOGUE

"Oh."

He stared at her for a moment, his lip curled into a mocking smirk, his cold eyes with pupils the size of pin pricks.

"Why don't you just piss off you do-gooding slag."

Sally opened her mouth to say something. Then she thought better of it. What was the point? It would just be a slanging match. She knew that she needed to be better than that.

"Just tell her I called will you."

"In your dreams. Go on. Piss off." The door crashed shut leaving the edge of a leaflet offering discount PVC windows poking out underneath.

The short walk back to her flat was more than long enough for Sally to be absolutely fuming by the time she unlocked the door and walked in. She threw her wet coat at the hanger in the hallway. For a second or two it looked as if it might stay hanging. Then it slipped to the floor. She considered picking it up and trying again but kicked it instead. The place was dark and she wondered where Lenny was. She had wanted him to be in so that she would have someone to get it all of her chest with. She marched straight into the bathroom and stared into the mirror. Christ, what a state. Her hair was plastered across her head. Her eyes blazed with the full heat of the Baxter temper. She grabbed at her hairdryer and held it close in so that the hot air burned away at her scalp.

Bastard. Arrogant bully bastard. The hot air soon frizzed up her hair and made her look even more ridiculous. Sod it. She tossed the dryer down and stomped into the kitchen and filled the kettle. Outside it wasn't even seven o'clock on a so called summer's day, but night was already settling into Sunnybank. She leaned forward with her hands on the edge of the sink and stared out into the rain whilst the kettle rumbled into life. These were the days when she wondered just what the hell it was she was doing. Days when a proper sensible job seemed like a really good idea. Proper house, proper boyfriend, a flat somewhere away from Sunnybank. Nights at the movies and meals out. No jumped-up swine like Kevin Peters calling her a do-gooding slag.

As she turned to get a mug out of the cupboard she all but jumped out of her skin. Lenny was sitting at the table. What was up? The lights were off. His sodden wet coat was on. His face was set somewhere between stone and ice. An open whisky bottle. A half-full tumbler. A fag that was more than half ash clamped between his fingers.

"Uncle Lenny, what is it?"

Nothing at first. Not a flicker. Her uncle was some place somewhere far away. Somewhere she had never been. Then he looked up and his eyes were terrible. Red-ringed and two lines of tears smeared his cheeks.

"Oh Jesus, what is it? What's happened?"

He got up slowly and wrapped her to him hard. His voice was flat. Completely drained. "It's Luke Crenshaw. He's dead."

It took Kevin a while to get Zoe up and ready. He had already dressed and the thought of the free heroin on offer round at Mog's was growing in his head. At first he couldn't get a flicker out of her. It took five minutes before her eyes dropped open, all bleary and confused. She was as floppy as melted rubber as he pulled her into a sitting position. He made his voice as kind as he could.

"Come on darling. Party time. Let's get some clothes on you . . . ."

It was like dressing a sleepy child. The T-shirt wasn't any great problem. No need to bother with knickers. He had to give up on the tight jeans which he couldn't get up any further than her thighs. He dug out a pair of joggers which were an all together easier proposition. He decided that socks were not required either and levered her trainers onto bare feet. When he got her up she couldn't stand. Her legs just crumpled. It took three goes until she managed stay upright on her own. Well, that was enough. Mog and Benny weren't wanting her upright. They would want her flat on her back. A coat? What was the point? It was only five minutes. The rain might bring her round a bit. She was certainly too far gone to notice. He pulled on his own coat and got his arm underneath her shoulder.

"OK sweetheart. Time to hit the town. Let's go."

Lenny had told it all in the same flat voice. He had offered Sally Scotch, but she had refused it. He drank mechanically in big gulps that burned all the way down. When there was nothing more to say they had sat in silence in the closing darkness. Eventually he felt that he should make an effort. He sat himself up and rolled his head on his shoulders.

"Anyway. What about you. How was Zone?"

Instead of reviving her it sent her lower. She told him about how quiet it had been. She told him about going to see Zoe. She told him about Kevin Peters. As soon as the words were out she realised she could have kept them in. His face turned hard. The raging anger that had been boiling up since the Pavilion suddenly found a focus.

"The bastard. Little piece of shit."

He was straight away on his feet and making for the door.

"No Lenny, please. Leave it. I'm not bothered, really, he's nothing. Not worth it . . . ."

She was talking to a wall. She caught him at the front door and grabbed a handful of wet coat.

"Uncle Lenny stop. Please."

He reluctantly turned and looked her in the eyes.

"Don't do anything stupid. You've had a few. You know what will happen if you . . . well . . . you know what will happen."

He forced a tight smile.

"Aye lass. I know what will happen. Don't worry. I'm not about to lose it. We'll just a have little chat, that's all."

She wanted to believe him but she could feel the rage that was running through him. She knew there was no point in going on. He was a stubborn old sod. Nothing she could say would change his mind.

He gave her a small nod and left. For a couple of minutes she didn't really know what to do. Then she bent down and collected up her coat and followed him out into the rain.

Kevin was more-or -less having to carry her. She was as limp as a sack of spuds. Normally the walk was just five minutes. Already it had had taken longer than that and they still had a couple of hundred yards to go and two flights of stairs.

"Come on you silly bitch, get a move on."

Zoe was just about able to speak now. The rain had soaked her T-shirt and the cold was beginning to bring her round.

"Where are we going Kev? I don't want to. I feel sick Kev. Let's go home . . . ."

He wasn't really listening. Instead his attention was fixed on the tall blond-haired figure marching towards him. Bollocks. All he needed. Lenny Baxter closing the gap in fast strides. He blocked their way.

"Come on Lenny. Move out will you. We're getting soaked here."

Lenny completely ignored him. All his attention was on Zoe. He gently lifted her chin up so he could see her face. Jesus. She was gone. All the way gone. Her eyes showed a flicker of recognition.

"That you Lenny? I feel sick Lenny. Bad sick. I want to go home Lenny. Make him take me home Lenny . . . ."

Lenny swung his gaze onto Kevin. He looked down at him from a height advantage of four inches. The weight advantage would have topped forty pounds.

"Just where the hell do you think you're taking her Kev?"

"None of your business Lenny. Just move, right."

Lenny reached out and took his upper arm and squeezed. Hard.

Kevin tried to shake it loose and gasped as the pain hit him.

"Get off you nutter. Leave us be. It's nothing to do with you."

A white anger was taking hold of Lenny. He was just seconds away from giving him the beating of his life. He never heard the small footsteps running toward him. He only knew that Sally was there when he felt her small hands pulling at the back of his coat.

"Leave it Lenny. There's nothing you can do. Just leave it."

Kevin's cockiness was returning now. "Aye that's right. Leave it Lenny. Got to haven't you? You can't do nothing can you? Not with your record. They'd throw away the key . . . ."

Lenny took long deep breaths of damp air and slowly released his grip. Sally was right. Even Kevin was right. Nothing he could do. Just like always.

Kevin dragged his arm clear as soon as he was able and barged past them.

"Head case."

Sally and Lenny watched him as he half carried the girl along the pavement and into the doorway to Benny's block. A minute or so later they saw the two figures emerge onto the balcony and knock the second door along. Then they disappeared from view.

Sally tried a soothing tone. "Come on Uncle Lenny. Nowt we can do here. Let's get home. Have some tea. Come on."

He slowly shook his head.

"You go lass. I'm waiting here."

"Why? What for? There's nowt you can do about it."

"I don't know why. I'm just waiting. That's all. I'll see you later."

She made no sign of moving. The anger was well away now. He smiled down at her. "Look don't worry. I'm calm now. Honest. I just want to see she gets home OK. That's all. I'm not about to do owt daft."

Eventually she decided to believe him. What else was there to do? She shrugged and walked away into the rain. Lenny followed the path of Kevin and Zoe and climbed the stairs. He took up a position at the end of the balcony and lit a cigarette. Just what the hell was he doing? He hadn't a clue. He just knew he wasn't about to go anywhere. Not until he saw the lass home. He pulled the coat tight around him and stared out across the deepening grey of the night. As he looked out the streetlights snapped on.

The Zoe that Kevin frog-marched into room and tossed onto the settee wasn't the fantasy Zoe that Mog had in his mind's eye when the deal had been done earlier in the day. She was soaked through, hair all plastered down across her face, an expression of half bewilderment, half fear. Her eyes flitted around the room and tried to make some kind of sense of what was happening to her. Her voice was flat. Very small.

"I feel sick Kev. Really sick. Just take me home will you. I just want to go home."

Mog had wanted the Hollywood starlet with the mischievous eyes and the overdone make up and the crop top. He hadn't wanted this. Not this bedraggled little lass about to cry out for her mum. Christ, she looked about twelve. No way. The image of the silhouette of his mum's boyfriend jumped into the very front of his mind. What the hell was he doing here? No way.

"Look Kev. Forget it. Look at her. She's a goner for Christ's sake . . . ."

"I just want to go home now Kev . . . I want to see my mum . . . ."

The lost desperation of her voice opened up a twenty-year-old scab on Mog's brain and the paralysing fear flooded over him. The landing. The care home. The orange light of the street lamp. The cracked tiles in the toilets with no doors at the care home. The tears as he tried to wipe at the blood pouring from his arse with cheap, scratchy toilet roll. No way.

"C'mon Kev, get her home. She's had it . . . ."

Kev's eyes lit up with sharp anger. "Piss off Mog. She's fine. Be fair. A deal's a deal."

"She's no fine Kev. She's gone."

"I just want to go home Kev. Please Kev."

For Christ's sake. Would the bitch never stop whinging? What a bloody joke. The cow moaning on. Mog getting cold feet. Bastards. All of them bastards. He slapped her hard across the face to shut her up. It knocked her onto her backside. It took a short while for the pain of the slap to work it's way through the fog of Valium and heroin. She was about to open her mouth to protest when he grabbed the collar of her T-shirt and pulled. He yanked her forward onto the floor as the shirt came off over her head and thrashing arms.

"There you go Mog. Delivered on time as promised. Look at that. Lovely tits or what. Come on. A deal's a deal."

Mog was losing control of the situation. This wasn't how it was supposed to be. He might have been the man of the hour, but it didn't make him hard. Kevin was getting scary. Something wild about him now.

Zoe was scratching about for her shirt on the floor.

"What are you doing Kev! Please Kev . . . ."

As she tried to unscrew the shirt, Kevin grabbed the legs of the joggers and wrenched them down beyond her knees. Her voice was getting louder now.

"No Kev!! Pleeease . . ."

Smack. Mog took a step forward, but Kevin pushed him back. Zoe tried to get to her feet but the joggers round her ankles tripped her and sent her sprawling on the filthy carpet. Mog tried to find some authority in his voice, appalled by the sight of Zoe's pale skinny legs and backside. So vulnerable. So helpless. Again. No way.

"Sod this Kev. You best get out. No way is this happening. She's not up for it. She's not up for anything. Here. Take a couple of bags anyway. Just go . . . ."

"It's not just your decision to make Mog."

Benny's voice was horribly quiet. "The deal was two of us. Remember. You might have cold feet, but not me. I'm having a piece."

Mog was feeling frantic now. "Come on Benny. This isn't right. Just look at her."

"Shut it Mog."

"Remember the home Benny. Remember what they did to us man. This isn't right . . . ."

"I don't want to remember the home Mog. Just shut up. If you don't like it then you can go."

Mog knew the expression on Benny's face. It was his ten seconds to blow expression. He knew that all of a sudden he was in danger. He held up his hands and took a step back. This wasn't any part of the plan.

"Cool it man. I'm not having a go. Easy."

Benny was on his feet, very still, coiled up and staring hard at Mog. After what seemed an eternity, he shrugged and bent down to the girl who was trying to drag the joggers back over her knees. He yanked her up and easily held her in a half nelson as she tried to cross her legs to cover up. Mog looked away and felt sick. Benny's voice was still horribly quiet.

"Shoot her up Kev. She's no good like this"

He sat down, easily holding Zoe with one arm whilst idly pawing her breasts and watching as Kevin did the honours. Zoe was near catatonic with fear now. No screams. Just tears and a tiny voice.

"Please mummy. Help me mummy."

Kevin roughly took her wrist and stretched out her thin white arm. He made the vein ready and shot home the bag. Benny casually tossed her onto the couch and started undoing her shoelaces. Kevin turned his back and lit up. What was coming next wasn't something he was much in the mood to witness. Mog watched as Zoe's eyes started to roll backwards. Oh no. Shit. Jesus. Her lips were already turning blue. No.

Benny already had one shoe off and he was starting on the next.

"Benny no. Look. She's going. Look. Look at the lips."

Benny stopped with lace and stood up. He bent over the naked girl and frowned.

"Bollocks. You're right."

He stood and spoke to Kevin.

"Get her out Kev. No way is she going in my flat."

Kevin had spun round and the vomit was rising in his throat at the sight of Zoe.

"What do you mean out. Come on Benny. We need to call am ambulance or something . . . ."

Benny wasn't listening. "No chance. Your bird. Your problem. Out."

He dragged Zoe to the door, opened it and tossed her out onto the wet concrete of the walkway. He returned and grabbed her T-shirt and the back of Kevin's neck.

"Jesus Benny . . . come on man . . . you can't just . . . ."

Before the sentence was past his lips he flew through the door and crashed into the wall of the walkway. Bang. The door crashed shut and suddenly everything was very quiet.

It took Lenny a moment to comprehend what he was seeing. One moment he had been finishing the last of his cigarette. The next moment the door flew open and out came Zoe, stark naked apart from the joggers round her ankles. What? A few seconds, then Kevin Peters was propelled out and into the wall. And then a wet T-shirt which hung in the orange grey light for a second before falling all the way down to the grass below. He was running before he knew he was running. She was so still. Horribly still. Not again. Please not again.

Kevin heard the steps and looked up fast, still fuzzy from smashing his head against the wall. Trouble. Lenny Baxter. Lenny Baxter pounding the walkway towards him. Coming fast. He panicked and ran. Down the stairs and onto the road and away.

Frank Dixon had just been about to pull his car away from the kerb when it all kicked off. What the hell was happening? By the time he saw Kevin hurtle through the front door he was still questioning himself as to whether his eyes were playing tricks on him. Had that been a naked girl? No. Couldn't have been. But it had certainly looked like a naked girl. Jesus H Christ. What the hell was going on? Now what. Another figure running along the balcony. Something familiar about the run. Couldn't be. Surely not. But it was. Lenny Baxter. Frank saw that run every Saturday through the summer as Lenny pounded in to open the bowling for his cricket team. What the hell was Lenny doing up there? He was trying to piece it together when the sprinting figure of Kevin Peters exploded through the doorway and out into the street. There was just time to get a glimpse of a thin pale face set in lines of terror before the boy was away and gone. Something was happening up there, but what?

Should he go and assist? Christ but it was big call. What if it were nothing? His presence would tip off Mog and Benny and they would be long gone before the four o'clock raid. Damn.

Damn. Damn. Damn.

What to do, Frank. What the hell to do.

Lenny was convinced that it had to be nightmare. Had to be. For the second time in three hours his mouth was clamped over another. For the second time he was trying to push life back into a failing heart. Please no. Please not again. He kept pressing with one hand whilst he made the call for an ambulance with the other. He didn't realise how loud he was shouting into the phone. Loud enough for Frank to hear that the girl was down. Down and dying. Jesus.

Loud enough for Mog to open the door to find out who it was out there. By the time the door opened, Lenny knew it was no good. Zoe was gone. Same place as Luke. Her naked flesh was dead and lifeless as the belly of a fish. Her breasts were filthy with the wet muck from his hands. Her pupils were lost high in the top of her head. Her mouth was still gaping open.

When Lenny saw Mog's head poke around the door he snapped completely. He sprang up from the dead girl and threw himself at the blinking rat like figure in the doorway. He took him in his chest and knocked him flying backwards on top of the needles and foil and ashtrays on the coffee table. Lenny didn't think. He was way beyond any thinking. He leapt on top of the winded man and grabbed a handful of hair. Mog's eyes were frozen in shock.

Lenny half turned him and crashed his face down into the coffee table, smashing his nose like a piece of meringue. He yanked the head back and was about to crash it down again when a fierce lancing pain shot up through his shoulder.

Benny had been as fast as a cat. In two steps he had crossed the room and buried his knife deep into the fleshy part of Lenny's shoulder. In and out. Lenny spun off the unconscious figure and scrambled for his feet. Benny had time for a small smile. Too slow big man. Way too slow. He prepared to spring. To bury the knife in deep. To finish the job.

Then the lights went out. Right out.

Lenny blinked in the sudden silence. Frank Dixon was standing over the prone figure of Benny. The knife had fallen to the floor. Frank had felled Benny with a big glass ashtray he had grabbed from the floor. He was gasping for breath. The sprint up the two flights of stairs had taken its toll.

"I don't want to know Lenny. Tell me later. Right now you don't need to be here. You know what will happen. Go on. Bugger off. I never saw a thing."

Part of Lenny's brain worked well enough to register a thought about what goes around comes around. Frank was doing for him what he had done for the Flint twins. He knew straight away that Frank was right. A court wouldn't be bothered about the niceties. Not with his record. He had felt the crunch as he had banged Mog's head into the coffee table. His face would be a mess. A real mess. It would be hard time and lots of it.

He held the big policeman's gaze for a couple of seconds then gave a short nod and made for the door.

"Thanks Frank."

"Forget it. Just go Lenny. Now."

Lenny took one last look at the wretched corpse on the walkway, and then he ran. He took the stairs two at a time and was back inside the flat before the sirens wailed their way onto the wet streets of Sunnybank.

Part One

Haddington,
South Yorkshire 1979

Whenever honesty persists –
you'll hear the snap of broken ribs,
Of anyone who'll take no more –
of the lying bastards roar –
In Chile – in Poland,
Johannesburg – South Yorkshire,
A stones throw away: now we're there.

The Style Council. 'A stones throw away.'

"How much do you want on it then?"

Lenny rolled his eyes. "Nowt. I don't want owt on it."

"There you go then. Tha knows I'm right."

"Who said I know tha's right? I just said I don't want owt on it."

Lenny was getting tired of the argument. It had been going on for ten minutes now, ever since Tommy Shilling had met up with him and his brother Frank for the morning walk to Haddington Comprehensive School. It was a morning routine that hadn't varied since they had moved up to secondary school five years earlier. The Baxters lived furthest from the school on Selby Street. Tommy's house was three minutes nearer. The three boys would then share each other's company for ten minutes which was long enough to cross more or less the full radius of the town to collect Roger Darnley at the end of the pit lane. Then it was only another five minutes to the big new school on the edge of the town.

They saw Roger now, leaning against the big sign. NCB Haddington Main. A tri-axle wagon rumbled down the pit lane and turned right, pointing another twenty-four tonnes of coal in the direction of Drax power station. As the wagon rumbled its way down Doncaster Road, Roger jogged over to his three mates.

Roger was the joker of the four with a grin never far from his heavily-freckled face. Nothing much got Roger down. Rain or shine, it didn't matter. This morning it was all shine. The sun had shone every day for over a week and already the flat fields of grain that surrounded the small town were starting to have a dusty look about them. Already it was easily warm enough for the boys to have taken off their jackets and put them along the top of the Adidas bags that hung from their shoulders.

PART ONE

"Y'alreet lads"

Roger's greeting was met by 'ayes' as he fell in with them. Doncaster Road was full of the pupils of the school making their way in for the last time for six weeks. The next day was the first of the summer holidays and the general mood was euphoric. For three of the lads it was to be the last time they would ever make the morning walk. Roger, Tommy and Lenny's twin brother Frank were all leaving. Lenny was going to be something of a Haddington rarity. He was going back into the sixth form to take three A-levels. By the time he sat down at the end of August for his first English class, the other three would be hundreds of feet below the ground in the pit.

Haddington wasn't a big town. Just over four thousand lived there, twelve hundred of whom worked at the Haddington Main colliery. Without the pit, the town would never have been there at all. Just like the neighbouring villages of Osthorpe and Kindon. Over ninety percent of the 1300 pupils of Haddington Comprehensive School came from mining families, and those who didn't came from households that were completely locked into the coal community: electricians, HGV drivers, newsagents, pubs, it didn't matter what, everything revolved around the coal.

All four lads had fathers and grandfathers who had spent their working lives in the depths of Haddington Main. Now three of them were going to follow the well-trodden family path. Maybe Lenny would be the exception. Maybe his A-levels would lead him away to college and into the big world beyond where everything didn't revolve around coal.

As soon as Roger fell into step with the other three Tommy was eager to sign him up to prove his point.

"Hey Rog, you know the final day Assembly?"

"Aye. It's this morning."

"Well. You know when they give the best pupils awards?"

Roger nodded. "Aye. I know."

"Well, don't they have to sit up on the stage for the whole Assembly?"

A nod. "Yeah."

Tommy clapped his hands together in glee as the point he had been hammering away at for ten minutes was confirmed. Lenny kicked out angrily at a stone which bounced away over the kerb and into the road.

He had secretly figured that Roger probably had it right. He just hadn't wanted it to be the case. He sensed his brother grinning at his side. Now the stick would begin in earnest.

They turned a corner and the school came into view a few hundred yards away at the end of a cul-de-sac. Now the morning routine took them into a disused yard that had once been a wagon park. The dry dusty ground was still covered with old diesel spills. Frank, Tommy and Roger all lit up their pre-school fags whilst Lenny threw stones at a rusty of sign hung on the fence at the edge of the yard.

'PRIVATE. NCB PROPERTY. KEEP OUT.'

Roger wanted to be brought up to speed. "Go on then. What you all on about?"

Tommy couldn't keep a smile off his face. "I've worked it out see. There's two best pupil prizes, yeah."

"Aye. Best student and best sportsman."

Tommy's voice now assumed of the air of a football commentator. He gripped an imaginary microphone in his fist. "Well after his spectacular efforts in taking Haddington Comprehensive to their cup victory in the All Yorkshire under 16's, who could possibly doubt that the new fast bowling sensation Lenny Baxter will be presented the coveted 'Sportsman of the Year' award. This boy, who is already spoken about as the next Freddie Truman, has attracted attention the length and breadth of Yorkshire, some say . . . ."

Lenny hurled a stone with a flat-armed throw. It clanged into the centre of the metal sign. "I told you Tommy. They won't give to a fifth-former. They never give it to a fifth-former."

"We never won the Under 16's cup before. Christ, we never got past the first round."

"That's why it'll go to the captain. It's obvious."

Roger hadn't really got a hold of what the dispute was all about.

"Hang on lads. I don't get it. You were asking if the students getting the prizes had to sit up for the whole of the Assembly. What's that got to do with Lenny winning or not."

His question was met with broad grins from Tommy and Frank. Lenny moodily snapped another hard throw to the imaginary wicket keeper. Clang.

PART ONE

Tommy took a long pull on his fag. "Think about it. Who's going to win the best Student award?"

That was easy. No need to consider that. It had been pre-ordained for seven years. "Beverly Morton. Who else."

Beverly Morton had become a legend within the small world of Haddington Comprehensive. She was of the minority. Her family owned a large grain farm a few miles to the north. Her dad bred horses and they won races. Her dad could be seen on Grandstand on a Saturday afternoon collecting trophies at Doncaster or Wetherby or Pontefract or York. All their dads put chunks of their wages on his horses. The Morton family was of a different world. A big Jag. Three holidays a year. A house rumoured to be a mansion. Stinking rich.

Beverly had been a legend from the very minute that her dad had dropped her off at the school gates at the age of eleven. Over the years she had blossomed into something the lads thought should be found across the centre pages of Mayfair. She was their Golden Girl. Their Ice Queen. Top of every class she ever walked into. The natural female lead in all the school plays. The first pupil from Haddington to sit four A-levels. The first ever to be offered a place at Cambridge University. The road from Haddington to Cambridge was about as well-trodden as the road to Mars. And Beverly Morton was as much of a nailed on favourite to win the Best Pupil award as Hitler had been when he sent his Panzer Divisions to invade Holland.

It wasn't just her looks and brains that made Beverly such a legend. It was the way she was. From the minute she had walked into her first classroom she had been aloof. In school she stayed among a tiny circle made up of the sons and daughters of doctors and dentists and solicitors and other landowners. The very few from the very small percentage of non-coal families. The rest of the school might well not have existed to her. All the lads responded with shouts in the corridors and playground. All around the school small pieces of graffiti gave out thoughtful messages such as 'I shagged Beverly Morton'. None of it ever seemed to have even the slightest effect on her. She met every comment with a roll of her eyes or a dismissive shake of the head. Outside of school she occupied a different planet with her riding and parties at the big houses of the rich people.

The more she ignored them, the more fascinating she became. The lads said they hated her because she was a stuck up cow but they all secretly fantasised about what it would be like to snog her. They fantasised a whole lot more than that. The girls loathed her with the pure passion of jealousy but they all wondered what it would be like to be her. To go to those parties, to get their hair done at that place in York, to wear her clothes, to live her life. Not that anyone had the faintest idea what Beverly's life involved outside of school.

Once she had entered sixth form the dress code changed. No tie required any more. And summer had brought short-sleeved shirts with the buttons undone far enough to stir endless debate about whether she wore a bra or not. When Beverly had arrived to start her final year, she had turned up in a small MG sports car which she had parked up in the teachers' car park. And the legend was complete.

Now at last the expression on Roger's face began to indicate that he was getting up to speed with the game of the morning. "Oh right. I get it now. Lenny's about to spend the morning up on stage with the famous Miss Morton."

Tommy once again was clutching the imaginary microphone and fell into his commentator mode. "What an amazing prospect we have here in Haddington this morning. Two plastic seats. Clipped together and in full view of a packed crowd of thirteen hundred. Close contact almost guaranteed. On the blue seat, Leonard Baxter, the sixteen-year-old fast bowling prodigy and famed throughout Haddington as a dirty, randy bastard. On the red seat, well, what can I say, the legendary Beverley Morton, the most shaggable thing on two legs this side of Sheffield. Maybe either side of Sheffield. Maybe even including Sheffield. What a prospect we have in store for the crowd this morning. Unbelievable. No wonder they queued all night for the precious tickets . . . no wonder touts are charging over fifty quid each . . . so many unanswered questions that will be answered in just a few short minutes . . . will he get caught looking down her shirt . . . and if he does, and my word this is the big one, will he get caught out with a storker on . . . ."

Lenny slammed a stone into the sign which had it been a cricket ball would have taken the wicket keeper's hands off.

"Look. Get stuffed will you Tommy. This is bollocks. I'm not going to win anyway. It'll go to the captain. He's in the sixth form they always give it to a sixth former."

Now it was his twin brother's turn. Normally the two lads were as alike as peas in a pod. Now they were easy to tell apart. Frank's face was wrapped in a gleeful smile whilst Lenny was all scowl.

"Oh aye Lenny. Dream on. Thirty-four wickets in cup. Eight for thirteen in final. And they'll give it to captain. Dream on. Tha's up there on stage and tha best lump it."

Lenny thrust his hands deep into his pockets and kicked at a stone. His brother was no doubt right. If there had ever been any doubt, it had probably been ended the day before. Staging the final of the All Yorkshire Under 16's Cup had been a rare red letter day for Haddington Comprehensive School. Never before had the school made it through to the second round. However, never before had they had a bowling attack spearheaded by Lenny Baxter. Lenny's reputation locally was already well-established by the time he was fourteen. The Baxters had three generations of tallness running through their family and the twins both topped six foot by the third form at school. It soon became clear to the junior coaches at the cricket club that the lad had a bit of pace. He was easy to teach and he soon had a classical, fluid bowling action. He modelled himself on his hero Michael Holding, the loose-limbed Jamaican who had hospitalised half the English middle order in a recent series.

Not only was Lenny Baxter quick, he had a mean streak. Growing up in the tough streets of a pit village had been the making of many a fast bowler. Lenny had no squeamishness when it came to slamming a cricket ball into a batsman's ribs. He enjoyed it. It was the way his people were in everything they did. Hard men working hard and playing hard. Everything was done hard. Football, Rugby League, Cricket, drinking, fighting, striking. It was their culture. In the Empire days, the public school culture had toughened young aristocratic boys to be sent out to all corners of Britain's disease-ridden tropical empire. The cold showers and institutionalised bullying of their schooldays prepared then to face up to any climate, any insurrection, any outbreak of contagion. The culture of Haddington and a hundred towns like it did much the same. Men had to be hardened off young to be able to face the endless shifts in the cold and the danger of the deep pits. So their kids were clouted around the ears and sent out in mid winter without coats. When any sport was played, it was played for keeps. Played proper.

Lenny Baxter had stood out even in this culture. The local junior teams quaked at the prospect of playing Haddington, especially on their notoriously lively wicket. Lenny made five balls of every over jump and rear up at the terrified batsman's chest and head. The sixth was pitched up for the stumps. He collected wickets for fun. At the end of most games, at least one batsman would have to be taken to A&E by a concerned parent to get a bust finger or rib or nose patched up. Most of the other clubs were from other local mining villages from around and about South Yorkshire, so nobody ever moaned about it. They would have been a laughing stock if they had.

However the public school from up north near Wetherby who Haddington were down to play in the final were not from a local pit village. They were from fifty miles up the A1. Too far to have heard of Lenny Baxter and Haddington Under 16's. Fothergills had a reputation as a cricket school. They had held the All Yorkshire Cup for six years straight and had come to treat it as a matter of right. For two of the past three years they had gone on to win the English Public Schools Championships. These triumphs had largely been down to their own prodigy, opening batsman and captain, Jeremy Feather. Jeremy's father, Sir Vic Feather, was of fourth generation textile wealth and he had been the Chairman for Yorkshire County Cricket Club for a decade. His son had been coached by the best and they had nurtured his considerable talent into a classical technique. He had represented England schoolboys for every age group from the under twelve's. He was said to be sure for Yorkshire in a year or two. Maybe even captain one day. Maybe another Hutton. Maybe another Boycott.

Haddington's Headmaster was a keen cricketer himself. On the weekends he kept wicket for the third team. He knew that the odds were against his school, Lenny Baxter or no Lenny Baxter. But the odds were evened up a little when they got a home draw. The wicket on the school playing fields was a miserably slow affair. Bearing this in mind, the Headmaster had told his opposite number that due to the historic nature that the final represented for his school, he was playing the match at the local club which would be able to better accommodate the expected large crowd. What he hadn't mentioned was the famous lightening wicket with the dodgy bounce.

The game was always going to be tetchy. The fees for a term at Fothergills represented four months of graft and overtime for a Haddington miner. The Fothergills eleven was made up of the sons of solicitors and doctors and landowners. The families of the

Haddington team worked in the pit. All of them. It was a time of tension in the country as a whole. Punk music was reawakening disaffected youth and it had got them out breaking windows and swearing at policemen. The Unions were locked into a twenty-year fight against the bosses. The political hard left was getting ever closer to the reins of power. All over Britain, the 'have nots' were beating at the door and the 'haves' were hanging on and considering life in Canada.

As soon as the shiny new minibus with 'Fothergills'written on the side pulled into the school car park, it was obvious to one and all that what was about to happen would be more than just a cricket match. It was miners' sons and bosses' sons. It was us and them. It was them and us.

The toss went to Haddington and the captain chose to bat on a burning hot day. The two openers seemed to be in control and every one of their thirty-three run partnership was roared by a crowd which was close to a thousand. Then Feather brought himself into the attack. He was an off spinner and he made the ball leap and spit off the wicket like an electrocuted frog. Thirty-three for none was soon forty five for five. Each of the Haddington batsmen returned to the pavilion fuming. The Fothergill close fielders were doing a fine job of winding them up.

"Toilets still outside down here are they old chap? Or do you still take a crap in the gutter . . . ."

". . . someone was telling me that you mining types still work for 10p an hour. Is that true? Sounds awfully reasonable to me . . . ."

". . . I suppose it must be true that all you chaps still marry your sisters . . . that's why you all look so weird. Interesting to see the results of good old-fashioned in-breeding at first hand. Might do a project on it for Biology . . . ."

First and foremost in the banter was Jeremy Feather. When Tommy had made his way to the middle when the fifth wicket had fallen, Feather had unerringly latched onto his weakness. The acne had taken a hold of Tommy's face soon after his fourteenth birthday and no amount of washing had been enough to hold it in check. As Tommy took guard Feather burst out laughing.

"Good lord lads. Take a look at that face. Never seen anything quite like it. Must be all the chips. Lots of lovely grease. I think this fellow must use the wrapper to wipe his face after he's eaten them. As fine a collection of zits as a chap could ever wish to see. My oh my."

Tommy had tried to keep his cool. He thrust his front pad forward and watched the first four balls carefully as they bit and spun.

". . . tell me batsman, do they allow you to sit in the classroom with everyone else, or does the school have some kind of quarantine policy . . . ?"

Cool Tommy. Stay cool Tommy. Ignore the toffee-nosed git. All about him the fielders crowded in and sniggered at his discomfort. After the fifth ball he'd had enough. The bastard was going out of the ground. Down the wicket. Head down. Put the ball straight back over his head. That was the way. Feather had been waiting for the charge. As Tommy moved towards him he speared the ball fast, flat and wide to the wicket keeper who had also been waiting for the moment. Tommy was stranded three yards out like a floundering washed up whale on a beach as the keeper flicked off the bails.

Sixty-three for six as Lenny made his way out. Batting wasn't his strongest suit. He had already made up his mind just to give it a go. No point trying to hang around. They were at him as soon as he strode to the wicket.

". . . heard the RSPCAwere down here last week. Apparently a lot of local cats are getting eaten. Hard times I gather. Not fussy about what they eat these coal mining types. Just so long as it comes with chips . . . ."

". . . this lad looks like he's been chomping through a few cats. My goodness, aren't we a big boy . . . ."

Feather's first ball was a rank full toss. Lenny was going to put him all the way out of the ground. He launched into his shot and somehow the ball seemed to dip on him and scurry under his bat. He closed his eyes in frustration as he heard the sound of it clattering into his stumps. The fielders mobbed their beaming captain as Lenny sloped off, clamping his ears shut to the mockery.

Ten minutes later the innings was all over. Seventy-nine all out. The lunch break was called early and it was a cold tense affair. All the teachers knew full well that a fight was just seconds away and if it got started it would become a mass brawl. Lenny barely ate a thing. He was filled with a cold murderous anger that he had never known before. All through the meal he sat very still and stared across the room at Jeremy Feather with unblinking eyes. It wasn't just what they had all said. It was the tone of voice. The idea of bosses and men was something he had been brought up with. The inequality of the capitalist world. His dad was a Union man and he had more or less weaned the twins on the fighting rhetoric of socialism. Frank had always been more of a firebrand than Lenny. Lenny was more laid back. He went along to the meetings and sat back rather than joining the cheering and stamping of feet. He had always thought a lot of the messages from the fiery speakers from Sheffield and Liverpool and Glasgow and Swansea were a bit overdone. Exaggerated. Words to heat up the simmering anger of a roomful of South Yorkshire miners already back end of eight pints each. It had always seemed a bit staged to Lenny. A bit artificial.

Now he felt different. Now he had been with the mocking contempt of the sons of the bosses for a couple of hours. He could have probably accepted them boasting about how much they had. Fair enough. It wouldn't have been nice, but it would have been understandable. What had got to him was the way they mocked him and his team mates for what they hadn't got. Mocked them for being poor. Laughed at them. As if they were all something that had crawled out from under stones. He had always taken the talk of the world capitalist conspiracy to keep the working man down with a pinch of salt. He probably still did. What he had just witnessed was that the young from the other side of the fence had been every bit as brainwashed as on his own side. Brainwashed into their arrogant superiority. Brainwashed into feeling they had the god given right to be cruel. He had seen the near tears on Tommy's acne-ravaged face as he had marched back to the pavilion. He had heard the amusement of Feather and the others about 'Pizza Face'. They obviously felt that cruelty was a birth right along with the big houses and the skiing holidays and the horses in the stables.

Well fair enough lads. Payback time.

As the Haddington Team took the field to hopeful applause, Lenny jogged over to his captain.

"If that Feather takes first ball open up with Ron will you."

The captain shrugged. "Aye. If you want Lenny. How come?"

"Stick me in at short leg. I'll have a word like. Before I have a bowl at him."

Feather and his partner strode out to the middle briskly; seemingly oblivious to the loud boos from all around the ground. Both brandished the new Gray Nichols bats with the scooped out backs. The closest any of the Haddington boys had ever got to one of these was to watch the tele, although one lad had had a feel at one in a big sports shop in Leeds once. Seventy quid. Seventy bloody quid.

Feather strode to the striker's end and held a vertical bat for the umpire to check. His cocky Sloane voice was like petrol on the flames.

"Middle peg please umpire."

He carefully took the mark and then slowly turned and took in the field around him with a cool amused smile. As he completed the turn he found Lenny standing no more than a yard away at short leg. Both boys were as tall as each other and their eyes were on the same level. Jeremy couldn't help but to flinch slightly as he turned into the implacable eyes.

"Bit close aren't you old chap?"

Lenny said nothing. Just stared. The umpire shouted him back a foot.

The first ball was wide and Feather left it elaborately then strolled forward to tap at the wicket. As he made his way back to get ready for the next ball Lenny spoke in a low voice.

"I hope you like pain Feather."

"What?"

"You heard. Pain. I hope you like pain."

Feather shook his head in annoyance and readied himself. The next ball was pitched up and Feather eased into a text book cover drive that split the field and sped away for four. He held the follow through.

"Not just a little bit of pain Feather. Proper pain. Can you take it?"

This time Feather ignored it. He left the next ball.

"Amazing what a cricket ball can do to a lad's face. Especially if it hits him smack on the nose. Know what Michael Holding calls it? The perfume ball. 'Smell de leather, man'. Smack. Crack. Feather"

Feather left the next ball alone.

"The sound of bone splintering Feather. Your bone. Your face. Nothing you can do about it. But can you take it Feather? Pain Feather."

This time the batsman spun around. "Piss off will you? Umpire tell this fielder to stay quiet please."

PART ONE

The Umpire at the bowler's end was the one from Haddington. He just smiled. "Two to play."

The fifth ball was short and Feather hooked gracefully for four.

"The clock's ticking. Just think. These are the very last minutes that your face is going to look this way. Enjoy it while it lasts. I'm going to re-arrange your features. Smack. Crack."

Lenny broke off and sprinted up to the bowler for a word.

"Sling it wide down leg. I'll have a word with the keeper."

The bowler duly obliged as did the wicket keeper who fumbled his take and allowed the batsmen through for a bye.

Lenny had Feather right where he wanted him. He slowly rotated his shoulders. Feather took his guard and examined the field. Lenny had made his mind up about his first ball over lunch. It wasn't something he had ever done before. Bowling a beamer was genuinely dangerous, the head high ball which didn't bounce. It was something that was universally frowned upon, even in the hard school of the South Yorkshire Leagues. But this was a special case. Feather had earned it. Feather deserved it.

When all of a batsman's focus is on the ball heading downwards to bounce off the wicket, it takes a fraction of a second for the brain to accept that the ball is in fact heading straight for their head without bouncing. So it was for Jeremy Feather. Not only was the ball a full on beamer, it was also quicker than anything he had ever faced before. He threw himself backwards just in time to get his head out of the way. In doing so, his pads got in a tangle and he fell over on his backside. Lenny followed all the way through and leant over him.

"Pain Feather. Pain. It's coming. Get ready for it."

Lenny quickly turned and before the livid umpire from Fothersgill could say anything he said in an exaggeratedly polite voice. "Terribly sorry about that umpire. Must have slipped out. Such a lovely day. My hands are sweaty."

All around the Haddington fielders sniggered. The umpire couldn't do anything but say a rather lame. "No more of those please bowler."

Feather picked himself up and dusted down his immaculate kit.

Lenny's second ball reared up off a length and arrowed in at Feather's chest. He actually played it pretty well, getting all the way behind it, but he couldn't get the bat high enough quickly enough and the ball smacked into his batting glove. A lance of pain shot up his arm and he whipped his hand off the bat and cursed.

"Bastard."

Again Lenny ran all the way through. "Pain Feather. Think that hurt? That's nowt. Poor old Feather. Got a sore finger. Ahhh. Diddums."

"Enough of that bowler. Back to your mark please."

Lenny stood and stared for another second or two. The fear was in Feather's eyes now. Good.

The batsman managed to sway back from the next ball that flew through at throat height.

He had no such luck with the fourth which climbed through his defences and slammed into his chest. Feather dropped to his knees and screwed his eyes shut against the pain.

This time Lenny followed through but didn't speak. He just smiled. It was worse.

Ball five followed ball four into the chest and the pain was more than double. Treble. Now the fear was eating the batsman. This was beyond anything he had ever known. The bowler was too fast. He could only just see the balls as they came at him. On the manicured flat wicket back at Fothersgill he would have been able to adjust and manage. There was no chance on this dusty, pitted track.

By the time he dragged himself back to his feet he wanted out. Surely he had a cracked rib. Had to. Enough to retire hurt and get the hell out of the nightmare that had come upon him so very quickly. Then he thought of his dad watching alongside the teachers. His dad would never forgive him if he walked. No way. No options. He had to stay and fight it out.

It wasn't for long. Ball six was quicker again. It spat up from a dent in the wicket and smashed into Feather's nose. Smack. Crack. Splintered bone. Feather didn't get up this time as the blood spurted out and down his immaculate whites. And Lenny's face was suddenly there. Looking down over his. Very, very close.

"There you are Feather. Pain. That's what you get for mouthing it off in Haddington. Go on. Bugger off"

After that it wasn't any kind of contest. The sight of their captain being taken to the infirmary by a headmaster white-faced with rage was too much for the batsmen who followed. All Lenny had to do was pitch it up and aim at the stumps. Nobody was about to get in line. 8 for 13. Fothergill were bowled out for 31 and the trophy went to South Yorkshire.

All the others had been hyped-up and couldn't wait to get changed and out to receive the acclaim of family and friends. Lenny sat quietly in the dressing room with a towel over his head. His team mates decided that the best thing was to give him a wide berth. At last his brother sat down and joined him.

"Getting changed or what Lenny?"

"Aye. In a bit."

"What's up?"

Lenny pulled off the towel and rubbed at his face.

"Don't know really. Suppose I scared myself a bit, that's all. Christ I was that mad Frank. I felt like killing him."

His brother laughed. "We noticed. Tha' damn well nearly did. Cocky bastard ad it coming."

"I just never knew I had it in me to get that mad, that's all."

"Don't be daft. We all get mad. Come on you soft git, tha'can't sit here all night."

But the feeling hadn't really worn off. He had ducked out of the celebrations and gone home early. The feeling had still been there when he had woken up and met the lads for the walk to school.

And all the joshing about Beverly Morton wasn't helping his mood any. He hurled one last stone and started to walk.

"Hang on Lenny. Give us a chance to finish us fags."

"Finish them on your own. I'm going."

Tommy was about to dock his cigarette and jog after his friend but Frank put a hand on his shoulder.

"Just leave him Tom. He's a weird old sod our Lenny. Best left on his own when he's wrong side out."

The Headmaster was waiting for him by the main door to the school.

"Morning Baxter." The smile hadn't left the man's face from the moment the last Fothergill wicket had been knocked from the turf. He had even slept smiling. The All Yorkshire Cup. To Haddington! Unbelievable.

"Morning sir."

"Lovely day."

"Aye. It's grand."

The headmaster smiled. He liked Baxter. Always had. Something about the boy. Of course there was the cricket. But there was more as well. Something indefinable. Something very decent.

"You're up on stage this morning Baxter. I dare say you're not surprised."

"No sir. I had an idea."

He followed the headmaster up the steps at the side of the stage and sure enough, there she was, already sitting there. Straight away his throat was as dry as sandpaper. Just like predicted, the metal chairs were clipped together at the legs. When he sat he was close. Very close. She smelt unbelievable. He had no clue what she was wearing to make her smell that good, but he was pretty sure it hadn't come from the small pharmacy on Haddington High Street. She was glancing down at a sheet of notes. A speech. Shit. He remembered now. There was always a speech. She had remembered of course. Miss bloody perfect Beverly Morton.

He took a peep at the paper. What was she going to say then? Soon the smooth skin of her arms distracted him from the notes on the page and he looked away. The lads were in the hall now and offering him up the full range of leering faces and hand signals. He tried to ignore them but their signals had worked. The thought of the blouse and the undone buttons jumped into his head. Ridiculous. Stupid. He stared up at the ceiling and tried to think about what the hell he could say in his speech. Why had he not thought about it? Stupid. And then, almost as if his head was outside of his control, it turned slightly and his eyes were drawn down to where the buttons were only done up so far. A slender neck and a sternum tanned to gold. No more than that. So the lads'theory was wrong. He lifted his head back to the ceiling.

Her voice came as an electric shock. Low. Barely audible over the hum of conversation in the fast filling assembly hall. If the sound of her voice had been an electric shock, the content of her words was a whole sub station's worth.

"If I lean forward a little you might be able to see better."

And she did. Only imperceptibly, but enough for her shirt to hang slightly forward and reveal a view down into the valley of her breasts. He snapped his head away and fought the fast spreading blush with everything he had. She chuckled.

"Your friends all seem very amused Lenny. Just look at them. Don't they remind you of chimpanzees?"

His mouth had gone beyond dry. He decided that dogged silence was the best approach to the situation. She gave a small smile and carried on reading her notes. A little after nine the headmaster rose to his feet and kicked off the business of the Assembly. Soon all rose for the hymn. As thirteen hundred unenthusiastic voiced droned away, she leant over again.

"I like cricket you know."

"Oh aye."

"Mmm. I was watching yesterday."

"Right."

"It was my kind of match. Nothing better than watching a quick bowler at full steam. Like Holding. Do you like Holding, Lenny?"

"Aye."

"We all think he's sex on legs. How about you Lenny?"

"Don't be so bloody daft."

Another small smile. "It's a girl thing Lenny. We tend to get sexually aroused by violence at times. It's the mammal in us I suppose. Like when you gave that opener such a pounding."

He screwed his forehead into a frown and tried to sing. This was an utter bloody nightmare. When the hymn drew to a close, the hall was filled with the muffled sound of thirteen hundred bodies resuming their seats. The headmaster talked a bit about the upcoming holidays and then he started with the end of year awards.

"It will come as no surprise to any of us here that Beverley Morton is the winner of our Student of the Year award. Beverley has been one of the most exceptional students we have ever had here at Haddington. Now she is about to travel a road never travelled before by one of our pupils: the road down the A1 to Cambridge University. All of us wish her every success with her career there which I for one am sure will be every bit as triumphant as her time here at Haddington."

Beverley rose to her feet to luke-warm applause and gave her carefully prepared speech. She was polite and crisp and thanked all the right people. Her voice easily carried to the back of the large room as six hundred male eyes mentally undressed her and about the same number of female eyes wondered what it would be like to be her. She wrapped it up with a small smile, took the small trophy from the headmaster and sat back down next to Lenny.

Now the head was starting his build up for the Outstanding Sports Pupil of the year award.

" . . . this was not a hard decision to make. Never in the short history of Haddington School have we seen such a dynamic . . ."

For Christ's sake she was leaning over again. Touching this time. Her shoulder against his.

"Do you know what my friends and I were wondering when you were thundering in yesterday, Lenny?"

"Bugger off will you."

She did nothing of the sort.

"I'm afraid it's terribly unladylike. I hope you'll forgive me . . ."

" . . . Lenny Baxter produced a spell of bowling yesterday that was at times . . ."

"Piss off."

" . . . well, I'm sure you will. You're a broadminded boy I'm sure . . ."

" . . . And so with no more ado, it gives me great pleasure to award this year's prize for sporting achievement to . . ."

" . . . we were all wondering how big your dick was . . . "

WHAAAAAT!!

" . . . Lenny Baxter . . ."

This time the applause was huge and prolonged. Lenny was one of theirs. A proper Haddington lad. His face was redder than an African sunset as he took the trophy. Speech. Oh Christ. Shit. Bollocks. He stood and faced the thirteen hundred faces, three of which were grinning like Cheshire cats. What to say? What the hell had she just said? Beverley Morton! Said that! No way. Shit. Bollocks.

"Aye . . . Well . . . You know . . . I'm proper thankful for this . . . And . . . well all coaches and that . . . and . . . well . . . thanks . . . ."

What a heap of undiluted crap. Jesus Lenny. What a performance. He sloped back to his chair and sat, trying to perch as far from Beverley Morton as he could. Not far enough.

"My goodness Lenny. For a moment there I thought I was listening to Winston Churchill."

He glanced round to her mocking smile. "Look. Get stuffed will you."

She never blinked. "Touchy, touchy. No way to speak to a lady Lenny."

"Aye. Well."

He concentrated on reading the engraved names of the previous winners of the trophy. Thankfully she seemed to have given up with the talk. The second doleful hymn and the assembly was dismissed. Thank god for that. Lenny almost leapt to his feet in his eagerness to escape. He was about to stalk off towards the stairs when a soft touch on the shoulder stopped him short. Again the small mocking smile.

"By the way Lenny. We all decided it was probably enormous."

With this she gave him a quick wink and then she was gone leaving him blinking like a paraplegic rabbit in a search beam.

Lenny was in no hurry to get out of his bed the next morning. To mark the end of the school year, and in the case of Frank, a school career, his dad had taken his two sons for a night out in the club with Tommy Shilling and Roger Darnley. None of them were strangers to a pint. Haddington wasn't the sort of place where too much notice was taken about how old a lad was. Just so long as he could hold his ale and not make a pratt of himself nobody bothered much. It certainly wasn't the sort of place where the police were about to raid a pub to flush out under-agers.

The night before had been a story of free pints and Lenny had lost count after six. For the other lads, it was the night that the stick started. They were due a fortnight off and then they would head out in the dawn light for their first day's work underground in the pit. The new boys knew full well that there would be a good few weeks of teasing to get through. However the prospect of no more maths lessons and Fridays with a wage packet made every jibe worth taking on the chin.

Lenny had no such problems. Word of his 8 for 13 had swept Haddington like a bush fire. The story of his over to Jeremy Feather was already well on the way to becoming local folklore. All kinds of wild stories were doing the rounds. His dad had told him that the boys had talked of nothing else all day in the pit. Word was that Feather would be in hospital for at least a week. There was talk of extensive plastic surgery. Even a chance of brain damage. If there were discrepancies on the details of the damage sustained by the visiting opening batsmen, there was complete agreement that it had served the upper class git right. The Haddington lads hadn't held back when describing the stuff that the visitors had been saying. Especially that Feather. Should have heard him. The bastard. Bloody hell though. You should have seen Lenny. At the lunch interval like. Just sat there he did. Dead still. Just sat and stared at that Feather. Like ice he was. Our Lenny. Ice. He'd made his mind up that he was going to crucify Feather before we even walked out to field. Bloody magic it was.

There wasn't a single ounce of sympathy to be found in the mean terraced streets for the boy in the hospital. Nobody came to Haddington and got away with that. Never had and never would. Young Lenny had taught him a lesson. The village was a place of deep pride that extended into many areas of the life of the community. The local pride was there in the well supported cricket club, the many times champion bowls team, the brass band that was always up there with the best in Yorkshire and more than anything, the local branch of the National Union of Mineworkers. The Coal Board never had anything to moan about when it came to the production figures at Haddington Main. It was one of the jewels in the crown when it came to throwing out endless thousands of tonnes of coal from deep under the Yorkshire earth. But the Board also knew never to mess the men of Haddington about. No way. Haddington was a 'one out, all out'place. The Union was everything. It always had been for as far back as everyone could remember.

Never, ever had a scab crossed a Haddington picket line.

Not in the General Strike of 1926. Not in the big strike of 1974 that had bounced the Tories out of power. Not once. Not one single, solitary scab in the seventy plus years that the union had gone out to bat for the coal miners of Haddington Main. The Union was their church. Men were brought up with its gospel from the day they could toddle around the living room floor.

It all made Haddington a place of ferocious pride. Pride that could easily turn to violence when the community felt a threat. Outsiders weren't much appreciated. Bosses were mistrusted at best, hated at worst. The likes of Jeremy Feather were scum. Simple as that. Young Baxter had done right. Not many would have shed a tear if he had killed the rich kid.

Lenny had fielded questions and thumps on the back all night. Everyone wanted to know about Yorkshire. When was the trial? When would he start? How soon did he think it would be until he would get into the first team? Lenny had smiled and shrugged. He didn't know. Not until after he had done his A-levels. Maybe then. He hoped to hear about the main summer trial which was due to be held at Headingley in a couple of weeks time.

Now Lenny stared up at the bedroom ceiling and thought about the prospect. Despite the spectacular progress that the school had made to the All Yorkshire Final, he had still been far from certain that he would get a call up for the trial. Haddington wasn't the easiest place to get spotted. A lad had a much better chance of catching the eye if he played up around Leeds and Bradford. But 8 for 13 in the final against Fothersgill wasn't something that could be ignored. For the first time he allowed himself to think that the trial was a real possibility. And then? Then he started to believe that he really might make it all the way to the Yorkshire first eleven. Jeremy Feather had come to Haddington with a big reputation as one of the country's foremost batsmen for his age group. Lenny had seen the fear in his eyes. Of course the wicket had meant that the odds had been stacked ridiculously in favour of the bowler. But Feather would still have been bothered by his pace regardless. Probably for the first time Lenny allowed himself to really start believing in the dream he had nurtured for ten years. To be a pro cricketer. To walk out at Headingley for the first morning of a Roses match. To follow in the footsteps of Truman and open the attack with the new ball. It was a dream that suddenly looked a lot nearer to coming true.

Sport had always been central to Lenny's life. Him and his brother Frank and Tommy and Roger. It was football in the winter and cricket in the summer and rock climbing all the year around. The climbing had come from his uncle Derek who would pick them up before dawn on Sunday mornings and drive down to the cliffs of the Peak District. His uncle reckoned that Lenny was a better climber than cricketer. He told him he should stop messing about on the cricket field and take the climbing up full time. There was more chance that Lenny would take a walk down Haddington High Street wearing a pink dress and an 'I love Lancashire' umbrella. Climbing was all right. Bloody good in fact. But it wasn't cricket. Not even close.

His teachers had managed to get through to him that it was important to get some qualifications behind him. They had explained that even if he made it into pro cricket he would still need something else. The money wasn't good. Rubbish in fact. It wasn't like a job down the pit with lots of overtime. He would have to do something else to keep himself going. Especially through the long winter months. That was why it would be a good idea to get some A-levels under his belt. Something to help him get a slot in sales or insurance or something.

They hadn't had to work too hard to persuade Lenny of the wisdom of the idea. He liked school well enough. He was down to study English and History to go alongside the mandatory General Studies at A-level. None of it seemed too much like hard work. Reading had always been a favourite pursuit. He didn't feel any envy for his brother and all the other lads from his year who were heading for a lifetime's work in the cold, damp bowels of Haddington Main.

The clock told him nine-thirty. Time to get up. The sun was gushing in through the window again. Not a day to loaf about in his bed, thick head or no thick head. No school. No exams to cram for. Nothing but a blank page and a warm summer's day. A contented smile sat on his face. Life was pretty damn good. He decided to lounge for another twenty minutes. Up before ten. That would do. Then what? Bit of fishing probably. That sounded a decent sort of way to idle away a summer day.

His ears registered the sound of a car in the street outside. Traffic was unusual at this time of day when the men were all away at work and the milk and post were delivered. It was the growling sound of a powerful engine. And then it stopped. A minute or so later there was a knock on the front door. Muffled voices. Then footsteps on the stairs and Frank burst into the room looking like a boy who had just seen the reincarnation of Christ.

"Bloody hell Lenny!"

"What?"

"It's Beverly Morton."

"WHAT!!!"

"It only is an'all."

Lenny was sat bolt upright now, eyes wide.

"What's she want?"

Frank grinned. "To see you."

"Me."

"Aye you. So you best get your lazy arse in gear."

Beverly Morton. Here. To see him. Unbelievable. But why? His brain was already filled with the sound of alarm bells. The girl was trouble. Big trouble. She had taken him to the cleaners on the stage the morning before as easily as if he had been some snot nosed kid in the first form. And now she was here. To see him. Shit. He threw on some clothes and made his way down the stairs with growing trepidation.

Beverly was sitting with his mum drinking tea looking for all the world as if she had been there a thousand times before. Frank was leaning against the sink with his arms folded trying to look cool and failing by about the same distance as the Trans-Siberian railway. Beverly looked as if she had stepped off the cover of Vogue in jeans, T-shirt and a soft leather jacket that had come from a shop with a postcode nearer to New York or Geneva than Sheffield or Doncaster. She turned and zapped him with a smile that almost removed his kneecaps.

"Morning Lenny."

"What are you doing here?"

His mum all but spat out her mouthful of tea. "Our Lenny! Where's your manners. Don't be so bloody rude."

"Why not. She's not bloody royalty or owt."

He made a point of avoiding the smile and switching on the kettle. As he walked by her he got another waft of the perfume from the day before. Bloody Nora. Focus on the usual. Tea bag. Cup.

"I don't know what's with you Lenny. Beverly's lovely. A proper treat. There's no need to be so ignorant. It's not like you."

So it was Beverly now was it? Sitting with his mum at the kitchen table and it was all cosy and call me Beverly. Bloody hell.

"I'm just wondering what she's doing here, that's all. Not one for slumming it in the likes of our street isn't the lovely Beverly. Bit off the beaten track I'd say."

He kept his back turned and focused on the gurgling of the kettle.

"I thought that we could go for a drive Lenny. It's such a nice morning."

Such a nice morning! What the hell was this? When did the weather have anything to do with Beverly Morton turning up and suggesting they go for a bloody drive.

"So what's brought all this on then?"

"Lenny!! Stop being so bloody miserable." His Mum turned to Beverley. "Eee I'm sorry love. Don't know what's up with him. His dad had them all out on the beer last night. Must have got out of his bed the wrong side."

"Oh it's fine Mrs Baxter . . ."

"Ethel."

"Yes of course. Sorry. Ethel. It's just that I think I owe Lenny an apology. I behaved rather dreadfully in the Assembly yesterday."

The blood running through Lenny's veins iced up. Christ no. Surely not. She wouldn't say anything. Would she?

"Oh aye?" His mum was intrigued now.

"I'm afraid so. I embarrassed Lenny just before his speech and it really wasn't fair of me. I decided last night that the least I could do was to come around and make my apologies."

"Embarrassed him?"

No. No. No.

A demure voice now. Christ if he had a gun he would put six bullets through her head one after another.

"Yes, I did rather. You see when my friends and I were watching the game against Fothersgill we . . ."

Lenny gave up on waiting on the kettle.

"All right. You want a drive? We'll go for a drive. Come on. Let's be off then. Sooner we're gone, sooner we're back. I'm off fishing later."

"Come on Lenny. Let the lass finish up her tea."

Aye mother. Finish up her tea. You're just gagging to hear what was so embarrassing. No bloody way. Not in a month of Sundays. "She'll be fine Ma. She's not about to die of thirst. Come on Beverly. On tha' feet. Let's go and take that drive shall we."

Beverly wasn't about to be hustled out of the kitchen like some Jehovah's Witness.

"Thank you ever so much Mrs Baxter. For the tea. And those scones of yours. Delicious. I hope we meet again."

"Aye lass. And me. Have a nice morning. I hope that miserable sod of a son of mine lightens up a bit."

"Oh he'll be fine. Goodbye. Bye Frank."

"Aye. See you then." Frank once again had the first hand witness of the Second Coming look on his face. Lenny marched through the door and waited impatiently on the pavement whilst Beverly said her farewells. At last she followed him out and closed the door.

"What the bloody hell...."

"Oh shut up and get in Lenny. You're acting like a big kid."

"No I'm bloody not . . . ."

"In"

She climbed into the driver's seat and gunned the engine. He stood there for a moment feeling like a spare part and could think of nothing else to do other than to get into the passenger seat.

Beverly gunned the engine and lit up a cigarette as she swung around the corner and headed toward the edge of town. Lenny gave the interior of the car a disapproving look.

"I see Daddy's girl gets everything she wants."

"Oh piss off Lenny. Try not to be so sad and predictable."

"Like what?"

"Like the silly Haddington chip on the shoulder. It's pathetic. Just get over it. It's boring."

"It's nowt to do with a chip on the shoulder. It's just I don't have much time for spoilt little rich girls who think they're God's gift, that's all."

"Oooh. Cutting Lenny. I might just come over all tearful and hurt." The grin on her face showed that she wasn't about to do any such thing. Lenny decided that he might as well loosen up. There would be plenty who would tell him not to be so soft. How often did a lad like him from Haddington get picked up and chauffeur driven around the countryside in an open topped sports car. Fair enough.

"So what's all this about then?"

"Abit of information and advice. I have decided to do you a favour. God alone knows why."

"Like what?"

"We'll go for a coffee. Little Chef on the A1. Push that cassette in will you. Just enjoy the ride. It won't kill you."

The softness of the June morning was broken open by the hardness of Joe Strummer and the Clash. The songs were of inner city London whilst the view was all ripening wheat fields and the winching gear of the surrounding collieries. No hills. South Yorkshire didn't have hills. Just acre after acre of grain and the scars of a century of coal mining. And a big flat blue sky that stretched all the way to Russia.

The air started to clear his head and he had to grudgingly admit that he was rather enjoying the ride. It was his first experience of an open top car and it wasn't a painful one.

He tapped the window ledge with his hands as the music told of a hairy night in a club on the wrong side of the tracks in Jamaica.

> " . . . I went to a place
> where every white face
> was an invitation to robbery
> sitting here in my safe European home . . .
> I wanna go back there again . . . . "

"Like the Clash do you?"

Beverly smiled. "Good God. He's decided to be civil. Wonders never cease. Yes, I do. You sound surprised."

"I am I suppose. Why do you like them?"

"Lyrics mainly."

He gave a derisive laugh. "Oh aye. Can't see you manning the barricades when the revolution comes. Tha'd be too busy doing your nails."

"That just goes to prove how little you know about it. Your lot couldn't organise a revolution in a chip shop. Rosa Luxembourg. Karl Leibknect. Illich Ulyanov. Carlos the Jackal. Bader Meinhof. Take a look at their backgrounds Lenny. Not like yours. Like mine. Spoilt rich kids. Not stroppy union types. Not piss and wind over their pints and fags in the club. Clean your ears out in history Lenny. You might just learn something. If you want a revolution, don't back a windbag like Scargill."

"That's what you want then is it?"

"Actually no, but at least I know something about it."

He decided that it was a pretty worthless pastime trying to hold his own in an argument. Best to stay quiet and enjoy the ride.

Quarter of an hour later she parked up and they took a smoking table in the Little Chef. Both ordered coffee. Another cigarette. She seemed so much more than two years older than him.

"OK. I'll get to the point. First of all I genuinely want to apologise about the way I behaved in Assembly the other day. It was immature and pathetic. Sorry."

That was a turn up. Lenny shrugged. "Apology accepted. I wasn't that bothered. You got me rattled mind. I never knew if I were coming or going. Why did you do it? I mean tha's never ever talked to me before."

"Oh it wasn't you in particular. I just can't be doing with boys like you."

"What do you mean boys like me. You don't even know me."

"I know your type. All sports and testosterone and fights on a Friday night after ten pints and a bag of chips. What really pisses me off is the way that most girls go chasing after the likes of you with their pathetic tongues hanging out"

He stirred his coffee and felt somewhat aggrieved. "Actually, that's not me at all. But I don't suppose you'll believe me."

"Well of course I don't. I saw you out there at the match. I mean the violence was dripping from every pore. I felt like screaming to the lot of you that it's just a bloody game for God's sake. And then afterwards I'm sure it was all pints and bravado and reliving every miserable minute."

"I didn't actually. Just went home. Didn't feel much like celebrating."

This caused a flicker of mild interest. "Why on earth not? You were the hero of the hour. A real Haddington hero. I assumed it would be all free pints and the girls queuing up for a celebratory snog."

"Tha don't think much of other lasses do you?"

She flushed with a spark of bright anger. "Not when they insist on behaving like pathetic tarts, no I don't. Get pregnant. Get a house. Get a fitted kitchen from MFI. No I don't."

"They don't exactly have a lot of choice. You don't get many chances to be a Charlie's Angel when you're born and bred in Haddington."

She gave a grudging nod to this. "Yes. True enough. Sorry. I can be a spiteful bitch at times. So tell me. How come you went home? I'm intrigued."

"I didn't feel so good about myself. With what happened."

"With Jeremy Feather you mean?"

"Aye."

"Go on." He was beginning to become mildly interesting.

"I didn't like the way I lost my rag. I mean really lost it. Real red mist. I could have killed him I were that mad. I scared myself I suppose. Didn't know I had it in me."

"So why? Because of his background?"

"No. Bloody hell. I'm not that much of a head case. No. It were what he said to Tommy. Tommy Shilling. You know Tommy, yeah."

She nodded.

"Well you might have noticed he suffers with spots. I mean really suffers. Has done for years. Well that bastard Feather went on and on about them when Tommy went out to bat. He were damn near in tears when he got out. Now I don't mind cricket being played hard. Course not. But that were completely out of order. When we had the lunch Tommy were dead quiet. It really gutted him. And I looked at Feather with his cocky arrogant grin and I just snapped. I wanted him to suffer. To pay. It wouldn't have mattered if he had come from wrong end of Leeds. Mind you, I won't lie. The fact that he's such an obnoxious toffee-nosed git didn't make it any better."

She sat back and looked at him rather approvingly. "Well, well Lenny Baxter. You're rather a dark horse. I seem to have misjudged you. More apologies are in order it seems."

He poured some more coffee. "Don't bother. I've got thick skin. Same with all us Baxters. Nowt much gets us rattled. Anyway. Let's be having it. Advice and information."

"OK. Information first. Then advice. You best brace yourself because you're not going to like it much."

Lenny sat back an folded his arms. He actually felt more intrigued than alarmed. She looked at him and wondered if there was any way of sugaring the bitter pill. There wasn't. Just get on with it and tell it straight.

"Vic Feather and my father are friends. They have been for years. They both share a passionate love of money. When it became clear that the final was going to be in Haddington, my father invited Vic and his family to stay."

"Bloody hell."

"Indeed. As you can imagine, the night after the game was somewhat tense. In fact we didn't see much of Vic Feather. He didn't get back from the infirmary until after midnight. Obviously I was away early in the morning for school so it wasn't until yesterday evening that I really saw anything of Mr and Mrs Feather. Jeremy had been discharged and they were all getting ready to leave. Vic was ranting on and on. As I said, he really is a truly horrid man. The trouble is that he is also a very influential man. Lenny, I'm sorry but there really is no easy way of saying this."

He already had half an idea of what was coming. "Go on."

"You know that Sir Vic Feather is the Chairman of Yorkshire Country Cricket Club?"

"I do." Lenny felt his world begin to collapse all around him.

"He has also recently donated £20,000 the cost of developing the Western Terrace. He has influence Lenny. Clout. And he has vowed that you are finished. No trial, not now, not ever. He swears that you will never play for Yorkshire just so long as there is breath in his body. You see, Jeremy has vowed to give up the game. Never again he says. I tend to think that he is just being dramatic and milking the situation. The trouble is that his father believes every word and the big dream of his son captaining Yorkshire has just been flushed down the toilet by a miner's son called Lenny Baxter. When he says there will be no trial and no future with the County, you probably need to take it seriously. I doubt if he's about to change his mind."

Lenny blew out his cheeks and slowly exhaled. It had been years since he had cried but now he could feel the weight of tears in his eyes. This in turn brought on a bout of panic. He couldn't let her see him cry. Unthinkable. He started to get to his feet muttering that he needed the toilet. She reached out and took his hand gently.

"It's OK Lenny. Come on. Sit down. Cry if you want. I think I understand."

If she had said that she actually understood, he would have stomped off. But she hadn't. She had said that she thought she understood and that was the right thing somehow. He slumped back to his seat and gazed out at the wagons thundering by outside. The tears rolled down his cheeks and he made no move to wipe them. Over. A dream that had grown and flourished for so many years and now it was over. Over with this strange girl in a Little Chef on the A1. And as he came to terms with it he realised that she still had hold of his hand. The Haddington thing to do would have been to pull his hand away and get the brave face on. But Haddington was ten miles away and he liked the feel of her soft fingers and so he left it be.

At last he said. "So what's the advice?"

"You need to bear with me here. Hear me out. Don't go all stroppy, OK?"

He managed a small smile. "I'll do my best."

"You should consider going the same route as me. Cambridge."

"Cambridge!!!"

"Just hear me out will you. Have a look in the papers. Every week the Cambridge University Cricket team side plays against County sides. Oxford as well. They are the only universities that do. That is why so many Oxbridge players go all the way and play for England. This has an effect on admissions policy. If you are an outstanding cricketer they take a different view on qualifications. Same with rugby and rowing."

Lenny was confused. "I don't understand."

"Basically, top sportsmen don't need fancy A-levels to get offered a place at Cambridge. A couple of E's would probably be good enough. You need to apply to Magdalene. The head of Admissions is supposed to be cricket mad. If he gets to hear that one of the most promising young fast bowlers in the country is considering a place he will jump at it. Instead of an interview it will be a trial with the college side. Like I said Lenny, I know a little about cricket. You'll walk in. Trust me."

"How do you know all this?"

"One of my friend's brothers is at Magdalene. I made some enquiries. I'm pretty good at finding stuff out."

"But I can't go there. It'll cost a fortune. My family could never afford it."

"Of course not. That's why they will make sure you get a scholarship. There will be a lot of politics working for you here Lenny."

"What do you mean?"

"Think about it. The Government introduces comprehensive education and tells the electorate that it is the best thing since sliced bread. The trouble is that the two top universities in the country never seem to take any one in from a comprehensive school. It's all Grammar Schools and Public Schools. Especially Public Schools. So the Government starts to feel angry and embarrassed, particularly when the papers start printing the statistics and asking why it should be. So the Government starts to threaten the universities. More students from Comprehensive schools or we'll cut your funding. No

more vintage port after supper. Then along comes a boy called Lenny
Baxter. A coal miner's son who happens to bowl like the wind. You're
their dream ticket Lenny. A high profile student from a northern
Comprehensive who will win them cricket matches."

Despite his instinctive urge to rubbish the whole idea he couldn't
help but see the sense in what she was telling him. He doggedly raised
objections out of blind habit.

"But how would I get down there for a trial, it's miles."

Now she smiled. He was listening. "Hitch hike."

"But what about somewhere to stay. I couldn't afford no fancy
hotels."

"I'll be in my second year by then. I dare say I'll have a flat. You
can come and stay with me."

"With you?"

"With me."

"But I just can't pick up the phone and ask for the admissions man
or whoever he is and say hi I'm Lenny and they say in the village that
I might be the next Freddie Truman."

"No. I can see that would be a difficult call to make. I'll do it. I am
actually very persuasive. I'll get you the trial but you'll have to do
the rest."

He wanted to object some more but already the idea was donning
the clothes of reality. Possibility. A new dream to work towards.

"Why are you doing this Beverley?"

"Mainly because I loathe Vic Feather. More than you will ever
know." Her face set in tight lines. She wasn't about to tell about the
afternoon when Feather had found her alone in the garden when she
had been twelve and got his hands inside her knickers before she had
escaped and run away. She hadn't told about that. Not ever. She
certainly wasn't about to start now. "That was why I started. However
after this morning there are more reasons. Against all odds I have to
say that I rather like you Lenny Baxter. You should be flattered. There
aren't many that I take a shine to. So. Tell me. Will you think about it?"

He smiled. It was the first time she had seen him smile and she
liked it. Liked it a lot. "How will I get in touch when I made my mind
up. Are you around for the summer?"

"Good God no. You won't be seeing me for dust. Tomorrow me
and a friend are hopping on a plane in London for ten weeks in India.

I get back a couple of days before college. You can write to me there. Beverley Morton c/o Trinity College, Cambridge. You'll find me."

He nodded. "Fair enough." He couldn't help but feel a sense of disappointment that she was disappearing from his life as quickly as she had come into it. "Happen you'll be around at Christmas."

She smiled. "Happen I will."

"Aye well, maybe we'll have another coffee or something."

"Aye. Maybe we will."

But they didn't. It would be well over two years before Lenny saw her again. But he wrote the letter. And he attended the trial. His dad gave him the train fare so there was no need for him to sleep on her couch.

Cambridge University
October 1981

It was standing room only in the debating chamber of the Cambridge Union. Not that there was even much room to stand. Barely room to swing a cat. The packed room was tensed up to the edge of violence. Lenny was impressed. He was no stranger to political meetings and debates. They were a fixture of Haddington life. His dad had taken him and Frank to meetings from the age or twelve. Part of their education he had told them. Never too young to learn how to be a proper Socialist. Lenny had seen most of the big names as they had come to talk to one of the Praetorian Guard Units of the left. The Haddington branch of the South Yorkshire NUM. Never a single scab. Not once. Not ever. Want a couple of minibuses full of flying pickets to show some solidarity with their working brothers? Ring the lads up in Haddington. They'll be there. And if it kicks off a bit rough, they'll stand firm.

Most of the big names had come to address them. Scargill, obviously. And Gormley. Foot. Grimond. And of course the man who dominated the massed ranks of students. Anthony Wedgwood Benn. The prince of the Left. The standard-bearer. He had impressed Lenny when he had come to Haddington. He hadn't ranted and raved like 'King Arthur' Scargill and his acolytes. Instead he had spoken quietly. Considered words of thought out revolution. Lenny had been swayed. They all had.

That had been a captive audience. Three hundred fully paid up members of the NUM on the right side of five or six pints of Tetleys. They weren't about to disagree with him. Tonight it was a different crowd. Half of the audience was clad in army surplus and old jeans and T-Shirts that demanded the release of Mandela. CND badges and spiky hair. Middle class revolutionaries who had signed up to the Militant Tendency and the Communist Party of Great Britain to get all the way up the noses of parents who managed banks and estate agencies. Then there were the ranks of those in the tweed jackets and the checked shirts. Some even wore cravats. Most of their parents did much the same kind of thing. They were the 'haves' and they wanted more and they didn't give a damn who knew it.

The debate was about one of the burning issues of the day: American Nuclear Weapons. Reagan had ridden his white horse into the White House and informed a trembling world that there was a new sheriff in town who was going to drive those goddamn Commies out. By this time, Britain had its new warrior queen who was ready to ride shotgun for the old gunslinger. By 1981, the first batch of cruise missiles was heading for their UK launch pads and the nation was split in half. The tweed half were adamant that the only way to keep the Russians in line was to hold the certain threat of wiping out their cities and make the twenty million that Hitler got rid of look like a side show to the main event. The army surplus saw the threat of full-on nuclear war as the greatest obscenity mankind had ever come up with in his long and savage history. It was an issue where there was no common ground. An issue that could easily lead to flying fists. And Lenny could feel that the room was ready to blow the lid.

The first speaker had been rather an earnest tweed with hair that was ridiculously thin for someone of his age. He already looked every inch a Tory and he was putting in the groundwork for a safe seat in a small town in Kent somewhere. Then came a girl from Cambridge University CND who was all red hair and passion. She was from Reading and she talked a lot about apocalypse and smouldering radio-active deserts and pointed with a bony finger at some of the tweeds who she said were about to slaughter millions of innocents. They in turn laughed in her face and shouted out that she was a Commie Dyke. That had nearly started a fight. But not quite.

The Conservative Party had put up one of their rising stars for the debate. A first glance had made Lenny fear for him somewhat. The build up had claimed he was a high flier, but he looked anything but. Sure, he was young enough, but he was one of those men who would have looked over fifty whilst they were still at primary school. He fidgeted and smirked all the way through the first two speeches and Lenny was somewhat astounded to notice that he was wearing a pair of brown hush puppies to go with his rather cheap looking blue suit.

When Kenneth Clarke, MP for somewhere in Nottingham, got to his feet he was met with cheers and boos that were no more than half hearted from either side. Here was a man who was neither villain nor champion. He was too bland. Too unthreatening. The tension started to drain from the room the minute he stood up. Lenny was intrigued. Appearances in this case were just about certain to be deceptive. No way would Thatcher send a poodle out to do battle with Tony Benn. Not a chance in hell. She would choose one of her best attack dogs and let it off the leash. This was going to be interesting.

Clarke started to rumble away like a favourite uncle at the bar. Soon he was cracking jokes and they were met with laughter from all around the hall. He chuckled merrily away himself. All of a sudden the near-violence of the night seemed far, far away. All of a sudden it was a light-hearted comedy show and even the most fervent found it hard not to be sucked into Clarke's easy going knockabout.

Lenny wondered where it was all going. Was this a softening up process? Would he suddenly switch and get fiery and serious? He didn't look as if he had it in him. He took a careful look at the face of Tony Benn who was sitting very still at his table waiting to bring the night and the debate to its climax. There was no laughter on Benn's face. He was white with anger. And Lenny sussed it. Of course. Benn thrived on addressing hyped-up audiences. He loved the heckling and undercurrent of tension. Clarke was popping his balloon. When he got up to speak he would seem boring and serious in comparison to the good old boy from Nottingham. He would look like a rather serious Maths teacher.

Lenny smiled. How clever. Really, really clever. He wasn't political himself. Never had been. He was a Union man of course. Every man, woman, child and dog in Haddington was a supporter of the Union. It wasn't something that was up for debate. To be against the Union was not even the faintest option. Secretly, he had come to resent the way the NUM was becoming hijacked by the far left. More and more their meetings were not about the issues of working conditions down the pit any more. The agenda was now the overthrow of the forces of capitalism, and this had accelerated rapidly from the day that Thatcher had walked through the door to Number Ten.

Lenny resented it. He feared that his people were about to be used. When the lid came off the simmering pot, the men from Haddington would be in the front line of an all out class war. They would be there because they always had been. It was their tradition. Their creed. In some ways they reminded him of the Spartans. They were brainwashed from the moment they could speak. They were indoctrinated into the proud history of Haddington. Never a scab. Not one. One out, all out. For years this fierce pride had been instrumental in forcing the bosses to improve the safety, conditions and wages of those who spent their lives underground. Now it was different. Now it was all politics. The agenda was different.

He had been taught that all Tories were pretty much followers of the Antichrist. But it was hard to think that way about Ken Clarke. And that of course was exactly the point. A look around the room told him that it was working. The faces of those in the jeans and army surplus gear were wrapped in laughter at his latest joke. Maggie had known better than to send down an attack dog. She was too cute for that. She had sent a Labrador instead, and it was working. He barely made a mention of nuclear weapons. Of course he didn't. Nothing much popped a feeling of cheer like the thought of world annihilation. He hinted that politicians on all sides were generally fairly decent sorts and the last thing they were about to do was provoke the end of civilisation as everyone knew it. To illustrate his point he told a story of a rollocking evening he had spend with a junior trade official over on a three day visit from Moscow who had set his heart on a night out in the strip clubs of Soho.

When he at last sat down he was cheered from all corners of the room. They had come to get fired up and angry at each other. Instead they had been entertained. Benn gave his fellow MP a rueful smile and a respectful nod and rose to his feet. The boos and cheering which would have lifted the roof a few minutes earlier were now as gentle as the those that had greeted Clarke. He paused for a moment and glanced down at his notes as the silence settled over the audience. Then he smiled.

"Well. I think the phrase is 'after the Lord Mayor's Show'. . ."

He took full advantage of the mellow mood Clarke had created.

There was no need to raise his voice to drill home his message. Instead he had the chance to be analytical. He used every second of his allocated twenty minutes and he wasn't interrupted once. Lenny smiled more or less the whole way through. As it turned out, Maggie had indeed dropped a clanger after all. Once anyone with even a pea for a brain sat still and listened to the cold facts, it was more or less impossible not to come to the conclusion that nuclear weapons were just about the most stupid idea that mankind had ever come up with. Benn quietly urged his young audience to see this as an issue where they needed to lift their eyes beyond the humdrum of party politics. This wasn't something that was about jobs and taxes and the movement of capital and wealth. This was quite simply a question of the future of mankind. And not only mankind. It was about every bird and beast and insect on the planet. Could it ever be right that the future of life itself could be left in the hands of such a very few men? He reminded the audience of the kind of men who had risen through the ranks to hold the reins of ultimate power. He had seen them in his own lifetime. Men like Hitler and Stalin. He asked the audience to close their eyes and imagine how things would have been if men like these had ever had the option of pressing the button. History taught a lesson that such men would always find their way to the top. It left the world with only one conclusion. One that every sane citizen of the planet would surely have to share regardless of their class, colour or political and religious beliefs. Nuclear weapons were abhorrent. An obscenity. And when he sat back down everyone clapped him and cheered him, regardless of whether they wore tweed or denim and none more so than Lenny Baxter who knew that he had just been privileged to watch genius at work.

Ken Clarke shook his hand with a wide grin and they shared a few words. The evening had started as a fight waiting to happen and the two men had ensured it had finished with an orderly exit to the pubs. The hall only had a couple of exits and there were already long queues filing out. Lenny decided to sit a while until things were a little clearer. He wasn't in any particular hurry. His only plan was to make his way back to his shoebox room in the eves of Magdalene's Elizabethan First Court.

His first three weeks at the university had certainly been interesting. Especially his college, Magdalene. Beverly had been right enough in all her theories. The admissions tutor had been delighted at the idea of giving the lad from Yorkshire a run out at one of the first team net sessions. He had been even more delighted to see his batsmen hopping and jumping as if they had live electric wires in their jock straps. Lenny was pretty sure that he would have been offered a place if he had failed every A-level out of sight. As it was, he did pretty well. Without the distraction of his brother and mates, he got immersed in his studies and in the end came out with two B's and a C.

What he hadn't expected was just how much Magdalene was just a natural extension of Eton and Harrow and Rugby. The beginning of term brought in an influx of students with voices from big houses in the shires who spent their days and nights getting indescribably drunk and talking about their school days and beagling. For a week he felt as if he had walked into a mad house. He decided to take his time with the whole thing. And so he stayed apart from it all and watched. He spent long hours walking around the place. It was mind-bogglingly beautiful. That was beyond argument. Fifty light years away from the dreary greyness of Haddington. The history of the place seemed to leak out from the old weathered stone. Here was where Great Britain Plc groomed its ruling classes. Had done for centuries. The ones who had gone out and overseen the building of the railways that had criss-crossed the biggest empire of them all. The ones who led the frightened ranks of the infantry into bloody skirmishes from Natal to the Punjab. The ones who led the cavalry charges of the nineteenth century to slash at the striking workers who were so close to triggering the British Revolution. He had come for a cricket career. Nothing else. Everything else was a surprise.

He hadn't made any friends. He hadn't particularly wanted to. After eighteen years of claustrophobic life in Haddington where everyone knew everyone and everything each other did, the solitude was a luxury. Others moaned about their poorly-heated little rooms. Lenny didn't. It was the first time in his life that he had a room of his own. He and Frank had spent a lifetime getting in each other's way in their boxy bedroom at the back of the house. He was more than happy to bide his time in this strange museum of a place. Everything was in a time warp. The buildings, the gardens, the students, the dons. It gave the place a strange fairytale quality. A place that had been left behind and never heard about the century when man had forgotten the ability to keep a leash on his dark side and had embarked upon the road to Paschendaele and Auschwitz. Cambridge was determined to stay rooted in a golden era of soft sunlight through the branches and drinks parties in gardens that looked like they were out of paintings.

What made it all so utterly weird was that just a few short months earlier the country had taken itself to the very edge. Riots which had flared up in Brixton had swept through towns and cities right across the country. In the end, the government had managed to muster just enough police to keep a lid on things. It had been a close run thing and there was a sense that it was merely a matter of time before the lid would get blown clean off. Unemployment was rocketing and people were getting angry. The British were famed for their patience and their ability to take it on the chin. But this was a different generation. This generation was no longer willing to doff the cap and accept it. Things were changing and Haddington had been full of talk of fighting back.

He had got on the train from a world of growing anger and got off on the platform of a town from Disneyland. He was still coming to terms with just how bizarre it all was.

Suddenly he was jumped from his thoughts by a light tap on the shoulder.

"Hello stranger."

He couldn't get over how different she looked. She had become one of the army surplus and denim brigade. The hair was cut very short now and she even had a nose ring, but the sight of her still made his heart start to try and climb up the back of his throat.

"Bloody hell. Beverly."

"Bev, actually. I stopped being Beverly ages ago."

He grinned. "Aye. So I can see. Bet Daddy's not amused."

"That's the understatement of the year. I thought you'd fallen out with me."

"Why's that?"

"I seem to recall that there was an offer of a couch to sleep on when you came down for your trial."

He was blushing again. Damn it. He hardly ever blushed and yet every time he was anywhere near Beverly Morton his face wanted to go off like a traffic light.

"Aye. I know. It were just that my dad gave me a train ticket see. A return."

"Oh well. If daddy came up with a train ticket that explains everything. What right has a girl to feel like she's been stood up. I also seem to recall spending several holidays at home and wondering if the phone might just ring. After all, I did go out of my way a bit you know. I bloody nearly got cramp of the eye lids from fluttering my lashes at your college's admissions tutor. You know what, he was even keener to look down my shirt than you were that morning in Assembly. And by then I had packed up wearing a bra. I had to put up with five minutes non-stop ogling to get you a shot Lenny Baxter. And what thanks do I get? Bugger all. Not a letter. Not a call. Shame on you. Any decent explanation?"

His mouth was working like a goldfish. As usual he was completely intimidated by her. It was laughable. He wasn't sixteen any more. He was a grown man and he was used to half the lasses in Haddington chasing him. And yet she made him feel like a kid. What the hell Lenny. Just tell the bloody truth. No point trying to be cool.

"I was going to ring lots of times. Whenever I saw that car of yours. Couldn't summon up the nerve. Too shy."

This won a smile. "My goodness. Such unusual honesty for a Haddington boy. There may well be hope for you yet Lenny Baxter. I suddenly feel lots better about that lecherous old sod peering at my tits for five minutes. How do you like Cambridge?"

"I don't know really. It's like Neverland isn't it."

She laughed. "Absolutely. I've never heard it called that before but how very right you are. It gets better though. Honest. How are you getting on with all those Magdalene Hooray Henrys?"

"You never told me about that part."

"Of course I didn't. You would never have come if I had."

"To be honest I've not had anything to do with anyone much. I'm just finding my feet I suppose."

A student in a bomber jacket and a Sandinista T-shirt came over and draped a leather clad arm around Beverly.

"Are you coming Doll?"

A voice from a suburb somewhere in Surrey. Raggy hair, thin face, earrings and designer stubble. Lenny hated him at first sight.

"Terry, this is Lenny Baxter. From Haddington."

Terry gave an off-hand smile and shook with a limp hand that hadn't seen a day's work in its life.

"All right mate. You the cricketer then?"

"Probably."

"Bev's always on about you. Apparently you're the next Johnny Truman or something. Can't stand cricket myself. Toff's game innit. Football's my gig. The people's game mate. The people's game."

Beverly rolled her eyes and suddenly looked a little embarrassed. "It's Freddie Truman you idiot and I wouldn't go accusing Lenny of being a Toff. He might just plant you."

Terry shrugged. "Fair enough. Sorry about that mate. Coal miner or something aren't you?"

"I'm a student. My family are coal miners."

"Fair play too. Comrades like. They'll be there when the day comes. When the bottles and the bricks get going. Always are, aren't they. Coal miners. Like in Russia back in '17. They'll be there when the working man has his day."

What a pratt. "Your dad a working man then?"

Terry's cocky veneer slipped a little. "Well not exactly. But my uncle's a bus driver. He's a Transport and General Workers Union man, my uncle. Used to be a shop steward."

"So what does your dad do then?"

"Well, he's an accountant but that doesn't matter. The movement has always welcomed comrades from the middle classes. Look at Lenin. Look at Trotsky. They came from the bourgeoisie didn't they?"

"I dare say they did." What in the name of Christ was Bev doing with this berk? He couldn't believe it. Terry in turn was visibly discomforted by his encounter with a real flesh and blood version of a working man from the north. He made a show of looking at his watch.

"Come on Doll. We need to go."

"You go. I'll catch you later."

"You can't just leave everything Bev. You're the organiser."

"And it's organised. All of it. From top to bottom. Don't get your knickers in such a twist. Everything will be fine."

He wanted to say more. Lots more. But Lenny's cold stare bothered him, really bothered him.

"Alright. See you in a bit. Don't be too long though."

He slouched away with a studied attitude that involved hands buried deep in pockets and shoulders hunched. Beverly watched him go with an air of impatience.

"So who was that?"

"Oh Terry's Terry. I know he seems a bit of a nerd at first sight but he's actually something of a mover and shaker round here."

"Doesn't look as if he could shake his way out of a wet paper bag."

She flared a little. "Hopefully when you spend some time here you will lose the tiresome Haddington habit of judging everyone on how much coal they can dig in a day and how many pints they can drink in the night."

He gave a sheepish smile. "Suppose so. Sorry about that. So what exactly does Terry do then?"

"He's Chairman of the university branch of Militant. He helps me a lot in CND."

"Your a member then?"

She smiled. "Chairman actually."

He whistled. "Bloody hell Bev. You're a dark enough horse to get a part in Black Beauty. Your dad must be spitting feathers."

"Just a bit. Especially when I jacked the family holiday last summer to camp out with the women at Greenham Common instead."

Now he was impressed. Properly impressed. He had a deep suspicion of students playing at revolutionary politics in the cotton wool safety of university. But Greenham Common was altogether different. A determined band of female pacifists had been camping outside the American airbase where the new Tomahawk Cruise missiles were deployed for some time now. The police had done their stuff. The tabloids had branded them all as 'Pinko Lesbians'. But they had sat it out through rain and shine.

He nodded thoughtfully. "I'm impressed."

"Good. So am I. I never really knew if I was the type of gal who could put up with taking a pee in a bush knowing full well some fascist from MI5 was probably staring up my bottom through a zoom lens. But I'm happy to report that I peed with the best of them for most of the summer."

"I went to Glastonbury. Me and Frank and the lads. Hell of a crack."

The Glastonbury Festival was CND's annual flagship event and number one fundraiser.

"In that case you better come along tonight. The University CND are holding our own mini-Glastonbury." She reached into a pocket and pulled out a piece of photocopy paper. "Here you go. One ticket. Two quid please."

He paid up and studied the paper.

"Christ alive. 'Pre-emptive Strike'. Are they still going?"

"Well obviously they are. They're here aren't they?"

'Pre-emptive Strike' had been a big noise in the summer of 1979, particularly their lead singer Reggie Philips who became known to the country by his stage name, Nuke. What the band lacked in musical ability, and that lack was considerable, they more than made up for with energy and attitude. They had a reasonably simple philosophy that they howled out to the nation over a blast of electric guitars. Number one in their creed was a fierce anti-nuclear message which was not uncommon and reasonably acceptable to an establishment that was still at odds about what to do about the growing phenomenon of Punk music. The band didn't stop with wanting to ban the bomb. They also wanted rid of the government. All governments. They wanted men in suits up against the wall and shot. They wanted the bosses hung from trees. They wanted America sunk under the Pacific. It was a wild anarchy that attracted a small but violently devoted following of skinheads who were fond of trashing the town centres of the small provincial places that staged 'Pre-emptive Strike'gigs when they toured.

The Tabloids had loved it. All of it. Especially Nuke. Three times during the wild summer of Thatcher's first year he was arrested and tried for inciting violence. Once he took the thing beyond the usual fine by greeting the decision of the Magistrate with a V sign and the words 'Shove it up your arse you wig wearing twat." That had earned him a month behind bars and an even higher perch in the firmament of tabloid bad guys. One of the things with Nuke was that he so conclusively looked the part. His head was shaven to stubble and his limbs were thin to the point of emaciation. The media snappers found him wonderfully photogenic. Hollow staring eyes and a twisted mouth with stumpy teeth. He was the perfect image to head up on any story warning the blue rinse generation that the youth of the day were wild, drug-crazed and a complete disgrace.

It had all gone wrong in October 1979 when the headlines of the tabloids had informed the nation that Nuke was in hospital trying to get over a massive heroin overdose. He had remained in the news for a few days and then disappeared from sight having enjoyed rather more than his fifteen minutes of fame.

Lenny was grinning." Stick it up your arse you wig wearing twat. Remember that?"

"Oh God. That's right. I'd forgotten all about that."

"So what's he like?"

"Nuke? More or less comatose when I met him. God alone knows what he was on, but he could barely remember his name. He was trying to work out how to drink a cup of tea. You'd have thought he was working at undoing a Rubik cube."

Lenny turned the ticket about with his fingers. "Are you sure this is a good idea?"

"What? Pre-emptive Strike? Course it is. We've sold two hundred tickets. They come bloody cheap you know. £50 for the night. Plus expenses. How the mighty fall and all that."

"Two hundred tickets. Sold where?"

"Record shops in the town. Why?"

"I thought you were smarter that that Bev. Think about it. Nuke. Cambridge University. Student audience."

"So?" Her face was slightly reddened. She didn't like the criticism in his voice.

"Oh come on Bev. It's a magnet for every self-respecting skinhead within fifty miles."

"Don't be so silly. That's all long gone. Nobody's bothered about 'Pre-Emptive Strike' any more. They're old news."

When they both stepped into the howling sound of King's Cellar bar twenty minutes later she found that he had been only too right. The cellar was low-ceilinged and it was clear that the numbers recommended for safety had been badly exceeded. The place was full to the point of being dangerous. Already many were leaving with expressions ranging from anger to fear. The audience was split into two distinct groups. The larger group was at the back of the room, furthest from the stage and it was made up of very much the same denim and army surplus as the crowd at the debate earlier. Lenny saw that many of the faces were the same. A few yards of clear floor space separated this group from group two who occupied the space in front of the low stage. This group was made up of sixty or so skinheads throwing themselves at each other in an imitation of one of the wilder tribal dances. Nuke was leaning out and over them, screaming into his microphone with his sheet white features contorted with rage.

Bev stopped and took in the scene.

"Damn."

"I'd say so. This place is about to . . ."

Lenny's next words were about to be 'kick off'. Before they could escape his lips, that was exactly what had happened. There was no way of telling what exactly had started it, but all of a sudden the thick warm air was filled with flying glasses and screaming. Lenny grabbed Bev and pulled her to him, dragging her head down so he could take the flying glasses on his back. By the time he half turned, three of the skinheads were on him. There was no time to think about anything much. His brain thankfully registered that none of them were very large. Number one's eyes widened in surprise as Lenny thumped him square on the nose causing a splash of blood. The second went down squealing like a stuck pig as his shin was cracked by the heel of Lenny's shoe. The third was paused in shock at the cold ferocity of the fight. This wasn't how it was supposed to be at all. The big blond bloke was some kind of psycho. He was sobering up fast from the four lines of speed snorted up in the car outside and he was just beginning to register genuine fear when Lenny's hand reached out fast and grabbed hold of his ears. Then his nose split under the sudden weight of the bigger man's forehead and he was out for the count.

It was all too fast for Bev. One minute there was a gig going on. The next she was buried under Lenny's well-built frame as glass shattered all around her. The next she was watching in astonishment as the three assailants met with an ultimate force. The next she was outside on the grass in front of the majestic shape of King's Chapel. Coughing and shaking. He had his arm around her and he was guiding her away from the gagging crowd that was spilling out from the below ground violence.

He looked down at her. "You OK?"

She nodded. "Yes. Just about. Bloody hell Lenny, I hope you never get angry with me."

He hung his head and nodded. It had happened again. This was the fourth time now. The red mist. The uncontrollable rage. The last time had been in a night club in Sheffield when three lads had jumped Frank at the bar. What was wrong with him?

She saw the hang of his head and immediately regretted her words "Hey, I didn't mean that badly Lenny. Just the opposite. You protected me, you . . ."

He shook his head. "I lost it Bev. Completely lost it. Christ knows what I've done to those lads. Specially the last un. Shit. I best go back and see if he's all right . . ."

"No you bloody well won't. No way."

"I can't just leave him Bev."

The night filled with sirens and the flashing of blue. Police cars and an ambulance swung through the magnificent arched gateway and rolled across the grass.

"There. There's an ambulance here now. Leave it Lenny. You'll just get in trouble."

A stumbling figure with wild eyes and a face full of blood joined them. Terry.

"Christ Bev. Did you see it. A bloody nightmare. Look at my face. The bastard glassed me . . ."

Lenny took his chin firmly and held up his face. There was certainly plenty of blood but the cut on his forehead wasn't all that bad.

"Tha'll be alright. It's clean enough, not too deep. Five or six stitches happen. Tha'll live."

There were four police cars now. Bev took his sleeve and pulled. "You need to go Lenny. Quickly. Before they seal the place off. Go over the river."

He nodded. Staying could mean big bother. He had no doubt that the lads he had injured wouldn't hesitate to ID him. She was right. Best away.

He ducked into an alley jogged clear of the scene.

Josh Ogilvy was drunk. Again. Beyond just drunk. Completely plastered. He had been at Magdalene for just over a month now and it was all that he had done. Get drunk. Get stoned. Snort cocaine. Deep inside he was disgusted with himself. He had come to Cambridge with high hopes of moving his life along to being something a bit more interesting. For eighteen years he had lived in the cocooned safety of his father's wealth. Prep school and Eton. St Moritz in winter and Antigua in summer. Hunting on Sunday mornings and the Lords test match. Friends from the same places and the same parents and the same well established money to open up all the doors.

At the age of thirteen he had decided that he had hated it all and he had made up his mind to be a rebel. The problem was that there were few things in life more pathetic that a rebel at Eton. He had spiked his hair and played his Clash records and smuggled in cannabis and taken his thrashings. His walls were a mosaic of Joe Strummer and Bob Marley and film posters. He was outrageous in the classroom and moody at home. But every weekend he still went to parties at all the same houses with all the same people talking about all the same old gossip and he tried to pretend that he was different by drinking more than anyone else and popping every pill he could lay his hands on.

His A-levels had been unspectacular. In fact, considering the frightening amount of money that had been invested in his education, they were pretty well pitiful. Not that it had mattered much. The track from Eton to Magdalene was a well-beaten one and poor results didn't matter a great deal.

From his first day at college, his cubby hole had been filled with invitations to parties and dinners filled with all the same old faces talking about all the same old gossip, and he had rebelled in his habitual way by making sure that he was always the drunkest and the wildest. The only difference was the cocaine. Cocaine wasn't something he would have risked at Eton. It was different here.

Tonight had been another dinner. In Trinity this time. A room full of hunting types in dinner suits desperate to get their trousers off and flash the bored-looking waitresses. He had drunk everything that was put in front of him but he had kept his trousers on. The fact that he never got the urge to flash anything in a skirt when three sheets to the wind was one of the very few aspects of his character that he had any respect for. It was late now. Past three. Four of them were making their way through the moonlit turrets and spires back to Magdalene and the undignified climb over the gates. There had already been a lot of falling down and Jocelyn Hollyoak had been thrown in the river. Their expensive dinner suits were in a state and bow ties were either lost or in pockets.

Josh had stopped and he was making a fumbling attempt to light a cigarette when one of the buildings of St Johns College jumped into his line of sight. Towering. Magnificent. All symmetric lines leading up to an elegant peak. Like a wedding cake. A picture in the chill of the autumn night.

The others had walked on a few yards before they noticed that he had lagged behind.

"Come on Josh. Stop arsing about. Let's go."

He shook his head. He wasn't about to go anywhere.

They turned and walked back to where he stood gazing up to the gothic peak of the building.

"Just look at that. Fantastic. Bloody marvellous."

Hollyoak made a drunken grab at his collar and pulled at him.

"Yeah, yeah Josh. Marvellous. Lez go. I'm freezing my bollocks off here."

"S'alright. Go. Couldn't give a hoot. You lot piss off. I'm going to climb the bastard. Look at it. Bloody fantastic."

This caused great mirth.

"Don't be such a wanker Josh. You couldn't climb into bed."

This riled him out of his reverie. "You don't think so, eh? Well stuff you. The lot of you. I'm going to climb the bastard." As he spoke he tried to pull off his dinner jacket in readiness for his attempt. Climbing was his one and only thing. The only time when anything in his life made a bit of sense. The only decent thing he had taken from his time at Eton. He had started when he was thirteen and he was good at it. The club at school went to Wales on trips and in his last year they had done Mont Blanc. He could do the ropes and the pitons and the ice work. So he could do this. Of course he could. Not a problem. And when he was up there he would find the peace that only a climb could give him. A respite when the self-loathing would leave him be for a while.

Two of them thought it was a bloody good laugh. One who, was marginally more sober than the others, wasn't quite so sure. "Come on Josh, you're pissed as a rat . . ."

"Go stuff yourself. I'm climbing the bastard. Bloody fantastic."

None of them had seen Lenny as he had approached out of the night. He stood a few yards back from the motley foursome. He had his hands in his pockets and he was following Josh's stare up at the building with interest.

"It's a bad idea."

His voice jumped them. Hollyoak spun around and screwed his eyes in recognition.

"Bugger me. It's the Narg."

"What Narg?"

"You know the Yorkshire Narg. You're the Yorkshire Narg aren't you?"

Lenny shrugged. "Sorry lads. You'll have to enlighten me. I've not got the foggiest what a Narg is."

Hollyoak giggled. It was a rather unpleasant feminine sound. "Course you haven't. That's because you are one. N. A. R. G. Not . . . A . . . Real . . . Gentleman. Narg. Buggers like you from dreadful places in Yorkshire. God knows what Magdalene's coming to. Never used to let Nargs in. Not a bloody chance. Now look. Bet your father's a bank clerk or something horrid."

"My dad's a coal miner actually."

This shook Hollyoak for a moment. A bank clerk father was bad enough. A coal miner was almost inconceivable.

"Bloody Grammar School boy I bet."

"Comprehensive actually. You're a grammar school boy I suppose."

Hollyoak wouldn't have taken more offence if Lenny had accused him of being paedophile. "Like hell I am. I'm a Harrow man you bloody Narg."

Lenny laughed. "Well surprise, surprise." His tone became conversational. "I really would never have guessed you know."

Hollyoak's rather cherubic face was clouding fast. His two colleagues were also less than amused. Josh was surprised to find that his attention was taken away from the building and it took a while for his vodka-sodden brain to register Lenny's speech. At last it got through and he cracked up. "Never have guessed . . ."

"Shut up Josh. I think we're going to have to teach the Narg a lesson. A lesson in manners." Hollyoak advanced unsteadily, closely followed by the other two whilst Josh was bent over laughing.

Lenny sighed. Some evening. It seemed as if everyone was wanting to give him a kicking tonight. The skinheads because he was a student. These clowns because he wasn't from the right school. It was a joke.

Hollyoak was close now and he stank of the stale water of the river. "Take it back Narg. Take it back before we . . .

Lenny slapped him hard with an open hand, the sound of his palm against the chubby cheek very loud in the still night air.

"Behave yourselves or I'll drop you. All of you. You're too pissed to stand up. Look at the state of you. He took a handful of Hollyoak's collar, turned him a hundred and eighty degrees, and sent him sprawling to the grass with a firm kick to the backside.

"Go on. Piss off home. The lot of you."

The two picked a near-tearful Hollyoak up from the grass and started to make an undignified retreat. Josh at last got over his mirth and watched his friends backing off with open amusement.

"Come on Josh. We're going. The Narg's a head case."

Josh waved them away. "Nah. Piss off. I'm not going anywhere. I'm going to climb this bastard."

Hollyoak wasn't in the mood to argue about it. "Suit yourself. You really are such a twat at times Josh."

Soon they were gone, their loud drunken voices floating away on the night air. Josh looked over to Lenny and shrugged his shoulders.

"Well. They're gone then."

"Aye. That they are. It's still a bad idea though. You're way too pissed mate."

This provoked frowning. "You really seem to think so. I don't feel very drunk at all you know. Not now. Did before. Drunk as a bloody Lord before. Better now. Going to climb the bastard."

Lenny sighed. This wasn't a man who was about to change his mind. He pulled off his jacket and dropped it to the floor.

"Come on then. We might as well make a start."

Josh's eyes registered a bleary surprise.

"Good lord. Climber are you? Bloody good man. All the best men are climbers. Every one of them."

They walked up to the base of the building and made a start. Lenny figured that the venture would fold before they made the third hand hold. He was wrong. Josh had been barely able to stand up on the grass, but as soon as he laid his hands on the wall he became cat-like. He was too fast for Lenny and it was immediately obvious that he had been much more formally trained. The whole point of the exercise for Lenny had been to try and make sure that the lad didn't fall off. The trouble was that he couldn't keep up to be of any use whatsoever as a chaperone.

"Hey pal. Slow down will you."

Josh took a look over his shoulder.

"Sorry old chap. Getting a bit carried away. Up you come."

By the time they made it to the gothic peak it had taken just over half an hour and Josh was twenty times more sober. He reached out a hand and pulled Lenny up to sit beside him.

"Good man. You're good. Bloody good."

Lenny laughed. "I shudder to think how good you must be when you're sober. For someone as drunk as you are, that was unbelievable."

Josh grinned and held out a hand. "Kind of you to say so sir. Josh Ogilvy."

"Lenny Baxter."

"And I gather from my dear appalling friend Hollyoak that you are a fellow Magdalene man."

"Aye."

"Splendid. Tell you something about Magdalene Lenny. No bloody climbing club. Umpteen drinking and dining clubs. Unbelievable really. Six hundred years old and no climbing club. I haven't climbed a thing since coming here. Miss it like hell. How about you?"

"I went last weekend actually. Peak District."

"And?"

"Aye it were alright."

"Bet it was. Bet it was bloody marvelous. I did bugger all. Got hammered and slept. No good." He dragged out a crumpled cigarette and lit it. "Tell you what Lenny. Why don't we form a climbing club? Two of us. 'The Magdalene College Climbing Society'. What do you think?"

"Sounds alright. I'm not in your league though. Tha'll have to do some teaching."

"Absolutely. It will be my pleasure. What have you done so far?"
The enthusiasm in his voice was infectious.

"Not a right lot to be honest. I go with my Uncle Derek. He's pretty good. He's been taking me and my brother Frank since we were about twelve. We've never done anything that fancy. Just bits and pieces in the Pennines and the Peak District. How's about you?"

"We had a club at school. We went to Wales mostly. I went in the holidays as well. The Alps. The Rockies last year. Can't get enough of it. It's the only time I feel right. If you know what I mean. Probably not. You look the kind of bloke who always feels right."

Lenny laughed at the thought. "Do I now. What school were you at?"

This troubled Josh. He really didn't want to say. The very mention of the word Eton could kill the friendship before it had chance to breathe. Lenny noticed and saved him the bother. "Summat tells me it wasn't a comprehensive."

Josh shook his head. "No it wasn't. It was Eton actually."

"You don't seem right happy about it."

A shake of the head. "No. Not happy. Never happy. We fall into two camps, the likes of me and the likes of Hollyoak. Rich kids born into everything. We either worship every ounce of our privilege and spend every second of our lives hanging on to it. Or we feel eaten alive by it all. Suffocated by our lives. Everything comes too easily. Our families think they are giving us everything when all they are doing is suffocating us in our tiny little world. Always the same people. Same faces. Same mindless crap."

"So you get drunk and climb high buildings."

"Yes."

"There's nowt like hanging off a hundred foot drop to make all men equal. We all turn into same kind of jam when we hit the deck."

Josh couldn't quite believe his ears.

"Good lord. You understand."

"Why not. I've got the same emotion somewhere. Just different circumstances. Look at me now. Down here with my own room. Graft means a couple of lectures a day and an essay every now and then. Then there's my brother Frank. And my dad and my uncle and all my mates. All down the pit. Down there in freezing cold and damp. Every day breathing in the filthy air that'll kill them off twenty years early." He took a glance at the luminous dial of his watch. It was close on six and the first light of a grey day was framing the old buildings all around them. "They'll be starting their shift about now. Down the lift and twelve hours before they come back up again. Twelve hours of noise and cold and filth. So aye. I know what it is to feel guilty Josh."

"Remarkable. The whole thing. If it isn't too rude, might I ask just how on earth you landed at Magdalene?"

"Cricket and a lass called Beverly Morton. Though now she's Bev. A long story that's best kept a while. It's getting light and if we get caught up here we'll be kicked out before the Magdalene College Climbing Society is owt more than a twinkling in the eye."

Their descent was uneventful. By now Josh was sobering up fast and Lenny was able to fully appreciate his climbing skill. He was not particularly tall and the first impression he created was almost of weediness. He had a mop of unruly black hair and a thin artistic kind of face with the pronounced nose of the Mediterranean. At ground level he seemed gawky, but as soon as he had his hands on the old walls he became lithe and graceful. By the time they reached the grass at the bottom it was light. A check at his watch told Lenny it was approaching six. Certainly an evening to remember. In theory he was due in a lecture about Chaucer at nine. Fat chance.

"Hungry?"

As soon as Josh mentioned it Lenny realised that he was.

"Starving."

"Let's go find some breakfast then. My treat."

Lenny shrugged. "Fair enough, but they don't start until half seven."

"Not college. The Newmarket. They kick off at six and a nod and a wink and a back-hander can rustle up a bottle of champagne."

Lenny shook his head and smiled. The Newmarket was a five-star hotel in the town centre. Not the kind of watering-hole that was his norm.

"Bloody hell Josh. You're like summat out of Chariots of Fire."

"One tries one's best. Come on."

The town was early morning quiet. Occasional bin men and paper boys gave Josh looks of loathing for his disarrayed dinner suit. Once they were seated in the near-empty dining room it became clear that Josh was no stranger to the waiter. A surreptitious fiver secured a bottle of Champagne that cost more that Lenny's brother Frank was about to earn that week. Josh poured with some ceremony and raised a glass.

"To the Magdalene College Climbing Society."

Lenny duly raised his glass and wondered if he was about to wake up. Two plates arrived heaped up with traditional British breakfast fare and they both dived in. Lenny speared a lump of sausage and waved it at Josh as he chewed through a piece of yolk soaked toast.

"No wonder tha feels guilty about life if tha makes a habit of this. Christ, my dad would have a duck fit if he could see me now."

"I dare say he would. Quite right too. They'll be down there now will they? Your father and brother?"

"Aye. That they will. Twelve hours straight with a flask of tea and corned beef butties half way through. How the other half live Josh. None of your champers and silver service."

Josh nodded. "Except it's not the other half is it? Its the other ninety eight percent. The ones the likes of me and my family try to pretend aren't really there. Just numbers on the balance sheet. Units of labour. If we drink enough and smoke enough and snort enough cocaine up our noses, we can just about convince ourselves that we are the beautiful people."

"You take cocaine!"

Another nod. "Fraid so."

"Bloody hell. What's it like?"

"For two hours you're superman. For the next day you want to jump off a high building. No guilt for a brief while and then about fifteen tons of it for ages. Stupidity. Just a way of punishing myself really. All of it is."

Lenny shook his head. "Mind my asking, but just exactly what does your family do. The way tha goes on about it you'd think they were axe-murderers or summat."

Josh smiled. "Maybe they were once upon a time. My father brokes stock. In London. And his father before him. And his father before that. Ogilvy and Simms. Stockbrokers. They shuffle the pieces of paper that make the capitalist world go round. Pieces of paper with lots of zeros. Enough zeros to make two or three percent commission worth a town house in Kensington and a country place in Shropshire and a villa in Antigua. My people have always been good at the two or three percent bit. It has got us into bother at times."

A rueful expression settled into his eyes. Now the penny dropped with Lenny. The olive complexion. The nose.

"Josh as in Joshua?"

"Indeed. Joshua David Ogilvy. Two great warriors of the Old Testament. Fine names for a spoilt rich kid who thinks snorting coke makes him some kind of a rebel. But yes, I'm a Yid if that was what you were driving at."

Suddenly there was an edge to his voice and Lenny leant back and raised his hands.

"Hey. I weren't driving at owt. I were just wondering that's all. We don't have any Jewish folk in Haddington. Plenty in Leeds mind.

Colour and creed makes no odds to me Josh. As me dad says, tha's either got summat or tha's got nowt."

Josh poured out two more glasses.

"Sorry. Just something I'm touchy about. Things used to be pretty bad at school."

"Because you were Jewish?"

"Of course. It wasn't the best of times."

Lenny wondered about it. "I don't suppose you'd have had a much better time of it at Haddington. Christ we all tried hard enough to make Beverly's life a misery, just because she was rich and had a BBC voice. Not that we got very far. It all just bounced off her."

"This is Beverly as in Beverly and cricket and the long story?"

"Aye. One and same."

Josh pushed his plate to one side and lit up and made himself comfortable in his chair. "Then my good man I'm all ears. I insist that you tell it. All of it, fully embellished with colour and detail. I for one have not the slightest intention of doing a damn thing today other than crashing out later on."

So Lenny told it. And it became a turning point. Without knowing it, they had reached the great fork in their lives where two roads offered different choices. By spending their day walking the quiet beauty of the ancient university they took their chosen fork and their destinies changed. Changed and became intertwined.

Not only theirs, but Beverly's too. She rose early that morning for an early lecture. She allowed some extra time and at ten past eight she was knocking on Lenny's door in the eaves of First Court. Her knocks were hollow sounding and unanswered. She knocked again on Saturday morning. And Sunday. But once again the room was empty. Lenny was staying up in a small pub in Buxton as the Magdalene College Climbing Society staged its first trip. Later, decades later, they were to wonder about it. If he hadn't made the climb, if he had returned to his room, then maybe he, maybe she, maybe they. Instead, a friendship was forged and a chance of love was lost. Only later were all three to know the cost. Later, when the skies turned dark.

After her third fruitless visit to Lenny's room Beverly felt a disappointed emptiness that annoyed her. What the hell was the matter? For two years she had enjoyed her pick of men. They had come knocking on her door as regular as clockwork. Not men. Just boys once she saw them in daylight. Pathetic most of them. Pathetic and predictable and boring. She had decided not to bother after the Easter of her second year and she had been single ever since. But ten minutes with Lenny Baxter had put paid to her game plan. What the hell was it with him? He had climbed clumsily under her skin from the moment she had teased him on the school stage all those years ago. She walked fast and tried to shake her head free of him. Magdalene bridge. A cluster of ducks on the flat water of the river. A cluster of Japanese tourists throwing bread. Elegant willow trees. A slight chill to the autumn air. And Lenny Baxter. Fair enough, he was handsome. No point pretending he wasn't. But so was his brother Frank. Identical twin handsome, and he did nothing for her. So it wasn't just that she fancied him. Something else. Something she had never really managed to explain to herself. She had never even noticed him before that bloody cricket match. Then he was there in her head and he had stayed there ever since.

That edge. It was something to do with the edge. The indefinable something he had about him. She had seen it in the shape of his body as he had leaned down over the bleeding face of Jeremy Feather. A dark hidden well of violence that seldom saw the light. On the surface he was all Haddington. Sport and pints and the lads. Underneath? Underneath was what intrigued her. Fascinated her. Underneath.

Oh for god's sake shape up Beverly. Like a bloody silly school girl.

Three days later she was again out and about early. She checked her watch. Ten to nine. She lengthened her stride and marched towards Jesus College and professor Reginald Simcox.

How long had it been now? No more than six months and yet it seemed a lifetime already. Six months since she had received an enigmatic invitation in her cubby hole.

Dear Miss Morton,

I have heard much. All good. Please join me for sherry. 7.00 p.m. if convenient for you. Please confirm.

RS

He was one of the Cambridge big hitters. His books on Hitler and Stalin were to be found in bookshops the world over. He was an authority who got plenty of TV work and lecture tours to America. He was tall and played squash four times a week and dressed in shabby cord jackets. More than one producer had deemed his leathery face to be good for television and many of his female students allowed their attention to wander from the history of the mid-twentieth century during his invariably well attended lectures. He was a maverick and Beverly had been intrigued by the invitation. Intrigued and wary at the same time. She had already had one so-called pillar of academic respectability leering down her T-shirt when she had negotiated Lenny's trial.

Simcox inhabited a small room of leather chairs and piles of books with a long dead plant on the window sill.

"Ah. Miss Morton. Goodness me. How right my informants were. What a lovely girl you are. Quite divine."

Instinctively she folded her arms to her chest. Not that she had taken any chances this time. This time she had chosen a polo-neck. Simcox noticed the defensive gesture and chuckled merrily.

"Oh goodness me. No need to worry about that. My word. The very thought. Please sit." He grabbed an armful of books and cleared a space on one of the chairs. "Here. That's better. I gather there has been some talk. A long way off the mark I can assure you. Let's put it this way. If you had that exquisite face and a different gender then you would probably be right to worry my dear. As it is, you need have no concerns. Queer as a bent penny as they say. So sherry is it? Of course it is. Where else on the this troubled planet would a man of my age offer a lady of your age a glass of sherry? Oxford possibly. Otherwise nowhere. But here it is the norm of course. Here."

He passed her a generous tumbler full and clinked it with his own glass.

"Your very good health my dear. Thank you so much for coming."

She took a sip and risked a small smile. She was no nearer to having even the slightest clue as to what her invitation was all about. She didn't study his subject, she wasn't from his college, and thankfully he didn't appear to have any aspirations to get her into bed.

"I can see that you are a little confused my dear. You have that what the hell does the old queen want look on your face."

"Sorry."

"No need. I was wondering if you would come at all. Plenty don't."

"So they never get to find out about their mysterious invitations."

"No" He sat now and fiddled with a pipe. She would have bet big money that he would smoke a pipe.

"So why am I here Professor Simcox? I must admit to being rather intrigued."

"Reginald please. But never Reg. Can't abide Reg."

"Fine. Reginald it is." She leant back in the chair which was surprisingly comfortable. Her instincts told her that this was a meeting that was going to be anything but short and succinct. She took a look around the academic chaos of his room and wondered if he had been in trouble for not tidying his bedroom as a boy. He was clearly comfortable enough with silence. For the time it took him to pad out his pipe and light it up the only sound was the ticking of the old clock on the wall. Beverly crossed her legs and waited. At last he was finished and puffed hard to get the thing going.

"That's better. Sometimes I need a pipe to get going. Ludicrous really. Right. Let's see. Beverly. Beverly Morton."

She considered telling him that it was Bev but decided that he might consider Bev to be as bad as Reg. She could be Beverly for a while.

"Our job here at Cambridge is to teach people. Obviously. I teach history as you know. And we like to think that we have a certain reputation for doing it well. However that is only part of the job. We wear other hats. Understand?"

She didn't, but she wasn't about to say so. So she nodded. "Other hats."

"Absolutely. Other hats. The other hat that I wear is that I look out for people. Spot talent as they say. You will find there is a lot of that here. You need to understand how Cambridge works. It's been the same for hundreds of years."

He suddenly felt the need to get to his feet and pace.

"When the place works best, we get in a high percentage of the high fliers of Britain. All kinds. Scientists and artists and engineers and doctors. The future cogs that will run the machine. Understand?"

She nodded. She did. It was something that was well enough known.

"Most of the process is pretty straight forward. A whiz kid mathematician will be thoroughly seduced and offered a Fellowship right here. He is given a life that is pampered and safe and he wants for nothing. The State has him right where they want him. The deal is that he uses his talents to further the interests of the State. The greater good. Enigma was the perfect example. Hear about it?"

"No. I'm afraid I didn't."

"1942. A dark year for the country. Never a darker one. The Nazi U-Boats were having a field day out in the Atlantic. Thousands of tonnes of shipping were being sunk every month. Thousands of men were dying badly. The country was on the brink of starvation. The key was cracking the code to the Enigma Machine. It was thought to be unbreakable. The Nazis certainly thought it was. Well, we had the mathematicians on tap right here at Cambridge and they broke the code, we won the war and the rest, as they say, is history. My point is that the University had done it's stuff and made sure the talent was ready and in place. Not in America. Not, God forbid, in Russia. With me so far?"

"I think so."

"Splendid. Right. Talent. The talent I look for is more unorthodox. Less obvious. Altogether less obvious. A question Beverly. What sets Britain apart from France and Germany and Russia and Italy?"

She shrugged. "Fish and chips. Cricket. Bowler hats."

He smiled. "Wouldn't argue with any of those, but not what I had in mind. Never had a Revolution. That's the big one. The one that sets us apart. Oh we've come close at times. 1842 with the Chartists, 1926 in the General Strike. Even last year. But it has never gone all the way. Somehow, by hook or by crook, it has always been stopped in its tracks. Ever wondered why?"

"I can't say that I have."

"There are lots and lots of reasons of course. The main difference is that Britain has never produced the revolutionaries. Not a Lenin or Leibknect or Robespierre. Not a Mussolini or a Hitler. Some would say it is the British personality, to which I would say bunkum. Not at all. Not even close. A big part of the reason is much, much more subtle. All the names I have just given you were excluded from the high table. They were made to live in obscure shadows and they hated it. They were kept from the centre of things and their resentment lit the flames that burnt everything down. Would Lenin have formed the Bolshevik Party had he been appointed as Dean of St Petersburg

115

University? Would Hitler have become what he did had he been given a senior teaching post at a Prussian Military School? Probably not. Almost certainly not. Britain produces it's share of these men. Of course we do. But we are very good at not excluding them. We tempt them with the dream of Oxford and Cambridge. We seduce them with the best that life in Britain can offer. And we make them want more. Much more. They crave to be a part of it all. And of course we let them in. We turn our poachers into gamekeepers before they have the chance to learn the art of poaching. Understand?"

This was getting much more interesting than she had anticipated. "Yes. I think I do."

He nodded and re-lit his pipe. "You've been noticed Beverly. Spotted. Not surprising I suppose. A pretty girl like you will always stand out. But colleagues tell me there is more. You have an interesting background. One level says you came here from a Comprehensive school in a South Yorkshire mining village. Very rare my dear. Like hen's teeth. But there are other levels. Your family are in fact not actually of the aforesaid village. Your family lives apart and is wealthy. Not so rare after all. And yet your father chose not to send you to Public School even though it is more than evident that he could have well enough afforded it. May I be so bold as to ask why?"

He knew a lot. It made her slightly uneasy but very intrigued. "I suppose you may. My father is very Yorkshire. He feared that Public School would make be soft. He thought that Haddington Comprehensive would be character-building for me."

"And was it?"

"Well, I'm here am I not."

"Indeed you are. I'll tell you why you have been noticed Beverly. Bright, beautiful and tough. Three words that have come up a lot. It means there will soon be a queue at your door. Suitors and recruiters. They will come from banks in the City and big business from both sides of the Atlantic. They will offer you treasure and lots of it, particularly the Americans. They always have more treasure than everyone else. You are a woman for the era we live in. Tough women are in vogue at the moment. Our gallant Prime Minister has set a trend. So it is my task to jump the queue before it has a chance to form."

"Do you worry that I might become a revolutionary professor?" She said it with a smile.

"Indeed I do. And a dangerous one to boot. Look at our new warrior queen in Number Ten. Just imagine how dangerous she might have become if Oxbridge had said 'no' and slammed the door in her face. One shudders. She would have had the greengrocers and the shipping clerks out on the streets with pitch forks and baying for blood."

"Like Hitler did?"

This made him cough on his pipe smoke. "Indeed. Very acute of you. Though not a sentiment that a respected don would necessarily air in public."

She decided to try to take a little control of the situation.

"So Reginald. Here you are at the head of the queue. You have already dropped some heavy hints that you have not arrived bearing treasure. You have spotted me. So what do you want from me?"

The smile was very sweet but her eyes were firm. They had been right about her. Formidable indeed. It was pop the question time.

"It is hard not to sound rather old fashioned and pompous, but I would like you to work for your country my dear."

Well, well, well. So this was how it was done. It was something that had often been debated. How did they pop the question? Where, when and how would the security services actually show their hands? And now she knew. She knew because amazingly enough it was her that they were asking. Her. Beverly Morton from Haddington. He had sat back now and was watching her intently. She decided to try and stall for a moment or two.

"My country you say?"

"I think that you heard well enough Beverly."

"Are you representing home or abroad?"

"Ah. Good question. Very practical. I'm from the home end of things. Some think that the abroad stuff is more attractive. More glamorous. Too many Bond films of course. I can assure you there is nothing remotely glamorous about eating over-cooked cabbage on a Tuesday night in Warsaw. It's all a long, long way from sun-kissed beaches and Nordic blondes bursting out of their designer bikinis."

"Are you suggesting that big bosomed-Swedish girls are my kind of thing Reginald?"

"Good lord no. Absolutely not." It amused her to see that he was suddenly rather flustered. Having dug himself into a smallish hole he dug deeper. " . . . of course there was nothing in our background investigation to suggest . . . ."

"Background investigation?"

He now wore a troubled sort of look. "Well yes. I'm afraid so. Nothing too intrusive of course. Basics really. Father. Mother. Finances. Friends and acquaintances. That kind of thing."

"And no lesbian links then?"

She was pleased to see that she had forced a blush. Splendid. She wasn't losing her touch. "No. None whatsoever."

He was about to try to change the subject but she wasn't ready for that just yet. "How much is my daddy worth?"

"I'm sorry?"

"I'm sure you understand Reginald. I dare say your investigations must have looked into the family finances. What did you find?"

Now the trouble lines on his face deepened a millimetre or two. "This is rather unorthodox I'm afraid. I'm not entirely sure whether I have the authority . . . and morally it is questionable . . .

"Don't give me silly morals Reginald." Her words snapped into him and he visibly winced. "You say you want me. England wants me. Well Reginald, here I am. You're actually doing quite well. In fact you have got me interested. The price. Answer the question or I'll walk."

He met the eyes across the cluttered desk. Christ, she was something this one. "Very well Beverly. You like to play a hard game, which of course is the very reason that you are here." He took a moment to choose his words diplomatically. "Nothing is as it seems I'm afraid. As you know, your father runs several companies and presents the world with an image of wealth and success. Underneath it is a story of re-mortgage and spiralling debt. Things are beginning to catch up I'm afraid. They have been catching up for several years now."

She say very still. She gave a slow nod. "I suspected as much. Daddy is very good of course. He can put on a hell of a performance. But there have been signs . . ."

He really didn't quite know what to say. This was not a situation he had any experience of. He was still weighing his options when she saved him the bother.

"OK Reginald. Here's how it is. I expect that your people get two types of recruits. Let's say idealists and whores shall we?"

"Well, I would hardly . . ."

"Save it Reginald. I dare say you will root out lots of over-pampered young men and women who will go all dewy-eyed with pride at the prospect of doing something for Queen and Country. Then there will be the other ones. The whores. The ones who do it for money and think of pounds, shillings and pence rather than England. I have no particular love of England, Reginald. Certainly not nearly enough to spend my days rooting through other peoples dirty laundry for a mediocre salary and a government pension. Not a chance Reginald. If you want me you're going to have to pay."

"You are very direct Beverly."

"I'm from Haddington. Don't ever get confused by the nice house in the countryside."

He fiddled about with his papers for a moment. He had never come across this kind of situation before and he found it extremely unpleasant. "I don't really know what you are driving at my dear. Well I do, I just don't know . . ."

She smiled and completed the sentence for him. "How much? You don't know how much. Am I correct?"

"Yes. Quite correct."

"Good. Then we are both on the same page. I have simple terms. You give me a clear concise analysis of the state of my family's finances. I don't want to work on the books. I will work freelance on a pay-by-results basis. The money on the table will always need to be enough to get the family back on its feet. Those are my terms Reginald. If your people can meet them, I am all yours."

Something about her made him feel old and sad and out of step. "You are a very direct young lady."

"It has always been something that Yorkshire folk have prided themselves on. I have no religion or politics. My world is really quite simple. I love my mother and father. Period. I have worried for some time that my family is in trouble. That is now confirmed. You have offered me an opportunity to solve the problem. It is as simple as that Reginald. I don't expect you to give me an answer. Go and consult. If I hear nothing more, then I know the answer is negative. If I hear, then we can negotiate."

She glanced at the old clock on the wall. "I'd better be getting along now. I have a lecture on Thomas Hardy and the rural dream. It has been a rare pleasure sir."

She reached across the desk with a slim hand. He took it and it was smooth and dry. Her eyes locked onto his and they had no relation to the smile on her face. There was a cold contempt there. She made him feel small. Dirty. She fired high velocity shells into his ivory tower.

She made it all the way down the stairs and out of the college before the tears started to burn their way down her cheeks like sulphuric acid.

It took less than two weeks for the second letter to arrive in her cubby hole. A careful analysis of her father's near bankruptcy was enclosed with another invitation to the cluttered room in Jesus College.

This time Simcox was not alone. He had a lizardy-looking man with a nobbly bald head and three piece suit at his side. The man was introduced as Latimer and he was up from London. The sickly sweet smell of his cologne was crawling into every corner of the room and when he leaned forward to shake her hands she felt physically sick.

Simcox was visibly uncomfortable with the whole situation. "Not really my thing today Beverly. Latimer here has some things to discuss. I'll leave it to him."

So no sherry this time. Obviously the sherry was only for the Queen and Country types. Latimer carefully placed his attaché case on his knees and removed some papers and a glasses case. He put on the glasses and shuffled the papers. Then he looked up at her with cold, empty eyes.

"We have listened to a recording of your chat with Reginald. People in London are interested. Extremely interested. I have been asked to investigate further and to accommodate you if possible."

"And you are?"

A smile all the way from the coldest bit of Siberia. "I'm Latimer."

"I mean where do you work? What department?"

"No department. I am the Chief Executive of a small company that co-ordinates public relations for corporations from the Middle East. We receive large fees from companies who prefer to remain anonymous and pay their bills via banks in Zurich or Nassau. In turn we make discreet payments to the various consultants whose services we engage on behalf of our clients. It is the kind of set up that would arouse great interest within the Inland Revenue. Our accounts of course are red-flagged for no investigation. The word used to describe our kind of organisation is 'deniable'."

"I see."

"Splendid. It makes things so much easier when people do. Shall I make my pitch, Miss Morton?"

"Please do."

"In a nutshell, we are interested. Very much so. We are willing to give you work that will pay enough for you to solve your family's financial problem. All family debt will be transferred to a bank in London where generous terms will be put in place. Once the sum is consolidated, we will ensure that it can be fully cleared over a period of ten years. You will be given specific targets for the work that we give you. These targets will be clear and achievable. So long as you meet these targets your family debts will be cleared within the agreed time frame. Over and above this, you will be remunerated at the level you could expect if you worked for one of the larger banks in the City. Am I being clear?"

"Extremely."

"Good. You will of course need to explain the situation to your parents in my presence . . ."

"But . . ."

"There is no but Miss Morton. You are a nineteen-year-old student. There is no possibility of our concocting any kind of cover story that would adequately explain the change in your financial circumstances. We need your family to have their eyes wide open. Of course this will also go a long way to ensuring your loyalty, commitment and silence. Shall I continue?"

He was the most appalling individual she had ever met. But what choice was there? The accounts had been brutally clear. Her father had less than two months before his creditors would beat down the gates.

"Continue."

For an hour he went through the small print. It was the following weekend that she had driven north with him in his Ford Granada. Her parents had been white-faced with shock and pretty well speechless. Latimer had allowed the family time to consult and her father had held her close and whispered to her.

"You don't need to do this Beverly. Really, you don't. We'll manage somehow."

Her mother was almost catatonic. She drank her gin and tonic mechanically. Beverly realised that she had been kept in the dark as to the dire financial situation. Somehow Beverly had dragged a smile from a cupboard she didn't even know she had.

"It's fine daddy. Really. I want to do this. I have to do this."

The house seemed to have died a little as the Granada crunched across the gravel yard and back onto the road south. She never spoke a word all the way back to Cambridge. Latimer played a Barry Manilow tape as the dreary flatlands of Eastern England blurred by outside.

Three weeks before the end of her second year she had signed away her soul and Latimer had started the process of creating a Beverly Morton to meet his requirements. Beverly the high-flying rich girl became Bev the disaffected rich girl. She cut her hair short, had her lip pierced, bought her combat jacket and joined a London branch of Militant Tendency. She spent a wet six weeks in a leaky tent with the CND women outside the US airbase at Greenham Common. When she had returned to college, she had immediately stood for election as the Chair of the University branch of CND and had won by a landslide. She had transferred her Militant membership to the Cambridge branch and her transformation was complete. Beverly had become Bev.

She met with Latimer on a fortnightly basis in a pub that was a twenty-minute train ride away in the small town of St Neots. By October he was happy that her transformation was complete. This triggered the first agreed reduction of the new family account at the bank in London. It was now time for her first task. He gave her a large brown envelope which contained a detailed description of the life and times of Terry Sanderson of Croydon and Trinity College Cambridge. Latimer explained that Terry Sanderson was a threat. He had spent two summer holidays on exchanges with students from East German Universities. First Magdeburg, second Leipzig. There were times when he had disappeared from their limited view. There was more money than there should have been in his bank account. Once he was back in South London in the holidays, he had spent evenings with a junior official from the East German Trade Mission called Schulman. Latimer explained that it was clear that Terry's East German handlers obviously rated him highly. Latimer didn't agree with their assessment at all. He thought that Terry was pathetic. Not that it mattered. He could be useful. Very useful. So long as the East

Germans retained confidence in their investment, they would ensure that Sanderson made progress in his chosen field. Latimer's people had decided to allow the progress and then turn him when the time was deemed to be right. Terry Sanderson wasn't the type who would tough it out when sticking to his ideals would mean a minimum of ten years in Brixton.

Beverly's job was to get close. All the way under his skin. She was to become his Lady Macbeth and ensure that he continued up the career ladder of the hard left. She was to become the power behind his throne. And yes, she was to take him to her bed if that was what it was going to take.

Things were very different now on the rare occasions that she visited Simcox. It had been the first time that his recruitment efforts had led to Latimer's door. Always before it had been the comfortable familiar world of his fellow Oxbridge colleagues in MI5. Latimer was from a different world altogether. He was the face of the cold future rather than the warmth of the past. The historian in Latimer found it all too easy to dress Latimer in the black uniform of Himmler's Gestapo or the coarse cut brown of Stalin's NKVD. Britain wasn't supposed to have men like Latimer. It wasn't on the brochure that Simcox had read before signing up to do his bit.

And if Latimer wasn't a part of the cloistered world Simcox wanted to reside in, then neither was Beverly Morton. The ease with which she had wrested control of the situation and sold herself so dear had stunned him. Of course it was silly to feel any sense of surprise. The increasingly bombastic behaviour of the dreadful woman in Downing Street was setting the tone for a new and dismal era for Britain. The land was being callously split down the middle and the next few years were not about to be pretty. The whole thing made him feel an empty sadness deep in the pit of his stomach. His field was the centre of the Twentieth Century and his hero, like so many of his generation, was Churchill. Churchill the man who had pulled every one of his citizens together and forged a belief in the power of good so strong that he had overcome history's most monstrous tyranny in under five years. For a moment Britain had become the beacon of light in a dark world that it had always claimed to be. Now he feared his country was sleepwalking into a time of darkness. A time of men like Latimer. A time of women like Beverly Morton.

Her tap at his door made him jump and he roused himself. "Come in."

How very different she looked now in the uniform of the left. Gone the cool girl of the middle classes with her careful hair and elegant clothes. The old American combat jacket looked as if it had swallowed her as she slept and it hung off her as though her shoulders were a twisted coat hanger. A student of his had once explained that this was the 'fuck you' look. How very extraordinary. As she sat he couldn't help but admire her acting ability. She had taken the role all the way down to the body language. When she had first sat in the chair opposite she had been still and erect. Elegant. Cool. Appraising. Now she lounged in the chair with loose limbs and a studied expression of light contempt that did as much as the nose ring to spoil her beauty.

"How are you Reginald?"

"I'm fine Beverly. Quite fine."

"It's Bev."

He sighed. "Outside it may well be Bev. Within these four walls it will continue to be Beverly."

She gave a dismissive shrug. "So what's with Latimer today. Off saving the world is he?"

Somehow she had eased some of the flat sounds of the London suburbs into her accent. It sounded dreadful.

"I am not party to Mr Latimer's diary. Nor would I ever wish to be."

This produced a small smile. A small window on the old Beverly.

"You don't like him do you?"

"No actually, I don't. But I don't have to like him. Liking him isn't part of the requirement."

She picked away at the frayed hole on the knee of her raggy jeans. He was appalled to see that her nails were filthy.

"So Reginald. I was summoned. All very dramatic too. Come this morning Beverly. Fly like the wind."

"Yes. I must apologise for the lack of notice my dear. It wasn't my idea, I can assure you."

"Ah. So the great Latimer is still with us in spirit. Well come on. Let's have it."

He sighed and opened the drawer of his desk. Inside were several photos which he took out and passed over. Beverly studied them with neither surprise nor interest. They were from a few nights before.

Photographs of herself and Lenny and Terry from the debating chamber and, later on, the lawn outside the Kings College Bar. She shrugged.

"So?"

"Who is the stranger? The tall one?"

"What. Fancy him do you?"

"Don't be ridiculous." But she held him with those unblinking eyes of hers and he had to concentrate hard not to squirm in his chair. She tossed the pictures onto his cluttered desk.

"It's Lenny. Lenny Baxter. Nobody to worry about. He's a friend of mine from home. Is there a problem or something?"

"Several I'm afraid."

A flash of anger flickered across her eyes but she kept it from her voice. How very good she was.

"Well you'd better do your job and tell me then."

He took a breath. "Yes. Of course. Number one is why was there no mention of Mr Baxter in your report."

Damn. She had hoped that by some miracle there may not have been a surveillance team at the debate. Fat chance.

"There was no need. Lenny is just a friend from home. He's not a part of the Militant scene or anything."

"You know him well do you?"

"Well enough. We were at school together, that's all. He was two years below me. That was all."

This was getting quite intriguing. Suddenly her poise was gone. It was the first time he had seen it happen.

"And you went along to the Admissions Tutor at Magdalene and flirted him into giving Mr Baxter a cricket trial I gather. Is this something you do for all your school friends?"

"How . . ."

"Oh come on Beverly, please don't underestimate us. This is a very small town and we are actually rather good at what we do. Don't for a moment believe that we proposition people without checking out all the nooks and crannies."

She nodded and looked young again. He continued.

"So Beverly. Why? People like Latimer say there are only ever two reasons. Sex or money. It doesn't appear that Mr Baxter has money."

"You bastard."

"Oh yes indeed. You can take that as written."

She wanted to buy some time but he was all over her now. "It isn't sex. Bloody hell, I've never even kissed him. He's a friend, that's all. Someone I like to spend time with."

"So much so that you cleared his path to Cambridge."

"It wasn't like that."

"Then what was it like Beverly?"

She jumped to her feet and went to stare out across the college gardens with her hands pushed deep into the pockets of the jacket.

"I really have no idea why Reginald. That's the truth. It was just something that I did. I couldn't really explain it, even to myself."

His voice was suddenly much softer. "Not sex then. Love."

She span round at this with look of something close to panic.

"Don't be so bloody ridiculous Reginald. I barely know him."

"Does it have to be anything more than barely? I think not."

She slumped back into the chair.

"I don't know. I really don't."

It wasn't a time to be sorry for her. Not with the ever present shadow of Latimer.

"I'm afraid that is no excuse for editing Mr Baxter from your report Beverly."

The anger was back again. "Oh for Christ's sake why are you people so endlessly bloody paranoid. Lenny isn't a threat to your precious ivory towers. He's a sportsman. Cricket. That is why Lenny is here. Cricket, not revolt."

"That, my dear, is not your decision to make. You forget that you are a junior. It is not for you to interpret information for the very simple reason that you are young and you know nothing."

"I know Lenny isn't what you seem to think." Anger now. Very real. The lioness defending her own.

"Oh do you? The young man's father is a local shop steward for the Yorkshire NUM, an organisation that is almost entirely at the beck and call of Moscow."

"Don't be so bloody silly . . ."

"He cut across her. " . . . not only that. His brother is in the union. His grandfather too. And you don't even deem it worthy of a mention in your report. Come on Beverly, grow up."

"How do you know all this about Lenny? You can't have found all this out since the other night."

"Of course we didn't. Think about it and stop acting like a love-sick schoolgirl. Student from Haddington comes to Magdalene and you think we don't run background checks. Well?"

She was livid with herself. Of course they would run their horrid checks. The Latimers. The men in the shadows. And they would assume all the wrong things. They were not men who would ever understand someone like Lenny. Not that she did. Not that anyone did.

It was hopeless. She looked so pitiful all of a sudden. Stuff Latimer. He softened his voice. "Look, Lenny Baxter is really just a small issue. This is the greater problem. These pictures. Look at Terry Sanderson's face. Here."

He passed the photos and she looked. There was no need for explanation. The expression was one that a blind man in a blindfold could have read. Jealousy. Pure, old fashioned and biblical. Oh no.

"You see don't you?"

She nodded. "I see."

"So you will understand why it is important that you don't see Mr Baxter again. At least not whilst your job is to get in close to Terry Sanderson."

Another nod. "Yes Reginald. I understand." It had only been a few days ago that she had heard the emptiness of his room as she had knocked on his door. How she had wanted to see him. How very much. How she had wanted him to take her and hold her and take away the nightmare she had allowed her life to become. And now she wouldn't see him again. Not for months probably. And he would think that she had snubbed him. And . . .

She hated herself for it as a tear broke free and ran down her cheek. Simcox pulled a handkerchief from his pocket and gave it to her. He took a deep breath and ground on with his task.

"I'm afraid there is something else Beverly."

"Is there." Her voice was now flat. Beaten.

"Mr Latimer is concerned about the slow progress you seem to making with Sanderson. Have you . . ." No matter how he tried he couldn't force the words from his lips.

She looked up with eyes that were now quite calm. "No Reginald, I haven't slept with him yet. Nor will I. Not ever. He disgusts me. Tell Mr Latimer not to concern himself. There are ways that a woman can achieve more by not sleeping with a man than doing so. It is a subtlety that men are incapable of."

This made him smile. "Most men yes. Not this one. I AM gay remember. Your strategy makes all the sense in the world to me. Get him to that frantic stage where the image of a naked you deprives him of his sleep and dominates his every waking hour. And then he will revert to being the animal that we all become when led by our genitalia. He will do just about anything to impress you. To make you think he is something special, something powerful."

"Of course he will."

"And that is when Terry Sanderson will tell you all his secrets. Clever girl. Clever, clever girl."

She shrugged. "Is that all?"

"Yes. That is all. I shall tell Mr Latimer not to worry himself."

She didn't bother with a goodbye. She just left, closing the door quietly behind her.

It would be several months later when the time came for Terry Sanderson to play his frantic card, at the end of March, just as the sun was finding the first hint of the warmth to come. By now Terry was completely overwhelmed by the ferocity of Bev's revolutionary zeal. Even more than this, he was hungry for her to the point of starvation. She had dismissed his every approach. She seemed to think he was nothing. Just another silly student playing Trotsky.

So he had told her, his words cascading out. He told her about a meeting with Schulman and an envelope full of cash. £10,000. He told her about a strike in Liverpool where the number of scabs was growing by the day. He told her of how men could be bought to smash the windows of the scabs and to slash the tyres of their cars and to take them into dark places and beat them into hospital for a month. He told her that Schulman had entrusted him with the cash and that he was to take it to the men in Liverpool who were behind the strike. He told her that he was to go to a small hotel in Old Swan and to wait for them to come to him. And Beverly had asked if he would be staying overnight and did he have a double room and could she come with him? And he had gasped at the look in her eyes, but he had been disappointed when she had told him that she would have to come up separately because if she missed her next tutorial she would be in danger of being thrown out of Cambridge. She said that she would arrive after the men had gone. When the deed was done. And then . . . And the next day they would go down to the picket lines and throw some bottles at the capitalist scum pigs.

After that it had all been so easy. She passed on the name of the hotel and the date of the meeting. When the men from the union came for their £10,000, the room was a hive of bugs and cameras. Terry had waited all through the night, but she hadn't come. He didn't bother with the picket line the next day. Instead he had packed his small bag and decided to take an early train.

He had been waiting on the platform when they came for him. Waiting and fighting back the tears of despair that had been with him all night in the bleak little room where he had thought he would find his very own piece of heaven. There were two of them. Non-descript men in anoraks. They took him to where Latimer waited in a small terraced house in Kirkdale. In a bare room with cheap furniture, Latimer had shown him the film and played him the tapes. He had shown him photos of Schulman passing over the envelope. He had shown photos of Schulman smiling and proud in his uniform when he had graduated from the Stasi training school. He had told him that the proof was absolute. Complete. There wouldn't be a judge in the land who would bat a eyelid at handing down fifteen years. He explained that a man lay in a critical condition in one of the city hospitals, beaten by the men paid for with the same East German money that Terry had brought to Liverpool.

There had been no fight from Terry. He signed all the forms.

Beverly never spoke with him again during the remainder of their final year. They attended the same meetings. They shared the same acquaintances. But they never spoke. Others smirked and read between the lines and figured out that she must have sent him packing. They said that Terry was never the same after that. He was always there, but in a way he wasn't. It was as if he went through the motions.

Christmas 1981

The end of term feeling was all over the town. Proud parents were down in their droves to collect their hung over offspring. Josh had said that he was in no hurry to rush back home. What was the point? The place was like a mausoleum. A smell of polish and a housekeeper. His mother had died when he was only three and his father had managed as well as he could. Lenny often tried to get Josh to talk about his father, but he met with little success. Josh never got obviously defensive about the subject; he just changed it. It wasn't a topic for debate.

On occasions he had told Lenny how much he envied him and the closeness of the Baxter clan. The boy from Eton and the boy from Haddington had become pretty well inseparable during their first term. It was something that caused no end of amusement and debate among Josh's more obvious contemporaries. They were the original odd couple. It soon became apparent to Lenny that the differences between them ran far deeper than mere class and background. He was all physical and his leisure time was dominated by sport whilst Josh played chess and auditioned for obscure productions of obscure plays. Lenny's childhood had provided a steel rod of confidence that ran through him. He had nothing to prove. He had nobody's approval to seek. He was who he was. The world could take him or leave him. Which meant that he was quiet. Often still. Never the loud one at the bar.

Josh was riddled by a million doubts. He was a sensitive Jew who had done the hard years of boarding school in the company of insensitive gentiles. He had a top layer that was the eternal life and soul of any party he was a part of, but underneath was the melancholy of his people. He buried it in alcohol and drugs and performing. Only when he was high up on a cliff face with the cry of a buzzard in his ears did he find any contentment. They complemented each other. For Lenny, Josh was a gateway to the world that lay beyond Haddington. Not just the material world which held little interest to him, more a world which went beyond digging coal, getting drunk and picking fights. Beverly's world.

For Josh, Lenny was the rock he had always sought. A friendship that wasn't a result of school or friends of his family. Most of all, there was no prejudice in Lenny Baxter. Not an ounce. For Josh that was everything. Several years of cannabis and cocaine had taken paranoia that was already there and nurtured it into something that all but consumed him. When he would at last collapse onto his bed after yet another night of destroying himself with drink and drugs, the paranoia would come and sit on his face like a fat flea-ridden cat. And no matter how hard he fought it, the image of his so called friends in full Waffen SS uniforms would leap into his mind and stay there, keeping his sleep at arm's length.

Lenny was the first real friend he had ever had who never fitted the black uniform of his imagination. Lenny's straightforward confidence rubbed off on him and for the first time in his life Josh Ogilvy stopped running and started to become the person he wanted to be.

Two days after term ended and Cambridge emptied out to quietness, Josh and Lenny made their way along the muddy path by the river to the Red Lion in Grantchester. It was a favoured place of theirs with its roaring fire and low ceilings. Their three-mile walk had been made in a thin rain and now their clothes steamed in the warmth of the flames.

"So when are you off home then? Is Yorkshire beckoning?"

Lenny stared into the flames with a smile. "Yes and no, I suppose. It'll be good to see all the lads and that, but I can't say I'm all that keen on the ten pints a night part of the job. Can't bloody afford it apart from anything else. I suppose I'll hit the road in the next day or two. How's about you?"

Josh shrugged. "I don't know. I might just stay here."

"What? Not go back at all. What about your family?"

"My family." Josh spat out the words like a piece of gristle and lit up.

"That bad then is it?"

"Worse. The festive season brings them out from the woodwork. Hundreds of them. All the aunts and first cousins. All of them spending their every waking hour talking about their money and the prospects of their children. Christ I hate it."

"And your Dad?"

"The worst of the lot."

There was a silence for a moment or two. Just the quiet crackle of the logs on the fire.

"Tha'never talks about him much."

Josh shook his head. It was very true. Lenny talked a lot about his own family. Josh felt as though he had already met them. The mother who was the lynchpin. The father who was the local union branch secretary. And a twin brother who was the joker of the pack, the happy-go-lucky one. Maybe it was time to talk about it.

"I don't know what my father was like when my mother was alive. I was too young to remember. But he died the very same day that she did. He died inside. And he replaced her with money. I was packed off to boarding school and he filled all the spaces with work. Thirteen, fourteen hours a day of acquiring and gathering and stowing it all away. It is as if there is some mythical amount of treasure that will make the memories go away. In a way we are similar. I drink and take drugs. He piles up his horde. Neither of us can bear to admit our pain to each other. My father stopped being a human being years ago. Now he is nothing more than a human calculator. He merely goes through the motions. Dinner parties. The Opera. Concerts at the Albert Hall. Just a front. Nothing more. His armour against life."

Lenny frowned. "Bloody hell Josh, that's all a bit hard."

"Just the truth. How it is. How it will always be. My father and I never learned to talk to each other. It is my destiny to be a disappointment to him. The hours together are a purgatory to both of us. So, no. I probably won't be going home for Christmas."

"What'll you do?"

"Stay here I suppose. Maybe I'll look up friends in London, but more likely I'll just stay here."

Lenny took a swig at his pint. Bloody awful. He could never work out why a hundred miles of the A1 made the difference between the good beer of the north and the rancid dishwater of the south.

"Tha'could come back with me if tha'wants. Mum wouldn't mind another mouth to feed. In fact summat tells me she'll be all over thee like a mother hen. It'll be a sleeping bag on the floor in mine and Frank's room, but . . ."

"Are you serious?"

"Course I'm serious."

"And what about your friends? I'm hardly standard Haddington fare I expect."

Lenny laughed. "Aye, you can say that again. Tha'll cut a dash down at club for sure. But it's nowt to worry about. They'll bark but they won't bite. You'll be right enough once they get to know you."

Josh thought about the offer for a long minute and then smiled broadly.

"Then yes please. I would love to come. Just so long as your family don't mind."

So they had gone. Up the A1 in Josh's Ford Escort with the music loud. For two days things had been better than Lenny could have hoped for. A mammoth bunch of flowers and ten gallons of natural charm had been more than enough for Josh to win over his mum. Frank had taken to him straight away as well, and with the two Baxter brothers in his camp, there was never any real doubt that Tommy and Roger would fall in line. Their first night was spent in the pubs and clubs of Sheffield and had ended in a three a.m. taxi ride back to Haddington.

The second night was Christmas Eve. It had started well enough, but things were going downhill fast. The five of them had made their way to the club via four pubs and had arrived at the club just after nine as the place was filling up. Their spirits were high and their laughter was loud. Word of Josh had predictably spread through the town and wherever he was sighted he was greeted with looks of fascination. An Old Etonian was viewed much the same as a lime green Alien from a flying saucer in the streets of Haddington. As the club continued to fill up, Lenny once again had the feeling of being some kind of circus act as glances from all over the room were cast in their direction. He took a deep appreciative swig at his pint and decided not to worry about it. It was so typically British, though nobody would be willing to admit it. The British and their endless fascination with fame and class. How many pints had they had now? His muzzy brain told him that it was already plenty. Must had been seven or eight and still hours of the night left. He was on course to be well and truly ratted come chucking out time.

The drinking bout had split the party in two. He was in the larger camp along with Roger and Tommy. Their camp was lolled back in their chairs with vacant lopsided grins and increasingly slurred speech. Camp two was altogether more hypo. Josh and his brother Frank were all energy. The night before, the pair of them had leapt around the Sheffield dance floor like primitive warriors going through some kind of frantic war dance. Now they were talking ten to the dozen and chewing through their cigarettes one after another. Lenny was far too drunk to question the shining gleam in their eyes. Frank had always been the live wire of the family and the smell of a night out was always all that was needed to spark up Josh.

There was something that warmed him deep inside to watch his twin brother and his friend. Not just friend. Best friend. Against all the odds. Against everything good old Britain could throw in their path. He was too far gone to spot the fact that the two of them had been in and out of toilets together all night to snort up lines of cocaine. Too far gone to see the blazing wonder in his brother's eyes. Too far gone to properly hear how loud they were laughing.

But not too far gone to spot the fact that Fred Church was approaching their table with a face brick-red with anger. Church was a big man in Haddington. In fact he generally went by the tag of 'Big Fred' or 'Big Churchy'. At six foot one he wasn't all that big. He just seemed bigger. He was a ferociously strong man with a reputation for seeing red very quickly, especially after a pint or two. Twenty years earlier he had been a nailed on certainty to carve out a career as a pro Rugby League player, but then a smashed knee in a game at Batley had put paid to all that. Instead it had been the pit and he seemed to have been angry ever since. Lenny knew him reasonably well as the number six batsman for Haddington where he brought his power to batting without much evidence of technique. If Big Churchy got in, then runs would come very fast. If he got out quickly, the opposition bowlers knew better than to take the piss.

As far as Lenny knew, Big Churchy was not a particularly political animal. His politics probably ran to an instinctive hatred for bosses and a murderous loathing of scabs. What was pretty certain was that he would have little time for Josh and his type. The look on his face as he advanced on their table certainly seemed to bear out the theory.

Bollocks.

"Frank."

His brother's head shot up as if it were on a spring. Lenny flicked his eyes in warning. His brother's head now spun round to be met with the sight of Fred standing a few inches away from him with his impressive beer belly level with his face.

Bollocks.

"Alright Fred."

"No it's not Franko. Not alright at all."

"What's up Fred?"

Frank's raging brain cells registered the fact that it was a pretty damn stupid question.

"Happen you remember what the sign over the door outside says Franko?"

Frank had twenty megawatts of energy but no clarity.

"How do you mean?"

"It says Haddington Working Men's Club, Franko. I look around the room and I see plenty of working men. But then I see one who isn't. One as doesn't belong here. One who shouldn't be here. One who some bastards should have known better than to bring in here. Getting my drift Franko."

Lenny rose slowly to his feet. The familiar anger was starting to surge. Seconds ago he had been eight pints muzzy. Now he was clear as a frosty day in January.

"Leave it Fred."

Church switched his attention from one twin to the other. He grinned with about the same warmth as an Alaskan outside toilet.

"So it speaks does it? Mr thinks his own shit doesn't smell Cambridge University twat."

Part of Lenny's brain knew that if it came to a fight he would get an absolute hiding. This wasn't an underfed skinhead brought up on chips and cheap brands of bread. This was Big Churchy. But the rage was taking hold fast. Logic was out of its seat and leaving the room.

"I said leave it Fred."

"Oh Aye Lenny. Or what are you about to do about it?"

Lenny kicked his chair backwards and out of the way but Josh was suddenly on his feet.

"Gentlemen, gentlemen. Let's not have any unpleasantness. It's Christmas!"

His eyes were glittering and his smile was ear to ear. Lenny's stomach knotted. Hadn't Josh any clue what was going on here? He started to move but Fred already had a meaty handful of Josh's shirt.

"And exactly what are you talking about you toffee-nosed piece of shite."

Josh winced at the waft or beery breath that hit his face from three inches.

"Snooker actually."

This knocked Fred off his stride for a second.

"You what?"

"Snooker my dear chap. I've been watching you play. You're actually rather good. Maybe we should have a game. How about it Frank? How about we challenge Fred and his friend here to a game?"

Frank's head was finally beginning to find some kind of cohesion. Plenty enough cohesion to know that a game of snooker against Big Churchy would be a fairly fruitless exercise, but it was preferable to a kicking which would mean Christmas in hospital.

"Want a game do you?" Fred was a little off balance. The skinny little upper class prick didn't seemed scared at all. And he was talking snooker? "Snooker's expensive in here."

"Really. How splendid." Josh's grin grew even wider, although that defied the rules of human biology. "My dear fellow, am I correct that you are offering a wager?"

"If tha means a bet, then aye, too right."

"Well that is absolutely terrific. I knew you were a sporting kind of chap. Now. To business. This is the festive time of the year so we should bear that in mind. Why don't we say three hundred pounds. Best of three?"

Frank's eyes nearly burst from their sockets. All of a sudden a couple of nights in Sheffield infirmary didn't seem a bad idea at all. Three hundred bastard quid. It would keep him in debt till the summer. So much for the planned trip to Majorca with the lads. Frank wasn't the only one feeling an onset of queasiness. Big Churchy knew that in a single sentence Josh had wrenched the rug from under his feet. All of a sudden everything had changed. He should have just thumped the bastard. That would have been straight forward. This wasn't. If he thumped him now people would say that he hadn't the bottle to take him on. But three hundred quid! Jesus H Christ. If he lost he would be up the creek without a paddle. He swallowed hard and knew he was hard up in a corner. No way he could say no because every pair of the eyes in the room was on him.

Bollocks.

He didn't lose many games of snooker. It was a game he played every night of his life after a few pints and he had once made a break of fifty-three. He would probably be all right. Then three hundred quid would be a bloody windfall and a half. Sod it.

"Aye all right then. You're on."

Frank took a miserable sip at his pint and cast a glance at his brother as he got to his feet. Much to his surprise he saw that Lenny had picked up his chair and had sat back down. And he was smiling.

It didn't take long for the whole room to fathom why Lenny Baxter's face was one big relaxed grin. Josh flicked the balls around the table with a careless nonchalance that made it crystal clear to everyone in the room that he wasn't just good, but bloody good. His first visit to the table yielded a break of thirty-four that was completely effortless. Big Churchy stood and watched white-faced. He'd been had. Completely had and there wasn't a thing he could do about it. Rules in Haddington were pretty clear on this kind of thing. If you got beat, you got beat. You took it like a man.

It was all over inside of half an hour. Josh shook the hands of his opponents and marched to the bar like a victorious matador. He peeled fifteen twenty-pound notes from his wallet and passed them over to the manager of the club.

"Here. Everyone can enjoy a drink on my good fortune. I'll start off with seven pints."

Frank delivered the drinks to their table whilst Josh went over to where Big Churchy sat apart from the room like a man who had just been handed down a sentence of fifteen years hard labour on a Mississippi chain gang. Josh sat down next to him on the bench seat and plonked a pint down on the table.

"Here. A drink."

"Bugger off."

Josh leaned close to ensure he wouldn't be overheard above the renewed hubbub of noise.

"Look. I'm sorry OK." The overblown public school act was back in the cupboard. "I was watching you. You can play, but I knew full well I would win. It was a stitch up and we both know it. I just didn't want to get a kicking. I have no intention of taking your money."

The anger was still in Fred's eyes but it was cooling. One the one hand, the fierce pride that had been bred in him shouted that he should react with rage. On the other hand, three hundred quid was an utter undiluted horrible nightmare. Instinct one won out, but only just."

"I said bugger off. I don't take charity from the likes of you."

"This isn't charity. This is just being fair. If you want to play me for three hundred pounds then you are more than welcome. We can play a fair game tomorrow and I will give you a start of thirty. That is fair. I know it. You know it. What just happened wasn't. I was talking my way out of a kicking and that was the best I could come up with at short notice."

Fred was confused now. It was getting harder to keep the hate going by the second.

"But tha's just handed three hundred quid to the manager. This lot'll have drunk half of it by now."

Josh shrugged. "Let's just say that I am happy to be here rather than home right now. Three hundred pounds is worth it."

"Home must be pretty crap."

"And then some."

For a few seconds Fred hung on to the hate and then he dropped it and smiled and shook his head.

"Tha's a proper lad tha knows. Proper. Tha'll do me."

"I presume that means that we are settled?"

"Aye it does. Done and dusted. Go on. Bugger off to your mates. Tha's all right by me."

Josh sat down next to Lenny whose grin hadn't slipped an inch.

"So you told him you didn't want the three hundred quid then"

Josh lit up and nodded.

"Very noble of you."

"Not really. Merely sporting."

"You should have taken it. The man's a lout. It would have served him right."

"No doubt it would. But it still wouldn't have been sporting."

Lenny shook his head and chuckled.

"You all right our Frank?"

His brother was just beginning to register the elation of what had happened.

"Too bloody right. Never seen owt like it. It were like playing with Steve Davis that were. Bloody magic."

All eyes in the room were on them. But it was different now.

"I don't suppose you realise that you have just become a Haddington legend do you."

Josh looked around the room and smiled.

"Really. What a very unexpected title. Thanks for inviting me."

"I'm glad you came."

"You probably won't be tomorrow."

"Oh aye? Why's that then?"

"You're just going to have to wait and see I'm afraid."

Lenny didn't much like the suspicion of a smirk that fleetingly passed across his friend's face. He liked the glint in his brother's eyes even less. He considered asking, but he knew both of them well enough to know there was no point.

The next day was Christmas Day and Josh broke a tradition of the Baxter household that had stood for as many years as any of the family could remember: after they had all finished their lunch he followed Mrs Baxter into the kitchen to help with the washing up. He didn't register the looks of astonishment from the male side of the family as he left the room. For a moment it seemed as if the Haddington matriarch might faint with shock when he tossed her the tea towel with the words, "I'll wash, you dry."

It took her a moment to find anything to say. Finally she managed. "Don't be so bloody daft love. Go and get thi'self back with lads. The men don't do washing up in Haddington."

He completely ignored her and rolled up his sleeves. "Well Mrs Baxter. I'm sure that is the case, but I am not from Haddington. Am I?"

"No but. Even so . . ."

"Even nothing. My mother died before I can remember. I never had the chance to help her with the washing up. OK?"

She couldn't begin to get her head around the strange friend her Lenny had brought to their home. She had never met anyone quite like him. By the time they returned to the front room with a tray of coffee and mince pies all three male Baxters were dozing in armchairs while the Queen told her Commonwealth that next year would be the golden one. Lenny dragged his eyes open and sat forward to take the coffee.

"Ta Mum."

"You'd best wake yourself up a bit sunshine. We're going visiting."

Lenny looked at Josh with a mixture of confusion and suspicion.

"Visiting? What you on about?"

Josh passed the cigarettes and lit one while Frank smirked and Baxter senior snored on.

"We have known each other for what now? Three months? Yes?"

Lenny nodded.

"Aye. Summat like that."

"And during those three months there have been several occasions when I have endured your company when you have been the wrong side of copious amounts of liquor."

Lenny shrugged. Josh forged ahead.

"And every time you hit those few minutes before the darkness closes in, it is always the same story that you tell. I am an expert of these matters as you well know. A man saves his greatest truth for those few minutes before he passes out from drink. These are the minutes for what is nearest to his inner soul Lenny."

Lenny rolled his eyes. "Very poetic I'm sure. What's all this got to do with going visiting when it's at home?"

"Because my friend when you reach those fateful moments in your life you only ever talk of one thing : the fair and elusive Beverly Morton."

Lenny just managed to stop himself spitting his coffee all over his new jumper. But only just. It wasn't only his brother who was smiling now. It was his mum as well. She had never quite forgotten the lovely polite lass who had called one sunny day in an open topped sports car. Lenny could feel the walls closing in on him.

"Oh sodding hell. No bloody way."

"It is not up for discussion I'm afraid." Josh jangled his car keys. "Finish your coffee and we're on our way. I cannot wait to meet this elusive angel who has such a vice like grip on your heart."

"Don't be so bloody daft. Anyway. Tha'll never find the place and I'm buggered if I'm about to show you."

"I showed him yesterday. Sorry Bro." Lenny was sure that if his brother grinned any wider he would split his face open. Keeping up the argument would merely make him look stupid. Besides, there was another nagging voice in the head that was singing songs of praise at the idea. He had summoned up the courage twice to visit the small house where Beverly lived in Cambridge. Both times she had been out, and when she had never been round to see him, he had been convinced that she wanted nothing to do with him. So he had let it be. But the thought of her had never been far from his thoughts. And now the chance of seeing her was a ten minute drive away. Maybe he wasn't so angry at being boxed in after all. He downed his coffee and pulled himself to his feet.

"Since I seem to have no say in this, we'd best be off then. Ready?"

"Never more so."

Outside the streets of Haddington were utterly deserted other than a couple of dog walkers and a few young boys trying out Christmas bikes. The weather was mild and grey and a thin rain eased down onto the sleepy town. Soon they left the winching gear of the pit behind them and struck out across the wet fields. It wasn't far to the turn off and the track down to the Morton stable yard. Lenny felt the huge Christmas lunch lurching around his stomach as they closed in on the big house and outbuildings.

Josh parked up in the yard and pulled up the handbrake with a flourish.

"You ready?"

Lenny nodded and swallowed down a dry throat. Josh rang the bell and they waited whilst the rain splashed into the puddles in the yard. The air was heavy with the smell of horses. It was Beverly's mother who answered the door, surprised to be receiving unexpected visitors on a Christmas Day.

"Hello?"

Josh was aware that Lenny had lost the power of speech. "So sorry for pitching up unannounced like this Mrs Morton. We were just passing and we wondered if Beverly was at home?"

"Beverly. Yes of course. Who shall I say is here?"

"It's Lenny. Lenny Baxter." The power of speech returned, though not very convincingly. Mrs Morton recognised him then.

"Of course. Sorry, I didn't recognize you for a moment. Please.

Come in. You can wait in the lounge. I'll go and tell Beverly that you are here. She's in her bedroom."

The living room was quiet. No sign of Mr Morton. An open paperback and a pair of glasses provided evidence that Beverly's mother had been sitting alone and reading. The house seemed to be cloaked with a heavy sadness.

When Beverly came in with her mother Lenny felt a calloused hand squeeze at his chest. She looked awful. She had lost over a stone since he had seen her on the night of the debate. Both her eyes were dark with fatigue. Pale. Terribly pale with her hair tired and lank. All the life seemed to have been sucked away. What on earth had happened? Their eyes were locked for a moment. His shock. Her despair. Their emotions met somewhere halfway across the room. It was Josh who broke the silence as he jumped to his feet.

"Well I can see that my friend here has no intention of introducing me, so I best do the honours myself. I'm Josh. Josh Ogilvy."

She took his hand and looked at him with mild confusion.

"You're from Cambridge?"

"Indeed. A Magdalene man like Lenny here."

"And you've come to Haddington? For Christmas?"

"Absolutely. Couldn't wish for a finer place or finer folk."

"Good Lord."

There was a silence that all four found hard to break. In the end it was Beverly who did the honours.

"Why are you here Lenny?"

He stumbled on the words. "Just thought it would be . . . well you know . . . I just . . ."

Josh rescued him. "My fault I'm afraid. I've heard so much about you ever since I met Lenny here. It's Beverly this and Beverly that. Never ends. Well since we were so close it seemed as if it would be a crime if we didn't stop by."

Her yes were still fixed on Lenny. "About me?"

"Indeed about you. Always in the hours before the dawn. The time when chaps talk of their hearts, secure in the knowledge that the world is asleep."

Her lost gaze moved onto Josh now. "And you're his friend?"

Josh's smile was slightly fixed now. What was happening here? It was if he was speaking to a ghost. He couldn't help but glance down to her thin pale arms to check for needle tracks. No. Not on the arms anyway. What on earth was wrong? Her eyes seemed to climb into him. Dark. Tired. Lost.

"I'm glad he has a friend. You're a good friend are you?"

He nodded, nervous now. "I hope so."

The gaze settled back onto Lenny. "Lenny, I can't see you. I'm sorry."

"What is it Beverly? What's happened?"

She gave a short shake of her head. "Nothing. I just can't see you. That's all. Things are different now."

"Different? What do you mean different?"

"I'm sorry Lenny. You need to go now. I can't see you. Sorry."

She left leaving the three of them terribly awkward. Josh could see that her mother was searching for something to say. Anything. He rescued her.

"It's OK Mrs Morton. We should have telephoned first. Awfully rude of us. We'll get on our way now. Come on Lenny. Let's be off."

He guided Lenny out through the door and back into the yard. As the car splashed up the drive Beverly watched it disappear into the grey flat horizon from her bedroom window. And her cheeks were drenched with tears.

And in the car so were Lenny's. Josh said nothing. They just drove.

Ulster
November 1982

Beverly sat in the cold of the whitewashed cellar room and shivered. It was the fourth time she had waited to play out her leading role in their sordid little drama. The fourth time she had hugged herself in the damp Irish cold and waited for the sound of voices and footsteps on the pitted stone stairs. And every time she had died a little bit. Every time took her a few miles further along the dark road from the Beverly Morton she had once been.

It had been four months now. Heart breaking months. Lonely months. Evil months. The first four months of the rest of her life. Life of the big boy's rules that Hendrick spat at her with his reeking breath and brown teeth.

They had planned things carefully when she had graduated in the sunny warmth of the Cambridge summer. Now that day seemed little more than a selection of snap shots. Her in her cap and gown and her parents smiling and proud and filling two films of photos to commemorate the day. After Cambridge it had been a plane ride to the heat and humidity of a refugee camp in Nicaragua. Nobody had been much surprised when Bev had announced that she was going to help out in the hospital of a Sandinista camp. That was typical Bev. Bev did the things the rest of them just talked about. So Bev took the plane to the frontline of the fight against the corporate Imperialism of Reagan's America.

She had found another piece of herself amidst the humidity and the gangrenous wounds and the flies that covered everything and everyone. It was a place where the sound of wailing grief from bereaved mothers filled the hot nights. It was a place where teenage boys came to sit as still as statues in corners, staring far into nothingness with eyes eighty years older than they should have been. It was a place of pain and filth and death and despair. A place where the flotsam and jetsam of the American war machine was washed up with festering wounds and minds that were lost for ever. A savage place where she worked thirteen hours a day with her T-shirt plastered to her skin with sweat. She mopped brows. She cleaned gaping wounds. She held hands. She cradled children all broken up by mines and claymores to her breasts. She cried. But she laughed as well. And over all, she thrived on every second of her life on the frontline under a canopy of emerald green tropical trees.

And then it came time for her to leave. A series of long bus and plane journeys took her from the bouncing heat of Central America to the bleak desolate farmhouse a few miles inland from the coast of County Antrim.

And Hendrick.

Bernard Hendrick. Ex 1 Para. Ex Flying Squad. Now Latimer's man in Ireland. Fifty years on the clock. Fifty cigarettes a day. Minimum. A bottle of vodka a day. Minimum. And every residual ounce of human compassion squeezed out of his spare bony frame many years before. Humanity wasn't something that he had been born with much off. His dad had got rid of most of it with his relentless beatings. What little bit that was left disappeared the day when Hendrick had opened fire during the search of a small shack amidst the dusty olive groves of Cyprus. He had been eighteen years old and green as May grass. Three months with 1 Para and trigger-happy. He had crashed in the door and sprayed the room inside and when the sound of the shots echoed away into the sleepy air of the siesta, a ten-year-old girl laid dead on the floor, her once pretty face a mask of blood and bone. He had thrown up outside and all the lights had gone out in his soul. His sergeant had covered it up in his report. An enquiry had exonerated him and he had moved on. He killed three times more. Once in Aden, twice in Ireland. Then he had left the Paras for the Metropolitan Police and the world of South London drugs.

Then Latimer came to call. He said he needed men like Hendrick. Not just himself. But also England. Men who would do the dirty stuff. The wet work. The stuff that had to be done to keep fifty five million

Brits in the style they were accustomed to. Men who were happy to work off the books. Off the record. Off the map. Men who would work for big lumps of tax-free cash and not worry themselves about a civil service pay grade and a pension enough to retire to golf in Bournemouth. Men like Hendrick. And Hendrick had been more than happy to go along with it. All of it. He was born to it.

Had he been drafted into one of the more orthodox areas of the Security Forces he would probably have had to attend mandatory sessions with one of the in-house shrinks. Maybe they might have picked up on the deep scars left by the brutal beatings Hendrick had received from his father during his childhood. Maybe they might have picked up on the raging anger that simmered close to the surface which was only ever seconds away from erupting into an explosion of violence. They might have discovered that the only way that Hendrick could sleep for more than a few snatched hours without nightmares was by dissolving his brain in vodka. But of course nobody ever did. It wasn't the way things were done in Latimer's little empire. All that mattered was that the job was completed. And that was something Hendrick was good at. Really good at.

A car had collected Beverly from a Little Chef a few miles north of Belfast on the road to Coleraine. The driver hadn't said a word other than 'You Morton?'when he had wound down his window on the car park. Their thirty-minute drive down narrow country lanes through fields filled with bored looking cows was a silent one. When he had pulled up in the small courtyard of the farm he had nodded at the front door and spoken his only other words. "In there."

Beverly had lifted her bag from the boot and he had driven away. It seemed so cold and dismally quiet compared to the bouncing heat and noise of the camp in the jungle. The door opened onto a bare kitchen with a table in the middle and Hendrick reading The Sun with a cigarette burning in the ashtray. He looked up with cold, dead eyes.

"Morton?"

"Yes."

"Sit down."

She sat. No tea offered. He folded the paper and threw it towards an old armchair by an Aga. He missed and the paper slid to the stone floor.

"I'm Hendrick."

"Pleased to meet you sir."

"No you're not. Nor will you be. I'm not a nice man Morton. Not even nearly. I'm a bastard. A through and through nasty piece of work. So don't expect any pleasantries. This isn't like drinks parties with your pansy Cambridge pals. Know what this is Morton?"

"No sir."

"This is a sewage processing plant. That's what we do here. We process shit. Stinking, festering shit. They bring it to us and we process it. We make it into our shit Morton. It still stinks. But it's our shit. Yeah?"

She shrugged. The man was unhinged. He lit up again and continued.

"That's Ireland. One big bastard toilet. Wall to wall shit. London has been shovelling it since 1969 and the pile just gets bigger and stinks more. Thirty thousand soldiers and they've managed toss all. They've tried the Mr Nice guy stuff and it's done toss all. They've tried the armoured cars and patrols. Crap. They've tried SAS killer squads in ditches. Crap. So now they want people who know about how to deal with shit Morton. And that's me. It's what I do. It's what you're going to do. You won't question it. We won't be friends. I don't want to know you. I told Latimer I didn't want no silly cow from Cambridge but he reckons he knows best. Well. We'll see. Until then, you do what I say. When you're working, you're working. When you're not, I don't want to see you. Just piss off somewhere. Anywhere. I don't care. I suggest you avoid the places where the green, white and orange flags hang from the lampposts. When I want you, I'll call. Are we clear?"

"We're clear."

So it had been a small flat in Larne and a second hand Cortina. And they had developed their very own little double act. Their sordid real life drama. The Eighties had brought a new front to the endless British war in Northern Ireland. It was the time of the Supergrass. Instead of the goal of the authorities being to catch and lock up their IRA adversaries, they now looked to catch them and turn them. Every low level offender was offered a new identity in some out of the way little town in England with a house and a moderate paying job and a few thousand quid in the building society. In return they were to publicly indict their comrades in the armed courtroom on the Crumlin Road. It was seen as a double whammy. Not only did the new strategy cut a swathe through the ranks of the Provisionals, but it also destroyed their morale, their pride, their self-belief. It was a policy that put neighbours at each other's throats. A policy to rip the heart out of Nationalist communities.

By 1982 the prospect of the IRA's infamous 'nutting squad'and the price they would extract from the families of those who turned Supergrass made it much harder to 'turn' the frightened young men who were lifted by the soldiers and hauled into the Castlereigh Interrogation Centre. Standard, 'on the record', methods didn't seem to work any more. And so the job was sub-contracted out to Latimer and his shadowy team. And in the late summer of 1982 Beverly and Hendrick developed their dark little play.

The footsteps were at the bottom of the stairs now. Heavy steps and dragging feet. And some shouting now. And crying. Painful sobs from all the way down the chest.

"Please . . . oh God . . . please . . . where are we going . . . ?" A young voice. She knew how old because the file had told her. Jerry O'Brian. Eighteen. From some small village in County Fermanagh. Picked up with a bomb in the back of his van at a routine roadblock. It would have been a good forty-eight hours since he would have slept. First the police station. Then a barracks. Then a long ride trussed-up on the floor of an army Land Rover. And now the stone steps and the cellar. The theatre. As she heard him being dragged past the door she caught a strong acrid whiff of urine. He had wet himself. It was just the same as the other three. Fear. Disorientation. Welcome to my world. Enter stage left. One young male. Probably in jeans and a shirt and a jumper. Wild scared eyes. Hit him with the bright lights. Two big guys with him. Guys in hoods and army uniforms. Manhandling him. Not a word from them. They would work in silence creating a picture for the audience. The voice was growing more hysterical now.

"Nooo . . . please . . . stop it will ya . . . Christ . . . !"

This was the part when the big men would rip his clothes from him and fix him to the chair in the middle of the room with brown leather straps. Screaming now. Terror in the purest form. Terror in the form of Hendrick. Enter stage right. Uniform. Hood. And a case which he opened and plugged in. Plugged in. Plug. Electricity. Wires. Scream.

Scream.

Cue Hendrick.

"Oh you'll scream in a minute you little piece of Mick shite. You'll scream until you rip your scrawny throat open. Because I'm about to clip this onto those nasty horrible bollocks of yours and you're going to know all the pain in world. Then you'll tell me everything. And then I'll switch it up some. Just to make sure you've told me the lot."

Cue Hendrick to lean in close. Close enough to breathe his foul breath into the terrified face. "And you know what? I'm going to love it. Every bastard minute. Every second. Because that's the type of guy I am . . ."

One . . . two . . . three . . .

Cue.

Beverly threw open the door. Smart. Straight back. Tall. Sharp creases all down her army uniform. Hair back. Just the right amount of make up to bring out the look of burning outrage on her face. A look to the bound and naked figure in the chair. A look to the hooded figure with the electrical wires. A look back to the chair.

And then a voice like a mountain stream.

"Just what the hell is going on here?"

The hooded man was too far over the edge for the cool authority of her voice. He lunged and pushed.

"Nothing to do with you, you interfering bitch . . ."

He pushed her hard in the chest and she fell back. And down. Such careful choreography. So perfectly executed. So utterly convincing to the audience as she fell to the floor and her back collided with the boy's legs. Her eyes never left her hooded assailant who was by now leaning forward and screaming out hatred that bounced around the stone walls of the basement room.

" . . . you've no business here bitch. It's war in case you hadn't noticed . . ."

She started to get back to her feet. Without taking her eyes from the man in the hood she reached her hand back to lever herself up and her palm landed in the sogginess of the young man's penis. Her head shot round. For the tiniest of seconds their eyes met. Regardless of the desperation of the situation, it was an inescapable fact that her hand was on his dick, accident or no accident.

This was the very core of Hendrick's dark little play. Lots of black psychological theories acted out in the cold basement of a farmhouse in the wet fields of Ulster. Women in uniforms are horny. No matter how shit scared a Boyo may be, his brain is still going to boil over when a woman in a uniform puts her hand on his dick. Sex and terror and disorientation. Hendrick's theories. Hendrick's drama. Hendrick's world.

The moment flashed by and Beverley was on her feet as fast as a cat, a gun in her hand.

"Out."

The eyes under the hood widened at the sight of it.

"I said out."

Slowly he raised his palms and took careful backward steps toward the door.

"One phone call bitch. One phone call and I'll have you out of here. I don't give a shit what your rank is. There are others who know this is a war. You best be ready bitch . . ." He twisted his hooded head to one side so that his blazing eyes met the eyes of the prisoner. " . . . and you, you little shite. I'll be back for you . . ."

Then he was gone. Exit stage right. Beverley's whole body sagged as the tension seeped out. She followed his strides and slammed the door closed. Then she turned back to the boy. All the severity was gone from her face now. In place was fear and disgust and worry. She took another long look at him.

"Jesus."

His mouth was working like a fish. " . . . Jesus Missus . . . he's mad . . . what's happening . . . Christ you've got to get me out of here . . . ."

She unbuttoned her tunic and laid it across him and took a seat at the table that held the box full of electrical pain. When she spoke her voice was calm. Clipped.

"Jerry. You need to listen to me very, very carefully. Can you do that?"

A nod. Eyes desperate for any shred of hope.

"Good. You're situation is very bad Jerry. This is what is known as a black programme. Nobody really knows much about it other than the fact that it seems to have been ordered from pretty high up. This is what is about to happen to you. You need to listen very, very carefully. OK?"

Another nod.

"The man in the hood will be making his calls right now. When he gets through to someone senior, there will be nothing I can do to stop this. Then he will come back and . . ."

She didn't say it. She just laid her glance on the machine in front of her. His eyes followed and his body shuddered.

"You will talk Jerry. And you will tell him everything. And when you have done so, he will throw you in the boot of the car and drive you to Rathcool. He will make a phone call to the UDA Brigadier there. He will dump you and if they put a bullet through the back of your head you will be lucky. It will be much worse if they decide they want to have some fun and do things slowly. Either way, you will be executed, and the UDA will make their announcement by the morning. That is what is about to happen. Understand?"

Again a nod.

"I can give you an option. Just one. And you need to make your mind up now. And I mean right now. Understand?"

"Yes." Just a croak.

"I have a colleague in the RUC. We are tasked to stop this. He is close by. Very close. One call and he will be here in five minutes. This is how things can play. I call. He comes. We get you dressed and untie you. You make a statement saying you will turn Queen's evidence against your colleagues and you say that you are willing to join the Witness Protection scheme. You say it on film Gerry. It is only way. The Witness Protection programme is still the number one objective of the British Government. Once you are in it you are not only safe from the IRA, you are safe from this."

She lightly tapped the wires. Her voice never wavered from its ultimate soft calm.

"There is no chance to think Jerry. You have a very simple choice. Live or die. Take the programme, and you can start again with a house and a job and some money. You can find a girl and get married and have a life Jerry. Otherwise all there will be is an ocean of pain and a bullet in the head care of the Rathcool Battalion."

And so the drama moved to its electrifying climax. The moment of life and death. The moment of yes or no. Her eyes locked onto his. All she found was a terrified teenager who would wake screaming in the night for the rest of his life as his memory replayed these moments of terror. Their drama always ended the same way.

He started to cry. And he nodded.

"Make the call. Please. Make the call."

Beverley picked up the phone and ran through the last of her lines.

Soon it would be time to stride to the front of the stage and take her curtain call. And the audience would clap wildly and shout 'Bravo'. Her fourth performance. Four frightened young men who months later would appear in front of the spitting hatred of the Crumlin Road courtroom and testify against a total of nine IRA members. All in all, their four dramas sent the enemy to the high security Maze prison for a total of over a hundred years.

And on each occasion another payment was made against the loan account in the discreet London bank.

And on each occasion Beverly died a little.

July 1983

Beverly watched the departure board in the terminal of Belfast Airport with mounting frustration. She had been fighting for almost a month to win this day off. She had wanted a week. Then three days. No chance. Hendrick had told her that there was too much happening. He had asked her if she thought she was on some sort of a picnic and he had called her a shirking bitch. But she had known that he was merely going through the motions. Things had changed. Hendrick liked her now. Not that he had ever said so. Not that he ever would. But his abuse no longer carried quite the same conviction. His star had risen very high during his two years in the Province and he knew full well that it wouldn't have happened without his ice queen from Cambridge.

In the end he had given her a day, just like she knew he would. The flight had been due to leave just before nine and to arrive at Heathrow for ten. That was without the fog that had come with the first genuine warmth of the summer. It was now twenty to ten already and there was still no word on the departure board even though the air outside was so much clearer. Surely it would be soon. It had to be. She forced her attention back onto the newspaper that was still filled with the news of Prince Charles and his bimbo wife to be. She sensed a sudden onset of shuffling movement all around her. Her eyes shot up to the board.

'Now boarding. Gate 3' Thank Christ. And as it became clear that she really was about to get on the plane and fly back to the mainland, the nerves once again got hold of her.

Two weeks earlier her heart had all but stopped when she had turned a page of her paper to find Lenny smiling out at her. The story was very

155

much in the human-interest section. It was about the son of a Yorkshire coal miner who had been made the captain of the Cambridge University cricket team. It was about a fast bowling talent that was getting the experts talking Truman. In the picture Lenny was standing casually with the green acres of the university cricket ground spread out behind him. Same old laid back Lenny Baxter. Easy stance. Easy smile. The annual Varsity match against Oxford was to be held at Lords in July and Beverley had made her mind up there and then that she was going.

From the minute she made the decision she started coming up with reasons why she shouldn't do it. But somehow she never got around to throwing the paper away. She wasn't about to cut the picture out and pin it on the wall of the little flat on the seafront at Larne. Not her style. But the paper stayed and every night Lenny's smile greeted her as she came in and unpacked her single person's shopping.

The plane bounced down into the best day of the summer. By the time she decided to hang the cost and take a taxi it was nearly eleven. The driver took the bait of the offer of an extra tenner if he could make it for eleven-thirty and he duly earned his reward.

It wasn't busy outside the ground. She carefully arranged her hat and put on sun glasses. She had decided to dress summer formal in a beige two-piece linen suit with a matching hat. A young professional woman on the sunny streets of London. No evidence of the darkness of the world she had lived in for over a year.

Inside, the ground was a little over a quarter full. Cambridge had lost the toss and they were bowling. Lenny was bowling. She took a seat in line with the stumps. In line with him as he walked towards her polishing the ball, his face all steady concentration. The batsman was ringed by close fielders and the scoreboard showed that Oxford were 14 for three after seven overs. Player 7 had taken all three wickets for four runs. Player 7 was Lenny Baxter.

By the time he reached the end of his run up he was no more than thirty paces from where she was sitting. She unconsciously tilted her hat a little lower over her eyes. She wasn't yet decided.

Lenny turned and started on his run up. Slow acceleration. Then a classical cartwheel of limbs. The ball thumped into the wicket halfway down and reared up at the batsman who was already rocking backwards. She heard the thump of the leather slapping into the wicket keeper's gloves.

"Nice one Lenny . . ."

"Keep it there . . ."

The fielders shouted out encouragement and worked the ball back to the bowler who was already on his way back to his mark. Beverley sat back and made herself comfortable. She was glad she had come. So glad.

Oxford had slumped to 76 for 7 by the time the umpire pocketed the bails for the lunch break. Lenny Baxter had bowled eleven searing overs and posted figures of 5 for 22. The captain had led his team from the front.

Beverly rose from her seat and took a walk. She bought a glass of Pimms and a chicken baguette and sat on the picnic lawn to watch the world go by. It was a world that was a normal world. A world that once upon a time she had thought that she would have been a part of. Smiling couples with linked arms. Proud mothers and fathers. Younger brothers with their carefully filled scorecards. Friends already the worse for wear from the drink. Grandfathers and great aunts. The sun beamed down on all of them. England showed off its best profile. The land of Pimms and strawberries and straw boaters. The cradle of democracy. The land of Wellington and Churchill.

She spent her days holding the line for these people. The haves. The ones with the nice houses which were doubling in price every two years. The ones with bank accounts filling up fast as Thatcher chopped away at their taxes. They were the reason that she held her post out on the border. On the edge. Little did these people know that their treasure was guarded by people like Hendrick. Like her. Like Beverly Morton.

Her mood started to slide. If only things had been different. Always the same. If things had been different. Maybe she might have been here in a different guise. Not the anonymous onlooker hidden under a wide-brimmed hat. She might have been the girlfriend. The lover. The fiancé. The mother to be. Another world. A dream. A mirage.

"It is you isn't it Beverly?"

The voice jumped her out of her reverie. She knew the voice. She knew the face as well. It took her a moment to place either. Then it came to her. The friend. The one who had come to the house that dark Christmas day. The friend who had come the last time she had seen Lenny.

"Yes. Yes it is. It's Josh. Yes?"

"Can I sit?"

"Of course."

He sat. Neither of them seemed to know where to start so they settled for silence instead. For some strange reason there was nothing uncomfortable about the silence they shared. Beverly took the opportunity to get a proper look at him. She had gained no more than an impression on the day that he had come to call with Lenny. The day she had sent them away. He wasn't tall. Nothing like Lenny. Slim without threatening being skinny. She liked his face. It was a face with character. Dark eyes under a carelessly kept mop of black hair. His nose was far too big for him to have much of a chance of getting anywhere near a boy band. The lines around his mouth ran in good directions. There was something about him that she liked.

They caught each other's eyes and smiled.

"You look different. It took me ages to properly recognise you."

"Do I? Oh yes. Of course. I've grown out of the spiky hair and nose ring phase."

"So I can see. So what is this phase? The go-getting business woman who takes no prisoners?"

She chuckled. My god if you but knew. If you but knew. "Hardly. I work in a refugee camp. In Nicaragua. With the Sandanistas. I'm only over for a brief visit. I have to go back tonight."

His eyes widened at this. "Good lord. Really."

She smiled at his open mouthed look. "Really. All this Pimms on the lawn stuff is something of a novelty." Which of course it was. Pimms on the lawn played no part in her life in Ireland.

"So when are you going back then?"

"Soon I'm afraid. My plane leaves at four." That much was true. Only it was Belfast, not Managua.

He dropped his head and flicked at some dead grass that had settled on his creased slacks. "That's a pity. He would have liked to have seen you."

More silence. Longer this time.

"Does he ever . . . ?"

Josh nodded. "Not often. But yes. He does. Not that he has to. You are always there you see. Always the figure in the background. The half-noticed person on the edge of the crowd."

Part of her soared at his words. A bigger part was despair. Despair in the knowledge that regardless of what he said she knew that in a few short hours it was her destiny to return to Hendrick and the dark places of his world.

"You are very poetic."

He smiled. "Thank you. It is one of the strengths of my people."

"And who might they be?"

"The Jews of course. The children of David. Who else?"

Ahh. Of course. The nose. And the dark eyes. It wouldn't have taken Hendrick so long to make the connection.

"What a strange pair you make. You and Lenny."

He shrugged. "Life is strange. Thank God."

"I think he is lucky. You seem to be a true friend."

"You don't know me."

"I don't need to. I'm a woman. We know about this stuff."

He flicked away the last piece of grass. "Actually, it is me who is the lucky one. Meeting Lenny saved me."

"From what?"

"From me. From myself. My upbringing. My school. My pathetic guilt. All of it. Not just Lenny. Haddington. His mum and dad. Frank. All of it."

This was a surprise. "You mean you spend time there."

He nodded. "More than I do at home. It has come to feel more like home than home."

"My, my. You must cut something of a dash."

"They're used to me now. I think I've become a part of the furniture."

She took a bite from her baguette and chewed thoughtfully. All this because she and Lenny had once sat together to receive their prizes. Another lifetime.

"So will you talk with him?"

She shook her head and swallowed. "I won't be able to I'm afraid. I'll miss my plane."

"You can. He fields out on the boundary when he's not bowling. We could see him there."

She shook her head, suddenly panicked. Talking was not part of the plan. She had come to see him. To watch. Not to talk.

"Please."

"Why?"

"I know he will want to. Just for a minute or two. That's all."

The dark eyes held her. Soft eyes. Kind eyes. Eyes from a better world than the one she had come to know. Eyes that still had some room in them for hope.

Slowly she finished her glass of Pimms. The eyes never left her.

"OK."

Lenny's first over after lunch brought him his sixth wicket as the batsman fended a ball headed for his nose to third slip. The cocoon of quiet concentration was still on him as he made his way to his position on the boundary.

"Lenny!"

He looked up at Josh's voice. First there was some doubt. Then there was none as he took in the figure in the linen suit and the hat.

"Hello Lenny."

"Hello."

She couldn't help but grin at him. Here he was with figures of 6 for 22 in the Varsity Match with every female in the old ground thinking unworthy thoughts about him and he was still as tongue-tied as that first day they had met.

"So it all came true. All the way from Haddington Comprehensive. I don't suppose I'll ever have my tits ogled in a more worthy cause. Did he ever tell you about that Josh? That the only reason he ever wound up at Magdalene was that the Admissions Tutor was a dirty old sod who . . ."

She turned to Josh but he wasn't there any more. It was just the two of them. She turned back to Lenny.

"You look better Beverly. Last time you looked ill. Ill and sad. At least now you only look sad."

Nothing like a bit of Yorkshire plain speaking. "Should I be flattered by that?"

He smiled and shrugged and turned to pay attention to the next ball which was played defensively out to cover.

"It's been a long time Beverly."

"I know. I'm sorry."

"So am I. Will you be about later? After we finish?"

"I'm afraid not. I have a plane to catch."

"Going far?"

"Nicaragua."

The pain flashed across his eyes and he once again turned to his fielding.

"Long way then."

She nodded. "Yes. A long way."

Another ball.

The over ended. His turn again.

"I'll miss you Beverley."

"I'll miss you too."

And then he jogged back to the middle and she left for the airport.

MARCH 1984

Lenny pushed his knuckles into the sides of his head and tried to force some concentration. In front of him the book he was attempting to read glowered back at him. That morning he had made all kinds of resolutions to himself over breakfast. February was over. March had started. He was just three months away from the final exams. It was time put in some long shifts in his room and get himself back on track. His last year had been a series of distractions and his studies had played a very modest role in his life. Two-and-a-half-years had been more than enough time for him to learn that failure was all but inconceivable. Cambridge University didn't fail people. That would have been too much of an admission that it had made some kind of failing itself. Instead it gave Thirds and 2-2s. Most of Lenny's sporting colleagues were more than happy to pocket their honorary 2-2s and head out into the world. He had thought about it, but he didn't want the talk. There would be plenty who would say that nothing much else could be expected from a Comprehensive boy from Yorkshire. Good at cricket. Bloody good. But not exactly an intellectual heavyweight.

Proving them all wrong was going to mean a few weeks of solid graft. Having completed the first four hours of his new regime, he envied the simplicity of his brother's task of digging coal. After a year of renting a house outside he and Josh were back in the college for their last year. Making a choice in the room draw had been easy. They had asked for Mallory Court and they had been granted their wish. It was appropriate. Fitting. George Herbert Mallory was one of

Magdalene's more romantic old boys. He was famed in his day as being one of the greatest climbers in the world. Lenny's favourite Mallory tale was the story of 'Mallory's Pipe'. The climber had resumed his way up a notorious rock face one day having paused to have a smoke of his pipe and take in the view. The section was so severe that the only way forward was for him to make a diagonal descent to a better section and then to resume the climb. Mallory had completed most of this manoeuvre when he realised that he had left his pipe on the viewing ledge which was now level with his position and forty feet or so across the rock face. Without thinking, he climbed over and retrieved it. Only when he had reached the spot did he realise the impossibility of the route he had just followed. Fifty years had passed and no climber had ever managed to retrace his steps. The section was duly named 'Mallory's Pipe.'

Mallory became a part of history in the 1920's. His name was to become known forever as part of the story of Mallory and Irving. One morning the two English climbers set out on the last leg of their very own Holy Grail: Mount Everest. They had made it to within striking distance of the summit and they were just a few hours climbing away from reaching the highest point on earth thirty years before it was eventually conquered in 1953. Their colleagues watched their progress through telescopes at base camp. When the two dots were just a couple of thousand yards shy of the summit, a violent storm swallowed up the mountain and they could be seen no more. Would they continue? Surely not. It would be madness. Their only sensible option was to try and ride out the storm and then get back down the mountain when things calmed. When the storm had raged for a few hours, the peak suddenly appeared through a brief gap in the clouds. Unbelievably, two tiny dots could be seen just a few hundred feet short of their goal. Then the clouds swept back in and neither man was ever seen again. It became one of history's great enigmas. Had they made it? Lenny liked to think that they had. On drunken evenings he and Josh would sometimes stand on the grass outside the building and study the shape of the roof against the moonlight and it seemed to them that it had been built in the shape of Everest. But by the time the morning came it was only ever a roof.

Bollocks.

His attention had wandered again. The coming weeks were going to be a torture. Now a further distraction got a piece of his attention.

At the end of the corridor outside the telephone was ringing. Was there anyone else about? Should he get it? It stopped after ten rings and he could hear a distant voice. Then footsteps. Then a rap at his door.

"For you Lenny. Your brother."

"Cheers."

Frank? Strange. He glanced at his watch and worked out that it was the lunch hour up in Haddington. A nagging anxiety. What was it?

"Hi Frank."

The pitch of his brother's voice immediately told him that this wasn't about bad family news. The voice was all excitement.

"Have you heard the news?"

"What?"

"Coal Board announcement this morning. The bastards are closing Cortonwood. Twenty pits in total. 20,000 jobs. We'll all be out inside a week Lenny. This is going to be the big one. We're going kick Thatcher's arse."

Lenny tried to make all the right noises, but all he felt deep down was a sense of foreboding. Things had nearly come to a head in 1981 but the Government had backed down and given in to the threats of the Union. It had been a time of celebration up in Haddington. The pints had flowed like water and there had been singing well past closing time. But Lenny hadn't been convinced. Josh certainly hadn't. Josh had seen the Government's decision as a strategic withdrawal. They hadn't lost a battle. They had merely chosen not to fight one. Thatcher was clever. She would fight only when she had selected the right time and prepared the battlefield of her choice. Was that going to be now? Certainly a whole raft of anti-Union legislation had crashed through Parliament over the last few years which would make it hard for any strike to be properly funded. A few months earlier she had hired the American Ian McGregor to head up the Coal Board. He had a track record of closing and privatising. He had fought the Unions in his native country for many years and he had fought them head on. And he had usually won.

Lenny had spent over two years in the company of the ruling classes. He had been at their drinks parties and their dinners. He had sat and listened in on their conversations. The sons of industrialists and bankers. The sons of politicians. Sometimes they had talked about the battle to come. The decisive battle. From the moment Thatcher had wafted into Downing Street the plans had been drawn up. The men who bankrolled the Tories expected a return on their investment. And a big part of that return was for the Unions to be broken once and for all. Then the money would start to flow again. And the only way to deliver a decisive blow against the Unions was to take on and destroy their Praetorian Guard: The Miners. And in the battle that was to come the fighting would be at its fiercest in Yorkshire. In Haddington.

At six o'clock he went and sat alone in the cold of the TV room. The news was all about Cortonwood. McGregor said that the only future for the coal industry was for it to match the efficiency of its overseas competitors. To become efficient long term would mean short term pain. His face was bland and he exuded the confidence of a man who held every card in the deck. Then Scargill was there. King Arthur. His eyes blazed from under a baseball cap. Lenny could see that he was on cloud nine. This was the moment that he had been waiting for. Craving. Arthur had been itching for his war for five years. Now he was about to get it. No way would the NUM accept 20,000 job losses. Not a chance. This wasn't about to be a negotiation thing. This was going to be all out and no holds barred. The fault line that had split the country apart for five years had suddenly become a chasm. Now the dice had been thrown. Now it would be decided.

Lenny never noticed the door opening. Josh fell into one of the armchairs and lit a cigarette. The news moved onto another story.

"So it starts."

Lenny nodded.

"Aye. So it starts."

All morning he had been reading up on the poets of the First World War. There had been some pictures of young men out in the streets waving their caps in celebration. That had been August 1914 when the news of war had been greeted as the start of a great European adventure and home by Christmas. Just a few years later young men were drowning in the festering filth of the battle of Paschendaele. Lenny had watched the faces of the crowd on the screen as they had roared out their support for the words of King Arthur and they had seemed like the faces of ghosts.

It took King Arthur less than a week to have the Yorkshire NUM out. All out. Every last one of them. The Scots followed within hours. The men of South Wales dithered for a short period, but not long.

Within days over a hundred thousand men were on strike and pits all over the country lay idle.

But not in Nottingham.

The men of Nottingham felt that there should have been a National Ballot. They were reluctant to fall in so easily with the fiery words of King Arthur and his warlike commissars from Yorkshire. Eventually the leaders of Notts branch NUM reluctantly announced their support of the strike, but thousands of their members chose not to hear them. More than half of them turned in to work every morning. The pits stayed open. The coal kept coming up from the ground and rolling out of the gates.

Lenny's life fell into a strange kind of limbo. His days were spent in the library, grinding his way through the books he had put off reading for three years. In between he grabbed fresh air with walks along the Disneyland riverbank. The sun was at last beginning to remember how to give off some heat and spring was poking its nose around the corner. He couldn't seem to escape the feeling of being some kind of deserter. Here he was living out his quiet life in this antique film set whilst a hundred miles to the north his people were fighting their war.

Every night he and Josh watched the growing violence on the evening news. King Arthur had been quick off the mark. Within ten days of calling his men out he was sending out thousands of flying pickets every day. They headed out from the small Yorkshire pit villages, five or six men packed into ten-year-old cars. Every day the men of Nottinghamshire had to be driven through a human wall of screaming hate. It didn't take long for these little battles to become the image of Great Britain 1984. Massed ranks of flying pickets, their faces twisted in loathing, their voices hammering out the chant of "SCAB!! SCAB!! SCAB!!".

Next were the lines of policemen, usually two or three deep. Hundreds of them. Thousands of them. Brought in from every corner of Britain. Their faces twisted in effort as they linked arms and held back the mob. "SCAB!! SCAB!! "

Flying bricks. Flying bottles. Faces split open. Crashing batons. Accusations of police brutality. Accusations of Union brutality.

Then the noise would hit new levels of hate as the coaches filled with working miners appeared. The bricks would crash into the meshed windows. "SCAB!! SCAB!!". Inside the men of Nottingham would meet the screaming mob with V-signs and waved £20 notes. The Coal Board were keeping the pits of Nottingham going with an open cheque-book. The workers who refused to strike were rewarded with huge overtime and bonus payments. The contract hauliers who ran the gauntlet with loads of coal for the power stations enjoyed rates ten times what they were used to and their invoices were paid as fast as they could raise them.

As the news moved on to the next item, Josh shook his head. "Set-up."

Lenny looked up. "What do you mean?"

"They've done the deal before the thing started. In Nottinghamshire. This hasn't just happened. They've paid them off. Lots of them. Think about it Lenny. Think about what Frank has been saying. Think about what happened to us last Saturday."

Lenny rang his brother every evening. Sometimes he was home. More often he was still away on picketing duties down South. His father had more or less left home for the club where he was in charge of co-ordinating the raiding parties. Frank told how hard it was to make it to the destination pit at all. Nottinghamshire was like one giant road block. It could take four and five hours to make a journey of forty miles. Josh and Lenny had driven North in the early hours of Saturday morning and met with Frank, Tommy and Roger at a service area on the A1. The target had been Ollerton Colliery. They hadn't made it. No matter how small the road, there always seemed to be a roadblock to turn them back. In the end they had given up at eleven and returned home to the club. They had tried for seven hours and achieved nothing more than to burn away half a tank of fuel and put another hundred and twenty miles on the clock of Tommy's creaking Cortina.

Lenny glowered at the screen. Thatcher was in America looking like a smug Grandmother gloating about how wonderfully her grandchildren were doing at school.

"Come on Lenny, look at it. You don't just organise that many policemen in a couple of weeks. Think about the accents we heard."

Lenny thought about it. Josh was right. The coppers manning the roadblocks had accents from all corners of Britain. Lancashire. Scouse. Cornish. Kent.

"They must have had the plans drawn up months ago. Maybe years. They knew the Nottingham pits would stay open. They knew that was where the battleground would be. They were ready."

Lenny nodded. Of course they were. They were playing Scargill every step of the way. It wouldn't have been all that hard to guess at his tactics. He had gained his legendary reputation in the early Seventies when his Flying Yorkshire Pickets had closed down the Saltley Gate steelworks in Birmingham. It had been the straw that had broken the back of Edward Heath's Tory Government. The beleaguered Prime Minister had asked the people of Britain to choose between him and the miners, and the people of Britain had kicked him out. He could see the cold hard logic of Josh's theory. Deals had been done in Nottinghamshire. The cash had been splashed around in brown envelopes. Once they had known the ground, they had drawn up their battle plan.

He nodded. "I can't argue with you. The bastards. They got it sewn up at every turn. I just feel that bloody useless. There has to be summat we can do."

Much to his surprise this brought a grin to his friend's face. It was the grin that he had become more than familiar with over the last two-and-a-half years.

"Well it's funny you should say that. You see, I have an Aunt in Mansfield and she's taken rather ill."

"What the hell are you on about?"

Josh explained and they embarked on a strange nocturnal life that was to last for the next three months. Frank would ring through at ten in the evening and let them know which pit the men of Haddington had been ordered to picket. Josh and Lenny would head out of Cambridge after midnight and make their way up to Nottinghamshire. All night long they would drive around the tiny back roads. They would be stopped constantly at road blocks. And Josh would wind down his window and run through his sick aunt story. The policemen would shine a torch into the car and see two young men in tweed jackets and the sound Rachmaninov would float out into the cold air of the night. The rounded vowels of Harrow were almost always enough. Sometimes a driving license bearing an address in Kensington was needed for final confirmation.

They were never turned away once. Most evenings they found a clear route through by two o'clock. Then they would head North to lay-bys on the A1 close to the Yorkshire border and pass on the information to the waiting car loads of Haddington men. Every night thousands of Yorkshire pickets failed to make it through the huge spider's web of roadblocks and were forced to turn around and go home. Others only made it after driving for hour after hour. Not the cars from Haddington. They always found a clear path and made it through to their nominated pit lane at the appointed hour. And their legend grew even larger.

Sleep became a snatched luxury to Lenny. A couple of hours here. A couple of hours there. He ached with fatigue and the books got more and more unreadable. When he eventually read the results of his final exams, it came as no great surprise that he managed no better than the traditional sportsman's Third. Not that it seemed to matter a great deal. Because by the time he read the news on the notice board bigger things were happening. Much bigger. Frank had rung with the news that there was going to be a family wedding. He was going to make an honest woman of his long time girlfriend, Sheila. He admitted that honesty was very much the word as Sheila had a two-month-old bun in the oven. Lenny had asked if he loved her and Frank had promised that he did. The big day was set for the beginning of June and Frank had asked Josh to be his best man.

It seemed to Lenny to be a small beacon of light in the great swathe of darkness that was closing in over the country. Amidst the sound of smashing glass and the thump of police batons on flesh, here was a sliver of hope. By the spring of 1984, the country was split all the way down the middle. The tabloid newspapers had conducted a master class. They made sure that the miners were hated across large sections of the community. Vilified. None more so than Scargill himself. He was painted as a puppet of Moscow. The flying pickets threatened all that was great about Britain. Headline after headline warned of the danger to the oldest democracy of them all. All over Britain the middle classes read about the threat to the lives they were accustomed to as they ate their Cornflakes and sipped their tea.

Three months in, the strike was seen as something more than men fighting for their jobs and homes. By the late spring the tabloids had convinced large chunks of the population that the Government was fighting an enemy at the gates. 'The Enemy Within' as Thatcher famously called it. The war against communism was to be fought on many fronts. The British Army on the Rhine stood their ground and stared with stiff upper lips at the massed ranks of the Red Army on the other side of the wire. The new Cruise Missiles at the US Airbases were presented as the last card to be played in the poker game for freedom. And the gallant policemen and Notts miners were all fighting on the very front line of the war for democracy.

Britain hadn't been so divided for half a century. And in the middle of it all, a Jew from Eton was to be best man at a wedding in Haddington. A lone shaft of sunshine forcing its way though a tiny gap in the dark clouds of hatred.

A week before the wedding, and the day that the exam results were posted, King Arthur marched out in front of the cameras and made his most fateful announcement. The time had come down for a showdown. A trial of strength. The time had come to stop breaking up his forces into small raiding parties of flying pickets. The army was to be brought together. All of it. And army of thousands was to be mobilised for a massive confrontation. Just like it had been at Saltley Gate all those years before. He was going to break the police lines by sheer weight of numbers. The ground had been chosen. The gauntlet was tossed to the ground.

King Arthur informed the country that his army was on the march. Through the massed TV cameras his words reached out through the lens and spoke straight to the Iron Lady in Downing Street. He threw out his challenge. He was ready for his Waterloo. One of them would be Wellington. The other would be Napoleon. And he named the place.

The British Steel coking plant at Orgreave.

It was one of those July mornings when there seemed no better place to be in the whole world than England. Even though the digital face of the Baxter kitchen clock read 5.27, the air coming in through the open back door was already warm. It was day five of a heat wave and the weathermen were fiercely confident that there was plenty more to come. Outside the sky was a rich uninterrupted blue broken only by the white slip streams of planes heading east to Europe and beyond.

All should have been buoyant and well within the Baxter household. The next day promised to be a great one in the history of the family. The next day was the wedding and all was in place. The bride was universally approved of. The dress from York made her look like something off the tele. Always had been bonnie that Sheila. Bonnie as a picture. More to the point, Sheila's naturally slender figure was still showing no signs of the package it carried within. The church was booked and the weather was set fair as fair could be.

For a while it had seemed that the financial aspects of the event were going to make it hard for both mothers to create the kind of day they had long dreamed about. The strike was into its fourth month and hardship was starting to bite hard into the people of Haddington. The union's fighting funds were being ferried about the country in suitcases as the lawyers hired by the Government chased every last penny. There was just about enough to pay for half tanks of petrol to get the lads down to Nottinghamshire, but that was all. There was just about nothing for the families. They had to manage as well as they could.

By that first blazing hot week of June, the pain was being well and truly felt. Mortgages were in arrears, HP payments had dried up, electricity and gas was on the point of being cut off. All over South Yorkshire families were eking things out with beans on toast and potatoes. The real hard times were still a few months away. The hard dark days of the autumn sent the men out with old prams to pick lumps of coal from the slag heaps. It was when the nights started to draw in that the marriages started to fall apart and the small houses were plunged into darkness as one red bill too many landed on the mat. Those dark days were still far out of sight as the summer sun shone down on Haddington, but belts were getting tightened to the last hole.

The Baxters were a prudent family. The mortgage had been paid off a few years earlier and the local branch of the Halifax had held a modest nest egg for a rainy day. The rain had fallen from the minute that the strike was called at the beginning of March and the nest egg was all but gone. There was still enough for food and the bills. There wasn't a chance in hell of paying for a wedding. Had Sheila not been up the duff, then both families would have applied pressure for the wedding to be put back until after the strike. But her condition had taken away that option.

The first two weeks of May had seen much agonised debate. Josh had been insistent that being best man meant that it was only right that he should be allowed to make a contribution. The contribution he had in mind was to basically pay for the wedding. The problem was a wall of stubborn Yorkshire pride that was about thirty feet tall. Luckily Josh was surprisingly stubborn himself. He argued late into the night that it served the Baxter family right. They had done everything to make him feel welcome, to feel part of the family. This had brought nods of acceptance. Well, in that case how could it be right that they refused to treat him as a proper member of the family by not letting him help with the cost of the wedding. It was the kind of eloquently argued point that appealed to the shop steward instincts of the father of the groom. Once Ralph Baxter had been won over, it had only been a matter of time until the rest of the two families had followed suit.

All Josh had needed was a foot in the door. To start with, there had been grudging permission for him to help out a bit with the buffet. He hadn't pushed it. He had quietly bided his time and taken opportunities as and when they came. By the time the sun started to rise over the ripening wheat fields on the morning before the big day, he had managed to pay for the dresses of the bride and bridesmaids, he had ordered a lavish amount of flowers, he had even managed to book a steel band. Helping out a bit with the buffet had turned into ordering a feast for half of Haddington. Never in his life had Josh had so much fun spending his father's money.

The Baxter kitchen really should have been a place of eager anticipation of the big day just a sunset and sunrise away. The mood should have been buoyant. It wasn't. Instead a heavy silence hung over the room. The men of the family sat around the table staring at half-drunk mugs of tea. Ethel Baxter and Sheila leant against the sink with folded arms and fierce faces. The argument had been bitter and unresolved. Sheila had said that it wasn't right that Frank should be going down to Orgreave on the day before the wedding. He had been out picketing every bloody day since the bloody strike had been on and she had never moaned once. So why couldn't he miss it just this once, just once, it wasn't asking a lot was it? What would happen if he got arrested? How would it be then? Her standing at the alter and him banged up in Sheffield nick.

Frank had said that he couldn't let the lads down. He tried to explain that this was the big one. This was the day when Arthur was going to need every man he could get. If it had been just another day down in Nottinghamshire, then fair enough, he would have left it alone. But it wasn't. This was the one that counted. This was when they were going to hit the bastards hard.

Ethel hadn't bought a word of it and she had said so. Don't try and pull the wool over my eyes Frank Baxter, don't even think about it. I gave birth to you and I've seen you every day of your sorry life. Arthur will have thousands down there today. Tens of thousands even. He doesn't need Frank Baxter on the day before his wedding. You should listen to Sheila because she's right. You just can't resist getting out there with all the lads and your cans of ale and your silly songs. Should be bloody ashamed of yourself you should.

Baxter senior had stayed quiet and hoped not to be asked. Fat chance. He attempted something along the lines of the lad being old enough to make his own decisions and got a torrent of abuse for his pains. Lenny in turn held up his hands and announced that he was staying out of it and he wasn't about to say anything either way.

In the end Josh felt that it was his place as best man to intervene.

"Look Sheila. I can see how you feel. Course I can. How's about this. I'm the best man here. I give you my solemn word that I will make absolutely certain that Frank gets back to Haddington tonight sober, in one piece, and at liberty. I'm sure you'll back me up here won't you Lenny."

Lenny was clearly surprised to find himself back in the spotlight. "Aye. No bother. We'll get him home Sheila. Promise."

At this Sheila had known that it was time to accept defeat. Big tears had burst down her cheeks. "You better bloody well had."

Then the silence had taken a hold on the room. It lasted for well over five minutes until Ralph Baxter squared his shoulders and assumed the role of the head of the house.

"Well lads. Time's running along. We best be off then."

Chair legs scraped on the lino floor and Frank made to hug his bride to be who pushed him away.

"You can piss off Frank Baxter. I hate your bloody guts."

Frank grinned. "Well tha best get over it before tomorrow lass. Don't get all lathered up. We'll be fine."

They climbed into the car and they were soon part of a convoy of similar vehicles leaving the town. All headed south. All headed for Orgreave in the crisp light of the dawn. Waves were exchanged. Clenched fists. Frank tapped at the arm rest on the back door.

" . . . here we go, here we go, here we go . . . "

Lenny found his enthusiasm anything but infectious. He felt tired and tetchy.

"I don't know what you're getting so bloody excited about."

Frank just grinned at his brother's mood.

"Don't be so daft our Lenny. This is going to be the big day."

Lenny shrugged. "Aye. It's always going to be the bloody big day. Come on Frank. We've been down at Orgreave for na' but a week now. What's happened? How many lorries have we managed to stop? Has the furnace at Scunthorpe been closed down yet? I don't think so. All that's happened is that we've had a proper kicking. That's all. So what's going to be so bloody different today then?"

"Numbers Lenny. That's what. Sheer numbers. There'll be thousands of us today. Too many. We'll break them by sheer bloody numbers. Come on. You heard what Arthur was saying yesterday."

Lenny blew out his breath in disgust. "Arthur. Bloody Arthur. Why the hell should I listen to a word that man speaks?"

"Steady on Lenny." His father this time, his voice alarmed at the blasphemy of his son's words. But Lenny wasn't about to be shut up.

"No Dad, I'll not steady on. I wish someone could tell me that King bloody Arthur has the first clue about what he is doing. From where I sit, everything he does gets our arses kicked. The leadership in Nottingham asked for a week to organise a vote and get the lads on board. Did he listen? Did he buggery. He sent the boys down to scream and swear at them. So instead of joining us, they stuck two fingers up at us. Every night he sticks his daft face in front of the cameras and puts the whole of the country against us. I didn't think all this was supposed to be about a revolution. I thought it was about keeping the pits open and keeping our jobs. Or did I miss something here?"

Nobody much wanted to answer him. He forged on, getting all his growing frustration off his chest.

"And now this. This Orgreave fiasco. Come on lads. It's a bloody joke."

Frank was getting angry now. "Look Lenny, just cos you've got some fancy degree from Cambridge bastard University doesn't mean you know better than everyone else. This is no fiasco. It's the same as it was at Saltley Gate the last time. We need to win a big one. And we're going to."

Lenny was having none of it. "Oh piss off Frank. It's nowt like Saltley Gate. That worked because nobody was expecting it. Nobody had ever heard of flying pickets then. They couldn't believe it when thousands of lads from Yorkshire pitched up in Birmingham. We caught then with their pants down and they couldn't do a thing to stop us."

They flashed past a cluster of police vans by the roadside. The constables were sipping at coffees from polystyrene cups. They looked amused at the V-signs from the cars of the passing miners. As the Baxter car drew level, Lenny looked out of the window at the uniformed figures. One of them grinned at him and drew a finger across his throat.

"There. See that Frank? Do they look as if they are about to be caught with their pants down. It's not just us that know today is supposed to be a big one. Think about it for Christ's sake. Think how it is when we try to get into Nottinghamshire. It's all but bloody impossible. Road blocks everywhere you look. Hundreds of the bastards. Why is that then Frank? Because they don't want us there. Because they need to keep us away and to keep the coal moving to the power stations. Do you see that happening today Frank? Have you seen it happening every time we drive to Orgreave?"

His brother just shrugged. He was starting to look uncomfortable now.

"Of course not. Just look at them. They are having a laugh. They make it as easy as they can for us. Come on dickheads. Come to Orgreave. Come to mummy Margaret. They even help us to park for Christ's sake."

Frank picked away at a hole in his jeans. He couldn't argue about it. They had all been talking in the club about the designated parking areas the police had provided for them in the fields around the coking plant. Lenny eased his voice a little.

"Orgreave is where they want us. No guess work. They have had a good look at the ground and they know just how to control us. And whilst we get a kicking every day at Orgreave they have gone onto double shifts in Nottinghamshire and coal stocks are going up. Orgreave has nowt to do with winning this bloody strike. It's about King bloody Arthur's dream of some kind of 1917 style uprising. He thinks that if the proletariat of Britain see the lads being beaten to a pulp by police in riot gear there'll be some kind of spontaneous revolt.

He lies in bed at night and dreams of mobs on the streets tearing down the gates to the big houses. It's bollocks Frank. All of it. This isn't Russia. It never will be. And we are all daft enough to follow him into the shite. Sheila was right. Tha'should have stayed at home. I should have made you. This is just bollocks."

That was it for Frank. "Oh aye. Bollocks is it? Well what are you doing in car Lenny? Why did you come home at all? Tha's not about to go down pit are you. Oh no. Not bloody Lenny. Pit's no good enough for Lenny Baxter is it? He's going to be some big fancy cricketer. So why come at all then? Why not stay away if tha knows so bloody much?"

Lenny smiled at him. No matter what, he could never stay mad at his twin brother for long.

"Hey Frank. Don't get yourself confused here. Just because I have a degree from Cambridge doesn't mean I'm not just as bloody stupid as the rest of you."

It took a second or two for Frank to realise that his brother was joking. Then he burst out laughing. They all did. And the smiling policemen politely waved them down the road to Orgreave.

From the minute they parked up and got out of their car it was clear that King Arthur had got his way. Everywhere they looked there were miners. Thousands upon thousands of them. The mood was buoyant. They were dressed for a summer day out in shorts and T-shirts and trainers. They were cracking jokes and singing. Already the cans were open. This was going to be their day. The day the tide was going to turn. The mood soon had hold of Frank and he joined in with the chants, clapping his hands above his head as he walked. Ralph Baxter was more pragmatic. But still he felt a swelling of pride every time he nodded at a familiar Haddington face. No other pit would have so many men down for the day. Win or lose, nobody would ever be able to say that the lads from Haddington hadn't turned out. Hadn't spilt some blood for the cause.

Lenny's mood was sinking with every step. Josh fell in beside him. "Not happy I sense."

Lenny shook his head. "I've got a bad feeling about this Josh. Stinking bad. Look at all these lads. They seem to think it's all some kind of game. Just a big laugh. Half of them are pissed."

Josh looked around at the teeming mass of red smiling faces.

" . . . *here we go . . . here we go . . . here we go . . .*"

" . . . *Arthur Scarrr . . . gill . . . Arthur Scarrrrrrrr . . . gill . . . we'll support you ever more . . .*"

"Surely you have to applaud their morale Lenny. Especially after everything they've been through."

"Course I do. Obviously. There's nobody like them. Never has been. It's just that it seems as if they're being used. A lot of lads are about to get the hiding of their lives today. And for what? A stupid pipe dream. That's what."

At last they came to the top of the hill where they could look down over the long field that ran up to the small road which was used by the trucks that came to collect their loads of coke. The crowd was huge. Twice as big as any day before. Three times as big. 10,000. Maybe even 20,000.

Frank gave out a cry of delight. "Christ all bloody mighty. Feast your eyes lads. Here we bloody go . . ."

But Lenny was looking beyond the great mass of miners. Beyond to the tightly packed lines of policemen. There were more of them too. Many, many more. And these were very different policemen from those who had held the lines outside the pits in Nottinghamshire. Gone were the traditional helmets of London postcards. In their place were motor cycle style riot helmets and Perspex visors. They stood in tightly packed lines behind huge plastic shields. Officers were marching them around in columns as if they were Roman Legionnaires. Showing off many hours of training. To the right and left were teams of dog handlers with snarling Alsatians straining at their leashes. And behind the lines the cavalry waited. How many. Ahundred. Maybe more.

As they made their way down the field they could hear the sounds from where the miners lines faced down the police.

" . . . *here we go . . . here we go . . . here we go . . .*"

" . . . *we're on the march with Arthur's army . . .*"

The police met the chants by creating their own sound of thunder by beating their plastic shields with their batons. The sound rolled up the field and made the hairs stand up on Lenny's forearms.

As they drew nearer he realised that the police were chanting as well. They were belting their shields and yelling *"Zulooooooooo!!! Zulooooooooo!!"*

Unbelievable.

And then the miners would growl with growing anger and scream abuse as the police waved twenty pound notes in the air over their shields.

"... *Here we go* ... *here* ..."

"*Zulooooooo!!!*"

Crash. Thunder.

"Christ Josh, just look at them. It's going to be ..."

His words were lost in the howl of twenty thousand voices. About a quarter of a mile away the first wagon of a convoy had appeared. Then another. And another. They looked almost military with their cabs protected by roughly welded mesh panels. Another. Ten now. Now fifteen.

There was no order. No battle cry. Just an instinctive surge at the trucks and the scab drivers who crossed their picket lines for a hundred quid a load. Cash.

And it was utter chaos. Those at the front of the mob never stood a chance. The weight of the thousands behind them pushed them onto the crashing batons and the wall of plastic. The ground was baked dry and soon the view was lost in clouds of dust. Screams of anger. Screams of pain. The policemen waiting in reserve beat away at their shields.

"*Zulooooooooo!!!!*"

And after a few minutes there were as many miners running away as there were trying to surge forward to stop the trucks. Lots of blood now. Torn clothes. Men dragging bruised legs. Men dragging semi-conscious mates. Men barely recognisable under spurting wounds.

"*Zulooooooooooo*"

Crash.

Not many going forward now. None at all. All running. Running hard for any kind of cover. The columns of police were moving forward now in tight formation. Batons hammering down on the backs of miners who had nowhere to run in the crush. Felling them. Trampling them. Lenny and Frank and Ralph and Josh were well back from it all. They were among the lucky ones who had arrived at the field late. Those who had got there first were getting a murderous beating. Then Lenny saw something new. Something different. Two of the columns were drawing apart. Creating a gap. And behind them the horsemen were grouping ready to charge.

"Oh no. Surely not . . ."

But the charge was already under way. The giant horses were slowly picking up momentum. The foot soldiers beat their shields and roared them on as they lumbered through the front lines. And within seconds the riders were cutting a swathe through the crowd, hammering down with their batons. Smashing heads. Smashing forearms held up to protect heads.

"Jesus. Come on lads. We're out of here."

The four of them turned and joined the wild retreat up the field. A small wood seemed the most obvious place to head for. It took them a minute and they reached the shade of the trees only to find that the police had planned for this avenue of escape. The wood was occupied by dog handlers and already there were men down on the floor screaming as the vice like bites of the dogs gripped into their unprotected arms. More batons. More kicks. More smashed faces.

Then they were out the other side. Another field. Not so many of them now. Not so many had made it out this far. Ralph Baxter was struggling already. His lungs choked up by years of coal dust and untipped cigarettes.

"Come on Dad. You've got to keep going."

Lenny was half carrying him. Ahead was a fence. And a railway embankment. Maybe some respite.

He risked a glance behind him.

Bollocks.

Six of them. Six in their helmets. Faces distorted and evil behind the Perspex. Six with batons raised and ready and screaming.

He almost threw his dad over the fence. Then he turned.

Oh no.

Frank had tripped. Frank was down. Frank wasn't getting to his feet quickly enough. And they were on him. All around him. Batons crashing down.

Snap.

The black killing rage was back again. No thought. No logic. No nothing. Just a killing anger. Lenny threw every ounce of his fourteen stones into the backs of two of them. They crashed to the floor hard. He sensed the wind bursting out as they hit the deck. The other four reacted fast. On him now. All of them. He didn't care. Didn't give a damn. The blows were nothing. The pain was nothing.

He was gone. All the way gone. Kicking. Punching. But going down all the same. Down and not able to get up again. Still kicking and punching but down . . .

Then for some reason it all stopped. His head was ringing from the blows. What the hell. He tried to see but his eyes were full of blood from a gash on his forehead. Josh? Was it Josh? Course it was. Had to be. No other bastard at Orgreave had an accent like that.

"There. Come on. Film it man . . ."

Through the blood that was pouring into his eyes he saw Josh at the other side of the fence with a three man camera crew. Where on earth had he found them? The policemen were hesitant. Nervous. Instructions had been made clear. Avoid rough stuff in front of the cameras. The sergeant hesitated for a second or two then issued his orders.

"Come on lads. Leave these. There's plenty more . . ."

And they were gone. All of them. Sprinting hard towards three limping figures fifty yards across the field.

Lenny was laughing as Josh hauled him up. Almost hysterical.

"Where the hell did you find them . . ."

He paused to spit out a tooth. Frank was dragging himself up. He was grinning through a split lip.

"Bloody fantastic. Bloody brilliant. Just wait till I tell lads . . ."

At this his eyes rolled up to the top of his skull and he passed out cold.

The madness was draining out of Lenny fast. Clarity brought pain. Pain all over.

"Christ I feel like I got hit by a bloody truck. Come on. Let's get him up. We're out of here."

Between then they managed to haul Frank over the fence to where his father waited on the other side. Lenny took a last look back over the field. All over there were prone figures being hammered by the black clad police. He looked to his side and into Josh's face.

"That was quick thinking sunshine. There's plenty who would have just legged it."

Josh shrugged. "Didn't seem as if I had a great deal of choice in the matter. I was on a promise remember. I dare say anything those policemen may have done wouldn't have been half as bad as facing Sheila."

He smiled. They both smiled. One with a face masked in blood.

The other now shaking as the shock of the violence set in. Lenny shook his head.

"Tha'll do me Josh Ogilvy. Tha'll do me."

Frank woke up as they were driving clear of the war zone. He reached up to his head and a red hot pain lanced down his neck.

"Bloody hell"

"Oh, he's back with us at last."

Frank was running his hands along his body and wincing each time he found a painful spot. Slowly the memory of what had happened came back to him. He reached forward and placed a hand on Josh's shoulder.

"Thanks mate. Really."

Josh grinned. "All part of the service old man. Let's just say you made a good choice of best man."

Half an hour later they entered the A&E unit of Sheffield Infirmary. It was like a scene from a war zone. The veterans of the battle of Orgreave took up every seat and had spilled onto the floor. Frank and Lenny had to wait five hours until it was their turn. All the while the crowd of injured men watched the pictures from the battle they had just escaped from on the television mounted high up on the wall.

The pictures told a very different story from what they had just witnessed. The police seemed to be using reasonable force in the wake of huge provocation. The men in the audience were too beaten up to get angry. It was what they were used to. After three months, they were coming to terms with how it was to fight the many and various battalions that Thatcher had marshalled against them. Even King Arthur himself had been lifted. He was frog-marched away from the battlefield by three policemen, his eyes blazing with anger. Maybe he thought that the pictures would stimulate the countrywide surge in support he had hoped for. Maybe a General Strike like in 1926. It wasn't about to happen. All over Britain people got on with their work. They watched the images of the battle of Orgreave over their lunch breaks and they had a laugh about it. Bloody nutters, those miners. Mad bastards. Had it coming. Especially that Commie bastard Scargill. Deserved all he got. Someone should stick him on a plane to Moscow and be done with it. And then the conversations moved on. On to the football at the weekend. On to the tits on Page Three. On to who her down the road was shagging. On to the price of fags.

Britain wasn't about to revolt. Not because of Orgreave.

The gash on Lenny's head needed thirteen stitches. Other than that, it was all bruising. Frank was in worse shape. He had a broken finger, two cracked ribs and concussion. The doctor was adamant that he should stay in overnight for observation. Frank hadn't been much impressed by the idea.

"Don't be so bloody daft. I'm getting wed in morning."

By the time they got back home, Haddington was reeling with the news of the day. Ten had been locked up. Thirteen were in the infirmary. Plenty hadn't made it back yet. One look at Frank and Sheila was ready to fire off both barrels. Ralph managed to calm her down and get her to put the kettle on instead whilst he told the story of Josh and the camera crew with huge relish.

The result of the story was that Sheila and Mrs Baxter fussed over Josh like a long lost son and completely ignored the others.

Lenny stirred his tea ruefully.

"That's what public school does for you our Frank. Here's us. All kicked to shite standing up for what's right and they don't want to know us. He comes back without so much as a scratch and they're all over him like a rash. No justice brother. No justice."

Frank was about to add a comment but the act of swallowing his tea set off the pain in his ribs and caused him to spit it out all over the table cloth that had only been washed that morning.

"For Christ's sake our Frank, you're like a bloody animal. I don't envy you Sheila, having to take him on. I don't envy you one bit."

But Sheila wasn't mad any more. She had realised just how close it had been to no wedding at all. Better to go up the aisle with a man who looked as if he'd done ten rounds with Mohammed Ali than not go up the aisle at all. And so what if he looked a bit bashed and bruised? When all was said and done, Sheila was a Haddington girl to her toenails and she would be proud as punch to go through the hoop with a man covered in the scars of the battle of Orgreave.

The next day saw the Haddington contingent down at Orgreave much reduced. Some were locked up. Others were in hospital. Many were sickened by what they had seen the day before. Most were scrubbed up for Frank and Sheila's wedding. The day was hot and perfect. It seemed as if half the congregation that packed the church were bandaged on one part of the body or another. Both of the groom's eyes had all but disappeared behind livid swellings of black and purple. Lenny looked little better with a thick roll of bandages around his forehead which made his hair stick comically up out of the middle.

Josh on the other hand looked a million dollars in his best Armani suit. By closing time the previous night, everyone in Haddington had become party to the camera crew story. He was one of them for ever more.

A large marquee on the outfield of the cricket ground hosted the reception afterwards and it was only then that anyone realised the extent to which Josh had exceeded his instructions. The drinks flowed until the early hours and the buffet was talked about for years. Josh's speech was something else that was never forgotten. He had his audience in stitches most of the time but there were tears as well when he talked about the way he had come to feel about Lenny and Frank and the family. They way he felt about the people of Haddington and their fight. He finished with a flourish as he lifted his glass high.

"Ladies and Gentlemen. May I propose a toast to the bride and groom. Ladies and Gentlemen, may I propose a toast to every man who turned out on that field yesterday. Ladies and gentlemen, may I propose a toast to VICTORY!!! NO SURRENDER!! HERE WE GO . . . HERE WE GO . . ."

The song seemed to threaten to lift the heavy canvass of the marquee clean off its pegs. And for a moment everyone believed that victory would be theirs.

As the singing filled the warm air of the night, Josh reached into his jacket pocket and passed an envelope to Sheila. Inside were two tickets for a plane leaving Manchester the next afternoon for Montego Bay, Jamaica. As soon as her brain registered the words she burst into tears and passed the envelope to her battered husband. All he could do was blink in dumb astonishment.

"Bloody hell Josh. I can't believe it. Thanks."

The next morning was all about thick heads and getting the newly-weds across the Pennines to the airport. Josh and Lenny broke the journey back with a couple of pints in the garden of a pub high on the hills overlooking the sprawl of Sheffield. They landed back in Haddington just after ten and things changed. Changed completely.

Waiting in the kitchen looking his usual stiff and quiet self was Williams. Williams was a Welshman who had worked as a groundsman at the Ogilvy house in Shropshire since 1969. He had immediately become a huge part of Josh's life. Up until that time, holidays had been a bleak period for young Josh. He had no friends to speak of and his father was almost always away in London. Josh would have liked to have gone to the house in Kensington with him, but they had no staff there. Instead he was left with Mrs Black, the dour housekeeper who seldom wasted more than three or four sentences a day. He spent his days in his room with books and Airfix kits and action men and vague dreams of playing out with other boys. Williams had changed all that. At forty, he had just left the army after twenty-two years of service. He could tell stories that brought the action men in Josh's collection to life. He soon took the youngster under his wing and the days of the holidays were all spent outside. He taught Josh to fish and shoot. He taught him the secrets of the countryside all around them, the names of all the birds, the places where the badgers made their sets, the way the kestrels hovered and waited for their moment.

As Josh had grown into his teens his relationship with Williams had never weakened. As he wandered off the rails at Eton and suffered the painful silences in his father's study as he read yet another letter threatening expulsion, there was always the tough Welshman as a fallback. Williams didn't speak much. But he could listen with the best of them. He had known plenty the same as Josh during his time in uniform. Young confused lads without any bearings in their lives. The army was pretty good at giving them some direction. Josh would just have to find his way. He had never worried about the lad much until the drink and drugs had started. Especially the drugs. For a while he had feared a full-scale addiction. He had seen that as well. Lots of times. Lads who hid away from the horrors they had seen at the bottom of a bottle.

Then Josh had met Lenny Baxter and everything had changed. Williams liked the big lad from Yorkshire the minute he met him. There was a steadiness there that was the perfect foil for Josh's wild side. Not just steadiness. Something else. Something that Williams had only ever seen now and then. It was that something that suddenly made men charge a machine-gun nest with a grenade to save their mates. A mix of courage and uncontrolled black rage. The stuff that usually lay behind the ones who won the Victoria Cross. And when these lads did whatever they did, they would never really be able to understand why.

When Josh headed off to Haddington, he had left contact details with Williams. By this stage the relationship with his father was all but over. It seemed that the old man couldn't begin to understand why his son had developed such a fascination with these people. Josh had been given everything. There could have been no more. The best of schooling. Introductions to the very finest of society. He could walk any road he wanted and for some strange reason he chose a road to a small mining town in Yorkshire. It was beyond his comprehension.

Josh knew that something was wrong the minute he walked through the back door.

"Hello Josh."

"Hello sir." It was always sir. Always would be. "What has happened?"

"I'm afraid it's your father. He's ill. Very ill. A stroke."

Josh felt all the strength drain from his legs. He sat. His father. His only real family. A relationship that had never had the chance to start. And now it looked as if it never would. He had never considered the prospect of his father being ill. It was inconceivable. His father was like a machine. He never drank. Never smoked. Took long walks every day and ate carefully. He couldn't be ill. It wasn't possible.

"I think you'd better come with me Josh. He's in hospital in London. The doctors don't know how it will be yet. There may not be much time."

"Yes. Of course I must."

Josh looked around the kitchen at the faces of his second family. They understood completely. They knew what family was all about. If only he and his own father had known as well. If only death had not had to come knocking to make the point.

"Do you want me to come with you?" Asked Lenny.

Josh shook his head. "No. It's OK. I'm sure everything will be fine. I'll give you a call. I expect he'll pull through well enough. He's a tough as teak you know. My dad."

He packed quickly and they were on the road before eleven. As things turned out, the old man was every bit as tough as his son had predicted. He fought death hard all through the summer and into the cool of October. Josh divided his time between the hospital and the empty house in Kensington.

Lenny managed to visit a couple of times, but his life had taken a different turn as well. The day after Josh had left for London, the telephone in the hallway had rung a little after nine. It was Warwickshire Cricket Club. They wanted to offer him a trial.

At first he wasn't about to go. How could he? It would be a betrayal. How could he go off and enjoy himself on the cricket field while the people of Haddington fought their increasingly futile war. His father had managed to persuade him in the end. He had explained that it had been a family dream for years to see Lenny make it as a cricketer. Sure, they had all hoped for Yorkshire, but Warwickshire were a decent lot. The strike changed nothing. The strike was the business of himself and Frank. They were the ones who made their livings underground. Lenny had already done enough. More than enough. He had said that he couldn't stand to see his son miss a chance like this. And his words had prevailed. Lenny caught a train to the Midlands and passed his trial with flying colours when his eighth ball in the nets all but broke the knuckle of the West Indian batsman who was the overseas player for that year.

"Jeeeesus man. That bowlin too quick for a white boy!"

The batsman's white teeth gleamed out of his ebony face in a big grin. Lenny was hired. The plan was to give him a couple of games in the second eleven and see how he got on. The first game gave him match figures of 7 for 64 and when he tore the ligaments of his left ankle in the second game, he already had figures of 4 for 21 in the first innings. The physio could do no more than give a weary shake of the head.

"Sorry Lenny. That's your summer up the spout. Complete rest for three months minimum. Then gym only till Christmas. You're not bowling anything till next year."

So Lenny was back in Haddington just three weeks after he had left. He did the driving, but he had to stay clear of the growing violence of the picket lines. For most of the summer it was back to Nottinghamshire every day. Back time after time and nothing seemed to make a difference. The Nottinghamshire scabs were being feted as national heroes in the tabloids by this stage. They were dressed up as the brave men who took no heed of the ultra-violent threats from King Arthur's marauding gangs of thugs. Men who overcame the fear to claim their right to go and do an honest day's work for their families.

They were the very best of British. The bulldog spirit. The reason why the Kremlin would never get its way.

It was a summer of envelopes stuffed with untraceable cash. Cash for miners to break the strike. Cash for the gangs of unknown masked men who appeared out of nowhere to beat and hospitalise car loads of pickets as they tried to find a way through the police lines to the working pits. Cash to the owners of the small private docks who unloaded the boatloads of Polish coal. Cash to the contract hauliers who covered their trucks in mesh and rode the gauntlet of spitting hate to get their loads out. Cash to everyone. Millions upon millions. In overtime for the police. In fat bonuses to the working miners. In huge pay settlements to the unions who may have shown solidarity and joined the strike. In purchases of imported coal at double the going rate. Maggie didn't care about the cost. It was an irrelevance.

As the summer eased into Autumn, Lenny fell into a black depression. The price that was being paid all around him was becoming too much. Marriages that had lasted for years were falling apart. Proud men were reduced to tears when they hadn't a penny to buy a birthday present for a young child. Houses were thrown into candlelight as the power was cut off. More and more, the people of Haddington had to turn to the great pan of soup cooked up in the club by his mum and others in order to feed themselves. They had become charity cases, eking out an existence on public donations. And Lenny could see no chance of victory. They were fighting an enemy that was utterly remorseless. The more they all suffered, the better. The greater their humiliation, the better. Thatcher didn't just want to defeat them. She wanted to destroy them. Obliterate them. Take away every last vestige of their pride. She was hell bent on complete and absolute victory and the sheer dogged stubbornness of the mining communities was making the most catastrophic of defeats almost inevitable.

October 1984

The tipping point of Trevor Beardsworth's life had come in the summer of 1979. Up until this point, his story had been the same as that of many lads from Haddington. Get born. Go to school. Down the pit at sixteen. There was nothing much exceptional about Trevor. He was popular. A good enough worker. He stood his rounds in the club on a Friday night. He paid his Union subs on time. We was well enough liked. Trevor was a regular guy.

In June 1979 the big moment of his life arrived. He was on a holiday to Benidorm with the lads. On the night of day two, they all ended up in a vast sprawling disco that was 99.9% British. Trevor had had a few. But he hadn't gone daft. He was certainly sober enough to be pulled up in his tracks by the sight of Tracey Heap on the dance floor. Tracey was a fine looking lass wearing very little of anything and moving like a cat. Trevor had never seen anything quite like her. He was entranced. And when he gritted his teeth and asked her to dance she actually said yes.

Tracey worked as a cleaner in the Co-op in Bury and all the lads from her school seemed to be on the dole. Everyone in Bury seemed to be on the dole. Tracey had set her sights on something better. She had decided she wasn't about to settle for a life of high rise council flats and Giros like her mum and two older sisters. She wanted something better. Lots better. And she had set out her stall to find it in Benidorm.

She actually quite fancied the miner from Yorkshire, though not half as much as he fancied her. That much was plain enough. What really impressed her was his wages. Unbelievable. None of the lads in

189

Bury could dream of getting anywhere near such wages. Fair enough, he wasn't a tall Texan with gleaming white teeth, cowboy boots and an open topped Cadillac like in Dallas. Tracey was a sensible girl. Realistic. She had come to Benidorm looking for something better and Trevor Beardsworth seemed a pretty good bet.

When they got home he drove over the Pennines every weekend to take her out. Drove. As in a car. Something else that was as scarce as rocking horse shit amongst the Bury lads. Her mum approved. Her sisters were jealous. Both of their men were Giro boys who smoked dope all night and slept most of the day. The cleaning job was an utter misery for a pittance that would barely cover a decent hair do of a weekend. Tracey made her mind up that Trevor was her bird in the bush and decided it was time to forget to take her pill.

They were married in November. Trevor couldn't care less about the unplanned pregnancy. In fact he was chuffed to bits. He still couldn't quite believe that a lass like Tracey would ever stick with him. As things turned out, the kid never arrived. Tracey miscarried one cold morning in February.

By the summer of 1980 she had found work waiting on in the Little Chef on the A1 and travelled there every morning in her car. Car. Her car. A yellow Mini with a cassette player. Two wages were considered enough by the Halifax for the young couple to be given a mortgage to buy a small terrace of their own.

And Tracey discovered the next great passion of her life. Building the perfect home. This meant serious graft for Trevor as it involved him taking every second of overtime that was available to keep up with the numerous HP payments for the carpets, the leather suite, the surround sound music system and the mortgage plus for the conservatory. From the moment that Tracey had completed one HPdeal it seemed that she was lining up another. She skated inches from the edge all the time. Every last penny seemed to be eaten up by all the repayments. At times it got Trevor down. At times it seemed as if he were little better than a slave working every waking hour in the cause of having a house that looked like something out of a magazine. But these days were not common. Most days he blessed all the gods and the stars in the heavens above for the miraculous fact that Tracey Heap was his girl.

Just before Christmas 1983 Tracey announced that she wanted to go on a Caribbean Cruise for her holiday. There was a special offer. It was a chance of a lifetime. It seemed all but impossible, but somehow his Christmas bonus covered the deposit and for three months they managed to make the payments.

And then King Arthur had called the lads out.

All out. Every last one.

Tracey hadn't seen it coming. She hadn't really looked. She had assumed that Trevor's income could only ever go on the up and up. Well, there would always be coal wouldn't there. She had read somewhere that the Yorkshire coal stocks were going to last for three hundred years.

And now her man was on strike and she had become the family breadwinner. Of course that was all her part time job at the Little Chef could do. They could just about eat and pay the bills and the Halifax were willing to re-schedule their mortgage payments. All the HP payments fell into a chaos of arrears and red letters. By a miracle of persuasion, Tracey managed to negotiate reduced payments on the cruise. She refused to give it up. It had become everything to her. The suite and the music system were carried out of the front door by bailiffs who had never been so busy, but Tracey managed to keep the dream of the cruise alive into the cool of the autumn.

By October the dream was fading fast. The cruise wasn't actually cancelled. But they were a mile behind the required level of payments and the lump sum that was needed to be paid before the end of November was the equivalent of the Crown Jewels.

It took a lot to get Tracey down. She was generally an irrepressible type of lass. But the sight of all her treasures being taken away by the Repo men had been too much. The prospect of the big white boat and the sparkling shores of the Caribbean had kept her going through the endless hard months of the strike. But now, as the thin rain of the Autumn came to the grey streets of Haddington, she knew that the dream was all but gone.

And the rows started. Endless screaming rows. She hadn't married him for this. If she had wanted this, she would have gone with any number of lads from Bury who all had bigger dicks than he could ever dream of. And what was the stupid strike all about anyway? They hadn't said they were closing Haddington had they? It was Cortonwood. Cortonwood and nineteen other pits. Not Haddington. Hadn't he always said that Haddington was one of the most modern.

Yes he bloody well had. She could remember him saying it in Spain. One of the most modern in Europe. Big, fat bonuses on production. Why couldn't he be like the Nottinghamshire lads. They weren't stupid. The Board were paying them a fortune.

He tried to explain how things were in Haddington. Why it was different to Nottingham. Why it always had been. What that meant. What the place was all about. Christ he tried. Night after night after night of screaming arguments that tore at his heart. And every night she would slam the bedroom door in his face and he would curl up on the old couch that had come out of his mum and dad's garage and try to find some sleep. But it hardly ever came. Instead he would stare at the gas fire they couldn't afford to run any more. And shiver. And curse the day that King bastard Arthur had ever been born. Trevor couldn't give a flying shite about solidarity and brotherhood. All he cared about was his Tracey. Making her happy. Keeping her. Being allowed in her bed. Everything else was bollocks.

Unknown to Trev and Trace, their reduced standing order payments to the Cruise company had been noticed. They had been noticed by Harry Grierson who was the proprietor of Grierson Investigations Ltd in Leeds. He was not only the owner but also the office manager, the investigator, the tea maker and the washer-upper. Harry was a one man band and he had set up his Agency after retiring from the CID after thirty years. Business hadn't been bad. Certainly enough to supplement his pension. Enough for a contented wife at home and two holidays a year. Then one night he had been invited out for a pint by an old colleague in August.

They had swapped memories for a while and knocked back a couple of jars. Harry had waited patiently for his old pal to come to the point. Patience was something he was good at. The pitch came at last when they were halfway down pint number three.

"I've got summat tha' might fancy Harry."

"Oh?"

"Aye. Discreet like. Hush, hush. But a good few quid in it."

Harry gave his nose a theatrical tap. "Tha knows me Gerald. I was born discreet."

"Aye. That's why I rang you."

"So. Come then. Spit it out. Is it kosher? I'm not up for owt that's bent Gerald."

His pal looked aggrieved. "Bloody hell Harry. I wouldn't do that. Tha knows me better."

Harry nodded. "Aye. Course I do. Just checking, that's all. No offence intended."

"None taken." Gerald took a careful sip of beer and wiped the froth from his top lip. "Always keep a belting pint in here, Harry. OK. Here goes. It's about the Strike."

"The Strike?" This was a surprise.

"Aye. The Strike. There's a lot going on. More than anyone realises. The Government are playing for keeps tha'knows. Obviously there's all the police stuff. Orgreave and that. But there's loads of unofficial stuff as well. They seem to reckon that they've got the Nottinghamshire bit won. Now they want to start winning in Yorkshire."

Harry was leaning forward now. This was interesting. Really interesting. He had no love of the miners. Once upon a time, a long time before, a miner had broken his ankle on the football field and ended his Sunday morning routine. He had voted Tory for three elections and he had no love for Scargill and his commie pals. "Go on."

"They reckon it's time to start to eat away at King Arthur where it hurts most. Hit him in his own backyard. They need to find men who will break the strike and go back to work. In Yorkshire. In the heartland like."

Harry blew out his cheeks. "Bloody Hell Gerald, they're not asking much then are they. Christ Almighty, any lad as goes back to work will be like a leper in those little places."

"Quite right Harry. Quite right. That's why they're paying top dollar. Paying in used notes in brown envelopes."

"Go on then. How much?"

"Two hundred a day. Plus expenses. No strangers Harry. You'll get paid by me and me only. There's a grand bonus the day any man breaks the picket line and goes into work in any pit in South Yorkshire."

"Bloody hell Gerald."

"Aye. Too right. It's a gravy train. They've got an open cheque book on this one."

Harry got up and took the empties to the bar for refilling. When he sat back down he had given it a bit of thought. Enough thought. He raised his glass for his old mate to clink.

"You're on. I'm in. Tell me how it's done."

Gerald touched glass and grinned. Recruiting Harry to the cause was worth another £500 to him. "We do it just like when we were CID Harry. We follow the money."

And it really hadn't been all that difficult. Harry had spent a day or two snooping about the small towns draped in a cloth of despair and decay. He had gone into the branch of the Halifax in Haddington to draw a tenner. It was a Tuesday afternoon and the place was deserted. Nobody had anything to deposit and anything that was available to draw out had been drawn out months earlier. The branch was manned by one member of staff, a cheery middle-aged woman called Liz and Harry got chatting. Liz it turned out was the wife of a contractor who made his living on a combine harvester, cropping the local grain fields. After twenty minutes of polite chatter Harry decided to take the plunge. If she got all appalled and indignant there was nothing much to lose. The account he had drawn on for his ten pounds was in a false name. If she got uppity, he would just leave and get in his car and drive out of town. There were plenty more towns like Haddington to go at.

But Liz didn't get uppity. Anything but. Her husband's business was three years into a rocky patch and bankruptcy was looming. She gave him her home address and told him to call round later. When he had found the small cottage out in the countryside she had been waiting with her husband with the kettle on.

The deal was done easily enough. For brown paper envelopes filled with used notes, she was more than happy to bring copy statements home for Harry to photocopy and take away with him. It took her a week to do the lot and it took Harry a further week in his office to file them and read them. And during that week he took Trace and Trevor's statements and put them on his promising file. And when he revisited the paper on his promising file, Trace and Trevor moved all the way to the top.

Perfect. Lots of HP. Then, one by one they had fallen behind on the payments. Fallen to nothing. Christ they had sailed close to the wind. Not a chance in hell once the lads were called out. And then just one payment left. A payment getting smaller and smaller, but there all the same. A payment to a small travel agents in Sheffield. The next day £50 got him the details of the Caribbean Cruise and the staggering sum that would have to be paid by the end of November if the dream was to come true. And Harry started to sniff the scent of a £1000 bonus.

The next step was a print shop in Batley. He ordered letterheads for a double glazing company with an address on an industrial estate on the outskirts of Rotherham. A few days later Trev and Trace opened a letter from Rotherglass telling them that they were the lucky winners of a special customer draw. The prize was a night for two in a hotel in Sheffield including a meal in the restaurant and a complimentary bottle of wine. There were no obligations. No strings. They simply had to ring and leave a message on the answer phone and turn up on the right date, The vouchers were right there in the envelope. Neither Trev or Trace could find a catch no matter how many times they read the letter. She had been due in Sheffield anyway and so she had called into the hotel to ask if the vouchers were real. And they were. And what a place it was too. It had everything. A pool. A Sauna. The lot.

Harry had watched them load their luggage into the yellow mini and drive away on the appointed evening. He had broken in through the back door and placed listening devices in the kitchen and the front room. And over the next week he had listened in on the tragedy of the cruise. Every ounce of spitting hate that flew from Tracey's mouth was patiently recorded on tape. Every ounce of anguish in the voice of Trevor. The slamming of the bedroom door. The sound of sobbing coming from the couch in the living room. After a week of listening to it, Harry felt that he had his man.

Gerald was in full agreement when he listened to the tape. He said he would have to go away and discuss it. The next evening he introduced Harry to a dour-faced man called Bill who had an Essex accent and a truly dreadful toupee. Bill said he had listened to the tapes and he liked it. He said he wanted Harry to make contact. He told him what he had at his disposal to make the deal.

The knock at the door had come as a surprise to Trev and Trace. They had been sitting in the cold living room watching the TV in icy silence. Harry smiled at Trev when he opened the door.

"Hello Trevor. I'm Harry."

"I don't know you." Trevor's yes nervously flicked up and down the empty street. Orange light. Light rain. Nobody about. Dead. Just like always.

"We should have a talk Trevor. Maybe you could invite me in."

"Piss off." But Trace was there now. Wrapping her thick dressing gown tight to her chest. Peering over his shoulder. Spotting the discreetly flashed wad of twenty pound notes. Trev was about to be angry, but she didn't give him the chance.

"Aye. Come in. Here. Have a seat."

They shared the sofa. He took the armchair. The curtains were drawn. His mind couldn't help but think that they were on the very same sofa. The one where Trev spent the long cold lonely hours of his nights. The one where he cried softly, heard only by the tiny microphone under the coffee table.

Harry gave an easy bank manager sort of smile. "I won't beat about the bush. I know all about the cruise. And all the other problems. I am the man who can solve them for you. All of them. Tonight."

It didn't take him long. He would accompany Tracy to the travel agents and pay the balance owing on the cruise in full. He would give them a thousand pounds of spends to take with them. He would catch their mortgage payments up. He would come up with a deposit on a new home in Leeds. He would arrange everything. What Trevor had to do was very simple. He had to move away from Haddington. And he had to go back to work. Time off for the cruise wouldn't be a problem. But they would have to put it off until February. He would cover all the additional costs of postponing it. All Trev had to do was to turn in to work for all of November and December and January. And they could go on their cruise in February. And they could have their dream. And £1000 spends. And a new house in Leeds and a guaranteed price for selling the house in Haddington. And Trace put an eager hand high up on Trev's thigh and sent a clear message that here was his ticket back to her bed. Away from the couch. Away from the damp cold of the living room. Away from the soft tears of despair.

Haddington had never had a scab.

Not one. Not ever.

Trevor Beardsworth was to become the first.

Josh awoke from a doze and struggled for a moment to find his bearings. Time? Just past three in the morning. Place. A private room in a private hospital. All very nice. En-suite bathroom. Carpet on the floor. A large TV. Fresh flowers replaced every other day. But it was still a place of death. Next to him his father seemed almost transparently frail as he lay and stared up at the ceiling with watery eyes. The weight had fallen off until there was nothing left to lose. The doctors hadn't really expected him to see out the summer. The fact that he had made it through to watch the leaves being stripped from the branches of the tree outside the window was testimony to the old man's stubborn will.

But it was becoming very clear that the time was drawing near. The curtains were slowly closing. Maybe another day or two. Maybe even a week. No longer than that.

His father noticed that Josh had woken. He slowly rotated his head so that he could see him. He managed a trace of a smile.

"You should go home. Really."

Josh tried to maintain his cheerful mode. "Don't be so daft. Here is where it's at. There are three nurses who I am definitely going to get a phone number from. They don't quite agree just yet, but give it time. They'll come round. How are you feeling?"

"How am I feeling? I feel like a man who is going to die soon."

"Dad . . ."

"No. Please. Don't misunderstand me. That wasn't meant as a complaint. It was no more than a statement of fact. Nothing dramatic. Most of my affairs are in order. Of course they are. I have always been careful. You know that."

"I know that."

"So very careful. Always careful. Probably too careful. Maybe I missed things by being so careful. I worry that I was never the father I should have been. I tried you know. It was just that after your mother died, I was never properly alive myself. All I seemed to be able to do was to be careful."

Josh wanted to say something. Anything. He didn't like to hear his father like this. He wanted to say something, but nothing would come. Instead he listened.

"I don't know why it was that we never really talked. My fault of course. Not yours. I was always so unapproachable. I regret it so much now. But that is all part of the process of dying. The regrets about what might have been. It is time for me to try and make you understand me Josh. I have watched the way you have lived your life. I suppose you must have felt only disapproval. How wrong. How very wrong. I treasure your wilfulness. Every time you got in some trouble,

I thought to myself thank goodness my boy isn't being careful. You have the ability to live Josh. I never had that. I hope that you treasure it. Just live for the sake of living."

Josh was still mute. The words astonished him. His father clearly wasn't finished yet.

"That week in June. When I had the stroke. You remember? I saw you Josh. On the television. I saw you in the crowd at Orgreave. You were running. You looked so afraid. And they were chasing hard. The police with their shields and their dogs. I saw you."

"Good Lord."

"I never told you about the other side of the family did I Josh?"

Where was this going? "No."

"When your great grandfather left Poland for Britain in 1882 he left a brother behind. Lodz. They ran a dress shop. A very fine one by all accounts. My father visited them once. In 1927. I saw photographs. Then we lost touch. Then . . ."

He took time to suck in the pure oxygen that hissed up a plastic pipe and into the corner of his mouth.

"They were taken from their home in 1942. They were murdered at the camp at Sobibor. All of them. There are none left. No a single relative. It is as if they never existed at all. All that is left are the photographs that my father took when he visited. They are in the drawer. You can look at them if you like."

Josh pulled the drawer open and took out five photographs. They were brown with age. A family group. Like something out of a history book. Big black beards and hats. The little boys in shorts. The little girls in frocks. Thirteen people in the photographs. They all looked very serious. Their faces concentrated hard on the job of posing for the photographer. And only fifteen years later they had been taken. All of them. On a train in cattle trucks. Taken and murdered. All gone. All that was left was this faint little echo in the quiet of a room waiting for death.

His father had recovered enough strength to speak again. His voice was getting fainter with every sentence. "I show you these pictures for a reason Josh. You see, that day when I saw you on the television, I thought of my lost relatives for the first time in many years. I thought of them because it came to me that they too must have been herded up by policemen with sticks and dogs. And I cried when the thought came to my mind Josh. I cried. Not with grief. But with pride. Pride that my son was in that field and fighting the men with the sticks and dogs. Yes. Pride."

Tears were pouring down Josh's cheeks now. Never before had his father told him that he was proud of him. Never.

"Our people have played a shameful part in what is happening in Yorkshire Josh. I have heard them. The men with the money. The real money. They have paid that terrible woman for the work she is doing on their behalf. Millions and millions. Money that will never be traced. Money that is to be used to pay for whatever it takes for her to win. For them to win. One day it will be seen as a dark time in our history. We have given Thatcher the tools to do the job. The men I talk to say it is all for the best. The Unions need to be destroyed. To destroy the power of the unions, the Miners must be beaten first. Beaten and eradicated. Only then will the men I talk to be able to make their money. It is all they care about. Money. Money and more money. They will never have enough money. I was becoming troubled with shame about what was happening. And then there you were. My own son. Out there fighting for what is right. My own son. And I didn't feel ashamed any more. Just proud. Very proud."

He reached out a thin pale hand and Josh took it. "There are some books at home Josh. You will find them in my study. You must read them. Read about the Warsaw Uprising in 1943. Read about the prisoners' revolt at Treblinka. Sometimes there is no choice but to fight for what is right. I hope you continue with your fight Josh. Soon the time will come when the fight will become more serious. Read the books. Read about how our people once fought even though the odds were impossible. If you want to make this fight yours my son, then you have my blessing. I ask only one thing of you."

"Yes?"

"You must allow Williams to help you. He knows about these things. I have talked with him and he has promised that he will help. Will you give me this last request Josh?"

Josh's head was reeling. "Yes. Of course. If that is what you want."

His father's eyes closed but the smile stayed on his lips. A small nod showed that he had heard his son. Once again the silence of coming death fell across the room.

The death duly arrived a little after five o'clock as the cold wind whistled through the bare branches of the tree outside the window.

Ralph Baxter finished what was left of his tea and checked the clock. Ten to seven. He already had his coat on. They had started burning the coal that he and Lenny managed to pick from the old slagheaps and it gave off barely any heat. Outside the light was coming on fast and the sky was a vivid blue. He could see a film of frost on the roof of his shed. Winter was upon them. All over Yorkshire men drank their tea in coats and scarves in houses where heat was a two-hour luxury to be enjoyed once a day in the evening.

The house seemed eerily quiet. Frank and Sheila had moved into their own place in September. Lenny was away attending the funeral of Josh's father. His wife had left at six to make a start on the huge pan of soup that had become the main meal of the day for so many. He was alone with the ticking clock and the dull glow of the scavenged coal.

Five to seven. Time to go. He ran his days on a strict routine. Some had allowed themselves to fall into lethargy. Some stayed in their beds till one and two in the afternoon, emerging to eke out a tiny tobacco ration and watch daytime TV whilst wrapped in blankets. The days of the mass pickets had passed. There wasn't the money now. Hardly a man in Haddington had a car that was road worthy any more. Tax discs were out of date. Insurance policies hadn't been renewed. MOT's the same. The police knew this and they carried out random checks on all roads out of Yorkshire. Any fault was prosecuted. Bald tyres. Broken brake lights. Anything. And a week later the letters from the court would land on the mat along with all the other red bills.

The Union was feeling the pinch too. The Government's lawyers had been remorseless in their pursuit of Union funds. By the end of the summer they had sequestrated millions. There was hardly any money for anything. Sometimes an emissary from Sheffield would arrive with an envelope. Then Ralph and the other local leaders would hire a couple of mini buses and a few Haddington men would travel out to some picket line or another. But it was rare. In fact they hadn't travelled for over ten days.

The only picket line they now manned was their own. They had moved a small garden hut to the entrance to the lane that ran up to the silent mine. It wasn't a mass picket. It didn't need to be. There was no traffic to picket. They always made sure there were at least two lads on duty. They kept the brazier going and drank cups of tea brought out from the houses nearby. By mid-morning there would be more. Sometimes ten. Sometimes twenty. Men with nothing to do other than to warm their hands over the flames and talk away the slow hours of the day.

Ralph's morning routine started with a visit to the picket line at seven in the morning. Seven was when the morning shift had once started. Hundreds of men had made their way into the changing rooms. Some had driven. Some had cycled. Most had walked as not many lived more than half a mile from their place of work. 7.00 a.m. had been the Haddington rush hour. Now he walked streets that were empty. Curtains were drawn. Nobody had a reason to get up and face the cold.

He turned a corner and saw a thin plume of smoke from the brazier threading its way up into the blue of the sky. Two heavily muffled figures stood close by, their gloved hands hovering above the barrel for warmth. Another day in the great strike.

"Alright lads."

"Aye. You well Ralph?"

"You know. Middling. Still all quiet on the Western Front is it?" Every morning the same question.

"Aye. I expect her from number 82 will be out with the tea in a minute. Good old girl. You can set clock by her . . ."

The sentence was left hanging in the air. All three pickets turned their faces to the sound of engines. Several engines. Close and running fast.

"What the . . ."

There they were. A police van. Then a coach with the windows blacked out. Then another police van. Coming on fast. All three. And then the vehicles were upon them. And then they were past and speeding up the lane to the pit. And then they were gone and out of sight.

"Oh no. Please Christ no."

Ralph Baxter felt as if he had been felled with a blow from an iron bar. So many years and never a scab in Haddington. Not one. Until today. Until now. Until this very minute and he had been there to witness the unthinkable.

"Who Ralph?"

"I don't know. But I'll find out. Then God help the traitorous bastard."

Chief Superintendent Jim Harris took a moment before he swung open the door into the canteen area of the old army camp at Simmington. He ran his hands down the front of his uniform tunic and checked the tilt of his hat on an old mirror. Throughout his thirty-year career in uniform he had hated briefings. Briefings on policing an upcoming football match. Briefings on safety aspects at a music festival. Briefings on speeding clampdowns in residential areas. Briefings on the annual attack on Christmas drink driving. A bloody pain. Better to let the sergeants do the job quietly. No need to get all the lads in and have them stand about like lemons.

But this was different.

This was like a proper war.

Jim Harris had been in South Yorkshire for five months in command of two hundred officers of the Greater Manchester Police. They had volunteered. Every man Jack of them. It had been made very clear that were they to volunteer for special duties it would mean being away for months at a time and living in an old army camp. It had also been made clear that there would be plenty of action and that the overtime would be massive.

He could have had over three hundred and fifty if he had wanted. Lots of lads had wanted a piece of it. It had taken him a week of interviews to get the number whittled down to two hundred. He had chosen the young lads. Fit. No wives mostly. Lots of fire in their bellies. Up for a good bit of aggro.

The two hundred certainly hadn't been disappointed on that front. The Harris squad had carved out a formidable reputation in the heat of the summer. The senior officers in charge of police deployment got in the habit of using them for the real flashpoints. They built a rep for themselves. No way was their line about to be broken. If they were attacked, they attacked back. Harder. Shoulder to shoulder, batons crashing on shields. They liked to let the pickets know who they were. The strikers knew them as the Manky Bastards in honour of their Mancunian roots. They left out the second part of the name and adopted the first. They became the Mankies. When they jumped down from their caged vans to fall into the battle lines of Perspex they would belt out their song.

"Manky boys, we are here . . . whooaaaa
Manky boys, we are here . . . whooaaaa
Manky boys we are here, shag your women
and drink your beer . . .
Whooaaaaa!!"

The song let the pickets know. Try it and you'll pay. The Mankies didn't do restraint. They hit hard. They resolved situations. And Jim Harris became the man who got the call when there was going to be a big one.

He had got such a call just before lunchtime. And he had been told that this was about to be the biggest yet.

He marched through the double swinging doors and stood in front of his army of two hundred. They stood seven deep in ranks. Chests out. Shoulders back. Very rigid.

"All right boys. At ease."

A general shuffling.

"OK. Tomorrow morning we've got our biggest yet. We're all seen a fair bit of aggro over the last month or two, but tomorrow it's going to be a whole new ball game. Make no mistake lads, we're about to go to war."

He tapped his pointing stick in his palm and then turned to the large map mounted behind him on the wall.

"Haddington"

He waited for the word to sink in. Every one of them had been at the front for long enough to have heard the name.

"Haddington. Population, 4000. Pit running since 1912. Over one thousand employees. They've got the reputation of being the most loyal of the loyal. The pit has been open for 72 years and there has never been a scab in Haddington."

He turned away from the map and faced his army.

"Until this morning."

A few whistles.

"This morning a single employee was taken into work. He will be returning to work tomorrow. This morning they were caught with their pants down. Tomorrow they will be ready."

Again, he turned to the map and tapped at two small clusters of houses a mile or two away from Haddington.

"Neighbouring villages. Osthorpe. One pit. Three hundred and forty miners. Kindon. One pit. Five hundred miners. No scabs at either. It means that they will be ready to join the Haddington lads tomorrow. That means we could have close on two thousand. I repeat gentlemen. Two thousand. And there will just be us. Two hundred. Like I said. This is going to be the big one."

The shuffling was a little more nervous now. Ten to one was serious. They hadn't done ten to one before. Harris grinned.

"Gentlemen, I refer you to the six P's. 'Proper Planning Prevents Piss Poor Performance'. First thing we do is to even things up a bit. We saddle up and leave here at 0200. That puts us in Haddington for 0300. We seal the place. And I mean wrap the bastard in Clingfilm. We keep Osthorpe and Kindon out. One, two, three, four, five." His stick tapped the map. "Five roads in. Five road blocks. One van on each. Ten men. Nothing goes past. Not a postman. Not a priest. Not a pregnant woman. Nothing."

He stared out into the eager young faces and found the understanding he needed. A nod.

"The rest of us deploy at the pit lane. Usual drill. The bus will be coming through at seven. So they will be out by then. And we need to expect all of them. Upwards of a thousand even without Osthorpe and Kindon. And these lads will do just about anything to stop the bus getting in. So again. We're going to even things up a bit."

Interest now in the two hundred pair of eyes.

"We expect they will gather from six onwards. Maybe earlier. Everything will build up to seven when the coach comes. At seven they will come. They'll come at us with everything they've got. So tomorrow we're not going to wait. It's not going to be all that easy. There's bound to be a stack of reporters on site. Tele as well. The whole world knows what's going to happen. At 6.25 a.m. there will be bricks thrown at us. And bottles. Be ready. As soon as the bricks and bottles come we go in. And I mean go in. We go in harder than we've ever gone before. We're going to clear the whole area. By the time the coach arrives there isn't going to be a picket within a quarter of a mile of that pit lane. Am I understood?"

Nods. Smiles. Eager faces. They were going to grab the initiative. Harris nodded back.

"6.25. Wait for the bricks and the bottles. Then take them out."

Harry Grierson was waiting at the bar of a town centre pub in Batley when he saw his man come in. The place wasn't busy. Just a few doleful punters putting off going home to their wives. He had first met the man thirteen years earlier. Rodney Gregson had been arrested outside Leeds United's Elland Road stadium as he had chased a Manchester City fan with a bicycle chain. It had been the first offence of many and it had led to six months in borstal. It hadn't done any good. No amount of borstal or prison or fines or community service were ever about to deflect Rodney Gregson from his preferred journey through life. His likes, dislikes and needs were very simple. He loved Leeds United. He hated Pakis. He loved a ruck on a Saturday afternoon. He liked lines of speed and pints until he was sick. He took a shag when he could get one. His preferred look was a skinhead and Doc Martins, but he'd had to give that up in the late Seventies when he couldn't get into the match looking like that any more.

He was thirty now and he had learnt that it was better to look neutral in jeans and an anorak. He had become a man of substance with a job and a car and a long-term girlfriend. But he was still a headcase.

He joined Harry at the bar.

"Pint?"

A smirk. "This is all very nice Harry. Aye. I'll have a pint, if you're in the chair."

Harry bought the pints and they took a small table in the corner. Nobody took any notice of them. Neither was on their home patch. Gregson took a long pull of beer and lit up.

"So. I don't suppose you're about to invite me to your daughter's wedding Harry. Spit it out."

Harry took a less exaggerated drink. "Did you know I'm private now? Retired."

"No. Why should I?"

"No reason."

"So you take photos of lads doing other men's wives. So what."

"So I have something you might fancy."

"I doubt it."

"It pays a grand. Cash."

Gregson's eyes narrowed suspiciously. "I'm not a grass Harry."

Harry smiled. "I know that. Think I'm some kind of idiot? You still National Front are you?"

"Might be."

"Well I'll take that as a yes then."

"Take it however you like."

Harry leaned back against the cheap plastic of the bench seat. He hadn't expected this to be a cosy chat.

"OK. I won't piss about. Have you ever heard of Haddington?"

Gregson shrugged. "Near Sheffield isn't it? Mining town."

Harry nodded. "That's right. Big Scargill stronghold. Not your favourite guy I wouldn't have thought, King Arthur?"

"He's a piece of Commie shit."

"Precisely."

"So?" There was more interest in Gregson's voice now.

"They had a scab in Haddington this morning. Just one. First there has ever been. Nobody expected it. Tomorrow it will be different. Tomorrow there's going to be a war down there."

Gregson chuckled. "King Arthur won't like that. Right in his back yard. What's it got to do with me?"

"The scab will arrive on a bus at seven. That is when everyone will be geared up for the action. There are those who want me to arrange something a bit earlier. It will have to look good. There's bound to be reporters and tele there. You get down there with a couple of your mates. I'll pay them £200 each."

He reached into his pocket and pulled out a wad of notes.

"At 6.25, and I mean exactly 6.25, you chuck some bricks and bottles at the police. They'll be waiting for it. Then you run because all hell will break loose. Come back in here tomorrow night and I pay you a grand. Simple. All I need to hear is that bricks and bottles get chucked at exactly 6.25."

Gregson's face was one big grin. Just like Harry had known it would be. He passed the wad of notes.

"Consider it done."

He buried the last of his pint and left. Harry took his time with his. Nice work when you could get it. Another £2000 in the coffers. He hoped the strike would last until 1990.

Lenny and Josh arrived in Haddington just after eleven. Ralph had broken the news of the scab when his son had rung home from the funeral reception. There had been no doubt that he would come straight back. A scab in Haddington. The unthinkable. The unbelievable. Josh had insisted on driving him. Why not? There was nothing to keep him any more. Not now that his dad was under the ground. All the way back up the M1 he had wondered whether he should tell Lenny about that last conversation. In the end he had decided to keep it to himself.

The club was bursting at the seams. Everyone was in. And of course there was only one topic of conversation. They knew who it was by now. It hadn't taken long. By two o'clock that afternoon every window of Trevor Beardsworth's house had been put through. The single word 'Scab' was daubed over his front door and garage. Dog dirt had been pushed through the letter box. And the neighbours had said that Trevor and Tracey had left in a taxi two days earlier. With bags.

By the evening it was generally agreed that it was that Tracey who was to blame. She was an outsider. And a greedy bitch. Always boasting on about what they had just bought for the house. And then it had been that Caribbean Cruise. Never shut up about it she hadn't. Jumped up little tart. That was what it was all about. The first scab Haddington had ever seen and it was all down to a cruise for a little cow from Bury. And if that Tracey Beardsworth ever showed her face in Haddington ever again . . .

But they knew that she wouldn't. Not a chance. Not ever. They had taken the money and they would be well away by now. There was only one thing that anyone could do about it. Stop the bus. Stop the bus, no matter what it took. The next morning was going to go down in the annals. It didn't matter how many coppers they sent. It didn't matter if they sent thousands. That bus wasn't getting through. The word had come through from Osthorpe and Kindon. The word had come down from all over Yorkshire. There would be thousands of lads out for the morning. And the bus wasn't getting through.

The word spread round in the early hours. Roadblocks. Every road in. Cops out already at the pit lane. It was a night when nobody slept much. Men gathered in small groups and made their way to the pit lane to take a look. By three the police lines were in place. Not that many though. Maybe a hundred and fifty. Well that was fine. Even if the lads from Osthorpe and Kindon couldn't get through they would still have over a thousand out. No way was that bus getting through.

By six, the pickets were already out. Not just the men from the pit. Their wives too. And those who had retired years earlier. And children. More or less the whole of the town. A great angry crowd in the starlight of a cold winter night slowly giving in to the dawn.

Frank went all the way forward to join his dad at the front of the crowd. Ralph was doing his best to maintain some kind of control. He had pulled a metal chair out from the garden shed that had provided shelter for those on duty at the quietest picket line in Yorkshire. Quiet until Trevor Beardswood had changed Haddington forever. Now he stood on the chair and tried to make himself heard over the chanting of the crowd. He had a loud speaker but his words were lost on a tide of angry voices.

"Here we go . . . Here we go . . . Here we go . . ."

Hardly any gap between the two sides. Just a few yards and the gap getting smaller all the time. The police were a solid wall of plastic. Dark helmeted figures in the gloom of the winter dawn. Slamming their shields. Practiced. Orchestrated. Meeting the chants of the miners with their own. Chants stolen and refined from football stadiums they had policed for years.

" . . . Everywhere we go – oh!
People wanna know – oh.
We are the Mankies
Mankie aggro – oh
If you don't believe us
Come and have a go – oh!"

Crash. The thunderous sound of wood on plastic sent a cluster of crows flapping up into the steel grey sky. Everyone knew it would be soon. Just over half an hour. All part of the ritual. Nearly two thousand waiting for the sight of a fortified bus carrying just one: Trevor Beardsworth. The scab. The traitor. Then it would be down to bricks and fists and helmets and shields.

Lenny and Josh hung back. They took up a position on a small pile of old rubble at the edge of the mob. It was getting beyond ugly. Both sides were stretched tighter than tight. Suddenly there was a movement to their left. A bottle flew high towards the police. Then a brick. Then another. Lenny was close by. Close enough to see a face he had never seen before. A very, very hard face. And a malicious grin. Who the . . .

The thought was still born in his brain. Killed dead in its tracks. Killed by the sudden battle howl from the police lines. Holy Christ. The reaction was instant. One moment and they were walled in behind their shields. The next second they simply exploded. Charged.

His elevated position gave him a grandstand view. With a gnawing horror he saw his father thrown from his chair as a burly young policeman took him in the midriff with his shoulder. Then he disappeared from view in the mayhem. For a second Lenny remained rooted to the ground. Long enough to see the three strangers dart through a gap in a fence and away. Who?

No time to think about it. He leapt down and pounded forward. The crowd had become liquid now. All running. Men and women and children. Screams. Swearing. The sound of wood on flesh. Wood on bone. Snapping dogs. Utter confusion. The crowd was running wherever there was a space to run into. And there seemed to be policemen everywhere. Hammering. Screaming. Baying. Hyped.

Lenny took a couple of glancing blows but the fact that he was running forward whilst so many others were fleeing gave him an edge. He covered the fifty yards to where he had seen his father fall in seconds. There was just one copper now. Kicking the prone figure on the ground.

"Have a bit! Have a bit! . . ."

Lenny took him by the shoulder and dragged him off. He gasped at the sight of his dad's face. Just a mask of blood. Barely human. He was about to reach down to him when he took a hard blow to the shoulder. He turned and ducked the next strike and leapt head down into the advancing policeman. His head plunged and drove out the man's wind. The man seemed to teeter for a moment. Then he fell as his legs went to rubber. Others had seen it and were turning. Two of them. Three of them. Raising their batons. Ready to dish it out. Coming in . . .

"For Christ's sake, it's his father. Do something man."

Josh's voice. Unexpected. Josh right up close to Harris. Pointing at the wrecked figure of Ralph Baxter. Demanding responsibility. A voice from somewhere else. Harris hesitated for a moment. Who the hell? Reporter? Some Trotsky type? No way of telling. Best to play safe.

"All right lads. Leave it. Carry on. Clear the area."

The four had formed a semi-circle around Lenny. They were itching to take him down. They were on the very edge of being completely out of control. Harris sensed it.

"GO!!"

Another beat. Another pause. Then they turned and charged off towards the retreating mob. Lenny fell to his knees and gingerly cradled his dad's head. The blood was pouring out of a gaping tear above his eye. He was out. Clean out. Harris stood over them and looked down.

"Best get him out of here. Johnson. Go with them. Is it far?"

Josh was breathing so hard he was on the verge of hyperventilating. he wanted to scream at the man. He wanted to rip his eyes out. Instead he managed to find a dull voice.

"No. Not far. Just a few streets away. Come on Lenny."

They got Ralph to his feet. Like a lump of meat. Not a flicker of life in him. They managed to half carry him with the nervous constable at their side. The ground was a litter of injuries. Men, women and children. All bleeding. Crying. Unable to comprehend what had just happened. Unable to believe that it had happened where they lived. In Haddington. In Yorkshire. In England. Not on the tele. Not in South Africa or Latin America. Right here. In the streets where they did their shopping and walked their dogs and stopped to talk about the weather.

It took Josh and Lenny a long time to cover the ground back to the house. As they turned the last corner, the coach carrying Trevor Beardsworth into the mine sped by them. It cruised past the smashed up wood of the old garden hut. Not a single picket was left to scream at the blacked-out windows. The Harris plan had worked to the last detail. By the time the coach bounced over the potholes of the pit lane the area had been cleared.

They got Ralph straight into Josh's car and an hour later he was rushed into theatre in the Sheffield infirmary. After two hours, a doctor told them that Ralph Baxter had a fractured skull. It would be a few days before anyone would know the full extent of the damage. He was out of immediate danger. Now it was a case of waiting. And hoping.

It was late by the time they made it back from the infirmary. The town was in a state of collective shock. All the confidence of the evening before was gone. All that was left was a growing sense of despair. Nobody in Haddington had been naive enough to think that the police would pussy foot around when they tried to stop Trevor Beardsworth. Obviously they hadn't. But they couldn't quite believe the way the police had attacked. Sixteen strikers had spent the day in hospital and it was rumoured that three of them wouldn't be coming home any time soon. The next day the coach would once again arrive at the pit lane. The next day the pickets would turn out to shout and scream. And the next day the convoy of police vans would trundle into the town. Nobody actually came out and said it, but everyone knew that the next day it would just be shouting and screaming. There would be no surge. Not when the price that would be extracted was so high. Harris's men had dished it out. Not many in Haddington had the stomach for more.

Lenny brought his mum and Frank up to speed with Ralph's condition and the family sat around the table in the kitchen and said little. Mrs Baxter went up for a night of no sleep just after midnight. Lenny and Frank and Josh sat. There wasn't anything to say and the quiet of the night ate into the room. It was Josh who broke the spell.

"My father had some things to say to me before he died."

Lenny looked up. "Yeah?"

Josh told them and concluded. "It seems like it might be the time to call Williams. Don't you think?"

Lenny had met Williams a time or two on his visits to Josh's house in Shropshire. He had found him to be a quiet man, but he had liked him well enough. The three of them had spent a night in the pub once. Lenny remembered a stillness that seemed to surround the Welshman. He had drunk a pint and a half of beer and eaten a bowl of soup. He had done the driving.

"Why Williams?"

Josh shrugged. "Because he was a soldier I suppose. I really don't know too much about it. It is ridiculous really. I've known him since I was seven and I really don't know him at all. He was forty when he came to work for us. That was in 1969. I know he had been a soldier since he left school. It was all he had done. Sometimes he lets a name out. Places from the old Empire mainly. Kenya. Malaya. Cyprus. I expect my dad knew more about it. I seem to remember that he took

Williams on as a favour to an old friend. Before he came my dad sat me down and said I should be nice to him. Said he'd had a bad time of it."

"Maybe he was in some kind of Special Unit." Mused Lenny.

Josh shrugged again. "So should I ring him?"

It was Frank who answered. "Aye. Ring him."

He had been very quiet all night. Now his voice was drained of all its usual life.

"You sure about this Frank? You're married remember. Young un on the way. Think about it. We're talking about crossing the line here."

Frank looked hard into his brother's eyes. "I've done enough thinking. Our Dad's fighting for his life tonight. Those bastards beat him like a dog. Thinking time's done Lenny. There's only you as should be thinking Josh. You sure this is a fight you want to pick?"

Josh nodded. "I'm sure."

"So make the call."

It was a call that came as no surprise to Williams. Old man Ogilvy had sat with him before he had died. He had said that young Josh might need his help up in Yorkshire and the Welshman had agreed to help out if he was asked. They all met up by the railway station in Leeds. Williams took in the story of the Mankies in silence and said he would have to go away for a few days. He said there was some stuff he would need to get. They went to the bank and Josh drew the cash he said that he would need.

He called in three days later and told them he had rented a cottage in the Derbyshire hills outside of Buxton. He asked them to drive down.

When they arrived he served up some soup and made tea whilst they brought him up to speed with how things had been in Haddington. The Mankies had fallen into a predictable routine. The first vans would arrive just after three to seal off the roads into the town. The main contingent would follow at five to set up their lines either side of the pit lane. There had been no violence after the first morning. On average, three or four hundred would turn out to scream at the bus. Neither side had left their lines. The men of Haddington had learned their lesson.

Williams nodded. "That's good. As I hoped. It makes sense to leave the same police unit on the job. They know the ground see. No point in someone else coming in and learning from scratch. Where do they park the vans?"

Lenny told him about the old compound at the side of the lane. And in a sudden flash he remembered the morning of his last day of school. A sunny morning when he had thrown stones at an old sign as the others had wound him up about sitting up on the stage next to Beverly Morton. Beverly. Where was she now? It had been years since he had seen her. A lifetime. The memory was an ache.

"OK then. Let's go."

"What. Now?"

"No time like the present is there."

They reached Haddington just after midnight. Williams had them drive him all around. They showed him which road the police vans arrived down. They showed him the compound and where the police lines would form the next morning. They showed him where the roadblocks would be set up a few hours later. After an hour he asked for them to drive out for a mile on the Kindon Rd. They pulled off the road into a long deserted pig farm.

"OK. What happens is this. We go back and you drop me and Lenny off. Then you come back here and wait. OK?"

"Fine, but why?" Asked Josh.

Williams smiled at him. "I only explain why when it is required. You'll get used to it. It's better that way. OK?"

They dropped the two men off on the edge of the town and returned to the piggery. When the taillights of the car had faded away, Williams gave his next instructions.

"OK Lenny. I want you to take us to the back of the compound you showed me. Where they park the vans. We'll go through the fields. OK?"

Lenny shrugged. It wasn't a problem. He had spent years in those very fields as a boy and he knew every inch. The night was very crisp and clear and the going was easy under the light of a fat moon. Their feet crunched on the frosted grass. When they were fifty yards short of the compound Williams stopped and squatted down for five minutes. Nothing. Just the twinkling of the street lamps the other side of the compound.

"OK. Let's go."

They moved up to the fence at the back of the compound and Williams took a small pair of wire cutters from the pocket of his old waxed jacket. He bent and cut the fence from the bottom and drew it open for Lenny.

"Through you go."

Once inside, he led the way to the remnants of an old workshop that had been demolished years earlier. He sat down in the shelter of a small wall and gestured for Lenny to do the same.

"OK. That's us. You'll be wondering what this is all about I expect."

Lenny smiled. "Just a little."

"Fair enough." He reached into his pocket again and pulled out a small metallic looking item. "Tracking device. When they arrive we get this onto one of the vehicles. Then you lead us over the fields to the old piggery. OK?"

"And then?"

"Then we wait for them to leave and we follow them. The first thing is to find their base."

"Where on earth did you get this from?"

Williams shrugged. "A friend from the old days."

"The old days?"

Lenny could sense the Welshman's smile in the darkness.

"Indeed. The old days."

Lenny was surprised at how undramatic it all was. The vans duly arrived a little after five and parked up in a neat line. One hundred and fifty officers. Ten vans. Two cars for the officers. Snatched conversations were of football and women and holidays as the policemen climbed out and stretched aching limbs. They were unhurried. Set into a well practiced routine. Williams waited for five minutes until the last of them had left the gate at the front of the compound and then he slithered forward on his stomach. He was back in less than a minute.

"OK. All done. We'll go shall we."

It took an hour to reach the car which was waiting at the appointed place. A further three hours later they followed the sound of a bleeping box up the A1 to the disused Army camp at Simmington.

Three days later Williams called and asked them to come to his cottage. Once again it was tea and soup. He said nothing until after the food had been eaten and cigarettes had been lit. Then he started to tell them how things were to be in a quiet voice.

"OK boys. Time for me to fill in a few of the gaps. Josh, you know that your father had a talk with me at the end."

Josh nodded. Part of him was still elated that his father had died feeling proud of him. Another part was growing scared by the terrible seriousness of the Welshman. This wasn't about to be any kind of game any more.

"What he told me, you will find interesting. Several of his friends were involved in providing the Government with funds to fight the strike. Discreet money. Untraceable. This is the money they have been using to fund all the unofficial actions. Your father was disgusted by them, but he played along. He even paid over some cash himself to make sure they put him on the inside. In the last weeks he learned that things on the Government side are not as strong as they like to pretend. The Cabinet is split right down the middle. All their projections were based on the strike being beaten by the autumn. Nobody considered that it could possibly last this long. They have all kinds of problems that they are not making public. There is the cost of course. Much longer, and there will have to be some pretty serious tax rises to pay for it all. Either that, or massive cost cutting. Either way, it could well kill off their chances in the next election. The coal stocks are hitting dangerously low levels. If the winter turns really cold, there could be power cuts soon after Christmas. There are all kinds of other issues as well. Crime is surging up all over the place. Not surprising really. The criminals are getting used to most of the police force being away in Yorkshire and Nottinghamshire. They've got a lid on it at the moment, but it will only be for so long. More than everything else, there are more and more in the Conservative Party who are becoming troubled at what they are doing. Thatcher likes to paint a picture of unity. It's not true. There are many who see what they are doing as morally indefensible. With me so far?"

Nods.

"Good. So you see, this whole thing has become a war of attrition. Both sides are running out of time and money. No different to any other war in that regard. A war comes down to two things. Resources and morale. Always the same. This is a war between the Miners and the Government. Over a hundred thousand strikers on one side, fifty thousand policemen and an unknown number of unofficials on the other. And we are four. So. What can we do?"

Shrugs. Williams smiled at their looks of incomprehension.

"We work on the morale. Here's how I see it. Haddington is special. All those years and never a single scab. It has the reputation as the heartland of fight. And now of course there is a scab. Only one, but one is vitally important. That is why the police were so brutal on the first day. Every time that bus is filmed going into the mine another blow is landed. But any day that the bus does not appear will have the opposite effect. Our job is to make this happen. We will re-kindle the Haddington legend. We will create a small beacon of hope. And if we do it well enough, we will give all the others enough hope to hang on that little bit longer. Enough time for the doubters in the Conservative Party to marshal their forces and end this thing. This is done in most wars. Most of the soldiers fight it out face to face on the front lines. But others go way back into the rear areas and try to wreak havoc. Disrupt supplies. Blow up communications lines. Attack command and control centres. Eat away at the morale of the men at the front. Take away their feeling of security."

"And you've done this kind of thing?" Asked Lenny.

Williams nodded. "Many years ago, but yes, I've done this kind of thing."

"So what's the plan then?" Asked Frank. He was leaning forward, completely hooked.

"We start in Simmington. A week from today. I have already spent some time there. I have a map of the lay out of the camp where they are billeted. We'll look at it in a minute. I have also spent time looking at the route they take when they go to Haddington. What we need now is a bit more knowledge about the village and the personalities. Your job Josh. You have five days then we make a start. OK with that?"

"I expect so. You'd best tell me what you expect."

Williams did so. All of it.

There was a cottage available for rent. In the summer it was let out a week at a time to families who would explore the coast and the Yorkshire Dales. There were seldom many takers in the winter and Josh got a special deal for a month's stay. He told the landlord that he was a writer working on the last few chapters. The landlord couldn't care less. A month's let at this time of year was a straight up and down bonus. Josh took an afternoon strolling about the small village until it felt familiar. Then he soaked in a bath and changed. At seven he strolled into the Green Man Hotel and ordered himself a gin and tonic. His accent attracted glances from a couple of the locals who were perched around the bar talking about farming and the weather. He met their hostility with an easy smile and took a seat in the corner of the room where he lit a cigarette and started to read the Times.

The first of the police came in just after eight. A group of five. Then another four. By nine the bar was full of Manchester voices. The beer was going down fast. Their entry was the cue for the few locals to leave looking resentful at the invasion of their space.

Josh took his time and watched. After half an hour he selected a group of five younger officers who were hammering through their pints in double quick time. He took a slow pull of air and got to his feet. For a moment his legs felt wobbly and he took a moment to calm his nerves. Come on Josh. Just a stage. Nothing else. Another part in another play. Just think of the lines. Just a play.

"Evening boys."

Looks without warmth. Faces reddened with beer. Auto-pilot hostility at the accent. None of them was about to answer his greeting. He fixed a smile and bashed on.

"So how was sunny Haddington this morning? Any action?"

He pulled up a stool and sat with them.

"What do you know about Haddington?"

Josh's smile widened a little. He gave the side of his head a gentle tap. "Oh you know. This and that."

"You a reporter?"

This made him laugh. "Good God, no. Is that what I look like. Come on lads."

He was so relaxed that they were intrigued. "So. Who are you then?"

Josh gave the question careful thought. A decent swig at the gin. Then the smile again. "Not all that easy to say really. Tell you what. How about if I just say cloak and dagger. Mmm? You lads wear a uniform, I don't. You lads hold the line, I knock about a bit on the other side. Get the picture?"

One of them found the idea hugely funny. "Aye. bloody right. With a toffee-nosed voice like that. Pull the other one sunshine. It's got bells on it."

The others were happy to join in with the mocking laughter until Josh talked to them in a different voice.

"Tha dun't want to judge a book by cover lads. I'd a'thought tha'd have known better like." Pure South Yorkshire. Not a trace of Kensington and Harrow. They were impressed.

"Bloody hell. That's not bad."

"There's plenty more where that came from lads. It's kind of a tool of the trade if you like." This time the voice was straight out of the mean estates of West Belfast. It put the hook all the way into them. Five minutes later he got his round in and for the next two hours he entertained them with fairy tales. The beer flowed and they wanted to keep up with his stories. They told him all about their part in the war. About the camp. About Haddington. About the first morning when they had let the bastards have it. About everything. And just after twelve he told them he would probably see them tomorrow night. They asked him where he was going the next day. He just smiled. He just gave his nose a gentle tap.

It only took him a few days to learn what he needed. Saturday night was the big one. No need to keep an eye on the ale on a Saturday night. There was no bus on a Sunday morning. Sunday morning they could lie in their beds as long as they liked. Saturday night was a coach into Leeds or York. They said that Josh should come with them. Bloody magic it was. A shag was more or less guaranteed. Nothing like a big fat wedge of cash in the pocket to guarantee that they all got their ends away. The older lads pissed off back to Manchester to see family. The younger ones preferred to stay and hit the clubs. Why go back home? Better here. Bloody magic. And it became completely clear that on a Saturday night there wasn't a soul to be found in the old camp at Simmington.

The night that the four of them started their own little war was dark and wet. Adismal wind blew over the flat fields. The camp was wrapped in darkness as they approached. Williams had been insistent that they took no chances. They wore black and their faces were rubbed with dark soil. He moved them forward a hundred yards at a time and then they would crouch and pause and listen. More silence. Then another hundred yards. Until they reached the thirty-year-old fence and wriggled through a gap that Williams had found three nights earlier.

Once inside they split into two groups. Williams and Frank headed to the main barracks. The door was locked, but it took the Welshman less than a minute to open it up. Another long wait. Nothing but silence. They moved swiftly. First the office area. Three telephones. Five desks with old metal chairs. Four filing cabinets. A radio base station. Williams took it all in with a few sweeps of his torch. High on the wall was an old ventilation grille. The screws were locked in place by thirty years of rust and it took Frank five minutes to prize it loose. Once the grille was lifted clear, Williams stood on one of the metal chairs and fitted a listening device as Frank found a small brush and swept the flaked chips of rust onto a sheet of paper and into his pocket. Ten minutes later they had fitted a second device in under the overhead light fitting in the small room that Harris had commandeered as his office. Before leaving the block Williams checked that they had left no trace. They hadn't.

Next they picked the lock to the small brick out building that housed the junction box for the electricity supply to the camp. This time the work took Williams ten minutes. Once the padlock was replaced they moved through the darkness and found Josh and Lenny where they were crouched by the eighth in a line of ten police vans.

"OK?" Asked Williams.

"Aye. Just two to do after this one."

"We'll get those."

Williams had noted down the make and year of the vans as he had watched them leaving and arriving at the camp over the previous few days. Lenny had toured a variety of motor factors in Leeds and gathered up a collection of spare keys for the diesel caps. Once they had the tank opened up they used a plastic jug to pour in a bag of sugar. By the time they had sorted out the last van they had been in the camp for just under forty minutes.

When the first of the Mankies started to return in dribs and drabs from their Saturday night revelling, Williams, Lenny and Frank were more than half way back to the cottage in Derbyshire. Josh was spark out asleep in his own cottage in Simmington.

Sunday was a lazy day for all concerned. There were lie-ins and sore heads in the camp. Lenny and Frank returned to Haddington via the hospital in Sheffield where their father had still not regained consciousness. Josh rose late and soaked most of the afternoon in the bath with a Thomas Hardy novel. Williams prepared his kit and left Derbyshire as dusk thickened over the dark hills. He parked up four miles from the camp and hiked over the quiet fields to a cluster of hawthorn bushes four hundred yards to the west of the barracks. He had cut out a hollow in the centre of the thickest bush the week before. Now he wriggled his way in and laid out his kit before climbing into his sleeping bag and dozing until his alarm woke him a little after two.

One by one he watched the lights coming on in the windows. By two-thirty the first figures emerged and made their way over to the line of vans. This was the first wave, the roadblock teams. It was too far for him to hear anything. He saw men trotting back from the vans to the barracks. Then more men. And then more. Until over a hundred were grouped in clusters around the vehicles. He put on his headphones and listened in on the boiling anger of Harris's voice.

" . . . What do you mean they're knackered!"

"I don't know sir. They just won't start. None of them. They all seem to have seized up."

"Seized up! For Christ's sake. Ten bastard vans don't just seize up. Find out what the hell is going on. Now!"

"But sir, there won't be anyone in the garage yet . . ."

"THEN RING THE AA!!"

The yellow van arrived forty minutes later. More conversation.

" . . . it looks like sugar." A Yorkshire voice with barely hidden amusement.

"What do you mean it looks like sugar."

"Sugar in the diesel. Mix the two and you seize up the engine. I think you might have been sabotaged."

"Oh for Christ's sake. How long to get them going."

Williams could picture the mechanic's shrug. "How long will it take you to get ten new engines."

"You ARE kidding I hope."

"Nope. Those engines are stuffed. Kapput. Totalled."

More conversation. Lots of swearing. Lots of calls. No police presence for Haddington. No, not a chance. By the mid-morning it was clear that replacement vans were going to be a problem. A big problem. Every van was being used. They would have to wait for new engines. No way around it. It would be at least two days. Maybe even three.

Williams smiled to himself. Round one in the bag.

Lenny made his calls just after nine that morning. The word had whistled around Haddington that the police hadn't arrived. The turnout at the picket line had been easily over a thousand. And for the first time the lads for Osthorpe and Kindon had been there as well. Seven o'clock had come and gone. No coach. No coppers. No scab. It was the best day in ages. Lenny called three newspapers and by noon the story was all over the wires. The picket line in Haddington had been re-established. No miner had gone into work. No police had arrived at the scene. A rumour spread that ten vans had been immobilised. The police met the rumours with tight-lipped lack of comment.

Williams listened in on the reaction. No way that a different force could be found for Haddington in the time available. Everything was stretched to the limit. They would have to leave things until the Mankies had their wheels again. Security around the camp would be put in place. Twenty-four hours a day. It would tie up twenty guys but that was how it would have to be.

Williams waited until the darkness was three hours old. Then he ghosted away from the bushes and walked back to the car. When he arrived back in Derbyshire he slept for ten hours straight.

For the next two mornings there were no policemen in Haddington. There was no scab in Haddington. And the word spread across South Yorkshire. Numbers were up on every picket line. At last there seemed to have been a little good news. And at three o clock on Wednesday afternoon Ralph Baxter woke up. He felt rougher than rough and his speech was slurred but he was still well enough able to smile at the news that there had been no coppers in Haddington for three days.

On Thursday the Mankies returned and they were ready for an all out scrap. They didn't get one. The pickets stayed well back and laughed at them. Every policeman was itching to charge in and smack a few heads but there were three TV crews there to cover the scene and Harris's instructions had been explicit. No aggro unless there was clear provocation. Not when the tele was there. The coach rolled past the screaming miners without incident and Trevor Beardsworth spent another day playing cards in the canteen.

At six o'clock that evening, Williams was listening to Harris making his report to his superiors. Yes, things were back to normal.

Yes, the coach got in and out no problem. No. No more problems at the camp. Yes. No problems for the next day. Yes . . .

Williams smiled to himself and detonated the tiny charge he had laid in the sub station a few nights earlier and put all the lights out. Now the voices in the darkness were once again furious. It took an hour for Harris to be properly briefed. Definitely some kind of explosion. The whole sub station was destroyed. It would be at least two days. And he heard the sound of Harris smashing a coffee mug against the wall. Lots of talk. No way they could go in the morning. All the heating was run on electric. No way of giving the lads anything to eat. The whole thing was knackered. Harris made his decision a little after nine. He ordered buses to take the men back to Manchester for the weekend. No choice. The contractors promised to have the power back up and running by Monday afternoon latest. Harris fixed for the coaches to collect at the station on Monday morning. He told his superiors that the charge must have been placed at the same time the sugar had been put in the engines. He told them there was nothing else he could do. He told them that the power was guaranteed for Monday afternoon. Yes, they would be back in Haddington for Tuesday morning.

The sound of the phone crashing back onto the cradle was enough to hurt William's ears.

The Mankies arrived back as planned on Tuesday morning. And Wednesday. But not Thursday. Thursday was the day of Josh's idea. Williams had noted that every morning the local milkman arrived at the camp to deliver two crates of silver top. He had jotted down the name of a local farmer who ran the round. He spotted that the camp was always the last drop and before making it the driver always stopped off for a bacon roll at a small cafe in a nearby town. Whilst he ate and read the morning paper, the milk float was parked in a small patch of waste ground. On Josh's Thursday, Williams crept up to the parked float while Lenny kept a watch. He had a syringe which he slipped through the caps of several milk bottles. He gave the plunger a slight push into each. It took just over thirty seconds to contaminate ten bottles with liquid LSD.

Williams listened in on the mayhem that lasted the whole night. The police returned from Haddington to cups of tea and a mince stew. The only ones who were not sent into ten hours of hallucination were the ones who took their hot drinks black. Harris had given up milk ten years earlier. It took him until after ten to work out what had sent over a hundred of his men into near psychosis. He made his report. There would be no police in Haddington the next morning. He didn't have all the facts yet. It looked like it was the milk. Samples had been sent for testing. It looked like some kind of drug. Yes, hallucinations. Yes, over a hundred. No, no idea how long it would last. His voice was Arctic.

Williams left him to it and faded into the night.

Round three.

That night Josh found the pub to be unusually quiet. The eight o'clock rush never happened. Out of the ten policemen who made it in, he had only ever spoken with two. The mood was subdued. Low.

"Bloody hell boys, you look down in the dumps. What's up?"

"Don't ask."

Josh smiled. "All right. I won't. Drinks?"

He tossed a twenty pound note onto the counter and the barman served up the round. The story came out slowly in bits and pieces. The three young constables who had joined him kept looking about nervously to make sure that they couldn't be overheard. Two of them took their coffee black. The third had never developed a taste for hot drinks and preferred coke. They said that things back at the barracks were an utter nightmare. They'd never seen anything like it. There were lads who were flipping out completely. It was like a madhouse. Some lads thought their arms had turned into snakes. Others thought they were on fire and stripped off all their clothes and were running about the place screaming blue bloody murder. There were lots of medics there now from the local hospital. Not the regular hospital. The sodding loony-bin.

The youngest of the three sucked at his cigarette and shook his head. "To be honest mate, it's getting pretty scary. I mean it could just have easily been poison couldn't it. I'm totally freaked out. Totally."

"So what are the brass doing about it?"

Three shrugs. "Who bloody knows. They've all got their tits stuck in the mangle haven't they. Harris is flipping his lid, I tell you. Some of the lads reckon that your lot will be brought in. Happen you'll get a call mate. I hope you do to be honest. I don't mind the aggro on the lines and all that. This is different. This is the sort of stuff that puts the shits up you."

Josh nodded and agreed. He bought a couple more rounds and then left and took the road south to the cottage in Derbyshire. It was well after midnight by the time he arrived to find the others in high spirits. Even Williams was all smiles.

"So. What are they saying?" Asked Lenny.

Josh tossed his coat down and took a cup of coffee. "They're worried. Really worried. There were only ten of them in. Apparently things are still pretty chaotic in the camp. Five have actually been put into straight jackets to calm them down. Sounds like there are some pretty heavy trips being had by all."

"How long will it last?" The duration of an LSD trip was something that was utterly alien to Williams.

Josh shrugged. "To be entirely honest, I haven't got a clue. The way they were talking I think I might have been a bit heavy on the dose. Liquid acid is supposed to be a very different animal from regular tabs. I doubt if any of them will be coming down any time soon. I can't imagine they'll be in any state to make it out in the morning."

"They're not. I heard Harris cancelling. He is one very unhappy individual by the way."

Josh grinned. "I gathered as much. The word from the lads is that they're about to call in the spooks."

Williams nodded. "Pretty obvious move. We've had an easy ride of it so far. Now things will start to get a little more interesting. This is where we all have to be very, very careful. If they catch us after tonight . . ."

He didn't finish the sentence. He didn't have to. Manchester's finest would be in no mood for any niceties if they got any of them in a cell. The stakes were going up very fast.

Latimer checked his watch and stepped up the pace of his walk slightly. He had five minutes still. Enough time. If he were a minute or two late then it really wouldn't matter very much. But he hated being late. Despised it. To the passers by on the quiet pavement in Knightsbridge he must have looked like any other city worker making his way to an appointment. Crombie coat. Bowler hat. Black umbrella. A man perfectly at home and at ease amidst the Bentleys and the three-storey town houses. He marched up the marble steps of the club a minute before the time of his appointment. The umbrella, coat and hat were taken by a uniformed attendant and he took the stairs two at a time. A door led into a smoking room that hadn't altered since electricity was introduced at the turn of the century. He paused for a moment to scan the room. It wasn't very busy. More than half of the deep leather armchairs were vacant. He spotted Reginald Tomlinson more or less straight away.

The last time they had met had been in Ireland two years earlier. Then it had been Brigadier Reginald Tomlinson of Military Intelligence. A uniform in a cramped office in Lisburn barracks and coffee in chipped mugs. Now Tomlinson was all Savile Row and cufflinks. Retirement was clearly treating him well. He was on his feet as soon as Latimer started towards him. The easy smile. A handshake that was as dry as sandpaper.

"Latimer. How good of you to come. You'll have a drink?"

"Whisky please. Straight up."

"Of course. Please. Sit down."

A uniformed attendant appeared out of nowhere and acknowledged that he had registered the order with a small nod. A couple of minutes later the drink duly arrived in chunky crystal. Tomlinson gently raised his own glass.

"Your very good health."

Latimer gave a small nod. He hated pleasantries. "So. I was under the impression that you had retired. I gather you didn't fancy the bungalow in Bournemouth much."

Tomlinson's smile was rigidly in place. "No. Not really. I fancied having a bit of a bash at private practice actually."

"Private practice."

"Yes. Freelance you know. All the rage these days old man. Big growth area since Margaret moved in to Number Ten."

"How very splendid." Latimer had little love for Thatcher's cowboys. It seemed as if they were everywhere. It was getting to the stage that there were as many bounty hunters as soldiers in Ireland. It made things confusing.

"I gather that you don't entirely approve."

Latimer shrugged. "I don't expect it matters a great deal what I think."

Still the smile. Annoying now. "Quite right. We never did like each other much did we?"

"No."

"So there seems little point in pursuing the pleasantries."

"I would prefer it that way. Why not get on with it?"

"We have a problem in Yorkshire."

"Who's we?"

"My clients. Margaret. Everyone."

"Go on."

Tomlinson ran through the problems that had beset Harris and his men. He reeled off statistics showing how numbers on picket lines all over Britain had started to swell. He gave an honest account of dwindling coal stocks. He said that there could well be power cuts before the spring. He explained that his clients were getting rather worried. They had come up with a lot of money and they had been assured of a result. And it wasn't pocket money either. It was serious money. Very serious money. Far too much money to lose. The problem was that there were growing numbers in the Cabinet who were getting cold feet. Not Margaret of course. Never Margaret. But even she could only hold the line for so long. The Haddington situation was becoming more than just an irritant. There were all kinds of rumours floating about. Word had leaked out that over a hundred policemen had been spiked with some kind of super strength LSD. It was eating away at morale. In fact it was beginning to put everything at risk.

Latimer listened with interest. Fascination in fact. Whoever was responsible was a class act. He found it hard not to smirk.

"How very unpleasant it must be for all of you. I can't quite see what it has to do with me. Maybe you might enlighten me?"

"Delighted. Another drink?"

"Yes. Thank you."

The waiter came and went. Tomlinson discreetly checked that he was well and truly out of earshot before continuing.

"Your team in Ulster. Headed up by that chap Hendrick. Something of a maverick if I remember correctly."

Latimer wasn't about to say anything. Tomlinson leaned forward and continued.

"I am rather confident that with a word here and there I can get things arranged for Hendrick and his team to be transferred to

Yorkshire. To the Haddington situation."

Latimer gave the expression of a man who had smelt something unpleasant. "You were always well connected."

"Quite."

"So. You can pull a few strings. Bully for you. Anything else?"

"Just this. My clients are keen to offer Hendrick and his team something by way of an extra incentive. If I remember rightly, all of your chaps are remunerated off the books, so to speak."

Once again Latimer wasn't about to help him. He stayed very still. Tomlinson was completely unconcerned.

"My clients would like to see the situation resolved conclusively. If this should be the case, I will organise a bonus of £100,000. I leave it up to you as to how the funds are distributed."

"Conclusively?"

"Yes. These people, whoever they are, might be seen as some kind of Robin Hood types. That won't do. Not at all. There is no point in apprehending them if they become some kind of working class heroes in the courtroom. I hope you understand."

"I understand. You don't want martyrs. You want bad guys."

Tomlinson beamed. "I knew that you would understand. May I assume that we have an arrangement."

"You may." Latimer didn't bother finishing his drink. He stood up quickly and left the room without a further word. Tomlinson watched him all the way out and sipped at his drink thoughtfully. A truly hateful man. But ever so good. He was perfectly happy that his clients would receive value for their money.

Beverly couldn't believe it. For the first time in eighteen months they had been given a fortnight off. Her ticket to Italy was paid for and her bags were packed. The phone rang ten minutes before she was due to leave her flat for the airport. She considered leaving the phone alone, but knew she that if it was Hendrick there would be no point. He would simply turn up at the airport and pull her off the plane.

"Hello."

"Sorry darling. Holidays are up the spout. We've a job on."

"Shit."

"Couldn't agree more. Get to the airport. Wellbank Hotel in Battersea. Tonight at seven. Latimer will be giving us a briefing."

"What. You mean something on the mainland?"

"Looks that way. No point worrying about it. We'll find out tonight."

"Yes. Of course."

She replaced the phone and sat very still. It was something that she had been dreading for several months. The mainland could only mean one thing. The strike. Yorkshire. Home. Ireland was bad enough at times. But at least there was some way she could make sense of the work she did. But now they were going to make her work against her own people. Maybe she was worrying unnecessarily. Maybe it was something else. But in her heart of hearts she knew it wouldn't be.

It was something of a rare event for the whole of the Hendrick team to meet up together. He wasn't much into team bonding. His people were in it for the money, full stop, period. If they didn't like it, or didn't think that they were being paid enough, they could bugger off. There were always plenty more to go at. As it happened, there were seldom any changes in personnel. The five members who currently made up the team had been together for the best part of two years. It was a pretty simple set up. Hendrick was in charge. Beverly was his main actress whilst the other three guys were basically techies. They could dish out a bit of stick if required, but their main role was bugging, tapping and keeping a watch. Most of the time if there was any rough stuff required Hendrick would pick up the phone to Latimer and guys would be arranged from the Army or some of the darker corners of the security forces. The Eighties had seen many off-the-books-type operators flourish, particularly in Ireland. It was never all that hard to hire in help for a bit of wet work.

Latimer himself was hardly a regular. They tended to see him once every couple of months or so. Most of the time they flew over to London. Every now and then he would make it to Ireland. The meetings were never very long and he never said a great deal. He left all the day-to-day stuff entirely to Hendrick. He did all his briefing and de-briefing with his man in charge on the ground. Beverly always guessed that the sole purpose of him meeting with them at all was to check that none of them were losing the plot. She had seen that losing the plot was getting pretty common in Ireland. It was a losing the plot kind of place. Ninety-nine percent of the time Guinness and blarney and one percent of the time ultimate savagery. It was the one percent that ate away at the sanity of those sent across the water to find answers to the seven-hundred-year-old Irish Problem, particularly in their line of work.

The Wellbank Hotel wasn't much of a place. The sign over the door had two rather faded stars but Beverly doubted if that assessment had been carried out any time recently. The lobby smelt of food fried in the cheapest oil on the market and re-used twenty-seven times. Behind the counter a very large Middle Eastern looking man who smelt like he hadn't showered since the last oil change. He barely looked up from his copy of the Evening Standard.

"Room 21."

The lift was bust. Two flights of stairs with frayed carpet. Half way up she passed a girl who looked barely more than fourteen. Chalk white stick legs and a mini skirt that barely covered her groin and hollowed out hungry eyes already eating the next hit of heroin.

She was the last to arrive. Room 21 was already a fog of smoke. Latimer had commandeered the single chair. Hendrick sat on the dressing table with a coffee cup full of vodka. The other three sat on the two single beds. All but Latimer were smoking.

"All right Bev." Hendrick's tone carried the merest trace of affection. The others just nodded. It amused Latimer. He had noticed some months earlier that Hendrick actually seemed to quite like the girl. Unbelievable. As a rule of thumb Hendrick never liked anyone. She took a seat at the end of one of the beds and didn't bother to take her coat off. It wasn't the kind of place where any great resources went into keeping the central heating up high.

Latimer didn't bother with any small talk.

"OK. A change of scenery for everyone. I'll start with the back story. You'll find it entertaining. Haddington, South Yorkshire. A small place with a very big coal mine. Beverly here knows it well. She grew up there."

She kept her face blank but she felt as if he had kicked her in the stomach. His dead eyes held her for a second or two and then he went on. He took well over an hour with the back story. He had mugged up well. He painted the picture of the town with the legend of no scabs ever. He explained how the men of Haddington had been in the front rank of every picket line battle of the ten months of the strike. Then he gave some details about the wooing and recruitment of Trevor

Beardsworth. It had been a pretty good piece of work, mostly done by a freelancer from Leeds. He ran through the 'hit them as hard as possible as early as possible'tactics adopted by Commander Harris on the second day that Beardsworth returned to work. Finally he told them about the series of calamities that had beset Harris and his fellow Mankies at their camp in Simmington. Each of the operations against the police was met with appreciative smiles from Hendrick and the guys. Only Beverly sat as expressionless as a marble statue. Latimer came to the wrap up.

"OK. So here is where we come in. We have semi-official sanction but basically we are pretty well off the books. I was approached from the Private Sector. There are a lot of rich people who have invested heavily on getting a result against Scargill. We're not talking peanuts here. We're talking millions, tens of. The word is that it's mainly Jewish money, not that it matters a whole lot. They are worried that if this Haddington fiasco continues much longer, the strike will get a big morale boost. The bottom line is that if they can keep going strong until the early spring they'll probably win. Right now there are not many who know just how weak the Government position is becoming. The Cabinet is all broken up. Even Thatcher is starting to twitch. So they want us to clean up. They've put up a hundred thousand for a conclusive outcome to the Haddington situation."

"So what's conclusive?" Asked Hendrick.

"Find who's doing it. Stop them. Make sure they're completely discredited. People are worried about martyrs."

"And the divvy?"

"Twenty thousand for you and I. Fifteen each for the team."

Hendrick shrugged and poured another drink. His body language said fair enough. "So who is in the frame?"

"Nobody has a clue. There are plenty who seem to fancy it's the Soviets, but I don't think so."

"Why not?" Beverly this time. Her voice very crisp.

"It's just not their style somehow. The main motive seems to be to humiliate. It's almost a piss taking exercise. There seems to be something very British about it. All I have to back that up is gut feeling. I just don't think the Sovs are in this. I don't think Scargill and his gang are either. Everything they have done so far has been as subtle as a turd in a perfume shop. No. My instincts tell me whoever is doing this are freelancers. Not many either. A small team with know how. They probably put some kind of tracking device on a van to find the camp. Then we have the disabled vans. A neat explosives job on the power supply. And then the liquid acid . . ."

Latimer actually smiled. It wasn't something he did very often. But every time he thought about the liquid acid he felt in the mood to smile. It was just so beautiful. Liquid acid in the milk. He loved it.

"We start with the basics. The Haddington connection may be an accident. If someone wanted a focal point for a counter offensive, then Haddington would make a pretty good choice. My judgement is that there is almost certainly some kind of connection to the town. Then we have the timing. Harris and his boys go in like a South American riot squad and all this starts up a few days later. Maybe co-incidence. Probably not. Think Ireland. Stuff like this is generally rooted in some kind of revenge. So here's how we do it. We have two start points. Haddington and Simmington. Beverly, you can't be seen anywhere near Haddington. You'd stick out like a sore thumb. I want you to take a look around in Simmington. The rest of you take Haddington. In two days time there will be a fire in the local council office. It will be electrical and it will gut at least three rooms. You will be the contractors with the job of fixing the place back up. That gets you in. You'll all stay in a B&B on the edge of the town. So that's your cover. The rest is down to yourselves. Expect a closed shop. These people are as tight knit as any Republican Estate in the Province. That's all of it. I want a result before Christmas. OK?"

Four nods. Nothing from Beverly.

"A problem Beverly?"

She had allowed her attention to wander. "No problem."

"I trust that you will let me know if there is."

"Of course."

"That's it then. Expenses are wide open. These are the kind of places where a few drinks can buy a breakthrough. Splash the cash all you like. Just don't be obvious."

"We're not dickheads." Hendrick was annoyed at the obvious being stated.

In the end it took the Mankies three days to recover from the acid attack. Twenty of them had to be sent home for psychiatric help.

Twenty had to stay back to guard the camp. Once the roadblocks were put in place, Harris was left with less than a hundred to man the lines. They were a pretty shaky hundred. The sight of their mates getting their brains cooked had taken a heavy toll. None of them were in the mood to bang their shields on the first morning back. Thankfully the pickets held back and settled for shouting. The mood was different. Instead of anger and half-bricks it was laughter and mockery that was thrown at his men. Every day they hadn't shown up had made them weaker. Every day the coach was stopped before it left Leeds was a defeat. It meant that the days when Beardsworth was successfully escorted into the mine counted for little. The crowd was happy to wait for the next disaster to hit the police.

Harris knew he had been put on the back foot and he hated it. The calls he had been receiving from his superiors were far from friendly. The pressure was being put on all the way down the line. The word was that London was livid. Harris was expected to make it stop and stop immediately.

It was a huge relief to get the lads back into the vans and back on the road as the coach took Beardsworth away from the mine and back to his place of hiding. It was an even bigger relief to get back to the camp to find all the lights working and the evening meal well under way. No unusual activity was reported. Thank Christ. A regulation day. Maybe the next day would be the same.

He tried to get an early night, but sleep was becoming elusive. He couldn't settle. His brain was permanently in overdrive. Waiting for something to happen. But what? From where? He knew that he was becoming paranoid and it annoyed him into full wakefulness. The bedside clock said twenty past one.

Shit.

Sleep wasn't even close and he was due up in under two hours. He gave up on the idea and got up and dressed. He took a cup of coffee outside and spent some time walking the perimeter, chatting with lads on guard duty, staring out into the inky blackness of the night. What was coming next?

At three he watched the first two vans depart with the roadblock teams. The main force now only needed six vans instead of eight. There was little banter as the lads climbed aboard. Morale was down low and there wasn't much he could do about it. Just a couple of weeks earlier his boys had joked about how brilliant it would be if the strike lasted another five years. Now they were ready for home. Two lousy weeks and so much had gone to rack and ruin. Christ but he was knackered and it was still only Wednesday. Another three days after this one before the relief of Sunday. Maybe he would find a game of golf somewhere. If only they could have three days without incident. That at least would be something.

He climbed into the passenger seat of his car and his driver watched in the mirror as the six vans lined up behind them. The gates swung open and they started out on the journey south to Haddington. It had been drizzling all night and now the rain was thickening up. His eyes were drawn to the steady motion of the wipers and they started to feel heavy. A nap was a good idea. Just half an hour or so. Enough to recharge the batteries up to about 20%. They were into a wooded area now. The road snaked through a dark wall of trees, a tunnel lit by the full beam of the headlights. Going from clear to blurred as the wipers swept the screen.

Sleep was all but on him when it was driven back as his driver slammed his feet down onto brake and clutch and drew the car to a skidding halt.

"Oh for Christ's sake."

In front, the narrow road was blocked by the trunks of three fallen trees. Harris jumped from the car to take a closer look. Behind the lead car the six vans jammed on their brakes and came to a halt in a close-packed convoy. Harris was about to go up to the fallen wood when he was startled by a sharp crack that snapped through the night air. Then another. Then two more. Instinctively he ducked down for cover behind the bonnet. Gunshots? Surely not gunshots. Then came the sound of something very, very heavy crashing down onto the road a few yards back from the last van. A wooden kind of heavy. A tree kind of heavy. Then there was another. And one more. His heart sank all the way down into his highly polished shoes.

Shit. Shit. Shit.

He walked back but he knew full well what he was going to find. Three more trees. Big trees. The road behind completely blocked. The road ahead completely blocked. Every bastarding direction completely blocked. No Haddington for them this morning. And the next time they went down the laughter and the mockery would be even worse.

Shit. Shit. Shit.

Two hundred yards into the darkness Williams once again smiled to himself.

Round four.

Beverly stared hard into her own face in the bathroom mirror. Christ she looked awful. Her skin was very pale and stretched tight across the bones. She was aware that such a bleached-out emaciated look was probably the very height of fashion. Appearance wasn't something that had been of any particular concern since she had crossed that small patch of miserable grey water to join the Hendrick team. In fact she took care to grey herself down. Most of her life was lived in a man's world and even a washed-out and grey Beverly had to deal with more-or-less non-stop harassment. She kept her hair short and deliberately left it unwashed and greasy. A pair of plain-lens glasses gave her a schoolmaam look to go along with dowdy clothes. Only when they played out their little dramas did the hair get a wash and blow dry. Only when she was due on the seedy stage did she try to look herself.

Right now she should have been in some tiny restaurant in Tuscany with a bottle and a book and the sound of crickets outside. Instead it was the en-suite bathroom in Simmington's solitary hotel. Through the open door she could hear Hendrick impatiently turning the pages of a newspaper while the TV droned away. She stepped back and took another look. It had been a long time since she had worn so much make up. Camouflage more like. Not bad. She decided she looked reasonably OK. A yellow striped shirt hung nicely from her shoulders, worn loose over a pair of jeans. Not too casual, not too formal. Not bad. Cool. Professional.

She put the items of her make-up away and clicked off the light. Hendrick tossed the paper and looked her up and down disapprovingly.

"What the hell are you supposed to look like?"

She gave a controlled smile. At times she could bury an axe deep into the top of his balding head.

"This, Hendrick, is how the professional woman of the mid-Eighties looks. Cool. Smart. In control."

"Well it's no use. Get changed. Show your tits for Christ's sake."

Beverly crossed over to the dressing table and took a cigarette from an open packet. "You know what Hendrick, it pains me to say this, but you are very good at what you do."

·Her words made him pull a face like a man inspecting a blocked drain. Hendrick didn't do compliments. She gave him a sweet smile and went on.

"At times this is rather surprising considering your relentless Neanderthal approach to life. Believe it or not, not every man is driven by your permanent desire to ogle the female form in general and the sexual organs in particular. Let me be very clear here. I am the young woman and you are the middle-aged semi-alcoholic man. When it comes to knowing how to play the male sex there really is no contest. I am very confident that you have absolutely no first-hand experience about how to create mayhem in a young man's underpants so, with the very greatest of respect, why don't you get stuffed."

She had pulled on a linen jacket by now and was ready to make her exit. He shrugged and handed her some paperwork.

"Here you are. You're Samantha Tate. Journalist on the Guardian. Features. You were brought up in Hereford. Now you live on the Wirral. Your dad's a teacher. Your mum's a housewife. Make the rest up."

She took the identity and slipped it into her handbag.

"Fine. I'll see you later."

He was already flicking through the TV channels and grumbling that it was all a bag of shit. He didn't seem to notice her as she left the room. Outside the night was crisp and clear. Very starry. In the distance the low hills of the North Yorkshire Moors were backlit by a rising moon. The pub was no more than a hundred yards down the small High Street and she decided to take a detour. The cold air would sharpen her up. Give her some bite. A bit of edge.

It was too cold for there to be anyone much about. She nodded to a solitary dog-walking pensioner. The rest of the town was tucked away inside the small postcardy cottages with early evening TV. Fifty yards or so down the road, a door to one of the tiny cottages was opening. She was allowing herself to drift a little. Another life, another time, and she might have lived in a place like this. Maybe she could have been a solicitor or even a journalist. Maybe she might have been married by now. She might even have been a mother. The thought seemed inconceivable. Pushing a pram around streets where there had never been a bomb warning . . .

The dream snapped shut. Thirty-five yards ahead the figure who had emerged from the cottage had turned to lock the door. He was clearly lit by a small overhead light. She ducked into a gateway surrounded by a high hedge. The figure finished locking up and headed up the pavement across the road from where she stood at a brisk pace. He was wearing brogue shoes and the click of the leather on concrete was clear and loud in the cold night air. As he passed her line of vision he was going fast with both hands buried deep in the pockets of an overcoat with the collar turned up. Every inch was familiar enough for there to be no doubt. The mop of jet black hair, the over large nose. It was Josh Ogilvy and the sight of him slammed her heart into fifth gear.

Hendrick looked up sharply from a documentary about flamingos as she came back into the room.

"Forget something?"

"No."

"What you doing back here then?"

She stood by the dressing table and folded her arms, head down. She felt like a Judas. She hated every molecule in her body. She made her report.

"I know who it is."

Three days later Williams moved silently through the buildings of NCB Haddington Main. The place felt as if it had been deserted for ten years rather than ten months. It was the third time that he had moved through the darkness to take up a position thirty yards from where the bus was parked up having delivered Trevor Beardsworth to another day of cards and magazines.

After the tree felling operation they had all decided that it would be prudent to leave Simmington alone for a while. Josh had reported that the place was beginning to feel as if it were under siege. The small town was filled with strangers and everything in and out of the old army camp was being checked three times over. It was all no more than Williams had expected. In fact he told the others that the Operation Felled Tree had been something of a bonus as far as he was concerned. News from the coalfields all over Britain where the pits were closed down had been encouraging. The word of what had happened in Haddington had drifted out. Nothing was confirmed, but a small legend was gathering pace. Whatever had been done and whoever had done it was making a difference. For the very first time, the police and the security forces didn't seem to be so indestructible after all. Every time the bus failed to arrive to carry the scab up the pit lane over a hundred thousand men took a little heart.

They had decided in the Derbyshire kitchen that it was time for phase two of their operation. The bus. The bus would lead to wherever they were keeping Trevor Beardsworth hidden. Once they discovered that, they could open up a second front.

For two nights the first real cold snap of the winter had laid bright moonlit skies over Haddington. When the bus arrived in the first light of dawn it was parked in the middle of an open area. Williams had waited patiently for the chance to get a tracking device on board but the chance had never come. It was too bright and the yard was never free of smoking policemen. Now on the third day things looked more promising. As promised by the weatherman the previous evening, a warm front had moved in from the Irish Sea. The wind had got up and brought thick grey cloud and lashing rain.

For three hours the only sound to be heard from where Williams waited was the moan of the wind as it clawed through the metal of the winching gear and the splash of rain in the puddles that filled up all over the yard. Then he heard the distant sound of shouts as the bus swept by the drenched pickets a few hundred yards away. It bounced into the yard a couple of minutes later and parked up. The door hissed open and Trevor Beardsworth and three constables sprinted through the soaking rain and disappeared through the door to the canteen where they would kill the hours of the day. A minute or so later the driver followed suit. Williams gave it a few seconds and then dodged forward in a low crouching run. The full light of the day was still a good half an hour away and it would have taken the most vigilant of guards to spot the brief shadow of movement as he flitted across the yard and back. The job was done in under twenty seconds and Williams slipped away into the rain.

By the end of the day they had the address in the outskirts of Leeds where Trevor and Tracey Beardsworth had been presented with their new home. Williams said he wanted three days to watch the place and to get a feel for the ground. They agreed to rendezvous on a small industrial estate in Bingley at 2 a.m. on Sunday morning. Williams headed for a small hotel in Bradford. Josh returned to his writer's retreat in Simmington. Frank and Lenny went home to Haddington.

Latimer had received the news that Josh Ogilvy was in Simmington two hours after Beverley made her report to Hendrick. By the next morning he had a reasonable file of information in front of him and he read through it carefully making neat notes. Once he had been over it twice, he started a diagram with boxes and arrows. Josh's name was at the top alongside that of his deceased father. An arrow pointed to a note that stated two words. 'Jewish Financier'. More arrows led to more words. Kensington. Shropshire. Cambridge. Magdalene College. Leonard Baxter. Frank Baxter. Ralph Baxter. Sheffield Royal Infirmary. Admission Date. Date of first Haddington Scab. And slowly the lines became completed circles and the picture emerged. He called Hendrick and gave his instructions. A two-man team was dispatched to the address in Kensington. Two were tasked to mount a surveillance operation on the Baxter household in Haddington. Beverly was sent south to the address in Shropshire. He demanded follow-up reports for noon the next day. Then he leant back and chewed at his pen.

Beverly felt low as she followed the lines of the Ordinance Survey map down a small road to the Ogilvy country residence. She was trying hard to come to terms with the frighteningly instant nature of her betrayal. She had done it without consideration. Without a second thought. For two days now she had been regretting her decision. Had she kept the sighting of Josh to herself would they have found out anyway? Probably. There was no way she could have gone into the pub without him seeing her. What explanation could she have possibly given to Hendrick for not going in? None. There wasn't one. And he would have smelt a rat straight away. Hendrick could smell a rat a hundred miles away. She tried to convince herself that she had done the right thing. There were still options after all. So long as Latimer and Hendrick were convinced she was onside, then an opportunity to do something might emerge.

She had thought of nothing else as she had crossed the country from Yorkshire. She knew that when it came to it she would do something. She couldn't allow Lenny to walk into whatever trap that was set for him without warning him off. There would be consequences of course. Consequences for her. Consequences for her family. But it wasn't really a choice. They would get by somehow. But Lenny wouldn't. She had seen enough in Ireland to know how it would be for him. And Frank. The gloves would be off. It was best that she stayed close and picked her moment carefully. It was impossible to avoid the gnawing sense that it was all her fault. But for her, he would have never gone to Magdalene. But for her, he would have never met Josh. But for her, things would have been so very different. She had caused it, even though it had been for all the right reasons. Now it was up to her to clean it up. She had no clue how. But when the time came she would find a way.

Once again she was Samantha Tate. A different Samantha this time. The new Samantha was a junior solicitor working for a small firm in Swansea. She told the housekeeper that she was looking for a Mr Williams. A relative of his had passed away. There was a bequest. And the housekeeper made the nice young lady tea and told her that Mr Williams had been away for some time. In fact he had left soon after poor old Mr Ogilvy had passed away. Such a shame. Such a wonderful man. And the nice young lady from Wales had made all the right noises. She had commented on how delicious the homemade biscuits were and taken her leave.

She updated Latimer on her findings from a payphone in a Little Chef on the outskirts of Shrewsbury and he told her to come to London straight away. Her instincts had urged her to argue. Her instincts told her that she should not be driving away from South Yorkshire, but there was nothing she could say. Latimer wasn't a man who encouraged any debate about the decisions he made. She told him she would be there by the early evening.

In London, Latimer allowed himself a rare smile. He pulled his page of arrows and doodles to the centre of the desk. He underlined the word Williams. Williams who had served the British Army from 1947 to 1969. Kenya. Malaya. Aden. Covert units that had been disbanded as the last outposts of the Empire had been signed away. Nasty little operations in places far from home. He had sensed that Williams was his man from the minute the file had been dispatched over from the Ministry of Defence. Williams was the last piece of the jigsaw.

The files he had requested were spread over his desk in careful piles. Files that told the stories that had led them all together. It was always the same. Random events. Chance meetings. Unforeseen outcomes. So much random fate that took people so far from the lives they had expected to live. And when it was all over and the cards had fallen to the floor, it would be the time for them all to say what if and if only. When it was too late. When Latimer had pulled his strings. Thrown the dice. He reached for one of the files. It was an old one. Forwarded from Simcox in Cambridge three years earlier. It contained a report about a Union Debate between Tony Benn and Kenneth Clarke. And there were pictures of students who might have become a problem. Two pictures of Beverly Morton with a tall smiling figure. Lenny Baxter. The boy from home. Simcox had written a few dry notes. Maybe she had been a little too protective of him. Maybe there was something more than mere acquaintance. Latimer drummed his fingers. It was all a long time ago. Beverly had been in Ireland for over two years now. But he had been in the game long enough to know that things went wrong for the most unexpected of reasons. There was no need to take any chances. He decided to play it safe.

He picked up the telephone receiver and started making arrangements.

When Beverly arrived in London that evening she was informed that her brief career as a nice young Welsh solicitor was over. Now she was to be Rosalina Gianni of Milan. She worked for an engineering contractor and she was due on the ten-thirty flight to Rome. A room was reserved. All the necessary would be waiting for her there. Latimer told her to call when she got checked in. There was no need to worry about the time. He would be awake. Again she was desperate to argue. Again she knew it was fruitless. London was far from South Yorkshire. Rome seemed like another star system. It had only been a few days earlier that she had been cursing her luck at having to cancel her holiday to Tuscany. Now she was booked onto a flight to Rome and she wished that there was any way she could remain in Yorkshire instead.

By ten a driver had dropped her at Heathrow. The banks of payphones stared at her wherever she walked. Should she? Not yet. Not until she had a clearer picture. Right now she was far too confused. Latimer had given her no clue as to why she had played the part of the nice young solicitor asking about a gardener. And now Rome. What the hell could Rome have to do with anything?

Her flight was called and she actually got as far as taking two fifty pence pieces from her pocket and standing right next to a phone. But what could she say? And would he listen? They hadn't exchanged so much as a word for as long as she could remember. How crazy would it all sound. The tannoy became more assertive. Would Miss Gianni please make her way to the departure gate. Last orders. Time gentlemen please. Time was all out. She pocketed the change and hurried to the gate. There would still be a moment. She would wait.

Rome was as wet as England. The taxi moved easily through streets filled with puddles. By the time she completed her check in and found her room it was past midnight. Latimer was obviously waiting for her call.

"Ah. Beverly. Good. No problems with your journey?"

"No. It was fine."

"Splendid. I suggest you get some sleep. You will have a long day tomorrow. You will be collected at ten by a man called Cabrini. He will take you back to the airport and make all the arrangements. You will be met the other end by another Italian. Salvatore Tucci. He will bring you up to speed. OK?"

"Not really. Where on earth am I going?"

"There is no need for you to know that yet."

She felt like putting the phone through the window. Instead she stayed calm. "I see."

"Good. I expect to see you back in London tomorrow evening. Sunday at the very latest."

"Fine."

"Jolly good. Have a good trip."

"I'm sure I will."

She stared down at the phone. He was keeping her in the dark. Why the hell was he keeping her in the dark? Every bone in her body sensed disaster. But what could she do. The phone was there. Right in front of her. The front desk could have her connected to the Baxter household within seconds. But she knew it would be a crazy option. Hendrick's team would already have the whole place bugged. One call and she would be out of the game. Could she make the call count?

It would be a gamble. If she could, then it wouldn't matter what happened to her. But if she blew it there would be no second chance. She took a gin from the minibar and splashed in some tonic. The phone seemed to stare back at her. It stared for two whole hours as the clock ticked on.

She never tried the call. If she had it would have been pointless. Latimer was far ahead of her already. The people on the exchange had already been fully briefed. Any calls from Italy to a certain Haddington number were to be blocked.

Although she didn't know it, Beverly Morton had already been taken out of the game. Her chance of becoming the loose cannon had come and gone. Latimer had found the threat in an old file and taken steps. As Beverly fell into a fitful sleep, she had no way of knowing that she was already out of the game.

Up in Simmington Josh had decided on a thoroughly restful weekend. He wasn't due to meet the others up in Bingley until the early hours of Monday morning. Two nights and two days of nothing seemed a hugely good idea. It was something of a relief not to have and go and play his part in the pub for a few days. The constant performance was starting to fray his nerves. It had all started as something of a game, but as the glowing anger of the Mankies grew more and more fierce, the game became more serious. The thought of being caught was a daunting one. They were all grand lads when he was in the chair buying rounds and cracking jokes. They wouldn't be such good lads if they found out that he was a part of the team behind all their problems. He was missing being with the others up in Haddington but Williams had been insistent that he should stay clear for a while. By now the place was bound to be under pretty intense scrutiny. Those who watched would be tasked with looking for anything that was unusual. Anything that didn't fit the pattern. There was little point in arguing about it. Josh stuck out like a sore thumb. It meant that for the next few weeks of their campaign he would be working pretty much alone.

Early in the evening he had driven to the nearest town and filled two bags or provisions from a supermarket. As a steak sizzled in a frying pan he opened a bottle of wine and played some music. The evening stretched ahead like an empty meadow in summer. Food.

Wine. Maybe some TV. Maybe a book. And sleep. A tonne of sleep. Another glass. More volume.

He never saw the back door opening. He was in the process of reaching out for the bottle when an arm clamped around his neck. And something over his mouth. Cloth? Cotton wool? And what was that cloying smell... He tried to thrash and kick out but already the lines of communication to his limbs were cut. The chloroform crawled through the passages to the brain and the lights went out.

Cabrini arrived at Beverly's hotel on time and walked her to where his Fiat was parked in a side street. It was another grey day and the people of Rome were slow off the mark filling the Saturday streets of their capital. By the afternoon the place would be packed with legions of Christmas shoppers. As the car wandered out of the city, Beverly stared out through the smeared window. She felt so jealous of the normality all around her. Men heading out for a Saturday paper. Conversations on street corners. Families planning for Christmas. Quiet routine lives filled with hope and love. So very far from the place she found herself in. Cabrini wasn't disposed to say anything. He switched his radio up loud, chain-smoked and occasionally cursed a driver who didn't meet his standards.

They arrived at the airport at nine-thirty and he simply passed her a brown envelope. There were no goodbyes. She climbed out and he drove off. Once inside the terminal she opened up the envelope. A return ticket from Alitalia. Rome to Tripoli. Tripoli to Rome. Departure from Rome at 10.20 a.m. She glanced up at the clock. 9.35. Just forty-five minutes. All planned down to the second. Five minutes to check in. Five minutes for cold feet. And her feet felt like ice. She had stared up at the ceiling for much of the night wondering where Latimer was about to send her. Wondering if he was sending her anywhere at all. Or was he merely getting her out of the country and out of the way. None of her nocturnal imaginings had taken her to the capital of Libya.

She made it to the check in desk on auto-pilot. A boarding card was issued. A departure gate named. 9.51. Twenty-nine minutes. Twenty-two by the time she made it to the gate. Still not too late. Still time to find a payphone and make a call. Still time to duck the flight and take a cab back to the city. Then what? She would be finished with

Latimer. No way would he allow her to walk away into some kind of Disney happy ending. Not if she missed the plane. Aborted. There would be a price to pay.

But calling was now a necessity. Since the assassination of Policewoman Yvonne Fletcher on a London street outside the Libyan Embassy in broad daylight, Colonel Gaddafi had become number one on the list of Britain's bogeymen. It was almost impossible for her to see where there could be a link between Tripoli and Haddington, but she knew with great certainty that it spelt the worst of news for Lenny, Josh, Frank and the mysterious Williams. She no longer had the luxury of time. Eighteen minutes now. Time to make the call. By the time she had the correct code and enough change the clock had ticked down to ten minutes.

Unobtainable. Maybe she had dialled wrong. She tried again, taking extra care when pushing the metal squares. Nothing. Maybe the Baxters had run out of cash and the phone company had cut them off. Or maybe it was Latimer. It didn't matter a great deal. She had ten minutes. Latimer would know if she missed the plane. She could try and make it back to the UK and warn Lenny. But Latimer wouldn't allow that to happen. By the time she tried to get back into Britain, the immigration men would have been issued with her photo and some story or another. She wasn't even Beverly any more. She was Rosalina Gianni of Milan. A fake woman from a fake address with a fake job. She was a non-person. A myth.

A single tear wandered down her cheek as she stared dumbly at the pay phone. There was no way back. Latimer had locked her in. The only option was forward. The only route to returning home and being Beverly again was to catch the plane to Tripoli. She made her way to the gate and presented her boarding card.

Latimer had managed a few hours sleep on the camp bed in his office. A shave and a coffee had restored him. He completed a call to Hendrick. No problems there. They had taken Ogilvy to an RAF base and caught a ride on a routine supply plane to Belfast. They had arrived at the farmhouse in Ulster just after three. The prisoner had slept the whole way. He was in the basement now. Still asleep.

Asecond call confirmed Beverly was on the plane. Yes she had tried to make a call from the airport. Yes, the Baxter house in Haddington.

He leaned back in his leather chair and stared out into the December sky. So he had been right. There was more. Not that it mattered greatly. It was a pity all the same. Beverly Morton had promised to become one of the greats. She had it all in spades. She would be of no use after this one played out.

Josh came awake into a world of cold. Terrible, awful cold that had already climbed all the way through his body. It took his brain time. All the messages it was receiving made no sense to him. A dim light from a small broken window. Stone walls. Old whitewash. The sound of crows somewhere outside. Flagged floor. And cold. So cold. Why? Because he was naked. Naked and strapped into a hard wooden chair. The sheer horror of it slammed into his consciousness and he screamed. He screamed like he had never screamed before.

The sound of the scream wandered up the stone stairs to where Hendrick sat reading the Sun at the kitchen table. He checked his watch. Nearly ten. He looked to the two men who sat with him.

"Give him till one."

They nodded and went back to the sports pages.

Salvatore Tucci was in his late twenties and dressed-up designer style.

"Miss Gianni. I call you Rosalina, yes?"

Beverly nodded. The airport around her was unbelievably modern. Modern and empty. Made to handle thousands and barely a passenger in sight. Just soldiers in every corner. He took her by the elbow and led her out of the doors into the warm air of North Africa.

"Come. I have a car. Not far."

She felt in a daze. It was all so surreal. More soldiers outside. And palm trees. And a big wide boulevard. And no cars. Once inside, he twisted in his seat and examined her with a smile.

"So they send a pretty one. Is good. You're going to like Tripoli Rosalina. Is OK. Is nice. We do the business and I buy you a nice food. No problem."

"Where are we going?"

"A place. Not far. They say I need take you to this place. Then I take you hotel. Then we go nice lunch. Nice place. On the beach. Is good. You no worry Rosalina. We have good time."

"Who are you?"

A big smile as he turned out onto an even newer, even wider road. "Me? me Salvatore. Salvatore Tucci. You know this. Why you ask this? We no ask these things in this business."

She felt numb all over. Her brain was fixed on the fact that he had said 'beezness'. 'Beezness'. Like something out of a De Niro film. Maybe she wasn't awake at all. Maybe it was all some bizarre dream. A smiling Italian who was undressing her with every glance and a highway with no cars. Just a dream. A nightmare. Small white villages. Olive groves. Huge construction sites with no workers and machinery standing idle. A dream.

The journey took forty minutes. They entered an industrial area. All new. All empty. Ghostlike. A film set ready for the cast. One of the warehouses had an open door. Tucci parked up just outside.

"So. We are here now. They say you need to see this. You need to, how you say, supervise? Yes? Is supervise?"

"Yes. Supervise."

Two men were ready for them. One exchanged a couple or sentences in Arabic with Tucci. The other opened the boot of the Fiat and lifted in a flat wooden crate which was clearly quite heavy. Then he closed the boot. There was a handshake.

"OK. Is done. We go."

A hundred yards away in a small cluster of palm trees, the motor-driven shutters of a Nikon camera whirred. Nice clear pictures in the crystal morning light of the desert.

"So where now?"

The big smile. "We take the package to the Consulate. Then you go to hotel. Then we have a lunch. Is OK?"

"Which consulate?"

"Italia. The British they have no place here any more. Is why they need Salvatore."

"Why do I need an hotel? I am expected back in London as soon as possible. My ticket is for this afternoon."

"No is not possible. There is no place for this afternoon. The plane is full. You going to have to stay till Monday. Maybe Tuesday. But is OK. You like it here. We going to have some fun."

Monday or Tuesday. Latimer had removed her from the scene.

Saturday morning in a frost-wrapped Ulster. But time meant nothing to Josh. Time was finished. All the normalities of life had been left behind. He had screamed and screamed until his throat felt red raw. He had screamed, but nobody had come. After the screaming it had been tears. Never, ever in his life had he known such utter desolation. The cold was only a tiny part of the misery, but it was almost unbearable. The temperature in the stone cellar was well below freezing and every part of his body ached with it. The terror and the pain of the cold numbed his brain. But he still had enough thought process to know that he was in a huge amount of trouble.

There could only be one reason for it all. They had found out. They. Men from the shadows. Men not shackled by rules and regulations. Men working beyond the safety fences of the law. Men who would stop at nothing to achieve their goal. But what would their goal be? That wasn't hard to figure out. They would be looking for betrayal. Confession. Facts. Evidence.

He knew that somehow he would have to find resolve. Courage. But how? In the past he had sometimes needed to find courage, usually when he was high on a cliff somewhere facing a difficult section of smooth rock. That was so different. All he was facing in those moments was the prospect of his own quick death. He had no wish to die, but it was guaranteed to be quick and clean. Honourable in a way. A fall then a silence. It was dealable with. Not this. This wasn't going to be about death. It would be about pain. A whole ocean of pain with no prospect of relief. And the only way for him to stop the pain would be for him to become a betrayer. He squeezed his eyes closed and searched inside himself for the courage he needed.

Instead of courage he found pictures from a nightmare. Snow. Pine trees. Electric fences. Guards in black uniforms and thousands upon thousands of men and women shivering with shaven heads. All emaciated. All naked. All petrified. It seemed so clear. He snapped his eyes open and tried to clear his brain. Reality was slipping away. His mind was closing down the shutters. He focused on the grey stones of the cellar wall. He knew the pictures. They came from books he had requested from the library near his father's house in Kensington. Poland. The death camp Sobibor. The place in the forest where they had massacred his family. And now forty years later he was about to be next. Naked. Bound. Frozen. Held by men with no concept of decency.

Oh God no.

Please no.

And the door crashed open.

Three of them. Uniforms. Masks. Figures from the ultimate nightmare. One face close in to his. Stinking filthy breath.

"Morning Joshua. Josh – oo – are. Josh – oooo – arrrrrr."

The man turned and chuckled. He had a case in his hand which he placed on a small lino topped table four feet in front of Josh. He opened the case. The case contained wires with small metal clamps on the ends. Josh screwed his eyes shut and twisted his head from the sight of it.

The man was talking. Conversational.

"I've been doing this for years Joshua. Many years. Lots of times. I don't want to sound arrogant, but I really am very good at it. You want to know why? Maybe not. I'll tell you anyway. I'm good at it because I enjoy it. I'm probably not right in the head. I accept that. A man shouldn't get his kicks from inflicting pain. I suppose it means I'm a sadist. Is that right Joshua? You would probably know. Clever twat aren't you? Cambridge University. It's a first for me you know. I've never had a clever twat from Cambridge in my chair. Do you know that?"

Josh tried to blank his ears to the voice. He tried to blank out everything. Hendrick slapped him viciously across the face.

"Manners Joshua. Don't ignore me. I really hate it when people ignore me. Now. I asked you a question. I asked if you realised that this was the first time I have had a Cambridge man in my chair. I expect answers when I ask questions. So. Answer."

Josh shook his head. "I didn't know that."

Slap.

"Nothing wrong with the answer Joshua. The answer was very good. The truth. I slapped you because I enjoyed it."

Slap.

"Marvellous. I don't know how to explain it. Have you ever caused pain Joshua? Well?"

"No."

Slap.

Slap.

Please God make it stop. Please. But Josh knew only too well that it hadn't started yet. He didn't want to think about the case and the wires, but no other thought could find any room in his head.

"It's not the only first you know. Guess what else is a first Joshua?"
Josh shook his head. "I don't know."

Slap.

"I'll tell you. All these years and you're my first Yid. The first Jew boy. I call it ironic. Think of all the Yids who have wound up in rooms like this in the last century. Rooms like this with men like me. Millions isn't it Joshua. Millions and millions. Isn't that right Jew boy?"

Slap.

"Yes."

Slap.

"I've read your file of course. This is something of a family tradition isn't it Jew boy. I read about Sobibor. I wonder if men like me were with your family before they offed them in the gas chambers. I wonder."

Slap.

"I'm going to have to change my routine this morning Joshua. I'm not sure I like that. I'm a man of routine. Are you a man of routine Jew boy?"

"No."

"Slap."

"Didn't think you would be. You're a spoilt piece of upper class shite from what I can gather. Who needs a routine when you're born with a silver spoon in your mouth. That right Jew boy?"

"Yes."

Slap.

Hendrick took one of the wires between his forefinger and thumb.

"Now Jew boy. This is a wire that delivers a strong electrical charge to this metal clamp. Doesn't look much does it? Like a bulldog clip in a stationary shop. And yet this little piece of metal can put pain into the human body unlike any other. The purest of pain. Now I was telling you about routine. My routine. When I question a man my routine is to start things off by clipping this onto my prisoner's foreskin. A lot of what I do is about psychology you see. I may be borderline psychotic, but I'm not stupid. I like to think things through. You understand that Jew boy?"

"Yes."

Slap.

Pause.

Slap.

"Good. All of this is psychology. The cold. The stripping of clothes and dignity. The hours to think about it. I wouldn't normally explain this. It would spoil the effect. But as a Cambridge man you will no doubt have worked it out for yourself. I don't get many chances to have a proper intellectual conversation. Mostly they send me thugs. Nutters. It is a treat to have a proper Yid intellectual. A treat. Anyway. My routine. I was telling you about my routine. I start off by clipping this onto the subject's foreskin. Why? Utter humiliation. A man can get no lower than to be stripped naked, tied up and electrocuted through his dick. It's the pits Jew boy. But you present a problem. We both know what don't we? No foreskin. Just a Jap's Eye. So I have to change my routine and I don't like that."

Slap.

Pause.

Slap.

Hendrick suddenly moved swiftly and reached down. Josh writhed at the pain of the clamp biting into the skin of his scrotum.

"No . . . no . . . NOOOOOOOOOOOO!"

A pure blinding pain climbed up through his groin and raced through his body. It went on and one and on and on. And then it stopped.

Hendrick had his face back close.

"Would you like to talk to me Jew boy?"

"Yes. Yes please."

"Good." Hendrick turned to one of his colleagues. "Bring his clothes. A blanket. Cup of tea."

He undid the leather straps and minutes later Josh was dressed and wrapped in a blanket. Head down.

"Smoke?"

Josh nodded and took the lit cigarette. His hands were shaking so badly that he could barely take hold of it.

"Now Joshua. Things are better now. You're dressed. You have a nice cup of tea. You have a fag. This does not have to change. To keep it like this all you have to do is to tell me. OK?"

Josh nodded.

"Tell me all of it and this is how it will be. Hold anything back and we go back to how it was before. Back to the pain. Understand?"

Another nod.

"And I'll know if you don't tell me the truth. Do you believe that Joshua? That I'll know if you're lying?"

"Yes."

"So tell me."

Josh told him. Everything. And Hendrick noted it all down carefully as they both smoked their way through a packet of Bensons and became intimate. The torturer and the betrayer. Locked together by pain and fear. He told about the cottage in Derbyshire and the meeting on the industrial estate in Bingley and the plan to stop the bus that took Trevor Beardsworth to his work. He told Hendrick what he had already guessed. Four of them. Ogilvy. Williams. And the two Baxter brothers. A four man team. Nobody else. Enough. More than enough.

At last he sat back. "Good. Very good. You can come with me now."

He led the way up the stairs. Then another flight. He opened a door into a smallish room with a bed and a wardrobe and a view across wet fields.

"You'll be staying here for a while. Maybe a couple of weeks. Maybe more. I'm going to take the pain away now Joshua. Roll your sleeve up."

Josh did so. He would do anything now. Anything at all. Anything to stay away from the chair downstairs. Hendrick chatted away as he produced a needle and found a vein.

"You'll be very damaged after this Joshua. Emotionally damaged. Anyone would be. It will mean that you won't be able to sleep much. You'll have nightmares. Flashbacks. You're lucky. We run a full service here. A comprehensive package. After the disease comes the cure."

He gave the needle a gentle tap. "You will find that this is the cure Joshua. A guaranteed cure. The preferred medication of millions who want to hide away from their nightmares. Heroin. God's gift to the abused. The tortured. The broken."

Josh felt a prick of pain and then a huge warmth wrapped him in its arms. His eyes closed and he sank back onto the bed. Hendricks words were still there but they seemed to be somewhere else.

"We'll give you medicine every day. Three times every day. And when we take you back to London you will need it. It will be your oxygen. Your life. A new start Joshua. A new life far from all the nonsense you have been involved in. You'll have no time for that any more. And you won't have to be out and about nicking from Woolworths either. Daddy has seen to that."

Hendrick realised that he was talking to himself. He sat on the edge of the bed and took a pulse. Slow, but no problem.

Job done. He went downstairs and passed what he had learned onto Latimer.

The wooden crate was transferred from Tucci's car to another in the underground garage of the Italian Consulate. The car took it out to the airport where it was put on the same Alitalia plane that had brought Beverly to Tripoli. It was loaded as a part of the Italian diplomatic bag. By four o'clock it was in Rome where it was transferred onto a plane to Heathrow, this time as part of the British diplomatic bag.

By early evening it was in the basement of the building where Latimer had an office.

Williams never heard the men who came in the night. Four of them. Two waited in their car at the end of the track to the cottage. Two walked. They came through the back door in silence. And upstairs. And into the room where he slept. The light woke him. Woke him to the sight of two guns pointed at his head by two men he had never seen before. Middle-aged men. Men with nothing in their eyes.

"Get up please Mr Williams. Turn around."

Handcuffs behind the back.

"Let's go."

One of them called in the car with a radio. They loaded Williams into the back. He was taken by the other two. They drove an hour until they reached a lay-by on a tiny road that wound over the moors. The night was very clear and moonlight bathed the hills in a silky white light.

"Get out please Mr Williams."

He got out and stood at the edge of the gravel. Such silence. Such silence.

He was executed by a shot to the back of the head fired from six inches. They took the body back to London where it was cremated without ceremony. Latimer had an arrangement.

The second pair of men cleaned the cottage and took Williams's car to a small breakers yard in Croydon where Latimer had another arrangement. Some weeks later the owners of the cottage decided they had better see if the Welshman was still there. He wasn't. He was gone without trace. They were angry at him for leaving without letting them know. There was a possibility that they had missed out on two weeks of rent. On the other hand they couldn't help but admit that they had never seen the place looking so clean.

The housekeeper in Shropshire had no idea what to do. Williams had gone away. Josh had gone away. But her wages were paid direct into her bank and so she turned in for work everyday and cleaned. When Josh at last came many months later he told her that Williams had gone away. He told her that he would be selling the house. He was very generous with her redundancy.

Lenny and Frank pulled into the industrial estate five minutes early. The night was clear and the place was predictably deserted. Lenny was checking his watch when they heard the sound of fast revving engines. And then lights. Lots of blinding white headlights. And flashing blue lights. Police cars skidded to a halt. Six of them. All around them. Officers jumped out and ringed them. And they had guns. Lots of guns. All pointed at Lenny and Frank.

"Holy Christ..."

"Hands in the air. Hands in the air."

Hendrick strode forward, his gun held casually by his side.

"Don't move.."

Hendrick passed them and popped open the boot. They looked around. What? A blanket in the boot. Not theirs. Not a blanket they had ever seen before. Hendrick pulled it to one side. Underneath were three guns. Automatic rifles. AK47. And packets of something that looked like grey play dough. And electric wires.

Hendrick waved over the senior officer. "Here you are. Like we said."

Frank couldn't believe what his eyes were seeing. No way.

"Wait a minute. This isn't ours. You've planted this you fucking bastards . . ."

Hendrick span around and smashed him hard in the face with the butt of his pistol. Frank took the hit completely off balance. He fell backwards. Fell hard. The back of his head cracked into the edge of the kerb. And suddenly he was very still. And his blood came out oily dark in the moonlight.

Lenny fell to his knees and tried to hold the broken head together with the palms of his hands. So much blood. So much.

"No Frank. Please no. Hang on Frank. Jesus."

The lights were going out in his brother's yes. And his lips slowly came to life. A fraction of a smile. And then the words that would haunt Lenny for the rest of his life.

"You'll look after our Sheila won't you Lenny. And little un, when it comes . . ."

And then there was nothing. Gone. His Frank. His twin. Taken. And the killing rage was on him before he knew it. Rage like he had never even dreamed of. One second he was on his knees holding the head of his brother. The next second he had hold of Hendrick. He had his hands on the man's thick neck. Squeezing. Squeezing with every ounce of strength he had.

And then he was dragged clear. Five of them. On his arms. On his legs. Hitting him. Hammering him. Handcuffing him. Throwing him into the back of a van. Latimer helped Hendrick to his feet.

"You OK?"

Hendrick was shaken. The cartilage of his neck was torn. But the pain was something that was secondary. He was shaking. For a moment he had arrived at the gates of death. For a moment he had thought he was about to go through.

"I'll live."

They looked over to the van which was rocking on its wheels as Lenny threw himself at the walls.

"NOOOOOOOOOOOOOOO!!!!!"

The senior officer joined them.

"He's dead."

Latimer shook his head. "Oh dear. How very unfortunate. Resisting arrest wouldn't you say?"

The officer shrugged. Nothing he could do about anything. Orders from on high. Take instructions from the man from London.

Latimer's tone stayed light. "Very good. Well we'll be off now. We were never here of course."

"No. That was made very clear."

"Excellent. I will leave everything in your very capable hands. We will bid you goodnight."

The policeman didn't reply. He felt sick to his stomach.

The red lights of Latimer's car disappeared behind the dark shape of a warehouse. Five minutes later the police van followed. One of his men had found a piece of plastic sheet in a nearby skip and covered up Frank Baxter. None of them wanted to look at the lifeless eyes staring up into the starry Yorkshire sky.

" . . . *Leonard Baxter, the charges of which you have been found guilty are some of the most serious I have ever had to preside over. The Miners' Strike brought a cancer to Yorkshire. I will not pretend that I do not have some sympathy for the miners and their struggle. I will also not pretend that I do not have some sympathy for the tragedy of your own family. It is sad that such an obviously fine man as your father should have sustained such an injury at the hands of the police. It is also a great tragedy that your brother Frank Baxter was killed whilst trying to escape. There are many victims in this terrible case. Your mother. Frank's young widow Sheila and her new-born baby. I can only imagine what dreams must come to you when you search for sleep.*

'However it is not my role to display sympathy. It is my role to uphold the law. We pride ourselves in this country that we have enjoyed democracy for hundreds of years whilst so many other countries have been plunged into the darkness of tyranny. Our democracy is something that must be treasured. Protected at all costs. Over recent years we have all had to face the threat of terrorists. A threat to our democracy. A threat to our very freedom. This threat has come from Ireland and other places. Libya is such a place. A rogue state led by a renegade who allowed his thugs to murder a young British policewoman on the streets of London.

'Leonard Baxter, there can be no excuse for the conspiracy that you entered into with the agents of this dictator. No cause or crusade can offer any justification. That is why you have been found guilty of charges of Terrorism. You took guns and explosives from an enemy of our country. An enemy of freedom. A man of pure evil. God alone knows what you and your brother planned to do with these weapons. There can be no leniency in such a case and none will be shown.

'Leonard Baxter, I sentence you to a term of twenty years imprisonment. Take the prisoner down please."

On the day that the great strike ended Ralph Baxter was back at home. Instead of marching back to work under the banner of his Union, he sat at the kitchen table with his wife. The doctors had told him that he would not work again. The damage to his brain was significant. If he took care, then there was no reason why he should not live for many years.

As he stared at his tea, he could find little point. One son dead. The other in Wakefield Prison. The strike defeated. Across the table the tears ran silently down the haggard face of his wife. It was very quiet in the kitchen. Outside was the sound of hundreds of work boots thundering down the tarmac. And a brass band. The men of Haddington marched back to work with their heads held high in defeat.

Six years later the shafts of Haddington Main were sealed. The pit was closed. Ralph Baxter didn't live to see it. He died less than a year after his son.

Josh watched the men march back to work on the TV in his father's house in Kensington. It barely registered. He was skating along the very edge of overdose. Just like every day. It was the only way he could survive. Without his medication the guilt ate him alive. Frank dead. Lenny away. His betrayal. The men on the TV screen seemed so alien. How could it have been that he had been a part of it all? Not a comprehensible thought. He switched over with the remote. Tom and Jerry. He could just about deal with Tom and Jerry.

Beverly heard the return to work on the BBC World Service. She was back in the camp in Nicaragua. Latimer had met her off the plane in Rome. He had told her that she was not welcome back in England for a while. It was the phone call. She should never have made the phone call. He told her that he had honoured their agreement. Her father's debt was cleared. If she went back to Nicaragua for a while then everything would be forgotten. He showed her the photographs. Her and Tucci and the two Arabs. Crystal clear in the morning light of the desert.

"I don't expect that I will ever need to use these Beverly. But if I do, I'm sure you realise that things for you would become rather difficult. You understand?"

"I understand."

"I knew you would. Stay there for two years. Then your life is all yours. A shame about the call Beverly. You could have been one of the best."

She had kept her head down. She didn't want to speak to him. She didn't want to look at him.

Now the crackle of the small radio told her that it was all over. The longest and most bitter strike of them all. Frank Baxter was dead. Lenny was locked up. God alone knew what they had done to Josh and Williams. And she was exiled to her jungle. The child she was holding was starting to wake. His eyes jumped open and for a moment there was sheer panic. Terror. The same five-year-old eyes had seen a squad of Government soldiers execute his mother and father. For a second it seemed as if he would scream. She tightened her grip around his chest and squeezed.

"There now. It's OK. I'm here Miguel. Beverly's here. Everything will be just fine. You'll see."

And his big saucer eyes slowly drained of fear as she hummed to him in the thick air of the night.

Part Two
Dumfries, Scotland 2005

*'There's a new Grand Design in case you haven't noticed, Edward.
It's called pre-emptive naivety, and it rests on the assumption
that everyone in the world would like to live in Dayton, Ohio,
under one God, no prizes for guessing whose God that is.'*

John Le Carré, *'Absolute Friends'*

Lenny had been to two funerals in twenty years. They hadn't allowed him anywhere near when his brother had been lowered into the ground. Things had been far too tense. The media were painting a picture of Lenny Baxter being the most dangerous man in Britain. The authorities feared it would take the merest spark to start an insurrection. He was safely locked away and out of sight as his brother was buried amidst scenes of huge security.

By the time his father died, things had moved on. The town turned out to pay respect to one of its finest sons. Over a thousand, far too many for the church. More than half of the mourners had to stand outside whilst the vicar told of a man who had spent his whole life fighting for his comrades. The men and women of Haddington followed the hearse to the cemetery on the edge of town in a slow, silent march. The banner of the Haddington N.U.M was held high and proud because for years Ralph Baxter had said that he wanted his coffin to be followed by the banner when the time came. Later, when pints were taken in a subdued club, many wondered if they would see the likes of Ralph Baxter again. He had been from the old school, a man from an era that had died the day they had all marched back to work in defeat. And then the conversation turned to his son. Lenny. The one who had survived. The one who had stood apart, handcuffed to a policeman. And for the millionth time the men of Haddington speculated about what had really happened with Frank and Lenny and the guns from Libya.

His mother's funeral had been an altogether more modest affair. Ethel Baxter outlived her husband by ten years. She outlived that hated Thatcher and was there to watch the tears of anguish as the destroyer of her family was at last stabbed in the back by her own party. She outlived the Haddington Main pit which was closed in the early nineties. The only focus of her final years were the fortnightly visits to her surviving son in prison. She watched him grow into his thirties. Prison treated him well enough. He obviously had enough to eat and he always looked fit. But his eyes carried the truth of a grief that never seemed to heal with time. When she tried to encourage him to move beyond what had happened he would smile and agree, but she knew there was no possibility that he would. When she had been buried next to her husband it had been a small affair. Neighbours and friends. No banner. And later that night the few who had attended reported that Lenny Baxter had looked older, but fit enough considering. The club was a quieter place now. Haddington was a quieter place. Once the mine had been closed down, there was no reason for the town to exist at all. Families moved away to the cities to seek work. The houses that were left were boarded up and slow to sell.

Lenny heard about the slow death of his home town from his mother during her visits. On the day of the funeral he had seen it for himself. Just a glimpse through the barred windows of the prison van. Closed shops. Empty houses. An overwhelming sense of emptiness. The five minutes it took for the van to cross the town to the cemetery was time enough for him to see that the place had died. It wasn't home any more. There was nothing left of the past. As the van had drawn away from the grave of his mother and headed back north to Wakefield Prison he had known that he would never return to Haddington. The town and all the memories it held was finished for him. There would be no more visits from his past. He would finish his time on his own and then find whatever life he could.

But then there had been a visit from the past. Sally. Fifteen years old and looking small and frightened in the hard bleak light of the visiting room. He joined her and couldn't begin to think what to say. It was Sally who broke the ice.

"Would you like a cup of tea? A coke?"

"Tea please."

He had gone for the tea and tried to control the blinding grief that had hit him like a train. Frank's lass. Frank's words. "You'll look after our Sheila won't you Lenny. And the little un, when it comes . . ." And here was the little un. Not so little. Nearly a woman already. Fifteen years of life already lived while he had been suspended in limbo. He felt terribly tongue-tied. What on earth could he possibly say to the girl? What had she come to hear? He covered his rising panic with the simple action of adding the milk and the sugar and offering a digestive biscuit from a packet that contained four of them. All the time her eyes were locked on him and when he glanced up he was hit by the train again. His brother's eyes. His Frank's eyes.

He had no skill for small talk.

"Why have you come Sally?"

"The pictures."

The pictures in her mother's album. Frank and Lenny. Lenny and Frank. Alike as two peas in a pod. Pictures she had stared at from as far back as she could remember.

"I never knew my dad. Maybe I can know him through you."

He smiled. "I can see Sheila has taught you how to tell it straight up like a proper Yorkshire lass."

This had brought a small hint of a smile and the ice was broken. After that Sally had become his fortnightly visitor. She took a job in McDonalds and earned enough for the rail fare. She refused point blank to accept any money for the tickets even though he fixed it with his solicitor who held the cash from the sale of the family home in Haddington. Every week a long chatty letter would arrive with news of life on the Sunnybank Estate in Dumfries.

Sally had come twice a month for the final seven years of his time behind bars. Over a hundred and fifty visits. Three hundred and fifty letters. And she had brought Lenny back to life. She had given him hope where there had only been black despair. She gave him a reason to try and live again. Sheila died six months before his release and when he finally emerged into a world he barely recognized, he had headed north to Scotland to look after his niece. But it had never been like that. Sally Baxter needed no looking after. By the time Lenny arrived in Dumfries she was twenty-two and fiercely capable. It was always the other way round. Sally looked after him though he hated to admit it. She helped to ease him back into the world. To de-institutionalise him. To shield him from the endless gossip and the occasional reporters. She gave him the time to put himself back together. To become twenty percent of the Lenny he had once been before.

Now after two funerals in twenty years he stood by his second grave in three days. Luke had been the first to be buried. It had been a huge affair. Sunnybank had turned out en masse. The funeral of an eleven-year-old boy was a thing that mobilised the neighbourhood. The two deaths had dominated the local media. They had been the topic of every conversation. Luke's smiling photo was front page news. And the people of Sunnybank had turned out in their hundreds to mourn the loss of a child.

The day had been baking hot and the great crowd had been sweaty and uncomfortable. The weather had turned grey for Zoe. Instead of hundreds, there was a mere cluster of family and friends. Of course it was sad, but it was different. Zoe was a junkie. Zoe had become a bad one. Zoe had hitched up with that Kevin Philips. Zoe had been a thieving little bitch. Nobody actually said that it served her right, but most thought it. Word had spread about her being naked in the flat. What the hell had she been doing? Well, it wasn't hard to guess was it? And with that Mog. Horrible. Unbelievable. Disgusting. And so the people of Sunnybank had stayed at home when Zoe was buried.

Beside him, Sally's face was terribly pale. They hadn't brought an umbrella and the rain soaked them through. She held his hand in a fierce grip and he could see that she was only hanging on to her emotions by a slender thread. The hollow sound of the soil hitting the wooden lid of Zoe's coffin was too much. Sally fell into him and buried her face as far as he could into the dampness of his coat. He folded her to him and stroked her hair. And the tears climbed out of his own eyes and mixed in with the rain that lashed his face.

They didn't stay long at the house when it was all over. The atmosphere was almost unbearable. Zoe's father was like a dead man walking. Every line on his face told the story of the things he had said. He had put his daughter out of his life. Cut her off. No daughter of his was going to shame the family. And now he had no daughter at all. His little Zoe. Gone. Gone, and he had driven her away. Refused to talk to her. Screamed abuse at her. Disowned her. Sentenced her. Now all that was left were memories and the look of slow hatred in the eyes of his wife. Lenny could see that the family was not about to be drawn together by the hell they found themselves in. They would be slowly ripped apart by blame and remorse. Zoe's brother sat alone in the corner of the room and stared dumbly at the bubbles rising up his glass of Coke. Thirteen going on ninety. Lenny knew him a little. The boy was an occasional visitor to the Zone. Always a quiet one. Never really part of the crowd. Zoe had been the one who had been born with the spark and life. Her brother Steve was the serious one. Now the boy was in a place that was beyond serious. A place Lenny knew only too well.

He squatted down next to the armchair in the corner.

"You all right Steve?"

A shrug. The eyes never moved from the glass.

"I lost my brother. Years ago. It's a hard thing. The hardest thing in the world. I never talked about it and I should have done. Talking helps you know. You know where I am if you want to talk. Yeah?"

A nod. Just a small one.

"Any time Steve. We can go for a walk or summat. Try not to keep it bottled. Come when you're ready. You'll do that will you Steve?"

Another nod. And more tears. Lenny laid a hand on the boy's shoulder and gave a small squeeze. Then he stood back up and went over to Sally. She was sitting on the sofa with Zoe's mother. Neither could think of anything to say to each other. Instead they held each other's hand and stared into space. Together they had tried to be a lifeline for the girl. Together they had failed and now she was dead. There were no words.

Lenny had watched the life dry up in his niece over the dark week that had followed the deaths. She had become a machine. He had suggested that she should take some time out, but she had refused. Every day she had been there to open up the Zone. She had mostly stayed in the office and hammered away at the keyboard of her computer. She couldn't face the kids. In every face she saw death. In every young body she saw a corpse. Lenny tried to fill in and do the talking. He tried to help the youngsters to make some sense of what had happened. He tried to answer questions that were unanswerable. And every night they sat together in silence. He had tried to get her to open up but on each occasion she had shaken her head and looked away. A letter from the Council had arrived on the morning of Luke's funeral. It said that a decision had been taken about the site at McIntosh House. It said that they regretted that it would not be possible. It said that it was not the appropriate time. It said that they would be more than happy to consider any future applications. Sally had read it and re-read it and re-read it again and then put it down on her cluttered desk.

Now when Lenny entered the kitchen to switch on the kettle he found that the letter had finally moved from Sally's small office. Now it was in the middle of the table. Quiet alone. Lying in splendid isolation, face up. Mocking accusing.

Accidental or staged?

Sally provided the answer. She picked up the letter and passed it to him.

"No."

He shook his head. "Sorry Sally?"

"You heard. I said no."

"I heard you well enough. I just don't understand."

She turned and left the room. Had she walked out on him? Surely not. He found her behaviour troubling. It was so unlike her. Usually Sally was an open book. He was about to follow when she came back in and presented him with a thick scrapbook. It was made up of over a hundred pages of lovingly glued newspaper cuttings.

Lenny turned over the cover and straight away sat down. Page after page of yellowing text. National papers. Yorkshire Post. Magazines. Twenty year old stories from another era. His story. Frank's story. And his father and Josh and Williams and a hundred and fifty thousand others who had taken on the Iron Lady and lost. For a while their story had become the Holy Grail for every investigative journalist in the world. Wild stories were everywhere. Stories about Gaddafi and the Libyans. Stories about the Soviets and the Bulgarians and the East Germans. Bits and pieces had leaked out from the Mancunian policemen who had been the primary target of their operations. Snippets of news bought for fat wads of cash. The people of Haddington had their say. They wanted to try to ensure that something approaching the truth would appear in the papers. Their version appeared in the publications of the left, mainly Militant and The Socialist Worker. Who was it that threw the bottles and stones on the second morning when Trevor Beardsworth returned to work? Was Frank Baxter really trying to escape? If there was a gang of four, who were the other two members? Where were the other two members?

Page after page. Words after words. Every other page he stared at himself. The papers had loved the picture that had been taken before his first Varsity Match as captain of the Cambridge University Cricket team. They liked to use it alongside shots of Burgess and McLean. Another Cambridge traitor. Page after page from a time when East and West had come to the very edge. The Thatcher time. The Reagan time.

Lech Walesa. Afghanistan. Beirut. A world of dark little men doing their dark work. And he and Frank and Josh and Williams had become a part of it all. Pawns in the great game. Fools.

"Where did you get all this?"

"Libraries mainly."

"It must have taken you a long time."

"Seven years. I started collecting after I first came to see you in prison."

"Why?"

"I wanted to understand."

"And do you?"

She didn't answer. Instead she went and stood by the window and stared down into the back yard where the wheelie bins lived. Lenny kept turning the pages. Every picture felt like a stab wound. His father. Frank. Memories. Obligations. "You'll look after our Sheila won't you Lenny. And little un, when it comes . . ."

"Why are you showing me this Sally?"

Still nothing. Still a frozen back. At last she turned, very pale. Ominously pale.

"I wanted to know. I wanted to know why Uncle Lenny. Why and what you did. Why my dad was dead. Why you were in prison. Why I never got the chance to see my Nana and Grandad."

"Tough questions."

"I still needed to ask them."

"So did I." He reached into his pocket and pulled out his cigarettes and lit two. They were the questions that had kept him awake staring at prison cell ceilings for year after year. Why? And for what? What had got into them? A kind of madness.

Sally sat and played with her cigarette. "It says in some of the articles that you nearly turned the tide. It says that the Government was nearer to throwing in the towel than they ever let on."

He nodded. It was something that he had found out in his seventh year in Wakefield. An older man had joined him at breakfast and held out a hand to shake.

"Hello Lenny. I'm Dick Rogers."

Lenny shook and looked the stranger over. Big. Nearly all bald. Not nearly fit. He was attacking the stodge of his breakfast with gusto.

"Well?"

"Happen we could have a walk together later. In the yard. There are some things I would like to share with you."

Quite a cultured voice. Not Yorkshire. Maybe Kent or Sussex. Educated. Enquiries before the exercise hour revealed that Dick Rogers had been a civil servant caught with his hands in the till. Pretty senior by all accounts. It had been quite a story for a while. That had been three years before. He had been transferred to Wakefield from Brixton.

They had walked the yard and the older man had said his piece.

"I was working very closely with colleagues from the Cabinet office back in eighty-four. I was Trade and Industry at the time. My days were taken up with handling the paperwork to bring in Polish coal. Lots of little ports that were on the brink of bankruptcy before the Strike. You'll remember?"

"Aye. I remember."

"Everything about the Strike was top priority. Nothing else mattered. It was Maggie's crusade. Money didn't matter. Nobody was counting the beans. Victory, whatever the cost."

Lenny gave a bitter smile. "Why not tell me summat I don't know."

"Quite."

They took a few yards in silence. "I thought you should know how close it was. In November and December 1984. The coal stocks were all but out. We were down to a week or two. No matter how many boats from Poland we brought in we kept going backwards. The Cabinet was split all ends up. Once you boys started up, there was near panic. Haddington looked like it was going to be the tipping point of the whole thing. That's why they went so dark."

"Dark?"

"Mmmm. They brought in some of the cowboys from Ulster. Wild types. They worked a mile off the books and they had no regard for any constitutional niceties."

"I guessed as much. You don't pick a boot full of Libyan registered weapons from Tesco."

"No."

"So what are you telling me Dick?"

"Nothing much. I just thought you should know how close you were to winning, that's all. Another two or three weeks . . ."

His words faded and they reached the high wall of the perimeter.

Did it make it worse or better? Lenny had no idea. But the man meant well enough.

"Was my brother's death an accident?"

A nod. "As far as I know. People were not at all happy about it. The whole idea of the operation was that were to be no martyrs. They wanted you both in court and on the front pages of the papers. I never heard the name of the man who did it. He was a complete cowboy by all accounts. Completely off the rails. I'm afraid there are lots like him over the water. I heard that they got him out of the country. The rumour was that he had emigrated down to South Africa. No shortage of work for his type down there."

"And the others? Josh and Williams."

Rogers was uneasy. "I don't know very much. I think that Williams was disposed of."

"Disposed of?"

"Yes."

"Jesus."

"It happens Lenny."

More silence. Lenny felt cold all over. "And Josh?"

"I really don't know. The word was that he wasn't going to be a problem any more. God knows why. I'm fairly sure that he lived."

"What do you want from me Dick? Or is this all just the milk of human kindness."

The older man shrugged. "You can probably guess. Prison is a hard place for someone like me. A man needs a friend."

"That he does. OK. I'll put the word out. You'll be fine."

For years he had been forcing the whole thing to the corners of his mind. Had what he he'd been told made a difference? Had it been important to know that they had so nearly won? Not really. There had been plenty of books in the prison library that told the stories of the inches that separated victory from defeat. The British Airborne units at Arnhem had been just a few hours from tearing a ragged hole in the German lines and wrapping up the war a year early. A few more hours, and the Western Allies would have been in Berlin before Stalin's armies had left their own soil. A few more hours and the Iron Curtain would have been drawn at the Russian border instead of Poland and Germany. A few more hours, and hundreds of thousands would have been spared the gas chambers of Auschwitz and Belsen. But a few hours might as well have been a few years, and the hundreds of crosses in Dutch graveyards were all about glorious failure. Glorious failure. Abject defeat. Dead was always dead. Frank. And Williams, if Rogers had his facts right.

And now his neice put it all back in front of him. Page after page. Pages from his past that refused to leave him alone.

"Why are you showing me this Sally?"

"Tell me uncle Lenny. Is it true that you nearly made a difference? There are lots who think that you did."

"What does it matter. Any of it. It was years ago. A lifetime ago."

"Tell me."

He looked into the eyes that were those of his brother. Straight forward. Passionate. Burning with a simple hope.

"OK. We nearly made a difference. Maybe a few days from it."

"How do you know?"

He told her about Rogers and the prison yard.

"So the articles in here are right?"

He shrugged. "I don't know. I haven't read them. But it was closer than anyone thought. The coal was running out and there was plenty of winter left. Maybe we were close."

She nodded and sat up straighter. Bracing herself.

"You took on the whole system. You and my Dad. Were there others?"

"Two."

"So four of you then."

"Aye. Four of us."

"Four of you and you came within a few days of winning."

"So."

She took a careful breath. "I want the new centre uncle Lenny. I won't accept this."

She spat out the word 'this' like a mouthful of sour milk. The letter from the council landed on the table between them. A gauntlet of headed paper.

"What are you saying to me Sally?"

"You know full well what I am saying Uncle Lenny. I want you to fight again. For me. For Zoe. For Luke. This is wrong Uncle Lenny. So wrong. I don't know what else to do. But I won't accept it. I refuse to accept it. I need you to fight."

His turn to get to his feet now. His turn to stand at the window and stare. Was he surprised? Of course he was. And yet he wasn't. She had merely spoken the words that had been screaming inside his own head. Twice he had watched the lights go out. Twice in a single night. First Luke. Then Zoe. Just like Frank. "You'll look after our Sheila won't you Lenny. And little un, when it comes . . ." And now after all these years, here he was with the very same little un who his brother had never lived to see. And she wanted him to go out and fight again. To take them all on, regardless of what the cost would be. Regardless of the damage. And slowly he started to feel the presence of his dad and his brother with him in the small Sunnybank kitchen. It was what the Baxter's did. Always had. They had locked him away from the light for twenty years and they thought that he was tamed. They had thought that two decades would be enough to bleed the Baxter out of him. And maybe if there had been no Sally, they might just have been right. But there was a Sally. A five-foot-two warrior queen. If she was ready to march out and fly the flag of the Baxters, then how could he run and hide. No way. Not a chance.

For the first time in as long as he could remember he felt properly alive. A hundred percent alive.

A smile. "OK."

"You mean . . ."

"Aye. If the lady wants a new youth centre, then the lady will have a new youth centre."

And to his amazement he suddenly felt better, better than in years and years and years. It would probably be another fight that he would have no hope of winning. Another tilt at another windmill. Another brick wall to beat his head against. But he was tired of going with the flow. He had followed the lines painted on the corridor floors of the prison for a long, long time. He had kept his head down and his nose clean. He had doffed his cap. He had behaved. Now it was time to shake the tree again.

Yousuf was an hour into the new routine of his mornings. A hated routine. A routine so very different from before. Before there had been a ride to school in the car driven by his father's chauffeur. Before had been a breakfast of yoghurt and fruit and fresh coffee prepared by the family servants while the music of the West hammered out from the satellite TV. Before, his father had been a big man in Famoudi. He had been in charge of industrial production for a region that stretched half way to Fallujah. Like all long-term members of Saddam's Baath Party, his father had enjoyed all the privileges that Iraq could offer. And so did his family, especially his oldest son who was his pride and joy.

Before, Yousuf had been a big boy. Overweight. Two or three stones overweight. Theirs was a household where food was always to be found in abundance, sanctions or no sanctions. Exercise wasn't something that featured in his life. He was taxied everywhere by the chauffeur. A clutch of servants undertook all the work of the household. Once upon a time he had played a little tennis, but it had become too arduous. Life was about eating and TV and the music from the ghettoes of America that was at the centre of his life. The faces of 50 Cent and Ja Rool and a host of other rappers glowered down from the walls of his bedroom. He had put in hours in front of the mirror, perfecting a blankly aggressive set to his face, working on the hand moves, learning every lyric until they were second nature. He and his friends turned their bedrooms into shrines to Hip Hop. They spent their evenings competing with each other to find who could remember most lyrics. Who could mimic the moves. Who would be the man. And his father had rolled his eyes and occasionally complained that his son listened to the music of the nation that had slaughtered so many of his fellow people. And in turn Yousuf had asked why it was that the family had an American music system in their huge lounge and an American washer dryer in the laundry room.

That had all been before. The time of Yousuf's first life. The time before he had stood and watched the Abrams tanks and Bradley fighting vehicles pull into the main square of Famoudi. His second life was very different. It had only taken a week for everything to fall to pieces. His father's name was passed to the Americans within two days of their arrival. They had come after midnight and tied his father's hands behind his back with plastic handcuffs and taken him away into the night in a convoy of three Humvees. Two days later the soldiers had returned and informed the family that their house was to be requisitioned for military use.

He and his mother moved into the spare room in his uncle's house in the centre of the town. They had been able to take only what they could carry. The posters and the widescreen TV had all stayed behind.

Yousuf's former life was reduced to a personal stereo and a carrier bag filled with his CD's.

On the final day of the first week the Americans had come for his uncle. More Humvees. More hard young faces with fingers itching on triggers. And suddenly Yousuf was the head of the family. Things got worse with every passing week. There never seemed to be any power. Food became all but non-existent. He was often left for days at a time to care for his three young nieces as his mother and aunt made the arduous journey to the prison at Abu Graib to try and find some news of their husbands. When they returned, they were always shattered and near starved with hunger. They said that the Americans wouldn't let them within three miles of the prison. There were thousands waiting outside in the blinding heat of the desert waiting for any snippit of information. But for months there was nothing, until a whisper reached Famoudi that both men had died. Nobody knew how or why or when. Just that they were not coming home.

In Yousuf's second life he was the provider. Every morning he was up early and out scouring the streets for food. Within a month the family had sold everything that had any kind of value. They were reduced to surviving on whatever aid the American soldiers handed out. Sometimes there was almost plenty. Rice and flour and dried milk and beans. Then the insurgents would let off a bomb or an RPG and there would be no food for a few days.

After three months Yousuf had lost all his puppy fat. Gone was the roly poly wanna be gangster in his designer street gear. The chubby cheeks became all bone. The designer street wear was soon dusty and frayed. His body became emaciated as he spent his days walking and queuing and waiting. Always hunting for food. Any food.

His aunt had fallen ill after six months. By this stage, water no longer ran from the taps in the kitchen and bathroom. Yousuf had to bring water in old plastic containers every morning. He filled it from a standpipe in the square and hauled it across town to the house. Sometimes the Americans gave out purification tablets to be added to the brown brackish water. Other times they were nowhere to be seen. It was after one of these times that his aunt became stricken with chronic dysentery. After three days it was obvious that it was serious. Yousuf and his mother had half-dragged her to the hospital where the doctors had tried their best. But there was no medicine to be had and death had come within hours. Soon his mother was ill as well and he took her to the same filthy ward where his aunt had drawn her last breath. His mother hung on and was able to come home after a fortnight. But she was only ever alive in a biological sense. Her spirit had died in the stench and misery of the overstretched hospital. She spent the hours of every day sitting in the darkness of the living room staring at the walls. Now Yousuf had even more on his plate. Not only did he have to scour the town for enough food for the family and carry the water, but now he had to try his best to cook as well and to see to his three young nieces.

Then one day an unexpected flicker of life came into the relentless darkness of his new life. He was on the edge of the town following up a rumour that there was to be a distribution of flour at one of the schools. By this time his walk had become little more than a trudge. He wore a frayed old coat and a woollen hat, for the cold of the winter had the town in its grip. Like everyone else, he had learned that it was wise to walk slowly with a bowed head. A fast walk could be mistaken for the walk of a suicide bomber. A raised head could be judged as that of someone guiding themselves to their target. Four had been shot down as they approached checkpoints in a manner that the soldiers had perceived to be threatening. Just like that. Pop. Gone. It was how life had become for the people of Famoudi.

The street he was walking down was very quiet. Far too quiet for there to be much hope that the rumour of flour had been true. If there was flour to be found at the end of the road there would have been hundreds of bowed figures moving slowly towards the roadblock with their heads down. Instead there was only Yousuf. Another wasted walk. Another hungry night. And suddenly his ears locked onto a sound that was familiar from his first life. The words of 50 Cent pushed their way out of an armoured car and hammered out across the empty space around the roadblock. He stopped and slowly raised his head. The roadblock was just thirty yards ahead. His stare was met by four Marines, all staring back at him down the sights of their automatic rifles. Another sat up high on the turret of the vehicle.

They didn't like it when he stopped to look at them. They didn't like the sharp bones of his cheeks. They didn't like the gleam in his deep set eyes. And in a moment he knew that his life hung by a slender thread. Only five of them. All black. Nobody else about. All the buildings around were cleared for security reasons. Broken windows. Doors hanging from their hinges. A steel grey sky and a world of silence. Five of them. One of him. No witnesses. And the fast banging words bouncing off the crumbling words.

Slowly he raised his arms. Shaped his fingers. Shaped his body. Carefully. Emphasising his empty hands. And then, as the soldiers waited on the kill order from their sergeant, he shocked them to mercy. He joined 50 Cent. Word perfect. Gesture perfect. Body perfect. And for a minute they seemed ready to kill him because it was just such a goddamn shock. Then slowly they stood and smiled and clapped and laughed. And they waved him over and gave him batteries for his stereo and they broke into the their C rations and told him to come back tomorrow. And they called him Bro. And that night the family ate some meat for the first time in months.

After that, he returned every day and the Marines looked forward to him coming. They brought food specially from the barracks. They gave him CD's. They shared their coffee with him. And soon his friends from the past would come along with him, and all of them would once again compete with each other in the dust of the deserted street. And the young Marines would whoop and clap and laugh and pass around gum whilst their sergeant scanned the alleys and shadows with eyes that never stayed still.

His time with the young Marines lasted for nearly a month until one morning the town shook with the sound of an explosion. A big one. Word soon flew around the small groups on the corners. A suicide bomb. The gate of the big base at the edge of the town. Seven Marines dead. Many more injured. Some were alight with the news. Others were terrified at the price they would have to pay. Yousuf and his friends had debated for nearly an hour as to whether they should go to the roadblock. Some had said that it would be better to leave it for a day or two. But others had been sure that it would be OK. The soldiers were their friends. They were their brothers. And so they had gone.

Just like every day they approached with the strut and swagger of their heroes. And they had thumped out the word of a chosen song in discordant harmony. But the soldiers didn't respond with grins and cheers and clapping. They waited behind the barrels of their guns with the stillness of death. The quiet of the winter morning was destroyed by the sound of a single shot fired by the sergeant. The boy next to

PART TWO

Yousuf fell in slow motion, a smashed up mess of blood and bone in the place where his face had once been. And they had run whilst the young soldiers watched with their faces set hard in the lines of revenge.

Yousuf had never returned to the street at the edge of town. He had resumed his daily routine of begging and scraping an existence for his mother and nieces. Now as he emerged into the heat of the spring morning, his mind was occupied with only two thoughts. Every day he only ever had the same two thoughts. Food and revenge. Revenge and food. Simple thoughts. Clear thoughts. Maybe there would be food today. Maybe not. Maybe the time for revenge would be today. Maybe not. He could wait for both.

Lenny walked for five days. He walked from the minute that he had told Sally that his answer was yes. He had given her a grin and left the house and walked. That night he had not returned until well after two. She was still waiting for him in the kitchen with a half-cold coffee and full ashtray.

"So, what are you going to do then?"

"You'll have to give me some time to think Sally. I've said yes, OK? Just be patient. I need to work it out."

She had nodded reluctantly. She had stood back for five days. On day two, summer arrived in Dumfries with a bang. The temperature shot up and the holiday clothes were pulled out from the back of wardrobes. High pressure settled over Britain and Lenny walked for miles every day, swallowing the ground with his long stride. He walked the narrow single-tracked roads that wound up into the low rolling hills around the town. He walked the Forestry Commission tracks through millions of pine trees. He walked the long beaches of the Solway Coast. And he walked back through twenty-five years of his life and trawled for answers.

He had been born into a long history of agitation. His family had always been ready to leave the house and man the barricades at a minute's notice. It was what they did. It was what Haddington did. All of which made him a dinosaur from an age that was now dead and gone.

He remembered the times of rebellion he had grown up through. Jerky images from the black and white TV of tear gas and riot police on the campuses of the American Universities where they burned the flag and demanded an end to the war in Vietnam. The rhythmic singing, running march of the students of Soweto as they chanted their defiance at the Apartheid police in their misshapen Land Rovers. Anti-Racism. CND. So many causes that had taken the people out onto the streets to knock down the walls brick by brick. And for a while it had seemed as if the great walls were destined to come down. He recalled the new colour TV showing the last Marines scrambling into the final helicopter out of the American Embassy in Saigon. The speakers who had come to the club in Haddington had told the packed, smoky room about the dawning of a new era. The age of capitalism and imperialism was all but ended. A new order was sweeping the world. It was to be seen in Central America and Asia. It was to be seen on the streets of cities all over Europe. The walls of the British Empire had finally collapsed after two hundred years. Now the walls of the American Empire were starting to crumble. The age of Empires was over. The age of the working man was at hand.

How very strange it all seemed now. The young people at the Zone looked at him as if he was some kind of lunatic when he talked about the times of his youth. Times when a generation marched onto the streets of the world to throw their stones and wave their flags and chant for a new order where the wealth of the world would be shared. He tried to explain that once upon a time people had believed that the guy in the boardroom in the five-hundred-pound suit was the enemy and the guy on the street in old jeans and an army surplus jacket was the good guy. The youngsters in the Zone would shrug and frown at the idea. They wanted to be the guy in the suit. So long as it was Armani or Hugo Boss. They were convinced that the coolest thing was to have it all. The right labels. The right electronics. The right everything. Every possession was coded and labelled. Their god and goal was the Nike tick. Rebellion meant getting the right stuff regardless of the cost. Look at 50 Cent. He was the man. His glowering face stared out from his CD cover. 'Get rich, or die tryin'. The gospel according to 50 Cent. Locked up by Federal America. Branded by Corporate America. Exported to the youth of the world care of the same guys who did Coca Cola and McDonalds and Wrangler. He did what was necessary to get the labels and the jewellery and the big cars and houses and the women. That was what it was all about. You do what you have to do.

PART TWO

Once upon a time the prize had been the release of Mandela and the withdrawal of troops from Vietnam and the scrapping of nuclear weapons. Great big ideas for badges and T-shirts. Now it was all about the T-shirts and whatever corporate label they sported. And trainers and personal stereos and mobile phones. Things. Things manufactured in Asian sweatshops for a few pence a day, branded by superstar sportsman and singers for millions, and priced up to be painfully expensive. Things were no good if they were cheap. Every item was judged on logo and price.

As he walked, Lenny marvelled at how the men in the boardrooms had staged the most bloodless coup in the history of the world. They had won out where tyrants and kings and governments of all colours had tried and failed. They had subdued the youth of the world. No religion had ever won over so many converts. On every continent the youth of the planet worshipped at the alter of the Nike tick. So clever. Mind-bendingly clever. They had developed a template and stuck with it. They would use their media divisions to discover and develop a suitable rebel, whilst at the same time making absolutely sure that the rebel in question had signed their life away before being given the opportunity to pick up a microphone. Then they could stand back and allow the rebel to rant and swear and take as many drugs as their body and soul could stand whilst the paparazzi snapped away. That was all part of the deal. They needed faces to fill the pages of their tabloids and chat shows and celebrity magazines. Every penny went down to the bottom line. And at the same time, other divisions dressed the rebel in their clothes and accessories. Mobile phones. Fragrance. Sunglasses. Cars. A fully integrated package labelled all the way down to the underwear. They had even persuaded their customers to walk the streets with the labels of their boxer shorts poking out of their similarly labelled jeans.

More miles. More hillsides of quiet pine trees. More hedges filled with chattering finches. More buzzards floating above on the thermal drafts from the baking fields below. He wrestled with the task at hand. He had made the promise. Now he had to deliver on the promise. The task was straightforward. The council had taken the decision to sell off McIntosh House to a property developer and bank the cash. Lots of cash. It would take a huge amount of persuading to get them to change their minds. Trying reasonable argument had failed. More or less blatant begging had failed. From the Prime Minister down, the community of Britain had declared war on its young people. They were addicted to their computer games. They were unable to talk properly. They were getting too fat. They didn't show any respect. They couldn't read properly. They were threatening to old ladies in their hooded tops and baseball caps. They needed to be kept in line. To be taught a lesson.

OK Lenny. So that is the prevailing mood. Young people are bad through and through. No decency. No manners. No respect. No idea. The prevailing mood that elected officials had to live with. So? So spending thousands of pounds on a nice shiny youth centre wasn't about to win them many votes. A political problem. It was why asking nicely and trying to argue sensibly had failed. These guys wanted to be voted back in next time. And who voted? The biggest percentage of those who voted in local elections were the grey-haired generation. The younger generation never bothered. Too boring. Why should they? And so to win a seat on the Council it was important to be seen as someone who was ready to teach those in the baseball caps and hoodies a lesson. To make sure they were kept in line and scrubbed behind their ears with a hard brush.

Asking nicely was a sure-fire loser. So that meant more forcible persuasion. And that of course was why Sally had asked him to take up the fight. She had done the asking nicely bit. She had done it to death. She had joined their clubs and talked their talk and doffed her cap and they had slammed the door in her face. And Luke and Zoe were six feet under. And enough was enough.

Forcible persuasion. How? Who? Where? When? How many? This time he had been handed the role of being the general. He was to play the part of King Arthur. And he had to make sure that he came up with a Saltley Gate and not an Orgreave. To be a King Arthur he would need an army. There was little point in thinking tactics until he had his army. Who would be his soldiers? Where would they come from? Why the hell would they want to join up? Come on Lenny. Take it step by step.

Number one. Who? Easy enough. McIntosh House would be for young people. If there was to be war, then it would have to be their war. If they were to sign up and fight, they would have to believe in the cause. Next. Where? Easy again. McIntosh House was in

PART TWO

Sunnybank Estate. It would be for Sunnybank. Those who would march out and fight for it would have to be of Sunnybank.

Fine. His army would need to be the youth of Sunnybank. That was blindingly obvious. The 'who?' bit and the 'where?' bit were not all that hard. The tough part was the 'why?'bit. Think posters on the wall Lenny. There are always posters on the wall. Every generation had its own posters. Martin Luther King. Malcolm X. Che Guevara. Jimmy Hendrix. Mandela. James Dean. Faces from the past. Rebels with causes. Or without. Rebels against the good and the great. Rebels against the men with the big money and the police forces who were bought and paid for. For twenty years he had grown up in a time when these posters had sent youngsters out on to the streets to be gassed and beaten. For millions there had been no greater fashion accessory than a black eye from a policeman's baton.

So what about the posters of today? The people of Britain had taken to the streets in numbers never seen before to tell their Prime Minister that his war for oil stank like a rotten kipper. Millions had marched. The trouble was that they had asked nicely. Politely. And the policemen had smiled and marched with them and had their pictures taken with toddlers and balloons. The people had asked nicely and Blair had given them his pained look and told them that his God had spoken and that his conscience demanded that the tanks should roll. And the tanks and Cruise Missiles and F16 fighters had gone out and done their stuff while the millions who had marched had politely taken the bus home and watched Eastenders. The greatest popular demonstrations in all history and they had failed completely. Why? Because they were too polite. Too nice. Too pathetically hopeful that democracy might actually stand a ghost of a chance against the requirements of the oil and weapons companies who had bought and paid for the war. And they had been middle-aged demonstrations. His generation. The ones who had once marched out to scream at the excesses of Thatcher and Reagan. And the generation had moved on. Now they had mortgages that were too high and good jobs that barely covered the payments. They had kids in public schools and private health care plans. Middle-aged Middle Britain. They showed their manners and marched in their designer clothes and they achieved a big fat zero.

So Lenny. Fine. No point in asking nicely. But, more than anyone

Lenny knew what happened when people took to the streets and didn't ask nicely. That was the road to Orgreave. The road to twenty years in Wakefield. Blair might look all nice and cuddly in front of the cameras, but he had signed the death warrant for umpteen thousand Iraqi civilians without batting an eyelid. The ones who paid all the bills had him in their pockets. They owned him. Just like they had owned Thatcher before him. They were people who didn't take well to those who didn't ask nicely. Somehow he would have to find the right balance between being too polite and seeing the whole thing go to hell in a handcart amidst the swirl of tear gas. Neither too nice nor ultra violent would work. Only some kind of middle way would stand a chance of success. Like the great Tony Blair who had stamped the words 'middle' and 'way' on his forehead and had won two landslides. Even now he was trying to explain that sending cruise missiles into cities where sixty percent of the population were kids was after all the most Christian and reasonable thing a caring father could do.

More miles. More long gulps from the bottles of water from his rucksack. A hilltop where the hazy view of the pale blue sea stretched all the way out to the murky shape of the Isle of Man. Lots of seagulls following a slow moving tractor in a field below him. Little shiny toy cars far, far below on the coast road. Microdot families from Airdrie and Dumbarton on the yellow sand of the summer beaches. For a while he focused on a chaffinch as it hopped from branch to branch in a hawthorn bush. A bush much like the one where Williams had listened in to the anger and panic of the Manchester police a lifetime before.

Again he pulled in his thoughts and lined them up. Stood them to attention. One, he needed an army from Sunnybank that was willing to march. Two, they needed to find a middle way. Just like Tony. He reached for the realities. It was all very well thinking of an army, but he had to be realistic. How many would there be? He wasn't about to muster the legions who had filled the fields at Orgreave. It wouldn't be thousands. It wouldn't be hundreds. It probably wouldn't even be fifty. His would be an army of tens. And there was no way he was about to take them down the dark road. Not after Frank. "You'll look after our Sheila won't you Lenny. And little un, when it comes . . ." He had walked the dark road. He knew the place where it ended.

His army would have to fight out in the open. It would have to apply pressure without giving those they fought the ammunition to put them in rooms with no windows. His army would have to punch far above its weight. So how Lenny? And slowly the answer pulled into the station. The first clear answer. The media of course. The media could make things look different from how they really were. He remembered all the men with bandages and bloody wounds watching the pictures from Orgreave in the Sheffield Hospital. The pictures told a story nobody had witnessed. The police became the force of decency and reason. The pickets became a wild uncontrolled rabble on the brink of rape and pillage. If he wanted his middle way, he would have to enlist the media to paint the pictures. The media could make his tiny army into a fighting force. A few could seem like many when they were beamed out into a world of twenty-four hour rolling news. That was after all what his gallant Prime Minister did. You take a company of Marines and a cluster of townspeople and pay them a few dollars to cheer. Then you tie a rope to a statue of Saddam and pull it down and let the cameras send the image out to the watching billions. And all of a sudden, an unimportant event witnessed by a crowd of a couple or hundred or so becomes an iconic image for the whole planet. A statement. A mirage. A lie. But a lie that did a job. Of course the people of Iraq are absolutely delighted to welcome in our soldiers and tanks. How could anyone possibly say any different? You must remember the statue. The image. Remember how they cheered when it crashed to the floor? Remember the crowd? Surely you do? And of course as time passed, people tended to forget that the crowd was only a small one and that it was an American jeep that pulled the statue down. All that was remembered was the simple image of the statue falling down. The middle way. So thank you Tony. Thank you for showing me the way. Because if King Arthur had pulled the statue down the cameras would have all been on the other side of the city.

Another hilltop. This time the view was into the north. A million acres of sun drenched nothing. Hills and valleys and barely a road or house to be seen. An empty quarter that stretched all the way to the Glasgow suburbs.

And his thoughts and plans were evolving into something that was nearly in reach. A small army from Sunnybank. An army that would find a kind of middle way. An army that would be multiplied by the media. But how would they win? What weaknesses could they find?

Whenever the masses stamped their feet and demanded more of the cake, the reaction of all British politicians tended to be the same. It always had been. Their instinct was to dig in the heels and tough it out. To give in once would open up a can of worms. Well of course it would. And it would always be so for as long as one percent of the country owned over half of its wealth whilst fifty percent owned less than a twentieth. The one percent needed to hold a firm line to make sure that the other ninety nine percent didn't get any ideas. That was why the dragoons had charged the crowds at Manchester's Peterloo Massacre two hundred years before. It was why the bills were paid so readily for the batons and shields of Orgreave. The perceived wisdom was that it was out of the question to ever give an inch. Don't be influenced by pressure. Never negotiate with terrorists. All those millions on the streets had beseeched Blair to stop and think it over and he had predictably chosen the Thatcher road and sent the troops in regardless. Of course he had. Just like Thatcher, his bills were all picked up by the one percent. You got the multi-million pound house in London Tony. We would rather like that big untapped oil well up near Mosul please. And we would certainly like it before the French get their hands on it. So come on Tony. Read the contract. Read the small print. Never mind all those people in their M&S rebel gear. Focus on the house Tony. Maybe we could help out a bit with the furniture.

Would his war be the same? In a way it would. The Council had made up its mind. They wanted cash in the bank. They wouldn't change their minds in a hurry. And if things got a bit too wild, they wouldn't change their minds at all. They would play the never negotiate card and they would pass the whole thing over to the police force. So he would have to find a different button to press. And it came to him that the one thing that the British always hated was to be embarrassed. As soon as something became embarrassing, the high and mighty British establishment would almost always capitulate. Not straight away. Not so that it would be obvious. But they would undig their heels and get themselves clear. The men of the Mau Mau had demanded independence for Kenya with threats of machetes and a bottomless well of killing. Where had it got them? The British had put hundreds of thousands of the Kikuyu tribe into camps ringed with barbed wire and sent the SAS into the Aberdare Mountains. They had dug in the heels and brought out the big stick. Ghandi on the other hand had put his lawyer's suit away in the wardrobe and gone for the guru look and put in the hours on the spinning wheel. When he had visited Buckingham Palace in his semi-naked state a reporter had asked him if he didn't perhaps feel a tad underdressed when he met the King. And Ghandi had replied that he was sure that the King had been wearing quite enough for both of them. And the men at the Colonial Office had wrung their hands and agonised deep into the night until the whole thing became such an unbearable embarrassment that they instructed Mountbatten to give the whole thing away just as quickly as he could.

Nothing much had changed. Tony found it easy enough to completely ignore the greatest street demonstrations the country had ever seen. No problem. He toughed it out boasted how he would never be influenced by pressure. But it all depended on the kind of pressure. Because when a few hauliers and farmers had blockaded a few fuel depots and the whole country had started to grind to a halt, the rest of the world watched the pictures and had a good laugh. And the laughter was loudest in Paris and Berlin and Dublin. And when it got really, really embarrassing he froze the rise in fuel duty and he hadn't dared to raise it since. So Lenny, find a way to embarrass them. Make them squirm in their seats.

This time he had taken a £3.50 bus ride to the past. Up the A76. Sanquhar. Kirkconnel. New Cumnock. Ochiltree. The Ayrshire coalfield towns. Small places with no purpose anymore. Not since the pits had been closed down. Places like Haddington. And Kindon and Osthorpe. Another day of hammering sunshine. It had been nearly a week now. He wandered the dusty areas of cracked concrete and broken bricks that were all that were left of the old mines. Rusty wire fences. Weeds sprouting up through cracks. A desperate empty hot breeze blowing through broken windows. Places of forgotten history. Places of thousands of lives that had come and gone. Places left behind. And the ever present ghosts of his brother and father and all the thousands of others who had been stupid enough to think that the one percent would allow things to be better one day. Dreams as smashed and broken as the shells of the old crumbling buildings. In a hundred years there would be nothing left at all and nature would have covered all the memories in a camouflage of weed and thorn. The old dreams had died that hot summer day at Orgreave. In their place were other things. Thatcher and Reagan had played their parts. Now the one percent of the world were sitting safer in their big houses. The mob had seemed to be close for a while. The angry shouts outside had been audible through the thick double glazed windows. But Maggie and Ronnie had pushed them back. All the way back. First it had been the tear gas and batons. Then it was supermarkets that stayed open 24/7 and a re-emergence of Bingo with even bigger prizes and great deals on remortgaging houses that had tripled in value.

They had even turned the rebels around. For years the rebel message had all been about how the ninety-nine percent should demand their share of the cake from the one percent. Now it was different. Now it was all about how the ninety nine percent could find a way of joining the one percent. And hang the cost. Get rich, or die tryin. Back to 50 Cent again. No matter how many miles he walked he always arrived back with 50 Cent. The black American Crack dealer who had got himself shot and done the hard time before he had risen like a tattooed phoenix from the ashes to cover himself in gold and join the one percent. So where did that put the promising fast bowler who had taken a road from Haddington to Magdalene to Wakefield Prison to Sunnybank Estate? If he wanted his army he would have to acknowledge 50 Cent. He would have to stop and look hard at the dead eyes and tough guy face that stared out from a million teenage walls. Because 50 Cent would have to be his man. There was no point getting all nostalgic for Che Guevara. The young soldiers of his army would probably think Che Guevara was a top-end cologne. His young soldiers would want to march to the banging sound of 50 Cent. Get rich or die tryin.

All he could see were the differences. He was white, 50 was black. He wore jeans and frayed shirts, 50 was all bling jewellery and designer wear. He wore sensible leather shoes that were good for walking, 50 wore $300 worth of trainers. He even had his name on them. He was single, 50 was never seen without umpteen adoring models on his iron pumped arms. He was old, 50 was young. He was poor, 50 was rich enough to be in the one percent club. He lived in a two-bedroom flat in Sunnybank rented from a local housing association, 50 had a string of mansions with swimming pools and security men in mirror sunglasses. He was good at cricket, 50 could rap.

All differences. No similarities. Lenny and 50. Chalk and cheese. Maggie and King Arthur.

Paul had been on the road to Damascus when the blinding light stopped him in his tracks. Lenny was three miles north of Kirkconnel. They did share something. Lenny and 50. 50 and Lenny. They shared notoriety. They were both the real deal. That was what was expected over and above everything else. The days when a pop star could make the front pages by throwing a TV through a hotel window were long gone. It wasn't good enough any more. The public wanted more. Sony didn't do games for forty quid that gave the young player the feeling of throwing a television from a sixth floor window. Of course they didn't. Instead they took their customers deep into the mean streets of badland urban America. They gave them the guns and knives and fast cars and 50 provided the soundtrack. Of course 50 could rap. He could rap with the best of them. And of course he had the right kind of action man prison-gym body. And he had the right tough guy look that ate the camera. But all of that was secondary. What had taken 50 and put him at the head of the queue was that he was the real deal. That was why it was his poster on the wall. He had dealt the drugs and discharged the weapon and done the hard time. 50 wasn't any pretend bad guy. He was a real bad guy. It was why the corporations paid top dollar for him. In a reality obsessed world, there was nobody who was a realer deal than 50. Drug dealer, gunman, rapper. Get rich or die tryin.

And of course Lenny was a real deal too. A fully accredited rebel with twenty years in Wakefield under his belt. A living breathing terrorist in a time where terrorists were all the rage. It was the other thing that Sony gave their customers. All the toys to fight the war on terror. Helicopters and F16s and Delta Force Units. Here was the place where he could take a lead from his six-packed Afro-American Guru. 50 had taken the street years and the prison years and packaged the whole thing up into an irresistible bundle. And neither the media nor the music industry had been able to resist. Instead they had all scrambled to grab a piece of the action.

Below him the sparkling waters of the Ninth slid quietly past the sleepy streets of post coal Kirkconnel. 50 had climbed down from the poster on the wall and exchanged high fives. Yo dude. Respect. Here's the road this white cricketing nigga's gotta walk down.

And as Lenny sat on top of the wall by the bus stop he felt that he had the answers. He knew where his army would come from. He knew the way they could win. He knew how to put the whole thing large and live on television.

And he had found the place when he and 50 could become brothers on the road from prison cell to the centre stage. 50 would get to be a member of the one percent club. And Lenny? Lenny would let the cards fall.

She looked up from reading the paper at the kitchen table.

"So. The wanderer returns. Seen the light yet?"

He ignored the dripping sarcasm and swallowed a glassful of tap water in two gulps.

"I have in fact. The light shone from the skies over the rooftops of Kirkconnel if you really want to know."

"Not quite the road to Damascus then."

"Not quite, but who am I to complain."

She tossed over her cigarettes. "Make the tea then. I'm all ears."

Every inch of her voice was all about doubt. Middle-aged men thinking things out in the countryside did nothing for her. It all seemed too much like some dodgy film on BBC2 on a rainy Sunday afternoon.

"Summer holidays start on Friday, correct?"

"Correct."

"Then battle will commence on Tuesday morning. Eight-thirty sharp."

Now she sat up. This was a time and a date. This was serious.

"Are you serious?"

"Of course I'm serious. I'm a serious guy."

"Go on then. What are you going to do?"

A grin now.

"I'm going to revert to type. I'm going to picket."

"Picket? What's picket?"

Tim or Barry? He still couldn't tell which. He doubted if he ever would. He had bought McDonalds. Big Mac with everything 'Maxed' up to the limit for them. A black coffee with three sugars for him. He should have made it five. He never managed to remember that a

McDonalds sugar was the equivalent to a quarter of a proper teaspoon. They had repaired to a bench on the edge of a stretch of baked grass.

It had come as a surprise to the twins when Lenny had come to call. At first they had been scared witless that he was about to tell them that he had changed his mind and was going to tell the police that they had been there with Luke at the Pavilion. It had been a bad couple of weeks. The Flint family always had a certain reputation on the estate. They had grown up used to the fact that they would never find their way onto guest lists for many birthday parties. But the last days had been different. Nobody had twigged that they had been with Luke when he died. But everyone seemed to blame them. The twins could feel it in the faces that suddenly turned hard when they passed on the pavement. The people of Sunnybank wanted scapegoats for what had happened and they hadn't taken long to find them. Luke had been a grand lad. Good family too. Hell of a footballer. Might even have made pro. He was always a good boy as well. Never in any bother. Not until he hooked up with those Flint boys. They had turned him bad. Of course they had. Well what else could anyone expect? That whole family was bad. And parents became serious about not having their children having anything to do with Tim or Barry. Not a chance. No way were they about to see their offspring go the same way as Luke. The Flint twins were poison. They were a complete no go area on pain of long term grounding and no pocket money and no time on the Playstation. The youngsters had done as they were told and the Flint twins had become separated and isolated.

Once they realised that Lenny wasn't about to march them into town to the police station their mood had brightened, especially when he had talked McDonalds. Once they had speared straws into their milkshakes and made a start on the maxed fries he had started with his pitch.

"You lads know I come from Yorkshire?"

Nods. 'Ayes' from mouths stuffed with food.

"We work to a set of rules where I come from. I reckon it's not all that different from how things are round here."

Quizzical looks now. Suspicion. A slow down in eating speed.

"In a nutshell, we remember when we owe somebody. Yeah?"

Grudging nods.

"So without going into things best left alone, shall we all agree that you lads owe me?"

The twins looked at each other quickly. Their eyes were used to speaking with each other without the need for words. Tim stepped forward as the spokesman.

"Aye. We owe you Lenny."

"Well don't look so miserable about it. I just wanted to make sure we're all on the same piece of paper. I told you about the new centre our Sally wants to get going didn't I?"

"Aye. Down at that old McIntosh House bit. The one with pool tables and basketball and everything."

"That's the one. Well the Council have knocked her back. They are selling it to build houses instead."

"We told you that didn't we? We said them at the Council would'nae give nothing. Not for Sunnybank. Not for the likes of us. They never do."

Lenny smiled. The two faces were like disgruntled little hamsters in baseball caps, their mouths stuffed to bursting point with their Big Macs.

"Well lads, you had it right enough. But that was just round one. It's time for round two now."

"Howd'ya mean round two?"

"You watch boxing? Course you do. Ding. Ding. Round two?"

Tim chuckled. "Aye. And a sign carried round the ring by some lass off Page Three."

"Well, Round Two starts on Tuesday morning and I expect you lads to be right there with me."

There was interest now. "What are we doing?"

"We're going to picket."

"What's picket?"

What indeed. Picket had become a forgotten word from a forgotten era. Tim and Barry had never turned on the news to see the massed ranks of pickets outside some factory gate. It was something from a bygone age. A word for the history books. Although it wasn't history any more. It was Modern Studies now. Picket had left the here and now and joined the ranks of other words from past times on the pages of history books that were seldom read. Boycott. Appeasement. Bolshevik. Colony. Socialist. Time to be the history master.

"OK. Picket. You know what a Union is."

"Not really."

"Right. This is what happens when you bunk school when there's no football. OK. Once upon a time there were lots of big factories all over Europe. Bad places. Dark. Cold. Dangerous. People worked there for sixteen, seventeen hours a day and got paid barely enough to eat."

"Like how much then?"

"In today's money, about £20 a week."

"They were stupid then weren't they. Better not bothering and living off the Social."

"There was no Social in those days. You either worked or you starved. Simple. So the bosses had it all their own way. They paid the workers just enough to keep body and soul together and not a penny more. Then some men worked out that the workers were in fact more important to the bosses than the other way round. No workers and the factories wouldn't run. If the factories didn't run, then the bosses wouldn't make any money. OK?"

"Aye."

"So the workers started to form what were called Unions. It meant all the workers forming a gang. All of them. And then they would vote on who would be their representative. And then they would go to the bosses and say you either pay us a fair wage or else. "

"Or else we'll smash your face in!"

"Not quite. Although that happened sometimes. No what they said was give us a fair wage or we'll go on strike. We'll put our tools down and walk out and you're factory will not produce anything and you'll stop making money."

"It would have been easier to just smash their faces in."

Lenny took a breath. "Aye, well maybe it would, but that would have meant people getting locked up. So instead they tried to do it peacefully. They went on strike. The thing was that sometimes they couldn't get everyone in the factory to agree. There were some who didn't want to go on strike. Some wanted to go to work as usual. And if there were enough who turned into work, then maybe the factory wouldn't shut down and the strike would be doomed. So the men who were on strike would all stand outside the gates and make sure they had the chance to persuade the ones trying to go in to work to change their minds."

He had to smile to himself. It was what could be called the edited version. The thought of the miners on the picket lines of

Nottinghamshire gently persuading their colleagues to change their minds was an amusing one.

"And what happened if they couldn't get them to change their minds. Did they smash their faces in?"

"Sometimes, but that was a last resort."

"A what?"

"What they did when all else failed. If a strike worked properly, then the factory would stay closed for long enough for the boss to start to feel the pinch. He would have no choice except to sit down with the union and pay some better wages."

"And did it work?"

"Aye. Most of the time. Things changed for the better. It took a long time, but they changed in the end. Take this place for example." He waved a thumb over his shoulder at MacDonalds. "If you lads get a job in there when you are sixteen, they have no choice but to pay you a minimum wage. Three pound something an hour. Anything less and they get taken to court."

"Three poond an hour's still crap."

"Better than three pence."

This cracked them up. "Aye. As if. Three pence an hour. Nobody would work for that."

Lenny reached out and took off Barry's cap. The front bore the proud red tick of Nike. "Know where this is made?"

"Aye. America. New York probably."

"Not quite. Sure enough, Nike is an American company. But they don't make their caps in America. They get made in other countries. Indonesia. Vietnam. Cambodia. China. Know why?"

Shaken heads.

"Because they only have to pay the workers three pence an hour."

"No way. That cap was ten quid."

"I'm sure it was. That's why they make so much money. The guy who does the stitching gets three pence an hour. Nike get ten quid. Big money."

The two faces were confused. "So why do the workers bother then? Nobody works for three pence an hour."

"Oh yes they do. Three pence an hour for sixteen hours is nearly fifty pence. Fifty pence is enough for rice and fuel for the stove. Enough to live another day. No work, no food. Three pence an hour is enough to eat."

"So why don't they start Unions then?"

"They are trying. But every time they form a union the bosses hire hard men to take the leaders away and beat them up or shoot them in the back of the head. One day they will have unions that are strong enough to make sure the workers get more than three pence an hour. Then Nike will close the factories down and move them somewhere else. Africa probably. Some place where people are that hungry that they will work for the price of a plate of rice. It's the price of the tick lads."

He mentally nudged himself. They had taken him right off track. The last thing he had intended was a sanctimonious lecture on the excesses of the Nike Corporation. He handed Barry his cap back and the boy examined the embroidered tick with suspicion.

"You've lost me now Lenny. You say you want us to picket, aye?"

"Correct."

"But we haven't got jobs. We're just kids."

"A good point. An excellent point. Let's get back to McIntosh House shall we. OK. Round One was Sally asking nicely. She filled in forms and went to meetings and smiled and was a very polite girl. Please Mr Council, will you give us the money to open a new youth centre at McIntosh House. With me so far?"

"Aye, and they told her to get lost."

"Precisely. So now we move on to Round Two. We have asked the boss nicely for more wages and he has had a laugh at us and told us to take a hike. Asking nicely hasn't worked. So we need to move things on a bit. We need to apply a bit of pressure. That means picketing."

"But we haven't got a Union."

"Not yet, but we will have in a few minutes. The Union of Sunnybank Youth. USY for short. You two will be the founder members. One of you will be President. The other will be the Treasurer. The subs cost a penny a year and you pay them to me. I will be the secretary. A paid position with a salary of a penny a year payable in advance. Got a penny each have you?"

Nods.

"OK. Cough up then."

Pennies were dug from pockets filled with wrappers and other detritus.

"Good. That is that then. USY is born. We have a membership of three. We start at eight-thirty on Tuesday morning."

"Start what."

"Picketing. We will picket the Council Offices on Buccleuch Street. We speak to every person who goes in to their work. We ask tell them that if they go to their desk they are crossing a picket line. Our picket line. The USY picket line. And we'll give them a leaflet explaining our manifesto."

"What's that?"

"It's a list of our demands. But it won't be a list. Just one demand. McIntosh House for kids not houses. We will ask people not go in to work until the Council changes it mind. We will ask people not to pay their Council Tax until they change their mind. And when they change their mind, we will stop picketing."

"Will it be just us three?"

"I hope not, because over the next few days we're all going to recruit new members. As many as we can. Because the more of us there are, the quicker they'll back down. But I am very realistic about this. There is a very real chance that to start with it might be just the three of us. And without you guys it would be just me. And I would look a right pratt."

Barry grimaced. "That's why you said all that stuff about how we's owe you and all that."

"You've got it."

The twins looked at each other and their eyes confirmed what they already knew. They were in a corner. Their dad had banged the idea of honour into them from the day they learned to crawl. This was an honour thing. Without Lenny they would have been dead and buried. They owed him pure and simple.

"Aye, we'll be there. But I can'nae see how it will make any difference. Even if there's more than three of us. Even if there's twenty. What do they care? They'll just have a laugh. Nobody will be bothered. Nobody will even notice. Not the likes of us."

Lenny lit up and shook his head when they held out their hands for one. This was about to be the tough part. He rolled the smoke out through his nose and made a start.

"They'll notice alright. They will not have time to think about anything else."

"How?"

"OK. Let's imagine that someone lets off a bomb in London. Right now. At this very minute. How would you lads know about it? It's three hundred miles away but you would soon know about it. How?"

"Cos everyone would be talking about it. Our mum and everyone."

"And how would they know?"

"They'd see it on the news. Or the papers. Or the radio."

Lenny smiled. "Very good. Move to the top of the class. The media. Bomb plus London equals story. Big story. Front page. First item. And everyone gets to know about it."

"Aye but that's different isn't it. That's a bomb. That's big news. The likes of us hanging around outside the Council offices in town is'nae big news."

"Not hanging around. Picketing."

"Whatever. It's still nowt. Who's going to care?"

Showtime Lenny. Take a long drag. Take a breath. And jump out of the trench and face the bullets again. Twenty years of hiding. Twenty years of blanking it all out. Twenty years of telling yourself never, ever again.

"If it was just the two of you, then you are absolutely right. Nobody would notice. They would have a laugh. But not if I stand out there with you. That will be news. Bigger news than you can imagine."

"Why?"

"You know I was in prison don't you?"

"Aye."

"Know why?"

This put their heads down. They shrugged. Of course they had heard the rumours.

"I'll tell you. Twenty years ago there was a strike where I come from. Yorkshire. My family are all miners. Everyone in the town where I grew up were miners. So when the Government threatened to close all the pits down the miners went out on strike. It was the biggest strike our country ever had. Two hundred thousand men fought it out for a whole year. And the bosses and the government threw everything they had at the miners. Fifty thousand policemen. It was like a war for a few months."

"What happened?"

"The miners lost. The pits all got closed."

"And you were in it?"

"I was in it. Me and my brother and two others. We tried to fight them at their own game. We tried to make a difference."

"What happened?"

"They killed my brother. They framed me. I don't know what happened to the other two."

This widened the identikit eyes of the twins.

"You're kidding. They killed your brother. How?"

"They hit him in the face with the butt of a rifle. He fell badly. He fractured his skull on the kerb. He died in front of my eyes. We were twins. Just like you two."

There was a long silence. For a few moments they stared out across the playing fields where a few youngsters played football in the sunshine. When Barry broke the silence his voice was almost awed.

"How did they frame you?"

"They broke into our car without us knowing. They put machine guns in the boot. And explosives. The stuff was from Libya. In those days Libya was like Al Qaeda. The terrorists. They said that I was a terrorist. They said that we were planning to blow things up. To shoot people. A jury found me guilty."

"How long did they give you?"

"Twenty-five years. I served twenty."

"That's no fair. When our dad gets the jail he only ever serves half. You should have been out after twelve."

Lenny smiled. "They don't do good behaviour for terrorists. Terrorists have a different set of rules."

"And they said that you were a terrorist? Really?"

"Yes they did. And they convicted me. So you can see why it will be big news when we go and stand outside those offices on Tuesday morning."

"Bloody hell"

"Absolutely bloody hell."

"But you weren't really a terrorist."

"No. Like I said. I was framed. Not that anyone believed me. Do you believe me?"

"Course we do. Our dad was framed the last time. He was never even there when they did that warehouse. He was with us. But nobody believed us did they. They believed all the other witnesses who only gave evidence to get themselves off."

Lenny nodded. "Aye. I heard as much. That's why I figured you'd understand. That's why I want you to be my main men. I hope that when we go to those offices every morning there'll be loads of us. But when all the stuff about me comes out people will get put off. So it might well be just the three of us. But that doesn't matter. Because the three of us will be enough. At the moment nobody knows what the Council have done. Nobody knows and nobody cares. It is just another secret. By this time in two weeks everybody will know. Not just here in Dumfries. All over Scotland. And that will put the Council in the spotlight. So lads. It's make your mind up time. In or out?"

Again they talked with their eyes. Again Lenny had to swallow down the acid memories of all the times when he and Frank had done the same. And the two little faces broke into smiles at the very same instant.

"Lenny."

Tim or Barry? No idea.

"Yes."

"Are we going to be on the tele?"

"Are you kidding? As the guys at the top of USY you'll never be off it."

The meeting outside McDonalds had been the easy part of his day's work. Then had come the nightmare tasks. He had completed the first. He had taken tea in the quiet piece of hell that was the front room of Luke Crenshaw's parents. He had seen the loss that would never heal in their blank faces. He had done his best to explain what it was that he planned to do. He tried to explain why he had decided to do it. He told them of his past and how the media would climb into it. He asked if he could use the name of their dead son in the battle he was about to fight. Most of the time he felt as if he was talking to himself. They were like two figures from one of the new reality museums where waxwork figures froze moments of history. Here is a front room from the first years of the twenty-first century. These parents have just lost their only son to drugs. Note the tidy surroundings. Note the cleanliness of the front room. Note the respectability of their attire. Remember that the drug epidemic that swept Europe in those years found its way into every corner . . .

He had stumbled after a while. Were they listening? Why the hell should they listen to him? But when he had stumbled Luke's father had slowly raised his eyes and nodded.

"You were there for him Lenny. We know that. Not just at the end. Before as well. When he was lonely and getting bullied. You made his life better. We'll never forget that you know. If you want to use Luke's name to help others, then fine. If you are going to picket those offices on Buccleuch Street on Tuesday, then fine. I'll be there. And I'll stay there for as long as you stay there."

He had reached out for his wife's hand and taken it. She hadn't spoken. Instead she had nodded, tears bursting out down cheeks that had been awash since the terrible news had arrived and destroyed their lives. She had gently released the grip of her husband's fingers and got to her feet. There was a photo album on the coffee table. Every page was filled with Luke. She looked through it slowly. Carefully. And at last she chose. It was a picture of a smiling Luke on the morning of the Under 14's cup final. A head and shoulders shot. His spirit seemed to explode from the shiny paper.

"Here. You can use this. Blow it up and put it on one of your placards. A picture paints a thousand words. Shame them Lenny. Shame them with my blessing."

Now it was the McGuire house. Another Sunnybank door. Another front room painfully spick-and-span. Another living nightmare. He sat and took his tea and told his story. Zoe's mother couldn't hold back the tears. She went through tissue after tissue and Lenny didn't know if he should go on. Roger McGuire was in another place altogether. A truly terrible place. It was written all over his face. He had betrayed his princess. He had allowed his pride and anger to prevail. He had walked away from her and now she was dead. She had begged and wept and he had turned her away. So many times he had said that she was no daughter of his. Not if she stayed with that Kevin Peters. And now she was indeed no daughter of his. No daughter of anyone. Gone. Gone and he had deserted her to keep face with the neighbours and the lads down at the club. Deserted so that he could hold his head up high. Gone. Gone and he had sent her away. And nothing would ever make it right. Lenny's words barely registered. Nothing registered any more. He couldn't work. Couldn't sleep. Couldn't do anything.

Lenny was about to get up from his chair and make an exit. He shouldn't have come at all. He shouldn't have intruded.

"I'm sorry. So sorry. It was wrong to come. I just felt that . . . well. I hope you understand."

On his feet now. Clumsy. Awkward. Incapable of dealing with the depth of their despair. Wishing that Sally was with him to find the right words. Zoe's brother Rory got up with him. He had stayed in the background whilst Lenny had talked, perched on a chair in the corner of the room. Now he stood and waited for Lenny to make his stumbling farewells.

"Sorry Rory. Really. I should have stayed away."

"No. It's good that you came."

Lenny barely had to look down to the boy's face. He was tall for a fourteen-year-old. And as their eyes met Lenny knew that the boy was carrying the wreckage of the family on his back. He reached out and held the boy's shoulder.

"You know where to come if you need any help?"

Rory nodded. "Thanks. I'll be OK. My uncle and aunt are coming down from Aberdeen at the weekend. He's taken two weeks off."

Lenny nodded and made to leave.

"You said eight-thirty? On Tuesday?"

"Aye. That's right."

"I'll be there. Maybe I'll persuade some mates to come along. You said that the Crenshaws had given you a picture?"

"Yes."

"Give me a minute."

Rory left the room and left Lenny alone with the tears of his mother and the vacant staring face of his father. He returned with a picture of his dead sister. Her last school photo. Sparkling eyes. A smile that predated the ultimate misery of her sixteenth year. Zoe from before. Zoe who might have been.

Lenny took the photograph. Lenny walked out of the house into the summer sun. Sally had asked him to shake off his twenty years in hiding and to go out and fight for her. For the family. For all the memories. And he had not had the strength to face up to the shame of saying no. But now it was different. No longer was Lenny the reluctant warrior. Not after the eyes he had looked into. The stale feted air of despair and loss. He had awoken as an army of one. Now it was an army of five. One ex-cricketer/terrorist. One pair of terrible twins. One bereaved father. One bereaved brother. A strange, desperate little army that was about to kick out at the might of the system. The very thought of it made him smile into the heat of the afternoon. He had slept for twenty years. Now he was awake again.

One or two pedestrians stopped and watched him as he strode by them. He was singing quietly under his breath.

"Here we go . . . here we go . . . here we go . . ."

They saw a tall man in middle age with a fierce smile and a straight back. They didn't see the ghost of the twin brother who marched beside him.

Sidney Nesbit's parents had moved up to Dumfries when he had been fourteen. His dad worked in a bank in the centre of London and had decided one morning that he could no longer tolerate the four hour daily commute from Bedford and back. He cashed in their detached house for a fortune and bought a cottage a few miles up in the hills above Dumfries. To supplement the pension that he took early, he set himself up as an independent financial advisor whilst his wife spent her days in the unaccustomed space of their half acre garden.

Sidney had felt utterly uprooted. He had just broken into the Bedfordshire under 17 cricket eleven and had got himself his first girlfriend. Every bone in his body resented being taken away to a place where cricket was as much of a joke as his southern accent. For two years his time at school had been pretty miserable. Mates were hard to come by, especially now that the family lived so far out in the middle of nowhere. For a while he had refused even to consider joining the Dumfries Cricket Club. It was a joke. Just like the whole town. He retreated to his room and spent his days cursing the world on his PS2. It had been the sight of Steve Harmison bowling like a Durham hurricane for seven match winning wickets at Sabina Park in Jamaica that had finally dragged him out of his two year sulk and delivered him for a Wednesday night net practice. It hadn't taken long for the ice to be broken. Sure he had been pretty rusty, but the speed of his bowling stood out as the farmers and accountants of the Dumfries middle order hopped and jumped. And as he had bowled he'd noticed a tall man who had stood to one side with arms folded and watched very carefully. After ten minutes the man came over and took his hand and moved his fingers into a new position on the seam. Not much. Just a fraction. Enough for the ball to feel awkward. But his next delivery was much straighter and the ball nipped away from the batsman. The man was waiting for him at the end of his run up.

"I'm Lenny and you're not bad."

Lenny had spent hours with him that summer and had done more than improve his action. He had listened to all of his anger. Soaked it up like a sponge. Drawn it out. And when it was out, Sidney had been calmer. Easier with himself. And his last year at school had been a whole lot better. There had been a steady girlfriend and invitations to parties and he had started to speak to his father again.

When the results of his exams landed on the mat everyone was pleasantly surprised. His mum and dad wanted him to head off to university. He wanted none of it. His long-term girlfriend was now on the verge of being a fiancé. She had got a job as a trainee manager in one of the shops on the High Street and her dad had bought her a flat. No way was Sidney about to jeopardise everything with another move. So it was that he applied for a job as a trainee reporter on the local paper and embarked on a career in journalism.

As the rain of spring had given in to the warmth of summer, all was pretty well perfect with Sidney's world. He had moved in with Elspeth who was now an official fiancé despite the misgivings of two sets of parents who agreed that they were far too young. The job at the paper was interesting enough and he had started the season bowling better than ever before.

Seldom had a pint of lager tasted better. It was seven o'clock on a Sunday evening. Dumfries Cricket Club had entered hitherto unchartered waters. They had put themselves into the fourth round of the cup care of 3 for 45 from Lenny Baxter and 5 for 27 from Sidney Nesbit. The evening sun was still full of warmth and he was sitting on the grass outside with his parents and Elspeth. Life hadn't been quite this good before. Not even close.

"Not bad for a southerner."

He hadn't heard Lenny approach. The older man passed him a pint.

"Thanks. You weren't so bad yourself. Considering your bus pass is due and all that."

"Cheeky sod."

Lenny sat down next to him and took a swig at his beer.

"I've got a lead for you."

"What kind of lead?"

"A journalistic lead. Be at the Municipal Chambers on Buccleuch Street at half past eight on Tuesday morning. OK?"

"Why?"

Lenny tapped the side of his nose. "All will be revealed good sir. Let's just say it'll be your first exclusive."

Sidney had done his best to find out more for the rest of the evening until the Yorkshireman took his leave from the bar a little after ten. Not a chance. All he got was an enigmatic smile which only made it worse. It bugged him all day Monday. Municipal Chambers at eight-thirty on a Tuesday morning? What for? What possible reason could Lenny have for asking him on such an errand? And he had said something about it being an exclusive. No matter how far he stretched his developing reporter's mind he couldn't begin to see what on earth could go on outside the Municipal Chambers at 8.30 on a regulation Dumfries Tuesday.

The alarm rolled him out of bed at seven whilst Elspeth cursed him in her sleep. Outside the hot spell had finally broken and rain splashed the bedroom window. Would it matter? Would it interfere with whatever Lenny had going?

He showered, made coffee and ate Cornflakes. Radio 5 informed him that three more Marines had perished in an ambush on the road into Famoudi. That was over twenty in the last three weeks. The reporter on the scene said that it was looking increasingly likely that Famoudi was about to become the next Fallujah. In the airwaves behind the reporter's voice it was possible to make out the distant crackle of small arms fire. Sidney digested the words from the radio along with his cereal. Nice and concise. Nothing too flowery. Competent. He listened and read news for how it was presented rather than the news itself. This guy was good. Superb in fact. Would he ever scale such dizzy journalistic heights? Well, according to Lenny he was about to get his first exclusive. The idea made him smile. Buccleuch Street today. Famoudi tomorrow. As if. He made a mug of tea and took it into Elspeth who peeled her eyes open to take in the rain outside and then buried her head under the covers with a groan.

Outside it wasn't as bad as it looked. The rain had come but much of the warmth had stayed. There wasn't much of a breeze and as

Sidney marched through the nearly empty streets he decided it was really quite refreshing. He reached Buccleuch Street bridge at 8.15. Too early. For what? Not long to wait now. He took a few minutes staring down into the swirling waters that rolled beneath him. Three swans looked mildly annoyed at the newly swelled river that bounced them up and down and made it tough for them to stay afloat with their accustomed dignity.

8.25. Rain in Dumfries. Gunfire in Famoudi. Five wickets in the cup. An exclusive to be written-up. Showtime.

He saw them as soon as he came off the bridge. A small group. Two adults. A teenager. Two kids. Lenny was head and shoulders above the others, very straight and tall in a blue waterproof jacket. As Sidney closed the two hundred yards of the street he saw that the others with Lenny had placards. Words on two. Pictures on two. At a distance of fifty yards the pictures came into focus. And as he recognised the faces, a small shock of excitement ran through him. Young smiling faces. Bright eyes brimming with hope. They were faces that had become burningly familiar to the town of Dumfries over the last month. They were faces that had stared out from his paper's front page. Luke Crenshaw and Zoe McGuire.

It had been the biggest story the paper had run during the course of his fledgling career. Sidney hadn't played any part in it. He had been left to cover the court page and the Council announcements whilst the more senior reporters had covered the agony of Sunnybank. For a fortnight the town had been wrapped in debate about death and drugs. But it had passed as the weather had stayed hot and the holidays season started.

Twenty yards now. Close enough to read the words on the placards held by two young ruffians whose faces were alike as peas in a pod.

"STOP THE DYING – GIVE US TOSH HOUSE."

Tosh house? What the hell was Tosh House? And what could it possibly have to do with stopping the dying? He didn't need a Pulitzer to work out what the dying bit was about. The dying was about the beaming faces of Zoe and Luke. Lenny was very still. Very tall. Smiling as he watched.

"Gentlemen. The media is with us. Morning Sidney."

One of the baseball-capped twins stepped forward.

"You a reporter then?"

"Yes."

A small hand was thrust towards him. "Barry Finch. Chairman of USY."

"USY? I'm sorry, I haven't . . ."

"Union of Sunnybank Youth. I've got an official statement for you."

Behind him Tim covered his mouth to try and stem the growing laughter that was welling up in his throat. Lenny cuffed him on the back of his head. Barry had sensed his brother's amusement at his formal air but he managed to keep it going and passed Sidney a piece of A4.

STOPTHE DYING

"On the night of June 14th Sunnybank lost two young people. Luke Crenshaw, 12 and Zoe McGuire, 16, paid the price of the Council's neglect. Over 3500 citizens under the age of eighteen live on the Sunnybank Estate. The only leisure facility provided for them by Dumfries and Galloway Council is the Zone Centre which can only accommodate twenty-five clients at any given time. Three months ago the Management Committee of The Zone applied for funding to develop the abandoned site of McIntosh House into a more appropriate facility for the district. The new centre would have over ten rooms and space outside and could accommodate over a hundred young people at peak times. The application was refused and it was the decision of the Council to sell off the site to a property developer.

It is in the light of this decision that the Union of Sunnybank Youth (USY) was formed on 11 July 2005. USY will contest the shameful decision in any and every way until the elected members and paid officials of Dumfries and Galloway Council reverse their shameful decision. All Council buildings and places of work will be targets for USY pickets. All Council staff will be discouraged from crossing picket lines. We urge all Council staff to withdraw their labour until the decision about the future of McIntosh House is reversed. We will lobby the local community to stop all Council Tax payments until such a time when the decision regarding McIntosh House is reversed. USY has the full support of the families of Luke Crenshaw and Zoe McGuire. USY is staging this campaign in the name of the dead and in the memory of the dead. Our campaign goes under the name of 'STOP THE DYING'. Our campaign will continue until the Council reverses it's decision.

For any further information please contact the USY Press Officer, Rory McGuire on 07764 467 345.

Sidney read through the statement. Then he shook his head a little. Then he read it again. When he reached the bottom of the page for a second time he looked up to Lenny who remained very still with the same big smile.

"Is this serious Lenny?"

"As serious as it gets."

"But there's only five of you."

"Aye. That's right enough. This morning we are five. Happen we'll only be five tomorrow morning as well. But then folk are going to go out and read all about it in the paper and come Thursday we'll be a few more. Anyway, this isn't just about numbers Sidney. It's about exposure. Coverage. You guys. Once we hit the front pages, the Council will be hopping about as if they're in the desert with no shoes."

Sidney's face became borderline miserable. He liked Lenny. The big man from Yorkshire had been there when his life had been bleak. He had always been struck by the quiet common sense of the man. And now this. It made no sense. Of course he could understand that feelings were running high after the two deaths. But Lenny was living in cloud cuckoo land if he thought that five crazies with a few placards and a half-baked Union were about to get anywhere close to the front page. The worst of it was that he was only too aware that he owed Lenny big time and now the favour was being called in. Didn't Lenny realise that he was just a junior scrubbing around in the dust at the bottom of the ladder? He had no clout. No say. The editor would laugh his socks off if he went into the office and tried to claim that this was front page news.

"Lenny . . . I think you've got the wrong end of the stick here . . . I mean there is a story here . . . especially with the families and that . . . but . . . well it won't be front page news. I'm sorry but it just won't."

Lenny's smile never slipped an inch.

"Aye it will. More than you can believe my friend. I promised you an exclusive and that is what you're about to get. Now. Take a few pictures. Get a few quotes from the lads here and get yourself back to the office. Say nowt to your editor just yet. When you get in switch on the computer, log on and get *Google* up on the screen. Tap in Lenny Baxter – Haddington – 1984. Then you'll find the story. OK?"

Haddington? 1984? What in God's name was he on about. Sidney was about to say more but Lenny stopped him with a heavy hand on the shoulder.

"Just trust me, OK? Now then. If I'm not mistaken, this is Mr Billingham on his way into work. Happen you should get a quote off him."

Sidney followed the direction of Lenny's gaze. A middle-aged man in a three piece suit was approaching fast with a briefcase. The young reporter spoke from the side of his mouth.

"Who is he?"

Lenny saw no need for secrecy. He spoke clear and loud so that his words would carry down the pavement to the approaching bureaucrat.

"Mr Walter Billingham is the business manager for Dumfries and Lower Nithsdale. I think it is a fair assumption that he will have strongly recommended that no funds should be made available for the development at McIntosh House. Is that correct Mr Billingham?"

Billingham had reached them by now. He wasn't a man who had much of a reputation for humour. He had a thin, rather Dickensian face was framed by a Bobby Charlton comb across job that emphasised rather than hid a pale bony crown. His eyes flitted across the figures who blocked his way into work with ill-concealed annoyance. Sidney waited whilst Barry stepped forward and handed him a flyer. As he read, the lines on the pale face of the suited man seemed to deepen into trenches. The day had started badly for Walter Billingham and it seemed destined to get about fifty times worse. The first setback to his day had been the bluntness of his razor which had left him feeling scraped and scoured. Then the post had come with a statement from Visa which revealed the stark facts of his wife's fun and games on Princes Street during a recent Ladies Club outing. It defied all belief. £187.47. Astounding. Didn't the damn woman realise that they were trying to put money aside for a new car. Was that such a difficult concept to grasp? Well obviously it was. £187.47

worth of difficult. He had thrown the statement to the breakfast table where she sat with one of her pathetic celebrity magazines.

"Well?"

She had taken the statement and glanced at it without much interest before tossing it back down.

"Well what?"

"You know full well what. £187.47. That's what. Clothes I presume."

"Yes. And cosmetics. A problem dear?"

He had nearly spat out his tea. "Well, actually it is, because I seem to remember that we were trying to put funds away for a new car, or am I mistaken?"

"Oh for goodness sake Walter, get a life. The car we have is less than two years old. The way you go on you would think it was a rust bucket. I really can't see what the hurry is."

Get a life! She had actually told him to get a life. And to make it worse the long-haired slob that was his son had started to snigger. The boy had taken to wearing idiotic baggy clothes, almost all of them black. Apparently it was the uniform of a Goth, whatever that was. Walter had turned to tell the little swine to shut the hell up when he had been stopped by an utterly unbelievable sight. The boy was wearing eye-shadow. Surely not. Impossible. Not for school. It had to be lack of sleep. But when he looked closely he saw that it wasn't lack of sleep. It was eye shadow. Make-up. On the face of his son.

"What the hell is that?"

A blank look copied from some CD case. "What?"

"That. On your eyes."

The boy shovelled in a spoon of Rice Crispies and shrugged. "Eye-shadow. So?"

"So? So it's school. That's what."

"They're cool about it. They like to encourage individuality."

"Well they might be 'cool' about it but I'm not. You can just get yourself up those stairs and wipe that muck off your face . . ."

"Don't be so Retro dad."

He had been about to completely flip when his wife chirped in.

"Walter. He's sixteen. He isn't breaking any rules. It's life darling. Get used to it."

He stared into her face and read the mockery in her eyes. He couldn't begin to remotely comprehend what he had ever seen in the ghastly, horrendous piece of humanity that was his wife. As he had crashed the front door he had heard the sound of their laughter and he could have gladly tossed a grenade back through the letterbox.

He had reached the outskirts of the town only to discover that a new set of roadworks had appeared that extended his journey by a quarter of an hour and meant that all his usual parking spots were taken. By the time he marched up Buccleuch Street he was twenty-five minutes behind his usual schedule and, more than everything else, he hated to be late.

And now this. This fiasco. This mockery. This . . .

He read the words on the paper as if they were poison. Then he screwed them up into a tight ball and dropped it into a nearby bin. The little rat who had handed him the paper was grinning. So was the other one. Two impudent freckled little swine in their matching caps.

"That's not very nice is it mister. That's our manifesto."

"Manifesto! It's not a manifesto. It's a joke. Now if you'll excuse me . . ."

But his path was blocked. A middle-aged man this time. No smile. A light golf jacket and shiny shoes and eyes that stopped Billingham dead.

"I hope that you are not saying that my son's death was a joke."

What? He took a look at the placard. He remembered the story in the paper. A dead boy. Glue sniffing or something. Oh Christ. And then he knew the other face as well. A dead girl. A bloody junkie by all accounts. Typical. A nasty thieving little cow when she was alive but the minute she was dead it was the old school photo and butter wouldn't melt in her mouth. He had been mad when he had read the stories. Mad about all the bleating. Always bloody Sunnybank. At times he wished that someone would bomb the wretched place flat. Do a Grozny on it. Flatten every drug-ridden stone of the wretched place. It was like a bottomless pit that the Council poured money into. Social workers, health visitors, police time, wardens, repaired vandalism, smashed-up schools, burnt out houses, God he hated the place. And now they were here pushing their silly bits of paper in his face whilst his wife and son tittered at him. But he couldn't say anything. Not when the boy's father was blocking his way and eating through him with those eyes.

"Look. I'm sorry for your loss. Really. I'm running late I'm afraid, I . . ."

He tried to ease past the man without it being aggressive. Tony Crenshaw was having none of it. He reached out and placed a hand on Billingham's shoulder.

"We're not going anywhere you know. We'll be here every morning. It doesn't matter how long it takes. Every morning until you do what is right."

To his horror Billingham realised that he was being photographed by a young man he hadn't noticed before.

"What the hell do you think you are doing?"

A cocky smile. Like his bloody son. "Sidney Nesbit. Dumfries Standard. I wonder if you have a comment sir?"

"Acomment? About this? No I bloody well haven't thank you very much."

He had left his tittering wife and son behind in the kitchen. He had pushed by the freckled twins from hell and the accusing eyes of the father. Now he brushed past the sneering reporter. The only obstacle left now between Billingham and the sanctuary of his desk was the tall blond man.

"You're aware that you are crossing a picket line Mr Billingham?"

Billingham had to look up a good six inches to find Lenny's eyes.

"This isn't a picket line. This is a bloody joke."

And with that he scuttled up the steps and away from the firing line. Lenny watched him go with an amused expression.

"And you have a nice day too Mr Billingham."

Sidney stayed for an hour and watched the looks on the faces of those who were stopped on their way into the Municipal Chambers. Some treated the motley band of pickets as if they were religious pilgrims on the High Street. Others paused and read the pieces of A4 that were presented to them with smiles and frowns. Three knew Tony Crenshaw and took time to talk and share sympathy. By nine- thirty every office inside the grand old building was aflame with the gossip about what was going on outside.

When he was happy that he had seen enough the young reporter jumped on his bike and cycled back to the office. His editor looked fraught and was doing the rounds. The same old Tuesday morning crisis in a town where midweek news was forever thin on the ground. Sidney said that he thought that he might have something and asked for an hour or so to put it together. The editor barely listened. The kid was hardly likely to come up with anything worth the ink.

His computer shook itself into life and joined the network internet. Sidney took a sip at his coffee and followed his instructions. *www.goog . . .* the machine's memory did the rest. For a moment he stared at the empty box thoughtfully. What was he about to learn? The past. Facts. Secrets. Memories.

'Lenny Baxter Haddington 1984'

Enter

Your search took 3 seconds and found 43,000 results.

Holy Christ.

" . . . Judge Fredricks summed up in the most forceful of terms before handing down a sentence of twenty-five years . . ."

" . . . Chief Superintendent Philips informed the court that the serial numbers on the Kalashnikov automatic rifles gave conclusive proof of a Libyan origin . . ."

" . . . a spokesman for the NUM stated categorically that they had no knowledge of the activities of the Baxter brothers . . . ."

" . . . Libyan Radio today has absolutely denied any . . ."

" . . . Prime Minister Margaret Thatcher made a statement yesterday in the House of Commons regarding the evidence of Libyan involvement in the recent arms find in Yorkshire, she said . . ."

Page after page after page. News items mainly. Snippets from a time when Britain had come close to the edge. Memories of a Cold War long gone. Memories of the greatest strike of them all. The facts about Lenny Baxter the terrorist. Another Cambridge bad apple alongside Burgess and McLean and Philby and Blunt. An enemy of the State. A bomber who had taken Gaddafi's gold. The kind of huge prison sentence usually reserved for Irishmen from the mean estates of Belfast and Londonderry.

Unbelievable. Sidney realised that he was shaking. He realised that his coffee had gone cold in the cup. He had been promised an exclusive. He had a story that was a primed bomb. Lenny picked up his call on the third ring.

"Hello."

"It's Sidney. I'm on *Google.*"

"Good."

"It says that you have always maintained your innocence."

"Yes. I'm like a record that has been stuck for twenty years. Not that anyone listens to me much. The stuff was planted. Who knows who did it. There were a lot of cowboys riding all over Yorkshire at that time. Freelancers mostly. Lots of cowboys and lots of cash. Me and Frank had become a thorn in their side. They got rid of us."

"They killed your brother."

"Aye. Not deliberately. It was a pure accident. But yes. They killed him. Maybe he was the lucky one. Look Sidney, don't get all hung about the guilt or innocence thing. You'll get one shot at this. Then the world and its dog will be all over it. Let the facts speak for themselves and don't forget to talk about what you saw this morning. That's all I ask."

"OK Lenny. I'll do my best."

"Good enough for me."

Sidney's best was plastered over the front page the next day. The story spread all the way to page six. The editor had a Wednesday beyond all his dreams as his phone rang hot with calls from colleagues all over the country. The headline screamed "TERRORIST FIGHTS OUTIN THE OPEN". The picture showed Lenny looking on as Tony Crenshaw gripped the shoulder of a rattled looking Walter Billingham. The front page hammered the basic facts. Guns from Libya. Twenty-five years. USY. McIntosh House. Inside were the back-up stories. "LENNY BAXTER – INNOCENT OR GUILTY?". The internet was full of sites dedicated to claims that the Baxter brothers had been framed by the dark forces of capitalism. Over the years there had been many who had taken up Lenny's cause. Two Labour MPs. Various civil rights groups. Campaigning lawyers. There had been several appeals, but none had been successful. The truth about the Baxter brothers was never teased out and the ranks of the establishment had remained closed for two decades. There was a picture of McIntosh House and quotes from the niece of the Yorkshire terrorist who ran the Zone youth centre in Sunnybank Estate. There were archive photos of the old battles on the picket lines of Yorkshire to go alongside the small band on the pavement of Buccleuch Street. Never again would the Dumfries Standard have an edition quite like it. Especially on a Wednesday.

The General liked the look of Dale Nash as he marched into his office and stood to rigid attention. Tall. Handsome. But some warmth about his young face. And intelligence. The files told the story of a boy from a small town in Virginia who had finished close to the top of most of his classes. A sportsman as well. College had seen him further distinguish himself both in the classroom and on the football field. His dad was a corn farmer with cattle and his mum kept house. The family never missed church on a Sunday. Dale married his high school sweetheart soon after graduation and she was as pretty as a picture. There had been no shortage of career options open to him but he had chosen the Marines and the General liked that. He liked anyone who chose his beloved Marine Corps, but he wasn't pig headed enough not to realise that it represented a third or fourth choice for most.

Not Dale Nash. He had joined because he was a patriot. Simple as that. The young man loved America and all it stood for. A genuine throwback. Those in charge of checking him out had been understandably suspicious. Obviously they had. Such motivation was generally confined to Hollywood at the dawn of the Twenty-First Century. Sure, patriotism was running high at home, but flying a flag on the front lawn and voting Bush was a far cry from signing up for the Corps. The investigators had been convinced that there would be some skeletons rattling around in the Virginian cupboards of Dale's youth. There had to be and they had to find them because if they didn't, then the press most certainly would.

Nothing. Not a single blemish. He was just a bright boy from the South with a pretty wife and a big heart. Once inside the Corps things had been outstanding. It took him less than five years to make Captain and all reports were A-Grade. His sergeants liked him. His men liked him. His superiors liked him. Everyone liked him. He seemed to have achieved the balance between the hard uncompromising discipline of the Corps with a closeness to his men that was needed to encourage them into harm's way. Nash had won his soldiering spurs in two tours of Iraq and one in Afghanistan. When war fighting had been required, his Charlie Company had secured objectives with maximum force. When a peacekeeping role was required, they kept the peace without leaving embarrassing corpses strewn about the place.

The files had been conclusive. Dale Nash was a young man on the fast track. In twenty years time he would have stars on his shoulder and a desk on one of the upper floors of the Pentagon.

PART TWO

Now the young Captain stood to rigid attention at the other side of the desk, his eyes fixed on a spot on the wall behind the General's head.

"At ease Dale. Take a seat. Want coffee? Maybe a coke?"

"Coke would be good sir."

The general shouted to his adjutant outside who duly delivered two cold cans from the fridge. The General lit up and gestured that it was OK by him for Dale to follow suit. The younger man shook his head.

"I gather you've been in Famoudi for a month now son."

"That is correct sir."

"How you finding it out there?"

"Our sector has been quiet sir. Three contacts. No casualties on our side sir."

"And their side?"

A slight shadow passed over the young eyes.

"Six sir."

"Any of those collateral damage?"

A slightly bigger shadow.

"Three civilian dead sir."

The general leaned back and blew a plume of smoke into the ceiling fan. The young man had gently picked him up on his military jargon. He liked that. It had been at the dawn of his own career in the Marines when some faceless desk jockey in Washington had decided they should describe dead Vietnamese civilians as 'collateral damage'. Was there a slight defiance in the young eyes. Maybe. He hoped so.

"Son, what's your evaluation of our situation here in Famoudi?"

"Sir I believe the situation is under control sir."

The General stood up and took a stare out of the window over the dusty parade ground of the command compound.

"And that of course is the right answer. The problem is that it is also a pile of crap. I know it. You know it. Every Marine out there knows it. You know that we're losing three men a day to combat stress. Shipping them out quietly. We're also getting reports of escalating drug use. Hard stuff too. It was the same in Nam. Men can only take so much stress. We know it, but we don't admit it. Every goddamn day wondering if every pedestrian is a walking bomb. That's 24/7 stress. Overload. So Captain, the situation isn't under control at all. The only way we're keeping a lid on things out there is by shooting first and asking later. The only way we're controlling a damn thing is by scaring the hell out of the people that live there. And the more we scare them, the more they hate us. And the more they hate us the more volunteers will stand up to become human bombs. I've seen it all son. Thirty years ago in Nam. And in the end we scuttled off that Embassy roof like guys caught with their pants down in another man's bedroom."

Dale was rather taken aback even though The General had a reputation for shooting from the hip. His commander turned from the window and ground out his cigarette.

"Famoudi is at boiling pot and the lid is bouncing on the steam son. We are a heartbeat from being another Fallujah. A heartbeat. What did you make of the Fallujah Operation son?"

Fallujah was a neighbouring town where the Iraqi rebellion had found a focal point. For a few months it had become a no go area until the Marines had been sent in and told to resolve the situation. They had employed maximum force, endured minimal casualties and killed a lot of people. Dale had watched the whole thing with a feeling of distaste.

"I believe we executed our mission with minimal casualties sir."

The General nodded. "Sure. We took the town. We didn't lose many guys, but that is about where the good news stops. God alone knows how many we killed. Nobody even tried to do a proper body count. It is my belief that we achieved four things in Fallujah son. One, we flattened the town and made it all but uninhabitable. Two, we played it safe and used as much ordinance as we could which meant that we killed far too many. Three, our tactics further alienated the locals and guaranteed the bad guys ten years worth of volunteers. Four, we were asked to do stuff that the US Marine Corps isn't supposed to do. I'm not dumb enough to buy into all the John Wayne stuff, but I don't believe it is the job of the Corps to flatten civilian areas to help politicians to look tough on the evening news."

"Sir."

The General smiled. What else was the young man supposed to say? He lit another cigarette.

"There are those of us who have convinced our masters that the Fallujah approach is doomed. Nobody likes to admit it, but the Brits have shown us up with the way they have done things down south. They run their street patrols without helmets and the locals actually seem to quite like them. They started to send out the right messages from day one. They talk to people instead of shooting them. Result? They ain't taking the casualties. Some of us figure it is time to learn a lesson or two. How do you feel about that?"

Dale wasn't sure what was expected of him. His father had always preached the concept of when in doubt tell the truth.

"Sir, I would fully agree with that evaluation."

"Good. I thought you would. That's why you have been chosen for a new mission. It is my belief that Fallujah was a disaster. That is not a thought I want sharing son. It is my thought and I am sharing it with you. Understood?"

"Sir."

"We need to send out a new message. We need to show Marines getting out on the streets and helping people, not shooting them. I'm talking about carrying bags for old ladies and kicking footballs with kids. Hell. I guess I'm talking about doing it the British way for a while. I have approval for Charlie Company to run a trial on a new tactical approach. You good for that son?"

"Of course sir."

"It will be dangerous, make no mistake. It will take a long time before the locals take much of a shine to us."

"I wouldn't have joined the Corps if I had wanted to avoid danger sir, None of us would."

And there it was. The shining eyes of the idealist. A young man who had put on the uniform to make the world a better place. A good choice. The right choice.

"There's more son. I have arranged for a camera team from ABC to shadow you for six weeks. You will become a regular on prime time. We need to put out a different message. The whole goddamn world is beginning to see us as some kind of bunch of savages. It's bad for business Dale. USAPlc relies on presenting the right image to our customers. We're supposed to be the good guys, the ones in the white hats. It's why people buy into Coke and Levi and Big Macs and Chevvys. The American Dream son. The American nightmare is bad for business. Bad for the stock holders. So the men upstairs want something different on the evening news. They want a bunch of baby kissing. They want a human face. They want some care and decency and less bodies on the streets. Son, your face has been chosen for the cameras. They want to make you into a good old-fashioned all-American hero. You good with that?"

Dale was knocked over. "Sir, I believe that Charlie Company is an appropriate choice for the mission you have in mind. I will try not to let anyone down."

A smile from the older man. "I don't believe you will son."

Middle age had tuned Josh Ogilvy into a creature of habit. It wasn't something that he had noticed. It wasn't a thing that anyone noticed because Josh had also become a recluse. Every morning he woke at six without the need for an alarm. Dressing-gown. Kitchen. Coffee into the filter. A CD. A look outside to see what the day would bring. A first cigarette and then onto the internet to find out what was happening in the big wide world.

Josh's heroin addiction had consumed him for seven years. What set him apart from so many of the other thousands of heroin addicts all over London was that he could afford it. His father had left him more than well enough provided for to feed his habit. For seven long years he had pumped a hundred pounds of heroin a day into his veins and blanked out the memories that ate away at his soul like hungry maggots. In seven years he had fed in excess of a quarter of a million pounds into the accounts of those who provided the powder to kill all the pain. They had been years of oblivion. Years of running ahead of a tsunami of guilt. Years of slow death.

Then one morning for no reason he could ever fathom, he had woken up to the feeling that it was time to change. More of his inheritance had paid for a year in a Californian rehab from which he had emerged three stones heavier and with a small desire to live out the rest of his life.

Next had been his wandering phase. Europe. Africa. Many, many months in India. He had dived into the still soothing waters of the East. Months of yoga. Meditation classes with monks high in the mountains. He had even shaken the hand of the Dalai Lama. And very slowly they had taught him how to find some peace. How to move the nightmares of his past far away and out of sight. He had pursued Buddhism through the humid forests of Thailand and Cambodia before swinging south to the islands of the Pacific. Then it had been a slow meander through the small towns of America. Bars and barbeques and straw-haired women who loved the way he talked. Aflat thirteen floors over the mayhem of Manhattan. A cabin for a snowy winter in the hills of Vermont. Then home to London after five years.

By this time all of the cash element of his inheritance was spent. He sold the houses in London and Shropshire and spent a fraction on a small cottage in the Dordogne. And his life had entered the fourth phase. Public school rebel. Heroin addict. Nomad. Recluse. He took his eastern tranquilities to three rural acres of Southern France and life became a model of simplicity. His days were spent with his vegetables and chickens. He chopped logs. He cleared areas that had been long overgrown. He did herbs and fruit trees. Life became slow and simple. His evenings were spent on a series of novels that were returned from publishing houses with polite refusals. But the quiet hours of the night now brought sleep without nightmares. It had been a journey from heroin through Buddhism to organic solitude, but in the end the memories had at last faded and he discovered a tranquility for the very first time.

The morning was his window on the world. An hour of the internet over coffee and cigarettes. Sometimes the hour stretched into two or three. Sometimes it was all day, particularly during the build up to the invasion of Iraq. In his nomad era Josh had wandered the world looking for something he could never really define. Now he allowed the world to come to him through his modem. He picked and chose. He sifted. He became an electronic nomad through the subterfuge and lies of the corporate world that he had renounced. But the routine never varied. Switch on. Log on. Enter *Google*. Light up. Type. Lenny Baxter. A habit. Athread all the way back to the end of the first era of his life.

As an addict he had still been torn apart by his betrayal. Sleep would never come without huge chemical assistance. Many, many times he had been on the verge of taking the train up to Wakefield for visiting. On three occasions he had actually made it to Kings Cross. But he had never boarded. What could he have said to his friend? I'm sorry I betrayed you Lenny. I'm sorry that they broke me. I'm sorry they killed Frank. I'm sorry I was the weak link. Because in the darkest, coldest, emptiest hours of the night he always knew that Lenny would never have given him up. They could have wired him from head to toe and he would have got through it. No matter what the cost. And the memories had eaten away at Josh until he was an empty shell.

For a while there had been a few hits during the morning routine. The papers devoted a few lines to the release of yesterday's man from his twenty years of penance. There were a couple of articles remembering the great strike and the part played by the infamous Baxter brothers. Far left websites provided eulogies to forgotten heroes to dwindling audiences. And then nothing. Only the old hits that he had already read. For a while he had considered going home and finding Lenny. He had mused about cleaning out the last of the poison. Where would he be? Maybe Haddington. Maybe anywhere. Maybe far from the land that had destroyed him. The thoughts had never come close to turning into actions. But every morning the routine never varied. Coffee. Cigarette. *Google*. Lenny Baxter.

But this morning, as the early morning heat of the French sun poured through his east facing window, it was different. New hits. Unexpected hits. Hits from The Dumfries Standard. Stories of a picket line outside some Council offices in a small Scottish town. The Union of Sunnybank Youth. A building called McIntosh House. Memories of a life from long, long ago. News of a terrorist from yesterday. And all of a sudden he was smiling like he hadn't smiled for years and years and years. Twenty years. Twenty bloody years and they hadn't managed to put Lenny Baxter down. Not even close. There he was looking older, but still tall as a tree. Standing with four others with their placards. Fronting up another lost cause with defiance written all over his face. And as he stared into the face of his only true friend, Josh knew that the fourth era of his life had come to an end. An hour later he had closed up the cottage and started a journey to Dumfries.

Morning two saw the ranks of the USYpickets more than double. Tim and Barry had forced agreement from Lenny the day before that the union would provide for rolls and crisps and drinks and stuff and they had used this as a tool to recruit four fellow members of the all conquering Sunnybank Under 14's. Lenny rather ruefully realised that the funds of the fledgling union were basically what he had in his pocket and that wasn't about to last very long as it was soon clear that picketing was going to be hungry and thirsty work. Bearing this in mind he instigated a new strategy and sent Barry off to *Poundstretcher* to invest in two plastic buckets to raise funds from passers-by. There was a marked increase in pedestrian traffic, but most of it was concentrated on the far side of Buccleuch Street. People walked slowly and gawped at the strange sight of the small group with their placards. The Wednesday paper had hit the streets in the early morning and by the time the journey to work had started the word was already well and truly out. Sales of the paper that morning were to become a record that The Dumfries Standard would never come close to beating. All over town only one conversation was worth having. It was the Lenny Baxter conversation. Miner. Terrorist. Cricketer. A man who had been caught with guns and explosives from Libya. Twenty years of time. Everyone wanted to get a look. They took different routes to get to work. Routes that included Buccleuch Street which became locked up with traffic soon after eight-thirty. Lenny decided that there should be a price for them all being goldfish in their bowl. Tim and Barry were dispatched across the clogged street with buckets where they made it more than clear that getting a look at what was happening carried a cost. By ten USY was in funds to the tune of £47.36 and bacon, egg and tatty scone rolls were served.

At 10.30 their numbers swelled by a further four. Not only did the new reinforcements add extra legs but they dramatically increased the average age of Lenny's embryonic army. The youngest of the four men who joined them was sixty-seven. The oldest was seventy-three and he was also the leader.

"You Lenny Baxter." Quite a small man. Five-foot-seven at most, but still with a boxer like pair of shoulders.

"Aye that's me?" Lenny was bracing himself for a tongue-lashing. The newcomers looked as if they could well be members of the bring back the birch club. He took a breath and waited to be told what young people needed was more discipline, a good belt about the ears, not some new fangled centre with pool tables and table tennis. In a way he was surprised it had taken until 10.30 a.m.

He couldn't have been more wrong. The tough old leathery face split into a grin and a hand extended.

"Good to know you Lenny. I'm Alex. Alex McCloud. This if Bill, Harold and Eric." The three stepped forward and shook Lenny's hand. All of them seemed pretty spry. None of them looked as if they were about to give him a lecture.

Alex resumed in his role as spokesman. "Read about you in the paper and we got the first bus. We're down from Sanquhar."

And it began to dawn on Lenny. Fit looking old boys. Firm handshakes. Something tough about them. Alex confirmed what he had already half figured out.

"Miners, Lenny. All of us. I did nearly forty years. The other lads all did over thirty. They shut down our pit in the seventies so we had to go and work up in Ayrshire. We were all out in 84. Same as your lot. We remembered you Lenny. And your brother. When we read about the picket we decided that we better come down."

Lenny grinned. "Bloody good to see you lads. We're a bit short of being another Arthur's army, but you have to start somewhere."

"Good enough for us comrade. It's been too long. Lads like us need a wall to have a kick at. Let's see if we can win this time. All four of us have our bus passes so you can count us in, rain or shine. Maybe we'll talk a few other of the boys into coming down. Good enough for you?"

"More than good enough."

By the time they packed up and left Buccleuch Street on the lunchtime of day two they were twelve.

Josh's journey to the fifth era of his life couldn't have been smoother. The internet got him onto an early morning flight from Paris to Prestwick Airport and he left the cottage with time in hand. As he drove north up the Auto route, he realised that he hadn't ventured outside France for over five years. He hadn't travelled further than the nearest town in a year-and-a-half. Without realising it, he had cut himself off from everything and everyone. It hadn't been something that had been particularly intentional. It had just happened that way. Such was life of course. And now a few touches on a keyboard had launched him out of his cocoon and back into the unknown.

The plane took off and landed on time. Prestwick Airport was surprisingly bathed in early evening sunshine and he made the sixty mile drive to Dumfries with the windows down allowing the warmth of the evening air to stream in. The countryside offered a stark contrast to the soft lines of the Dordogne. Hard stark hills and mean struggling towns. He noticed the overgrown slag heaps and old machinery, idle and rusty from years of redundancy. Ochiltree. New Cumnock. Kirkconnel. The ghost of King Coal embedded everywhere in the bleak landscape. Tiny towns that must have been like Haddington once upon a time. Now they seemed to be spent. Washed out. On the scrap heap. The landscape could not have been more appropriate. It was a window on the past that he had gone to such lengths to block out, a past that had now snapped its fingers and summoned him back.

As he came to the outskirts of Dumfries he started to feel uneasy for the first time. Packing and leaving had been pure instinct. The journey had been enough to hold all his attention. But now the journey was almost over. He had arrived. All that was left was to find Lenny. And then after two decades of hiding it would be time for the truth. For confession. Time to lance the boil that festered on his soul.

There was no need to ask for directions as he soon picked up a sign for Sunnybank. For ten minutes he drove around the pebble-dash houses and flats and took the place in. It was a place like hundreds all over Britain. The wrong side of town. The place at the bottom of the housing list. A postcode that didn't do any favours on job applications. Most of the houses were being used, unlike similar places in city centres where broken and boarded windows were the norm. There was some graffiti but it wasn't overwhelming. At least it was framed by a backdrop of gentle hills rather than more urban sprawl. It certainly was a far cry from Moss Side or Peckham. He was about to make his way back to the parade of shops to start to ask for Lenny when he spotted a sign saying 'The Zone'. In an instant everything was clear. He parked his hire car and considered the size of the estate all around him. Not enormous, but big enough. One of the articles on the internet had mentioned that Sunnybank was home to over three thousand under-eighteens. What was overwhelmingly evident was that The Zone wasn't very big at all. It was the end unit in a line of three shops and he didn't have to be a quantity surveyor to see that it wasn't remotely big enough to cater for the needs of the surrounding area.

He pulled up across the road and sat for a while, staring down the dusty dryness of the street. He didn't have to go in. He hadn't called ahead. The moment he had been putting off for twenty years could still be put off again. It could be put off for a lifetime. There was nothing in the world to stop him driving back to the airport and heading back to his sanctuary. And then what? Sanctuary would never be the same again with the knowledge that he had come so close and been too frightened to get out of the car.

Lenny had been hiding away in the office for hours. The calls from reporters had been pretty well constant from the early afternoon onwards. It had caught him on the hop. He had been expecting at least a day before the real deluge started, but Sally had explained how it was all down to the internet. The story was on the Dumfries Standard website and all over the country it was the job of junior staffers to trawl the local news for stories with the potential to go national. It meant that everything now happened faster. Had he been at home the constant ringing phone and the knocking door would have driven him round the twist. It wasn't so bad hiding out in the Zone. He had twenty youngsters who were more than happy to open the doors and send the hopeful reporters packing. No, Mr Baxter was not available. News of a Press Conference would be announced the next morning. No, they couldn't come in. The youngsters had been well trained on how to deal with the pressing urgency of the reporters as they had seen it done a thousand times on films and soaps and celebrity shows. They loved every minute of it.

Lenny had now been sitting in front of Sally's PC for three-and-a-half hours. He'd had umpteen goes at the promised press release and deleted every one of them. The ashtray on the table was a filthy sight and his head was spinning slightly from a surplus of caffeine. Maybe he would put it off until the morning. It would be quieter then. No distractions. He could get up at six and come in on his own before anyone was around. That would give him time to sleep on it and write it in his head. On the other hand . . .

Barry stuck his head round the door.

"Nother man to see you Lenny."

"You know the drill Barry. Tell him to get lost. News on a Press Conference in the morning . . ."

"He says he's no a reporter."

"Aye and I'm a one-eyed monster from Pluto."

"Says he's a mate of yours so he does. Dead posh sounding, ken. Says I've to tell you he's from a climbing club or something."

This froze Lenny into stillness. No. It couldn't be. Impossible.

"Some climbing club?"

"Aye. Moredin or something. I cannae remember like. Shall I tell him to go?"

A slow shake of the head. And the beginnings of a smile.

PART TWO

"No I'll come Barry. I reckon I know who it is."

"Is he all right?"

"Aye. He's all right."

And still he couldn't really believe it. Not after twenty years. Half a lifetime. But when he got to the door he saw it was true. The man waiting for him didn't have a great deal of hair left and the lines on his face ran in the same pained directions as his own. But it was still undoubtedly Josh. And there was some kind of fear in his eyes, nerves, he was about to speak but Lenny didn't let him. He took a step forward and embraced him before they shared any words.

"Christ Josh. Where the bloody hell have you been?"

The fear was still there when Lenny told him to come in.

"Actually can we walk a bit? There are things I need to say. Things I've needed to say for too long. It would be easier outside."

"Sure. Let's go."

There was too much to say for either of them to say anything. They walked for five minutes until they came to the open green of the playing fields where the death of Luke Crenshaw had started the whole process that had brought them together again. Josh pulled out his cigarettes and lit up two and took a deep, deep draw. The next few minutes would decide the next era of his life.

"There's no easy way to say any of this Lenny so I'll just say it. When I'm done all you have to do is to tell me to go and I'll go."

"Don't be so daft . . ."

"Just let me say it Lenny. Please."

"OK. Fire away."

"They came for me in the house in Simmington. I didn't know a thing. One minute I was cooking a steak, the next minute I was out cold. It must have been chloroform or something. When I woke up I was strapped to a chair in a basement of a farmhouse in Ulster."

He faltered at the memories he had spent so very long trying to kill. Tears broke free and started to slide down his cheeks. Lenny was about to say something but Josh shook his head angrily.

"I was naked. Cold. And scared. I've never been so scared. When they came they had balaclavas on and uniforms. The main one, the boss, he . . . his breath stank. I'll never forget that. Stank like a sewer. And he talked about my family. The ones who were killed at Sobibor. Called me a Yid. Said I was going to get what they got. Then he fixed wires onto me. Onto my balls and . . ."

He screwed his eyes shut. A quarter of a million pounds of heroin had never taken the memory from his brain. It had never lifted the sheer godforsaken terror. Lenny reached out but he pushed his hand away.

"And I told them. All of it. Every last detail. They broke me with one hit of the electricity. I told them about our meeting in Leeds. The time. The date. Everything. They showed me the papers about you and Frank. I kept asking about Williams but they said nothing. They kept me there for three months and every day they dosed me up with more and more heroin. And the more they gave me, the more I didn't really care any more. When they dumped me back in London I had a habit. A big habit. Hundred pounds a day. And the only way I could survive the guilt was to take more. And I'm sorry Lenny. So sorry . . ."

The tears were pouring out. Lenny reached out and put a hand on either shoulder and waited until Josh lifted his head and met his eyes.

"There's no need Josh. I worked it out you know. All of it. Hell, I had enough time. Twenty years of it. Of course you told them. I would have done. Frank would have done. Christ, even Williams would have done. We all knew full well we were playing a dangerous game. Me. You. Frank. Williams. We were stupid to think we would ever get away with it, but that is hindsight. Everything is easy with hindsight. At the time we did what we felt was right and we did it with our eyes open."

"But Frank . . ."

"Frank would never have blamed you. Not in a thousand million years. I know that Josh. Just like Frank could have told you the same if it had been me. This has destroyed you hasn't it?"

"Pretty well. I've been better the last few years."

"Tell me."

They walked all the way out of Sunnybank and into the countryside. They walked through the thickening warm dusk into the darkness of the crystal, starry sky. They walked and shared twenty years of aching despair. Lenny told of the funerals and the slow death of Haddington and the numbing regularity of the prison and how he had come to Sunnybank to keep his final promise and look after Sally. And Josh told of the three eras of his life and how he had spend many thousands of pounds on private investigators who had tried without a glimmer of success to discover the fate of Williams. And by midnight they had brought their meandering lives to the same place and Lenny told about the night when Luke and Zoe had died and how Sally had demanded that he should fight again. And he described the birth of USY and the first two days back on a picket line made up of twelve. And at last Josh began to smile in the darkness as Lenny ran him through his 50 Cent theory.

"Christ Lenny, that's just about crazy enough to work."

"It is working. We've had reporters pounding the doors of Zone all afternoon. That's what I was trying to do when you landed. I thought we should have some kind of press conference or something. Not that I got very far. It was like walking through a treacle puddle. All I managed was to stare at the screen and chain smoke."

"Well no need to bother now. How much is your salary as USY General Secretary?"

"A penny a year."

"Holidays and pension scheme?"

"Nope. Unpaid public holidays."

"Nice. Quite a result for a convicted terrorist. Your probation officer must be over the moon. Rehabilitation works after all. It'll be a mortgage next. Do you reckon I might be able to land the Press Officer job on the same terms?"

Lenny grinned. "It would be down to the President and Chairman, but yeah, I reckon that's a decent chance. USY's in the money at the moment. We pulled in over forty quid today from public donations. More than half of that went on bacon rolls, but I think we could run to another full time salary if push comes to shove."

"Splendid. Here endeth a lifetime of unemployment. Do you realise this is my first ever proper paid job? Will I get a contract?"

"Not a chance. Welcome to the black economy."

"You've got a computer and stuff at the Zone I presume?"

"Sure."

"Best get back then. Things to do. Lots of things to do."

Josh made to head back towards the orange lights of the town but Lenny stayed still.

"Josh, are you absolutely sure about this. Things could easily get a bit ugly again."

"Oh for Christ's sake don't go all mature on me man. Let's go."

DS Frank Dixon's day started with a major surprise. A note on his desk requested that he make his way across to Police HQ for an audience with the Chief Constable. Straight away his heart started banging away at the ribcage. What? Why? He had exactly the same feeling in his stomach that he had once known many years before when summoned to the headmaster's office. He was pretty sure that he hadn't done anything remotely wrong enough to warrant a summons to the top man. He knew that he hadn't exactly been following the book to the letter. Nothing new in that. He hadn't been near the book in his whole career and it had never meant a visit to the office on the top floor. His bollockings were always dished out by immediate superiors. But there could of course be one thing that would send him up in the lift. Could anyone have got wind that he had cut Lenny Baxter loose on the night of Zoe McGuire's death? Maybe. No, not maybe. It had to be. It must have been statements from Mog and Benny who were both on remand up at the prison waiting on heavy time. Damn.

His brain was racing as he decided to take the ten minute walk to HQ rather than driving. His instincts as ever were to come clean and tell it how it was. It was his style. The trouble was that he knew in his heart of hearts that such an approach would go down like a lead balloon. What option was there? Only the obvious one. Brick wall denial. Shoulders back and stare at the wall at the back of the room and lie through his teeth. Make it his word against Mog and Benny's. The word of a respected copper with twenty years under his belt against the word of a couple of dealers with almost as much time inside the nick under theirs. With a feeling of gloomy regret he decided that the stonewall approach was his only real option and he rode up to the third floor with a heavy heart.

The condemned feeling lifted slightly when the Chief met him at the door with a smile and waved him to one of the easy chairs by a coffee table.

"Morning Frank. Thanks for coming. You'll have coffee? Tea?"

"Coffee please sir." Promising. Very promising. Bollockings generally didn't come with coffee. A secretary was summoned by intercom to take the orders and she was also smiling. Good news? Had to be. She would know if he was for the high jump. Secretaries always did.

PART TWO

The Chief joined him. "Well it's another splendid morning Frank. Good for the cricket no doubt?"

"Yes sir. " Good for the cricket! Things were looking up fast. They had to be.

"OK. I'm not going to leave you in suspense. Lenny Baxter."

Bugger it.

"Sir."

"I believe that you play cricket together, yes?"

"Yes sir."

"What do you make of him?"

Maybe it might be OK after all. Careful Frank, the ice is thin. "I've always liked him sir. He's a good lad. Hell of a bowler. I reckon he'd have made pro if he hadn't." He allowed the sentence to trail away.

"Yes. If he hadn't chosen to be a terrorist instead. You've read all the papers of course."

"Sir."

"Quite a story wouldn't you say?"

"Aye. I suppose so."

The secretary returned with a tray of coffee and biscuits. Chocolate too. The perks of office. Chocolate biscuits were as scarce as hen's teeth in the drug squad. Sugaring and stirring gave Frank time to review the situation. Maybe things might still be OK. Once the coffees were ready to drink, the Chief resumed.

"A lot of journalists are in the town Frank. Every one of the Nationals. TV and radio as well. Our Press Office has been swamped with calls since yesterday afternoon. Do you know much about the press Frank?"

"Not really sir. I read the papers. That's about it."

The Chief took on a thoughtful expression. "If you look at the papers from the last week or so, the thing that stands out is how little there is going on. I believe they call it a quiet news time. No Pope to bury. No Royal wedding. No politicians getting caught with their pants down. All reasonably quiet in Iraq. Dead. It means that this Lenny Baxter story is probably going to be just about the biggest thing around. Terrorists fascinate the media Frank. Now more than ever before. We've had a few years of the Muslim Menace. This whole business offers them a refreshing new angle. The home grown item. Tall. Handsome. The 'words working class hero'spring to mind. And emerging from twenty years of hard time to stand on a pavement an fight for a youth centre. Imagine if you were a journalist Frank. You have to admit it's heady stuff."

"Sir." Now he was confused. He had no clue where this was heading.

"It's my job to take a look into the crystal ball at times. Where will all this lead? What on earth are we supposed to do about it? So let's start with this morning. Will there be more pickets on Buccleuch Street? Or will there just be a few? What do you think Frank?"

The older man took a gulp of coffee. "Best guess sir. I'd say there'll be more. I have to say that Lenny has a bit of a point here. There really is nothing for the youngsters to do up on Sunnybank. Our lads know it more than most. They'll turn out on Buccleuch Street for something to do. Especially if the TV is there. Kids will travel a long way for a chance to get on TV."

"I agree entirely. Early reports suggest there is already a crowd of over fifty. I estimate that will at least double. Maybe treble. What about longer term Frank? The next two to three weeks."

More coffee. On the spot. "I figure it will keep growing sir. Once there are more than fifty it becomes a social thing. The wardens won't allow groups of people to congregate up there in Sunnybank. So the picketing gives them a chance they don't normally get. Aye. It'll keep growing. Definitely."

"Agreed." The Chief got up and started to pace. "The lawyers are trying to unpick the law. Nobody seems to have a clue if this Union of Sunnybank Youth is remotely legal. It appears that they have elected representatives and the members pay a subscription. A penny a year I gather. If the thing is halfway legal, it will present us with a few problems. Between you and me I've already had a lot of calls from the Council. Not happy. Not happy at all. Well of course they aren't. That's the whole point. They want Baxter and his little group dispersed. Not easy Frank. Not easy at all. If this Union is remotely legal, then peaceful picketing is also legal. So if they behave themselves and don't go and breach the peace there is nothing we can do. To be honest Frank there is nothing that I personally would want to do. We're both long enough in the tooth to remember 1984 and the strike. The whole lousy business did the force no favours."

PART TWO

The Chief allowed the sentence to drain away and took up a station at the window which looked out onto the car park. He had lain awake for most of the night considering what on earth he should do about the bizarre situation that was developing on Buccleuch Street. The whole thing was about to go very political and there was no way that the force would be able to stay out of it. His gut instinct told him that this was about to become one of those situations where there would be no easy answers. It was all very well for the jumped up bureaurocrats in the Municipal Chambers to demand that he cleared the street. It just showed how pathetically out of touch they were. The surest way to escalate the situation would be to try to ban a gathering. That would attract a crowd like nothing else. Ban anything for young people and all you ever did was glamorise it and make them want it all the more. The long hours of the night had provided no certain answers. All he knew was that the next few weeks were about to be very difficult and they would almost certainly determine if he got the next career move up to Glasgow or Edinburgh. He sat back down.

"Sorry Frank. You're obviously wondering where on earth all this is leading. This is how I see it. It is likely that USY is illegal and if it was proved so we could no doubt find a reason to clear the street. As far as I am concerned, such a course of action would mean time and court and it's a no brainer. Maybe the Procurator Fiscal will disagree, but I doubt it. So I have decided to treat USY as a legal union mounting a legal picket. The Council won't like it, but that's tough. Our job is to maintain public order. Pure and simple. That's the book Frank. What's more, we're going to have a tonne of journalists out there watching our every move. So Frank, I'm going for the light touch. A really light touch. You."

"Sir?"

"You know this Lenny Baxter. You play cricket with him. I want you to get down there and stand with him. Just you. I'm moving you off the drug squad for as long as this takes. Stay close. Smile for the cameras. Keep a close eye out. One way or another, this whole business will sort itself out in a week or two. It is your job to try and make sure things stay calm. OK?"

Bloody hell. Complete bombshell. No options though. "Of course sir. I'll do my best."

"I know you will Frank. You always do. I can only hope that it will be good enough."

"In uniform sir?"

"Absolutely."

"I best go and get changed hadn't I?"

Walter Billingham turned the corner into Buccleuch Street and gritted his teeth. Despite the coverage on local radio he had still hoped that maybe the picket lines may have thinned a little. Instead he saw that they had multiplied. Not only was there a considerable crowd bearing their placards on the pavement outside the Municipal Chambers, there was a mob of journalists of almost equal size further down the street.

"Christ."

He paused a moment, using a doorway as cover. He saw that pickets and reporters were all intermingled. There were camera crews out and radio reporters holding out microphones. It was a bloody jamboree and there was no other way into work. His heart sank. The only thing for it was to get his head down and walk through it. He took a couple of deep breaths and started off briskly. Lenny spotted him from fifty yards and bent to whisper in Barry's ear. The youthful USY President darted over to the nearest cluster of reporters and told them that a senior Council man was approaching. The bowed head and fast walk never stood a chance. Billingham was ringed by questions and microphones and he had to push out his briefcase to force a path. He closed his ears to the frantic questions and battled his way through. Five minutes later he was at his desk and actually shaking. And this was only day three. For the first time he felt the slithering worm of fear in his guts. When was any of this about to stop?

Outside Josh was moving among the reporters. He was all smiles.

"Ok Guys. Best introduce myself. I'm Ogilvy. Josh Ogilvy. USY Press Officer. I'm going to be your man. All dealings through me OK? It's me or nobody. Simple as that. Here you go. Press Conference at 2.00 p.m. this afternoon in Sunnybank Labour Club. Before that, you can beg and plead all you like but we're saying nothing. So take your pictures and do your background and try to be patient. OK?"

They all wanted to know who he was and where he came from. All they got was a smile and a Press Release that told them what they already knew. Wait till two. Not long. By quarter to nine the workers were arriving. For the first time the chants of "We want Tosh Hoos" had a bit of body behind them. Placards were held high. Some of the staff pushed through with heads down. Others stopped to talk. They said they had no choice. If they didn't go to work they would be in trouble. Some were aggressive to the youngsters and told them they should get themselves back home and behave themselves. Others said they understood, but what could they do? And over fifteen saw the crowd and turned around and went back home. They made calls to line managers and said that they didn't feel safe coming into work. They said that it was too much to ask that they should run the gauntlet of reporters and pickets.

By nine-thirty a livid Walter Billingham found that his department was thirty percent below strength. A few phone calls confirmed that he was not alone. He placed a call through to Police HQ and demanded that something be done. He said that it was an outrage. A disgrace. And in turn the policewoman who fielded his call assured him that they were watching the situation carefully. She said that there had been no intimidation and that the picket line had been orderly at all times. She said that in the opinion of the Police there was no reason why any of the staff should fear coming to work and she suggested that he contact absentees accordingly. Billingham actually cracked the plastic casing of his phone as he smashed it down.

It was a nightmare. An utter complete nightmare.

The function room at the Labour Club was filled to standing room only by one thirty. A clutch of microphones were clustered in front on the tables where the USY officials would sit at the appointed hour. Either side, cameramen from BBC. ITV and SKY made sure that the light was crisp and even. Frank Dixon took up station with folded arms against the back wall and refused every question with a genial smile. Josh was everywhere, making sure spare seats were brought in from the storeroom and checking that the tea and coffee didn't run out. Every reporter was a presented with a media pack that contained photos of McIntosh House, photos of Luke Crenshaw and Zoe McGuire and a USY mission statement signed off by the President and Chairman. At three minutes to two, the officialdom of the Union entered through the door at the back of the room that led into the kitchen area. They took up their posts. The Chairman and President took the centre chairs. Both Finch boys looked mildly agitated following some heated moments backstage. Lenny had insisted that it was the role of either Chairman or President to make the first statement. Neither had been at all happy at the prospect of addressing the crowd outside. Showing front in the playground was one thing. This was quite another. They told him there was absolutely no chance and he leaned in close and reminded them that they still owed him big time and they realised there was no way out. The decision was eventually made when Lenny took a ten pence piece and held it behind his back. Barry chose left and Lenny revealed the coin in his right hand. Barry thereby assumed the role of speaker number one.

Roger Crenshaw and Rory McGuire took their seats to the left of the Chairman and President. Lenny sat to their right with Josh next along. Josh watched the hand of the wall clock click into place and stood.

"Right Ladies and gentlemen. A little hush if you please. Thank you. Welcome to this, the first USY Press Conference. Most of you have met me. For those of you who haven't had that pleasure, my name is Josh Ogilvy and I am the USY Press Officer. This means if you want to know something then it comes through me. You can duck and dive all you like, but you will find that USY maintains a strict discipline. OK. I have one or two formalities before we kick things off. If you take a look around the room you will see that there are three exits to use in the event of a fire. One where you came in. One there on the side wall. And one behind me. OK? Got that. Splendid. Now for the running order. Our President Barry Finch will be getting the ball rolling. Then Mr Roger Crenshaw and Mr Rory McGuire will be saying a few words. Then we will be taking questions. Good. No more ado then. Barry?"

Josh sat and Barry stood very slowly, blinking frantically under the rim of his baseball cap. Lenny gave him a light tap on his back.

"You'll be fine Barry. No fear."

Barry discarded the paper that Josh had given him. The words were too hard to read under such pressure. He thrust his hands into his pockets and took a steadying breath.

"Aye. Well thanks for coming and all that. You've read all the stuff ken. Well. It's pretty simple ken. They lot at the Council are out of order. There's nothing for us to do here. They wardens won't let us do

nothing, ken. Luke was my pal. And Tim here. That's what it's all about like. Luke. And Zoe. So that's it really. We want Tosh Hoos and we're no going to give in."

He looked about the faces of all the reporters, many of whom were scribbling away.

"Aye. Well that's me I suppose."

Barry sat and Lenny leaned over.

"Nice one pal. Perfect."

The room was filled with a stunned sort of silence. None of the journalists quite knew how to respond to the small figure in the cap. Then from the back of the room there came the sound of clapping. Heads turned to find that it was Frank Dixon who couldn't maintain the required level of professionalism. Slowly his applause was taken up by the rest of the room and Barry gave a grave nod.

Next Rory and Roger made their statements. Very simple. They said that they would stand out on the picket line for as long as it took. They said that their families had paid the ultimate price. They said that they would do what they could to make sure that no other Sunnybank family would have to endure the nightmare they found themselves living. This time there was no need to start the applause. This time it was instantaneous and generous. It wasn't hard to respond to the simple dignity of the father and brother who had the courage to stand before them.

Then Josh was back up on his feet. "Thank you all for your attention. We'll have some questions shall we? Let's try and keep a semblance of order. OK. There at the front. That's right."

"Tom Garrett. Sky News. Question for Lenny. Lenny, do you think it is right that you should be working with kids as a convicted terrorist."

Lenny swallowed a mouthful of water. So Lenny. It starts. You set this up. So ride the wave. He gave the journalist a steady gaze.

"I would like to say something before getting into that Tom. Obviously there will be questions about my past. I expect it. But please don't get away from the main issue here. The main issue is McIntosh House. That is the reason why we are all here. I would like you all to take a moment to remember your own childhood. How was it? Did you get to play out? Football? Cricket? Did you get to spend time just chatting with your mates? I did. I bet you did. It's what kids do. Not just here. Anywhere in the world and for as long as man has walked on top of this earth. Kids are not that different to adults. They enjoy company. Human beings are social animals. Sadly that's not allowed here in Sunnybank. If you are between 12 and 18 you are presumed guilty. You are not allowed to spend time in a group of mates because you are deemed to be threatening. You get moved on. You are told you're not allowed. Football in the street. Forget it. Hanging about with pals in the sunshine? Not a chance. So why on earth are we so surprised when our young people take a few wrong turnings? We all love to preach on about how different it was in our day. And so it was, because we were given the space and freedom to grow up. The reason we are all here today has nothing to do with what went on in my past. It is because of Luke Crenshaw and Zoe McGuire and the courage of their families. So. I simply ask that you all remember that. Write about it. Don't just ignore it."

He took time to look slowly around the faces of his audience. Maybe they would. Maybe they wouldn't.

"Anyway Tom wasn't it? Your question. Should convicted terrorists work in Youth Centres. Of course they shouldn't. You have two words there, Tom, 'Convicted' and 'Terrorist'. I plead guilty to being convicted, but for twenty years I have never once wavered from my stance that I have never been a terrorist. I am innocent of the crimes of which I was convicted and therefore I can see no good reason why I shouldn't work at the Zone."

"Zak Brown. ITN. Come on Lenny. They caught you and your brother cold with Libyan guns and explosives."

"I am fully aware that there were guns and explosives in the boot of our car Zak. I am also fully aware that neither myself nor my brother had ever seen them before."

"Tina Philips. The Daily Mirror. How do you expect the public to accept your conspiracy theory? Wouldn't it just be better to admit it and get on with your life?"

"Quite right Tina. It was made more than clear to me in prison that all I had to do to get out early was to make a statement of remorse and regret for what I had done. I could have been out after ten years."

Tina dived in for another go. "But do you seriously expect anyone to believe you?"

Lenny shrugged. "Seriously expect? I don't know. But if you mean will I ever stop trying, then no. Not a chance. You are very young Tina, but a little research will tell you about the Guildford Four and the Birmingham Six. Who would ever have thought they would have managed to prove their innocence after so many years? But they did. And one day so will I. Sadly it is one of the problems of being framed by the state. It takes time."

Questions, questions, questions.

Did he? Why? Did he ever have any contact with Gaddafi? What was his opinion of Al Qaeda? How had he felt when the IRA prisoners were released during the Peace Process and he still remained locked up?

Lenny kept his cool and answered each and every one in turn. Nothing they asked was unexpected. He had each and every answer planned. Then the man from the Times spoke. He had an old face, grey from years of sixty-a-day smoking which had also taken rather a toll on his voice.

"Jake Hollins. The Times. Let's take what you say at face value shall we Lenny. Assuming you are indeed innocent, don't you feel what you are doing is a little risky?"

This wasn't a planned question. "Sorry Jake. You better flesh that out for me."

"Sure. You are very focused on the skeletons in your cupboard Lenny. So are we. Are they real or were they planted? The thing is, if the guns were indeed planted, then they are in fact the skeletons in somebody else's cupboard and they might not be all that happy to have the cupboard doors opened after twenty years. Especially when it is so public."

The man was right. It wasn't something that Lenny had even begun to consider. He gave a shrug of his shoulders and spoke with an indifference that he didn't really feel.

"All I can say Jake is so be it. What USYis doing here is important. I can't allow myself to be deflected by things I can't prove."

He carried on for another fifteen minutes until Josh brought the curtain down. Then came the photo call. At last the function room began to clear until the only journalist left was Jake Hollins who had ignored all the signs on the wall and lit up. He was all but at the end of his cigarette and was using his saucer as an ashtray. Lenny went over and sat next to him and lit up himself. Jake looked straight ahead as he spoke.

"There were a lot of cowboys around Yorkshire in 84/85. Most were freelancers but some were on the books. The men who were in charge were on the books. They did their bit and the Government was grateful. There were lots of promotions. A few knighthoods. Lots of well paid non-exec directorships on various boards. These people went from strength to strength. Next came victory over Communism. Then the IRA. They have risen far Lenny. All the way to the top. I dare say they will be less than amused at . . ." He took a slow look around the empty room with a smile full of yellow teeth. " . . . all this."

Lenny shook out a couple of cigarettes and lit. "You don't think I did it do you?"

This prompted a bark of a laugh. "Of course I don't. Nor would any halfway sensible person. What age were you both. 21? Two twenty-one-year-old coal miners for South Yorkshire cuddling up with Libyan intelligence? I don't think so. I was well-connected with a source high up in the Union. Nobody had ever heard of you when it happened. So you must have been completely freelance. So no. It never washed as far as I was concerned."

Lenny took this in silence for a while. "Any idea who it was?"

"The usual suspects. MI5 may have been in there somewhere, but I doubt it. The establishment has never really trusted the security services properly since Burgess, Philby and McLean. Then when MI5 made plans to overthrow the Labour Government in the 70's politicians became very wary of them. My guess is that they would have used freelancers. Safer. I heard a whisper that a team was brought over from Ireland around that time. Very dark people who worked off the charts. A week after I heard that whisper, two young lads turned up with a boot full of Libyan weaponry. It always seemed to me that two and two made four, but I could never prove it. Never got close."

"And you think some of these people might still be about."

"Maybe. Maybe not. But any who are still in the system somewhere will be pretty high up. And they won't be amused Lenny. Not at all."

"What will they do?"

The older man gave him a flash of his terrible teeth. "Now that is the interesting part. Normally they would start digging and do everything to discredit you. But that isn't all that easy in your case. There isn't a lot they can dig up that will be worse than serving twenty years as a terrorist. That is what makes all of this so very, very interesting."

"Thanks."

Jake chuckled. "Pulling the tail of a tiger is always a dubious idea Lenny. No point in getting cold feet now. You've damn near yanked the thing off. Now you better get ready for it to bite your arse. I'll be seeing you. My card by the way."

Lenny sat and watched Hollins take his leave of the room. Josh had been tidying up, gathering papers and stacking chairs. He joined Lenny.

"That looked interesting."

"It was." He told him and Josh couldn't help a shudder when he heard about the rumour of a team from Ireland.

"Did you say anything?"

Lenny shook his head. "No. I didn't think it would be all that wise. It's still early enough for you to walk Josh. Why not jump in your car and go and catch a plane. I'll find you when all of this is done with. One way or another."

Josh stared down at the floor for a while. "No. I don't think so. All I've done for twenty years is run away. I've had enough of it. Anyway, it's different this time. We're older and wiser."

Lenny chuckled. "Older maybe. I don't see any of this as wise. Ah what the hell. Let's go grab a pint. The bar should be open by now."

Sir Edward Cardigan Latimer watched the press conference on BBC News 24. He had left the office early so that he could watch it at home. He was quite alone. His wife was away visiting her sister in Spain and the maid was done for the day. Outside the street where he lived in Kensington was quiet and bathed in sunshine. A clock ticked away on the wall and the ice in his whisky rattled when he lifted it to his lips. The anchor team in the studio told him they were going live to Sunnybank Estate in Dumfries. And then he was there with them. Baxter looked annoyingly well for a man who had spent twenty years away from fresh air. Introductions were being made and he stiffened at the sight of Ogilvy. Holy Christ. The last he had heard of him he had been buried ten feet deep in heroin. What the hell was he doing there? Press Officer? For Christ's sake. The camera panned the ranks of journalists. Damn. A coach load of them. Well of course there was. The story was as juicy as a big fat steak. Baxter was cool. Far too cool. He had a TV face, all earnest cragginess. He looked like an American Senator from way out West somewhere. Easy and relaxed. Born to the bloody job.

He reached out for the remote and snapped off the screen. Somewhere outside some children were playing in the sun. The sound of a car horn floated across the rooftops from a street or two away. Another sip. The story was too good. Far too good. The press were going to be all over it. They were all terrorist mad these days. Everybody was. The news, paperbacks, computer games, movies. Terrorists, terrorists, terrorists. Not that they had done his career any harm. He had been rewarded handsomely for his intervention in the strike. The private sector had filled up his Geneva account to the extent that he could look forward to a life of ease. The Public Sector had welcomed him in from the cold and granted him a corner office that looked out across the Thames. The knighthood had come along in the late Nineties and he had been lucky enough to be well away from the Iraq desk during the Kelly fiasco. Other heads had rolled and he had moved up another few notches. At sixty he was almost at the very top rung of the ladder and all good things awaited him. And now this.

He drummed his fingers on the leather arm of his chair and started to break the whole thing down into bite sized pieces. Problems. Lots and lots of niggling problems. The first problem was that the damn business was going down in Scotland. The root of the thing was a purely Scottish issue, first for the local Council, then for the Executive in Edinburgh if they dared to touch it. It wasn't remotely a Whitehall thing and nor would it be. The London politicians would run a mile from it and pass the buck. He could almost hear glasses being raised to Scottish Devolution in the Commons bar. Leave the bloody Jocks to sort it out. Which of course meant that he wouldn't be able to easily use the resources of the Department. Not easily. But it wouldn't be impossible. No reason why it wouldn't be appropriate to take a look around the background. Why not? There was still the Libyan connection. But anything direct would have to be done off the books. Not a great problem. He knew people. Plenty of people. And he could afford it easily enough.

The question was what and how. What and how. He rewound the video and studied the pictures of the picket line carefully. It certainly seemed peaceful enough and the police had made it more than clear that they were going to stay well back in the shadows. Baxter certainly wouldn't be daft enough to want the thing to get out of hand which of course would mean that the police would in all likelihood continue to stay back. And that wouldn't do. Not at all. If things stayed peaceful, the thing would only grow and grow. And that would make Baxter's credibility grow and grow. And the damned journalists would become more and more nosy. And?

He needed to think of the weak places. Three of the Hendrick team had died. One of cancer, one in a car accident and one in an undercover operation with the drug squad. Which left Hendrick himself and Beverly Morton. He had cut Hendrick loose after the Yorkshire Operation. The man had become too much of a loose cannon, even for Ireland. He had paid him handsomely and looked on as Hendrick had taken a plane down to Pretoria to work for the South African Security Services. He had kept a distant watch on him. Rumour had it that he behaved with predictable beastliness in the death throes of the Apartheid regime. Then he had disappeared from view entirely only to re-emerge surprisingly at the Truth and Reconciliation Committee to tearfully confess to all the horrible things he had done to the blank faces of the families of his victims. For a few months Latimer had been genuinely nervous. Hendrick had swallowed a bible and found God. If he was in the mood to confess his sins in South Africa, then maybe he would decide to hop a plane home and do the same in London. Latimer had made a few tentative arrangements. A modest sum would have paid for a car-jacking had it come to it. Another random crime of violence leading to another fatality. It hadn't been necessary. Hendrick headed off into the hills of Swaziland and started a new life in a mission home for those dying from Aids. Latimer had kept a cautious eye on him for a couple of years and then he had lost interest. Hendrick's hold on basic sanity had always been pretty weak. Now he had obviously let go and immersed himself in some kind of born again Disneyland.

Then there was Beverly. He had kept an even closer watch on Beverly, especially when the second anniversary of her exile came around. But Beverly hadn't caught a plane to London. Instead she had stayed in Central America patching up the victims of the CIA killer squads. In 1990 she had made a move, but again it was not to the UK. Instead she had headed into the primordial carnage of Rwanda and planted herself in the midst of the flying machetes. It hadn't been hard for Latimer to work it out. He had worked it out when he had paid her a visit in the Sandinista camp. The guilt was eating Beverly Morton from inside. She was to be one of the ones for whom guilt would become a cancer. Coming home to a job and a husband and a happy ending wasn't going to be an option for Beverly Morton. Instead she would try and purge her soul in the hell holes of the world, and there were more than enough of them to go at. She had been injured in Rwanda, and for a while it had seemed as if she wouldn't make it. A crazy had burst into the makeshift ward where she was working and taken a lump out of her face with a machete. The wound had gone bad and fever had got a grip. But she had come through it and she had moved on. Over the next few years she had turned up in Bosnia, Chechnya and East Timor. The last he had heard she was somewhere in the Sudan. No. Beverly wasn't about to be a problem. Neither was Hendrick. The past was reasonably secure. Trying to make it more secure would be a waste of time. It would be better to focus on the present.

He decided that he had two options. He could allow things to run their course until the whole thing fizzled. Or he could take a look at it and see if events might be influenced a little. It wasn't his style to sit back and wait on events. It never had been. Better to see if he could nudge things a little. Who and how? Or more to the point, how and who? There really was only one way on the how side of the equation. So long as the thing stayed calm and peaceful, then Baxter and his past would be the main story. But if things started to get a little wild, then things would be rather different. He took another sip at his glass and allowed himself a grim smile. Oh dear, oh dear Lenny Baxter. It looks as if history might just be about to repeat itself. He picked up his phone and rang a mobile number in Cumbernauld.

Jed Thompson had been an odds on candidate for a life of fruitless crime at the age of sixteen. He had already come within an inch or two of borstal. At this point his dad had given him the hiding of his life and he had run away to join the army. He had done six years before coming out in the early eighties with great hopes of getting a job and a wife and a proper life. It only took a matter of weeks to find out that jobs for ex-sqaddies were no part of Thatcher's Scotland. He drifted in and out of temporary stuff. Bouncer. Security man. Once even a spell on the bins. Then one of his old sergeants got in touch and told him there was good cash to be made having a go at the pickets at the Ravenscraig Steel Plant in Ayrshire. He put in a couple of weeks. It was easy work. He headed up a team of five ex-soldiers who were given names and photos of men who they were to take down alleyways for a good kicking. Shop stewards. Militant types. He enjoyed it and got a holiday in Spain on the proceeds. When the big strike got going he had a whole year of similar stuff and had plenty of cash left over to pay a deposit on a house in Cumbernauld, to put himself through his HGV, and to buy a wagon. Life as a self-employed haulier was OK, but rather boring. By the late eighties he had got into the long haul game and was doing regular runs into Europe.

This was when Mr Latimer had come to call. This time the work was different. Instead of breaking heads, he drove his truck on a regular run to a component factory on one of the sprawling industrial areas of Leipzig. Soon his face was known to the border guards and he became a regular source of jeans and American cigarettes. After six months Latimer gave him the first box to deliver. There was a rendezvous in a lay-by sixty miles down the Autobahn east of Eisenach at three o'clock in the morning. It was all very quick. A man with a cap pulled low over his face climbed out of his Trabant which was belching fumes into the clear night air. The man took the box without a word and chugged away. No words were exchanged. No words were ever exchanged as the process was repeated thirteen times over the next two years until an astonished world watched the Berlin Wall crash down on prime time TV.

There had been no need to deliver boxes into the newly unified Germany, but Latimer's golden handshake had been enough for Jed to buy two more wagons and increase his fleet to five. He gave up driving himself, found a wife, and settled into the rest of his life. Latimer's call took him completely off guard, but it wasn't at all unwelcome. Before the phone rang he had been at his desk staring at a monthly fuel bill from his diesel supplier that absolutely beggared belief. Things had been bad enough before the diesel price had taken off. More and more he had found it impossible to keep up with the joke rates bandied about by the cowboys from Poland and Hungary. For five years he had seen costs shoot up and income fall down. The bank had a claim on every penny of equity in his house and wagons and he was getting the feeling that they were about to call it in. And now this. A bill that bordered on the obscene. He didn't even have the energy to screw it up and throw it across the room. Instead he had merely laid it down and stared out of the dusty window to where two of his wagons were parked up for lack of work.

Then Latimer had called with a lifeline. And he had reached for it like a drowning man. Half an hour later he was on the M8 heading south. He rang his wife and told her that something had come up. He told her that he would probably be a day or two.

Yousuf was killing time with friends when the word came that something strange was going on at the north of town. There was food. Not like the usual food, the sacks of flour and rice. This time it was hot food. American food. He had wanted to ask the young ragged boy who had brought the news more, but the boy was gone in a scamper of callused bare feet. Such an event was headline news in the daily grind of Famoudi life. Certainly not to be missed, whatever it was. Initially Yousuf was convinced that the boy had got the whole thing wrong somehow. Hot food? Ridiculous. But as they made their way through the town they found that they were among a growing number of people who were headed the same direction.

They smelt it first, long before they had turned the last corner. A smell that in an instant took him back to his former life and gave him a jab of pain. His father by the pool in an open white shirt with the cuffs rolled back. Friends of his parents sharing a joke. The sons and daughters of the friends splashing in the pool. And a fine array of different meat sizzling on their huge barbeque. Meat. Something he hadn't had in his mouth for nearly two years, and now the baking air of the late morning was filled with the smell of it.

As Yousuf turned into the street he was met with a sight that made him doubt whether or not he was actually awake. The Marine Corps had created a barbeque with a difference. Halfway down the street two Bradley fighting vehicles were parked at ninety degrees to the pavement, leaving a gap of about six feet between their front bumpers.

This created an opening for a queue of more than five hundred to shuffle into. Either side of the armoured vehicles, a wall of sandbags blocked off the rest of the street. He could see that a further two Bradley's were arranged in similar fashion down at the other end. In the middle of the carefully erected strongpoint, a column of smoke wafted lazily up into the burning blue sky. He could hear laughter and loud voices within the compound. And he could smell meat.

He and his friends joined the queue which took more than half an hour to reach the gap in the defences. Here everyone was head to toe searched before being allowed to move forward. By the time he was halfway down the line Yousuf sensed something different. The soldiers up on top of the vehicles behind the big machine guns were certainly watchful, but they were not the same as usual. No flak jackets. No helmets. And smiling. The ones doing the searches were the same, almost casual in green T-shirts with 'USMC' on the front. Once inside the compound, he saw a sight that was beyond bizarre. The queue curved round to line up along a long line of trestle tables and oil drums cut in half and filled with glowing charcoal. The tables were filled with piles of unleavened bread and bowls of salad which were constantly being refilled. First he was presented with a paper plate. Then a plastic knife and fork. He followed the lead of those in front and filled his plate with bread and salad. And the soldiers grinned at him as they doled out the miraculous food. Then he came to the drums. An Iraqi in uniform told everyone that the food was good food. Halal food. Chicken. Beef. Lamb. A mountain of it. And everyone was piling their plates as high as the laws of gravity allowed, and none of the soldiers seemed to mind. The ones who threw the meat about over the heat of the charcoal were dancing to a tune from the East Coast which Yousuf had once known, but now couldn't remember the name of the singer.

Madness. One day they shot us with faces like stone. The next day they smile and dance and give us a feast fit for a wedding. His friends had caught the mood and were laughing with each other almost hysterically at the sight of their piled plates. Yousuf drifted away from them. How easily they buy us. How easily we dance to their tune. He wandered to the edge of the area where many sat eating and talking. He found a patch of shade. So what are you doing then Yousuf? Too proud to smile at them, but not too proud to eat their food. He hated himself a little with every mouthful. In front of him a tall man stepped out of a tent closely followed by a woman in civilian clothes and another non-soldier with a camera. The tall man was dressed different to the ones on the guns and behind the cooking drums. He was bare headed, but smart in a pressed short sleeved shirt. He took a moment to check the scene with a back as straight as an ironing board and thick arms folded. Officer. A man in command. Yousuf was sitting no more than six feet from where he stood but he knew he was as inconsequential as a piece of litter.

The woman smoothed down her shirt and fiddled with her blond hair before striking a pose in front of the man with the camera. She lifted a microphone to her lips and revealed a mouthful of snow-white teeth. On the side of the camera were the letters ABC. The woman suddenly became animated and started to speak with exaggerated movements of her heavily lip-sticked mouth.

"I'm Peggy Hill and for the next month I will be spending time with the men of the Marine Corps. Charlie Company. And for the next month we will all be seeing something different. This is Famoudi. A small town just an hour down the road from Fallujah. Here in the Sunni Triangle there has been a lot of blood spilled over the last two years. American blood and Iraqi blood. Hatred on both sides has run deep. Suspicion on both sides has run deep. However, rather than allowing the divide to get so deep that it becomes a chasm, Charlie Company here has started to build bridges instead. This is Captain Dale Nash who is instrumental in this new approach. Dale, there sure seem to be a lot of happy people here with you this morning."

Dale turned an earnest face to the camera. "I would agree with that assessment Maam."

Peggy's smile got even wider. Jeez the viewers were going to love this guy. He was just about the most all American thing she had ever seen. The men would see warrior. And the women! The women would eat him with hungry eyes.

"So Dale. A barbeque? Tell me about how this all came about."

"Maam, it's my mission here to show the real face of the Corps to the community. We have some work to do. Back home in Virginia we all come together on a sunny day and we barbeque. It's a sunny day, maam, and we're all barbequing here."

"And what other plans do you have Dale . . ."

PART TWO

Yousuf chewed quietly at his meat and made no sign that he understood the words they spoke. He kept his eyes down and took it all in. And when he finished his food and left the compound he didn't choose to walk with his friends. Instead he weighed the words he had heard. The cameras were in Famoudi for a month. The soldiers were planning to start being nice. He spat in the dust at the thought. They came to his town and killed so many and then thought they could turn everything around by giving a barbeque. And memories started to re-emerge. He recalled an interview with a rapper from LA. There had been much talk of a man called Rodney King. Poor quality shots had shown a group of policemen kicking a black man down on the ground. Then there had been footage of a huge riot, and people carrying TVs and sound systems through the broken windows of shops. At the time he had found it amusing. Every day a man was beaten to death on the streets of Iraq by the police. It was nothing unusual. People merely turned the other way and carried on with the business of their day. And yet these Americans had smashed up a whole city. He had decided the Americans were weak. So much rage at one criminal getting what he probably deserved. But two years of watching the Americans in Famoudi had shown him that they were anything but weak. They were every bit as strong as those who had followed Saddam. The only difference was that their weapons were bigger. The Americans were killers with no god. And yet they had gone crazy when they had seen what had happened to Rodney King. He knew it meant something, but he couldn't work out what.

Then lyrics from another song bounced into his head. Not clear any more. Blurred from all the months since the batteries for his Walkman had run out. Something about a gunfight in the hood. The police outnumbering their enemies. The police ready to kill. That was it. Death by cop. And then a camera team had arrived overhead in a helicopter. Yes. He remembered the video now. The twisted anger of the policemen as they squinted up into the cameras hovering above them. Then the face of the rapper saying there would be no death by cop today. Not when the TV had come to the party. Because death by cop was to be played out behind closed doors. No death by cop on prime time. No more Rodney King. And that was it. The Americans had no fear of killing. Obviously they hadn't. They had a fear of being seen by the cameras as they killed. No death by cop on prime time. He had heard the name ABC. It was a big channel. Bigger than Al Jazeera. And now they were here in Famoudi for a whole month filming the soldiers. And suddenly the soldiers had taken off their helmets and flak jackets and cooked a barbeque.

And Yousuf smiled because he knew that for a month they would be weak.

As Frank Dixon struggled to button the collar of his uniform which had become too tight in a matter of six months, he wondered what effect the blanket news coverage from the previous evening would have on the numbers of pickets. He parked up at Loreburne Street Police Station and strolled down through the town centre. He heard the answer to his self-asked question before he saw it.

> *"We want Tosh Hoos!*
> *We want Tosh Hoos!*
> *We want . . ."*

Had he been a betting man, it was what he would have put his money on. All of a sudden the pavement outside the Council offices had become the number one place to be. Two days earlier, the presence of the retired miners from Sanquhar had lifted the average age on the picket line well to over thirty. Now as he turned the corner, he saw that the average age had plummeted down to nearer sixteen. Maybe even fifteen. Buccleuch Street was a sea of baseball caps. How many? Had to be well over three hundred. Far too many for the pavement to accommodate. They had covered half of the road and it was obvious that more youngsters were arriving all the time.

He couldn't help but smile. It was a sight nobody in Dumfries could ever have dreamed of. The street was absolutely bouncing. Three camera teams were doing the rounds. Reporters spoke live to their breakfast shows as small faces were jammed in behind them pulling comical expressions. An ice cream van and a burger van were ignoring the double yellow lines and doing a record trade. And right in the middle of it all Lenny Baxter stood head and shoulders above the youngsters who had joined his cause. Frank stood back and watched with a small smile. Lenny was firing off instructions and trying control the chaos all around him. Not a chance. It wasn't a picket line. It was a picket sprawl. Some had placards. Others chanted. Others knocked about in groups and talked. Frank eased his bulky frame through the throng to join Lenny.

"Morning."

"Aye. Another belter Frank. Wicket'll be a tad zippy on Sunday with a couple more days like this."

"You're playing then?"

"Course I am. No picketing on Sundays."

Frank scanned the packed street.

"Fair turn out I'd say."

Lenny smiled. "Aye. Not bad for a bunch of beginners."

"I hope things stay calm Lenny."

"Does it look as if they won't?"

"No. Not right now it doesn't. Try and help the poor sods who work in here to get in without too much aggro."

"I'll do my best."

As things turned out Lenny didn't have too much to do on that front. Most of those who worked in the Municipal Chambers had watched the news the evening before and decided to stay at home. Others had come in to town out of basic nosiness, but had progressed no further than the end of the street. Only four actually made it in, one of who was Walter Billingham who barged through pickets and reporters with a face like chalk and sealed lips. For the first morning of the campaign the administrative function of the Council started to hiccup like an old engine.

A hundred miles up the road in Edinburgh, Scotland's First Minister snapped off his TV and tossed the remote. His private secretary was perched anxiously with an undrunk cup of tea and averted eyes. She could tell it was about to be long day.

"Just what the hell is going on down there?"

"We're looking into it sir. It seems at this stage as if everything is more or less as it seems. The local Council took a decision to sell off some property for a housing development rather than fund a youth facility. It would appear that the local community are not accepting the decision."

"Not accepting it! For Christ's sake there's not accepting something and there's bloody anarchy. Did you see those pictures?

The road's blocked. It's a damned mob. Ridiculous. What are the police saying about it?"

"The Chief Constable says that so long as the picketing remains peaceful he sees no need for his men to intervene. They are of course on hand and keeping an eye on the situation."

The First Minister slapped the table. "I wonder what the bloody man considers to be under control. In my book a mob and a blocked road and all of it on live TV is anything but under control. What about the blocked road? Surely that has to be against the law. People can't just go around blocking roads. Can't the wretched man see that?"

"He says that there is a diversion in place sir. He says traffic is moving normally. No delays."

"He might as well admit he's on their side. I don't know why he doesn't get dressed up like a Ned and go and join the rest of the mob. What about this so called Union? USY or whatever. That can't be legal. You can't just scribble a bit on a piece of paper and call yourself a union. It's outrageous. And if the union is illegal, then the whole thing is illegal and he can get the place cleared out."

The secretary stared hard at some notes written in a neat hand.

"Sir. He says that his legal team are looking into it. He feels that to prove legality one way or another would mean court and it could all take several months if they decide to drag their heels."

Now he leaned back in his swivel chair and screwed his eyes shut. "And the Council. What the hell have they got to say for themselves? I hope to Christ they're not blaming us for this fiasco."

"Actually sir, it seems they might be. They're suggesting that central funding for education and social services has declined in real terms. They say that they are having to cut their cloth accordingly. That is why the decision was taken to sell off the site."

This brought him jumping to his feet. "What! Please don't tell me that they are saying this in public."

"Not yet sir. But I think they are warming up to it."

"The swine. The bloody wriggling swine." He had to take a few long deep breaths to calm himself down. "Get a team looking into how we might be able to make some funds available for this centre on the quiet. And if we do it, and that is the biggest bloody 'if' there has ever been, I will want this doing quieter than the grave. If there is even a whisper that we are giving in to this kind of thing we'll have demonstrations from Gretna to Inverness. I want to be very, very clear on this. What I am asking is for the possibility of finding funds to be looked into. Only that. The possibility. Until further notice we tough the thing out, we make no comment and we confirm the whole affair is an entirely local issue to be dealt with by local government. Is that crystal clear?"

"Yes sir."

"Well get on with it then."

The Private Secretary was blushing as she scuttled from the room. Normally her boss was such a nice man. She had never seen this side of him before. As soon as she had closed the door behind her he ripped open the bottom drawer of his desk and pulled out cigarettes. He hadn't touched one for four months. Stuff that. He opened his window, lit up and took in a huge draw. Better. Heaps better. He leaned in close to the gap in the window and blew the smoke outside in a long plume. It seemed typical of everything. He was supposed to be the most powerful man in Scotland and here he was sneaking a fag at the window like a fourth former.

Jed Thomson mingled easily with the swelled ranks of pickets. Outwardly, he strolled with hands in pockets and an easy smile. Inside he thought the whole thing was a joke. It wasn't a picket line. It was a free for all in the sunshine with ice cream and burgers. Eighty percent of those on Buccleuch Street were kids on a day out from their normal tedium. Every now and then one of the chants would take hold and reverberate around the street. Then the placards for the two dead ones would be waved. But it would soon die back down and everyone would get back to loafing about. The adult twenty percent was an equal split between pickets and reporters. These were more earnest as they gave and took interviews.

Jed had little sympathy for the cause. The army had taught him to put up and shut up. He couldn't abide do gooders. The country was awash with cut price Polish hauliers working with their tachographs switched off and nobody was much bothered about that. If he was to go to the wall and thousands like him, nobody much cared. It certainly wasn't an issue the media were about to get exited about. But fill a street full of kids under the orders of some mad terrorist Pinko from the past, and they were out in droves.

Business was business and money was money, but he was going to enjoy this one all the same. Stuff the lot of them. The nicey, nicey time was coming to a close it was going to be as easy as shelling peas. Once he got to his car he sent Latimer a text before heading back north. It comprised of just one word.

Monday.

For five days Yousuf had shadowed Charlie Company and the ABC camera team. Each new day brought a different activity. Had he been party to the jargon, he would have known it was a campaign to win the hearts and minds of the locals. For some reason today they had arrived at one of the town's disused schools. It had been quite a modern three-story structure before the invasion. On the day that the Americans had come to Famoudi, two snipers had taken up a position at one of the windows on the third floor. They had fired off five shots which had all missed their targets but been enough for the soldiers to fix their position. The officer in charge had made a tactical decision from what he saw as two available options. One, he could send in an assault unit to neutralise the threat. Or two, he could remove the third floor and neutralise the threat. He had chosen option two and duly passed on the order to the commander of one of his Abrams tanks which had duly removed the third floor of the school with three depleted uranium shells. His decision had consequences for the long-term viability of the site for educational purposes. First and most obvious was that the third floor was now largely removed to the playground area in the form of rubble and broken glass. Second, the shells soaked the area with radioactivity which would make the pupils of the future as likely to get leukaemia as maths should the school be reopened in the future.

Yousuf sat on a large chunk of rubble to one side of all the activity. The officer was in a T-shirt today. They all were. For some reason they were clearing the mess away from the playground. A small group of locals looked on with blank expressions. By the late morning, the old playground had re-emerged from under the debris and the squad of sweating Marines paused to drink cans of Coca Cola from an ice box at the back of one of their Humvees. The officer waved over to the watching Iraqis and held up a can and shrugged. Several children bounded forward straight away followed by more suspicious adults. Yousuf followed suit, walking slowly with his head down.

"There you go man."

He was handed an ice-cold can by an enormous black Marine.

"Coke adds life. Even to ragheads."

Yousuf gave an ingratiating smile and nodded eagerly which made the marine laugh.

"Stupid goddamn gooks."

Once Yousuf might have flared up. Not now. Like everyone else he had learned. He kept the stupid smile on his face and sipped the ice-cold drink with grovelling gratitude.

The woman was a few yards from where he stood. And the other civilian with the camera. As usual she was talking with the officer. The same every day. Yousuf understood the routine now. He had been collecting up snippits of their conversations for several days. Peggy Hill was excited about the whole Famoudi thing. She had told Nash that it was playing out like a dream Stateside. Ratings for the evening news slot had sky rocketed. Focus groups had confirmed that people were tuning in to see what was happening with the young captain who had a smile like Brad Pitt and Charlie Company.

"So Captain. Tell me about today?"

"Maam, today the guys are clearing this playground area. As you can see there is still damage from the combat phase. Once we have the area clear, we will be erecting basketball nets. We anticipate completion before O eleven hundred on Monday maam. Then some of the guys will be available to teach the game to any kids who want to give it a try."

Yousuf felt the eyes of the towering marine on him and dutifully shuffled back to his perch. So now it was basketball. Barbeques and basketball. Burgers and ice-cold coke. First they come and murder us and destroy our homes. Then they think they can make us love them for burgers and basketball. On the outside he was just another ragged youth with deep set eyes and tattered clothes. Bent and beaten with nothing better to do than to sit and watch the soldiers crack jokes with each other as they dragged away the debris. Inside his anger was moving from hot to cold. He was finding out how things stood. The woman had been flushed with excitement. Ratings were soaring. He was pretty sure he knew what that meant. Lots of people were watching in America. Every night she had said. On the news. For the last three days he had been certain that this had to make his enemies weak in some way. He knew that everything depended on the cameras. And now at last he understood why. And now he understood how. And on Monday the fight back would start.

The start of the week was forecast to be the end of the heat wave. Lenny strolled towards the town centre with Josh and felt like the Pied Piper. Just a few days ago this had been a walk taken by the gallant few. Himself and the twins and Tony Crenshaw and Rory McGuire. The famous five. Now there was Josh by his side and a throng of Sunnybank youth at his back. An army on the march. A fine Sunday which had restored his spirits. His prediction about the wicket to Frank Dixon had been spot on. He had lolled about in the sun as the home batsmen rattled up a total of 211 for 3. The Sunday papers had been fascinating. Every one carried lengthy pieces on the USY protest. Many said how it was a throwback to days gone by. Focused direct action. Youthful protest. Something that seemed to have been put away in the same drawer as workhouses and whooping cough. The politicians were clearly ill at ease with the whole thing. They were in a tough position. Political correctness was all about encouraging communities to have their say on how they wanted things run. It was a thing that sounded great on paper. In practice the government had found a comfort zone. The opportunity was always given to the public to turn up to small rooms to give their opinion on any policy to junior bureaurocrats who would make copious notes. These were inevitably one man and his dog affairs which duly got the boxes ticked. Once they could claim that a full consultation with local stakeholders had been undertaken, the politicians could then get on and do pretty well what they pleased.

Then, just when it seemed like nothing like it could ever happen again, the public had taken their leaders by surprise. Firstly, a gang of wagon drivers and farmers nearly brought the country to a halt over petrol prices and the people cheered them on. Next came the millions who marched against the war and ensured that their Prime Minister was tarnished forever. And now a man from the mists of the past had done the impossible. He had harnessed the energy and passion of hundreds of kids and sent them out onto a small Scottish street to get into the faces of the politicians. Tony Benn produced a long piece praising USY and all it stood for, and as he read it, Lenny felt a familiar coldness in the pit of his stomach. His mind slipped away from the words on the page and away into the past. A night at the Cambridge Union. Tony Benn and Ken Clarke and Nuke and Josh. And Beverly. Always Beverly.

"You OK?"

Josh's voice pulled him back.

"Aye. Fine. There's a piece from Tony Benn here. Took me back. That's all."

When Lenny had taken the field he had bowled better than at any time since his release from prison. His six wicket haul was much photographed as many of the journalists had decided to kill their Sunday at the cricket. After the match he didn't pay for a single drink. The pints were sent over to him from all quarters. His side. The opposition. The press. And all his instincts told him that the public were behind the USY campaign.

By the time Walter Billingham stomped up the steps to work, the street was packed. There were many, many more. He tried to guess how many. Certainly more than five hundred. There were more on the street and less in the Chambers. He had only seen two others go in through the front door after Billingham. So far the Council had stayed tight-lipped. A couple of terse Press Releases had made statements about not making policy as a result of threats. Other than that, the beseeching questions of the journalists had been met with a wall of silence.

Lenny had been trying to work out what on earth they could say. He certainly didn't envy whichever poor sod drew the short straw to be wheeled out in front of the cameras to explain why a new housing development was more important than a youth centre. Maybe, just maybe, they might see that the easiest option would be to do a U-turn and give Sally her money after all. Maybe. Maybe this time they might be allowed to win.

Jed had found the spot on the Friday morning. It was a yard at the back of a disused office block that seemed to be undergoing some kind of renovation. It was obvious that there must have been problems. Money probably. All kinds of old wood had been stripped out from inside the building and had been dumped in a messy pile by the back door. There was a texture to the rubbish that suggested it had been there for a while. The place was certainly very much deserted when he had picked the lock of the door and took a look round. The workmen had left their chip wrappers and half-drunk coffees in polystyrene cups. Old newspapers were all at least five months old and turning to yellow. Someone had run out of cash and the workers had packed up their tools and moved on. There was a 'To Let' notice in the front window.

It would do. He had returned to the yard a few minutes after nine o'clock once the street outside was full enough to give him plenty of cover. He removed a small back pack and took out a two litre plastic Coke bottles that he had filled up with unleaded petrol. He pulled aside some broken pieces of plasterboard so that he could reach all the way into the middle of a stack of old wood. Then he emptied the petrol into a nest of screwed up newspaper that he had prepared on his first visit.

A glance at his watch told him 9.15. On target. On the nail. Showtime. He lit up a crumpled page of the Sun and shielded it for a moment until it was well and truly lit. Then he tossed it into the petrol and jumped back as it lit up with a thump. He didn't bother checking that his fire had caught. No need. There hadn't been a drop of rain for days.

He ducked out of the alley and joined the crowd before the first of the smoke carried up and over the line of the rooftops. Ten minutes later he was back at the mini bus he had hired from a pal the day before. OK. Stage one. Stage two was down to Ally.

Ally McCrone was fifteen years old and he was a hoodlum to his dirty toenails. His school career had been a litany of failure, suspension and expulsion. In the end, the local authority had given up trying to find anywhere willing to take him. They had cut him loose to roam the streets of Cumbernauld with his band of cronies. They stole and swore and smashed windows and were the town's number one target to be ASBO'd. Jed's dealings with Ally and his crew had started when he had caught them climbing the fence into his yard. He had caught the young tearaway as he had dropped to the ground and given him a good slapping. Then he had given him a tenner and told him not to come back. The cheeky little sod had come back the next day and had shown the cheek to offer protection at the rate of twenty a week. The front of the lad had amused Jed who had haggled him down to a tenner's worth of booze to cover the contract.

Ally had been true to his word. There had been no vandalism at the yard for well over a year and Jed had got to throwing a few packs of cigarettes in with the carrier bags filled with cheap lager. There had been no doubt that Ally's team would jump at the idea of a day trip down to Dumfries, especially for the unimaginable sum of five hundred quid cash. Now they maintained a tight group as they mingled with the crowd. Ally checked the time on his mobile phone. 9.25. Sure enough, there was smoke now. Lots of smoke. It poured up from behind one of the buildings in a thickening black column. He could hear sirens. He was good at guessing the distance of sirens. He needed to be. These were a bit off yet. A mile or so. Five minutes probably. He gave the others the nod and they pulled off their backpacks. Eight packs, each containing a weighty load of seven half bricks. A total of over fifty.

Jed had been very clear in his instructions. The police station was much closer than the Fire Station. The cops would arrive first. Get in close, but not too close. Throw the bricks fast. Really fast. Then get back to the minibus. Don't hang about. Throw and go. Simple. Five hundred when it's done.

9.31. There it was. One police car. Lights flashing. Siren on and off, forcing its way slowly through the milling crowd, an officer hanging out of the passenger window screaming for people to get out of the way. Close to the burning building now. Close enough for the driver to stop and the doors to open. The passenger door first. Then the driver. Ally gave the word.

The Cumbernauld crew drew their hooded tops over their heads and started their barrage. All fifty six bricks were fired off in less than thirty seconds. One caught the driver high on the forehead and felled him like a sack of grain. Three turned the windscreen of the police car into a spider's web of broken glass. One took the passenger on the elbow and cracked the bone. Another flew high and broke the nose of a thirteen year old who had come down to Buccleuch Street because all of her mates had said it was brill.

Complete bedlam broke out in seconds. Everyone was trying to run in different directions. Two more police cars drew up and the officers started throwing bodies out of their way as they fought to get through to their injured colleagues. By now flames were shooting out of the front windows of the disused offices which had gone up like a well-built bonfire.

Lenny stood at the top of the steps and felt a familiar helplessness. For a while he had believed that for once things were about to turn out. What a fool. What a complete and utter fool. He remembered the hard faces of the strangers he had seen on the morning they had fractured his father's skull. Strangers throwing half bricks at policemen. Strangers setting buildings alight. He had wanted to believe that the USY campaign would be allowed. What a fool. Of course it wasn't. Nothing was allowed. Not ever. He knew he should have been doing something to help, to try and put some semblance of order into the growing chaos all around him. But he couldn't. Suddenly he was tired. More tired than he had ever been in his life. Tired of smacking his stupid Yorkshire head into the bricks. He knew he should do something but he just stood as still as a statue and watched as Buccleuch Street went berserk in front of him.

And in the midst of all the bodies running in all directions he sensed a stillness. A body that wasn't moving. A body that held a camera which was pointing up from the bottom of the steps. Pointing at him. Zooming in. Accusing. Damning.

Sir Edward Latimer leaned back in his chair and allowed a smile to take a hold of his cold face. The image zoomed in. There he was. Baxter. What on earth did the man think he was doing? He just stood there. Watching. Unemotional. And all of a sudden the tall Yorkshireman looked every inch a terrorist. Perfect.

He picked up his phone and dialled a number from his Filofax.

"Thomas. Edward Latimer here. Are you well? . . . splendid . . . yes, good order thank you . . . Thomas, I gather you're in charge of the building project down at the naval yard at Rosyth. You are? Excellent. Thomas, there's a haulier I would like you to use. He's from Cumbernauld. Thomson. Jed Thomson. Pay him the rate for the job plus £20,000. Don't be so silly man, of course you can swing it, yes, yes, I will make sure that funds are transferred into your budget . . . you know better than that Thomas. Need to know and all that . . . terrific. Absolutely. Dinner would be great. Let me know when you are back in town. Bye for now."

On the TV, the street was more or less clear now. Two fire engines were pumping water into the blazing building. A shocked reporter was telling it with gusto. And the producer in the studio replayed the shot of Lenny Baxter standing so very still at the top of the steps watching it all happen. Like a statue. Like a terrorist.

Latimer snapped off the screen. End of problem.

Yousuf had spent his weekend talking hard. Persuading. Cajoling. Almost pleading. Most of his contemporaries thought that he had gone plain crazy. Others had no interest in joining him. Why should they? Why would they antagonise the Americans when they had finally started to treat the people better. It made no sense. For two years everyone in Famoudi had all but starved and now at last there was food to eat and people could walk the streets with less fear of being executed by the trigger happy Americans. Why choose the very moment that things seemed to be getting better to provoke them?

Those who had been willing to listen to him had been sceptical. What could a few kids do to change things? The whole of Saddam's supposedly invincible army had been crushed by the Americans in a matter of days. Not just once, but twice. They were too strong. They were indestructible. Yousuf talked and talked until his voice was hoarse and cracked from talking. He tried to explain why the reporters made it different. He tried to explain why the Americans had suddenly started to be so nice. It wasn't because they had changed their minds and decided that they liked the people of Famoudi after all. It was because the news people were showing it all to the people at home. It was like all the posters there had once been on the buildings of Famoudi showing uncle Saddam with his hands on the shoulders of smiling schoolchildren. A lie. Propaganda. He tried to show them how this made the Americans weak.

Finally he had found a way of making a few of them understand. He talked about the children of the Intifada in Palestine. Everyone had watched them when they had taken to the rubble-strewn streets with scarves wrapped around their faces and thrown stones at the Israelis in their tanks and armoured cars. Night after night it had been the number one item on the news. The heroes of the Intifada. Only then did the ones Yousuf talked to begin to understand. If the children of the Intifada had stepped out into the streets with machine guns, then the Israeli soldiers would have cut them down within seconds. And the Israeli government would have gloated about it. But children throwing stones was different. No way could the soldiers open fire and cut them down, no matter how much they must have wanted to. And so the soldiers had to hide behind their vehicles and their riot shields and take it. Sure, they fired rubber bullets and tear gas, but they hardly ever fired real bullets, and never when the news cameras were on the street to bear witness.

Yousuf told them that they could do the same. It was their opportunity to pay the hated Americans back for what they had done to Famoudi, to Iraq, to their fathers, to all of them. He told them that the ABC camera team would mean that the Marines would be as helpless as the Israeli soldiers had been. He told them they had a chance to fight back. To be proud. To escape the shame of begging every day from the invaders who sneered and laughed at them.

In the end he gathered together a group of ten. They were all boys who had lost family to the Americans. Some were like Yousuf who had seen their fathers and brothers taken away in the night to the prison at Abu Graib. Others had seen mothers and younger brothers and sisters eaten away by diseases and lack of medicine. Others had lost family in the first days of the war when the helicopters and fighter planes and huge tanks had pounded the town as the rampaging Americans had raced for Baghdad. Every one of his nine comrades had two things in common. They were bound by a burning desire for some kind of revenge for what had been done to their families and they felt that they had nothing to lose. Death was nothing much to fear for life had become barely worth living. They were ready to listen to Yousuf and his plans. They were ready to avenge their families.

The Marines arrived at the old school playing ground a few minutes after nine. It was all usual, the routine that Yousuf had watched carefully for three days. The soldiers liked to get most of the heavy work of the day done before the sun became too hot. At eleven they would down tools and return to their base to sit out the heat of the day before returning for more work in the late afternoon. The woman from ABC came in the morning. Yousuf had worked out that the afternoon would be too late for her to send her pictures back for America to watch on the evening news. Her van parked up with the Humvees and the armoured cars. The playground was now recognisable as a basketball court in the making. The rubble of the war had been cleared and the surface of the playground had been patched up so that it was now clean and smooth. One pole and net had been completed. Opposite a hole was half dug ready for the second pole to be cemented into place. Yousuf saw that they had some paint this morning to mark out the lines of the court. By tomorrow the work would no doubt be complete and then they would bring cans of Coca Cola and chocolate bars to bribe the younger children to come and play basketball with them while the woman from ABC filmed it all and sent her pictures back to America. Her lies.

Now that the hard work of clearing all the debris had been completed, there were less Marines than there had been. Yousuf counted twelve. Four started digging the hole for the second net. Three started marking out the lines. Five took up a casual watch on the small crowd that had gathered to watch the work. It was now usual that they wore caps instead of helmets and T-shirts instead of full body armour. They cradled their weapons casually as their eyes scanned the watching Iraqis and the buildings overlooking the playground. The tall officer was once again talking into the microphone. Yousuf was too far away to hear what the man was saying, but he found it easy to guess. It would be the same as the day before and the day before that. He would be boasting about how people of Famoudi were coming to accept and respect his men. How there had been virtually no incidents since the new tactics. He would be describing in sickening detail how easily he and his men had bribed those they controlled. A few burgers and cans of coke and everything was forgotten.

Not any more. Yousuf had explained his plan until the others had been sick of hearing it. They would spread out into three groups. They would stay back until the woman in civilian clothes started to talk with the tall officer. Then they would strike. Their target was the officer and the woman. Not the cameraman. Absolutely not the cameraman. As long as he was able to shoot his film they would be safe. His film was their shield. As long as his camera saw everything the soldiers would be helpless. Only the camera would save them from execution.

The woman was animated now, taking in the almost built basketball court with a sweep of her arm. Her words were louder now and they carried to where Yousuf waited.

"Only a few days ago, this playground was a memory of the fighting which swept through Famoudi two years ago. Now it has become a small image of how things are getting better here every day. A small piece of America on the streets of the Sunni Triangle. When do you anticipate the court will be finished Captain . . . ?"

Yousuf pulled the scarf around his neck up over his nose and mouth. All the others had been waiting for his lead and they followed suit. One of the Marines on the perimeter saw them and stiffened. His gun was coming up automatically and Yousuf could see he was about to shout. No time to turn back now. Already he had a stone in his hand. A nice stone. An easy fit. Perfect for throwing. He stood up fast and threw.

Even though he was no more than fifteen yards from where the Captain talked with the women, it was still a magnificent shot. The jagged stone hit the woman high on the cheek and drew an immediate spurt of blood. Every one of the others followed his lead without hesitation. Nine more stones rained down. Five missed. One hit the woman on the arm. Two hit the marine Captain as he reacted fast to cover the falling woman with his body. Yousuf threw a second stone which missed and a third with hit the captain on the back of the leg.

And even as he focused on aiming his missiles, Yousuf was aware that death was now a fraction of a second away. All the guns were on them now. Raised and ready. Fingers on triggers. Bullets in place. Eyes staring down sights. He braced himself for the red hot tearing of his flesh. The smashing of his bones. The blackness of death.

All the other watching Iraqis had reacted instantly and now they were fleeing the street. The soldiers who had been digging and painting were scurrying for their weapons. Those on the perimeter were about to fire. And then he heard the captain's voice. Loud but calm. Clear. Commanding.

"Hold fire. Repeat. Hold fire. Apprehend only."

And for a second he felt the hesitation of the soldiers with the guns. Like dogs told to sit when all they wanted to do was to chase the sheep. Training and discipline stretched tight. Again the voice.

"Apprehend. Now. Move!"

The camera panned fast from soldiers to stone throwers to the captain to the bloody and shocked face of the woman and then back to the stone throwers. And still no gunfire. No killing. And a feeling of triumph filled Yousuf because it was all as he had told them it would be. Time to leave now.

"Go!!"

And at the same instant the ten masked figures were running, fast as stray cats through the rubble of the deserted street. Too fast for the big Marines who lost ground straight away. Nash took it in quickly. He registered the possibility that pursuit could mean planned ambush.

"Stop!!"

Again the soldiers started to raise their guns towards the stone-throwers who were darting away down the street.

"No firing. I repeat. No firing. Move back."

One last hesitation. Movement that was not instant.

"Back!!"

His master's voice. A command to be obeyed. The hundreds of hours at the boot camp kicked into play. They lowered their weapons. They moved back to the perimeter. Nash waited a few seconds to ensure that his orders were properly in place then he turned to the woman on the ground. Jesus. What a mess. The stone had taken her on the forehead and left a big gash which was pumping out the blood. She was just beginning to come clear from the initial shock. He could see it in her eyes. Realisation. Fear. In a second or two she would be screaming. He aimed a level stare at the cameraman who was in the process of zooming in on the gore which he knew would play out like a dream on prime time.

"Maybe it would be appropriate to stop filming now sir." Nash's voice was very calm. The cameraman wanted to tell him no goddamn way. Tell him that this was the stuff they were here for. And he was going to until he caught the hard blue eyes. The captain was in no mood for kidding about here. The captain was just about as serious as serious got. He lowered his camera and clicked off the power switch. Nash gave him a nod.

"Marines. On me. Now."

They fell in around him. He snapped out his orders clean and quick. Within five minutes they were clear of the playground and heading back to the base. To assess. To evaluate. To plan. And as their small convoy bounced through over the potholes, Yousuf and his friends whooped and laughed in triumph as they ran without being followed.

No death by cop. No death by soldier.

Frank Dixon stayed on Buccleuch Street until the fire engines had completed their work. Officers had blocked the street at either end where crowds of passers by and reporters looked on as the police and firemen restored an element of normality to proceedings. A forensics team with expertise in arson investigations had arrived from Glasgow in the middle of the morning and already the word had come out that they were pretty sure that it had been deliberate. A strictly amateur affair. Petrol by the looks of things. A couple of witnesses had stated the yard was filled with timber, stripped out of the place by builders before they had been taken off the job. Once the fire had got going it had taken no time for it to sweep right through the building. The word was it could easily have been kids. In fact it was almost certainly done by kids.

Frank had an uneasy feeling about the whole thing. Of course he was too long in the tooth to be surprised at what the little toe rags could get up to. But this time it just didn't fit somehow. He had been on the street with USY from Day One. Nobody had been excluded from the party. It had been an open house. Free tickets for anyone who fancied turning up. He knew that mindless vandalism generally found its roots in boredom, exclusion and anger. Which made what had happened illogical. Nobody had been bored on Buccleuch Street. Most of the kids had been having the time of their lives. Nobody was excluded either. The bad boys and girls were allowed to mix freely with the good boys and girls. And anger? Well the whole point of everything that had happened was that it gave the kids a decent channel for their anger. So who in their right mind would want to start a fire and blow the whole thing out of the water?

His radio had buzzed and the Chief Constable's secretary had told him that he was expected as soon as he could get himself up to Police HQ. On his way across town he considered what he was going to say. It might not be the wisest thing to share the edgy gut feeling he had about what had happened. On the other hand he wasn't much in the mood to nod his head like a puppet. As he rode the lift up to the second floor he decided the best thing to do was to play it by ear.

PART TWO

The Chief was extremely unsmiling as he waved Frank to a seat. No coffee on offer this time. A biscuit was about as likely as peace in Palestine.

"Not good Frank. Not good at all. Tell me please."

He didn't mention the fact that he had just come off a phone call from the First Minister up in Edinburgh which had been little more than a ten minute rant. Why had he allowed the situation to develop so far? Why hadn't the street been closed off earlier? Why hadn't the so called picket line been deemed illegal? Did he have the faintest idea how all of this made the country look across the rest of the world? Had he never heard of tourism? And on and on it went until the Chief had confirmed that from here on in the street would indeed be sealed. There would be no more USY pickets on Buccleuch Street. And yes, he would be investigating whether there would be criminal charges against the leadership. And yes, he would be announcing the new approach as clear as clear could be to the assembled media at an early afternoon press conference. And when he had put the phone down he had known without the faintest shadow of doubt that his chances of making the move up the road to Strathclyde or West Lothian had all but vanished in the haze.

Frank could see that his boss was a bomb itching to go off. Maybe for once in his life it would be wise to box a bit clever.

"It's hard to say at this stage sir. I gather that the team from Glasgow think it was purely amateur. Petrol and a match. Nothing suspicious."

This brought a snort. "Oh nothing suspicious at all. A building in the centre of town gets burned to the ground in broad daylight and there's nothing to worry about. Bloody marvellous. What about the ones who threw the stones. Anything on them? The first pictures from the cameras appear inconclusive."

This was the part that had been bothering Frank Dixon. Oh what the hell.

"Something stinks sir."

"Go on."

"Timing first of all. It was as if they were waiting for our lads to arrive. The bricks were thrown as the lads were getting out of the car. Then there was the bricks."

"What about the bricks? Bricks are bricks as far as I'm concerned.

Especially when they are thrown at my officers. Rogers has a fractured cheek you know."

Frank swallowed and ploughed on. "I heard that sir. The thing is, where did they come from? Think about it. Buccleuch Street isn't the sort of place where there are convenient piles of rubble lying about the place. They must have gone out of their way to find them. I can't think of anywhere where anyone could come up with a few half bricks within a few hundred yards. It seems as if the fire had been going less than half an hour when the lads were attacked. The timing doesn't stack up. These lads must have seen the fire before anyone else, had a chat about it, decided to brick the police as soon as they arrived, legged it off to find a few missiles, come back to the street and done the deed. Pretty good going for an off the cuff."

The chief drummed his fingers on the desk. He was itching to tell Frank not to be so damned stupid but the argument was compelling.

"Continue."

"Sir, I'm finding it hard to see that the fire and the attack were not linked. The only logical reason for those lads having bricks ready to throw is that they knew the fire was about to happen. That means that they knew our lads would turn up and . . ."

He paused and wondered whether to keep going.

"I gather there is more?"

"Sir."

"Well spit it out then."

"I got a look at the lads who threw the bricks. Not much of a look. Just a glimpse. There's two things. Number one, the cameras won't give us a thing. All of them had their hoods up. There won't be a prayer of making an ID. Number two. I don't know sir. There was something about them. They just threw the bricks and legged it. I tried to get after them but there wasn't a chance. It was like it was planned. I just got a real feeling that they knew exactly what they were doing."

The Chief shrugged. "I can't say there is anything all that surprising in that Frank. USY had shown that they can organise things pretty well."

"But why on earth would USY do it?"

Another shrug. "God knows. Publicity probably."

"But that makes no sense, sir. They couldn't get much more publicity. They've been all over the news for days. More to the point, the media have been on their side. Look at the papers yesterday. Three of them were asking questions about whether Lenny Baxter might just have been innocent after all. Look how he looks today. Why the hell would he want that?"

The Chief was getting more and more wound up. "I don't know Frank. I haven't got the first clue. Maybe you have a theory to share with me?"

Time to shut up Frank. Time to shut up, shake the head, button the lip and bugger off. Time to show some savvy. As if.

"Sir. If those papers were right and Lenny was framed, then someone out there must be getting a bit nervous. The last thing they would want is for him to look good on the tele every night. They would want it stopped as soon as possible. It seems to me as if that is exactly what is about to happen. I expect there will be no more picketing?"

"Of course there won't. Do you seriously expect me to allow this to continue after what has just happened?"

"No sir. Which means that someone must be pretty happy with their day's work."

Frank thought for a moment that the chief was about to throw a coffee cup at him. The man was wound up all the way.

"Than you Frank. I'm grateful for your input. I will consider your thoughts, but I can't for the life of me see what on earth I can do about it. One thing however is absolutely clear. I DO NOTwant any of these thoughts sharing with the media. Under any circumstances. Is there anything else?"

"Would you allow me to look into things? Quietly of course."

A long, long pause. The chief's instincts urged him to send Frank to watch the traffic but it was hard not to see the logic in his thinking. He weighed the pros and cons. The damage was already done. That had been made abundantly clear by the First Minister. And if someone was responsible for the damage, he wasn't averse to the idea of finding out who they were. In fact if he could find out who it was, he might actually be able to undo some of the damage. So why not?

"OK. Have a go at it Frank. But keep it to yourself. Report to me and only me. Understood?"

"Of course sir. Thank you sir."

Frank left the office amazed that for once in his career things had actually gone better than expected.

By the time Frank made it across town to The Zone, Lenny was in deep hiding. The doors were shut tight on a pavement full of eager journalists. A hard bang on the door drew forth a youthful reply of "Piss Off"

"No can do I'm afraid. It's the police. Open the doors."

The door opened to reveal the deeply suspicious face of Barry Finch.

"What d'yu want then?"

"Where's Lenny?"

"He's in the back but he's no seeing anyone the now."

Frank eased the door open with one hand and with the other he eased Barry to one side.

"Down here is it?"

"I'm no saying nothing."

Frank chuckled. "Like father like son."

The main room was filled with a set of rather disconsolate looking figures. In the main it was the early USY members who had returned to the sanctuary of The Zone to lick their wounds. The whole place felt low-key. Deflated. Beaten. For a while everything had seemed to be going like a dream. Now it was just another nightmare. Frank nodded as he passed and made his way to the small office at the back of the building. He knocked and opened the door without waiting for permission. Inside the space was filled by Lenny, Josh and Sally. Josh stopped in mid-sentence and was about to complain at the intrusion when he took in Frank's uniform. Sally's face paled. Lenny barely registered anything. He was behind the desk sitting with a bent back and slack shoulders. Frank guessed that the other two were trying to pick him up, but by the look of him it didn't seem as if they were having a great deal of success.

"Hello Lenny."

Lenny's eyes came up slowly and took in his presence.

"Frank." Lenny started to pull himself to his feet. He half turned to collect his jacket from where it hung on the back of the swivel chair.

"Going somewhere are you Lenny?"

"I presume I'm going with you. That's why you're here. Well isn't it?"

"And why would I want you to go with me Lenny?"

"Not hard to figure out. I'm on parole. Because of me we had a riot on Buccleuch Street this morning. Two policemen injured, one quite badly from what I gather. One young girl in hospital. One office building burnt out. So, yeah. I expect that you want me to accompany you to answer some questions."

"Well that shows how much you know doesn't it. Sit down Lenny."

Frank started hauling piles of paper off a chair in the corner of the room and once he had an armful, he looked around rather helplessly until Sally snapped out of her pose of frozen panic and took them off him. Once he sat, he pulled off his hat and wiped at the sweat on his brow.

"Hell it's hot again. Too bloody hot. Not used to it, I'm not. Look Lenny. Sit down, settle down and lighten up. I don't suppose there's a chance of a cup of tea is there?"

Sally looked for somewhere to dump the pile of papers and in the end decided to take them out with her having established that the requirements were milk and two sugars. Lots of milk. Lenny had fallen back into Zombie mode and was staring vacantly down at the clutter on the desk. Frank could see that it was going to be on him to make all the running.

"Lot of unanswered questions this morning Lenny. Too many for my liking."

Lenny didn't look up. "Like what?"

"Like where did the bricks come from? Like how come the lads were ready the minute the squad car pulled into the street? Like where did they vanish to once they chucked the bricks? Like who the hell were they anyway because none of them were familiar to me. What about you Lenny?"

A shake of the head. "I've been asking all morning. Nobody has a clue. One minute they were there. One minute they were gone. People are saying they must have been from out of town."

"People are probably right."

This brought Lenny's head up. "You think so."

"Aye. I think so. What's more I've got permission to look into who they were. So what am I going to find Lenny? Any ideas?"

A grim smile. "I appreciate it Frank, but you won't find owt. Not a chance."

"And why might that be?"

"Because they'll have covered their tracks. Just like always. Just like back in 84. It's what they do."

"And they are?"

Lenny shrugged. "Who knows. The powers behind the throne. The ones who stitched me up. The ones who killed Frank. And Williams. The press have started sniffing about what went on back then. Somebody isn't happy. Somebody has decided to close us down. Well. Looks like they've done a pretty decent job doesn't it."

Lenny allowed his gaze to wander back to the desktop. Despondent. Frank felt a stirring of anger at whoever had orchestrated the events of the morning. There was something about Lenny Baxter. The poor sod deserved better.

"I might look like a big daft copper Lenny, but don't be deceived. I'm actually not a bad detective when I put my mind to it. And I'm a stubborn old sod to boot. I'll get to the bottom of this. Just watch this space. Now. You'll not be surprised to hear that the pickets are banned from the street tomorrow."

"I heard."

"So you'll stay away?"

A nod. "Aye. I'll stay away. You have my word on that."

"And the kids?"

Lenny shrugged at this and looked uneasy. "I'll do my best Frank. I guess most will stay away. But you know how they are. There might be a few . . ."

"Aye. I know that Lenny. Just do what you can. Let's try and not let things get worse."

"Fair enough."

Sally returned with a mug of tea and the four of them passed the time by running over the events of the morning. When Frank had finished he put the empty cup on the desk and got to his feet.

"I'll try to keep you posted."

"Cheers."

When he left Josh checked his watch. "Sorry to be the bearer of the news but we have a Press Conference in fifteen minutes. Time to go."

Lenny pulled a face and got to his feet. "What am I supposed to say Josh? You saw the way I looked on the television. I'm me, and even I think I looked like a terrorist."

Josh met his friend's anxiety with a grin. "You'll think of something. At least you better had or those boys outside are going to chop you up and eat you piece by little piece. Come on. No use moping. Sooner it's started, sooner it's done with. Then we can grab a pint or three."

The press conference was everything Lenny had expected. It was like feeding time at the zoo and he was the food. He gritted his teeth and kept his cool and stuck to the simple truth that nobody within USY had any idea who had been involved in the events of the morning. The more he denied everything, the more they attacked him with their barrage of questions. Later when he watched himself on the news he couldn't get over how guilty he looked. Same old, same old. There would be no more sympathetic good old Lenny coverage the next morning. He had reverted to type. He had brought the old anarchy to the streets. He was the disease from which Britain had been sure it had been cured. He was the enemy within. And he looked it as he moodily insisted again and again that USY had nothing whatsoever to do with any of the events of the morning. And as he watched he could barely believe his words himself. The editor had been very clever. Words were suddenly missing. Sentences came out in the wrong order. There was no way that anyone watching would be in any doubt that here was a man who was guilty as sin.

Sheila Finch still found it hard to get used to the new six o'clock routine her twins had fallen into. For some years any request that she had made that they should be home for a certain time had been made in hope rather than expectation. Of course it was different when their father was enjoying one of his brief periods of freedom. Then, if she said eight o'clock they would be at the front door of the flat for five to. But as soon as he was locked away again they would fall into their same uncontrollable routine. She had pretty well given up on having any control on them whatsoever from the day they moved up to Sunnybank High School. And yet this was the fourth day on the trot that they were inside the house for quarter to six. Not only in the house, but on the settee in the front room with their eyes locked on the news. A few days earlier she had sat with them and watched in utter amazement as Barry gave out his prime time statement.

That had been a fine night. It had been just about the greatest night their family had ever known. A few minutes after the news piece the telephone had rung and her husband had demanded to speak with both boys from a payphone in HMP Kilmarnock. He had told them that he was the proudest man in the nick. He told them that all the cons were talking about them. Even the screws were. He told them to keep it up. He told them to make sure that they didn't let the coppers stop them. Sheila had been on cloud nine as they had marched down to McDonalds for a celebration. And the five minute walk had taken half an hour because everyone wanted to stop them and tell them how well Barry had done and how it was brilliant. That night she had lain awake almost to the dawn relishing the fact that for once their family wasn't the centre of attention for all the wrong reasons. And she had wondered if for once things might just get better rather than worse.

Tonight the mood in the front room was different. The pictures told the story of the morning madness on Buccleuch Street. There was the image of the officer being half carried to an ambulance with blood streaming down his face and uniform. There were shots of the panic on the street as the crowd streamed away. There were pictures of the flames breaking through the front windows of the disused offices. And there was the image of Lenny standing like stone on the steps of the Council Offices with an unreadable expression on his face. The studio interviews were all in agreement. Things had gone too far. It was a case of going back to the bad old days. To make the point the editor threw in a few archive shots of the great riots of the early eighties. Toxteth. Handsworth. Brixton. The Poll Tax demonstrations. Grave-faced experts pondered on whether or not the bad old days were on their way back.

Then the newscaster turned away from her hired in experts and moved the show along.

" . . . *Dumfries wasn't alone in experiencing a riot today. For the last two weeks the Marine Corps in Famoudi have been involved in a dramatic change of tactics. In a surprise move they have adopted many of the tactics employed successfully by the British Forces in the south of Iraq. They have discarded their helmets and flak jackets and made efforts to engage with the local community. The new approach has been filmed by an embedded news team from ABC and for some nights the exploits of Captain Dale Nash and his Charlie Company has been watched by record audiences in America. However things have changed today. John French reports from Famoudi . . .'*

Scene. A team of Marines in T-shirts clear rubble in the morning sunshine as others look on in relaxed fashion.

'Another morning of winning hearts and minds here in Famoudi. Last week Charlie Company put on a barbeque and invited the whole of the town. For the last few days they have been clearing this old playground ready to build a basketball court.'

Scene. Dale Nash looking on as his men work away with small crowds of onlookers watching their every move.

'We believe that sports can be a bridge between ourselves and the local community here. That is why we are constructing this basketball court. Once we have finished, we will be looking for young people to come forward to play the game. We will of course be offering them instruction . . .'

John French voice over.
'However things changed dramatically this morning. For a while it seemed it was to be business as usual until a small group of young men suddenly stepped forward from the watching crowd and pelted the Marines with rocks . . .'

Scene. Yousuf and his comrades with scarves pulled high over their noses hurling rocks and rubble at the shocked Marines. A jagged rock hits the ABC reporter square in her face and draws blood. Another missile hits Nash on the back of his leg. The Marines on the perimeter raise their weapons ready to exact revenge. Nash's voice rings out loud and clear and commanding. The camera watches the ragged band as they skip away from the scene and melt away into an alleyway.

'As the events of the morning unfolded, it was impossible not to be reminded of hundreds of similar scenes we have witnessed over many years on the streets of Gaza and the West Bank. Now the question

here in Famoudi is whether or not this was a one off event. The Marines are saying little. In words of Hollywood, tomorrow is another day.'

Scene. A live satellite camera image of John French. Jerky. A little blurred. A caption reading 'John French. Famoudi.'

The newscaster again.

"How are things now John? Is the town calm?"
   "Very much so. To be honest the town has been calm all day. This was clearly something that involved only a very small number of people."
"And has there been any comment from the Marines yet."

A jerky shake or the head. Time delay as the words flew up from the studio in London, bounced off a satellite, and flew back down into French's headphones.

"Not really. They are very tight- lipped about what happened. The trouble is that this new strategy has been so very public. The nightly reports of Dale Nash and Charlie Company have been watched by millions in the United States. Nash himself has become something of an icon. The US military has been spinning the operation for all it's worth. It will be very hard for them to change course now, especially as those involved were little more than children and no shots were fired. To be honest, they have backed themselves into something of a PR corner. There is no way they can remove the ABC team at this stage and so long as the cameras are present they have few options in terms of their response. It has been said in many quarters that the Americans have tended to shoot first and ask questions later in this campaign. As yet, no American soldier has faced trial for killing a civilian. That of course is one of the main reasons why the occupation is so unpopular throughout the country. It is clear that the Americans have invested much in this new approach. It will be very hard for them to change things now. Many, many millions of people will be watching what happens tomorrow."
   "And is more violence expected?"

PART TWO

Again the time lag.

"Impossible to say. The Marines will be sincerely hoping that this will be something of a one off. If it isn't, it is hard to see that they will be able to respond with a great deal of force with the cameras watching."

"Thank you John. There has been better news today for all of those hoping that there may still be a future for the Rover plant in Longbridge"

Neither Tim nor Barry were much interested in the future of MG Rover. They exchanged a glance and it was enough. There were many times when they were able to communicate with each other without needing words. Files up in the offices at Sunnybank High School held assessments that showed that both boys were a minimum of four years behind where they should have been in terms of reading and writing. But when it came to the ability to spot an opportunity they were light years ahead. The two news stories merged into one and the same thoughts formed in their minds at the same time. Cameras. Reporters. Stones. Famoudi. Dumfries.

They got up and told their mum not to bother with tea. They said they weren't hungry. Maybe they'd get something later on. They said they had things to do.

Peggy Hill swallowed a handful of paracetomol and stared angrily into the small mirror she had taken from her purse. Oh sweet Jesus. Her right eye had morphed overnight into a rainbow of colours, mainly along the lines of blue and purple. Her cheek was covered by an ugly great plaster. The rest of her face was all puffed up. She looked in a complete and utter state but there wasn't a damn thing she could do about it. Her boss had cried his crocodile tears over the Sat-phone from Washington and told her that everybody would understand if she didn't feel safe enough to go back out with Charlie Company again. He told her that they could rotate her back Stateside if that was what she wanted and that they would pick up the tab for plastic surgery if that was what was needed. And Peggy had read between the lines because that was what she was good at. The subscript wasn't hard to decipher. Her bosses wanted her back in front of the cameras looking like the wounded heroine because it would be great for the ratings. Of course she could go home. And if she did they would all be really nice about everything and pack her off to cover the prom queen in nowhereville Idaho. Not a chance. Not a chance in hell. Peggy had scrapped her way to the top for ten long years and had spent every spare cent she had on having her face reconstructed for the camera. She had paid the cash and now she had the lips and the cheekbones and the nose. Many thousands of dollars more than she cared to count. So she was one hundred percent godamned if she was going to blow it all away because some rag-headed punks had smacked her one in the face with a half brick. And if she looked like all kinds of hell on prime time news, then so be it. And she would make sure one hundred and fifty percent godamned certain that if her cheek bones needed putting back into place, then the network would pay top dollar to get the job done.

Same street. Same burning blue sky. The Marines had their helmets back on their heads. No laughing and kidding around. No onlookers either. Just an empty street with all the windows shot to hell and a stray cat that flitted from one side to the other.

"Everything seems very quiet this morning after yesterday's incident. Captain Nash. Has what happened yesterday changed your tactics in any way?"

"No Maam. It is our judgement that yesterday's problem was a result of a minority of citizens. We are confident that a clear majority of the people here in Famoudi are behind our new tactics."

"Do you expect more trouble today?"

"The Marine Corps always expects trouble Maam, It's what we do."

"And will you continue to exercise restraint?"

For a moment the handsome face stiffened slightly. "We intend to maintain the integrity of the operation Maam."

She was about to ask her next question, but she saw that he was distracted. A shadow had flitted momentarily out of one of the alleyways.

"Excuse me Maam."

As he marched towards the men on the perimeter of his position, the waifs appeared from the alleyways like ragged ghosts. More today. Maybe twenty. Within seconds the air was thick with stones. The Marines crouched down in the face of the barrage. It was nothing like the day before. This time the stones were thrown from over forty yards and they landed with little power. Dale wondered whether to simply let them keep throwing until their arms ached. It seemed the best thing to do, but his orders had been fairly specific. He had been told to be proactive whilst maintaining the integrity of the mission. Bearing this in mind he had placed three of his quickest Marines on the perimeter. Now he set them running.

"Alpha Squad. Apprehend."

The three took off like Olympic runners, but to no avail. The waifs were primed and ready for the charge and started to melt away into the ruins as soon as the three soldiers rose from the blocks. The incident had lasted less than thirty seconds and there had been no casualties on either side. Elsewhere in Iraq three suicide car bombs accounted for seventeen trainee policemen in Mosul, four civilians in Tikrit and two American contractors on the road to the international airport. None of these attacks made the evening news. Once again that was dominated by Dale and Charlie Company and their efforts to build a basketball court.

Yousuf's second strike was carried out at 9.30 Iraq time. Tim and Barry launched their campaign half an hour earlier. Their efforts the evening before had gathered in a small but dedicated team of six, all with chequered records in the early years of Sunnybank High. They had collected stones from a building site and placed them under the bridge at the bottom of Buccleuch Street. A reconnaissance at eight o'clock had revealed that there were two uniformed policemen manning barriers at either end of the contested street. Another was diverting the morning traffic. A clutch of a dozen reporters and photographers waited nearby sipping at coffees and wondering if there would be anything worth covering. There was a slightly gloomy mood among the media ranks. The previous day had been a bonanza. Now it seemed as if the party was fizzling out. The word was that USY was licking its wounds and there would be no action for the day. A Press Conference was scheduled for the early afternoon when an announcement would be made. The majority of the reporters had decided to take an easy morning and have a lie in.

Initially, neither policeman nor journalist noticed the first tiny figure emerge from the small street by the bridge. It was only when a particularly well-aimed first shot sent a stone squarely between the shoulders of one of the constables that anyone became aware of the action. Suddenly there were eight small figures with hooded tops and scarves around their faces, all of them hurling stones at the policemen who instinctively backed away from the attack. Motor drives hummed on cameras as one of the officers made a report into his radio whilst crouching low behind the metal barrier. Before he had finished his second sentence the attackers had melted away.

The morning raid of the Finch twins was recorded by a single video camera. It was used to surprisingly good effect by a young cameraman from Rotherham who was just a month out of college and waiting on Buccleuch Street more out of hope than anything else. As soon as the last stone bounced along the road and settled against the kerb he knew that he had found his big break. An hour later he had sold the pictures for a sum that easily cleared his student loan. By ten the pictures from Buccleuch Street were all over the news channels. The attack had been launched by eight assailants with an average age of twelve and it had lasted for a matter of seconds. There had been no injuries. But the media took it as clear evidence that USY was taking their actions to a new and dangerous level. Earnest experts with worried expressions gave out grave warnings about how the situation was starting to escalate. Once again the archive pictures from the ravaged streets of the eighties were rolled out.

The Chief Constable received another call from the First Minister late in the morning. He was told in no uncertain terms to contain the damned thing. Lenny recognised the two leading hooded figures straight away, despite the fact that they had taken the precaution of wearing borrowed tops. He considered trying to find his President and Chairman but knew straight away that it would be a complete waste of time. When the Finch twins wanted to disappear, they disappeared, and there was no point in looking. Instead he tried to get his head around the Press Conference which was going to be another nightmare of the first order.

All around Sunnybank Estate young eyes recognised the small band and the consensus was that they were completely cool. The word whistled round. The next morning there would be more. Plenty more.

Asif Mohamed was enjoying a rare morning of leisure. Very rare. The momentum of his life offered virtually no leisure time at all. His regular morning routine saw him out before five-thirty in the morning. Five days a week he was on the shop floor of his Bolton factory as his workers made their bleary-eyed way to their stations. He was there to do the rounds. Crack jokes. Poke a bit of fun. Flirt a bit. Talk football a bit and generally get the show on the road. Start the money machine humming.

Asif had left Bolton Grammar School with three solid A-levels and he had disappointed his father by deciding against college. His mum and dad had arrived from Pakistan in the early seventies and had carved out a decent living in their adopted Bolton home. The family shop on the corner of one of the few remaining terraced streets had sold everything from cigarettes to scrubbing brushes and it was open from dawn to dusk and beyond, long before 24/7 retailing was the norm. For his father, there could have been no greater vindication for leaving the mountains of his native Kashmir for the grey hills of Lancashire than to have seen his eldest son collect a degree from a British University. But it was the last time that he was to be disappointed by Asif.

Asif had been in too much of a hurry for more study. From the age of twelve he had helped out his uncle Sadiq on the market where he sold cheap clothes from factories back on the sub continent. Sadiq prided himself on knocking out the cheapest denim in Bolton and trade was brisk. But as Asif grew older he realised that his uncle was missing a trick, though he never told him. Cheap was one thing, but his uncle's stuff was also naff. Seriously naff. All Asif's English mates told him so when they came down to the market for a crack. Most of Asif's mates were white. It was nothing to do with any disrespect for his own community, it was just that most of the pupils at his school were white. He grew up speaking like any lad from Bolton. He played cricket for the school team and like thousands of Bolton lads, he took the short train journey every other Saturday to watch Manchester United. The summer of 1990 saw him turn seventeen. It was his big time. The time when his life took off. He had finally persuaded his uncle to lend him the money to rent his own stall and stock it. Turnover was easing up and the he was making reasonable inroads into the loan. He focused on selling gear that was cheap enough but not naff and it was going OK. Unlike most of the other Asian stall-holders he had the patter and he spoke like a native. It gained him a toehold into the younger market. Instead of selling cheap jeans to hard-up mums who insisted that their sulking kids had to wear them, he sold jeans to the kids themselves. Sure they didn't have the labels but look at the cut and the price. Who notices a label at two in the morning after ten pints? And little by little he inched his way forward.

And then as the sun shone down for a whole long summer, everything changed. Manchester became Madchester, and for a while the eyes of the world were on the twenty-four hour party city a few miles up the road from Bolton. Every weekend thousands upon thousands descended on the city to dance through night to new music filtered through minds loosened by a new drug. Ecstasy. For a few magical months Manchester was the centre of everything and the whole country bounced to the sound of the Happy Mondays and Asif was slap, bang in the middle of it all. Night after night he sweated with the multitude. His faith kept him clear of the ecstasy and kept his brain clear enough to look and learn and turn the great party into profit. His stall was soon filled with party clothes; casual and baggy and easy to get produced back in Pakistan. By the time 1990 became 1991 he had seven stalls on markets all over Greater Manchester.

It was at this time that he stopped being Asif Mohammed. He took the first two letters of each of his names and became Asmo. And for many, Asmo became the man with the plan. The man with the gear. A man on the ball.

By 1995 Asmo was well and truly on his way. His comprehensive range of party and street wear had crossed over the racial divide and was sold by Asian and indigenous Brit alike. He dominated the northern market scene and somehow it seemed as if his energy took him everywhere at once. Then in 1996 he did something that united the whole community of his native Bolton. He took a decision that left the Pakistani elders shaking their heads and saying that the boy had gone too far, too fast. Crazy. Too much time at the white man's raves. The boy had clearly lost his head. On the other side of the fence, the born and bred white community of the town snorted with contempt at the jumped up little Paki who though he was God's bloody gift. The cause of such an outpouring of opinion was Asmo's most daring business move. He bought himself a disused cotton mill and vowed to have it back up and running within eighteen months. Some, like his bankers, took a look behind the scenes and saw that the majority of the cash required for the unlikely project was coming from a new regeneration fund from the EEC. They saw that maybe Asmo wasn't quite so crazy after all.

Fothergills Mill was four stories of Victorian red brick on the edge of the town centre. When it had been opened by the Mayor in 1892 it had provided jobs for well over a thousand and a sprawling mansion on the edge of the moors for the Fothergill family. When Asmo re-opened the doors in 1997, the workforce was somewhat less expansive, but two hundred new jobs in a blighted inner city area in the north was still enough to draw a Trade Minister up from London to do the honours. The clothes that started to roll out of the mill in the run up to Christmas actually cost Asmo a few percent more than those he had imported from Pakistan. But what he lost in terms of bottom line cost price he more than made up for in terms of speed and flexibility. Now he was able to use his nose for street trends to better effect and catch each new wave of fashion at an earlier stage. Fothergills gave him a three month advantage over his competitors and that was as good as a lifetime.

Eight years later the Asmo who lounged in his five star Glasgow hotel room was a man well and truly in his prime. The eight years of Fothergills had taken him far. He was a millionaire several times over and his range of street wear dominated markets from Inverness to Penzance. He also wholesaled to a growing number of independent shops and his website was moving along to something more than tick over.

And yet the burning desire that had taken him so far had barely been quenched. It hadn't taken him long to learn that it wasn't about money. Money was something that he found little personal desire for. Most of what he made found it's way back to his sprawling family back in Kashmir. He had a nice flat in the right part of Manchester but he was hardly ever there. If he wasn't at the mill, he was on the road. Seven days a week. No holidays. His work was his life, plain and simple. The problem was that he had peaked a good three years earlier. His sky rocketing turnover had finally reached a plateau and it gnawed at him. His life had become consumed by the next task. He was a rich man. A very, very rich man. There was barely a Saturday night street in Britain where his clothes were not to be found. And yet he had reached a glass ceiling. His clothes looked right and felt right. They were always there. In time. Right. But they were still lacking. Lacking what was needed to take them all the way to the premier league of his business.

He still had no label. And the label was all.

Designing and printing a label was easy enough. He had done that four years earlier. His label was Koz. But a label meant nothing unless it meant something. Unless it had that intangible something that would take it up the elevator to the top floors where the Nikes and Reeboks and Armanis had set up their camps.

Asmo was a very wealthy man, but the ticket for that elevator was a million miles and umpteen million pounds beyond his reach. The next level was the greatest step of all and finding a way to take it had become the Holy Grail of his life. The answer was always hidden around a corner that he could never quite reach, but never once did he lose the faith that he would one day get there.

And now all of a sudden he suddenly realised that he might just have arrived. He sat up sharply in the deep armchair in front of the hotel TV. It was so clear. As clear as the morning air over the snowy peaks of the mountains that cast their huge shadows over the village of his family in Kashmir. And as he watched a small group of twelve-year-olds throw their stones at three bemused-looking policemen he knew that the door of the lift had just opened and the way ahead was clear.

Half an hour later he had checked out and tipped extravagantly with his Amex Platinum and he was working his way out of the Glasgow's busy centre following the signs to the south.

Beverly Morton had come home to die. In the twenty years that had passed since she had taken the plane to Rome and her exile, she had only once returned to Britain. That had been in 1993 when she come back from the refugee camp in Goma to bury her father. Her mother had wanted Beverly to stay, but there had been too much work to do. Strangely enough the reason for her fast approaching death had at the time seemed to have been the thing that had prolonged her life against all the odds. When the blood-crazed young Hutu had stormed into the packed infirmary, it had seemed all but certain that Beverly would become just another statistic among the million plus who perished in Rwanda'a machete genocide. She had seen it in his eyes. Empty eyes filled with death. As clean, clear and deadly as a pan of boiling water. As she had stood to bar his way her brain struggled to dig out the lessons in self-defence she had once learned during her training for the Hendrick team. Her fuddled mind was still reacting as his machete had sliced through her face. It had been pure luck that her Kenyan assistant had been outside when the attack had happened. He had carried Beverly to the Belgian hospital over his shoulder as her blood had gushed down the back of his shirt. Later the surgeon told her that at first he had thought there wasn't even a sliver of a chance. But he tried all the same. He gave her priority because he was full of respect for the

English woman who had ignored all advice and stayed to try and do what she could. He sewed her face back together and filled her back up with blood and piled in the antibiotics. It had been touch and go for over a fortnight, but in the end she had pulled clear. When she at last left the hospital the killing fever had at last abated. She took the road east and started work in the black volcanic dust of the camp in Goma.

When she had returned for the funeral there were not many who could bear to look her full in the face. The scar ran from her left ear all the way to the centre of her chin and somehow her face had never quite regained its shape. She was a different Beverly from the one everyone remembered. Her hair was cropped short and her clothes were dowdy. She was all bone and her eyes burned with all the horrors she had witnessed. Her mum had pleaded that she should stay for a while at least. Rest up. Eat well. Put some weight back on. But Haddington was too cold and full of ghosts. The empty streets were as empty as her life. She had only stayed for two days before catching the plane south to the shores of Lake Kivu.

After Rwanda she had moved north to villages on the rocky hills of Bosnia. Then it had been east to Chechnya. It had been in the hospital in Grozny that her health had started to fall apart. The senior doctor from Iran had taken her blood and his eyes had gleamed with tears when he told her that she was HIV positive. He told her that it was already full blown. He told her that new medicine meant there was at least a chance. And that was when she remembered the huge blood transfusion that had saved her life in 1990. But it hadn't saved her life after all. Merely prolonged it for a while. She had worked on for as long as she could in the refugee camp in Sudan's Darfur region, and then she had said her goodbyes and taken her final plane ride back to Haddington. At first she had hoped she would be able to pass her last months at home, but after a few weeks her condition had deteriorated so dramatically that her mother had no option other than to transfer her to the infirmary in Sheffield.

As the chill of the spring had given way to a surprise early summer heat wave, she had felt the life slowly draining away from her. And then one morning against every expectation, Lenny's face was on the TV, and a last breath of life came into her. For days she watched the news for twenty-four hours a day and read every paper her mother brought in. For a while she allowed her hopes to surge. It was magnificent. Outrageous in its typical simplicity. A poke in the eye for the good and the great at a time when they thought they had finally bolted the doors forever. And her skeletal face smiled for the first time in many months at thought of how Latimer must have been squirming every time Lenny spoke into the camera. And then stones flew and an office burned and everything changed.

Outside the blue sky had finally gone away and the trees were framed by a backdrop of grey. On the screen she watched a very different Lenny. He was trying to keep his head high, but it wasn't hard to see that his neck was struggling with the task. For a while he must have thought that he was about to be allowed to win. But of course they would never allow that. They. Latimer and all the other Latimers who ran Britain like a private estate. She knew that there would have been nothing accidental about the bricks and the flames. Just like when the office in Belfast holding papers that proved collusion between the army and the loyalists hadn't burned by accident. Just like David Kelly hadn't been driven to suicide by accident.

But was it Latimer? Or was it just another cold faceless man making down payments on a knighthood and non-exec seat on the board of Great Britain Plc. She switched on her brain and worked it through. It wasn't hard. Of course it was Latimer. In the end the whole thing was about whether or not a derelict building in a small Scottish town was used for a youth centre or a housing development. Of course no government ever liked young people taking to the streets and demanding a share of the cake. They hadn't in 1968 or in 1981. But this was hardly a big deal. It was a little local issue. If any pressure from the top was going to be applied, it would be for the Council to do a quick U-turn and resolve the thing before it went any further. It wasn't the kind of thing that would persuade anyone of the need to let the dark roaders off the leash. Unless, of course, somebody had something to hide. And Latimer had plenty to hide. She had learned to use the internet since she had returned home and she had spent many hours reading of how Sir Edward Latimer had emerged in the highest branches of the Civil Service tree. Every time Lenny's face appeared on TV or in the papers, Latimer must have been taken by a cold sweat.

Lenny had become the story of the hour and people were starting to turn over the stones. There had been those who had fought to prove his innocence for years. A couple of left wing MP's from the ranks of

Old Labour. A couple of dogged lawyers. A few civil rights groups. Nobody much had noticed them for the twenty years that Lenny had been kept from the fresh air. But all of a sudden everyone was noticing now. Because Lenny was news. Big, big news. And Latimer must have decided to play it safe just like he always did. The thrown bricks and the burning office had his name written all over them. He had moved the prying eyes of the media away from those dark days of the winter of 1984. Suddenly Lenny looked every inch a terrorist as he stared out from the steps of the Council Offices. The tide was turning and Lenny Baxter was once again being made the bogeyman.

And now he was on the TV again. The questions rained down harder than the stones that had pelted the policemen. And the more he denied any knowledge of what had happened, the more it looked as if he had issued all the orders. Her mind was filled with the image of the Latimer she had first met all those years ago at Cambridge. Cold. Machine-like in his ambition. Quite willing to kill for his career. The web had thrown up photographs of the Latimer of 2005. The knight of the Realm. All Savile Row and lizard smile. A sixty-year-old with a year-round tan. Every inch of him spoke of a man who was convinced that he was indestructible, untouchable, an establishment Capone sure in the knowledge that the law of the land was not a thing to fear. A man who knew he had the sanction of the great. A gatekeeper. An executioner.

As she saw the pain in Lenny's eyes she felt a last gasp of life flicker through her. The ghost of the old Beverly was back. There was time. Not much. But enough. She reached out to the table by her bed. It was on wheels and she pulled it to her and switched on her laptop. *Google* took her to the BBC. BBC took her to Panorama. And then she clicked onto the contact button and found a phone number.

Alison Hammond was convinced after less than five minutes of listening to the small voice on the phone. Within an hour she was on a train headed north out of Kings Cross. Within four hours she was by the bedside of the dying woman with the wrecked face. She was back in the office by the evening and her boss was waiting for her in a fair degree of ill-humour. He had been looking forward to the theatre and was not remotely amused to have been harangued into cancelling.

Half an hour later he knew he had a story of weapons grade quality on his hands. By midnight Alison had gone all the way up the chain to the very top of the Corporation. It would need to be done in a hurry: a record-breaking hurry. She committed herself. As long as she was given the resources, she promised she could have a Panorama Special filmed, edited and ready to roll for Sunday evening. OK, it might be a little rough at the edges, but the content would more than make up for any lack of polish. Lawyers were summoned to give their £500 an hour advice and by one-thirty it was concluded that although the legal ground was shaky it was just about firm enough. The government would hate it of course. Hate it with a passion. But there wasn't anything new in that. The BBC had been seething ever since Lord Hutton had whitewashed his Whitehall cronies and placed the blame for the death of David Kelly squarely at the their door. Good men had fallen on their swords and the Corporation had patiently waited for its moment. Now it was clear that the moment had arrived.

The Director General finally gave a wintry smile. Revenge he decided was always a dish best eaten cold. Alison Hammond was told she would have whatever resources she needed. They were going to put Sir Edward Latimer in the dock. And everything he stood for.

Lenny breathed a huge sigh of relief when Josh put him out of his misery and stood to bring the curtain down on the press conference. A disaster. Complete, total and utter. He had tried to stare down the questioners and keep his face expressionless. Had he managed it? Maybe. Josh would know. The fact was that he had watched the TV the same as everyone else. Like most of Sunnybank, he was only too aware of the identity of the two small figures who had thrown the first stones. And if he could get himself clear of the pack of reporters and photographers who followed his every step, he was going to root out the Flint twins and ring their scrawny necks. The problem was that he had a horrible feeling that it might already be too late. The mixture of chucking stones at policemen and getting on the tele was a heady brew. The more that serious-faced commentators talked about the grave escalation of events, the more youngsters would be itching to be a part of it. He knew that it was on him to try and get the whole thing back on track but he hadn't the faintest idea how to go about it.

At least he was done with the press for an hour or two. All gone except one. There was always one who had to try their luck and look for that extra comment. He gently put the lid down on his rising temper as the young Asian approached him.

"Sorry lad. We're all done here. There'll be another conference in the next day of two."

The young Asian grinned. "You're all right mate. I'm not a reporter." A confident outstretched hand which Lenny took and shook out of habit. "Asif Mohammed. Call be Asmo though. Everyone calls me Asmo. Fancy a pint? Let me buy you a pint."

"A non-reporter who is offering me a pint. Am I supposed to jump up and down? You might have noticed there are one or two things going on at the moment."

Asmo never batted an eyelid. Like all truly great salesmen he was well enough used to rejection. "This'll be a pint you'll never regret. A pint you'll remember all your life. Have a bit of faith Lenny. Faith moves mountains."

Lenny couldn't help a small smile. The enthusiastic northern accent reminded him of home. It reminded him of the young boxer from Bolton who had come within inches of winning Olympic Gold the summer before.

"Aye. And when the mountains move they go to Mohammed, yeah?"

This brought a laugh which was infectious. "Too right they do. I hadn't thought of that. Nice one. So Mr Mountain. Come to Asmo and we'll talk."

"About what?"

"About how I can deliver you victory on a plate all wrapped in ribbons."

"Oh really. And are you a modern day prophet like your namesake, though I seem to remember he wasn't a pint kind of guy."

"Well he wasn't from Bolton was he? But no. I'm not a prophet Lenny. I'm a businessman. I make clothes."

"You make clothes and you can deliver victory. Well I can't say that I'm not just a bit intrigued. Josh!"

Josh had been stacking chairs. He dragged a pile of six to the edge of the room and joined them.

"Josh Ogilvy, USY Press Officer. Asif Mohammed, non-prophet clothier from Bolton who prefers to be called Asmo." The two men shook. "Josh, Asmo here says he can deliver us victory and he wishes to discuss it over a pint. Can we squeeze him in?"

"Oh I dare say we might. Victory is always worth a look. Shall we drive?"

Lenny nodded. "Yes. Let's duck town for a while. I'm getting the goldfish feeling again. Is your car round the back?"

Josh rattled his pocket to check that he had the keys. "It is."

"Come on then. A bit of slick driving and we can drop the pack."

Twenty-five minutes later the long stretch of empty road in his mirror confirmed to Josh that they had successfully lost the press.

"OK. Where next?"

"Take the next left in about half a mile. The sign says Carsethorn."

The wet and wind of the morning had finally abated and the grey skies were breaking up into patches of blue. The sun was pouring through the gaps and lighting up the waters of the sea. They took a small road down to the shore where a cluster of houses stared out over to the hills of the Lake District. They parked up at the Steamboat Inn and Asmo stretched and took a long draw of fresh sea air.

"Nice view boys. Very nice."

Ahead of him a few oystercatchers filled the air with their chinking cries as they hopped across the mudflats seeking a fish supper. A solitary dog-walker had twenty acres of beach all to themselves and suddenly the drama of Sunnybank seemed a long way away. Lenny pulled an old newspaper from a bin and started to wipe away the day's rain from a bench and table by the pebbled beach. He couldn't help a small smile when his own face once again stared out from the front page. It was the Lenny the terrorist photo from the steps to the Council Offices. He screwed it up and used it as a sponge.

"One pub Asmo. Mine's a pint. I dare say Josh is the same. It's your gig, so you're buying. Fair enough."

"Fair enough."

Asmo vanished through the door with the bounding stride of a man who was used to making things happen. Josh followed him with his eyes.

"Who on earth is he Lenny?"

"No idea. He says he can make clothes and help us win." He shrugged and lit up. "I suppose I just liked his accent."

Asmo returned with a tray of three pints and grin firmly in place. "Sound boozer lads. Here you go."

He placed the glasses and lit up himself. Lenny tut-tutted. "Pints and fags Asmo?"

"Me and Allah have a working arrangement. If I lived in Saudi or something it would be different. He knows I live in Bolton and so he cuts me a bit of slack."

"Very decent of him."

"Course it is. That's why he is the one God. Here's to him." Asmo tipped his glass in a toast to the one God and the others joined him. Lenny wiped some froth from his top lip with the back of his hand.

"So my friend. Maybe you better get on and make your pitch. What are you selling here?"

"What do you lads know about branding?"

"Retail goods or cattle?" Like Lenny, Josh was becoming rather intrigued. Such confidence was rare.

"Retail."

Both gave Asmo a 'not much'shrug.

"OK. Potted history. We've always had brands right? Hoover. Heinz. Ford. Nothing new in them. Things used to be simple. The brand was the way to the product. Wrangler make good jeans that last. They let the public know this by showing cowboys roughing around and the jeans not getting torn. So when you need a pair of jeans you think a few key words. Strong. Quality. Lastability. Wrangler. And that's it. The brand leads you to the strengths of the product. OK?"

Nods.

"Then it all changed. The Nike Corporation changed it in the eighties and nineties. They broke the mould. Instead of Nike leading customers to their footwear because of messages about the quality of the shoes, they got their customers to buy their footwear just because it said Nike. Customers don't think words like quality, lastability and value when they shell out seventy quid on a pair of Nikes. They just think Nike. They think the label. The brand. So how did this happen. Come on class. Give me something."

Lenny held his hands up. "No point talking about the eighties and nineties to me. I was banged up."

Josh was the star pupil. "Michael Jordan."

"Good lad. In one. Michael 'Air' Jordan. A one in a million basketball player who Nike made into the most famous face on the planet. Now Jordan would have been the best in the world if he had played barefoot, but Nike made it seem as if his genius flowed from the shoes he was wearing. A partnership made in heaven. He got mega, mega rich and Nike moved all the way to the big league and became blue chip. With me?"

More nods.

"Not surprisingly everyone jumped onto the band wagon as soon as they could. It's a hell of a way of making money. Selling goods on their quality is an expensive business at both ends. At one end you have to buy top dollar raw materials and employ top staff to make a sound product that lasts. At the other end, if a product lasts, then it takes a while before the customer needs to buy another one. That is why the label game is the biggest game in town. It means you can charge a fortune for fairly low quality goods which barely last at all because you have trained your customers not to care about quality because all they care about is the label itself."

He paused to swig his pint.

"The thing is, there aren't that many Air Jordans on the block. Certainly not enough to go round. More to the point, every top sports or pop star soon got themselves an agent and realised what they were worth. That of course meant that the iconic faces to launch the labels could only be afforded by the blue chip boys. Look at how it is now. Who bought Beckham and 50 Cent? The blue chip brigade. Vodaphone and Reebok. Which brings me onto someone like me. I have a cracking factory in Bolton. I have a cracking range of street wear that can kick it with anything. I'm in the vanguard and I'm bloody rich. The problem is that I'm not even close to being rich enough to fork out for a Beckham or a 50 Cent. So the big question is how do I do a Nike? Lots of middle-sized businesses have the same problem. We need to show imagination. Think out of the box, as they say."

"How?" Josh was becoming more and more intrigued.

"OK. Let's say you own a little whisky distillery up the road. You make great Scotch but how do you let everyone know? Bells can afford Jools Holland playing the piano on an advert. Glenfiddich can run to a deer walking through New Orleans. You can't afford TV advertising. Not in a month of Sundays. So how do you make your pennies go further and still give out all the messages? Well maybe you might sponsor a Poetry Festival. You don't do that just for the few punters who turn out, you do it because every review of the festival will say it's the Josh Whisky Poetry Festival. And every poster. And every mention on the TV and radio. Sure, it's not the same as sponsoring a sports event, but it's ten times cheaper. And the message?"

Josh was getting there now. "Poetry. Sophisticated? Deep thinking? Romantic? Black clothes and brown bread"

Asmo beamed. "Ding! Correct answer. Ten points. So when a lad orders a glass of Josh, he is giving out a message to the whole bar, especially the females. Look at me. I drink Josh. I'm not a lager lout. I'm the thinking type who you will find deep and interesting. Yeah?"

Lenny was well on his way as well by now.

"So you reckon that people don't always buy a thing because they want that particular thing. They buy a particular labelled brand of thing because they think it will do something for their image."

"Not think my friend. Know. Stone cold know it."

"Well it's all very fascinating Asmo, but I can't see why we are talking it through over a pint."

"That's because I've got a way to go yet. Still sitting comfortably? OK. The biggest marks out there for brands are young people. They always have been. This is where the big players traditionally have a problem. They want the money out of young people's pockets, but for most of history the young people haven't wanted to give it up. For quite a while it was the norm for young people to detest big capitalist business, yeah? Especially American firms. Do you know the worst case scenario? It's when youngsters take to the streets to vent their rage in clothes that look like they have come from a jumble sale. Maybe they **have** come from a jumble sale. It's the dreaded moment when they care more about what they think and do than how they look. It's the nightmare zone when they smash the shop window and nick the trainers rather than working a few shifts throwing burgers in McDonalds to shell out £70 for them."

Lenny was really getting there now. "Like 1981."

Asmo nodded. "I was just a young un myself, but I've heard to tell. So the big boys have been pretty clever. Now they buy up troublemaking types and shape them like play dough. Take Eminem as a case study. For a while he was all over the gossip pages. How could he say that! How could he do that! Moral outrage. What's becoming of the youth of today? But when you think about it, what did he actually do? Bloody nowt. He pulled tough guy faces for MTV and pocketed the cash. He was the right kind of bad guy for the tabloids and nobody smashed any windows. And let's never forget who owns the tabloids. The same people who own the big brand boys. The same people who own the retailers. The same ones who own everything. The institutional investors. The engine in the back of every PLC."

Lenny smiled at the younger man who was getting more and more animated.

"Hey Asmo. No need to go through the whole capitalist conspiracy bit with me and Josh. I did twenty years of the hard stuff because of a capitalist conspiracy. I was weaned on it. I'll get a round in and then you can get to the point"

By the time Lenny returned Asmo and Josh were locked in conversation with heads down low. By the look on Josh's face, Lenny could tell that he was beginning to see where it was all leading. By the look in his eyes he could see that he wasn't all that upset to be on the bus. Once he was sitting back at the table and the new pints were started, Asmo resumed.

"OK. Me. What about me? I've done good guys. Really good. My mum and Dad have a corner shop in Bolton and my uncle has a market stall. I've got it in my blood. I started with a market stall myself and now I have a factory with two hundred people in it. I make clothes. Cool clothes. Hip clothes. Street clothes at a price that people on the street can afford. My clothes are sold on market stalls and small shops. They look and feel like Nike and Reebok and they cost a quarter of the price. It's made me a rich man. Really rich. But I'm still down there at the bottom of division two and it's a hard league to get out of. The only way I'm ever going to get promoted to the Premier League is if I become a brand. But becoming a brand means paying out cheques which are more like telephone numbers and I'm nowhere near rich enough to manage it."

"Does it really matter that much?" Asked Josh who knew more than most that money brought nothing much other than disappointment.

"The money doesn't. Not at all. Honest. I mean look at me. Clothes? Car? Jewellery?" Josh and Lenny looked. Fair enough.

Nothing brash and flash. Asmo careered on. "It's the game lads. That's what gets me. It's like a sport. Like climbing a mountain. I want to get up there with Nike and Armani like some people want to get to the top of Everest or walk to the South Pole and back. Can you see that?"

Lenny smiled. "We can see that. Go on."

"I've already got the range. Street gear. It's banging. I've already got the brand. Koz. K . . . O . . . Z. And I've got two hundred top people back in Bolton ready to roll the stuff out twenty-four hours a day, seven days a week. Everything is ready and waiting. All I've been waiting for has been the right wave to jump onto."

Suddenly he slowed right down and looked at them carefully before continuing.

"The wave's here guys. Right here, right now."

Lenny thought he should have been on the stage. Seldom, if ever had he seen such a magnificently executed dramatic pause. "Fashion is all about what went around before coming around again. Hippy look. Punk look. Bloody flares even. Yeah? Think youth rebellion guys. Think thirteen year cycles. Late sixties, student revolt all over the world against Vietnam. Late seventies and early eighties, ban the bomb, riots in the streets. Late eighties and early nineties, the rave time. We're a couple of years overdue. All over Britain kids are fed up with spoon-fed rebellion imported from America. Who cares if Eminem struts about the stage on MTV with a chainsaw? What does it mean? What's it got to do with them? They're ready for their own proper rebellion. Not a pretend one. They want it, they just don't know it yet."

Now the penny found the slot in Lenny's head and dropped. "So if you want to buy a brand that says deep, cool and philosophical you buy Josh's Scotch and the poetry. And if you want to wear a brand that says you are a real McCoy James Dean of the twenty-first century you wear Koz?"

"I'm impressed Lenny. Proper impressed." Lenny bashed on.

"Josh uses the poetry festival as a vehicle because it is within his price range. Koz needs something the same. It needs to sponsor a real rebellion. And that's why you're here isn't it? You want USY to be your Michael Jordan?"

"Bet your life on it."

"Is this about money?"

"No. I told you. It's about victory. You can have money if you like, but I think you're more interested in winning."

"And how do you help us to win?"

"Easy. Numbers. Sheer massive numbers."

"How."

So Asmo told them.

And two pints later they shook on it. But Asmo was no longer his normal beaming self. Before shaking on the deal Lenny had thrown in an extra clause to their agreement. It was the clause which would send Asmo and his Koz range all the way to the stratosphere. The problem was that Asmo had a horrible feeling that it might also send him to his grave.

When Frank Dixon had told his boss with such conviction that his detective skills would find out the truth of the Buccleuch Street arson and brick throwing, it had been more bravado than conviction. But much to his own surprise he had managed to make real progress quite quickly. He started with CCTV. Nothing much there. He knew that much already. Hoods up and faces hidden. But he stuck at it. Five hours of screen staring later he found it. Hooded figures running in a tight group down a small street two hundred yards and three minutes away from the incident. A further three hours back tracked them to a mini van parked up and waiting. He watched them climb inside and the van make its way out of town. Heading north. He also got the licence plate.

That got him an address in Cumbernauld. He arrived the next day to find the van in question parked up in the drive or a ordinary kind of house. The man who answered the door was all aggression until Frank pointed out two bald tyres and reminded him what they would cost if reported. This gave the man something to chew on, enough to explain that he had rented the minivan to a mate. Jed Thompson.

Frank found Thompson's yard late in the afternoon. He sat and watched four wagons return one by one and park up for the night. The drivers took their paperwork into the Portacabin that was obviously the office. One by one they came back out and drove away. Then a woman of middle age followed suit. Secretary probably. Last out was a fit looking man of about fifty. He locked the office and padlocked the gates to his compound before heading home. Thompson.

Next came some time at a borrowed desk from a sergeant in Falkirk who he had put time in with at the bar at various conferences. Bit by bit the computer told the story of Jed Thompson. Bad, bad boy to start with. Within an ace of serious time at a Young Offenders Institute. Then into the Army before it all got completely out of hand. A good army career then out with a splash into the icy waters of the early eighties. Periods of unemployment. Periods of short contract stuff. Security work. Bouncing. Bailiff's heavy. Then back on the dole in 84. Then? Then interesting. From dole to HGV licence and a wagon in a year. Now how did that happen? He was on the dole the whole year. Maybe a rich auntie from Australia died or something. Or maybe he did something well paid and naughty. Steady tax returns for a while then steady growth into the nineties and then marriage, a fleet of five trucks and entry into middle class respectability and years of regulation life. His attention was waning when he saw that the turn of the new millennium marked a sharp decline in fortunes. Companies House showed three years on the spin of losses, with each year getting worse than the one before. Frank knew about that. He had a couple of pals at the cricket club who ran wagons. He had heard their tales of woe more than once after a few pints. Diesel through the roof. Cheap jack teams over from Poland and Hungary. Regulation after regulation from Brussels. And Jed Thompson had felt the same cold wind. The numbers suggested the brink of bankruptcy. And Frank had been a copper long enough to know that when men with mortgages and families and businesses found themselves at the gates of going bust, they were often willing to take a ride along the dark road.

He doodled, making lines and pictures of a life. Childhood bad-boy redeemed by the army. Good soldier. No reward. A period of hand-to-mouth. Then a turnaround. Ten years of unexpected success. A business. A wife. A house. Then all of it under threat. So what happened in those middle years of his life to turn things around? Maybe he had been smuggling in drugs? The information said that he had been doing long haul stuff. It didn't really make sense. There wasn't a sniff of it as far as the police were concerned. And if he had wanted a good drugs run he would have chosen Holland or the Middle East. Plenty of big money Saudi runs in those days. And if it had been drugs and the police had never got a sniff, then why wasn't he still doing it? Why was he so clearly on his uppers? So if not drugs, then what? In the late eighties he had been on a constant run in and out of

East Germany. Not West Germany, East Germany. All the way from Cumbernauld to Leipzig and back. This made Frank sit back and tap thoughtfully at his teeth with his pencil. Leipzig and back. Late eighties. A couple of years before East Germany became the first of the communist dominoes to topple and fall. Maybe. Just maybe.

The next morning he was waiting across the road from Thompson's depot from four-thirty. The first of the drivers arrived at quarter past five and his truck trundled out of the gates fifteen minutes later. Frank followed. He really had no idea why. It was just a gut feeling. Frank Dixon had always been a gut feeling type of copper.

The truck headed out of Cumbernauld to a sprawling yard filled with all kinds of giant creations made from poured concrete. From where Frank watched and waited he could see ten, eight foot tall wall panels being craned onto the back of the truck and strapped down tight. Ten minutes for football gossip and paperwork and the wagon was back on its way.

From the moment it became clear that they seemed to be following signs to Rosyth, Frank's brain started to ponder. When he watched the wagon being checked through the condition black security on the fortified gates it was in overdrive. Over the high fences he could see the shape of cranes down by the water's edge. Some kind of building going on. Building that needed concrete panelling. Concrete panelling delivered by Jed Thompson who happened to have been driving a minivan filled with young hooded stone throwers on the morning that it had all kicked off. He didn't bother following the empty truck when it left. Instead he strolled over to the guardhouse and went in. A hard-faced type in naval uniform gave him a less than welcoming look. The look hardened a notch or two when he took a look at Frank's Police ID.

"Sorry sir. You'll have to report to the office. Nothing I can say."

Frank gave him a 'we're all lads together' type look.

"Cut me a break will you pal. It's only a detail. That truck you just checked out. From Thompson's in Cumbernauld. How long's he been on the job?"

A shrug. "Not long. A week. No more than that."

"And how long has the job been running?"

"Got to be six months now."

Frank smiled. "There you go. What did I say? Just a detail. That's me all done."

PART TWO

The navy man watched him all the way back to his car then picked up the phone and asked for his details to be checked. Five minutes later it was confirmed that he was indeed Frank Dixon of the Dumfries and Galloway Police Force. Frank decided it was time to head back down the A74 and did so with no thought that his name was already speeding its electronic way into the office of Sir Edward Latimer with the view of the Thames.

Asmo had made calls on his mobile from the beach at the front of the pub. When he snapped the phone closed on the last call he rejoined Lenny and Josh at the table.

"OK. Done. Give the lads three hours and they'll be here."

"What? Photographer as well?"

"Photographer, video man, the whole shebang."

Lenny was impressed. "No hanging around then."

Asmo gave them a self satisfied smile. "You'll find out that hanging around isn't my thing."

Once they were back in Dumfries they found Asmo a room in a B&B and left him to more work on his mobile. Josh went back to the flat whilst Lenny took the long way round to the Finch household in order to stay well clear of the reporters who still hung around in small knots wherever they thought there was a chance of a photo opportunity. By the time he knocked on the front door it was well past ten and the light had all but drained from the sky. Sandra Finch was a woman of thirty-seven who looked nearer fifty. Bringing up the twins on her own while her man was forever locked away had taken a toll. As she edged open the door Lenny saw an expression of permanent anxiety. At ten o'clock it would only mean a visit from policemen or debt collectors. She showed a quick flash of relief when she recognised Lenny, but it was soon replaced with cold hostility.

"What do you want?"

"Are the lads in Mrs Finch?"

"Aye."

"Any chance of a word?"

For a moment he was sure she was about to tell him to get stuffed and to take a hike. Instead she muttered. "Stay here."

He waited as she made her way to the foot of the stairs.

"Tim! Barry! Someone here for you."

Instead of returning to the front door she went inside the lounge from where Lenny could here the sound of a studio audience laughing out of the TV. The two boys came down the stairs a few seconds later and stopped up short of the door when they saw who had come to call.

"Evening lads."

Both faces were small replicas of shared guilt.

"Alright Lenny."

"We need to talk."

A swift exchanged glance. No words needed. Tim took on the role of spokesman.

"Aye. But we cannae now Lenny. It's late ken. Our Ma won't let us out ken. And she does'nae let anyone in, ken. Not when our Da's away."

Lenny smiled. "Nice try boys. Come on. Let's take a walk."

Another shared glance. A shared realisation that they were backed into a corner. They both shrugged acceptance in the same instant. Barry leaned around the door to the lounge. "We're going out Ma."

He received no reply as another cascade of laughter flowed out of the TV. For a while the three of them walked in silence, the twins almost having to run to keep up with Lenny's long stride. Only when they reached the edge of Sunnybank where the street lights stopped and the dark hedges started did Lenny ease his stride. He paused and checked behind to confirm that the late night road was empty. He pulled out a cigarette and lit and took a seat on an old water trough.

"It would have been nice if you'd told me lads. I though we were a team."

This made them bow their heads. This time Barry took on the front man role.

"You would'nae have let us go Lenny."

"No. I don't suppose I would. May I ask why?"

"It was the news, ken. On the tele. It showed those boys in that town in Iraq. Ken the ones. They've been chucking stones at the soldiers. And the man said that the soldiers couldn't do nothing because there were cameras watching. And we thought there are plenty of cameras here as well. And we thought that the policemen couldn't do nothing either. And so we just thought . . ."

His voice drained away into the night air. Lenny knew the rest well enough. Once the idea was in their heads it would have been impossible for them to resist the chance of having a pop at the police.

"Watching the news? I'm impressed."

"Aye well, we were watching the riot and the Iraq stuff came on straight after."

"And can we expect more of the same?"

Nervous glances. Shuffling. Heads back down.

"I see. Where are you all meeting?"

"The old Pavilion. Seven o'clock."

"How many?"

"Dunnae ken. A few more boys say they fancy coming. Maybe fifteen I suppose. We'll no go if you dunnae want us to Lenny."

Lenny took a hard thoughtful pull on his cigarette. Once again he had arrived at a step over the line moment. A moment to accept responsibility. It hadn't been his idea that they should throw stones at the policemen, but it had been his actions that had given them the opportunity. What was going to happen next would be all down to him. If it went right, then it would be fine. If it went wrong, it would take an awful lot to live with it. What had seemed such a good idea over a pint earlier in the evening now seemed to be bordering on the crazy. The trouble was that in his heart he knew that this was also the moment to make the choice of whether to go forward or to give in. Throw in the towel. Surrender. Let everyone down.

He made his mind up with a familiar sense of dread.

"I'll meet you there tomorrow morning. There's a new plan."

He committed.

The next morning brought a light wind and thin rain and a world of grey. Lenny, Josh and Asmo were at the Pavilion by 6.30 a.m. With them were two other young Asians who had driven up the M6 from Bolton the evening before. Hamid carried a small video camera while Tariq was armed with two cameras which hung around his neck. Asmo had brought along a large holdall which had weighed him down as he lugged it across the playing field. Tim and Barry had arrived a little after quarter to seven and by five past they had been joined by eight others. Every face was a picture of suspicion when they saw that adults were present, especially the three Asians with the Bolton accents. Most were about to leave straight away but Tim and Barry did their stuff and persuaded them to hang around and listen to what Lenny had to say. He knew all of the faces well enough. Seven of them came from the ranks of the all conquering Sunnybank Under 15's. If he had set himself the task of guessing the names of ten candidates who would set their alarms for the crack of dawn to go and throw stones at policemen, he would have got at least eight and maybe all ten. They stood in a resentful, suspicious group and their shared body language said they were not at all happy with the new turn of events. Lenny decided that it didn't look as if anyone else was coming.

"OK lads. I have a proposal. I'd like you to consider it. This is Asmo. He makes clothes. Street clothes. He has a bunch of them in his bag. The proposal is that you all change into his gear before you go off into town. It's yours to keep. Whatever you want. When you chuck the stones, Hamid and Tariq are going to take a few pictures. That's it."

This left eight faces wearing expressions of extreme suspicion. They were a long, long way from being convinced and Lenny was struggling for anything else to say. Tim and Barry were in the same boat. The whole thing was on the verge of collapsing when Asmo stepped in.

"Come on lads. Check it out. You won't see better gear than this. Seriously. All of this is massive down in Manchester. See these? I bang these out for £49.99. And I mean bang. Hundreds. If these were G-Unit, you'd be looking at a hundred and fifty quid. But people don't want to be seen in G-Unit down Manchester any more. No chance. It's just mainstream innit? Lads who want to be out there on the edge all go for Koz. Check these . . ."

Lenny stood back and left him to it. It wasn't hard to see how Asmo had become a top dog in the markets of the North. To say that he was a born salesman was as big an understatement as suggesting that President Bush didn't like Arab terrorists much. It took him three minutes to have then eating out of his hand. Within a few more minutes they were changing, every one of them convinced that they were donning gear that would retail for two years worth of pocket money and then some. When they were all done, Lenny had to admit to himself that he was impressed. Koz was about bagginess and dark colours. The label was reasonably discreet rather than being emblazoned across every available inch of space. The lettering mirrored the style of the graffitti artists. Once all ten Sunnybank youngsters were kitted out from top to toe Tariq and Hamid got to work. Tariq had already chosen the rear of the pavilion where the rotten timber was daubed in spray paint as an ideal back drop. Whilst Hamid arranged the models in a series of frames he kept up a running commentary and he ducked and stooped in and out firing off, shot after shot. Hoods were up and caps were on. Scarves covered the lower half of faces. As Lenny hung back and watched, he couldn't believe how much older they all looked. The oldest boy in the pictures was thirteen and the youngest was just turned eleven, and yet as a group decked out in their urban uniforms they all looked at least sixteen. The photos took up fifteen minutes until Tariq stood himself up straight and gave a thumbs up to Asmo.

"And dusted. It's a wrap guys. Time for the main event."

Lenny and Josh had decided the evening before that there was no way they could go along. Even if they tried to disguise themselves, the risk was far too great. The merest suspicion that either of them was anywhere near the action would be plenty enough for them to be picked up and locked away for a couple of days. As the newly-uniformed Sunnybank rebels marched off towards the town centre with Tariq and Hamid bringing up the rear, Lenny and Josh headed for the Zone to get a guaranteed alibi from the reporters who would already be waiting outside. Asmo returned to his guest house for a full Scottish breakfast minus pork. He was always pretty confident that Allah would forgive him a pint or two, but pork was a completely different matter. Pork would be pushing it.

Once again the attack of the Sunnybankers was shown live on the morning news. This time the police were ready and waiting and they ducked clear of the stones as soon as they left the hands of the assailants. A squad of four younger officers had been allocated to the task of giving chase should hostilities be renewed. They were fast off the blocks in pursuit of their small adversaries but they never really stood a chance. The attack team vanished within seconds of their attack and the policemen pulled up after less than a hundred yards. The pursuit had never been particularly serious. It was primarily for the cameras. At least twenty photographers and two film units were on hand to record the action for the media. It meant that nobody took the slightest bit of notice of the two Asians who were new to the story. Nobody noticed the way the kids were dressed either. They clocked the hoods and the caps and the scarves. Nothing else. Kids were kids.

It was how they all dressed. The attack had started at 7.51 and it was all over by 7.52. The men and women of the media took their leave to find coffee and phone sockets to send their images in to the office. The police also wound down and went into killing time mode.

Later that morning Lenny Baxter once again told a Press Conference that he had no knowledge about what had happened that morning. He also said that USYwould be resuming picketing the next morning. No. It wouldn't be in Buccleuch Street. USY had no wish to enter into conflict with the police force who had made it clear that the street was closed. He pointed out that the Council worked out of many different locations. From now on USYwould target all Council offices. No notice would be given. When the reporters asked if he would tell them where the action would be the next morning he merely smiled and said that he was sure that they would find out soon enough.

Tim and Barry were waiting for him when he got back to The Zone. He said nothing until they were safely in the back office with the door closed.

"OK. Good job lads. No problems?"

This brought a joint laugh. "Course not. Them coppers couldn't catch a cold. Did you see them Lenny? Talk about slow or what."

Lenny tried to keep a stern expression in place. "Good. So tomorrow it's back to picketing, correct. We have a deal?"

Their nods were slightly reluctant. Suddenly the picketing had become a bit boring. Lenny held them with a stare until he felt reasonably confident that they would stick to their agreement. "OK. I trust you. I must be bloody tapped, but there you go. Get the word out that tomorrow morning it is the Education Offices. Eight o'clock sharp."

"Is that out by the big Mercedes garage?"

"That's right. And remember. Don't wear the Koz gear. Keep it in the cupboard until I tell you. And make sure all the others know it as well. Clear?"

"Aye."

Frank Dixon had received another summons. It was almost becoming a routine. For as many years as he could remember he had seldom been in the Chief Constable's office more than once every couple of years and now it was becoming a daily event. This time he was glad of the summons. He'd stayed up late when he arrived back from Rosyth and he'd taken great care over his report. It had been his intention to call the Chief to ask for a slot and so it had merely saved a job when the top man had beaten him to it. As soon as he was shown into the office by the secretary, he could tell that the Chief was no calmer about what was happening. In fact if anything he looked even more wound up. The good news was that the secretary had once again offered coffee and Frank was happy to take that as a good sign.

There was no beating about the bush.

"Maybe you should have told me that you were going up to Rosyth, Frank."

Frank was stunned for a moment. How the hell? He hadn't even made his report yet and he hadn't mentioned the Rosyth thing to anyone. Then he remembered that all of his details had been taken by the security guy on the gate. But even so.

"I'm sorry sir. I assumed you wouldn't want to be troubled with details."

"From here on in take it as written that I want to know every move you make Frank. Understood?"

What the hell was happening here?

"Of course sir, but maybe you could explain why."

The Chief took up his favoured position at the window. His hands were deep in his pockets and he rattled his car keys with his fingers.

"I'm going to gamble on you Frank. We've never really worked together but everything in your record suggests that you can be trusted. Tell me I'm right in this assessment please Frank."

"Of course sir."

The Chief spent a few more seconds staring out into the morning rain. Finally he gave himself a small nod as he made his mind up. Then he turned and sat down opposite Frank.

"I received a phone call this morning and I am not at all happy with it Frank. In fact I am extremely angry."

Frank's mouth was drying out fast. He took a quick gulp of coffee and burnt his lip.

"Sir."

"The call was from London. Whitehall. Some cocksure hooray bloody Henry who sounded as if he had a pack of apples in his mouth.

He said that you had been asking inappropriate questions up at the Royal Navy Dockyard in Rosyth. He told me that I should be very careful. He made noises about sensitive areas and National Security and treading lightly. He dropped some very heavy hints that the best thing for my career would be if I had a quiet word and suggested that the Royal Navy Dockyard was not the best place for one of my sergeants to be spending his mornings. He dropped even heavier hints that if any of my people were to continue making a nuisance of themselves in and around sensitive military installations then there would be implications. He reminded me that all issues of defence are still the responsibility of Whitehall and that the Official Secrets Act is a very serious piece of legislation."

Frank hadn't the first clue what to say and so he decided to say absolutely nothing and took another sip at his coffee, much more careful this time.

The Chief seemed to consider getting to his feet but thought better of it. He fiddled with a pen instead. "I don't like getting phone calls from Whitehall Frank. I don't like it at all. I like it even less when people from semi-detached Tudor-fronted houses in Surrey try to push me around. So let's get down to it shall we. What took you to Rosyth? What did you find there? And why the hell are faceless people in London starting to jump up and down."

Frank forced down another mouthful of coffee. He reached into his case and pulled out the carefully typed report that had kept him at his desk almost until midnight. He walked his Chief carefully through his investigation. The CCTV. The Cumbernauld registration. The leading out to a Mr Jed Thompson. A life history. Mysterious turnarounds in fortune in the eighties. A regular run in and out of East Germany. Then seeming security and success until hitting a five year long skid row all the way to the edge of bankruptcy. And finally a big fat contract to run building supplies into the Royal Naval Dockyards in Rosyth. The Chief seemed to become more and more still as he took in each element of the investigation. When Frank finished he looked up sharply.

"You're holding back Frank. Those are the facts. Let's have the theory. I know where my mind is going. I'm more than a bit interested on where you are up to, having slept on it. Come on. Spit it out. I'm not about to bite."

"Fair enough. Three things rattle me sir. Number One, 1984. He started the year on the dole and finished with an HGV licence and his own truck. How did that happen? We both know that there was money to be made for ex-sqauddies at that time helping out with the Miner's Strike. Happen a mate of his found him a piece of the action. That would have meant that his name went on list somewhere. Number two. By the late eighties he's on a regular run in and out of East Germany. Maybe that wasn't a complete accident. Maybe someone was delivering something other than industrial goods. Maybe they were happy to pay good money for it too. And maybe that was how he managed to go from one truck to five and buy himself a house. Number Three. By 2005 he's slid all the way back down the slippery slope. He's in debt up to his eyeballs and the bank is ready to pull the plug. Let's say that someone from the past had a sudden problem in Scotland. And let's say that problem was called Lenny Baxter and let's say that the media were all getting far too interested. Then let's say someone felt that a spanner needed sticking in Lenny's spokes. So what do they do? They need a man in Scotland. They need him in a hurry, they need him to have a bit of track record behind him, and they need for him to have a reason to stick his neck out and do the dirty. So out come the old lists from the cold war days and lo and behold there is Jed Thompson, one time soldier, picket-basher and Iron Curtain runner. Well qualified and desperate to make a quick buck to save his business. All of a sudden a mystery team of kids arrive in town in a minivan from Cumbernauld fully armed with half bricks that they had brought along with them. A building burns down, two coppers are injured and Lenny Baxter is back to being a bad guy again. Payment by way of a nice fat Government contract to run building materials into Rosyth. So if you want my opinion sir, I think the whole thing stinks like last week's fish."

The Chief was back still again. He was never a very ruddy-featured man at the best of times but now his face was like marble.

"If you had come with all this before my phone call Frank, I admit that I might just have had a problem in swallowing it all. But in the light of this morning's little chat, I am inclined to agree with you one hundred and ten percent."

Frank allowed out a small sigh of relief.

"What do you want me to do next sir? I suppose you want me to ease off?"

"Are you mad Frank? One of our men is still in hospital with a smashed up face. It appears the reason is someone in London is trying to cover their nasty little tracks. Well whoever it may be, they have chosen the wrong town. What I want you to do Frank is to get straight back up to Cumbernauld and arrest Jed Thompson on suspicion of arson and inciting riot. I want him in custody in Loreburne Police Station and I want him charged under the new anti-terrorism legislation which will give us plenty of time. Call in at Falkirk on the way and I will make sure that there is back up waiting for you. In the meantime I will make a few calls. We are going to go through that office of his with a fine tooth comb. I want to look at every tachograph record. I want to see copy paperwork for his bid for the Rosyth job. I want tax records. I want VAT records. I want vehicle maintenance records. In my experience there isn't a haulier in Scotland who doesn't break at least ten laws a week to keep their noses above water. Once we have enough to shut him down and bankrupt him I expect he'll be ready to talk with us. Is that clear enough Frank?"

"Crystal sir."

"Splendid. Off you go then."

"Sir."

The elation that Frank felt all the way up from Dumfries to the yard in Cumbernauld collapsed the moment he entered the Portacabin to be confronted by the panic-ridden face of Thompson's secretary. She was almost hyperventilating as she told him that Mr Thompson had gone away for a short break with his wife. A cheap flight from Prestwick with Ryan Air. Milan, so it was. He would be away all weekend. Back on Monday morning, so he was. And she hoped that he wasn't in any trouble. And she would help in any way she could. The poor woman was so stressed at their arrival that Frank had to make her a cup of tea and leave her for a few minutes whilst she calmed herself down.

The next morning brought yet more wet and windy weather. Lenny had made sure that word about the picket at the Education Offices had been spread as widely as possible. Late in the evening Tim and Barry had arrived at the Zone looking rather down in the mouth. They said that not many would be coming along the next morning. Most had been banned by parents who were scared by the pictures of the Buccleuch Street riot. Others reckoned that picketing was boring and said they couldn't be bothered. Lenny could tell that his

Chairman and President shared that particular view and every bone in their bodies wanted to put their new Koz gear on and go and throw a few more stones.

"Come on lads. A deal's a deal. It won't be for long now. Just a few days whilst Asmo gets things moving."

Their heads were down as they studied their trainers with deep concentration. All of a sudden eye contact was a really big problem.

"Well?"

"Aye. Fair enough like."

Still no eye contact. Lenny leaned back and sighed.

"OK boys. Let's put it another way shall we. A little birdie let me know something this morning. The little birdie said that your dad has just been transferred down from Kilmarnock pending his release. Now if by any chance you decide to give the picketing a miss tomorrow and head off to chuck a stone or two instead, then I will be forced to pop along to HMPDumfries and have a little chat with him."

They both flared up at this, faces all indignation but real fear in their eyes.

"Go and see him if you like. He won't be bothered. He'll just tell you to get lost, so he will."

Lenny reached carefully into the top drawer of his desk and took out a folded piece of A4. "This is a letter that I received about a month ago. From HMP Kilmarnock. I'll read it out.

> *Dear Lenny. The word in here is that my lads were there when Luke Crosbie died. It seems to me that you must have known that. You must have decided not to grass them up. Thank you. If you ever need a favour all you need to do is ask. I owe you one. All the best. Roger Finch*

So lads. Maybe he won't tell me to get lost after all. Now I'll ask again. Do we have a deal?"

Now he had his eye contact. Two pairs of startled eyes met his with an imploring look.

"Aye Lenny. Nae bother. We'll be there. Honest."

"Excellent. I'll expect you at eight o'clock sharp." He tossed over a five pound note. "I'll leave it to you guys to bring the bacon rolls."

"Aye. Nae bother Lenny. We'll be there."

And they were at eight sharp, looking for all the world like a pair of drowned rats with cold bacon rolls in drenched paper bags. The USY picket line was all but back to square one. Tony Crenshaw and Rory McGuire were there. As were the contingent of retired miners from Sanquhar. In total, they were less than twenty and the Council workers hurried past them with their heads down under umbrellas. A few journalists had given up waiting for more action on Buccleuch Street and wandered along to see if there was anything worth writing about. The bedraggled group outside the Education Offices with their soggy placards were anything but headline news. One or two stayed for a few minutes. Others took one look and drove off to the warmth of their hotel rooms. Many phone calls were made that morning. Editors told their people to check out and make their way back to base. The Dumfries story had been great whilst it lasted, but it was obvious that it had all fizzled out to nothing. Maybe they would get their youth centre. Probably not. That morning most of the workers in the Buccleuch Street offices had made it into work. They had received phone calls from management telling them in no uncertain terms that now the police had the situation under control there was no excuse for absenteeism. For a while the USY picket line had captured the imagination of the public. Not just the Dumfries public. The British public. But things had moved on. No longer were there dramatic pictures to be had of hundreds of chanting youngsters in a street bathed in sunshine. Now it was just a tired group of less than twenty looking lost and beaten in the rain. The Lenny Baxter story had run its course. He had got a heck of a sight more than fifteen minutes. But now the game was up. Time to get back to base before the weekend. By eleven, the rain was easing and Lenny decided it was time to call it a day. A car pulled up at the kerb and Jake Hollins of the Times pulled himself out of the door creakily. He shook out a cigarette for Lenny and took one himself.

"After the Lord Mayor's show, hey Lenny. They did a job on you didn't they. I told you to be careful my friend."

"That you did. Are you away now?"

"I suppose so. The word is that the story is dead."

"Really?"

Something in Lenny's tone made the older man look up with new interest. "Or maybe it isn't. Maybe I should hang around for a day or two. What do you think Lenny?"

"I think the forecast says the weather should look up a bit over the weekend. Dumfries and Galloway is nice this time of year, especially when the weather looks up."

"So I've heard. Maybe I'll take an extra day or two. Why not. I'll see you around Lenny. You have my card still?"

"I have it."

Yousuf was troubled. It had been the second morning when they had run into problems. All of them had known that the element of surprise would not last for very long. The day before they had barely thrown a stone before a wall of screaming Marines had exploded at then with a roar that had almost made him wet himself. He had got away, but three had been tackled to the ground and had not been seen since. The cameras only offered a defence so long as they were all out in the open and on the street. Once they were arrested and taken away anything could happen. Numbers had been steadily growing but this morning the ranks had been noticeably thinner. At first he had thought it would be better. There had been no charge from the Marines, instead they had crouched low under clear plastic shields like a unit from a Roman legion. Yousuf and the others had been encouraged to edge nearer as they pelted them. Then three small squads of Marines appeared from hiding places at the edge of the street and once again there was a chaotic frantic retreat. One of them had actually got his hand on Yousuf's arm but thankfully the bigger man had tripped and been unable to hang on. But it had still been far too close for comfort. What if he had been taken? By now he would have been on his way to Abu Graib.

The next day was a real problem. Numbers would be lower again. Bravado was one thing, but the prospect of torture and humiliation in Abu Graib was a daunting prospect. Yousuf had to admit that he really didn't want to go himself. Maybe they had all done enough already. They had seized the initiative and for once stopped the American murderers in their tracks. Maybe it was time to call a halt for a period.

He was wrestling with these thoughts as he turned a corner close to his uncle's house and found that the world had been plunged into darkness. His senses struggled to get a line on what was happening to him. Someone had hold of him from behind. And in front. His feet were off the ground and he was being carried. Then manhandled into a small space. And it was all dark because there was something on his head. Thick cloth that smell faintly of petrol. A metallic bang and he was bouncing hard on metal.

A car boot. He was in a car boot. A hood on his head. No room to move. No air to breathe. He shook his head to try and remove the hood but all he managed to do was to bang himself on a wheel arch. His hands were cuffed behind his back and every time the car hit a pot hole he was slammed one way or another.

He was right on the edge of screaming for all he was worth when the movement stopped. He heard doors opening. Then he sensed a rush of air on his skin as the boot was popped. Once again he was lifted, but to his feet this time. Hands had a hard grip on both of his arms and he was forced to walk. Where? Who? His ears strained for any sound that might give him a clue as to what was happening. Every second he expected the twang of American voices. He must have been betrayed somehow. This was a snatch squad like the one that had come to their house to take his father to his death at the dawn of the war.

He didn't have to walk far. Just a few seconds, although the huge levels of adrenalin that were gushing through him made it seem much longer. Pressure was applied to his shoulders and he was forced down onto a chair. Then the hood was yanked off. Not Americans. Arabs. Four of them standing with guns levelled at his face. One sitting behind a small table nursing a glass of tea. Behind his back the handcuffs were unlocked and he was able to bring his arms back in front of him and rub at his bruised wrists.

"Please don't be alarmed Yousuf. You are quite safe." It was the older man who spoke. Now he was pouring a second glass of tea and sliding it across the table. "Here. Drink this. You must be thirsty. We are all thirsty after a shock."

"Who are you?" Yousuf's voice was dry and cracked. The man was right. His mouth was as dry as the desert. He took a sip of tea and to his surprise found that it was hot, sweet and delicious. The man obviously had better luck than he when it came to finding sugar.

"You do not need to know my real name Yousuf. It would not be safe. Not safe for you. Not safe for me. It is enough to say that I once knew your father. He was a good man. A truly loyal man. We all grieve at what was done to him. Once I had a name, but it was never a famous name. My work was discreet and it was always best that my name was a thing to be known by as few as possible. Now people call me the Colonel. You will call me the Colonel. You will have some more tea? Good."

The Colonel gave a small nod which brought forward a man from the back of the room to refill Yousuf's glass. Then he continued in his calm clipped voice.

"Yousuf, all my life I have fought the enemies of our country. Like your father. The Iranians, the Kurds, the traitors in the south. And now for the second time I have the honour to fight the greatest enemy of them all. Just like you Yousuf. And how they underestimated us my friend. The fools really believed they would be welcomed into our towns and cities with flags and flower petals. They believed the Shia traitors who ran away into exile and pretended that the Iraqi people would open their arms and welcome the infidel into our holy land. Like me Yousuf, you know this will never happen. Every day American soldiers bleed into our holy soil. Every day the Shia scum who join their police force pay for their treachery. Now you understand who I am Yousuf?"

"I understand." All fear had washed clear of Yousuf now. He had heard the Colonel's name whispered in hushed conversations for over six months now. He was the great man who took the fight to the Americans all over the country. Some even said that he would be the new Saddam. Others said that he would save the Sunni people in their darkest hour. Again his calm voice almost hypnotised Yousuf.

"I have watched you and your friends Yousuf. Many have watched. We have watched your courage and your commitment to the cause of our people. You must tell me how it was that you chose this course."

Yousuf was glad to. He told of the video he had watched before the invasion and the words he had overheard from the woman reported on the day of the barbeque. And he told of the Hip Hop song that said there would be no death by cop when the TV was there. And all the time the Colonel nodded and made sure that Yousuf's glass was refilled.

"And tell me Yousuf. What have the infidels done to stop you?"

He explained about how things had got harder for the last two mornings. He told of the snatch squads and how his people had been fewer than the previous morning. More nodding. Very quiet. Very controlled. And then a pause for consideration.

"You know Yousuf, it is strange. Since the first morning when you and your friends attacked the Americans with stones, our forces have had many successes. A total of over forty enemies have been killed by those who have gladly given their lives into the hands of Allah. Three Americans and tens of Shia and Kurd traitors. But all the world sees is you and your friends and a handful of Marines. Those of us who bear the task of leading our people in their struggle have watched with great interest. Maybe some of us are too old to understand the weaknesses of these Americans. Maybe it needed a young man to see. You see, none of the old men like me could ever understand the importance of this no death by cop song you tell me about. So you must tell me what you worry about now Yousuf? You must tell me what it is that you need to continue your fight."

That part was easy. Yousuf explained that many were terrified of being arrested and taken to Abu Graib. He said that he feared that the next morning they would be too few and that the marine snatch squads would carry even more of them away. The colonel continued to nod at his words while never taking his eyes off Yousuf's face. When Yousuf had completed his report, the Colonel wasted no time.

" These are things we can help with my young friend. For two days you will stay away from the Americans. Give them a false sense of victory. I will bring many more men into Famoudi. Young men. Like you. And on the third day you will be many. Too many. For every one they take, there will be two more to step into their place. Is this enough to help you to continue your fight my friend?"

"It is enough."

"Then Allah is indeed great."

It only took the Colonel a few hours to issue his orders. Then he left Famoudi as dusk fell, and took the small roads of the desert. Before the light of the following dawn he had crossed over the border and returned to his flat in Damascus. He was part of a small group who had known that Saddam's taunting of the Americans was something that had been close to madness. They had made their preparations carefully and when the disaster had come they had quietly escaped the country and waited patiently to take the fight to the infidel. Some had been caught and imprisoned and executed. Not the Colonel. The Colonel always stayed many steps ahead of those who pursued him.

PART TWO

By Saturday morning Jake Hollins was beginning to wonder if he was on a wild goose chase after all. Friday's picket had been another sad little affair and Dumfries showed every sign of a small town getting back into its normal dreary routine. No stones were thrown. No new revelations had come forth. All signs were that the story was dying, but still his instincts were nagging at him. He had got out of bed at seven because it was what he always did. The nearest newsagents to his hotel was three hundred yards away and he used the stroll to get in the first two cigarettes of the day before returning to a leisurely cooked breakfast with a comprehensive selection of the morning papers. Firstly he flicked through them all to make sure that there had been no Dumfries stories that any of his competitors had dug out and he had missed. He was more than confident that there hadn't been but he checked all the same. A habit of a lifetime. Nothing. The media circus had moved on. Lenny Baxter was yesterday's news. As was USY and McIntosh House and two young people who had died in a place where there was nothing for them to do.

After three cups of coffee and an equal number of Rennies, he moved into the lounge where smoking was permitted and sat down to go through the papers with greater care. He was half way through a feature on the problems that the now famous Charlie Company were wrestling with in Famoudi when his mobile phone took his attention. The screen told him that it was his editor and he couldn't avoid a sense of disappointment. No doubt this would be the recall.

"Yeah."

"Hi Jed. How's Scotland. Plenty of fresh air and old malt?"

"Something like that."

"Good man." His editor was less than half his age and it irked Jed that he insisted on the buddy buddy tone. When Jed had been watching the last helicopter off the American Embassy roof in Saigon his editor had been watching the Klangers. "Has your hotel got Sky Jed?"

"It has."

"Good. There's something odd going on. Check out the MTV Base channels. Let me know what you think."

"What exactly is MTV Base when it's at home?"

"Urban Music. Hip Hop mostly. Take a look at the adverts."

"Why?"

"Just watch it OK? Then call. One more thing Jed. There's a hell of a lot of talk down here about tomorrow night's Panorama. The Beeb is just starting to trail it. The truth about Lenny Baxter. They're dropping all kinds of hints that there will be startling new revelations but no facts whatsoever. Nobody seems to have a clue what they are going to be saying. Broadcasting House is battened down tighter than the Kremlin. See if you can find anything out at your end will you?"

"Of course."

"Ciao then. Bell me when you've watched the tele."

Jed rode the lift and opened the door to his room. Why on earth did his editor want him to watch a music channel? In twenty plus years of news-hounding he couldn't remember anything quite so bizarre. He lit up and switched on and scrolled through the channels to unfamiliar territory. A huge tattooed black man surrounded by models in bikinis was hammering out words like machine bullets whilst the girls focused on being sultry. Behind them all was a rather unconvincing studio set ghetto that was about as threatening as an episode of Emmerdale Farm. Jed had an uneasy feeling that he was being played in some way. He couldn't help but form a picture of his editor sitting at his desk back in London having a good laugh with some of the younger reporters at the thought of miserable old Jed up in Scotland watching MTV. He decided to give it another ten minutes and then the hell with them all. With a final gesture of the fingers, the rap star ended his song and all the girls joined him in a tough stare at the camera. Adverts. Bacardi first. A bouncing dance floor filled with shining oiled bodies and a Latino model grinning as she poured down into a circle of waiting glasses. Welcome to the Latin Quarter. Jed's Latin Quarter had been a piece on the American-backed Contra's in Honduras in the early eighties. Then it had been burnt out villages and death squads working to the orders of shadowy figures with Texan accents. Next was yet another magic deodorant that attracted women for less than two pounds a can. Then an Italian looking guy who preferred to drive his shiny car round the deserted streets of Rome to watching the football. Then . . .

He sat forward as if a bolt of electricity had run up his spine. He knew that view. Surely not. No bloody way. Buccleuch Street. A little blurred. A little stylised and in black and white. The footage was jerky, matching a flat threatening beat in the background. Zoom. Policemen.

PART TWO

Three of them. Zoom. Small figures in hoods and caps, masks over their faces. Zoom. A policeman ducking. Freeze frame. Close up on hooded figure. A slow motion throw. Freeze frame at the moment of release. Zoom. Close in on the masked face. Writing on the cap. Koz. Pan backwards. Eight figures now. All bent into their throw. Freeze frame. Writing and voice over.

Koz. Sometimes you gotta fight.

Next was the Renault Megane shakin'its ass but Jed wasn't watching any more. What the hell had he just seen? All thoughts of being wound up by his editor vanished. What on earth was Koz and what on earth had it to do with Lenny Baxter and USY and Buccleuch Street? It was the most utterly weird thing he had ever seen in his life. He dialled up London.

"OK. Seen it."

"What do you make of it?"

"I haven't the first idea. I'll go and ask about. I'll let you know as soon as I find out more. Any more on this Panorama thing?"

"Not a thing from the BBC. Lot of twitching in the civil service though. The word is that there might be some dark stuff from the eighties."

"OK. Keep me posted."

"Will do."

Jed drove across Dumfries and was relieved to find that The Zone was open for business. The youngster on the door was in no mood to let him by.

"You ken the rules. No reporters."

"Is Lenny in?"

"How should I know?"

Jed recognised the glint in the eye well enough. He reached into his pocket and passed over a fiver. "I just though you might have an idea, that's all."

"Aye well I suppose he might be." The note disappeared into a pocket. Jed pulled out another. "Take him this card and there's another fiver in it."

The sentry reached for the note but Jed whipped it back and out of reach and gave him a business card instead. The boy studied it for a while before slamming the door in Jed's face. Three minutes later he was back.

"Aye. He says he'll see you. That's a fiver."

Jed passed over the second note which disappeared into the same pocket and followed the boy through an excited crowd to a small office at the back of the building. Inside Lenny was waiting with his press officer. Josh's face was all smiles as Jed came in.

"Ah. The last of the Mohicans. Good things come to he who waits, wouldn't you say Jed?"

"Maybe."

The desk was filled with open magazines. In each was a full page black and white image along similar lines to the MTV advert. As Jed leafed through he saw there were three different captions. One was the already familiar, *Koz. Sometimes you gotta fight.* Then there was *Koz. No surrender.* Finally there was *Koz. You're sick of getting pushed around.* He flicked to the front covers to see that the magazines were a varied selection. Music magazines. Teen magazines. Extreme sports.

"What does it all mean Lenny?"

Lenny gave a theatrical shrug. "Your guess is as good as mine. It seems that some of the lads have become a brand."

"A brand? What do you mean, a brand?"

" Everything is a brand Jed. It is the beating heart of our fine modern world. Sportsmen. Models. Film stars. Cars. Clothes. Mobile phones. Nike. BMW. Armani. New Labour. Books. Films. Climbing Everest. Whatever happens, it has a corporate sponsor. Well it looks like a few of our tearaways just got branded."

Lenny was smiling a smile that told Jed that he knew a whole lot about what was happening here.

"You knew all about this didn't you? That is why you hinted that I should stay."

"Maybe. It's not the sort of thing I feel I should comment on."

Jed was getting mildly angry. "Well if all you're going to do is to sit there and look smug I wish you'd let me bugger off home for the weekend."

Lenny was unfazed. "Why do people pay for advertising Jed?"

"Don't play silly games Lenny."

"I'm not playing silly games. Just humour me a while."

Jed pulled out his cigarettes and took a moment to calm down a little. He tossed one to Lenny and lit up.

"OK. People buy advertising to make people aware of their product so that they go out and buy it. OK?"

"Fine. And why do people choose specific brands?"

"Because they want to give out a message about themselves. It's all about image as far as I know. Christ Lenny, I'm an old crocked reporter. What do I know about it?"

"You'll soon get the swing of things. A few clues. Where does a punter go to buy Koz clothing? And why? And who? Your paper must have a few reporters for the younger reader. Another clue. Get them to sniff around Greater Manchester, maybe on the Sunday markets."

Jed was exasperated. "I have no idea where you are going with this Lenny."

"But you will have. And when you get up to speed, you will be out in front and clear of the rest of the pack."

"And you want me to get the story out?"

"I might."

"Because it's all part of the plan?"

"It might be."

Jed gave a sharp laugh. "OK. Fair enough. It's puzzle time. I'm not going to embarrass myself any more by asking questions you're not going to answer. What about this Panorama business. Are you going to give me anything on that?"

"What Panorama business?"

"Oh come on Lenny. Panorama. Tomorrow night. The real truth about Lenny Baxter. All kinds of dark hints. It must be pretty damned hot because the BBC is locked down tighter than tight about it."

Lenny wasn't smiling any more. "Honestly Jed, I have no idea what you are talking about."

Jed decided that Lenny would make the worst poker player in the world.

"Bloody Hell. You don't know do you?"

"No. Not a thing."

"Well that's pretty bloody odd if you ask me. The truth about Lenny Baxter and nobody asks Lenny Baxter about it."

All the upbeat optimism was draining out of Lenny. "For Christ's sake. It doesn't stop does it. Not ever. One step forward and bastarding four back. Every single time."

Josh's voice was more thoughtful. "It doesn't necessarily have to be back Lenny."

"Oh sure. Please tell me how."

"Think about it. All the bad news about you is right out in the open. The guns. The explosives. The twenty years in prison. The only stuff that is still a secret is the truth. You know it. I know it. All the people who tried so hard to prove your innocence knew it. The only ones who don't know it are the people of Britain. So if the BBC are making a big thing of this and keeping a big secret it seems to me as if the most likely thing is that somehow they have also found out the truth. It is the only logical reason."

Lenny was determined not to allow any hope to wheedle its way in. "It sounds good Josh. It always does. It always has. But when you get there all there ever is yet another kick in the ribs by some big bastard in hobnailed boots."

But Jed had no such doubts. Ogilvy was right. He had to be. That was why his editor had been picking up bad vibes from inside the civil service. Things seemed like they were getting interesting. Really interesting.

By the early evening he was beginning to get the picture. The editor had sent a team of reporters out to find out what they could about Koz. By the mid-afternoon they had discovered that the range was manufactured in Bolton by a high flying Asian businessman called Asif Mohammed. It became clear as the day wore on that there was already a lot of street talk about the new brand. However, what was mysterious was that nobody could find where the clothes were on sale. Extensive phone calls to all the major retailers bore no fruit. There didn't seem to be a single shop on the High Streets of Britain that stocked the Koz range. Already it was clear that managers and buyers alike were trying to find the distributor as their shops were filled with people asking if they had the range. A couple of managers said that they didn't know if the customers were actually wanting to buy the stuff. Well, how could they? Nobody had a clue what any of it cost. People just wanted to look at it. See what it was like. Lenny's clue sent a freelancer on a tour of the markets of Manchester and he came up with the first piece of pay dirt. Several stalls had opened up with Koz gear, but not a lot. By the late morning they had all sold out and none of them had any idea when they would get any more. All of the stall holders were Asians.

Then at five o'clock Jed took a call from one of the reporters in Manchester saying the word was that there was a website that gave details of where people could find the range. He went downstairs to the hotel's small business suite and logged on to *www.koz.com*. The site opened to the familiar frozen image of a young hooded figure caught at the moment of throwing his stone. *Koz. Fightback clothing*. He clicked on the 'outlets' icon and found two entries. One was for Dumfries Market, Whitesands, Dumfries. The other was for 'The Zone', Sunnybank Estate, Dumfries.'

He sat back away from the screen and allowed himself a smile.

"Lenny Baxter, you clever old sod."

Whoever was calling the shots here was tapping into the oldest rule in the capitalist book. Scarcity. Nothing worked quite like scarcity. Diamonds were the classic case in point. He had once read that if every diamond mine in the world worked at full capacity, the price of diamonds would collapse so far that they could appear on jewellery in Christmas crackers. And then of course nobody would want them any more. It was only their scarcity and expense that made them worth having. Look how much I love you. Here's a diamond. Just imagine how much that cost. For centuries diamonds gave men the chance to show their desire in terms of pounds, shillings and pence without actually doing so in hard cash. Jed now saw where Lenny had been coming from. Everything was a brand. Everything said something. So what would wearing Koz say about those who were about to adorn themselves in the new brand? Look, I'm a rebel. Look, I come from the streets. And more. Look, I'm so streetwise and cool that I managed to find these items. More. Look, I went to Dumfries to find these items.

Now he sat forward. Of course. Not just I've been to Dumfries. More. I've been to the front line. Because the core message of the Koz campaign was that people who wore Koz were the people who had the bottle to walk the walk. *Koz. Sometimes you gotta fight*. And there were more carefully thought out old messages. Women like men in uniforms. The heroes from the front line get the girls. And that was why the new range could only be purchased right here in Dumfries.

That would mean that it would work like a uniform for those who wore it. A combat badge. Attire that shouted 'I was there'.

The next morning he was out of bed good and early. At first the town was predictably quiet for a Sunday morning. But as he approached the river he found that there were a surprising number of people out and about. Young people mainly. The large car park was already nearly full and more cars were parking up all the time. Small cars. Old cars. Cars filled with five and six bodies which spilled out into the early morning sunshine and stretched their cramped limbs. Jed checked the number plates for garage addresses. Liverpool. Hull. Newcastle. Kirkaldy. Maidenhead. The whole of Britain was represented in the car park by the river. The entrance to the market was already a magnet. Most of the stall holders still setting up their stands, bemused at the unaccustomed throng. At the back of the market, a large articulated lorry was parked tight up against the wall. In front was a large stall a good fifty feet long and twenty feet deep. Sure enough the side of the cab confirmed that the haulier was from Horwich near Bolton. The customers leaving the stall bore carrier bags with the graffiti style *Koz* written large and bold.

From the market, the next destination was easy to predict. It was like a pilgrimage. Just a couple of hundred yards led the crowds to Buccleuch Street. Some had their magazines open so that they could pick out the landmarks from the adverts. The metal fences that the police had left across the entrance to the street gave the scene credibility. They confirmed that this was the right place to be. There were no policemen because it had been established that USY didn't picket on a Sunday. Jed found a low wall and sat and smoked and watched as the street filled up. By ten it was heaving with people. By now, two police cars had arrived and the officers looked on with bemusement. But they were relaxed enough. What was happening here was strange but not threatening. Buccleuch Street was infused with a party atmosphere. People had driven through the night from all corners of Britain to be there. To say they had been here. To have the uniform to prove it.

Jed knew with utter certainty where it was going finish up. The value was always going to be in the 'being there' factor. Which of course begged the question of being there for what. Something had to happen. The event needed to be finished and framed. By noon the street was becoming dangerously full. More police had arrived and it was clear that their radio conversations were becoming more and more agitated. Jed could guess at what was being said. Someone back at the station would be saying that the street should be blocked off and then cleared. The officers on the ground would be saying that they needed back up and that they needed it fast. Back up arrived in the shape of a van that brought reinforcements of four. This took total police numbers up to nine. They deployed along the metal fences and started the task of blocking the way of the new arrivals. Within minutes there was pushing and scuffles. Tempers became frayed. A baton flashed. Angry shouts. A surge. And then all was a massive swirling chaos as the policemen beat a frantic retreat to their vehicles and forced a way clear through the shouting crowd that beat away on the metal roofs.

By twelve-thirty Buccleuch Street belonged to Koz. The battle had been fought and won. And every single person who stood and raised their fists in triumph would be able to return home and tell all their friends that they had been there for the first battle of Buccleuch Street. In the vanguard. At the dawning. Already their clothes had become a uniform. And already a legend had been born.

Jed had noticed the two Asians as soon as he had taken up his position. Both were decked out in the new uniform. One had two cameras. The other had a videocam. Both wore scarves over their mouths so the CCTV would not give them away. They captured images of the morning for posterity. For the Koz gallery of the future. These would become the images for the adverts that would appear in the days to come. This time it would be *Koz. It's time to be heard.*

Jed left soon after the policemen. The afternoon was warm and he felt strangely elated. He broke his walk to Sunnybank Estate with a couple of pints where the talk of the pub was all about that was happening. He was surrounded by excited accents from all the regions of Britain. All the years of his work had shown him the sickening results of the unrestrained capitalism that had conquered the globe after the collapse of communism. Once upon a time the young people of the world had rioted and burnt flags in protest at the killing zones of Vietnam. Jed had seen it first hand as a cub reporter covering the near anarchy on the streets of Paris in 1968. The Corporations had licked their wounds and learned their lessons. It had taken them thirty-seven years to fully tame the youth of the planet, but tame them they had. They had given young people new gods to worship. Items. Labels. Expensive things. Things that meant money was the greatest god of all. But now, against all odds, a scarred old warrior from the last gasp of the Socialist Dream had come back from the dead to turn the weapons of the Corporations back onto the men in the boardrooms. Lenny Baxter had turned a brand into a weapon. He had made rebellion the coolest game in town.

The Zone was surrounded by a wall of bodies as a ragged queue waited in the sun for the chance to buy. Jed didn't bother trying to find a way inside. Instead he called up Lenny on his mobile and waited. A few minutes later Lenny appeared to sustained cheers from all who recognised him. He forced his way through, a big daft grin on his face, shaking hands, getting his back slapped. The unlikely Messiah of the twenty-first century. And again Jed felt a surge of elation. He recalled the old black and white film of Lenin arriving back in Russia on a train laid on by the German High Command to lead the people's revolution. Another middle-aged man in the right place at the right time.

"Glad you stayed then?"

"Oh I think so."

"Can I look forward to reading the paper tomorrow morning then?"

"I think so."

The next morning the Times carried one of its more unusual headlines. 'The dawning of the era of Koz.' People in the office could not believe the style adopted by grumpy old Jed Thompson. It was as if he had lost thirty years during his trip to Scotland. They said that he wrote like a young man. All the cynicism that generally accompanied his usual biting prose was absent. In its place was a picture painted in bright vivid colours about a morning when the young people of Britain at last woke up to what it meant to be young again. He recalled 1968 and 1981. He recalled the campaigns to ban the bomb and free Mandela. At first the editor was going to pull it completely. Then he was going to edit it down. Then he decided why the hell not. The piece ran in full.

Lenny, Josh and Sally finally locked the doors at The Zone and headed out of the back door at eight-thirty. Three journalists had second guessed their intentions and were waiting, and duly trotted after them all the way back to the flat. When Lenny finally closed the door on them he leant against the wall and blew out his cheeks with relief.

Ten to nine. Plenty of time. Sally offered tea, but both men preferred the idea of a can of lager. By the time the news started to wind down they were all sitting ready for the Panorama programme that had been at the front of their minds all day.

'So that's it for us on a day when the news was once again dominated by quite extraordinary scenes from Dumfries. Now stayed tuned for a special edition of Panorama. Over the last few days millions have joined the debate on the question of Lenny Baxter's innocence. Stay tuned for a truly extraordinary story . . . '

The newscaster was gone from the screen. In his place was a young man in jeans and casual shirt. He was outside and it was sunny. In the background were non-descript industrial type buildings. The scene was utterly ordinary, it could have been any small industrial area on the edge of any British town and yet Sally felt her uncle tense beside her. When she glanced at him she saw his face was suddenly quite white.

' This is a very ordinary place. Willow Lane Industrial Estate on the outskirts of Bingley in West Yorkshire. They repair cars here and assemble computers and distribute soft drinks. Yet twenty years ago the eyes of the nation were fixed on this place. On the night of November 23rd 1984, officers from the West Yorkshire Police and the Special Branch lay in wait for the Baxter brothers – Frank and Lenny. Despite a public enquiry, the truth of what happened when the brothers arrived has always been shrouded in mystery. On that night Frank Baxter met with his death as the police found automatic weapons and explosives in the boot of the brothers' car. During the ensuing trial of Lenny Baxter it was established that the guns and explosives had come from Colonel Gaddafi's Libya. The jury found Lenny Baxter guilty and sentenced him to twenty five years in prison.'

Now the scene changed. Bleak high walls with wire on the top. The reporter stood in front of a daunting high gate and a sign that read.

'HMP Wakefield'

THE POISONOUS PAST

'This is where Lenny Baxter spent twenty years of that sentence. Never once did he even come close to admitting his guilt. His story remained perfectly consistent for two decades. He and his brother knew nothing of the guns from Libya. They were planted by the security forces. They were planted by men working for a Government that would stop at nothing to beat the Miners in the greatest and most bitter strike our country has ever known. Politicians and lawyers and civil rights groups all tried in vain to prove that Lenny Baxter was innocent, but unlike the Guildford Four and the Birmingham Six, he served his full sentence.

'When Lenny Baxter walked free in 2004 it seemed as if he would live out the remainder of his days in obscurity. He went north to Dumfries to stay with his niece, Sally. As we all know, for the last few weeks Lenny Baxter has once again been in the full glare of the media. Once again he is fighting the odds. Instead of the future of the coal industry, this time he is demanding a youth centre for the young people of the Sunny-bank Estate in Dumfries. Old wounds have been reopened and once again the debate about what really happened in 1984 has filled many column inches. When the demonstrations in Buccleuch Street turned ugly last week, there were many who believed a point had been proved.'

Images of the riot. A bleeding policeman. A burning building. A fireman hosing the flames. Newspaper headlines. 'Lenny the terrorist!'. 'The enemy within?'. 'Same leopard. Same spots.' And footage of Lenny on the steps of the Council Offices, face frozen.

'Tonight Panorama will present new evidence. Truly extraordinary evidence that once again casts doubt about what really happened twenty years ago. More than this, the story we are about to tell casts doubt about the very integrity of our democracy. Our story raises many, many questions . . .'

The Panorama music pulled the viewers into the programme: A school. Rather faded looking. A vision of the flawed architecture of the 1970's. Concrete and peeling wood.

'This is where our story starts. Haddington Comprehensive School. It was here in 1979 that a seemingly innocuous event changed the lives of so many . . .''

PART TWO

The hall now. Rows of empty plastic seats. A stage. And Roger Darnley. A man in his mid-forties with receding hair and a warm smile of memory.

"It was end of year prize giving. We were all giving Lenny Hell. Day before he's won us the Yorkshire Cup at cricket. Bloody brilliant he were. Took seven for nowt. Well, we knew he were a shoe in for sportsman of year award. It meant he were going to have to sit up on stage with Beverly Morton. She were . . . Well you know. Good looking, top o'class, posh family, we were all in awe of her which is why we took the mick out of Lenny cos he were going to have to sit next to her"

A school photograph. Beverly smiling into the camera. Young. Assured. Confident.

New scene. A hospital room. Flowers. An open laptop. A terribly thin woman on the bed with a livid scar that ran from her ear to her chin. A small smile. A small voice.
    Lenny's eyes widened with horror.
    "Oh please Jesus no."

Beverly's voice was tiny. *"Oh yes. I remember that day. Poor old Lenny was so nervous. I was completely horrid to him. I'm amazed he ever forgave me. But he did."*

    More pictures with voice over. Beverly on the road to Cambridge. The star pupil. Beverly the young woman with the world at her feet.

"There was nothing unusual about my first two years at Cambridge. It was in my third year that things changed. I received an invitation to tea with professor Simcox . . ."

An outside view of Simcox room. A description of Beverly's entry into the secret world. Archive shots from the eighties. Militant Tendency banners. CND marches. The women at Greenham Common. A thin-faced Terry Sanderson.

" . . . I actually believed that Beverly liked me. We arranged to go up to Liverpool together. I was with the Militant Tendency at the time. I was helping the local union up there. I waited for Beverly to come in an hotel. She never arrived. Instead I was lifted by MI5 and tortured. They made me work for them as an informant. It was either that or ten years in prison. When I went back to Cambridge, Beverly acted as if nothing had happened. She was frightening to be honest . . . ."

Now the images changed dramatically. A jungle scene. Archive shots of wounded children. Archive scenes of Sandanista Guerrilla fighters. Archive pictures of Reagan and Thatcher. The story of a cover story. The girl who left the security of her middle class life for the violent front line of the fight against the guns and napalm of American Imperialism. Now there was a farmhouse in the Ulster countryside. Dilapidated with boarded up windows and grass growing out of the gutters. The story of how Beverly was brought home once her cover life was in place. The small voice recalled how it had been in Ireland at the time whilst old images of soldiers on the streets of Belfast came to the screen. Stone-throwing crowds. Tear gas. Rubble from a recent bomb. She described how everything had changed under Thatcher. How the gloves had come off. She told of how the Hendrick team went about their work.

Now a man whose face was just a black shape spoke in an accent from County Derry. He told of his time in the basement with Beverly and Hendrick. The psychotic man in the balaclava and uniform. The promise of torture and death. Then promise of a new life if he would give evidence against his comrades. Beverly's voice was even smaller now.

"We did truly terrible things. But it was a terrible time. Everyone said that it was a war. A dirty, filthy war. Some did it because they were patriots. Others did it for their careers. Some actually enjoyed it. I was the very worst. I did it for money. I did it so that my family could keep a nice home in the countryside. So my father wouldn't have to know the shame of bankruptcy. I was the worst of all of them. I was a mercenary. Nothing more, nothing less. I have had to carry the guilt all of my life. I'm so sorry. So, so sorry . . . ."

Her face seemed to collapse like a wet cardboard box. Very slowly she lifted a skeletal hand to her eyes to wipe at the tears. Tears were streaming down Lenny's face now, but he didn't seem to notice.

Now the programme moved to South Yorkshire. Familiar shots of the early days of the great strike. The milling ranks of police and pickets on the pit lanes of Nottinghamshire. The battle of Orgreave. King Arthur being arrested in his baseball cap. And then it was King Arthur twenty years on. Older. No longer familiar. He told of how near they had been in late 1984. Just days from victory. And what had happened in Haddington had nearly made all the difference.

Now the story moved to the sorry shell of what was left of Haddington Main. Just a few buildings, all but demolished and overgrown. Closed-up shops. And then a very old looking Jim Harris, the long retired Chief Superintendent of the 'Mankies'. He said when they were deployed to Haddington they all knew how it would be. Haddington was the heart of the heartland. There had never been a single strike breaker in the history of the town . . .

Old news footage of the battle of Haddington. Bloody faces. Writhing figures on stretchers. Streets filled with debris. Police lines crashing their batons on their plastic shields. 'Zoolooo!!!'Harris again.

He told of how things had started to go wrong up in the old army camp where they were billeted. First there was sugar in the engines of their vans. Then all the power was cut. LSD in the milk. Felled trees blocking the roads. A nightmare. They couldn't seem to stop it. And every time that something happened and they couldn't make it down to Haddington, the bus with the scab would have to be turned back . . .

King Arthur again. A rare smile at the memory. *"None of us had any idea who was behind it all. Seriously. Not a clue. But by God it didn't half make a difference. All over Yorkshire there were more lads out on the lines. And Scotland and Wales and Durham. Everywhere. Whoever was behind what was going on was turning the tide . . . ."*

Now a retired executive from The national Coal Board remembered how they had warned Downing Street that stock levels were collapsing. The amounts being imported or produced in Nottinghamshire were not going to be nearly enough if it turned cold in January or February. He remembered that they had told the government that power cuts would be inevitable by March at the latest. Unless the strike was broken. And with everything going on in Haddington it had seemed as if the strike was getting stronger all the time . . . .

Beverly again. *"They called us over to London. I had waited for months to go on holiday and then the very day before I was due to leave we got the summons . . ."*

Shots of the small hotel in London.

"All the team was there. Me. Hendrick. All of us. And Latimer. He was calling all the shots. I had been hoping against hope that it wouldn't be the strike. But in my heart I knew it would be. What else could it have been? Of course I had no idea what had been happening to the police in Haddington. Nobody did. I remember that my blood turned to ice when Latimer explained what was going on . . ."

Beverly's voice became very flat when she explained their mission. Find who was responsible. Achieve a conclusive outcome. Leave no martyrs. Now the reporter again, this time outside the mighty edifice of one of London's grand government buildings. The Latimer of 1984 is now Sir Edward Latimer, a senior officer in MI6.

"We have not been able to get anyone to comment on the allegations that Beverly Morton has made regarding Latimer's involvement in any operations against the strike of 1984. However we have received leaked documents from within the security forces. The first is a file on Beverly Morton which came from inside MI5. The file contains intelligence about Beverly's activities within the Militant Movement of the early eighties. There are surveillance photographs of her at the peace camp at Greenham Common. There are also photos of her with alleged Soviet advisors in Nicaragua. The file claims that Morton was a known agitator with clear links to the Soviet Bloc all the way through the 1980's. A second leak from within MI6 shows that Edward Latimer was working in Pakistan for the duration of the strike.

'In the light of new evidence these leaks appear to have been a deliberate smokescreen."

Beverly again. *"I hardly ever came back home to Yorkshire. On one visit on the way from Rwanda to the Balkans I had a letter with a South African postmark." She held it up for the camera. "It was from Hendrick. I hadn't ever heard from him after what happened in Haddington. Things had changed by 1994. He had changed. He said if I ever needed help all I had to was to call . . ."*

Archive shots of Hendrick as a boy. As a young paratrooper. Posing with fellow soldiers in shorts and T-shirts in the dusty heat of Cyprus. Old news footage showing the small farm in the olive groves where a young girl had been killed in cross fire between a squad of paras and the insurgents. Shots of Hendrick in dress uniform emerging from the ensuing hearing having been exonerated. And over the photos the reporter told his story from the army to the drug squad to Hendrick. After Haddington, Latimer had disbanded his team. Hendrick and the others were paid off handsomely. There seemed little for him in the UK. He had only ever known one life, and to continue it, he had flown south and started work for the South African Counter Terrorist Forces. When the apartheid regime had collapsed with the release of Mandela, Hendrick had become a man whose skills were suddenly redundant. Surprisingly he stayed in the country and bought a small vineyard on the edge of Table Mountain near Cape Town. It was at the Truth and Reconciliation Commission that his life turned on its axis. Like hundreds of others, he found the experience of facing the wives and families of those he had interrogated and tortured to be something that reached into the very depths of his soul.

Now an older Hendrick was on the screen. Very tanned, but much more at peace with himself. All the old burning anger was gone from his pale grey eyes.

"I don't know what I expected really. The Government had said that so long as we told the truth we would be forgiven. I didn't believe them. But I knew that I didn't deserve to be forgiven. Not after all the things I had done. I didn't want to run away any more. I had been running all my life. First from my father. Then from the guilt at what had happened to the little girl. I don't know. I suppose it just seemed as if it was time to face the music."

Apause. The tanned face stared out and the camera followed his gaze. An unending line of dusty brown hills burning up under a ferocious sun.

"It wasn't what I expected. There were so many of them. Mothers. Fathers. Sons and daughters. They all just sat and stared at me and wiped their tears. And one by one they came forward and forgave me. I remember one grandmother in particular. She pulled me to my feet and embraced me. It seemed like she held on to me forever. It was the first time I could ever remember anyone doing that. I had been there when her grandson had been beaten to his death and here she was holding me and filling me with love. I think that was the moment that I found God. I think his presence came out of that wonderful woman and filled me. All of me. And I felt bathed in his light."

Voice over:

"Hendrick had sold his vines and headed east to the dry hills of Swaziland to help out in a Missionary-run Aids hospital. And this was when he had started to think about Beverly. All the others from the Latimer team were nothing to him. They had all been mercenaries just as he had been himself. But Beverly had been different somehow. Better than the rest of them. He could see now how everything they had done together in Ireland had slowly rotted her soul. He had never found out what had become of her. All he had was an address for her parents in Haddington and so he had written and told her that he was there if she ever needed help."

"I never trusted Latimer. Not an inch. I knew the things that we were doing were wrong. OK, the Government knew full well what we were up to. They were more than happy so long as we got results. But I also knew they had never committed anything to paper. We were working out of the system. That was why they paid so well. I knew that if anything ever went wrong, we'd all be hung out to dry. So every now and then I made sure that I collected up bits of insurance. Just in case."

He reached into the breast pocket of his shirt and pulled out a small cassette and held it up for the camera to see between his thumb and forefinger.

"Insurance like this. This is a recording of the meeting we had in the hotel in London when Latimer brought us back from Ireland."

Again a picture of the outside of the small hotel. There were voices which were slightly fuzzy and it needed sub-titles to ensure that the viewer missed nothing. Each voice was labelled. Hendrick. Morton. Latimer.

" *. . . so they want us to clean up. They've put up a hundred thousand for a conclusive outcome to the Haddington situation."*

Hendrick: *"So what's conclusive?"*

Latimer: *"Find who's doing it. Stop them. Make sure they're completely discredited. People are worried about martyrs . . ."*

Beverly in her death bed again:

"Hendrick and I were sent to Simmington. That was where the Manchester police were billeted at an old army base outside of the town. My job was to play the part of a reporter in the local pub. Keep my ears open, flirt a bit, see if I could pick anything up . . ."

Once again tears made their way down the bony ledges of her near lifeless face.

"I never even went to the pub. I didn't have to. On the way I saw someone I knew. It was Josh. Josh Ogilvy. A friend of Lenny's from Cambridge. And I knew for certain that it had to be them. Why on earth else would he be in Simmington? I knew he had to be involved. I had a decision to make. There was no way that I could go into the pub because Josh would recognise me straight away and then my cover would be useless. But I couldn't go back to Hendrick and say that I just didn't want to go into the pub for no reason."

Her head slowly lowered and her voice fell to a whisper.

"So I told them. It was me you see. I was the betrayer. I didn't know what would happen. To Frank. To Lenny. But I knew the men I was working with. I knew what they were capable of. Especially Latimer. I knew all this and still I told them. So it was me you see. I was responsible for Frank, for Lenny, for all of it . . ."

THE POISONOUS PAST

It took a huge effort for her to get her head back up.

"Latimer knew that I was no longer properly on the team. He kept me out of the way. First he sent me to ask questions in Shropshire where Josh's father had a house. Then he sent me out of the country. First Rome. Then Libya. I had to collect some boxes from an industrial area with an Italian Agent. In the end I was stuck in Tripoli for nearly a week. The whole place was in uproar when the story broke that Libyan weapons had been discovered in the boot of a car in Yorkshire. I had tried to call Lenny from the airport in Rome but Latimer had been way ahead of me. The call was blocked. He knew I had tried to warn Lenny. When it was all over he told me that I wasn't welcome in the UK any more. He told me to go back to the camp in Nicaragua for three years. He said that if I ever revealed anything about what happened he had files on me that would send me to prison for the rest of my life. I didn't care. I wanted nothing of Britain any more. People have no idea what goes on. We like to pretend that we are so wonderful. The oldest democracy of them all. A land of freedom. And yet men like Latimer are always there in the shadows, pulling all the strings. I never came home. Not until now. I really don't know the exact details about what happened in the end. Latimer made sure that I was thousands of miles away. I assume that the boxes I collected and delivered to the Italian Embassy contained the guns and explosives that were found in Lenny's car."

A new view. The postcard beautiful horizon of Tuscany. Medieval towers and olive groves. A terrace. A distinguished looking Salvatore Tucci in a snow white shirt to go with his dazzling teeth. He took a sip of coffee and gave a very Italian shrug.

"Sure. They tella me to meet this Beverly. Very pretty. We go and collect boxes and take them to our consulate. Is all I know. Later I think maybe when they come to Rome they handed to the British. Maybe somebody they once tell me this. Maybe not. And maybe the boxes they have guns and explosives that get found in the boot of a car. Maybe. Maybe not. The woman Beverly, she all the time very sad. I try to cheer her up OK. I buy her dinner and she no eat. After a few days she get a plane and she go. I no see her any more."

PART TWO

A final that's it shrug. Back to Swaziland. Back to Hendrick.

"Once Beverly tagged Josh Ogilvy it all went pretty quick. We lifted him and got him out of the country on a military plane. We took him to the house in Ulster. Gave him the treatment."

A question from an unseen reporter *"Treatment?"*

Hendrick nodded. Once he would have found it harder. The Truth and Reconciliation Commission had taught him not to fear the truth any more.

"Yeah. Electric shocks. Not many. He wasn't made for it. He told us everything. That was how we knew where Lenny and Frank Baxter were due to meet up with the others."
  "Others?"
  "Ogilvy and Williams. Williams was an ex-soldier who worked as a gardener at the Ogilvy house in Shropshire. He was the brains behind all the operations against the police. Once we knew, it was pretty simple. We broke into the car and put the guns and explosives in the boot. Then all we had to do was to set things up for a raid by the local police."
  "Were you there?"
  "I was."
  "Do you know what happened to Frank Baxter?"
  "I do."
  "And?"

Again the serene grey eyes took in the empty spaces of the African horizon.

"When he saw the guns he just flipped. I mean really flipped. I hit him with the butt of my rifle. I hit him too hard."
  "And was he trying to escape?"
  "No. No he wasn't. Latimer sorted everything out with the senior officer at the scene."
  "So Latimer was there."
  "Oh yes. He was there. He wanted to be there for the kill."
  "What about Ogilvy and the man Williams."
  "We kept Ogilvy at the house in Ireland for several weeks. We

injected him with serious amounts of heroin. Got him addicted. Latimer thought that it would ensure that he wouldn't cause any trouble when we let him go. Who believes a junkie?"

"And Williams?"

"He was the problem. He was a tough guy and nobody could predict what he may or may not do. In the end Latimer decided to play it safe. He had him terminated."

"As in executed?"

"As in executed. I wasn't there. Latimer used specialist contractors for that kind of work. Williams had no family. Latimer assumed he wouldn't be missed. He wasn't, as far as I can tell."

"And then?"

"You know the rest. Everybody does. It was all over the papers. Frank Baxter and Williams were dead. Me, Beverly and Ogilvy disappeared off the map and Lenny Baxter was locked up for twenty years. And Latimer became Sir Edward Latimer, knight of the realm."

Back to Beverly. Now her head was up again, her deep set eyes staring hard into the camera from their sunken sockets. A small light of brightness flickering for a brief moment.

"I have had to live with what happened for most of my life. It is why I have always tried to help people. I hoped that one day it might wipe the slate clean. Nicaragua, Rwanda, Bosnia, Chechnya, Darfur, all those people, children, all broken . . ."

Her voice trailed away as the images of thousands of ghosts marched through her tortured mind. At last she seemed to steel herself.

"But it never did. Never a day went by that I didn't think of Lenny. Locked away for something he didn't do. Branded as an evil terrorist. A whole pyramid of lies. It got a little easier when I knew that he had been released. Then all of a sudden when I had come home he was there again. On the television. In the papers."

The merest thread of a smile.

"Same old crazy Lenny. Tilting at windmills and chasing rainbows. I knew they would never allow him to win. And of course they had to start it all up again. The burnt building and the riot and those pictures *of him standing there looking as if it had all been at his bidding. Of course it wasn't. I know Lenny. He knew that it was all starting again. Just like always. If it wasn't Latimer himself it was somebody like him. Because there's always another Latimer. The hired hands who keep everything in its proper place. That is how Britain is. It's how it always has been. We're just better than most at keeping it hidden away."*

All of a sudden the programme was no longer for the watching millions. It was down to two people joined up through the lens of a camera. Her eyes reached out.

"I know you're watching Lenny. I hope you can forgive me. Don't give up. Never, ever give up. I know that this time you'll win. You have to. I really am so very sorry."

Back to the reporter in front of the government building. Serious-faced.

"This story asks many questions of our country. It asks questions about the relationship between governments and their security forces. It asks questions about the relationships between corporate wealth and elected politicians. Where did the money come from to pay for the Latimer team to resolve the Haddington situation all those years ago? Who benefited? Edward Latimer became Sir Edward Latimer. But who else? Maybe the answer lies in a look at how the Stock Market took off on a fifteen year long explosion in the wake of the defeat of the Great Strike of 1984. This story illustrates how our liberties are under constant threat when the interests of great wealth are allowed to infiltrate the highest echelons of government. For many years we have heard alarming stories of how the security forces behaved in the long war in Ireland. Now we know that their tactics were imported onto Mainland Britain to help defeat the strike in 1984. Once again we are all told that we face a threat from terrorism. Once again our government is using this threat to erode liberties that have taken hundreds of years to be put in place. My grandfather died on the beaches of Dunkirk. He and many hundreds of thousands of others died to save the liberties that every single one of us are born to. What was done to Frank and Lenny Baxter, and Josh Ogilvy and the man known only as Williams is the kind of thing we used to see in the old Soviet Union. The kind of thing we see

today in places like Zimbabwe. It isn't only Lenny Baxter who deserves answers to these questions, it is every single citizen of these islands."

Music. Titles. Complete stillness in the small Sunnybank lounge. Then Lenny slowly aimed the remote control and sent the screen to black before rising to his feet.

"Are you driving Josh?"

"To Sheffield?"

"Where else."

Sir Edward Latimer didn't switch off his TV. The next programme came on but he was not aware of what it was. Just sound and noise. He hadn't moved from the moment that he had heard his voice from twenty years past. He had known that Beverly Morton was talking. Questions had been asked. It had been something that he had anticipated many years earlier. There was nothing to be too concerned about. He had duly leaked the file that he knew would completely discredit her. Similarly his Pakistan alibi had been something that had been patiently filed away in case of a rainy day. He had guessed that there might be a few awkward days ahead, but nothing he couldn't handle. Just crazy allegations from a bitter woman nearing her death with a long history of militancy.

The bombshell had been the tape. Hendrick. How could he have been so careless? He had completely lost track of Hendrick. He had heard that the man had purportedly found god and vanished into some godforsaken African wilderness. And yet all that time Hendrick had carried a tape with him that would one day become dynamite. The tape changed everything. There would be no point in any denial. Already someone in some department or another would be checking the voice recognition. And the voice recognition would be conclusive.

Latimer knew he was at the end of the road. Not that it was the end of the world. Not remotely. He had plenty of his own insurance in place. There was no way that anyone would dare to ask him too many questions. They all knew that if he went down, a whole host of the great and the good would go down with him. But he had no future in the department. It was time to pen his letter of resignation. It would take most of the next day to clear up his affairs. Then he and his wife would leave for their villa in France. It would take a while for things to blow over, but in the end it would all be forgotten. He had hoped that he might go a little further, but it was not to be. He had always rather looked forward to his retirement in France. It would just have to be sooner rather than later.

His wife hadn't spoken a word as the programme ended. He saw that there was a slight shake to her hands as she poured herself a gin and tonic and dropped in some ice.

"I think it might be a good idea if you spend the morning packing darling. We'll be going out to the cottage for a while. Let things blow over a bit. It won't take very long."

She turned on him with a flash of anger.

"Is that all you can say Edward?"

"What do you expect me to say?"

She took a gulp of her drink, draining all but the ice. Then she made him jump by hurling the glass against a print that he had only bought the week before.

"Were you not listening Edward? Did it really all just wash over you? Well I was. I heard what the man said. Specialist contractors. For that kind of work. The whole country has just learned that you are the kind of man who uses specialist contractors to murder people. And you say that things will blow over a bit. Well you go and hide away in France if you like Edward. But you go alone. My solicitor will be in touch Edward, and don't you dare argue about a single thing. You make my skin crawl. You really do."

He was on his feet now. Suddenly blazing in his anger. More angry that he had ever been in the whole of his life. Angry at Hendrick and Morton and the BBC and the pampered bitch of a wife who all of a sudden felt she had the right to be holier than thou. He reached out and gripped her wrist to stop her running from the room. He twisted and forced her to face him. Even though the rage was all over him his voice was as quiet and calm as ever.

"Oh yes. So easy for you to say. You and all those like you. Look at you. Nice home. Nice public school. Daddy in the City. Never wanted for anything have you. Never one day in your over pampered life have you had to step out of your front door and feel fear. Ever wondered why? Because of men like me who spend our lives up on the ramparts. The ones who keep things as they are. Has it never entered your pitiful empty little head why we don't do revolution here in Britain? Is it because the people in places like Belfast and Liverpool and Glasgow are really, really happy with their lot? Is it? Or is it because people like me are there to stop them before they get started. You all love the results of our work. You love your big country houses and the fat, share dividends that you spend on skiing holidays. You just don't want to know who makes sure that it all stays in its proper place. Disneyland Britain. The rich get richer and the poor put up and shut up. You might just have noticed that we've never had a Robbespiere or Trotsky or Mussolini or Hitler here. That is why mummy and daddy live in a nice big house. That is why our two sons went to Eton. It is because men like me do what needs to be done and we always have. We do it quietly and we get on. No great song and dance. No tawdry American drama. We resolve things. And life goes on. Get used to it."

The cold contempt never left her eyes. When he had done she pulled her wrist and he released it.

"If you've quite finished Edward, I would like to go to bed now. Like I said. My solicitor will be in touch."

She didn't bother to slam the door. Latimer sat and took a sip at his whisky. Maybe he would get blind drunk. It had been many, many years since he had. Then again maybe he wouldn't.

All because of a single lousy tape.

There were no thoughts of Panorama programmes in the Marine base on the edge of Famoudi that Sunday night. Dale Nash had completed a tactical meeting with his sergeants and corporals. They had worked through ideas on how to combat the stone-throwers in the coming week. Orders from Division were still very clear. The Famoudi initiative had to continue as planned. The men of Charlie Company were only to discharge their weapons as a last resort. ABC had confirmed that their team was remaining in place. Not just America was watching. The whole world was watching. The situation had to be resolved in a manner that showed the US Marine Corps in a good light. The week before they had made several arrests each day and by Friday it was noticeable that the crowds were thinning out. Dale was confident that their snatch squads could carry on making arrests for the next five days. He was also confident that the stone throwers would soon lose heart, especially when they saw more and more of their friends being arrested and taken away. The biggest problem would be if Charlie Company escalated the situation by shooting. Dale had requested that Division find a copy of one of the films that had been made to commemorate the twentieth anniversary of the Bloody Sunday incident in Ireland. He had sat the whole of the company down the evening before to watch how it was that the British Paras had lost control and killed thirteen demonstrators. After the film was finished he had reminded the men of how this single incident had fanned the flames in Ireland and guaranteed that the Brits would fight the war for another twenty-five years. He had talked to all the men and explained the significance of their work. He told about how it was about a whole lot more than a few dusty streets in Famoudi. It was about the whole world watching America. Watching the Corps. Watching them. Charlie Company. The sergeants had given him feedback that the guys had gone for it pretty good. They had enjoyed the film, maybe because they were all heartily sick of hearing how goddamn perfect the Brits were. All of them were confident that the guys would continue to keep it tight.

Once the junior officers had left him, Dale settled into his paperwork. For once there wasn't too much of it. Half an hour would be enough to kill it. Forty minutes tops. Then he promised himself an early night for once. He was aware of a deep fatigue that was all over him, brain and limbs. It was the kind of fatigue that lay behind horrible mistakes. Errors of judgement. He needed a sleep catch up. Not a chance of any leave with everything going on the ABC. He was just getting down to his work when his CO knocked and walked in.

Dale shot to his feet and into ramrod attention.

"At ease Dale. Sit back down son. Sorry to butt in"

Dale sat. What now? His CO was with a civilian he hadn't seen before. Mid-forties maybe. Terrible, terrible hair like some seventies singer in a sequinned suit. Safari suit. Toothy grin and eyes like buckets of ice. Daytime TV meets the killing fields. The tone of his CO's voice spoke of annoyance that he was having to do this.

"Division requested that I brought Mr Walters here along for a talk Dale. Walters, captain Dale Nash."

Walters extended a hand and shook with a workman's grip that belied his bizarre appearance.

"Good to hook up Dale."

Dale gestured to the two metal chairs the other side of the desk. He asked his CO a question with his eyes and received no response. It was Walters who took things along.

"Well son. I've been watching the Charlie Company show. Sure as hell. Who hasn't? Biggest show in town. Join the Marines and become a pin-up boy for middle America. Hell, we live in a crazy world Dale. Crazy, crazy world."

` Dale had no inclination to join in the conversation. There was something about Walters that made his skin crawl. He wasn't buying the cosy good ole boy from the South act. Walters kept the smile on his face but the ice never left his eyes.

"Guess I best tell you what this is all about. War's changing son. Like everything else. Folks in Washington are always looking for new ways to make their tax dollars go that bit further. Hell, why not? And there ain't nothing that the U S of A spends more tax dollars on than the glorious military. Hell no. Guys in Washington are always looking for ways to get a bit more bang for their buck. It's why Wolfowitz projected that USAPlc would break even on this little adventure. It all means new trends Dale. Trends that come from the guys with the big brains thinking all the way out of the box. You with me Dale?"

"I don't know sir."

"Sure you don't, son. Who the hell would? I'm talking outsourcing Dale. All the rage. Think a hospital. Someone has to clean the goddamn place. Once upon a time the government used to use tax dollars to employ the cleaners and it cost a fortune. Then they decided to out-source and got the private sector to bid against each other. If someone does a shitty job it is easy to cancel the contract and hire in another company. No problems with employment law and stuff. If some Latino cleaner slips on a wet floor and breaks her back, it is her company who needs to worry about the health care. You with me Dale?"

"Sir."

"Then that is good Dale. Real good. This here is the first outsourced war. Not all of it. Not like the old Renaissance Popes who used to pay for Swiss mercenaries to fight their wars. We've not got that far yet. Not yet anyways. No Dale, instead the government is outsourcing parts of this war. Transport. Supply. Security. You know where I'm at here?"

"I do."

"OK. Now. The company I work for doesn't do security and supply. We do getting bad guys. Targets. The Pentagon and Langley get their heads together and try to work out who the biggest targets are. The guys who are a real royal pain in the ass. Then they get the private sector to bid for getting them. You have to admit it's pretty cool. Companies bid for the price on a bad guy's head. The lowest bid gets the tender. That's capitalism in the purest sense Dale. Now let's not get any false ideas here. When I say lowest, we're not talking a few hundred dollars. We're still talking huge piles of dollars. But it's a whole lot less than training and running a Delta team. The cutest bit of all is how much the big investors like it. Think about it. Think if you were managing some great heap of investment fund. Pretty boring job, huh? All ten year bonds and shit. Then you get the chance to make an investment in a few bonds in a company like the one I work for. You don't have to watch trends on the dollar to get your returns. You watch to see if guys like me can get the bad guys we've tendered for. It's good old fashioned bounty hunting gone corporate. That's America son. We've even made a tradeable market out of eliminating bad guys." This made Walters chuckle. "But we always loved Westerns didn't we. You like westerns Dale?"

"Not really sir."

"Pity. You'd make a pretty damn fine Sheriff. That's what you are son. Gary Cooper comes top Famoudi and god bless America."

The CO was clearly getting a little threadbare.

"Captain Nash has things to do Mr Walters. Maybe you could come to the point."

"Oh sure. I would hate to hold you back any, son. Ever heard of 'The Colonel' son?"

The switch was instant. No good old boy from the south now. And Dale had heard of the one known as 'The Colonel'. Every US soldier had. Rumour had it that he had been behind the deaths of many of their comrades.

"I believe I have."

"Sure you have Dale. We all have. That's why my company has put in a record bid for the rights to nail the sonofabitch. That's why I can retire to a big condo in Florida on the commission if I make the hit. We've had word that he has been in Famoudi, Dale. Within the last few days. We heard the word because we were listening. As soon as Charlie Company started playing to the prime time millions, 'The Colonel' was always going to get interested. Your CO here will confirm that you are to render me any assistance that I may require. OK?"

"What kind of assistance sir?"

"I need immediate access to the prisoners as soon as they are apprehended by your teams. I need a discreet space to use to interrogate them."

"Discreet."

"Sure. Discreet. I guess you wouldn't want your guys to listen in on the sound effects. I like to outsource too, Dale. I don't speak Iraqi none and I lack the expertise to get information quickly. So I outsource. I hire in experts. Plenty of that kind of expertise round these parts Dale. Comes real cheap too."

Dale was about to lose it. The fatigue of course. The fatigue and the smugness of the killer across from him. His CO's voice was hard.

"It's non-negotiable Dale. Right down from the top. I don't like it either."

Walters had given up on the act now. "Bring me prisoners Captain Nash. It's all you have to do."

"Then what?"

"No rocket science. Someone out there must be running this stone throwing gig. We find where they live. That's where 'The Colonel' will turn up. Then . . ."

"You outsource that work too?"

A big cold smile. "Sure I do. It's all about team building and delegating Dale. Team building and delegating."

By the time Josh and Lenny reached the M6 it was after eleven. The road was quiet and the night sky was a sea of stars. Lenny's phone trilled. It was Asmo.

"Bloody hell Lenny, that Panorama stuff was out and beyond. You must be made up mate."

The ever-enthusiastic Bolton voice never failed to put a smile on Lenny's face.

"Let's just say it was a pleasant surprise. What impact will it have on our plans?"

"Bloody magic plus a hundred percent. All publicity is good publicity my friend. What we've just got tonight would have cost us six figures if we'd had to buy it off the shelf."

"And how are sales?"

A chuckle. "Sales don't matter Lenny. Sales aren't what we're about right now. That's why the gear isn't on sale anywhere but Dumfries.

Demand is what we're interested in Lenny. Demand. Demand that grows and grows and outstrips supply by a thousand to one."

"So how's demand then?"

"Spectacular. Monumental. I've not got words to talk it up."

"Bloody hell Asmo. I'm lost now. Fair enough, there's been a decent enough crowd here in Dumfries, but I can't see how you can tell all that much from one day."

Again the gleeful chuckle. "You're a dinosaur Lenny. That's why I love you. Too long out of the fresh air. This is 2005 my friend. Measuring demand is easy. Click. Click. Measured. It's called *Ebay*. Heard of it?"

"Some kind of online auction isn't it?"

"More than that Lenny. Much more. It measures value. It measures how much people are willing to pay. It measure what things are worth. For someone like me it is the best tool in the box."

Lenny shook his head. At times talking to Asmo was like doing a Rubik cube. "Let me see if I've got this. You've been putting items of Koz clothing up for auction on Ebay?"

"That's it. Not many. Not in my name. Just enough to see how many bids they attract."

"And?"

"You wouldn't believe it. It's everything we hoped for times five. Best of all. I think our timetable might just get brought forward. Don't you?"

"I hadn't really thought about it. Why?"

"Come on Lenny. Get with the programme. If the government were embarrassed before, just imagine how they feel now. After all this. The last thing they're going to want is hundreds of kids wearing Koz and reminding everyone about what went on twenty years ago. I think it might be time for me to get my friend to make the call. How about you?"

Lenny stared out of the window at the dark fields outside the window.

"When?"

"Tomorrow morning. OK?"

"Yes. OK. Get it done."

"Where will you be?"

"I'm not really sure."

"Just keep the mobile charged."

"No problem. What about stage two Asmo."

Lenny could sense the mood change on the other end of the line. Tense now. Fearful.

"Better than I thought. My contacts are making progress. There might be a way. I'll know in a day or two."

"This is going to happen Asmo. You know that?"

"I know that."

It was gone two by the time they parked up outside the hospital in Sheffield and made their way inside. More ghosts. The ghosts from the burning heat of the battle of Orgreave. The ghost of his father lying as still as stone for days. And now another ghost. A living ghost. Beverly was the ghost of everything that might have been if things had been different. And now things could never be different. Not ever. Because Beverly had come home to die. All that was left was to say goodbye. And to try to tell her despite everything that had happened, something good was going to come. Something better than any of them could ever have dared to dream about. A victory that was so great as to be almost beyond comprehension. Something that would make it worth her hanging on to life for a few extra weeks.

The first woman on the desk was having none of it. She asked if they were actually mad. She asked if they actually knew what the time was. She managed to maintain politeness and basically told them to hop it before she called in the security.

The second woman took no notice at first. She was fully-focused on completing entries into her computer. But when she looked up from her work she started taking a great deal of notice. Her shift had started at midnight which meant that at ten that night she had been glued to her TV screen along with the great majority of the population of South Yorkshire. She recognised Lenny straight away. She knew exactly why he was waiting at the front desk. Three hours earlier the sheer pain of what had been done to them all had brought tears to her cheeks. Her husband too, and he wasn't the crying type. She didn't need to think about the situation for very long.

"Sheila. It's OK. I know about this. Come on lads. I'll take you up."

Long empty corridors with only an occasional cleaner providing any sign of human life. Empty trolleys and wheelchairs. Strip lights. Staff notice boards. A wide eyed nurse on the desk to the ward. A brief hushed conversation, and then on quietly past dark rooms to the door to Beverly's room.

The nurse eased the door open and peered inside. The bedside lamp was on and a discarded book lay on top of the sheets. Beverly was wide awake and staring up at the ceiling. Her head eased down at the sound of the voice.

"There are some visitors love. You alright to see them?"

A nod.

"She's awake. You can go in. She's not very well at all, so don't tire her."

The nurse stepped back and made the way clear for them to go in. And Lenny didn't think that it was possible to take the next step. He was paralysed. Awash with emotion. And scared of what he was about to find. Josh lightly took his elbow and steered him forward.

It wasn't a surprise to Beverley. She had tried so hard not to expect him. But she had failed. She knew Lenny Baxter. She knew him better than she had any right to know him. She knew that it didn't matter how she had hurt him. He would still come through. Through rain and shine and thick and thin and war and peace and day and night. He would come through because he was Lenny and there was only one Lenny and there could never, ever be another. She could have probably even predicted his time of arrival. A few minutes for the programme to finish. Two and a half hours to drive down. A few minutes to blag his way past the front desk. And hey presto. An open door. And there he was.

Neither was surprised at the other's appearance. They had both watched each other on the TV that very evening. Lenny had spent two hundred miles bracing himself for the reality of seeing her at the gates of death. She had braced herself not to be broken into pieces at seeing him still looking like the same old Lenny. Seeing Josh guide him in was a surprise. No reason why it should have been. She had seen Josh on the TV too. And she had been glad. Glad for both of them that after so many years they had been able to find each other again. She should have realised that they would have come together. Because it hadn't only been Lenny that she had betrayed. Josh had been her first betrayal. She tried to keep her head up but as soon as she saw Josh, a memory speared into her. Simmington. An hour shy of closing time. Josh coming out and turning to lock the door. Josh's face caught in the light from the lamp above the door. The sound of his footsteps clacking up the pavement. The sound of the steps fading away into the silence of the small town night.

"I'm sorry. So sorry."

The sound of her voice energised Lenny. He was at the bed side in two strides, taking her bony had between two of his.

"Let's get that bit done and out of the way shall we Beverly. You've done the sorry bit already. In fact you've done it in front of about ten million people. Now as far as I'm concerned that'll do. One word. Accepted. OK? Let's do it Yorkshire and keep it simple. Josh?"

Josh was standing close behind. There was nothing false about the smile on his face. Nothing false about his eyes either. "Of course. Accepted. Hundred percent."

"But . . ."

"There are no buts Beverly. We don't have time for buts. I can't be doing with them anyway."

Typical Lenny. So like his father all of a sudden. No time for bloody moping.

"OK. Sit down. Please. There are chairs."

They found them and took up station by the bedside.

"They don't sell grapes at all night garages. But we found this at a service station."

Lenny reached into his pocket and pulled out a small pot figurine of a coal miner complete with helmet and lamp and pick. "Asouvenir from South Yorkshire. An extinct species I believe. Seemed like it had to be bought."

She smiled as she held it up to the light to examine and the tears started.

"I can't begin to tell you how much I've missed you Lenny."

"Tha doesn't have to. I know it because I guess it's about half as much as I missed you. We had our chance Beverly. We had it and we blew it because other things seemed more important at the time. We were young and daft and if we had our time over happen we'd do things differently. In fact I'm sure we would. Neither of us has exactly had the best of it. But moping about was never our style, so there's not a lot of point starting now. The way I see it we've still got some time. Best thing is to learn our lesson and take it. I'll be going away in a while. Until then, I'm right here. We'll catch up."

"You can't stay here Lenny. What about USY and the centre and everything. You can't just leave it. Not for me. I won't have it."

"From where I'm sitting you're the one in the bed and I'm the one on the chair. I don't fancy your chances of kicking me out so tha might as well give in quietly. You know how stubborn I am."

"Yes. I do."

"So live with it. It's not for negotiation. Everything up there will be fine. I've done my bit. Josh can keep an eye on things. He's off back tonight. We reckon everything will be done and dusted by tomorrow anyway."

"You're going too fast for me Lenny. How? What has happened?"

"You know what has happened. The thing is what's about to happen. That is what I'm going to tell you. That is why you're not allowed to even think of dying. Not yet. Not until we get to the end of the final chapter."

There was a strange gleam in his eyes. What was it? A fervour. A light that wasn't quite sane. Something she had never seen before. Part of her was frightened. Another part was almost exhilarated. Both parts fused together and she felt another faint surge of life. A final twitch on the thread. Once upon a time she had heard how swans made a quite unique noise in their last seconds of life. Their swansong. Her swansong was beginning. Her completion.

The whole concept of the basketball court had become symbolic. Dale Nash knew full well that there was no possibility any more that his men would be running any training workshops with local kids. The idea had gone west from the moment that the stone-throwers had arrived. Now it was all about a trial of strength to be played out in front of the cameras every day. The stone-throwers wanted to provoke the Marines into losing it and firing into the crowd whilst the cameras recorded the crime. In turn the Marines were about proving that their discipline and training was more than enough for them to endure the daily pelting. After a week of fighting out their daily battle for the street, both sides had developed and refined their tactics. The throwers advanced and retreated in small bands of ten or twelve, whilst the Marines were now fully kitted out with Perspex riot shields which they used to make a solid see through wall from which fast snatch squads would emerge to grab the slower running stone-throwers.

Dale always made sure that he had his insurance policy ready and in full view for all to see. Two Bradley Fighting Vehicles always took up a position a few yards behind the Marine lines with their machine gunners primed and ready in the turrets. The message was clear as crystal. If for any reason the stone throwers escalated the action, then the gunners could go through them like a harvester through a ripe field of Kansas wheat. The machine guns acted as a fully visible reminder of where the real power lay and guaranteed the rules of the game.

For a few days Dale had actually got to quite enjoy it. In a way it was as good a thing as the barbeque and the basketball project. If the disillusioned youngsters of Famoudi could get things off their chests by throwing a few stones, then that had to be better than allowing themselves to be talked into becoming suicide bombers. But Walters had changed everything. Dale was sickened by the thought of what would happen to any of the kids his squads managed to catch. Just kids. Many of them looked like they were barely teenagers. And yet he was completely helpless to do anything else. Walters had insisted in coming along as an observer and his CO had made it more than clear that Walters had backing from way on high. All that Dale had been able to do was to send the word down through the sergeants that none of the younger ones should be lifted. It wasn't much, but it was all he could think of.

Charlie Company arrived at the half built court at their usual hour. Nobody bothered making a start on any work. Instead, the men got themselves ready for the arrival of the stone-throwers.

Peggy Hill was growing rather anxious at the new turn of events. To start with the stone-throwing had made great TV in every way. Split heads and lots of movement. Then for a day or two there had been an intrinsic interest in watching the young captain refine his tactics to deal with the new situation. But for several days now it had all become the same and there was an imminent danger that it was about to become boring. She struggled through her accustomed pre-action interview with Dale and was frustrated that she couldn't think of any fresh angles. A few more days like this and the whole thing would start to die on its feet. As she was about to ask her final stale question, a radioman came over to Dale and passed him a headset. As he stepped away and held a conversation her hopes started to lift a little. His face clouded as he glanced up to where a helicopter hovered a few hundred feet above them. After a few minutes he handed the headset back and came to her.

"I need you and your people to get behind the Bradleys maam."

"Is there a problem?"

Dale gave a grim smile. "No problem maam. That was the chopper on the line. Looks like we have extra guests coming this morning. Things might get a little choppy for a while."

As the ABC team retreated to the relative safety of the Bradley's, Dale called his sergeants to him. By now the crowd was already starting to fill the far end of the street. He gave his instructions fast and they nodded their understanding. They sprinted back to their platoons and passed on their orders.

Dale gave all his attention to the far end of the street. The chopper pilot hadn't exaggerated. There were several hundred already and they just kept on coming. At first he had been highly dubious of the pilot's estimate of two thousand. Not any more. In fact it was starting to look more like an underestimate. He took a look back to make sure the camera team was as safe as was possible. They were. And as he glanced he caught an amused stare from Walters who was standing by the second Bradley with his hands in his pockets. Sonofabitch.

He wiped the thoughts and focused back in on the street. It seemed as if most of the stone-throwers had arrived now. They were coming on fast, chanting with their fists held high. He checked his line. Not bad. Forty wide, two deep. Three four man snatch squads in reserve ready to make their move. The crowd stopped thirty yards short of the line of Perspex. Instead of immediately starting up with the stones they paused to run through a series of chants. They certainly made an impressive noise. The sound of their voices bounced up and around the broken buildings that closed in the street.

At last the first half brick flew in from the back of the crowd and smacked into a shield. It started. The sky was suddenly filled with a rain of stone. The Marines crouched low and ducked under their shields. Instead of the sound of chanting voices, the street was now filled with the sound of stone on plastic and the wild battle cry of the crowd. Coming forward now. Twenty yards. Ten. It was what he had feared. The size if the mob would give it a new momentum. Those at the back would give no choice to those at the front. Today things would go hand to hand. And once their lines became blurred the insurance policy of the guns atop the Bradleys would mean nothing. Five yards now and he could see the terror on the faces of those at the front of the mob who were being pushed onto the shields. It was about to happen. Just a few seconds. Nothing would stop it.

Dale was at the centre of the lines, a few yards back.

He waved in the snatch squads to him and turned to the sergeant next to him.

"Ready?"

"Sir!!"

"OK. Let's go"

The sergeant held a flare gun with straight arm and fired. As the red explosion burst above them, the front line of Marines parted five yards and Dale lead the snatch team forward in a head down screaming charge. They hit the front wall of the crowd like a runaway truck and smashed forward with flailing batons as the rest of their lines started to advance. Dale's team cut into the crowd like a sharp wedge whilst the solid line of shields pushed and opened up the breach. It didn't last long. Those at the back of the crowd felt the pressure turn around on them. The helicopter had swooped down low to fill the street with noise and dust. Panic set in fast and soon the crowd was streaming out of the street pursued by the Marines.

Dale had hold of the collar of a writhing young rioter. He ignored the wild kicks and wrenched the scarf from the boy's face. Terrified eyes no more than twelve years old stared back at him. He released his grip and sent the boy packing with a hefty kick to his backside.

All around him he saw that his men were repeating the process. In the end they only came back with three prisoners, all of who seemed to be in their early twenties. Walters had joined him now.

"I don't remember anybody saying anything about throwing fish back into the river son."

"Go to hell Walters."

Dale barged past him. Walters just smiled and shouted after him.

"My oh my. Ain't it just dandy to see some real corn-fed American idealism. You're in the wrong war Dale. Guys like you went west with John Wayne."

Jed Thompson stepped off the plane into fresh morning air. The wind was straight off the Irish Sea and he felt instantly energised. The break had done him a power of good. He had been running on tanks that were lower than he had allowed himself to admit. The battle at the gates of bankruptcy had raged for almost five years and it had taken a heavy toll.

But now, as he paused at the foot of the steps and took in the crisp blue of the sky, he had a warm feeling that the corner had at last been turned.

The feeling stayed with him all the way to the entrance to the baggage reclaim area and then it ended abruptly. His path was blocked by a huge lump of a man with a identity badge that said policeman.

"Jed Thompson? I'm Frank Dixon. Dumfries and Galloway Police. Would you come along with me please. Just a few questions."

Jed knew the tone well enough. This was a case of being nice in a public place, but he had a distinct feeling that the big man would be more than happy to stop being so nice if that was what was required.

Beside him his wife looked as if she had just been force-fed a month old kipper. Jed tried to keep his voice light.

"It's OK love. Probably just some mistake. Has to be. You grab the bags and go and get yourself a cup of tea. I'll meet you in a few minutes."

"But . . . ."

Frank could see from her body language that a scene was mere seconds away. He took Thompson firmly by the elbow and whisked him through a door marked 'Private. Staff Only.' No care had been taken over the corridor behind the door. Grey breezeblock walls and bleak strip lighting. Frank led the way and opened the fourth door and waited for Jed to go inside.

Once again he found himself in a non-décor area. The room was again breezeblock, this time whitewashed. Strip light. A simple metal table with three chairs. Acouple of rather frayed posters warning everyone to stay alert to the terror threat hung somewhat dolefully on the wall.

"Have a seat Jed."

It was all very strange. This didn't have the feel of a room used for routine police interrogation. There was no tape on the table. The second copper had called him by his first name. And the second copper didn't fit either. It was the uniform. Jed was no expert, but the man's uniform seemed to speak of high office. He was in the middle of this thought when the Chief Constable introduced himself and confirmed his suspicion.

"You lads going to read me my rights?"

The Chief sat back and tapped away with a pen. Frank took up a station perched on the edge of the table so that he stared down into Jed's face as he talked.

"Not yet Jed. Maybe later. That will be down to you."

By now a cold fear was creeping through Jed. This could only be about one thing. This was about Buccleuch Street and it was serious. It was time to shut up shop and say nothing. He was fairly confident that Latimer would turn up with the cavalry at some stage. Frank started talking in a matter of fact tone.

"The bad news Jed. We've got you stone cold pal. I'll take you through it. No need to go into great detail. You're not a fool. We got a warrant Jed, to search your offices. I suppose you'll know well enough what we found. Enough for quite a lump of time. Forged Tachograph records. Drivers' hours sheets that looked like adverts for Tippex. A big tank full of red diesel. And a couple of grand's worth of fags that didn't seem to have the 'Duty Paid' label anywhere to be seen. Not good Jed. Not good at all. Now maybe with a decent lawyer you might manage to beat a charge or two. But not all of them Jed. And it will only take one or two for your bank to come piling in and grab what they can while the going is good. We've seen the books Jed. Rocky. Very rocky. It will mean no more trucks and no more house and no more car. Not a happy prospect Jed, especially for a man of your age. The world can be unforgiving on our generation when we find ourselves on our uppers. Are you listening to me Jed?"

"I'm listening." Jed was focusing very hard on keeping his expression blank. But the colour was draining out of him with every fresh revelation.

"All of that is fairly trivial Jed. The bigger stuff is what went on down in Buccleuch Street. Arson and grievous bodily harm done to a colleague of mine. We take that very seriously Jed. We take it seriously enough to do everything in our power to make sure you'll be in the nick until you're eligible for a bus pass. So I suggest you keep on listening Jed. OK?"

Jed nodded. He wondered if the senior officer was going to say anything. Now the older man had linked his fingers together and stopped with the pen tapping. Frank kept on.

"I've spent my weekend reading all about your life Jed. It's a good story. Interesting. Especially all the parts that don't quite add up. And there are a few of them Jed. Let's kick off with 84. You come out of the army and fall straight onto the dole. A few months drifting from dead end job to dead end job until all of a sudden you've got yourself an HGV licence and a wagon. Now that seems interesting to me. How could that happen in the middle of a recession? Maybe a rich aunt from Canada died? Or maybe some of your old army mates got you a bit of work as a strike breaker? The record doesn't mention any rich aunts. Now. Fast forward. After a few years of very modest accounts you suddenly find the cash to extend your fleet. Now this is the kind of thing that jumps out at me Jed. I'm a drug squad man you see. I just hate anomalies like this. I get to thinking about where you were going to at that time? And where you were coming back from? And what might you have been coming back with that enabled you to buy all those new wagons? But when I looked, it wasn't like I thought it would be. Not Amsterdam or Istanbul. Leipzig. Leipzig a year before the wall came down. Hardly one of great drug capitals of Europe Jed. So where did all the money come from? If it wasn't something you were taking out, then maybe it was something you were taking in. Now that would be interesting, wouldn't it? But I expect you must have fitted someone's bill pretty well. Ex-soldier. Done a bit of strike breaking. Hungry for cash. Not averse to a risk or two."

Frank paused and ran his fingers through his hair before moving on.

"Which brings us all the way to where we are today. Business has been bad Jed. Not hard to see that. Not having spent a bit of time with your books. You were on target to go pop before the autumn. And then lo and behold, you get a nice fat government contract to haul building materials into the Royal Navy Dockyard in Rosyth. Quite a break Jed. Almost as if somebody was repaying you for a favour. Somebody with an office right up near the top floor. Because you need an office up at the top of the building to be able to pick up the phone and persuade someone to give out a nice fat government contract. So I wrote down all the facts and I think I have an inkling as to what is going on here. Would you like me to tell you Jed?"

"I can't wait."

"You don't have to. I believe that what was going on in Buccleuch Street was in danger of opening a few cupboard doors that had been locked for many, many years. And I think there were rather a lot of skeletons in the aforesaid cupboards. Somebody decided it was time to protect themselves. For whatever reason, they didn't want Lenny Baxter and USY looking good for the cameras. So they picked up the phone and dialled rent-a-riot. You Jed. Just the man. Reliable and discreet. The right age. Asteady hand. And my word you made quite a job of it."

"Sounds like a fairytale to me."

"Yes. I suppose it does. In fact I dare say we wouldn't be too bothered about putting any of that in court. I think we would probably just stick with the Tachograph records, and falsified drivers' hours, and the red diesel, and the contraband cigarettes, and the arson, and the conspiracy to riot. Yes. I think we would be inclined to keep it pretty simple Jed."

Jed couldn't help but wince. If the cavalry didn't come riding over the hill he was all washed up and finished. Maybe it was time to try and find out just what was happening.

"What do you want?"

Finally the Chief leaned forward and spoke for the first time. "I think we all know what is happening here Jed. Someone called you and did a deal. Turn Buccleuch Street into a blazing riot and you get a big Government contract. I would dearly love to put you somewhere far away from the sunshine for a long, long time. But not half as much as much as I want to do the same and more to whoever it was who made the call. Simple deal Jed. Co-operate and tell us all of it, and there will be no charges. You can even keep the Rosyth contract. I want the man who made the call. Right now, he will be sweeping every shred of evidence under the carpet. So I'm not hanging around for an answer here Jed. I want it now. Yes or no. It's a one time offer. I want a name and a statement or I will personally make sure that the rest of your life will be a prolonged misery."

Jed knew that these were words without bluff. The policemen knew well enough that they held every card in the deck. The only decision that was required of him was whether or not he was about to fall on his sword. It wasn't a decision that took him long.

"OK. Here's how I'll play this out. I give you the name. You take me to my lawyer. Then I make the statement. I want the immunity offer signed in my lawyer's office before I make any kind of statement."

A slow smile spread across the Chief's face.

"That sounds reasonable to me. Name please."

"Latimer. Sir Edward Latimer."

The First Minister was in his office before seven that morning, a good hour and a half before Jed Thomas's plane hit the tarmac at Prestwick

Airport. Like the rest of the country, he had been glued to the TV the night before to watch the Panorama programme. There would be all kinds of fallout and all his instincts told him that he should be worried about it. He had barely slept at all as his brain tried to spot the bear traps that would be waiting for him. But the more he thought about it, the more it seemed as if it might not be such a problem for him after all. It was going to be a hell of a problem for someone down in Whitehall. Latimer was about to be served up on toast. The man would be lucky to escape being locked up in the Tower of London. And London was the key. This was a London problem from to top to bottom. Not Edinburgh. The only reason that he would be drawn in at all was that the whole USY business happened to have gone down on Scottish soil. All of a sudden all the fuss about the youth centre would take a back seat. The story had moved on. If he played his cards right, he could keep all the heat a good three hundred miles away from where he was sitting.

Already he had made a call to Dumfries to find out how things were looking. The Chief Constable was out of the office and was not expected back that day. Bloody ridiculous. The whole world was going crazy and the man had buggered off. The second in command had informed him that cars had been turning up in the town all through the night and already Buccleuch Street. was packed. The cars were heading in from all over Britain apparently. Kids mostly. They were coming to buy clothes.

The First Minister sat for a while and stared at the phone in confusion. Why in God's name would anyone in their right mind drive through the night to buy clothes off a market stall in Dumfries. It was completely beyond him. If they would be happy enough just buying clothes then he would have been happy enough to say why not, fair play to them. But buying clothes was only going to be a part of the experience. The other part would be throwing a few stones at the police. He had seen all the adverts. In fact he had already requested that his legal people should examine the adverts and see if some sort of case could be built against the manufacturer of the Koz range for inciting violence. The problem with that idea was that it would take ages. Anything involving courts and lawyers took forever and a day. And he certainly didn't have forever and a day.

His intercom buzzed and he picked it up.

"Yes?"

His secretary sounded nervous. She had sounded that way for days. Ever since he had started biting her head off every time she spoke and that had started when the good folk of Dumfries had gone crazy.

"There's a call sir."

"For God's sake woman. Didn't I make myself clear. No bloody calls Not until after seven-thirty. Not even if it's the damned Pope."

"It's Mr Iqbal sir."

"Oh." Mr Iqbal was a completely different proposition to the Pope. He was a man who could call the First Minister any time of the day or night. The Pakistani had settled in the First Minister's Glasgow constituency in the early sixties and had gone on to become one of Scotland's most dramatically successful entrepreneurs. His empire was centred on a factory that manufactured a range of microwave curry dishes which employed over six hundred of the First Minister's constituents. More than this, the tycoon had taken up the cause of the politically ambitious shop steward many years earlier. He had supported him onto the local council. He had come up with campaign funds to see him elected as one of the first intake of MSPs into the new Scottish Parliament. And now by some distance he was the largest financial backer of the First Minister's Party in Scotland. So when he called the First Minister was in. Always.

"Put him through . . . Omar . . . Good morning to you . . . how's business my friend?"

"Allah continues to be generous. And you First Minister? You are well? And all of your family?"

"Absolutely. All thriving thank you. How can I help?"

"Well, maybe I can help you."

"Nothing new in that Omar. Fire away."

He sat back and waited to see what it was. At least it didn't look as if it was going to be a problem. The polite voice at the other end of the phone continued.

"I think I am right in assuming that events in Dumfries must be somewhat embarrassing at the moment."

Interesting. Where was this going? "Alittle. Nothing we are losing too much sleep over."

"Would you like it to stop?"

Very interesting. "Yes. Of course. Do you have something in mind Omar?"

"In fact, I do. I have spoken with the young man behind the Koz clothing range. An interesting young man. Rather a fine future ahead of him I would think. He has rather an interesting proposal which he requested that I might put to you."

"I see."

"He feels that the main reason young people will be coming to Dumfries is to purchase Koz items. He has ensured that this is the case by restricting sales of the new range. Dumfries is essentially the only place in the world where one can find the goods on sale."

"Yes. I had heard as much."

"It really is very clever you know. There is always value in scarcity. Very clever indeed. Anyway. I digress. Obviously the crux of the issue in Dumfries is the building known as McIntosh House and the demands of local youth that it should be converted into a leisure facility. Correct?"

"Yes. That is correct."

"Well I am in a position to help you to resolve the situation. Conclusively and quickly."

Unbelievably interesting. "Indeed. Pray continue."

"My friend is willing to provide funds to enable the Dumfries Council to change their minds. He will double whatever the property developers are paying as well as providing cash to convert the building. However he is adamant that this must be entirely confidential. As far as the public is concerned, the money will be coming from the Council."

"Oh dear."

"Yes. I thought you would see it that way. It is why he has chosen this approach. He thinks that the Council will dig their heels in and be stubborn. Such a course of action would ensure that the situation in Dumfries continues to escalate. Such an outcome would have an increasingly damaging effect on your administration First Minister. None of us want that. Especially those of us who have invested in you."

"I see."

"I hoped that you would."

"What do you have in mind Mr Iqbal?"

"My young friend will pay the money over to me and I will in turn feed it into you. You can find an appropriate channel to send the money down to the Council in Dumfries. Your main task of course will be to pressure them into changing their minds. I have every confidence that you are more than capable of achieving such an outcome."

The First Minister drummed his fingers and considered. It wasn't much of a choice really. He wasn't about to upset his number one benefactor. Not over this. If it meant knocking a few heads together then so be it. It was something that he did most days.

"OK. Mr Iqbal. Consider it done. May I ask why?"

"Why what First Minister?"

"Why does the money have to come from the Council. Why doesn't he just want to build a place himself and get all the plaudits."

"Because it is important that the young people feel that they have been victorious."

"Oh yes. Of course. This could open up a can of worms you know."

"I am an old man who can remember how it was to be young. Maybe this is a can of worms that should be opened. Maybe we need some angry young people feeling that they have the power to make changes. I think that you might feel the same First Minister?"

Sudden images of marches and protest banners and T-shirts demanding no more atomic weapons and freedom for Mandela. Iqbal was probably right. In fact he was definitely right. Too many around the First Minister spent too much time forgetting how it once had been when they were young. Before they allowed their lives to be ruled by choosing the right pension package or BMW car or villa on the Algarve. Yes. Maybe it would be a good thing to allow the youth of Dumfries to win for once.

"Give me twenty four hours Mr Iqbal."

Lenny woke when the late afternoon sunshine found the right angle to slant in through the window onto his sleeping face. For a moment he was completely disorientated. He was in a chair. White walls. Medical equipment. But when he turned his head he found that Beverly was smiling as she stared down into his face from the bed.

"I think you needed that."

He rubbed at his eyes and pushed his hair back into place.

"How long have I been asleep?"

"Nearly six hours."

"Bloody hell."

She could see his brain switch into instant overdrive. "I can give you an update if you want."

"Oh. Yes. Please do."

"Buccleuch Street. has been one big log jam all day. The police have actually had to set up some road blocks on the edge of Dumfries as the town is so full that public safety is threatened. Certain parts of the media are reporting that they have received a leak that the Council is about to do a U-turn and grant funds for a new Zone Centre at McIntosh House."

Now he was smiling. "Did they say where the leak came from?"

She matched his smile. They had talked through the quiet hours of the night and she was fully up to speed with the USY battle plan. "Edinburgh."

"Perfect. It looks like Asmo's man has come through. Bloody hell Beverly we might have the thing in the bag by tomorrow."

She picked up his mobile phone from where it lay on top of the covers.

"I have been fielding calls for you. Asmo is here. He rang a few minutes ago. I told him that you were asleep so he said he would go and find somewhere to get a coffee. He said to call him when you resurfaced."

"I'll go and find him."

"Bring him here Lenny. I would like to meet him."

"You don't want to overdo things Bev . . . ."

"Lenny. I'm dying. What I do or don't do won't alter that. Now you have chosen to bring me in on this thing of yours. OK. I'm in. One last task. But you can't have it all ways. If you want me in on this you get the old Beverly, not a fading cripple who you have to wrap in cotton wool. That's the deal Lenny."

He stood and looked down at her ravaged face. Had he been right to come? Should he have left her in peace? At first he had come on the spur of the moment. But there had been two hundred miles of night road for him to change his mind. But instead of changing his mind he had realised that he still needed her. She was the last piece in the jig-saw. In the game he was about to play he was going to need someone who he could trust. Absolutely trust. Not only that, he needed someone who would carry things through in spite of the consequences. Beverly was the perfect choice. The job he needed to be done was perfect for someone at the gates of death. It was the only place where the consequences wouldn't matter. He smiled down at her pale face. The disease was eating her alive and yet a fierce spirit still burned.

"Of course. No more cotton wool talk. I'll go get him. It's good that the two of you can meet."

They returned together a few minutes later. Asmo was a bundle of barely contained energy. He never missed a beat at the sight of death staring him straight in the face. He reached out to shake her thin hand and was soon into his fast talking stride.

"I reckon the job's all but done. My man had a talk this morning and he got the nod. I fired off the cash just back of twelve and he rang me before to say he'd done the same. Did you hear the stuff about the leak from Edinburgh."

"Aye. Beverly just told me."

Asmo gave a shrug. "My man reckons they'll announce tomorrow morning. End of story. Koz will be out Nationwide by the close of play. All wrapped up. Not bad if you ask me."

"You mean Plan A all wrapped up. I presume you're not about to forget Plan B."

The idea of Plan B clearly took all the wind from the young Asian's sails. He slumped down into the chair by the bed.

"You really sure about this Lenny?"

"Never been surer. I do hope this isn't the start of a cold feet speech."

"Course I've got cold feet. Who the bloody hell wouldn't have cold feet? I mean there's close to the edge and there's over the edge. And this is about ten miles over the edge. I don't know Lenny. I really don't. I mean I've just got there haven't I. After all these years I've made it. Koz is going massive. Bigger than massive . . ."

Lenny's voice became very firm. "Think back Asmo. Think back to when we shook on this thing. Remember what you said. You told me that you wanted to take Koz all the way. Right up there to the top of three with Nike and Reebok. Remember?"

"Aye, but…"

"No buts Asmo. It's what you said. It's what we agreed. It's what we shook on Asmo. Your word. I shook because I trusted that word. Please don't tell me that I was wrong."

The younger man bowed his head. "You weren't wrong Lenny. I'm not backing out like. It's just . . ."

"Just what Asmo?"

"Bloody hell Lenny, I just don't want to die, that's all. That's not so bad is it?"

"It isn't bad at all. I'm not over keen on the idea myself. Neither is Beverly. Cliché time Asmo. We're all dying every minute of our lives. We know it, we just don't like thinking about it. Tick, tock, oops-a-daisy, another minute closer to death. The only variable factor is the timing. We're all dead men walking. It's merely a question of how long we walk for. And how we walk. Heads down and frightened. Or heads up and kicking."

Asmo's head sank lower and lower.

"I don't know if I'm ready for all this Lenny."

"You're ready Asmo. All your life has brought you to this moment. So you can either play it safe and become another rich boy trying to find a few kicks by throwing cash around in places where they sell champagne for £300 a bottle. Or you can become a someone. A real someone. A someone who will get talked about down the ages. And one day you will be a dead someone. The day may be soon. Or the day may be sixty years away. But you'll always be that someone."

Asmo still didn't want to lift his head back up. "I think I have some news. From Pakistan. It looks like there might be a way. I'll hear more later tonight."

Lenny's eyes lit up bright. What had been a crazy pipe dream had just come nearer to reality.

"Will it be soon?"

"If the information firms up it can be as soon as the next few days."

"Soon enough then. Soon enough."

Asmo looked into his eyes to try and find a trace of fear. None. Lenny Baxter had moved away from where he lived his life. He was already in another place. Asmo had seen other men who had found the place where Lenny Baxter had reached. He had seen them in the videos from Gaza and Iraq. Young men with an eerie air of placidity. Contentment. Ready to blow themselves to kingdom come for a ticket to Paradise. His faith fell a long way short of that kind of certainty. He couldn't help but wonder what kind of Paradise was drawing Lenny Baxter forward. And he realised it was something that he would never know. Only two people seemed to understand the road he was so determined to walk down. Josh and Beverly. Three people all broken up by life. Three people determined to chase one last rainbow.

It was after six o'clock by the time that Latimer had cleared up all his affairs. He had written his letter of resignation and had it sent into the office via a courier. Then he had taken the phone off the hook and closed his mind to the mayhem that was sweeping through the corridors of Whitehall. It took most of the afternoon for him to move his funds around into places where the money would be easily available and safe from prying eyes. Then he packed a single case and booked a taxi to take him to the airport.

He was sipping at a Scotch when the front door announced the arrival of the cab. He knocked the drink back and took a last look around his office before heading for the door. He had hoped to go a little further, but all in all he didn't have many complaints. His career had been long and satisfying. He was a very wealthy man, and he had made his money without having to endure years of tedium like most of his contemporaries. Years of dry paper pushing in law offices or the City. He had spent forty years in the fast lane and he didn't regret a single minute. Some rode horses and chased foxes. Others slaughtered pheasants. Others knocked lumps off each other on the rugby field. But he had played the real game. A deadly game all the way from Ireland to Leipzig to Haddington to the Middle East.

He opened the door and froze. Not a cab driver. Two policemen. A sergeant and someone more senior. What the hell was this?

"Edward Latimer?"

"Yes."

"Sergeant Frank Dixon. Dumfries and Galloway Police."

"What…"

"Edward Latimer, I am arresting you on suspicion of . . ."

"Excuse me, but have you any idea whatsoever who I am?"

The second man spoke this time "I think after last night's television the whole of the country knows exactly who you are. And what you are."

"And who might you be? Another lackey?"

"Not quite. I am the Chief Constable of Dumfries and Galloway Police Force. Carry on please Frank."

" . . . of arson and inciting violence. You do not have to say anything . . . ."

"Where are you taking me?"

"The police station of course."

"I demand a call to my solicitor."

The Chief smiled reasonably. "Of course you do. Remember to tell him that it is Dumfries Police Station. I expect he will want to pack some overnight things."

Latimer was suddenly finding it quite hard to get his breath. Anger was taking hold. Anger like he could never remember. Who the hell did these people think they were? Two bit nobodies from some hick town in Scotland. They were going to pay for this. Really pay.

"You have no idea of how much you will regret this. I will destroy you. Annihilate you. It will take three telephone calls. Just that."

The Chief stepped in a little closer. "Oh really. It rather seems to me as if you are all out of friends Sir Edward. You'd better get used to being yesterday's man. Yesterday's man and today's news. So don't get your hopes up. Not that you are going to be making any calls for a while."

Latimer was red-faced now. "I will be making calls within 48 hours. That's how long you have Chief Constable. Forty-eight hours and I will be on the phone. You think I don't have files. I'm not about to call in favours. I will demand them. Because you had better get your thick provincial head around the fact that I know where the bodies are buried Mr policeman. All of them. Thirty years worth. I can bring down careers faster than you can write your name. So dream on. Take me if you want. I'll stare at you for 48 hours and then you will let me go and I will take you apart piece by piece."

"And who said anything about 48 hours Mr Latimer?"

Latimer gave an icy smile. "It's called the law of the land. You either charge me or release me. Even if you charge me do you seriously think that I am not about to make bail?"

"Oh. I see. That is where you get this 48-hour idea from. I must remind you however that only applies in the case of normal, run of the mill criminality. You might have forgotten that the new Anti Terrorist Legislation gives me the power to hold you for as long as I want . . . ."

"The Anti Terrorism Law!! Are you absolutely barking mad?" He was losing it now.

The Chief stepped in even closer so that his face was no more than three inches from Latimer's. "When highly paid officials from the security forces of another country conspire to burn down buildings and incite riot in my town, yes, I consider it to be an act of terrorism."

"What the hell are you talking about, another country . . . ."

Now the Chief smiled. "It's a country called England. I live in a country called Scotland. Some might call it small print. I call it history. So yes Mr Latimer. You are now held under the Anti terrorism Act. And when I'm done with you, I've also had a wee chat with my colleague in South Yorkshire who looks forward to asking some questions of his own. Finish up and cuff him Frank."

" . . . but anything that you do say may be used against you. Hold your hands out please sir. Thank you."

Frank Dixon snapped on the handcuffs and guided a suddenly bewildered Edward Latimer to where their car waited.

Walter Billingham was in the mood to kick something. Anything. Preferably something about twelve years old in a baseball cap. He had left the office on Friday fully confident that the whole thing was in the process of fizzling out. Buccleuch Street was at last effectively sealed off and a couple of calls to colleagues in the education offices had conformed that there were no more than a handful of pickets outside. Friday had been the first day when attendance of the Buccleuch Street. staff had finally got more or less back to normal.

Some colleagues had actually shown some sympathy for the USY campaign. They made Walter sick. As if throwing good money after bad would make the slightest bit of difference to the offspring of the human offal that resided in Sunnybank. As far as he was concerned, the whole miserable place was a festering pit of benefit cheats and drug addicts. He saw it first hand. He saw how that lousy few acres ate up millions upon millions of council resources. Social work, criminal justice, parole, community service, housing benefit, sickness benefit, community care grants, it never, ever ended. Every time anyone wanted to invest in something to take the town back to the place it had once been they were told that there was no way that the money could be found. Forget any cash going on a new Arts centre, every last penny was always hoovered up by the scrounging masses of Sunnybank.

Watching Baxter march his legions of baseball capped acolytes into Buccleuch Street had made Billingham feel almost physically sick with anger. And just who the hell did the man think he was anyway? He wasn't even local. A bloody Yorkshireman. A pinko relic from the bad old days. For Billingham the principle of the fight against USY had always been far more important that any practicalities. Councils couldn't make decisions on the basis of being threatened by teenagers with half bricks in their hands. It had been tough, but he had won over a majority of his senior colleagues. This was a time for the Council to dig its heels in. To show a bit of resolve. To remind everyone who was actually in charge.

He had left the office on Friday evening with a warm glowing feeling of achievement. USY had thrown everything they had at them and they had stood firm through it all. By the time he made his way into work on Monday morning that feeling had become a very distant memory. Buccleuch Street. was a seething mass of bodies. As he forced his way through he heard accents from all over Britain. The whole thing had spiralled completely out of control. It was the bloody Panorama programme of course. That and the whole Koz business. He couldn't begin to get his head around what that was all about. He had seen the adverts of course. Who hadn't. He couldn't see anything different about the Koz clothes and all the other clothes that young people seemed to want to wear. The afternoon before he had gritted his teeth as his son had flounced in with a stupid grin on his face and a Koz top on. He had actually done a twirl in front of his mother who had coo cooed like some idiotic moron. His son hadn't even acknowledged the presence of his father in the same room. Walter had pulled his paper closer to him and done his best to ignore them.

His day had started badly and gone downhill from there. Other than himself, only two others had bothered to make it into work. He had hammered away at the phones to try and hound in a few others, but he had no success. At eleven he had a totally unprofessional blazing row with a union official who said that his members couldn't possibly be expected to put themselves in danger by coming to work. Billingham had screamed down the phone. Where did the cretin think Walter Billingham was? In work. In Buccleuch Street. And he had arrived at eight-thirty just like he did every day of his life. The voice on the other end off the phone had been condescending. Of course it was up to the management to make their own personal choices. He would advise all his members to stay at home until their safety was clearly guaranteed by the police.

The police! Another joke. He had blazed away at the Chief Constable's secretary. The bloody man was away for the day. London. Buccleuch Street. looked like something out of 1968 and the man had swanned off to London on a jolly. Swine. Complete and utter swine. He had set up a portable TV in his office and tried to get some kind of handle on what was in store for the rest of the week. All any of them seemed to want to talk about was the Koz phenomenon. Every time they mentioned the word they couldn't keep stupid grins off their faces. They took reports from all over the place which all told the same story. Groups of teenagers from Bristol to Inverness were interviewed. Koz was it. Koz was the business. And all of them said that they would be heading to Dumfries to get a piece of it. Camera shots of clapped-out cars packed full of grinning youngsters giving the thumbs up to the cameras. Unbelievable. Completely unbelievable.

And then the news was full of the story that the Council was about to cave in. That set him off on another raging round of phone calls but nobody seemed to know anything. And yet the reporters all seemed sickeningly sure of their ground and then in the middle of the afternoon it became clear that the leak had started up in Edinburgh. Typical. Absolutely typical. That lot up in Edinburgh had about as much backbone as a jellyfish. As five o'clock approached Walter Billingham was sick of it. All of it. He was going to go home and sit in the garden and drink about half a bottle of Scotch. The hell with USY. The hell with the gutless wonders up in the capital. Sick of his pathetic spendaholic wife. Sick of his insolent swine of a son. Sick, sick, sick.

As he was rising to go the phone rang. Leave it. Everyone else did. Everyone else had stayed at home and pottered about in their gardens. Why should it always be him? But he picked it up on the seventh ring.

"Yes." He snapped out the greeting.

"Walter Billingham?"

"Yes. Who the hell is this?"

When the First Minister announced himself it was like a punch in the stomach. Billingham sank back down. He had made the mistake of thinking that the day wasn't going to get any worse for the simple reason that it couldn't get any worse. Wrong, wrong, wrong Walter. Things could always get worse because life was an unrelenting bitch of a business. The voice on the phone told him that enough was enough. What was going on down in Dumfries was making Scotland into a worldwide laughing stock. The time had come for a line to be drawn. Funds would be made available for the Council to develop McIntosh House as a new youth centre operated by The Zone. The Executive would transfer twice the amount that the developer had offered for the site. Billingham had tried to argue that backing down would be a mistake. It would send out the wrong kind of message and the First Minister had told him that such policy decisions were for elected politicians working at national level. They were not decisions to be made by local civil servants. He made it very clear that it was Walter Billingham's job to act as a tool of government. It wasn't for him to think about policy. He was to do the paperwork and make sure that the policy of the government was carried out. He asked Billingham if he understood what it was that he was saying as if Billingham was some kind of moron. And Billingham said that he did because he sensed something dangerous in the man's tone.

It was nothing less than a complete railroading. He had been set up. As he had been working the phones in his office all day whilst the mob outside had chanted and bayed, people up in Edinburgh had been carefully putting together the jig-saw of his humiliation. A room had been booked at the University. All reporters in the area would be informed at five o'clock. Informed that Dumfries and Galloway Council would be holding a Press Conference at six o'clock. And Dumfries and Galloway Council's position would be explained by Mr Walter Billingham. He would inform the media that after great consultation and consideration the Council had decided to reverse its decision with regard to the site at McIntosh House and that full funds would now be made available for the Zone Project to develop the site. He wasn't to worry about circumventing normal due process. All of that would be smoothed over. The First Minister took great care to assure Billingham that conducting the Press Conference would do nothing but enhance his career. He also made it very clear that he would personally make it his business to ensure that Billingham would never even get a job as a dustman if he wavered a single degree from the agreed plan.

By the time Billingham put his phone back down he felt as if he had been assaulted. Violated. He felt sick to the stomach and he knew he had absolutely no choices.

An hour later he got to his feet in front of the TVcameras and flash guns. A speech had been waiting for him when he arrived at the hall. Viewers all over Britain agreed that the man from the Council looked like he was involved in a lemon sucking competition.

But he made the speech.

And he conceded the defeat.

Josh had arrived at the hospital in the late afternoon. He confirmed that he had acquired everything on the list that he and Lenny had put together on the drive down from Dumfries. It was all packed away in the back of a white Mercedes van that he had purchased from a garage in Barnsley. The technical stuff had taken a bit of tracking down, but he had got there eventually. The people in the shops had given him a pretty good run-down on how everything worked. Nothing was all that complicated. He assured Beverly that all the stuff he had left at her mother's house was simple enough. Not that she had to worry about it. Asmo was going to send a mate round when the time came.

He laughed when he explained that the hardest part had been the passports and went on to describe a distinctly hairy half hour spent in the dodgiest pub he had ever walked into. But yes. No problem. He had both of them. Done and dusted.

They all settled down to watch the live coverage of Walter Billingham telling the world that Dumfries and Galloway Council had changed its mind. The man looked as if the words were like sulphuric acid in his mouth. Josh and Lenny both remembered him clearly from the days when he would push by them on Buccleuch Street.

"They couldn't have given the job to a better guy." Lenny was grinning with delight as Billingham angrily pushed his papers into his briefcase and informed the reporters that there would be no opportunity for them to ask questions.

And then Lenny suddenly realised that this was the Press Conference that should have happened twenty years earlier. It should have been a man from the Coal Board speaking the words that felt like poison in his mouth. It should have been McGregor or Thatcher who had to face the massed ranks of the media and admit defeat. Maybe somewhere his dad could see the TV screen. And Frank. Even Williams. And maybe seeing this small victory might just make it feel better somehow.

The news moved on, giving him a small jolt. He leaned forward to the screen. Famoudi. Heat and dust. Huge billowing clouds of dust thrown up by the low hover of a helicopter. A much bigger crowd today. A huge crowd. More than they had ever seen in Buccleuch Street. Advancing and chanting. Every face covered with a scarf.

Camera close ups showed fists held high and dark blazing eyes. Then the camera swung round to take in the double rank of Marines, waiting with set faces behind their Perspex shields. Closer still to where Captain Dale Nash stood a few feet behind. The close up on his set face looked like something straight out of Hollywood.

Josh chuckled. "No wonder they love this guy. He'll be straight onto the silver screen the minute he hangs up his uniform. Remind you of anything Lenny?"

"What? Orgreave?"

"Of course Orgreave. I reckon those lads are singing 'We're on the march with Arthur's army in Arabic."

"No. It's different to Orgreave. It was more or less even numbers there. Look. Those Marines must be outnumbered twenty to one. You've got to give them credit for bottle."

"Something else is different to Orgreave." The two men turned to the small voice from the bed. "Look. There. Behind the lines. Two armoured cars. If anything starts to go wrong they know full well that they can drop every body in the street in about twenty seconds. And that's not counting the machine gun in the helicopter. This is beyond boots and truncheons. The stones and the shields are all just a charade. If any of those children carry things too far there will be a massacre. They know that. The soldiers know that. That makes it different to Orgreave. It is like the places I have been. Nicaragua. Bosnia. Grozny. Orgreave was never going to become a killing field. This could."

They turned back to the screen and watched in silence as the stones started to fly. They saw the dramatic shots of Nash leading the surprise counter attack that cleared the street. Then it was all grinning faces and back slapping. The Marines had done it the all American way.

"Are you both really going to do this?"

Again they turned to her and one look at their faces told her that they were. Where there should have been features etched with tension there were smiles. The answer to her question was in their eyes. Crazy, crazy eyes. The prospect of another thirty years of so called normal life was a nightmare to the pair of them. All they wanted was a big ending. Against all their expectations she started to laugh.

"What?" Lenny was almost put out.

"Sorry. It's just you two. Bloody idiots. I got a picture of Butch Cassidy and the Sundance kid. You know. At the end when they're outnumbered about a million to one."

Now both Lenny and Josh were smiling too. Josh picked up the dialogue.

"Call that shooting . . ."

Lenny picked up the thread. "Call that running . . ."

For a while they laughed together until it became strained. Beverly broke the painful silence before it had much of a chance to take root.

"Look. I'm not doing any goodbyes. Sorry, but no way. Would you both just go now. Just get up and walk out and close the door. Only that. Do it right now. Don't look back. I'll be there to do my part. That's all you need to know. So go. Please."

Lenny was about to argue but Josh didn't let him. He took him by the arm and led him out of the door. Neither man looked back and the door clicked shut leaving Beverly alone on the bed with tears rolling down the sharp bones of her cheeks.

Dale Nash pushed his food around his plate and tried to summon up some appetite. He took a glance around the room they had chosen as a chow hall. Once upon a time it had been part of a warehouse of some kind. Business couldn't have been all that great as the walls were peeling and the metal brackets holding the strip lights to the ceiling were all but rusted through. The room was a micro-version of the whole wretched country. Rusty, dusty, peeling and picked clean by thirty years of Saddam and his vultures. Normally the hall was a hubbub of sound. Jokes. Arguments. The traditional soldier's complaining about the muck sent out from the cook house.

Not tonight. Tonight he could hear every scrape of every knife and fork. And he wasn't alone in finding it hard to eat what was in front of him. More than half of his men seemed to be in the same boat. It wasn't very hard to guess why. The only place he had been able to allocate for Walters to undertake his interrogation was a small outbuilding that had once been used as some kind of tool storage area. It was a good hundred yards away from the chow hall but it was easy to hear every one of the agonised screams that drifted across the dusty yard where they practised their drill. The screams had started late in the morning, just a few minutes after three Iraqis in civilian clothes had arrived and asked for Walters. For seven hours the sounds that came out from the small building spoke of the outer limits of human pain.

Now he could see the toll it was taking on his men. There were many faces cast down. Young faces who had been told what they were doing was for God and freedom. Young faces from small bible belt towns where torture was something that was unimaginable. Young faces from places where over eighty percent of the population met at the church on a Sunday. Where weekend afternoons were filled with the sound of lawns being mown. Barbeques and junior league and summer camp. Not this. Not this utter filth.

"Sergeant Jimenez."

"Sir."

"I do believe that I have seen that you have a boom box in your quarters?"

"Affirmative sir."

"Then please bring it the hell in here and play the loudest goddamn thing you own."

"Sir."

The swarthy Latin sergeant returned a few minutes later and flooded out the sounds of hell with full volume Gipsy Kings.

"That's a whole hell of a lot better Jimenez. I thank you. Tell the men to be out on the parade ground at twenty hundred. We're going to do some drill sergeant. Drill with a difference. Understood."

"Sir."

Dale got to his feet and took a tour of the tables before returning to the sanctuary of his room. His father, who was a veteran of two tours of Vietnam, had found it highly amusing when his son had packed his notes from Officer College to take all the way to Iraq. Now Dale allowed himself a small smile at his old man's expense.

"You see Daddy, you never know when a bit of history comes in handy. He sat on his bed and started flicking through the notes he had made as a bright-eyed teenager. Old classic campaigns. Great generals all the way from Alexander to Rommel. The campaigns that forged history. He made notes. Leonidas at Thermopylae. Augustus in Gaul. Wellington in Spain. He was still making notes when there was a rap at his door.

"Yo."

It was Walters. The older man took a look at the notes and smirked.

"Little old for homework aren't you son?"

"Can I help you?"

"Not really. Thought I'd bring you up to speed. We're all done with our questions."

"You must be proud of yourself."

Walters pulled a hip flask from his pocket and took a hard pull. He offered it to Dale who refused with an angry shake of his head.

"Don't get preachy on me Dale. This is how it is. The rest is for the comic books and the smaltzy movies. War is a place where you need to get things done. Sooner you learn that, sooner you get the oak desk in the office on the top floor."

"I don't need any lessons from you. Just get on with it."

"OK. Not in the mood for cosy chit-chat. I'll go with that. We got three guys. Two from out of town who didn't know much about anything. They got word to come along and throw a few rocks. Much as we expected. The third guy was the pay dirt. He comes from here. The whole gig was kicked off by a Yousuf Habiri. Sounds like some kind of punk. Nineteen years old. Daddy used to be a local player in the Baath Party. Once upon a time they had a house with a pool and satellite TV. I figure he doesn't much like coming down in the world. Hence the stone-throwing. To start with it was just him and a few of his buddies. Then he got a visit. Sure sounded a heavy duty kind of deal. Two cars and nine guys armed like something out of Rambo. Yousuf spends some quality time with an older guy and hey presto you got two thousand bodies out there today, every last one of them twitching for a reservation in Paradise."

"The Colonel?"

"Sure as hell sounds like it."

Dale could feel the excitement coming off the bounty hunter.

"How much are they going to pay you for bringing them this guys's head on a plate?"

"What? Thinking about cashing in the commission and getting a taste of the private sector, Dale?"

"I asked you a question."

"Yeah. And the answer is a corporate secret buddy. I wouldn't want you sharing anything with that nice tight piece of ass from ABC. Let's just say we're talking a cliff top condo in Hawaii and dancing girls on tap."

Dale shook his head. Every morning, rain or shine, his father went out to the front of their home in Virginia to raise the Stars and Stripes. For what? For blue chip killers like Walters to play their filthy games. He felt sick to his stomach.

"Not part of the Boy Scout, handbook Dale? Well ain't that just a sad and sorry shame. Anyways. I'm going to need some assistance tonight."

"Like what."

"We got an address on this Yousuf cat. I want you run a patrol into his street. Run everyone out of every house. Check them over. Papers. Quick body search. You know the drill. Normal routine. I'll get a guy into his place to plant a few devices. And then when the Colonel comes to call we can be all ready and waiting with a kettle on the stove."

"And is that work that your company handles?"

"Hell no. We sub that out to a Delta team. Like I said. We're all about outsourcing Dale. You give me list of what you want for your guys for helping out tonight. Seriously. T-bones. A movie screen. A couple of thousand Buds. You just name it. We look after our contractors."

Dale's first instinct was to smash his nose half way through the other side of his skull. But that wouldn't have been the brightest call. If he told him to stick it up his ass all it would mean was that he would get a call from his CO in an hour or so. If his company was paying, then it wasn't really fair on the guys to get all principled. He went for the T-bones and the movie screen. And when Walters left the room he felt somehow dirty.

After a moment or so he picked up his notes and headed for the makeshift parade ground which was now lit up by floodlights. A hundred very suspicious Marines were waiting for him. They were a whole hell lot more suspicious when he started telling them the story of Augustus and his classic march into the badlands for pre-medieval Germany. Two hours later they were bouncing with anticipation. There was a unanimous feeling that Captain Dale Nash had to be just about the best goddamned officer in the whole goddamned US Marine Corps.

By the time Lenny and Josh reached the junction where the A1 met the M62, a curtain of rain was pelting the north of England. In the early dusk the great ghostly towers of Pontefract power station loomed over them. Like always the sight reminded Lenny that the steam that poured up into the dark sky had once come from water heated by coal dragged from the earth by his father and brother. Another lifetime. And now this brief era was drawing to a close with every mile the Mercedes covered as they headed east. He knew now that the USYcampaign was never going to replace all that he had lost. Victory had made him smile. Nothing more. The final drops of real life that flowed through his veins had been all wrung out at the sight of Beverly's destroyed face on the Panorama programme. No matter how he had tried to be positive during the time following his release from Wakefield, he had found nothing that even began to fill in all the empty spaces. The guilt. The lonely regret. Being re-united with Josh and Beverly had only sharpened his sense of having reached the end of the road. Beverly would be dead within weeks and Josh was every bit as much an empty shell as he was himself. Life might have been so different for all three of them. But it hadn't been. They had been mere pawns in a game that was greater than they had ever known.

Hindsight showed him that his fight had always been futile. He and thousands upon thousands of others had been encouraged to believe that life might one day be better. It had seemed logical that mankind would one day wake up to the fact that the endless desperate pursuit of wealth would most surely end in tears. Now the planet was dying like an old leper and yet the billions of the world still scrambled like frantic ants to collect up things that were supposed to answer their prayers. It would never change. None of it. Nothing could have been more obvious. And he knew deep in his bones that he wanted no part of it.

Outside the hills of the Pennines were left far behind as they drove straight east towards the North Sea. It would probably be the last time he would lay eyes on his native Yorkshire. Once upon a time his only dream had been to pull on a county cap and run in from the Football Stand End at Headingley in a Roses Match. Such a simple dream. A simple dream from a time when things had been less complicated. He had been lucky enough to grow up in a time when the winds of hope blew fresh and clean. It was a hope that had died in him a long, long time ago. It died a little at Orgreave. A little more when the Mankies came to Haddington. After holding his brother and watching the light leave his eyes there had barely been any left. Twenty years of prison had killed off the last fraction of what remained.

"Penny for them?"

Josh stared straight ahead down the middle lane of the motorway, a slight smile on his face.

"Nothing much. I was just thinking I should feel more sadness at leaving."

"Neither of us are leaving much Lenny. This isn't our place any more. I don't suppose it ever was."

Lenny lit up two cigarettes and passed one over.

"I'm glad you turned up Josh."

"Yeah. And me."

A few hours later they stood out in the rain at the rail of the North Sea ferry as it slipped slowly away from the orange lights of Hull. Normally the lights would have stayed out on the horizon for a long time. But it was a night of no stars and low clouds. Ten minutes after the ship left the quay, all visible evidence of Britain had been swallowed up by the night. They went down and bought coffees. Lenny dug in his pockets for change. Not enough. Josh coppered up and gave him a couple of pound coins. Sally picked up on the third ring.

"Hello love."

"Hi uncle Lenny." Her voice was buoyant. She told him about how it had been since the announcement in a frantic tumble of words. Her bubbling hope made him feel even older. At least she might get the chance to lead a life without torment. She was so lucky to be driven by a manageable dream. A building. A place to change the lives of a few young people from a small estate in a small Scottish town. Bite-sized dreams were the best type.

"How is your friend uncle Lenny?"

"She's not well. Not well at all. I'm afraid she doesn't have very long left."

He could tell from the silence that Sally was struggling to know what to say.

"Will you stay with her? I mean until . . ."

"No. I have said my goodbyes now."

"Oh. So are you an your way back?"

This was going to be the hard part. "I'm afraid not Sally. This is a goodbye call. I know I should have done it face-to-face, but I have had too many goodbyes. I couldn't face it. Sorry."

His words tore at her.

"But I don't understand. What about The Zone and the new building and everyone is going to be looking for you now that we have won and . . ."

She ran out of steam. Somehow she knew that all of her words would be futile. She had never begun to understand the air of doomed sadness that wrapped itself around her uncle. She had tried and she had believed that one day she would find a way through to the inside of him.

"The Zone is in good hands Sally. The best. I couldn't be more proud of you. Your Dad is too, wherever he may be. He's there, Sally. Watching with that big daft grin on his face. Never forget that. Never forget that giving up isn't an option. Not that you needed me to tell you that."

"Are you going away?"

"Aye. That I am."

"Where?"

"It's a sturdy stride. You'll find out soon enough."

The silences were getting a little longer every time their conversation paused.

"Will you be coming back?"

"Maybe. But to be honest I doubt it. You should take this as goodbye."

She was crying now. He could hear the hard sobs and could picture the tears on her young face. He hated himself for destroying what should have been her greatest moment.

"Look Sally I . . ."

Nothing. Not a thing. Just like always.

"Just take care Uncle Lenny. Wherever you are going. And remember how much I love you."

"And I love you Sally."

He put the phone back on the hook and killed the line. The last thread was cut clean through. Out in the dark night the shores of Britain were sliding further away. Only the final chapter remained. Then he would find some peace at last.

For several days the media was near frantic in its search for Lenny Baxter. He was the undisputed man of the hour. He had brought the walls tumbling down. The Council had caved in. A Knight of the Realm was in custody having been charged under the Terrorism Act. And within twenty four hours of Billingham's tight lipped speech, the Koz range had gone national. Store managers fumed at the limited stock levels that were delivered. The stuff was always sold out within minutes of hitting the shelves. All day long their phones rang with enquiries. Shop floor staff were sick of the constant stream of eager youngsters who poured in through the doors in search of the brand that had become their Holy Grail. In Bolton the old mill hummed twenty-four hours a day and the staff were on a constant high. Asmo had done the impossible. Asmo had found his way all the way to the top of the tree where the view went on for hundreds of sunlit miles. And yet they all noticed that he wasn't his normal self. His moment of complete triumph seemed to have left him somehow listless and rather drawn. He spent most of his time up in his office, and when he walked the shop floor he seemed unusually distracted. It was decided that he was probably just tired. Not surprising really. Not after what he had just achieved.

When he was alone he was eaten up with fear. When he had made his deal with Lenny Baxter he had never really believed that the man was serious. Of course he wasn't. Nobody could be that crazy. So he had given his word. Of course he had. Who wouldn't when the dream of a lifetime was on the table and just asking to be picked up. But as he had come to know Lenny Baxter, he had begun to realise that the man was actually going to do it. And with every phone call the sense of foreboding had grown in him.

Lenny had called from the ferry. They were on board. They would be there in no more than four days. And was everything in place? And were there any problems? And was everything going according to plan? And Asmo had said that it was. And he had told Lenny to call him in a couple of days. Because by that time everything would be fully finalised. When he put the phone down he tried to tell himself that there was still time to back off the whole crazy idea. But in his heart he knew that time had passed many days earlier. He had lit a fuse that wouldn't be put out. All there was now was to sit and wait to see just how loud the bang was going to be.

Walters joined Dale Nash to watch Charlie Company climbing on board their transport for the early morning journey to the basket ball court. Despite his ingrained cynicism, he couldn't help but be impressed by the evident high moral of the young soldiers. Idealist or not, there could be no argument that Nash knew how to get his soldiers to follow him. He was the type to take his company into a situation where seventy percent casualties were a near certainty and not one of them would bat an eyelid.

"Thanks for your help last night Dale."

"Get all your bugs in place?"

"Sure did. Now we can listen in and see if our man sings when he takes a dump."

"How wonderful."

There was still a bitter set to the young officer's mouth.

"We picked up intell that might be useful for you this morning."

"Really."

Walters was finding that his patience was getting slightly stretched.

"Jesus man. I'm trying to cut you a break here."

"Then cut it."

For a moment Walters considered walking away and leaving the arrogant sonofabitch to his own devices. Then he decided that would mean he was behaving like some kind of schoolgirl.

"OK. Looks like there are a lot of new faces in town this morning. Yousuf was talking about over four thousand being out there this morning."

He had expected some kind of concern from Nash. Instead the young captain merely smiled.

"That's OK. We've been working on some new tactics."

"Like what?"

"Come and watch if you like. You might learn something. It's called real soldiering."

Walters hadn't been going to go, but now he was intrigued.

"OK Captain Nash. I'll take a ride."

An hour later the helicopter pilot confirmed the intelligence. It was going to be a big one. A really big one. Dale took a last walk round his men and confirmed that they were all on top of the new strategy. When the crowd started to pour into the street it was a truly ominous sight. They came and came until there was barely room for them all. Chanting. Much longer this morning as if they had decided to savour the moment. From the roof of one of the Bradley's the ABC cameraman felt as if he was about to hyperventilate. He had been in the TV game for a lot of years, but this was something else. This was hardcore TV. Next to him Peggy Hill tried to keep it cool but her voice was only barely under control. A few seconds earlier the tinny voice of the controller back in the States had informed her that the audience figures were out of sight. The image of the thin line of Marines facing down the baying mob that outnumbered them by forty to one had captured the imagination of the nation. She was instructed not to go heavy on the machine gun option. The idea of the Marines being the underdog was playing like a dream with the advertisers.

" . . . this really is a truly awesome sight. And yet still Captain Nash and Charlie Company are standing firm. It is hard to put into words the hostility in this street. You can almost touch it. Again we have the chants. Again we have the fists held high. And soon the fighting will start. There must be twice as many demonstrators out there today. Maybe three times as many. It seems as if this whole mighty conflict has come down to a single thin line of a hundred Marines. Not just this conflict. This is the front line in America's struggle against an increasingly hostile world . . . ."

The tinny voice in her earpiece was back again.

"Go Peggy! This is great. Keep hitting it . . ."

" . . . Ever since our Independence, the people of America have turned to the Marine Corps during our very darkest moments. When you look at the faces in this street it is impossible not to think that we are once again facing an implacable enemy. These people want to see our way of life destroyed. Smashed into a million pieces. And we have a hundred young Marines out there. Holding the line. Young men from small towns most of us have never heard of . . . ."

Just as Peggy hit the greatest roll of her broadcasting career, the first stones started to pelt down. For a long moment the great crowd never moved. They merely poured down their barrage. Then almost imperceptibly the crammed ranks started to inch towards the thin line of Perspex. Dale didn't wait. He gave the sergeant next to him a small nod. The sergeant from the wrong end of Detroit had a well-earned reputation for having a voice that could carry the length of any parade ground in the world. Now his big voice threw out a single word over the tumult.

"Leonidas!!!"

The reaction from the ranks of Marines was instantaneous. They had practised the manoeuvre for several hours the evening before. The hundred split into five groups of twenty. Within seconds each group slotted onto a tight square. There were four Marines on each side of each square presenting a tight Perspex shell. Four Marines in the centre of each square held their shields above their heads to seal the space. Before the drill, Dale had sat the men down and given them a half hour lecture on the tactics of the square. The idea was to present a tight wall to the enemy and he explained how numbers became unimportant so long as the square retained its integrity. He told them about the way the Roman legions had made a hard shell with their shields. He told them of how the British squares had destroyed Napoleon's much vaunted cavalry on the field of Waterloo. And he stood up the hairs on their necks with the legend of how the Spartan King Leonidas and three hundred warriors had stopped a Persian army of a quarter of a million cold in its tracks at Thermopylae.

Once the squares were formed, they moved into a diamond formation of four with Dale's square placed in the centre. Then they began a slow advance that moved inexorably up the street until after ten minutes they had once again cleared the area.

By the time the action was complete Peggy Hill barely had a voice left to speak. Fantastic. Unbelievable. And all of it watched by one of the greatest audiences that the news had ever pulled in. And all of it commentated on by her. By Peggy Hill. Once the Marines reached the end of the street they formed back into two lines and moved carefully back to their start position.

She bounded over to the heavily sweating Dale Nash.

"What was it that your sergeant shouted Dale?"

"Leonidas Maam."

"Could you explain that Dale?"

"Search engine. Enter Leonidas Thermopylae. Return. Let's just say that sometimes soldiering don't change all that much."

Josh and Lenny watched the whole thing later on the BBC 24 channel in their hotel room in Vienna.

"Come on then Josh. You're the one with the disgustingly expensive private education. I expect you did all the classical stuff. Who the hell was Leonidas?"

"At times I worry about your ignorance. I really do. OK. We're talking a few hundred years BC. In those days the two great superpowers were Greece and Persia. Greece was all about philosophy and trade and culture. You know, pretty temples with white columns and Socrates and all that. King Xerxes and the Persians were about war, conquest, rape, pillage and all things nasty. Xerxes decided that the next item on his conquest list was Greece and so he spent a few years putting together the biggest army there had ever been. And I mean monumental. Hundreds of thousands drawn from all over Asia. The Greeks were scared witless, especially when they realised that negotiation wasn't going to be an option. As the Persians rolled towards them, they argued and bickered and couldn't make their minds up what to do. Within the Greek alliance, the Spartans were the warlike guys. Please tell me that you have heard of the Spartans?"

"Yes. Brought up to be warriors from the age of two. No luxury and frills and all that."

"Quite. Well, they were not a hundred percent committed to the idea of throwing in their lot with Athens who they had little time for. As a half way house sort of measure they decided to send King Leonidas along with three hundred of his top lads to the straits of Thermopylae to hold the line whilst they decided on strategy. The ground was well chosen. There were just a few hundred yards of flat land with the sea on one side and cliffs on the other. The odds looked pretty bad, I mean two hundred and fifty thousand against three hundred Spartans and a few hundred allies were about as bad as odds could ever get. But the thing was that the battle came down to a few hundred against a few hundred at any given time. There just wasn't room for Xerxes to bring his numerical advantage into play. So for three days he threw his soldiers against the wall of Spartan shields. It was much like throwing lumps of beef at a mincing machine. So long as the Spartans kept the integrity of their lines, there was no way past. In the end they were betrayed and Xerxes was shown a path round to the rear of the Spartan lines and then it was all over. Legend had it that the three days that Leonidas held up the advance was enough for the Greeks to get their act together. A while later they defeated the Persians at the battle of Marathon and the runner who legged it twenty-six miles back to Athens gave the news and keeled over. You probably know that bit as well. You know. Race. Olympics."

"Yeah. I know that bit as well. Young Captain Nash is going to be playing to full houses after this."

"God bless his cotton socks."

They both took a stroll down the street to a bar and raised their glasses in toast to the young Marine Captain who was playing their game better than either had dared to hope

Jake Hollins had stayed in Dumfries for a day and waited along with all the other journalists for some kind of appearance from Lenny Baxter. Nothing. The man seemed to have simply vanished into the ether. All the talk in the hotel bar was that he was deliberately waiting to milk the moment. The media attention was huge on several fronts. There was all kind of speculation about the career of Sir Edward Latimer and the astounding decision taken by the Chief Constable of Dumfries and Galloway to lock him up using the Terrorism Act. A major spat had broken out between the Government in London and their opposite numbers in Edinburgh. Those in London insisted that Latimer be returned south as soon as possible. Those in Edinburgh dug in their heels and backed their policeman all the way. Law and order was a reserved issue over which London had relinquished all control when they established Scotland's devolved Parliament. It wasn't hard for the media and the public to guess where the majority of the skeletons were to be found.

The Koz phenomenon was another blinding story. All over Britain were a thousand and one tales of high street stores swamped by the demand for the elusive range. *Ebay* got more free publicity that it had ever known.

And finally there was the great 'Where is Lenny Baxter?' story. The man of the hour had disappeared in a puff of smoke. Word soon got out that he had spent two whole days in the hospital room of Beverley Morton, the dying woman from the Panorama programme. Then nothing. Not a trace. Not in Dumfries, not in Sheffield, not anywhere. None of the many reporters who waited in Dumfries had any doubt that he would return. But Jake wasn't so sure. Lenny wasn't the sort to play silly games. If he had vanished, then it was probably for good reason. The man from The Times decided that the Dumfries end of things had gone cold. He packed his bags and took the train back to London to pick up on the steady flow of twenty-year secrets that were leaking out from all over Whitehall no matter how hard the

Government and its civil servants tried to plug them.

Like Lenny and Josh, he too had been watching the extraordinary scenes from Famoudi. The last month had brought scenes that he had never believed he would see again. It was as if time had shifted like some sort of tectonic plate. First Buccleuch Street. Now an unknown street in Iraq. Two small towns thousands of miles apart where young people had forced themselves into the forefront of the news. Angry young people who had at long last decided to stand up and be counted and to demand a change in the agenda. Many of the younger reporters couldn't begin to grasp the importance of what was happening. They had been drilled into seeing every story as a five minute event. In the sound-bite era of the twenty-first century it was hardly surprising. But Jake had been around the block a few more times. He had been there in 1968 when young people all over the world had found their voices. To start with it seemed as if the establishment had shut them up with clouds of tear gas and water cannons. But just a very few years later a grim-faced President Nixon had to eat humble pie in front of the eyes of the world and pull his troops out of Vietnam and admit to America's first and only defeat.

Was it really happening again? Probably not. There was no ideological connection between the young people of Sunnybank who had occupied Buccleuch Street and those who waged their prime-time war with Charlie Company. If there was, then it could be the start of something huge. Something that might turn the world on its axis. He sat and smoked his way through a whole packet and tried to make a connection. Tried and failed. It was nothing more than wishful thinking.

Then his mobile phone rang.

"Jake?"

Holy Christ. He knew the Yorkshire twang straight away.

"Is that you Lenny?"

"It certainly is. Keeping busy then?"

"I'm doing all right. How about you?"

"Oh, you know. This and that."

"I gather you have decided to keep a low profile."

A laugh at the far end of the line. "Just for a while Jake. Fancy another exclusive?"

It was a gift horse Jake had no intention of looking in the mouth.

"Always. Just tell me where and when. I'll be there."

"Aye. I'll bet you will. Ankara. Three days time. I'll call you to arrange a place. Do it off your own bat, Jake. Don't tell the office where you're going, OK?"

"OK." Jake spoke the word slowly, every journalistic instinct in him exploding like a sky full of fireworks. Could it be? Ankara. The capital of Turkey.

"Seriously Jake. Not a word. I promise you won't regret it."

"No need to worry Lenny. I'll see you right. Can I ask something?"

"I kind of expected that you would."

"It occurs to me that Ankara isn't a million miles from Famoudi."

"Not a million miles, no. I'll see you in a couple of days Jake."

Jake called the office the next day and told his boss that he was feeling a little frayed at the edges after all the drama up in Scotland and that he was going to take a few days to go and do some fishing. Then he packed the old leather bag that had accompanied him on so many journeys. He killed two days wandering the baking hot streets of the Turkish capital and tried to understand what Lenny Baxter was about to do. That he was going to Iraq now seemed to be almost certain. But for what? He had sensed something from the man during those crazy days up in Dumfries. On the surface he was all bluff Yorkshireman. Plain words and an easy smile. A man who it was hard not to like. A Pied Piper for the new Millennium. And yet underneath there was something that Jake could only guess at. Something doomed. A feeling that the man knew that his time had been and gone. He was a man who had lost all interest in his own future. It meant that trying to guess what on earth he was about to do was all but impossible.

The call came as promised three days after initial contact. They were staying at one of the new hotels out by the airport. The three Englishmen met for a couple of beers and small talk in the bar along with air conditioning, canned music and complimentary peanuts. Then they took the elevator to a room on the third floor. Lenny flicked on the kettle whilst Jake took in a view over the long flat plain of Central Turkey. Josh busied himself in setting up a small video unit on a tripod and arranging two of the chairs. Lenny passed him a cup of tea.

"I hope you don't mind recording our interview Jake? I'll give you a copy of course."

Jake shrugged. "You're calling the shots. Want to start?"

"Why not."

They sat and Jake was suddenly a little awkward. He wasn't used to going about his work in front of a camera. He cleared his throat and was a little self-conscious when he started.

"For the record, we are in a hotel in Ankara, Turkey and it is now four days since the Dumfries and Galloway Council gave in to the demands of USY. I am here with Lenny Baxter and Josh Ogilvy who were two of the main instigators of what happened up in Scotland. Does anyone else know that you are here Lenny?"

"Not many. A handful of people, that's all. We're not advertising our trip."

Jake ran through a few background questions asking how Lenny had felt when he realised that USY had won through and what he thought about Latimer and his prospects. Then he cut to the chase.

"So Lenny, where now?"

"Famoudi." It was the answer that Jake had been expecting but the sound of the name still sent a small shiver through him.

"May I ask why?"

"It's why you're here Jake. I thought it best to get summat down on the record before all the propaganda kicks in. They're all going to have a field day on this one. If it were Lenny the terrorist up in Dumfries, just imagine what it'll be like now." Lenny paused to light a cigarette. "My life has been a journey Jake. Same as everyone. Sometimes you don't realise where you're headed until near the end. That's how it has been for me. Most of my life has guided me along to the place where I am right now. I just never realised it. Bloody Hell. This is sounding like a right load of twaddle. Tha'd never guess I was from Haddington. That night when those little buggers broke ranks and started chucking stones on Buccleuch Street I was really down. Flat down. Everything was falling to pieces. I were just sitting feeling right depressed in front of the tele. Everything looked bad. Me on those steps looking like I'd planned the whole thing. The lads with hoodies and scarves. It had only taken about ten minutes for all of us to become bad guys. I'd been there before. Orgreave. One minute I was watching the coppers half kill my brother and thousands of others. The next minute I'm watching pictures on the tele that made the whole thing look as it were all our doing. They say a picture paints a thousand words. A thousand lies more like. And then there was Famoudi. And it hit me that it was just the same. Angry kids. Kids with no voice. Our lot were mad because they wanted a place to go and something to do. These kids were mad because a bunch of foreigners had come to town and killed their dads. It suddenly seemed very, very clear. You see Jake, when I thought about it, I knew exactly how they felt. I remember the day when the police came to Haddington. Strangers who had no business to be there. Men waving twenty pound notes over their shields and having a laugh."

He paused and stared into space for a moment.

"They fractured my dad's skull. Just like that. All he was trying to do was calm things down. He was a truly good man, my dad. He spent his whole life trying to make things better. He was a proper socialist from the time before they made it a dirty word. Thirty years of helping his community and they sent strangers to town to smash his skull. Never apologised. Not a word. He never worked again. He never really lived again. He might have lived a while longer but they basically murdered him that morning. Well you know what me and Frank did after that. And Josh and Williams. Because there comes a time when you are just not willing to be polite about it any more. And suddenly I saw the truth of what Famoudi was all about. The government wants us all to think what a load of Arab nutters. And the media were happy enough to help out. But I suddenly realised that it was just the same as Haddington. And Sunnybank. And just about every place in the world."

"Realisation is one thing Lenny. Doing something about it is another. I can't see what you can possibly think you can achieve. There are over 150,000 American soldiers in Iraq, every one of them armed to the teeth. This is a bigger game than policemen with dogs and truncheons."

Lenny smiled. "Aye you're right there Jake. Two middle-aged losers against the last of the Superpowers. Not great odds, I agree. And up until a couple of weeks ago I wouldn't have given it a thought. But now? Now I think there might be a way."

"Do you now." Jake was getting the uneasy feeling that the man might have actually slipped over the edge.

"I know. Sounds barking mad doesn't it. Humour me Jake. Tha's come a long way. Keep your mind open for a while. Brace yourself. I'm going to go philosophical on you. When the big Empires collapse it is always because their enemies learn to copy them. For a while Hitler caught everyone cold with Blitzkrieg. Then the Russians managed to copy him and then do it better. Us British were the first to build an Empire on the back of industrial progress. Then the rest of the world learnt to do it better and now we're left with Belize, the Falklands and a chunk of Ireland. It took Wellington ten years to work out how to play Napoleon at his own game, but he got him in the end. It's the same every time. Empires come and Empires go. What makes them strong turns them weak. So what has made the American Empire Jake?"

"You're in the chair Lenny?"

"They conquered the world with their brands. They didn't need to send soldiers and officials to run their colonies. Too expensive. So they sent Coca Cola and McDonalds and Levi and Ford instead. They didn't ban the press, they took it over. They hard sold their American Dream to the young people of the whole damned planet through Hollywood and slick advertising. And by Christ, did the world ever buy it. Lock, stock and bloody barrel. And for a while it looked as if they were indestructible. Just like the Greeks and the Romans and the Brits and the Third Reich before them. But nothing is forever Jake. I have learned big lessons. USY changed in a few days. One minute it was me and Josh and one or two others hanging around looking like a bunch of planks. Next minute there were cars pouring into town from all over the country. Why? Well you know full well why. It were Koz. A brand. All of a sudden being a street rebel was the coolest game in town."

Now Jake was leaning forward intently, a new light in his old cynical eyes. "Christ Lenny. You're talking about taking Koz to Famoudi aren't you?"

Lenny smiled. "Hey Jake. You've arrived. Nice to see you've got here at last."

Jake's brain was clattering round. Trying to weigh it up, trying to split madness from brilliance. He forced old reporting habits onto himself. Take it step by step. Despite the quiet presence of the camera he pulled his notebook from his pocket and started to scribble in a shorthand unique to himself.

"OK. One. Just how in the name of hell do you expect to get there.

You might just have noticed the US Army runs Iraq, and they're hell bent on stopping troublemaking foreigners from getting in and raising hell."

Lenny shrugged. "We have help."

"What kind of help?"

"No comment. Let's just say it's from people who know the ropes around the border areas."

"And was Asif Mohammed instrumental in arranging that contact?"

Lenny's face glazed over. "No comment."

Jake stared at him for a moment and knew that this was a case of no comment meaning precisely that. "OK. How much gear have you brought?"

"Enough. A van full. A couple of thousand of everything."

"And what is your plan when you get there? If you get there?"

"Nowt that complicated really. We'll try to persuade the kids to wear the clothes when they go and have a pop at the soldiers."

"But what if the US Army embargoes the pictures. It's happened all the way through the war. What good will it do then?"

"Aye we thought of that. We've got some equipment of our own. Satellite phone. Fat laptop. Digicams. We can get the images out."

"But even if you do there will be enormous pressure to lock them down once they make it back home. Nobody is going to want these pictures seen."

"Too right they won't. That's the gamble. Those back home will have to try to have the pictures out all over the place before the authorities have cottoned onto what's going on."

"But . . ." Jake paused. He was so hell bent on the fact that the idea was plain crazy that he was in danger of missing the fact that it might just work. Rather than another question he started to work the thing through aloud. "OK. IF you manage to get the images out, and IF those at the other end manage to get them into the public domain before anyone can stop them . . . Christ Lenny."

"It's called the toothpaste coming out of the tube. Once it's out tha can't get it back in."

Jake sat back and worked it all through. Lenny started again, his voice quiet to the point of dreaminess. "Everything right now hinges on the fact of those kids in Famoudi being perceived as different to the kids at home. They are painted as wild-eyed religious freaks whilst Nash and Co are the square jawed all American heroes. Everyone likes to forget that Nash can radio his man up in the helicopter and reduce the whole area into a slaughter yard in a matter of seconds. But if people begin to see that the kids in Famoudi are just the same as kids everywhere else, well then it gets interesting. Think about it. Think music industry. Bad boys sell records. But the badness has to get badder. It's evolution. The Rolling Stones got busted. The Sex Pistols used the F word on prime time TV. Eminem waltzed around the stage with a chainsaw and said he hated gays. And now we have 50 Cent. The baddest of the bad so far. Proper real life crack dealer, all full of bullets. Back at home kids are queuing up to buy Koz because it identifies them with the ones who took on the cops in Buccleuch Street. A progression from hanging about in shopping centres acting tough to actually doing something. Koz equals action. Proper action. Direct action. Call it what you like. So think about the far end of the rainbow. Think of the hardest, baddest, most in your face thing a kid could do on this whole planet. When it comes to being a street rebel it doesn't get any bigger than getting out there and throwing stones at a Marine Corps Company backed up by two armoured cars. We thought we were having a go at Orgreave, but let's face it, it's nowt compared to these kids."

Jake had arrived. "And by dressing them in the Koz range you make the link. You make the kids in Famoudi the same as the kids in Sunnybank. Jesus Lenny"

"Koz. Sometimes you gotta fight."

The room fell silent for a couple of moments. Jake was beginning to realise that he had been given the greatest, most outrageous story of his whole life. He should have been elated. He should have been dancing around the room and punching the air. Instead he felt only an overwhelming sadness.

"You know they'll never let you get out of there."

There was no hint of fear in Lenny Baxter's eyes. "Aye. We worked that one out. But you never know. Funny things can happen. This isn't meant to be a suicide mission. Just pretty high risk."

Jake didn't say any more. They both knew it was a lie. They were pulling the tail of the greatest military tiger the world had ever known. The tiger was hardly going to be philosophical about what was about to happen.

"What do you want me to do with all this Lenny?"

"Wait until the adverts are out in the open. Wait until it is unstoppable. Then you can play it how you like. Make sure you tell people that this is all dedicated to my dad and my brother Frank. They came from a time when people believed the world could be a better place. Everyone mocks the old socialists now. They call them idiots and dreamers. They say the only thing that counts is how much profit is left at the end of the day. Well happen my dad had it right all along. Happen folk can get sick of blokes in suits and fancy cars telling them what to do."

That was it. A plan that was outrageous in its simplicity. Two victims from a poisonous past that had all but destroyed them. Two men who had dared to fight for a dream that powerful men had decided not to allow. Many had said that Orwell had it right in his book 1984. Big Brother had won the day and Big Brother seemed destined never to lose. But the past always spawns the present. Lenny Baxter and Josh Ogilvy were Thatcher's wayward children and now they were about to turn the world on its head.

"Good luck guys. For what it's worth, I reckon you'll do it."

Beverly's mother was almost inconsolable. So long as her daughter was in the hospital she had been able to hang on to the hope that she might yet survive. Modern medicine achieved miracles every day. Was it too much to hope for her own daughter to be a miracle? She knew why Beverly had checked herself out and come home. She was coming home to die. There was no other reason. And soon the house in the middle of the wheat fields would be a place of emptiness and ghosts. What made it worse was the strangers who came to call. Young Asian men with high tech equipment that soon filled her daughter's room. When she questioned Beverly about it there were no real answers. It was something that was important. Something that had to be done. A promise that she had made. Physically, Beverley was little more than a breathing skeleton. But ever since the Panorama programme she had been energised. She was hanging on to life with a ferocity that shone from her eyes.

Late one night she turned her bleached face to her mother and found a smile.

"I'm sorry mum. But I know you will understand. I need to make sense of everything. My life. I've seen far too much suffering. I've caused it too. Maybe I can help make some of it stop. You have to know how lucky I feel. Privileged. I was so close to dying all empty. Now I can die with a song in my heart. We all need our lives to mean something mum. I promise that you will understand. I promise."

Her mother didn't believe that she would. She never had. Her beautiful daughter had always been an enigma to her.

Once Jake had left for the airport, Josh wandered down to the business suite on the ground floor of the hotel to check an email account in which neither name Josh or Ogilvy played any part. A message gave details of an overdue account from a plumbing firm in Huntingdon. Back in the room they pulled out the middle four figures from the invoice and translated them into a map reference on their Michelin Map. The fifth figure given was 11. A rendezvous time. The map reference showed a small town a hundred miles or so short of the Syrian border. Quite a trip. It meant an early start.

They took the evening checkout option and prepared to hit the road no later than four in the morning. Both men took long soaks in the bath and privately wondered when they would have the opportunity to do the same again. Maybe they never would. It was the start of the land of question marks.

Getting through the deserted streets of Ankara was no problem and soon they had a long straight road all to themselves. East and east. A vivid moon lit the long flat plain in silver light. By day the horizon was all the way yellow with sunflowers. Now it was shades of dark. They played unintelligible Arab stations on the radio and said little as their van patiently ate up the miles. Lenny's mind wandered aimlessly as he focused on following the straight white line in the middle of the road. Nash had talked about Thermopylae. It must have had the American public scrambling for their encyclopaedias. This was probably the road that where many of Xerxes men had marched down to join what at the time was the greatest army in history. After Xerxes came Alexander the Great, only he was headed the other way. Churchill had harboured great dreams of sending a British force up the road only to see them wiped out on the beaches of Gallipolli. The quiet emptiness of the night gave him a feeling of being close to history. Here was the crossroads where the east had met the west for as far back as man could remember. Hadn't he once read that Nostradamus had foretold that the east and the west would come together at the end of the world. Maybe that was why he and Josh were heading out across the empty plains of Asia. They were about to try and bring the east and the west together with a couple of thousand hooded jackets. The thought made him laugh.

"What's up?"

"Ah nowt. Just dreaming that's all."

"Me too. Know what has just occurred to me?"

"What?"

"Right now the storm has closed in and we're in the clouds. Hidden from view. We've actually gone and bloody made it. Against all the odds."

Lenny looked across. "I haven't the faintest idea what the hell you're on about."

"I didn't for a minute think that you would. You never could manage a cryptic crossword could you."

"Well come on then. Plain English."

"I was thinking about Mallory and Irving. Remember. The shape of that rooftop in the courtyard at Magdalene. You know the story well enough. They vanished from view in the storm and everyone at base camp was waiting for them to come back because to go on would have been crazy . . ."

Now Lenny was there. ". . . but when there was a gap in the storm they saw them. Just shy of the summit and still climbing. Then the clouds came back over and that was that."

"Well. Think about it. Everyone sees us the day before the Council caved in and everything was on course and going to plan. Then we disappear into the clouds. When we reappear it will be in Famoudi. Looks like we've finally found our Everest doesn't it?"

"Aye. It does."

And still the humming engine of the Mercedes carried them through the night and into the east.

As promised, the town they pulled into at ten-thirty was a one street affair. Certainly there was only one café, a mean sort of place with a few old men staring into glasses of thick sweet tea. Nobody seemed over surprised when two Europeans sat down and ordered coffee. On the dot of eleven a grumpy looking man in overalls came in and scanned the room. When he saw them he nodded and went back out. They settled up and stepped into the blasting heat. The man was waiting by an eight wheeler truck that had more miles on the clock than Xerxes had men in his army. He made no gesture to them. Instead he climbed into the cab and gunned the engine which caused a plume of oily black smoke to fly out of the exhaust and float lazily up into the heat of the sky. They started up the van and followed him as he pulled off the car park. Twenty minutes later he turned off the main road onto a rutted track that eventually terminated in the yard of a long disused factory.

There was another vehicle waiting for them. A 4x4 with a long trailer. There was also a fork lift truck which must have been the reason for the trailer. And there were two more men. Lenny and Josh got out and stretched their weary limbs whilst the others unloaded the truck with the fork lift. Once the load of pallets was spread out across the dusty yard, the wagon driver tossed a spare pallet to the floor behind the Mercedes and made a gesture with his thumb.

It only took five minutes to hump all the boxes of Koz-wear and video equipment onto the pallet. Then the driver lifted it into the centre of the wagon behind the cab. He then placed pallets either side of it and then a further two which left a gap. Then he gave another of his trade mark thumb gestures.

"Looks like it's all aboard time. Christ, it's going to be hot."

They stood in the gap between the pallets and the men below threw up a couple of rather oily blankets and a canvas bag which held several plastic bottles of water and some pitta bread and houmus. Loading up the remaining pallets and fastening down the curtain sides took a further twenty minutes. By the time the process was completed they were in total darkness. The bag held a lamp and a spare set of batteries. They folded up the blankets and sat on them whilst trying to take their minds off the sauna like heat of their hiding place. Josh pulled out a bottle of the warm water and raised it in an ironic toast.

"Baxter and Ogilvy enjoyed luxury all the way on the road to Famoudi."

Then the battered old truck started down over the potholes and they both knew it was going to be journey to remember. Lenny was convinced that the next twelve hours seemed just about as long as the whole of his twenty years in prison. The heat in the small space between the pallets was something that seemed to be almost alive. It climbed all over them and sucked them dry. At first they had talked, but they soon found even that was exhausting. Eventually they both collapsed onto the blankets and tried to sleep, though the deterioration of the roads made that all but impossible. After four hours the truck slowed and stopped. Then every three minutes or so it eased forward a few feet. They deduced that they were probably in the queue for the Syrian border. The edging forward cycle continued for just over an hour and then the truck was motionless for longer. Now the seconds dragged by at an even slower crawl. Both of them knew how it would be if they were discovered trying to smuggle themselves and their unusual contraband into Syria. Muffled voices drifted in through the gaps between the pallets and then silence once again took over. At last the floor shook as the engine belched back into life and they were on their way.

When the truck next stopped it was journey's end. As a forklift lifted away the pallet adjacent to their hide, a heavenly gush of cool night air poured over their sweating bodies. They were given no time to enjoy the cool of the night. As soon as they jumped down from the truck they were firmly led to a car which was waiting with the engine idling. Before getting in they both had bags of thick, rough cloth pulled over their heads and then they were on their way. This time the journey was less than half an hour. They were walked along with the bags in place and were guided up a set of steps. Only when they were inside were the bags removed to reveal a bare room with peeling paint on the walls. The only furnishings were a metal table and three chairs. One chair was occupied by a man in his mid-fifties. He was well dressed and sported the moustache of a Battle or Britain pilot. He looked amused at the sight of the two bedraggled figures who had come to see him.

When he spoke his English was clear and clipped though fairly heavily accented.

"So. The crazy English have come. You sit, OK?"

He barked out a couple more sentences in fast Arabic and one of the men darted from the room. It was clear enough who was in charge. He filled the next minute by reaching into the breast pocket of his shirt to remove Lucky Strike cigarettes and a gold lighter that looked like it had come from the kind of shop that could make a profit on two transactions a day. The man returned with a tray that contained a jug of water which rattled with ice and a plate heaped with dates.

"So English, you drink. OK?"

The English drank as requested. Three glasses each which chilled their gullets and made them feel halfway human again. The whole thing seemed to amuse the man who proceeded to pass out Luckies and light them up.

"Your journey, it is fine, yes?"

"Couldn't have been better actually." Josh fielded the question as Lenny was draining his fourth glass.

"Well. Welcome to Syria my friends. I think it is good that you are here."

"Thanks for inviting us. I'm Josh by the way. This is Lenny."

"Yes I know. I have seen the television OK. I watch the story. Is good. I like it."

"And might I enquire who you are?"

This brought a laugh. "He is always so polite the English. So polite and then the knife between the shoulders yes? So you want to know me. Let me think. OK. I watch your BBC all the time. They say people like me are insurgents. Is long word for sure. I never know this word but they say that is me. Insurgent. I think they mean this word as a bad thing. Bad people OK. Me? Maybe I think I not so bad. Maybe I think I not like all this foreign soldiers coming to take my country OK. People call me the Colonel. Once I was real Colonel. Yes. For Saddam. Now I am still Colonel. For insurgent. I say is both the same. For Iraq. For my country. Always my country OK?"

Lenny nodded. "Did you ever hear the definition of the word terrorist, Colonel?"

"Sure. Why not. I hear many. You have one?"

"A terrorist is a man who throws a stone at a tank."

The Colonel weighed this for a moment or two, arranging the words carefully until their meaning dropped into place and he grinned. "So my English friends. You want me to take you to Famoudi. Is OK. Is normal. I take many men into Iraq. They are from Saudi and Yemen and Egypt. Is good. They are men of Jihad. But you are different. People tell me you want to give clothes for the people in Famoudi. They say that when these clothes are on the TV many people say OK, we understand now, we see that it is good to throw stones at these Americans. And I tell them it is all crazy but they tell me I need to see you English. So OK. I see you now. You tell me. Why, English? How?"

Lenny was feeling himself again. The water had restored him completely. "Ever heard of Vietnam, Colonel?"

"Sure. I hear of this place."

"Hundreds of thousands of American soldiers. Millions and billions of dollars. Tanks, planes and napalm. And still they lost. Know why?"

"You tell me English."

"Because the young people at home said no way. They did like the young people in Famoudi. They took to the streets and threw stones and petrol bombs. They took the batons and the water canon and the CS gas. And it wasn't just in America. It was everywhere. The whole world. Wherever you looked there were young people burning American flags. The government tried to persuade people that the war was all about truth and justice and holding back the advance of communism. But the young people refused to buy it. They said it was all about brutality. And the cause joined them all together from California to London to Paris to Berlin. They became united. And you know what happened in the end?"

"The Americans went home."

"The Americans went home. They won every battle they fought in Vietnam but they lost the battle at home. To start with the parents were willing to take what their government said at face value. They argued it out with their children at the breakfast table. But slowly everyone came to share the truth. Dropping napalm on villages where children are growing up is just plain wrong. It has nothing to do with stemming the tide of communism. It has everything to do with plain old-fashioned killing. And once the truth was out, the war was lost."

"And you think bringing these clothes to Famoudi make people see the truth?"

"It makes the link. It makes young people in Britain and America and France and Germany remember that they are no different to the young people in Famoudi. As soon as they feel the same, they share the anger. The way for them to feel the same is to share the same clothes. The same brand. In England, wearing Koz gives a young person a special identity. It says they are willing to fight it out. It says they are sick to the back teeth of being ignored. It says they want a better slice of the cake and they are willing to fight for it. Think about it. Why do armies wear uniform? Why do football teams wear kit? People are tribal animals. We all need something to bond to. A gang. A cause. An identity. Koz can reach out and join the kids in Famoudi to kids all over the world."

"Big, big words English."

Lenny jumped to his feet and started to stalk the room with his arms waving about. "Fair enough. Big words. But big words are always the best words. Did Ghandi or Martin Luther King or Mandela speak small words? Did Mohammed speak small words? Small words allow small men to do big evil. Small words make up big lies. And we are all drowned by small words. Twenty-four hours a bloody day. Seven days a week. Year after year until we can't see past the small words. On and on and on. Words to make us blind and greedy and happy to turn away from the truth when it stares you in the face. Maybe nobody will listen to these big words. Maybe it will all come to nothing. Maybe the time of big words has passed. But I am damned if I'm ever going to believe that Colonel. The world might be on its last legs but it doesn't seem to me as if the time has yet come for us all to give up and watch the TV."

The sudden outburst of passion took the Colonel somewhat by surprise and his expression of mild amusement was replaced by a deeper look. His dark eyes were suddenly filled with a new respect. If the Colonel was surprised, Josh was nothing short of astonished. It was almost as if his friend had been storing up his speech for the whole of his life. And it had suddenly all come out under a bare light bulb in a room with peeling walls somewhere in Syria. It had taken over forty years for Lenny Baxter to throw away his reserved Yorkshire cloak and allow the fierce passion out. For the whole of his life, the only outlet Lenny had for what burned within was to hurl a cricket ball through twenty two yards of space with as much ferocity as he could muster. Only now as they approached the end of the final act were the gates thrown open. Josh couldn't help but feel a huge sense of loss. For the first time he truly saw the man who had been the greatest friend he ever had. He had always seen Lenny as the ultimate steady hand. He was like all the sergeant majors who held British lines for hundreds and hundreds of years. Calm and unflappable. Facing down the advancing hordes with an even stare. But now he saw just how much more there was to Lenny Baxter. If only he had allowed himself to unlock the passion sooner then how far could he have gone? Instead he had kept it all bottled and waited until he reached the gateway at the end of his life to allow his inner self to escape.

Lenny stood in the middle of the room clenching and unclenching his fists, waiting to hear his fate. The Colonel carefully stubbed his Lucky Strike and resumed his smile.

"Now I know you English. You are not the first. Once there was another English like you. We call him English Lawrence. You call him Lawrence of Arabia. There is big film OK. He was a man of big words. Good words. Not like this Bush and Blair. Maybe your big words are good words. That is for Allah. So I send you to Famoudi English. And yes, the people in Famoudi will wear these clothes that you bring. For me, OK, is all crazy. But sometimes crazy can be great. You can go. May Allah bless you English."

"Thank you."

Dale was listening to his Walkman and on the edge of sleep when Walters tapped him on the shoulder. Wearily he killed the sound and opened his eyes.

"What is it Walters?"

"We're getting some kinda weird stuff out of the house."

"Like what?"

"That's the thing. We can't make much of it. Not yet at least. They're all pretty excited about something, that's for sure. I get the feeling they're picking their words in there. Maybe the Colonel has warned them we might get bugs into the house. It seems like someone's coming, something's going to happen, hell it's hard to tell."

Dale started to put his headphones back on.

"There's always something happening Walters. It's called being in a war."

"Yeah, yeah. Like I'm some kind of schmuck? Look, I can't make it yet, but there is something strange here. Something has got them all wound real tight. It's like they've all just got tickets for the Superbowl in there. Then there was something else."

"Go on."

"One of the kids started talking. Real, real excited, yeah? Yousuf shut him up so he only got halfway through what he was saying. It didn't make sense. But you should have heard how he got slapped down. He was saying something about English Lawrence."

"What?"

"Yeah. That was what I thought. I talked it through with my guys. That is what they call Lawrence of Arabia down here. You heard of him?"

Dale pulled himself up from his bed and reached over to a line of books. He chose a well thumbed paperback and tossed it over to Walters who read the title aloud.

" 'The Seven Pillars of Wisdom'. T. E. Lawrence. You've read this?"

"I've read it. Maybe if Bush and Rumsfield and Wolfowitz had done the same we wouldn't be in such a mess down here. It isn't such a surprise that those kids are talking about him. They still revere him. I don't see it as any big deal."

"Maybe I wasn't clear. The kid wasn't just mentioning him in passing. He said he was coming."

"Coming?"

"It's what he said. Then Yousuf shut him down. Hell, it's probably nothing. I just figured you should know. It's a good idea to stay alert."

"We always stay alert Walters. It's how we try not to make like dead guys."

The final leg of the journey to Famoudi took Josh and Lenny two days. After eating well at the table of the Colonel, they were driven for two hours into an arid and empty area where they were met by on old man with many lines on his face and barely a tooth in his mouth. Under a blanket of stars he led them on a five-hour hike that took them over the unseen border from Syria to Iraq. He called a halt half an hour before the break of dawn. They hid in a shallow cave in the side of a rocky outcrop. The old guide curled up and was fast asleep before the fat red sun slid up and over the edge of the world. Josh and Lenny watched the vivid reds of the dawn light up an area of desert that didn't seem to be the world of men. They pulled off their boots and nursed blisters and talked in quiet voices. It wasn't that there seemed any danger. It was just the sort of place where it seemed right to speak quietly. Like a million acre church. After chewing through a couple of dry pitta breads, they followed the example of the guide and slept. The toll of the long journey all the way from the hospital in Sheffield ensured that they slept right through the burning heat of the day. They woke in the late afternoon feeling parched but more energised. As soon as the blanket of the night was thrown down on the desert they resumed their hike. This time it was only four hours until an unexpected flash of a torch flickered for an instant in the blackness.

Five minutes later they found a Toyota 4 x 4 pickup and two more middle-aged men with blank expressions. The guide disappeared before either of them had the chance to thank him. He hadn't spoken a single word in the twenty-four hours they had spent in his company. The two who took over seemed unlikely to be more chatty. One spat out a short sentence of machine gun Arabic and gestured to the back of the pickup and dropped the tailgate.

It was another slow night under the canopy of stars as the pickup moved cautiously across rough ground without lights. Sometimes they would arrived at the top of a ridge and the view ahead would open up. They were in a world devoid of human light. Devoid of humanity. A land where nothing had changed for millions upon millions of years. It was as if they were sliding back into the depths of pre-history when the planet had been a quiet place uncluttered by the misery of man. Once they saw the winking lights of a plane high in the dark sky. Movement without sound. Distant evidence of the crazy world that lay beyond the stillness of the desert. By dawn they had reached a long straight road where trucks rumbled by every five minutes or so. A little after six one of the trucks stopped on the edge of the road a hundred yards from where the Toyota was parked behind an outcrop of rock. One of the men pointed and nodded.

Time to go. They jogged over to where the driver waited and were instructed to climb over the sides and join a crowd of just under a hundred goats in the open back. The driver directed them through gaps in the planks that contained his bleating cargo. He waved them to the area behind the cab and urged them to sit and pull a tarpaulin up to their necks. More gestures suggested they should pull it all the way over their heads if anything happened.

But nothing did. The tired engine ground up and down the gears for the next eight hours as larger vehicles rumbled by. Once again, plastic bottles of rancid warm water had been left for them and once again there didn't seem to be enough. At last they felt the truck swing hard to the right and the road underneath them was bumpy. After five minutes they stopped and the driver waved for them to climb out.

This time they had arrived at a long deserted factory of some description. All around them were square concrete buildings and an array of rusted pipework. Two figures were waiting in the doorway of what must have once been some kind of office. The driver was true to local custom and he jumped into his cab and departed in a billowing cloud of dust without a word. Their new guides did not step forward until the truck had clattered out of sight.

This time they were younger. Teenagers. They approached with smiles which made for a welcome change.

"I am Amir. He is Yousuf. You are welcome here. We are waiting now. Come. You coming away from sun. Too much hot yes? Iraq he is too very hot now he is summer, OK"

"Too very hot seems pretty on the mark to me guys. Got any water in there?"

"We have these water, yes please."

They had set up camp in what looked to have been a reception area. There was a blanket and more bottles of water. And food. Dates and a plastic box filled with rice and plate of flat unleavened bread.

"So now you sit."

They sat. Both faces were beaming with excitement. The two boys exchanged a couple of fast sentences whilst the dusty Englishmen drained two bottles of water each.

"Yousuf who is my friend is asking me which one is the English Lawrence?"

Josh returned the smile and nodded to Lenny. "He's your man. Visionary and dreamer. Rebel, fast bowler and moderate rock climber."

"Is very good you are coming Lawrence. You are making these Americans to go home for sure. We not wanting no more Americans in this place. They make too much bad. All the time bad."

Lenny finished his bottle and wiped his lips with the sleeve of his shirt which smelt of old goat. "How far is Famoudi?"

"Yes please Lawrence. Famoudi he is close now. Only five kilometres and he is coming here."

"Is he now? Tell me Amir. Have some other things arrived for us?"

This brought an eager nod. "This thing it is yes Lawrence. He is here last night. Many boxes. They are in very safe place. In Famoudi. No Americans can see them there."

Lenny reached down for a piece of bread and chewed through a smile.

"So it was a hot dusty afternoon when the Magdalene Climbing Society finally arrived on the outskirts of Famoudi . . . ."

"Please Lenny? I not knowing about this thing you say."

"Sorry Amir. When do we go into the town?"

"Yes. OK. This is when the night he is dark. We can walk this time. It is only maybe two hours."

"And in the morning you will fight with the Americans?"

"He is every morning we fight with the Americans. Now we are too many OK. So every morning we can go and do this."

Once again Yousuf spoke fast to his friend.

"Please Lawrence. My friend he asks me to tell you why it is that you bring these clothes."

Lenny blew out his cheeks and lit a cigarette. This was going to be tough one. The Colonel had promised an interpreter who would make sure that everything could be explained. Amir was a thoroughly likeable lad but Lenny had grave doubts in his ability to understand the concept of Koz.

"I think that a few props might be a decent sort of idea." Josh pulled his rucksack to him and started to drag out items of Koz clothing which he duly tossed across to the two Iraqi's. They were all smiles as they pulled on the hooded tops and baggy black pants. They arranged each other's baseball caps and to the complete amazement of the Englishmen Yousuf fell into his well practised 50 Cent imitation whilst Amir mirrored his exaggerated hand gestures. The only area where they were not able to properly ape the great man himself was that they couldn't wipe the grins from their faces as the ran through the performance. Yousuf had barely a word of English but he was all but word perfect in his rendition of the rap. As Lenny watched, he felt a superstitious prickle run through him. 50 was back again. 50 his multi-millionaire soul mate who he had never met and never would. 50 who had been locked up in America at the same time that Lenny had been in Wakefield. 50 who stared down at him from the walls of the Zone. 50 who had given him the inspiration for the USYcampaign during the long walks through the countryside around Dumfries. And now here was again. The words from New York which had flown all the way up to a satellite orbiting the globe and back down again into a dish in Famoudi. 50 and Lenny. Lenny and 50. Still in step.

When Yousuf had finished, Amir applauded enthusiastically and translated.

"Yousuf he is say he knows these clothes. He says they are like the G Unit OK. Like 50 Cent. We all like the 50 Cent. He very great man OK. This Koz he is G Unit yes?"

"You have it my friend. This Koz he is G Unit."

"And all these Koz we put on like clothes to fight Americans?"

"Yes."

"And many people they see Famoudi boys all in these Koz from the television of satellite OK?"

"Millions and millions and millions."

More fast words from Yousuf. Amir passed them along. "And you think that 50 Cent he is watch these satellite in New York City?"

This time Yousuf chipped in with carefully chosen words of English. "He is Big Apple. 50 Cent. Is good."

Lenny was more than happy to go along. Why not? The whole of America was supposed to be tuning in every night to watch the exploits of Captain Nash and Charlie Company. Why not 50 Cent?

"Of course. I heard that 50 Cent sees you every night. Never misses."

"And he likes OK? He likes Famoudi boy OK?"

"Course he does. But he hates your clothes. That's why he told us to bring Koz. Koz is good. Everyone wears Koz in New York City."

"So Famoudi boy he is like New York City Boy?"

"The very same."

This prompted a vigorous and intricate high five routine between the Famoudi boys. Josh leant over and spoke in a low voice. "You forgot to tell me that Koz was quite so big in New York. Funny that."

"Aye. Must have slipped my mind. Must be getting old."

Amir was back in question mode.

"He is why you bring these video camera yes? So you make pictures for 50 Cent? For New York City boy?"

"Of course. 50 Cent told us we had to. He said he needed to see the Famoudi boys looking good. Really good. And he said he needs to hear you."

"How you say hear us?"

Lenny stood and pointed to his ear. "Hear. Yes?"

"OK. You say make the noise. Big noise."

"Big, big noise. Yes. You make like this . . ."

He held his arm up high with a fist clenched like he had seen the crowd in the street as they chanted at the Marine lines.

"Is OK. This is how we make it for American soldier."

Both boys raised their arms. Lenny tapped Josh on his shoulder and he stood as well.

"OK. Great. Then we shout."

"Yes. He is always shout. Too loud shout."

"We shout KOZ!! KOZ!! KOZ!! KOZ!! . . ."

Both boys caught on fast and Josh joined in. They shouted as loud as they could for a whole minute and then Lenny lowered his arm.

"Oh yes. Perfect. Couldn't be better. Just like 50 Cent said it should be. Tomorrow we make very loud OK?"

"Big loud Lawrence. He is bigger loud than these American he have ever see."

Lenny held out his hands and fumbled his way through the high five routine. It was far from perfect but it did the job. He felt more than confident that 50 would have approved.

Dale Woke up feeling in better spirits than he had known for several weeks. For the last three mornings he and his men had employed different tactics, all of them drawn from the battles of history. The men were loving every minute of it. For the first time in his army career he had soldiers showing real enthusiasm on the parade ground. Drill suddenly had some sense as they practised falling into different formations in seconds. The evening before he had presented a lecture on the history of the British Square. He had described many high moments and one or two low ones. The highs included Waterloo and an epic encounter against the Mahdi's horsemen in the Sudan campaign when two thousand British infantry had defeated a force that outnumbered them by fifteen to one. The greatest catastrophe had been in 1879 when the square at Islandwana had broken and the warriors of the Zulu army had slaughtered every white man on the field of battle.

Once he had completed his history lesson, they had headed for the floodlight parade ground. Two solid hours of intensive work left the men of Charlie Company bathed in sweat, but in the end they could manage a pretty good imitation of a British infantry unit from the nineteenth century. As the men fell into lines around him, Dale had stood in the centre of the forming square with a stop watch. When they broke the thirty second barrier he had called a halt. Then he made good on the promise he had made to them as they had filed out into the warmth of the evening and he ordered his sergeant major to break out four cases of beer.

It was not only the planning and training which lifted his spirits. He had also come to look forward to the hours at the end of the day when he could retire to his quarters and immerse himself in the history books that had been the cause of so much amusement when he stuffed then into his kit bag. After his talk with Walters, he had settled down to re-read 'The Seven Pillars of Wisdom'. By the time his eyes had grown too heavy to hold open, he had raced through more than half of the book. As he drifted into sleep he felt a vague sadness. Why the hell hadn't anyone who counted taken the trouble to read what Lawrence had to say? Back in 1915 the tyrants in place were the Turkish colonists rather than Saddam Hussein. The British hadn't sent a whole army to throw them out. They couldn't. The lifeblood of the nation was being poured down the drain in the slaughter of the Western Front. Instead they had sent one man. Lawrence. A dreamer who most thought was borderline crazy. The dreamer persuaded the Arab Sheiks to join together and throw out the Turks. Surely the same kind of thing could have been by uniting the Shia in the south and the Kurds in the North. Instead Bush had sent 160.000 soldiers and about a trillion dollars worth of ordinance. And every day he and his men had to go out and face the consequences of the President's decision whilst the Arabs still spoke of the English Lawrence with something approaching awe.

Awe. The word stopped the sleep in its tracks. Walters had told him that the word was that the English Lawrence was coming to Famoudi. It wasn't a title that would be offered up lightly. So who was it? And what were they coming to achieve? And the sleep that had been so close was driven away and Dale lay in the darkness wondering what the next day was about to bring.

When he awoke the book was still open on the top of his sleeping bag and the thought was still in his head. In the dark the thought had made him feel uneasy, but with the morning sun streaming in through the window he only felt a sense of excitement.

The men of Charlie Company jumped up onto their transport with genuine eagerness. He had to smile. They would actually be disappointed if the stone-throwers didn't bother to show. In the midst of all the killing they had all discovered a game that both sides seemed to enjoy as much as each other. In the weeks of stones, his company had received just two light injuries, neither of which were serious enough for the Marines involved to be removed from the line. No doubt there were plenty of sore heads and bruised ribs on the other side, but he was pretty sure that nothing would have been life threatening. Except for the unlucky three who were delivered up to Walters and his sub-contracted torture team.

Of course it was only the television that made the whole thing possible. His orders were crystal clear. Show restraint. Keep the cool. Don't let anyone lose it and fire off any rounds. The US Army had been a panned for the whole of the occupation and here was a chance for them to show a better side. No doubt the mysterious Colonel had issued similar orders to the stone-throwers. No suicide bombs. No RPG's. Just stones and kids. The whole thing had become a bizarre PR exercise and neither side was at all upset about it. Was the man they were calling the English Lawrence about to change all that? And if so, how? And when?

His Humvee was about to lead the convoy away from the compound when the passenger door swung open and Walters jumped in.

"Morning Dale."

"Any more news?"

Walters gave him a smug smile. "Well, look who is suddenly on board with our intelligence thing."

"I have no objections to intelligence Walters. It is torture and behaviour beyond all levels of acceptability that I object to."

"Yeah, yeah. You've done that gig Dale, give it a goddamn rest. There's nothing all that clear, but there sure as hell is something. We swung a chopper over town last night with some night vision capability. It looked like something was being handed out. There were kids all over the place queuing up to be given something. Plastic bags. Nothing heavy. You could tell that much. Something real light. Maybe some kind of material. Cloth? Hell. I don't know. We got nothing from the house. Yousuf was out all night. All the others were a skittish as hell but they said nothing. I figure it's nailed on that they know we've got the place bugged."

"Any more about the English Lawrence?"

"Nah. Not a thing. Probably nothing."

There was nothing different about the street when they arrived. The same broken windows stared out at the same dust and rubble. The routine was by now completely familiar. The men laughed and joked as they jumped down and fell into their starting positions. Peggy Hill took up her normal station and messed with her hair whilst her cameraman checked his light-meter. The men on top of the Bradleys ran through last checks on their guns to make certain there would be no jamming if the moment came.

There were sounds of the approaching crowd, but still distant. It would be a few minutes before the first of them appeared at the other end of the street. Dale heard the tinny voice of the spotter up in the helicopter through the earphones of the radio man who stood beside him. The man frowned slightly then turned to speak to Dale.

"Sir. Chopper reports there is something different about them today sir."

"Different. What is different?"

The radio man relayed both question and answer. "Sir. He doesn't know sir. He says they look different sir."

"Jeezus. Give me that mike . . . this is Captain Nash. Clarify your report please."

The voice had to fight with the roar of the rotor blades.

"Sir. It's hard to say sir. They seem to be wearing different clothes. I can't really see properly from this elevation sir. All the clothes look the same. Like uniform sir."

"Thank you."

He passed back the headset and considered the information. There had been unusual activity last night. The streets had been filled with kids queuing up to be given some sort of bags that looked as if they were light. Like they contained cloth or something. Or clothes. Uniform. Was this why the one they called the English Lawrence had come? To bring uniforms? No way.

The sounds were much nearer now. Just a couple of minutes and he would be able to see with his own eyes. The chanting was already pretty loud and they hadn't even got to the street yet. Something had got them all fired up. Uniforms maybe. But why?

At last the first figures marched around the corner and into view. As ever, they held their right arms high with fists clenched. And yes. They looked different. No doubt about it. Beside him one of his sergeants was watching through binoculars.

"Jesus H Christ . . . "

"Report please Sergeant."

"Sir. They're dressed like they come from the hood sir."

"The what?"

The sergeant was a towering black man from Philadelphia who looked as if he could walk into the defence of any NFL team he chose. Now the big face was a picture of bewilderment.

"Like I said sir. The clothes. They look like the guys from the hood back home. Here. Take a look."

Dale focused the binoculars and sucked in a breath. Now he knew what they had been saying. Baseball caps. Baggy tops and pants. Hoods. What the hell?

He passed the binoculars back and tried to work it out. All of a sudden there were thousands of Iraqi kids who had been dressed up in urban street wear that would have looked the part in any city from Detroit to Los Angeles. By who? By this English Lawrence? It had to be. But why?

"Sir!! Caucasian at eleven o'clock. Has a camera. Looks like video. He's filming sir."

Again Dale took the glasses and soon found the man in question. Unlike the kids, the man made no effort to conceal his identity. He was tall. Maybe six two. Blond hair. Hard to tell how old because his face was hidden by the camera. Then for a moment the camera dropped and the man stared straight over to Dale. By now the mob were no more than sixty yards away and the binoculars sucked the man's face in close enough for Dale to see every feature as if he were just a few feet away. Not all that young. Somewhere in his forties. And smiling. Beaming. What the hell was with this guy?

Without taking his eyes away Dale once again passed the binoculars back. He needed no magnification now to see the man. He was just fifty yards up the street now and still looking straight at him.

Like he knew him. And then Dale realised that the man probably did know him. Thanks to Peggy Hill and ABC, half of the world knew him. Once the man knew that Dale was staring straight at him he lifted an arm and waved. What the hell . . . ?

"Sir. Another Caucasian at two o' clock sir. Same thing. Taking pictures. Looks like a digital camera sir!!"

Dale snapped himself back into focus. Whilst he had been staring at the stranger like a rubber necker at a crash site, he had barely noticed that the crowd had all but reached his lines.

"Form the square Sergeant."

"SQUARE!!!!!!!" The big man's voice soared up over the cacophony and the Marines reacted instantly. Dale forgot the men with the cameras and took out his stop watch. All around him his men moved without either panic or hurry. Click. Twenty-three seconds and a perfectly formed square had formed around him. A record.

The crowd flowed around the soldiers like a fast flowing stream around a rock. They ringed the wall of shields leaving a gap of about five yards. Dale calmly turned a full three hundred and sixty degrees, all the way round meeting dark eyes that gleamed with excitement. It was a new chant today. What was it? A short word, repeated over and over and over. Like hot, hot, hot.

"What do you think they are saying sergeant?"

"Sir. Check out the label on the clothes. Here. Take a look."

Dale zeroed in on a nearby cap with the binoculars. 'Koz'. What the hell was 'Koz'? But now he could recognise the chant.

"KOZ!! KOZ!! KOZ!!"

They were taking their time this morning. Normally they would have started the stones by now. Things were obviously different. Today they wanted to take their time and do a whole lot more chanting. Well, it was fine by him. They could chant all day if they liked.

"KOZ!! KOZ!! KOZ!!"

Loud. Really, really loud. Masked faces. Dark gleaming eyes. And suddenly he could see the blond stranger again. The man must have climbed up on top of a burned out car that had been there in the street from day one. The extra height meant that he had a clear line of sight over the heads of the crowd and all the way down to where Dale stood at the centre of the square. Dale knew the lens was pointed straight at him. Behind the camera the man was smiling like he had just hit a home run in the World Series. And then he dropped the camera so that his eyes could meet those of the young Captain. Who the hell was he . . . ?

Suddenly Walters voice was very loud in his ear, straining hard to be heard over the deafening chants that filled the dusty air.

"We have a problem Captain!!"

"What!!"

"You need to snatch the white guys . . . ."

The remainder of the sentence was lost as all of a sudden the air was thick with stones. He turned to the sergeant.

"Roof please sergeant."

"ROOOOOOOFFFF!!!"

The Marines reacted instantly. This was the toughest manoeuvre they had attempted to date. The night before it had needed well over an hour's practice until it was anything like right. The four sides of the square were each made up of twenty two men. 'Roof' meant every other man taking a step backwards with those left in the line closing the gaps immediately. Three seconds after the sergeants mighty roar, the size of the square had exactly halved. Those who were now in the middle lifted their shields above their heads to form a solid roof of Perspex. Now the street was filled with the thunderous sound of hundreds and hundreds of stones and bricks crashing into the locked down square.

After the barrage had come down for just over a minute Dale was happy that the square was secure. Now he could sit and wait to see how long it would take for the new tactics to bear fruit. Today the men of Charlie Company had no intention of making a charge. Today the plan was to remain in their locked down roof formation for as long as it took for the stone throwers to get sore arms. The barrage never eased for a whole ten minutes by which time the arms of the Marines were throbbing and their ears were all but deaf. But then the intensity gradually eased until the mob got the message that a stalemate was in place.

At last the youngsters started to withdraw. Now the chanting resumed as the crowd moved slowly back down the street. Once they were fifty yards away Dale again issued his instructions.

"Re-form the square please sergeant."

"SQUARE!!!!!!!!"

The stop watch this time showed twenty-eight seconds as the levels of adrenaline had eased off somewhat. Still pretty darned good, especially as the guys had just had about a million rocks bounce off them. Without the roof of shields, Dale once again had a clear view of the street. He saw the cameraman shoot the crowd as it moved past him and then he jumped down to the street and carried on filming the withdrawal.

"KOZ!! KOZ!! KOZ!! . . . "

"Line please sergeant."

"LIIINNNNE!!!"

Now the Marines dropped back into their two line start position. They were all dripping with sweat but the cast of their bodies was triumphant. Peggy Hill blustered over from where she had filmed the whole thing from the cast-iron safety of the Bradleys.

"Wow Dale. That was un – bel – eeevable. People are just going to love it. That square thing was just the coolest thing I ever saw. Are you good for an interview now?"

"Not just yet Maam. We're not all done yet."

Most of the crowd had disappeared around the corner now and yet the sound of their chanting was still loud in the air.

"KOZ!! KOZ!! KOZ!!"

At last the only figure left at the far end of the street was the tall cameraman who was filming the crowd as it marched away. Then he turned back to the two lines of Marines and pointed his camera in their direction.

"We'll have the final phase now sergeant please."

"SING!!!!"

The street was now filled with the sound of a hundred voices of varied singing ability, every one of them forcing out maximum sound. They were filmed from back and front. Lenny Baxter took in the spectacle from two hundred yards whilst the man from ABC came up from the Bradleys. Now the sound was as American as pancakes and syrup with bacon.

> . . . *From the Halls of Montezuma*
> *To the shores of Tripoli*
> *We fight our country's battles*
> *In the air on land and sea . . .*

Dale hammered out the Marine Corps hymn with the rest of his men whilst the cameraman came in close to his face. Peggy was all but beside herself. Fantastic TV had just turned into over-the-rainbow-brilliant TV. Once this little lot hit the airwaves she was guaranteed her place on the fast track for as long as she wanted. Her mind was spinning with visions of the glittering career that was laid out ahead of her like a red carpet without an end.

The man at the far end of the street waited until the last line of the song was thrown in his direction then he carefully laid his camera on the floor and clapped his hands above his head. His applause was sharp and clear in the sudden silence that followed Charlie Company's battle song.

And then he shouted something, collected his camera, and jogged away after the crowd.

"Who on earth is that?" In all the excitement, it was the first time that Peggy had noticed that there was a white man with the mob.

Dale hadn't really listened to her.

"Did you hear what he said, sergeant?"

"Sir. I think it was 'Bravo' sir."

"Who was it Dale?" Peggy's voice was no insistent enough to get his attention.

"Maam. I do believe that is The English Lawrence."

"What? But who . . . ?"

But Captain Dale Nash was already walking towards his men. She was about to follow him when a hand on her shoulder restrained her. It was Walters. The man had never spoken a word to her and now he was laying his hands on her. Now that was something that Peggy Hill would not stand for, war zone or no war zone.

"Excuse me. Please take your hand away."

"I need you come with me please. And your cameraman."

"Are you crazy. No way. I'm going to my vehicle and I am going to file my copy. Now if you please . . . ."

She tried to pull herself clear of him but his grip only strengthened. Suddenly she was shrill. "Get OFF me!!"

Dale turned around to the sudden outburst.

"Is there a problem here?"

"The lady needs to come with me. And the cameraman. No need for any drama. Let's just go shall we."

Dale was clearly confused by the bizarre scene that was beginning to unfold.

"This lady is under my jurisdiction. Explain please."

Walters rolled his eyes and used his free hand to wave his phone at Dale.

"This comes from Washington Captain. High up Washington. The film goes nowhere. And I mean nowhere. The lady and the camera guy go with me. Right now. Come straight over once you get back with the guys. I'll explain."

The cameraman was now being held in restraint by one of the Iraqi sub-contractors.

"What in the name of hell is happening here! Captain Nash. Tell this sonofabitch to get his goddamn filthy hands off me."

Dale was about to issue instructions to his sergeant. Enough was enough. Walters might think that he had sanction for high places but there was no way this was going to continue to happen.

"Sergeant . . . ."

Walters spoke in a very quiet voice that got everyone's attention. "Captain Nash. Right now your career is at a crossroads moment. You better believe me here. We have a major, major problem and I AM going to resolve it. If I have to shoot these people to ensure that the film does not leave the can, then I WILL shoot them. Now back off Captain. Get your men saddled-up and back to base. I assure you no harm will come to either Miss Hill or her guy. I only need to take control of the film. Now I suggest that you make the smart call here and I will explain everything as soon as we get back. OK?"

"Dale, you can't!!"

Dale had absolutely no idea what was happening, but he was in no doubt about the tone Walters had used. This guy wasn't kidding around and there was no way he would be man handling high profile media people unless he was pretty sure of his ground. Decision time.

"OK. Take them Walters. Miss Hill, I apologise for what has happened here. My sergeant will ride with you to ensure that you are comfortable at all times. I expect that all will become clear once we get back."

Peggy was almost apoplectic. "You can't do this. No way. That film is going and it's going now . . . ."

"Maam. Please. Stay calm. Take a ride. We'll straighten things out."

There was no way Peggy Hill was about to calm down. She had just shot the greatest ten minutes of film that TV had seen in years and some spooky creep with a haircut from 1975 was about to screw the whole thing up. She kicked and screamed all the way to the Humvee like a hyperactive child overdosed on E numbers whilst a hundred Marines looked on with dumbstruck expressions.

As Lenny jogged to catch up with the rear of the crowd he was filled with a euphoria he had never known before. What had seemed a lunatic dream had come unbelievably true. The dire luck that had dogged his entire life had finally turned. Against all sensible odds he and Josh had managed to find their way to Famoudi and make take their pictures.

Now one last task remained. They needed to get the pictures out before the Americans woke up to what had happened. For the first time since making his deal with Asmo he allowed himself a small feeling of confidence. The time difference was now all in his favour. It was just past ten in the morning which meant that it was 2.00 a.m. in Washington. Dale Nash was clearly a very fine infantry officer, but he would not be the one to pick up on the consequences of Koz coming to the streets of Famoudi. The men who would analyse that particular threat would in all likelihood be tucked up in their beds in the American capital. The only unknown factor was how quickly people would get a close look at the ABC pictures. No doubt they would be flying up to the satellite already. He had to assume that someone in the ABC headquarters would be connected in some way to the Administration and that meant that he could take no chances. The trouble was that once he caught up with the crowd it was almost impossible to move at all. He was engulfed by masked figures, every one of whom was talking ten to the dozen and want their picture taken. After fifteen minutes he had barely moved and the frustration was growing.

He forced his way through the crush to where Josh was experiencing similar difficulties. Thankfully Josh was with Amir and Yousuf.

"Josh. Leave this lot to me. You get back and start sending. We probably haven't got all day. Will you go with him Amir? Help him OK?"

"OK I can make to go. And Yousuf he is OK too much as well."

PART TWO

"Great. Give me that spare camera Josh. You take the video. I'll be back as soon as I can."

Yousuf was shouting something to him which he didn't get at all other than the word Lawrence. Amir leaned in close and translated.

"Please Lawrence, Yousuf he says that street was very nice today. He says all pictures must be too much nice. He says will 50 Cent see these pictures today?"

"Tell him no problem. Tell him that 50 called me on my mobile phone whilst we were out there and told me to be as quick as I can. That's why you need to get Josh back to the house OK?"

"He is OK and very good. We going now very straight."

Lenny took the spare camera from Josh and started taking a variety of small group photos. They posed in twos and threes and tens. They arranged themselves like sports teams. Some beamed for the camera. Others adopted tough guy expressions. Thankfully the camera contained plenty of extended memory. He had no clue how he was ever going to get the finished photos back once they were developed. It was a job for another day. Now he just wanted to ensure that every one of them had the chance to have their moment recorded. Those who managed to survive the war would always talk about this day. These would be the photos for the walls of the Famoudi of the future. Small groups of boys of young men, their eyes shining with pride. These would be pictures of one of those 'I was there'moments in life. So strange to think that decades in the future these boys would be proud old men who would sit their grandchildren around them and tell the story of how the Americans had come to Famoudi. And how they had gone out to fight them with nothing more than stones. And how men from far away had come with clothes called Koz. And maybe Asmo's brand would still be found at the back of cupboards, lovingly wrapped up and passed down the generations.

Josh, Amir and Yousuf went straight to the roof. Everything had been set up before they had left for the confrontation with the Marines. They had brought three satellite telephone systems. Two were already hooked up to high speed laptop computers which were powered by a small humming generator. Josh quickly got both machines online and plugged in the camera he had used and Lenny's video. He tried to stay calm and take on each task carefully. It didn't take long to transfer the images onto the computers. Next he attached the files onto emails and hit send and the screen started to feed back information about how quickly it was getting through the task.

He sat back and wiped the sweat from his face. "Come on you bugger. Come on . . . ."

Then the blue line moved. Not far. Almost too little to notice. But he knew it had moved because underneath the line the screen told him that the file transfer was now 1% complete. And 1% meant that at least one picture had arrived at its destination. And he knew that a picture could paint a thousand words. He stared at the screen as if his was hypnotised. The clock at the bottom of the screen moved steadily along. 10.51. Still 1% complete. 10.52. 10.53. And then the line nudged along another fraction. 2%. It had taken three minutes for another percent. A hundred and eighty minutes for the whole shooting match. He checked the second machine which was firing off the video images. It hadn't made it to 1% yet. The files were far bigger. To transfer the whole lot would probably take the best part of a whole day. Well it was no more than they had expected.

Next he logged on the third computer and logged on. Straight away a ping informed him that an email had arrived. He clicked the read icon and opened the file. It had been sent at 5.51 a.m., 10.51 Famoudi time. It wasn't a long message but it was enough for him to spring to his feet and grab a bemused Amir in a bear hug.

"He is working very good yes?"

"He is working like a bloody dream my friend. We're in business."

"These are pictures of Famoudi boys for 50 Cent OK?"

"50 Cent, the Queen, George Bush and whole planet. OK. Is the man ready to take a message to the Colonel?"

"He is too much ready and he is down in the stairs."

"OK. Give me a few minutes."

He returned to the three laptops. Another look at the message confirmed that it really was true.

"The first file has arrived. I have opened it and it is perfect. B."

For the umpteenth time in his life he marvelled at the mysteries of computers. Here he was on a roof in Iraq with three plastic boxes and somehow he had just managed to send photos of something that had only happened a few minutes earlier all the way to Beverley's house in Haddington. Crazy, crazy, crazy. But then the whole world was barking crazy. Two of the computers had Zip drives and now he transferred all the files onto the over-sized disks and ejected them.

"There you go Amir. Two disks. Big, big important OK. Tell your man that the Colonel he is very angry if he doesn't get these disks. Big, big angry. And 50 Cent."

Amir was suitably solemn. "The man he is too much good man. He make this job finish. Is OK."

11.00. 4% complete. The disks were on the way. Nothing else to do. He sat back and closed his eyes for a moment. In his mind's eye the icy summit of Everest was no more than a few hundred feet away. Nothing would stop them now. Mallory and Irving. Lenny and Josh. So long since they had watched the slow Cambridge dawn from the rooftop in St. Johns. So long to reach the end of the road. Just like Mallory and Irving they would not be going back to England. Not without an absolute miracle and in his bones he knew that they had used up every miracle in the locker. 4% complete was enough of a miracle. The future could probably be measured in hours but it really didn't matter because there was plenty of time to make the last short journey to the summit.

Asmo lost all the feeling of terror that had taken root for days the very minute that Beverley opened up the first file. A dusty street under a burning blue sky. Smashed windows. Peeling walls all smashed up by bullets. A line of young men all dressed in Koz. His Koz. Their arms were raised and they stared defiance over the scarves that masked their identity. Another image snapped open. A sea of baseball caps and raised arms. Then a small gap where street could just be seen. Then a square of Marines locked down behind a wall of Perspex. Then another. Boys in Koz, stones in the air, Marines behind shields. And it was real. It was actually happening. There were two young Asians in the room with Asmo and Beverley. As soon as the first picture landed they started their work. They were graphic designers from the advertising agency who had taken Koz to the magazine pages of Britain. After five minutes of feverish key board tapping then first sample was ready for approval.

"Check it out Asmo."

He leaned over to look at the screen. The designer had fused two images together. On the left were three small Koz figures with their backs arched into throwing their stones whilst a few yards distant two policemen were ducking the shots. On the right the Marines of Charlie Company braced themselves for a similar onslaught. *Koz. Fight for every street.*

Asmo only needed a few seconds.

"Bloody Hell. That's perfect. Get it sent. Let's go."

He was about to start work on the phone when he caught Beverley looking at him from the bed.

"No. Hang on. Do a print for Beverley first. Then send." He looked back to her. "They've only gone and bloody done it haven't they."

She smiled. "Of course they have. Did you really think for a minute they wouldn't."

A few minutes later the first image was in the system of a popular skate boarding magazine which would be printed ready for distribution the next day.

Dale Nash had built up a full head of steam by the time Charlie Company made it back to their base. He jumped out of his Humvee and stormed across to the building where Walters and his team had established themselves. From behind a closed door on the corridor he could hear the near-hysterical anger of Peggy Hill who was hammering away at the wooden panel. He followed the sound of Walters voice and found him in his command centre talking furiously into a Satphone. He was about to start when Walters held up a single finger to indicate that his call was all but dome. Thirty seconds later he was true to his word and killed the conversation.

"You better have proper explanation for . . . s"

Walters held up both hands to stop the flow of angry words.

"Dale! Stop. We don't have time. Trust me OK? Now just stop and listen. I'm going to take a couple of minutes to explain what happened out there. Then I've got some stuff for you to check out. Then we try and work out what the hell we do. OK?"

"OK."

"Take a seat. You're making me nervous."

Dale bit down on his lip and sat. He was itching to fire off both barrels and throw in a grenade for luck but there was something about Walters that made him pause.

"Thanks Dale. Look, I apologise for the way I behaved earlier. Just hear me out and you'll see where I'm coming from here. I is my belief

PART TWO

that we have a major situation and just about no time to solve it. By my reckoning we've got less than an hour to get Washington to play ball or it will be too late. I'll give you the bones right now. Then you can flesh the thing out some whilst I make some calls. OK. As you know, three days I flew down to Saudi for a briefing. I hooked up with some Brits I know. Guys in the same line of work. We all headed back to a room to nail a few drinks. They all wanted to watch the TV. There was some crazy assed story going down back in Britain. And I mean crazy assed Dale. Some whacko had fired up a bunch of kids up in Scotland to riot about some Youth Centre. I didn't seem much of a deal to me. Sure a couple of cops got a bang and an office got toasted. What made the thing play big was that the cat involved had once been indicted as a terrorist twenty years ago. Him and his brother were caught cold with a trunk full of semi-automatics from Libya during a Miner's Strike back in 84. The brother got whacked and the guy from the TV got twenty-five years. So when he turns up like some kind of Pied Piper firing up a bunch of kids the media were all over the thing. Then things got really weird. Some BBC documentary dug out a whole load of stuff that seemed to prove that this guy and his brother had been innocent all along. They got set up by the spooks and all of a sudden some big wheel got arrested and locked up. Sir Edward Latimer. The guys I was with said he was from way up high on the top floor. That's why they were so keen to watch. None of them were crying much at his fate. Sounds like a real piece of work. Then the whole thing got even weirder. Just as the whole street riot thing was fizzling out a bunch of kids turn up in some new gear and throw a few stones at the cops. Next day there are pictures of them all over every bill board in Britain. Want to have a guess at what it said on the clothes?"

"You're kidding. Not Koz?"

"In one buddy. Magazines, TV, every damned place. The thing was that the guy who made the gear was pretty cute. The only place a kid could buy the stuff was in Dumfries which was where the whole gig kicked off. Well next up, every goddamned kid in Britain was heading to Dumfries for a piece of the action. The Council ran for the hills and gave them the Youth Centre. Mr Terrorist come Pied Piper disappeared off the planet . . ."

"No!"

515

THE POISONOUS PAST

"Oh yes. Mr Pied Piper terrorist come folk hero come English Lawrence. That was him Dale. Up close and personal grinning like a Cheshire cat and pointing his camera in your Hollywood face my friend."

"But why? I don't understand."

"Maybe I don't either. But I think I do. And I think it is serious as all hell. Why did we pull the boys out of Nam in 73 Dale?"

Dale was knocked back by the sudden change in direction. "Hell I don't know. The government came under too much pressure from the people at home I guess."

"Bingo. We lost that war in 68 when every damned student in the United States started burning flags. Think of what they are making this Koz thing mean Dale. Here. Take a look."

He leaned over a keyboard and brought up one of the original adverts. "There you go. Koz. Sometimes you gotta fight. Damn it man. This is all about going back to 68. And this sonofabitch Baxter is putting Famoudi kids alongside his Scottish kids. He's working on getting every lousy kid in the world out there throwing stones at cops. And where the hell will that leave us Dale?"

Nash shrugged. He had a feeling that Walters wasn't really looking for an answer.

"Screwed. That's where. The American people are already on the fence about the whole gig down here. It won't take a whole hell of a lot to push them over to the other side."

"But what are we supposed to do about it?"

"We're going to have to stop the pictures getting out. No pictures, no ads, no nothing. We can shut them down Dale before anything gets the chance to happen. That's why I've got the ABC people locked down. Now I need to make more calls. Take ten to check the thing out on the web. Then I need you to start planning how to throw a cordon around Yousuf's place."

"What? You mean that's where they are?"

"As of ten minutes ago. Maybe not Baxter. The other guy landed up just before eleven. I swung the chopper over and they reported men on the roof. My guess is that they are using satellite communications. We're counting in minutes here. OK. You have the bones. Work on having the guys rolling in no more than thirty, OK?"

"OK." Dale felt as if he had been run over by a runaway truck. He could get a cordon around the place at a push, although he had a nervous feeling that the whole thing could be an elaborate ambush. But then what? Was Walters going to want Charlie Company to take these guys out? Jesus.

He sat in front of the screen and started working the keyboard. In a moment Google Images gave him a full screen head and shoulders of Lenny Baxter. He stared for a moment into the same face that had smiled at him just a short while before.

"Well I'll be damned."

The time difference factor that Lenny and Josh had relied on would have worked much better had Walters not been on the scene down in Famoudi. He dragged his boss from his bed and managed to convince him that here was a major opportunity. Gerry Hunt had put in thirty years with the CIA before moving over to the fat bucks of the private sector. He had guided the corporation to a number of massive contracts and had been instrumental in convincing the military to adopt the bounty concept as a key strategy in the war on terror. Now he was soon awake enough to smell a huge opportunity. If the corporation was responsible for stopping this thing before it happened they would pick up a whole handful of bargaining chips for future use. It took Walters ten minutes to ensure that his boss was all the way with the programme. Hunt needed only fifteen minutes to get some of Washington's bigger hitters scrambling from their beds and heading for a three o'clock meeting in the White House.

By the time the meeting kicked into life, there were several four star generals round the table and a collection of representatives for the upper echelons of the CIA. Gerry Hunt's PA had graduated in the top ten of her year group at Yale and she won her spurs by putting together a full PowerPoint presentation of the Lenny Baxter story in record-breaking time. The last to arrive was the assistant to the Secretary for Defence who was clearly far from amused about being dragged from his bed for some kind crazy fairytale. Normally he would have told anyone who had brought such a pile of junk to his bedside to take a hike. A very long hike. But Gerry Hunt was one of those Washington insiders who knew everyone and everything and even the President himself would think long and hard before telling him to take a hike. So the deputy pulled on a favourite woollen jumper, slapped some cold water in his face and made his way down to the situation room.

He made no effort to conceal his foul mood when he arrived. Several greetings were ignored and he fixed Gerry Hunt with what he hoped was a withering stare.

"Is all this really necessary Gerry?"

"Bill, if I didn't think so you know that you would still be getting your beauty sleep. Get yourself a coffee and I'll bring up into the loop. Sarah."

The PA was on hand with a coffee which Bill Muir took grumpily. "Don't need cream. Just black."

Gerry waited until the coffee was stirred then started his pitch. He clapped his hands together in the attention of the room.

"Thank you for coming at such short notice gentlemen. This is a tough situation. If our assessment is correct, it will require a decision within the next half hour. It also our judgement that this decision will have major implications on the future of the whole Iraq project."

Muir butted in. "Who's we Gerry?"

"Myself and my man on the ground in Famoudi. Walters."

"And the pair of you think that you can get us all out of our beds on some wing and a prayer?"

Hunt sighed. "Look Bill. I know you're pissed about this but if you keep interrupting we're all going to miss our window here. And I promise you there will be a lot of people who will want to know why. Hear the facts. Make a judgement."

"And why the hell should I?"

"Because we might just have half an hour to stop Iraq becoming this country's next Vietnam. That's why."

The very sound of the name Vietnam caused shuffling around the table. Every one of the Generals had started out their careers in the heat and misery of the that war. Muir was clearly desperate to shut Gerry down, but his instincts sensed that doing so might bring his promising career to a very sudden end.

"OK Gerry. We're here now I suppose. Just make it quick."

With no more ado Gerry flew through the bones of the Lenny Baxter story. Sarah had worked miracles and had a series of images that illustrated the extraordinary events that had taken Baxter from Haddington to jail to Dumfries and finally to Famoudi. She had several examples of the Koz adverts and media coverage of the huge crowds of buyers that had descended on Dumfries and forced a Council U-turn.

"Normally I would have brought in experts from the commercial sector to assess the potential reach of this Koz brand. But we have no time for that. All we can go on is what happened in Britain. The only evidence we have suggests that kids are going to buy into the whole thing big style. I believe that the theory runs that the whole fashion business runs in cycles. 1968 was thirty-seven years ago. The guys behind this whole Koz thing obviously believe that rebellion is about to be the next big thing. But they're not just waiting for it to happen. They're making it happen. What happened in Dumfries was nothing. The media lapped it up because of Baxter's history. But if they manage to link kids throwing stones at cops in Scotland with kids throwing stones at Marines in Iraq we could have a problem. That's why I'm talking Vietnam gentlemen. But for the riots in 68, we might have kept the people on side. And if we had kept the American people on side we might just have won the war. We didn't and we lost."

Several of the generals were nodding their heads now. They could remember all to clearly the desperate images of soldiers returning home frrom tours of duty to be jeered and spat on and called baby killers. The agitation at home had destroyed the morale of the army in the Nam. Things were already shaky out in Iraq but the American public was still more or less behind its soldiers. But if the wind changed and young people started rioting for peace then things could change very, very quickly.

Muir was suddenly very glad that he had decided not to tell Gerry Hunt to take a hike.

"Let's accept your assessment for now Gerry. What are our options here."

"Bill, as you have seen, Koz relies on pictures. Images. Kids throwing stones at cops. The real deal. Not just pretend stuff on Playstations. That is why Baxter and his sidekick went down there themselves. That's why they took the pictures themselves. Without the pictures they've got nothing. And they also know this is a real one-shot deal. No way would we allow any one else to get in there. I still can't quite believe that Baxter managed it. So the decision is a simple one. We need to stop them getting their pictures out."

"And have we any idea how they plan to do this?"

"I think so. We got a report from one of our helicopters that the other guy, Josh Ogilvy was seen up on a rooftop with electronic equipment. We need to assume that they plan to send the images out of Iraq electronically. By my estimation they might have been doing this for the last fifteen minutes or so. The good news is that this kind of data transfer is pretty slow. If we can stop them straight away then we might be able to limit the damage."

"Gerry, it seems like you have already come to some provisional conclusions."

Hunt paused. Now for the big pitch. "That is correct. Gentlemen, I have three proposals. Number one. The man behind Koz is based in a town called Bolton in the North of England. We need to pull strings and get the Brits to raid his place of work. There has to be a chance that they are sending the stuff to one of his computers. Once they take control of the computers, they control the pictures."

Muir threw a question at the table. "Who has a line into the Brits?"

One of the CIA men put a reluctant hand up. Muir nodded grimly. "Get onto them. Get them to raid the place and get them to do it by yesterday. And don't take any of their Limey crap. Lean as hard as you have to. OK Gerry. Next."

"The captain in charge of the Marine Unit in Famoudi believes he can get a cordon around the house in thirty minutes from us giving the word. It might be soon enough to stop anyone getting away with a disk."

This time Muir looked over to the Marine general who nodded and got to his feet and left the room.

"Good. Number three. The reason my guy is in Famoudi is that we are working on a contract to take out a top twenty target. Guy known as the Colonel. We have intelligence that the Colonel paid a visit when the whole stone-throwing thing kicked off. It seems fair to assume that he played some role in getting Baxter, Ogilvy and a whole bunch of clothing and equipment into the place. We interrogated a couple of kids and got the address of the leader of the agitation. Kid called Yousuf Hamid. Ogilvy is sitting on his roof right now. We got into the place and fitted it out with surveillance devices." He paused to clear his throat. "We also covered the eventuality of the Colonel returning to the house at a future date."

"How did you do that Gerry?"

"We installed tracking apparatus."

"You mean we are placed right now to guide in a smart bomb?"

"That's affirmative Bill."

Muir sat back. Hunt had said that decisions were going have to be made. What he had meant was that they might have to order the execution of two British nationals. "That's a hell of a big ask Gerry."

"It's why I called the meeting. We believe the thing can be covered. There is no hard evidence that either of these men are in Famoudi at all. They entered Iraq illegally and without our knowledge. If they happened to be victims of a surgical strike then two things can be made certain. One, the Marine team on the ground can remove all physical evidence of their presence in the area."

"By which you mean scrape up what little bits of them are left and incinerate the evidence."

"That is correct sir. Secondly we announce that the air strike was targeted at known insurgents with clear Al Qaeda connections. With what we already have of on Yousuf Hamid that shouldn't present any difficulties. His father was senior Baath Party and it won't be hard to put him next to the Colonel. Sure there will be a few crazy rumours, but without bodies we'll be pretty well fireproof."

Muir looked now to the CIA men who gave the plan thoughtful nods. "So you recommend that we hit hard and fast and tough it out?"

"Yes Bill, I do."

Muir stared down at the doodles on the pad in front of him. One thing was for certain. Hunt was right that there was no time to sit about and ponder. Every minute meant that the pictures from Famoudi could be flying their way through cyberspace.

"Gentlemen. I'm not willing to make this decision on my own. There is clearly no time to take the thing upstairs. I think that I would like to see a show of hands. The question is should we authorise an immediate air strike. Please raise your hands all that say aye"

One by one the hands went up until every one was raised. Muir nodded and raised his own. "Well we have a clear decision." This time he looked to the man from the air force. "Give the order please. Come straight back when you have a time."

Nobody was in the mood to talk once the decision had been taken. The air force man returned in five minutes. "We'll have an F16 in the air in fifteen minutes. The flying time to Famoudi is ten minutes. My people will set up direct comms with your man on the ground Gerry. Half an hour and it's done."

Later it was mentioned in the enquiry how well the Marine communications had worked. It only took fifteen minutes from the moment that the General departed the situation room in Washington to Charlie Company climbing back onto their transport and rolling out. Dale took in the detail of his town map as his lead vehicle bumped along the pitted road towards the centre of Famoudi. There was a small park about five hundred yards from Yousuf's house and he directed his driver accordingly. At the same time he used the radio to brief his platoon leaders. The map showed that there was a clear box of streets making a rough oblong around the target. He allocated each of his platoons a street each and received conformation from each platoon.

Privately he had his doubts as to the viability of the mission. Only an hour before there had been in excess of three thousand in the mob that had pelted them with stones. They would hardly have evaporated into thin air. The target area would still be milling with bodies, all of then highly excited by the morning's action. His orders were to seal off the area and search anyone leaving for hidden computer disks. It probably sounded pretty good back in Washington. In the morning heat of Famoudi it sounded like a wild goose chase. His real concern was that the plan meant that he was going to have to stretch his forces and that meant they would lose control. The key to their morning fights had been that they had been able to fall into tight defensive formation within seconds. Now he was being ordered to split his force into four and he knew that would mean vulnerability. He thanked his lucky stars that they had worked the four square move a few days earlier. Now each platoon leader had a practised option of falling into defensive mode within seconds. The Bradleys would be his reserve. The map showed that if the two armoured cars maintained a post in the park they would never be more than four hundred yards from any of the platoons. A matter of seconds at worst.

He duly passed the order of battle out through the radio. Then he checked his watch. Not bad. They were on target to be fully deployed within half an hour of receiving the order.

Omar, the young man who had once been a trainee solicitor from Baghdad and now played the role of courier to the Colonel, was just passing the park when the vehicles of the Charlie Company roared into view. He stepped back into a door way as the Humvees and trucks rumbled by and crashed over the kerb and onto the long dead grass.

He lowered his head and focused on walking without any sign of urgency. It was how people were all over Iraq. They had learned to ignore the Americans. To stare down at the floor. To pretend they were not there at all. He counted his steps ten at a time. The fourth set of ten took him to a corner. Before he turned he stole a backwards look. All of the soldiers were out of the trucks now and they had fallen four groups. He could see that they were receiving orders from gesticulating sergeants. Then they departed at a jog.

They didn't come towards him. Instead they moved away towards Yousuf's house. His heart had accelerated to what felt like thrice its normal speed. Now it slowed back down and he pulled in a few deep breaths.

Twenty minutes later he reached the truck which waited for him with the engine quietly grumbling.

Lenny heard the Marine vehicles when they were a few hundred yards away. He was still a good quarter of a mile from the house and it was time to get a move on. He fired off a final group photo and then started to jog away from the sound of the approaching engines. Five minutes later he joined Josh and the others on the roof.

"How's it going?"

"The photos are 22%. The video footage is still only 3%."

"And the disks?"

"Already away."

"When?"

"About quarter of an hour ago. Maybe twenty minutes."

Lenny blew his cheeks out in relief. Almost certainly long enough. Nash still had to unload his guys and deploy. He felt quite confident that the courier would already be well clear of the area.

"Anything from Jake?"

"Yes. An email has just come in. He's in place and ready to roll."

"OK. We best do it fast. They're here already."

"Do you think they're going to come in?"

Lenny shrugged. "Who knows. We have to assume they are, though I think they'll want to check things out first. They're bound to be worried about some kind of ambush."

Josh started work on the third computer and three minutes later he had completed a satellite link with Jake Hollins. The man from the Times had been good to the word he had given in Ankara. When he had returned to London he had made contact with Alison Hammond from the Panorama team. He had told her enough to get her interest and not enough for her to have clue what was about to happen. He had explained that there was about to be a major break in the Lenny Baxter story. It was going to be bigger than anything that had gone before. It was going to be huge.

Her part of the deal was to arrange for Jake to set himself up in the BBC 24 studio with a variety of computer equipment. He explained that Baxter would be getting touch via a satellite link. By the time an email popped onto Jake's screen, Alison Hammond was all but beside her herself with curiosity.

Now at last he could let her in on what was happening.

"OK my lovelies. At last we can arrive at the kiss and tell moment. Lenny Baxter and Josh Ogilvy are in Famoudi." Blank stares. It was so far from anything they had been expecting that the penny didn't come close to dropping. Jake hurried them along. "As in Iraq? As is Charlie Company and the Brad Pitt look alike and the pesky locals with their masks and stones. With me now? Excellent. Well the news is that as of this morning the pesky locals threw their stones decked from head to toe in Koz."

Alison looked as if he had just slapped her across the face as hard as he could. "You ARE joking."

"I'm not known for it. I'm Mr Grumpy remember. This email should have a couple of pictures attached. Let's check them out shall we."

He opened the message and sure enough a selection of four photos told the story of the battle of the morning. Jake was rather impressed with the quality. He wondered which one of them had been on the camera. Each image caught the heat and the dust and almost the noise. The great difference of course was that the world had become accustomed to seeing pictures from the Marine side of the lines. These pictures were from the other side of the tracks. Now the men of Charlie Company seemed threatening and shadowy behind their wall of shields. The stone-throwers looked completely different as well. Where they had seemed so alien, the familiar style of clothes suddenly made them seem closer somehow.

Alison's mouth was working hard but she didn't seem able to find a thing to say. Finally she almost spat out a sentence in a jumble.

"What else is about to happen?"

"They'll be through on the Satellite link in a minute or two. I rather thought you might like to do a live interview."

This prompted a flurry of discussion which resulted in the producer deciding that there was no way in hell she was about to miss such a chance. She briefed the anchorman of the development and he glanced quickly in her direction to make sure that she hadn't suddenly gone round the bend. She nodded eagerly and thrust a thumbs up at him.

"It's game on then is it?" Asked Jake who was by far the calmest individual in the room.

"Absolutely." replied the flushed producer and a team of technical types descended onto Jakes laptop to link it into the rest of the planet.

Before letting them have their way, Jake quickly typed an email and sent it away south.

"Live interview on BBC 24 as planned. It goes as soon as you link up. Good job and good luck. J"

Lenny was watching the Marines from the edge of the roof. It was hard to see much, but it seemed as if they were sealing off the area around the house. They certainly didn't seem to be making any imminent preparations to launch any kind of attack. From the northern side of the house he got a clear view up a street. At the intersection the soldiers were in the process of setting up a makeshift checkpoint. Already they were stopping and searching.

"Look pretty good Josh. They're setting up checkpoints. It doesn't look like they're coming in just yet. How near are you?"

Josh turned found with the expression of a man who had just landed a lottery jackpot. "We're bloody on. I've just got the word from Jake. As soon as we link up we're live on BBC 24."

And there it was. Just a couple more digital links and the thing that had seemed to be a five hundred to one shot would have come to fruition. Lenny crawled back over and positioned himself next to Josh in front of the small web cam which stared back impassively. It was impossible to comprehend that this modest piece of plastic was about to take their faces all the way around the world.

The screen informed them that they were almost there. Josh passed a pair of headphones over.

"We should hear them as soon as we go on line."

"I reckon this is the summit and we're on it. Should have brought a flag."

Josh grinned back. "The Magdalene Climbing Society gets there in the end."

At that moment a disembodied voice squawked in his ears.

"Are you there Lenny? Can you hear me? We can see you. This is Kate Whittaker of BBC 24 . . . "

"Loud and clear. Are you getting me?"

"100% Good picture too. OK. Thirty seconds and we go live. You ready down there?"

"Ready and raring. "

The anchorman took in the updated instructions and assumed a suitably grave expression.

"We have some remarkable breaking news coming in. Many of you will have watched the events in Dumfries over recent weeks. An extraordinary sequence saw what started as a local campaign for a youth centre become something that grabbed the attention of the world. The upshot was that the young people won their battle and the Youth Centre Project was given the go ahead. A senior member of the Security Services, Sir Edward Latimer remains in custody under charges relating to the Terrorism Act. And a remarkable new brand of street clothing – the Koz range – has become a 'must have' for millions of youngsters. At the very centre of the story from beginning to end was Lenny Baxter. Baxter was convicted under the Terrorism Act in 1984 for the part he played in the Miner's Strike. A recent Panorama programme however has cast many doubts as to whether he was ever guilty of the offences. He orchestrated the Dumfries campaign and it was rumoured that he was instrumental in the introduction of the Koz clothing to the affair. This morning it appears that we have proof of this link. This morning the demonstrators in the Iraqi town of Famoudi took to the streets wearing Koz clothing. We have learned that it was delivered by Lenny Baxter and his Press Officer, Josh Ogilvy . . . "

As he spoke the four pictures appeared on the screen one by one to confirm his words.

" . . . and we can now go live to Famoudi to talk to Baxter and Ogilvy. Lenny, can you here me?"

"Aye. Clear and sound."

"Lenny, what exactly are you doing in Famoudi?"

"Delivering clothes. It's gone well. The kids certainly seem to like them."

"What is your thinking in taking the Koz range to Iraq?"

Lenny smiled at the serious voice. "As you know, the kids up in Dumfries found that Koz helped them to get their message across. We thought we should give this lot in Famoudi the same opportunity."

"But surely the circumstances couldn't be more different."

"Aye. That's for sure. I'll be telling our lot that they don't know they're born. Having nowt to do is one thing. Having a bunch of soldiers and tanks come to town is a whole new ball game. What's your name by the way?"

"Peter."

"It's not good here Peter. No power most of the time. No clean water. Next to nothing to eat. It seems to me that these kids have every reason to throw a few stones. I thought it was rough when the Greater Manchester Police came to Haddington back in 1984. But this is on a different level. People get killed here every day and nobody gives a damn."

"And how do you think you can change that?"

"Simple. Kids in Dumfries wear Koz. Kids in Famoudi wear Koz. Then they look at each other and think hang on a minute here, we're all the same boat. Time to make a stand. Time to stick together. Show unity for your comrades all over the world. Sounds bloody old-fashioned doesn't it? It's what my dad used to say. Brought us up on those words. Well they killed my dad and they killed my brother and no doubt it won't be long before they get me as well. But they won't kill the thought. Koz means if it's wrong don't put up with it. And if you have to throw a few stones, then throw them. These kids have thrown stones at a hundred American Marines armed to the teeth. That's what Koz is all about. That's . . . "

He stopped in mid-flow and turned to look behind him.

"Lenny . . . "

The door to the situation room in the White House crashed open and a panting Captain charged in.

"We have a problem. "

Muir spun around in his seat. "What is it?"

The Captain grabbed a remote and pointed it at the bank of television screens that played silently up on the wall. CNN disappeared to be replaced with BBC News 24. And the face of Lenny Baxter. Every body around the table stiffened.

" . . . these kids have thrown stones at a hundred American Marines armed to the teeth. That's what Koz is all about. That's . . . "

"NO!!" Muir was out of his seat, suddenly frantic. He looked to the man from the air force with beseeching eyes. "Call it off!! CALL IT OFF!! NOW!!!"

"Sir, I think . . . "

What happened next was played over and over for several weeks. The few seconds of footage were watched like the images of the planes hurtling into the Twin Towers. Lenny Baxter half turned his face away from the camera. Enhanced sound picked up the distant roar of a low flying jet. Then there was a small flash far away in the sky. It wasn't something that anyone noticed at the time. It was only later when the boffins got hold of the picture and did their stuff.

Baxter turned back to the screen. Suddenly the frantic enthusiasm was gone. In its place was a strange air of calm. What he said next was talked about for many years to come. In its way it was a bit Kenneth Wolstenholme's legendary words from Wembley in 1966. " . . . there are people running on the pitch . . . they think it's all over . . . it is now."

When Lenny spoke his voice was resigned but not at all desperate.

"I think they've just fired a missile. Looks like the game's about up. Sally, Tim, Barry, Jed, Asmo, everyone. Keep the faith. And you too Beverley. Happen we'll be seeing you soon . . . "

Then the screen went blank.

Dale Nash heard the roar of the F16 at the same moment as Lenny. He turned in time to see the flash of light.

"Holy Christ no, they couldn't . . . ."

He saw the missiles. One a hundred yards or so in front of the other. Fast. Searing fast. Many thousands of dollars worth of death delivered at supersonic speed. As the first missile screamed by no more than fifty feet above his head he had an image of the face from the street. Smiling. Assured. A man who had found the place that he wanted to be. The English Lawrence who had returned to Arabia.

The first missile was sucked into the house at the bottom of the street. A second ticked by. Then the second missile struck. And then a tiny pause that he had become familiar with. And then the fast expanding yellow orange ball of light as the house was thrown high into the sky. Another pause and then the thunder rolled back down the dusty street and hammered into his eardrums. The F16 screamed over him and climbed up high into the rich blue of the sky.

The Air Force man put his phone down carefully. It wasn't the time to crash it down. He pulled himself upright in his chair and looked over to where Muir sat with an ashen white face.

"The target has been eliminated sir. Confirmed."

Muir hung on. He gripped the side of the table and tried to calm himself. All eyes were on him. He was the senior man present. They had all voted but they all knew where the buck would stop. He got to his feet very slowly and ran a careful hand through his thinning hair.

"Gentlemen. It appears that we have just executed two British nationals live on the BBC. I hope that the Lord will forgive us."

He carefully screwed the top back onto the fountain pen his wife had given him at Christmas. The he took a last look around the faces at the table.

"Because I sure as hell know that nobody else will."

Asmo found that he was crying the moment the screen went blank. The anchorman didn't seem to have realised what had happened. He looked like a man who had been frozen in a science fiction movie.

"We might have lost our connection I think . . . "

Asmo screamed at the TV.

"You haven't lost the bloody connection you moron. They've killed him. The bastards have murdered him."

He turned to Beverley with tears pouring down his cheeks. He was surprised to see that she was strangely calm. She was just like Lenny had been in the last seconds. Her voice was as calm as a summer dawn.

"It was what he wanted Asmo. Both of them."

"But why? How?"

"They were tired. They didn't fit. They both knew that the world had just moved on too far and left them behind. Don't try to understand it. You won't because you are young and full of life and hope. And so you should be. Lenny and Josh and me . . . They killed the light a long, long time ago. This was the last flicker. The last twitch on the thread. Think of it like a firework. We don't cry when a rocket bursts in the sky. We cheer. We let it lift our spirits away from the grind of life."

Asmo stared through blurred eyes at the dying woman who was already letting go. She smiled at him.

"It is all down to you now Asmo. And Koz. And a whole new generation. Maybe this time you might even win."

She closed her eyes and allowed her whole body to relax. She had been true to her word. She had seen it through to the end. Images flickered through her mind. Images of the public telephone at Rome airport. The camp in Nicaragua. The basement in Ulster. The rivers of blood in Rwanda. The ice in Latimer's eyes. And a fifteen-year-old Lenny Baxter running in to bowl in the All Yorkshire Cup Final. A sunny day from a time before everything went dark. She enlarged the image as he hit his delivery stride and slammed a ball by the batsman's nose. Applause from all around the boundary edge. And Lenny took a moment to stare down at the batsman before pushing his hair back and marching to the end of his run up.

And Beverley Morton kept her eyes closed and smiled.

THE END

Other titles
by Mark Frankland

One Man's Meat
£5.99

The Cull
£5.99

Terrible Beauty
£6.99

Red Zone
£6.99

The Drums of Anfield
£4.99

Target One
£6.99

**To order copies please complete the order for
at the back of the book or tel. 07770 443 483**

All prices include P&P to customers in the UK

www.thecull.com

One Man's Meat by Mark Frankland

"Frankland turns crisis into drama"
Sunday Telegraph

November 1997 and British Farming
is being ripped apart by the BSE Crisis.
Vast areas of the countryside are facing devastation.
Finally one man decides that enough is enough.

Sir Alistair McIntyre, owner of the vast McIntyre
Holdings Corporation, makes the fateful decision to
save the Beef Industry. He hires a team of Mavericks
who claim to be able to solve any problem.
Their prize is massive. So is their task.

As their campaign gathers momentum
thousands of angry farmers at last start to fight back.
The story sweeps across the globe at breathtaking speed
from Argentina to Matabeleland,
from the windswept Scottish hills
to the shanty towns of Brazil,
from the Cabinet Room in Downing Street
to the Boardroom of a supermarket giant.

Every step of the way the team are sucked into ever
greater danger until their path inexorably leads them
to the lair of one of the most dangerous men on earth . . .

**To order a copy complete
the order form at the back of the book
or tel. 07770 443 483**

£5.99 (incl. P&P to customers in the UK)

www.thecull.com

The Cull by Mark Frankland

"Mark lifts the lid on Drug Town" **Sunday Post**

"Everyone who has lost a child to heroin will want to be Jack Sinclair. Tragic, thrilling, captivating." **Simon Houston, Daily Record**

Will Sinclair is dead. It seems as if he will be just another statistic. Another young man dead before he reaches twenty. Another Scottish junkie unlucky enough to shoot-up a bad bag of heroin. A few column-inches in the local paper. Ten seconds on the radio news. And then he will be added to the long, long list. Just another dead junkie.

But this time it is different. It is different because Jack Sinclair will not accept his son's loss with resigned grief. He refuses to forgive and forget. He was once Major Jack Sinclair of the Scots Guards. In three tours of Northern Ireland he learned all about fighting an unseen enemy. Then there were rules. Regulations. Restrictions. Red tape. His war against the drugs gangs who killed his son will be very different. This time the gloves are off. This time he has a free rein.

As Jack Sinclair lights his small fire, the story sweeps from the empty wilderness of the Galloway Forest to the war-torn streets of West Belfast, from the mean council estates of West Scotland to the Cabinet Room of 10 Downing Street. And the fire becomes an inferno.

"Like 'Trainspotting' before it, 'The Cull' takes the reader into the darkest corners of the Scottish drug world. Compelling. Harrowing. Always gripping. Nothing will stop you turning the pages."

**To order a copy complete
the order form at the back of the book
or tel. 07770 443 483**

£5.99 (incl. P&P to customers in the UK)

www.thecull.com

Terrible Beauty by Mark Frankland

" Gripping and horribly realistic." **Glasgow Evening Times**

It is the story of the making of an outrage. An outrage which will be the greatest of them all. An outrage that will make Omagh and Enniskillen look like mere sideshows. An outrage that will blow the Good Friday Agreement into a million pieces.

It is the story of two men from West Belfast. It is the story of how their lives are swallowed up by the endless war of their peoples. Sean O'Neil travels the road of the IRA. For Davie Stanton it is the British Army and the UVF. Their journey carries them through thirty years of pain – Burntollet, the riots of 1969, the Battle of Ballymurphy, Internment, Bloody Sunday, Warrenpoint, The Hunger Strike, Loughgall.

Slowly their lives become intertwined. They become puppets in the dark game where their strings are pulled by the shadowy forces of the British Security Forces. And their destiny becomes one. In the end one man can no longer stand the Peace that he sees to be a lie. The Peace he sees a betrayal of his people. He plans an act so appalling that the fragile Peace will be shattered beyond repair. And there is only one man in the world who can stop him.

"A compelling read. Terrible Beauty is lovingly written, imbued with compassion, humanity, and great attention to detail. It will keep the reader entranced from the moment they pick it up." **An Phoblacht – Republican News**

"This book identifies the murky world of terrorism, it also shows how in more cases than not, an incident opens the path towards vio - lence." **David Ervine – Leader of the Progressive Unionist Party**

"Frankland shows insight and authority about the perennial problems of the Province. It is also a rivetingly good read!" **Rt Hon Sir Robert Atkins MEP, Minister of State, Northern Ireland Office, 1992 – 1994**

£6.99 (incl. P&P to customers in the UK)

www.thecull.com

Red Zone by Mark Frankland

"An unrelenting pile driver of a read"

An asylum seeker goes berserk on the late night
streets of Sighthill. Three local teenagers are hacked
to death. The worst riot Glasgow has seen
in a generation rages through the night.

The Israeli Defence Forces stage a dawn raid
on a house in Gaza city. Mahmoud Bishawa,
the most notorious of all Palestinian fighters,
is taken into custody to await trial and execution.

Two events. By pure accident they happen within hours
of each other. Two events that are in no way related.
Two events in two cities thousands of miles apart.

It is the plan of one man which draws the two events
together. Khalil Bishawa will go to any lengths
to secure the freedom of his brother.

He brings the savagery of fifty years of fighting
between the Israelis and the Palestinians
to the towering blocks of the Sighthill Estate.

He takes the people of Glasgow into the Red Zone.

*"You watch the news and see the pictures from Gaza
and the West Bank and think it will never affect you.
You won't feel the same after you turn the last page."*

**To order a copy complete
the order form at the back of the book
or tel. 07770 443 483**

£6.99 (incl. P&P to customers in the UK)

www.thecull.com

535

The Drums of Anfield by **Mark Frankland**

"A fantastic adventure book for all young
football lovers – even one as young as me!"
Sir Tom Finney

Once in every generation a great new star emerges
into the world of football. Out of the slums of Sao Paulo
came Pele. Out of the bullet-scarred streets of Belfast
came Georgie Best. Out of the shanty towns of Buenos Aires
came Maradona. When Liverpool's veteran captain,
Tony Hobbes, suffers a crippling injury and receives a long
ban for violent conduct, he decides to take his son to Africa.

He expects to find lions and elephants amidst the Dark
Continent's endless wild plains. Instead, far away in the East
of Uganda under the shadow of the Mountains of the Moon,
he finds a boy called Simon Matembo. He knows that the
boy's talent is so huge that he could become the greatest
of them all. He knows that this boy can take Liverpool back
to the great days. But first he has to find a way to take him
back, and to do this he must overcome many huge challenges
from the tribe, the club, and even the forces of nature.

"Anyone who loves football will love this book.
Football is about passion, unrelenting excitement
and, more than anything else, it is about dreams.
Exactly the same can be said about 'The Drums of Anfield'.
Gerry Marsden, from 'Gerry and the Pacemakers'

"Genuinely hard to put down", **FourFourTwo Magazine**

**To order a copy complete the order form
at the back of the book or tel. 07770 443 483**

**£4.99 (incl. P&P to customers in the UK)
www.thecull.com**

Target One by Mark Frankland

'A head-spinning "Day of the Jackal" for the Twenty-First century. The pages almost turn themselves'

Roland McMillan is 95 years old and his doctors see little chance of him making it to 96. In 1926 he fled the desperate misery of his life in the mining town of Kirkonnel and emigrated to America. Over 79 years he has built up a colossal family fortune. Now it is time to tidy up his affairs.

McMillan's greatest treasure is his gallery of paintings which is reputed to be the most valuable and extensive private collection in the world. He has always known that one day he will bequeath it to the nation. The question he needs to resolve is which nation – Should it be Scotland, the land that bore him? Or should it be America, the land that made him?

His solution is an old-fashioned one. The fate of the McMillan collection is to be decided by a game of golf played by modern day gladiators. America's number one golfer will challenge Scotland's number one over Turnberry's majestic Ailsa course for the greatest prize in the history of sport.

George Albright the Third is one of the greatest sportsmen America has ever produced. A world figure. A sporting icon. The undisputed Number One in the world with a fortune fit for a king to his name. to his name. Archie Banks is an unknown. A hard-smoking, hard-drinking nobody from ttorious Sunnybank estate in Dumfries who is only his country's number one as a result of a fluky streak of results.

The twenty-first century version of David and Goliath catches the imagination of the world and sends the lives of both players into chaos. It is an event that everyone wants a piece of. Even the American President will be there to watch.

As the eyes of the world are fixed on the event, unwanted guests plan a dramatic intervention. When the news of the President's intentions reaches Al Quaida, they put in place a plan to assassinate their TARGET ONE.

**To order a copy complete the order form
at the back of the book or tel. 07770 443 483**

**£6.99 (incl. P&P to customers in the UK)
www.thecull.com**

Order Form

Name --

Address --

Telephone --

Email --

Please send me ----------------- **Copies of**

Please send me ----------------- **Copies of**

I enclose a cheque for ----------------------------

Please make cheques payable to:
'Glenmill Publishing'

Return this form to:

> **Glenmill Publishing**
> **Glenmill**
> **Dumfries**
> **DG2 8PX**

Or Telephone   07770 443 483